REDEMPTION

by
Fernando Gamboa

Translated by Christy Cox.
Edited by Peter Gauld and Anne Crawford.

To my uncle, Carlos Miguel.
RIP

Guilt

Barcelona
August 17, 2017
4:48 p.m.

As she strolled idly, hands in her pockets, window-shopping on Pelayo Street on that hot Barcelona afternoon, Nuria Badal could not have imagined that in exactly two minutes and thirty-nine seconds she would make a dramatic decision that would change her future and the fate of an entire country.

Perhaps forever.

Nuria had lost sight of her friends but decided to follow her own path instead of looking for them. Stopping in front of the Zara shop window, she compared her own reflection with the silhouette of the slim mannequin and wondered whether those white linen pants would look as good on her.

Cocking her head, she concluded that the legs were too straight, and besides, they would make her ass look flat. The only way to find out would be to go in and try them on, but at that particular moment the downtown shop was crowded and she guessed that the line outside the dressing rooms would be never ending. She lowered her gaze to the white tag with the price—€39.90—and told herself she really didn't need another pair of summer pants.

Just then, a jingle from the cellphone in the back pocket of her jeans alerted her that she had a message on WhatsApp. Taking out her smartphone, Nuria opened the app. Laura had sent her a message, telling her they'd taken shelter in Sephora, which had air conditioning and was on the other side of the street.

"Coming," she typed rapidly, adding a smiley face at the end of the message. Abandoning the pants, she made her way to the crosswalk just behind her and waited for the light to turn green. To her right, a group of rowdy British teenage girls were on their way back from the beach, towels slung over their shoulders and cheeks as red as if they'd been slapped, while on her left a Sikh with a white beard and an ostentatious turban was shouting at the phone he was holding out in front of him. Presumably he was recording a voice message, but his actions had the amusing effect of making him look like he was yelling at the poor phone itself.

Nuria looked around her, distractedly taking in the diverse crowd defying the humid midafternoon heat around her. Most were foreigners: blonde, blue-eyed, Nordic families, Japanese tourists newly disembarked from a cruise, German retirees wearing socks and sandals, Pakistanis offering trinkets with

7

flashing lights for sale, Nigerians selling knockoff handbags from the blankets they'd spread out … Nuria smiled happily. She loved all this diversity, the babble of different languages and the fact that no two faces were alike. Each person dressed, spoke, and did exactly as they pleased.

The light turned green and she'd started to cross when a white van that was going too fast stopped with a screech of brakes. Nuria turned toward the driver, urging him with her eyes to calm down.

He was a young North African with a scant beard and sunken eyes fixed on the ceiling of the van rather than on the traffic light, murmuring to himself as though praying. As Nuria stepped into the crosswalk and passed in front of the white van, the young man raised his hands to either side of his head, then covered his face with them, jogging a memory in her mind: a movie she'd seen days before in which a jihadist with a suicide vest had made the same gesture a moment before killing himself in front of a mosque in Iraq. Nuria froze.

The young man in the van did not appear to be wearing a suicide vest, though, only a wrinkled white shirt with horizontal black stripes. Nor could she see a detonator in his hand, as in the case of the terrorist in the movie. She suddenly felt annoyed with herself for allowing a poor young man who was just praying in the middle of traffic to alarm her. If it had been a white man crossing himself, she wouldn't have given it a second thought. Shaking her head, she reproached herself for that glimmer of xenophobia.

The young North African moved his hands away from his face. Nuria averted her gaze with a hint of shame and their eyes met. As the light turned green, the young man's sunken eyes fixed on her with indescribable hatred. Though streaks of sweat were running down his forehead, not even the afternoon heat could justify that look. His hands gripped the wheel so tightly his knuckles whitened and a cruel grin appeared on his face as he savagely bared his teeth.

Nuria knew at once there was something wrong with him. It was only when the other drivers began to lean on their horns, urging her to move out of the way, that she realized she was still in the middle of the street. The young man, seeming not to care that she was in his way, went on glaring at her as if trying to strike her dead with his gaze.

The honking of the other drivers was now joined by indignant voices yelling at her to get out of their damn way. Nuria was aware of the growing crescendo of insults, but she couldn't take her eyes off that sweating young man, who very slowly started to shake his head.

Even if he wasn't wearing a vest loaded with dynamite, she was sure something was wrong with him. Something terrible, something that was making him look at her as a predator would a cornered victim.

Unexpectedly, somebody grabbed her arm and she jumped. "Are you all right, child?" an elderly woman beside her asked.

Nuria turned to her as if awakening from a dream. "Huh?" she asked blankly. "Yes, yes, I'm fine, thanks. It's just that … that man is up to something." She pointed at the young North African.

"You're stopping the traffic," the kind old lady pointed out, tugging at her and ignoring the warning. "Come to the sidewalk, my dear."

"No, ma'am." Nuria pulled back, straining her neck in search of a police officer. "I've got to warn someone. He's up to something, I'm sure of it."

"Come on, child," insisted the old woman, determined to get her out of the way. Nuria couldn't spot an officer anywhere, only casual strollers and irate drivers, honking their horns.

"Move over, you moron!" one of them yelled at her, leaning out his window with his fist raised. Could nobody else see it? How was it possible? The young man had the word *danger* written on his forehead. And his eyes: those sunken black eyes could only belong to a madman or a murderer.

"Get out of the street!" someone shouted.

"Out of the way, you lunatic!" another added amid a sonata of horns and angry gestures.

The old woman's bony fingers clawed at her arm, insistently trying to pull her back to the sidewalk. "Come, child," she urged her. "Come away from here. These people can be rough, you know."

"But …" She pointed at the white van, still stopped in front of her. "The driver … I …"

"Yes, yes, dear," the stubborn old woman insisted. "But let's keep moving."

The situation was making Nuria feel impotent, unable either to make people see what she saw or to maintain the precarious status quo any longer. There was no sense in staying there blocking the traffic. All she would accomplish was to make some unhinged driver get out of his car and shove her out of the street.

"Fine," she said at last, giving in. Without taking her eyes off the young man in the striped shirt, she regained the safety of the sidewalk just as the traffic light turned yellow.

Nuria memorized the name of the rental company displayed on the side of the vehicle, but the light turned red and the van moved forward just as she was about to look at the license plate. She raised her gaze to the van. For the last time, her eyes met those of the boy, who gave her one final scornful look as he slammed his foot down on the accelerator and, with another screech of tires, shot past her in the direction of Las Ramblas.

At the sound, those around her finally turned to look. Together they watched as the Fiat van gained speed and jumped the curb of the pedestrian

9

walkway, then plowed into the hundreds of strolling people, flinging them into the air and driving over them, crushing them mercilessly.

A second later the screaming began.

1

Eleven years later

A mass of Saharan air saturated with suspended dust and sand particles hung over Barcelona, enveloping it in a dense, hot, ocher mist. It had swept in from the south the week before like an intangible tsunami. Upon reaching the city the mass had found the Collserola mountain range barring its way and had remained trapped there ever since. It had been so long since there had been any wind or rain that the sticky mist ended up adhering to every pore of the city: cars, streets, clothing, and even the pedestrians' hair, like a layer of dirty makeup that had to be washed away every evening when the residents got home.

The combination of the dirty mist, the contamination, the humidity, and the intense heat was becoming intolerable, and it was no longer news that the hospital emergency wards were flooded with children, old people, and asthmatics, clinging to oxygen masks in the corridors and waiting rooms.

Nobody debated any longer whether global warming was a real threat. Instead, they talked about how far-reaching the effects would be and what could be done to reverse them. On social networks the phenomenon had even been given its own hashtag: *#TheRevengeoftheEarth*.

Swarms of motorbikes, bicycles, and electric scooters zoomed nervously along the Gran Vía, snaking through the jam of buses and electric cars along with the few conventional vehicles that had permission to drive in the city center on days like this. The old gray Toyota Prius, scratched and dented, was just one of many—except for the fact that it was an undercover car used by the police. It currently carried two undercover agents.

Corporal Nuria Badal brushed a lock of hair from her forehead and looked around with her almond-shaped green eyes. She couldn't remember a worse summer than the one they were still enduring. Recent summers had been hot, hotter each year, it was true. But they were already almost into autumn and the police cruiser's dashboard display showed an unbearable one hundred eleven degrees. Nuria shivered at the prospect of leaving the vehicle and facing the outside temperature, though she knew that sooner or later she would have no choice.

"As if we didn't have enough with the pollution," she muttered angrily. "This was all we needed."

"They say it's because of the thermal inversion," Sergeant David Insúa said from the seat beside her as he leaned forward to look at the sky through the windshield.

"And what does that mean?"

"Not a clue," he admitted, still looking at the yellowish sky. "I heard it on Google News this morning."

"Wow, you're a fount of knowledge."

"At least I follow the news."

"As if that were any use," muttered Nuria. She was watching a man with his hair gelled back reading the newspaper in the back seat of a streamlined Mercedes as it passed them, an invisible driver at the wheel. "We should have waited till evening to go out. We could have spent the rest of the day at the air-conditioned station."

"We couldn't do that," David argued, knowing she already knew what he was about to say. "Vilchez's message was urgent."

"Do you think he's decided to talk?"

"I don't know. But if he has, we can't risk him changing his mind."

"Even so," Nuria insisted, her tone teasing, "I'm sure a couple hours more wouldn't make him change his mind. I don't see the urgency, and we could have spared ourselves the traffic."

She wasn't really serious. At least, not completely. For several months they'd been squeezing information about Elias Zafrani out of Vilchez drop by drop, and the fact that Vilchez had called them to his own house was so risky for him it could only mean he'd decided to come clean. After almost two years of fruitless investigation, Wilson Vilchez's testimony could finally send one of the biggest kingpins in the Barcelona trafficking business to prison.

"That's enough out of you," David quipped with a smile. "If you're bored, turn off the autopilot and drive yourself." Nuria grunted in protest, but took the wheel with both hands, deactivating the self-driving function.

"Which way do you want us to go in?" she asked. "East or west?"

David took a moment to decide. "East. If we drive through Villarefu, they'll send out a warning that we're there immediately. We'd better go through the east entrance and walk to the house."

She raised her eyebrows. "Walk?" she snorted. "All right … your call." Her partner glanced at her out of the corner of his eye with a conspiratorial smile. Although he outranked her, years of being partners in a string of investigations had forged a bond of trust and respect between them that went beyond official rankings. For all practical purposes they treated each another as equals, and very rarely did David impose his opinion by pulling rank.

"Headquarters," Nuria said, raising her voice to activate the communication system. "Corporal Badal calling, ID 2117."

"Sergeant Insúa, ID 5862," said David.

"Headquarters, go ahead," replied the impersonal voice of the AI through the loudspeaker.

"Is the subject still stationary?"

"Affirmative. His activity bracelet indicates he hasn't moved in the last two hours."

"Okay, thanks. ETA ten minutes."

"Copy."

"Headquarters, do we have an aerial visual?" David asked.

"Negative," the voice replied. "No support drone has been authorized."

"What a surprise," Nuria muttered under her breath.

"Request corporal to repeat, please."

"Nothing. It was nothing. Stand by," David said, cutting off the call.

Nuria glanced at the dashboard screen, checking the signal of Vilchez's bracelet coming from the slum around them. "Why do you bother asking about the drone?" she said. "You know there's no budget. They'd never authorize one just to go talk to a possible witness."

"I feel more comfortable when there's one over my head, covering my ass."

Nuria winked at him. "Don't fret. I'll make sure nothing happens to your ass."

David eyed her speculatively. "I'd rather have the drone."

Nuria clicked her tongue and her angular features widened into a broad smile. "Jerk."

David had turned forty the month before, but if it weren't for his silvered temples and the hair that was beginning to thin on his crown, nobody looking at his youthful, unlined face would have thought him over thirty. Not quite her height, he must have squeezed into the *Mossos d'Esquadra* by a hair, just before the reunification of all the security organizations under the umbrella of the new Unified National Police. His friendly face and the ever-present smile in his gray eyes had little to do with the supposed image of a tenacious detective, but this fact had proved useful to him, allowing him to pass unnoticed. Many tended to underestimate him because he looked like a timid encyclopedia salesman. Suspects often tended to realize their mistake too late when, without quite knowing how it had happened, they found themselves with their faces pushed into the ground, hands cuffed behind their backs. David was an excellent officer, and together, he and Nuria were one of the finest teams in the department.

He pointed ahead. "Take this way here, and let's cross through Hospitalet. It'll take longer, but it'll be less conspicuous."

"Good idea," Nuria agreed. She turned the wheel.

As soon as they left the highway, the urban landscape changed dramatically, as if they'd landed in a completely different city: neglected blocks of public housing, dusty streets, jellabas, scarves, and turbans framing darker-skinned faces. Through the tinted windows, Nuria contemplated the transformation of a neighborhood she remembered visiting frequently ten years before. It had been around 2019, when she hadn't yet joined the Police Academy and one of her best friends would invite her to free drinks at the disco where she worked from Thursday to Sunday. Another time. Another life.

A life that had begun to change not long afterwards when the Coronavirus pandemic had relegated them all to their homes for months. By the time they were allowed back in the streets the pandemic had devastated the health, the economy, and the freedoms of the entire world, especially Spain. A red line had been crossed that ill-fated year after which nothing had gone back to normal: tens of thousands had died as a result of the virus and millions had lost their jobs and were forced to survive on the paltry income provided by the government. The cuts had swollen the rolls of the welfare system as never before, and the temporary social control measures—the use of surveillance cameras and mobile devices—though at the time gladly accepted in the fight against the epidemic, had become a permanent part of people's lives and online presence.

Only a few years later, adding insult to injury, more than a million terrified refugees from North Africa, fleeing the atrocities of the Islamic State of Maghreb, had crossed the Strait of Gibraltar in less than a month on board anything that would float.

At the time the Spanish government, weakened, its resources depleted, overcome by the scale of the avalanche, could do no more than attempt to contain the uncontainable. By the time the controversial orders were issued from Moncloa Palace to stop any ship, barge, or boat that came near the beaches—using force if necessary—there were already hundreds of thousands of refugees wandering the Iberian peninsula with nowhere to go—until they began to erect shantytowns next to the country's largest cities.

In Barcelona, many had congregated and built a camp, consisting of tents and shacks, in what until then had been the Llobregat Agricultural Park, a mile and a half to the south of the city. Six years later, the slum was still there. Nobody believed its inhabitants would ever return to countries that no longer even existed, countries sunk deep in the chaos that was now North Africa, the result of an identical process that had begun twenty years before in the Middle East. History was not only repeating itself, it was getting worse.

Now that improvised refugee camp had mutated into a slum consisting of shacks built of wood and cinderblock, and the initial twenty thousand refugees had grown into more than sixty thousand men, women, and children who threatened to spill across the boundary line of the Llobregat River.

Faced with the impossibility of fencing in a space that was growing like a cancer, the only solution the government had come up with was to seed the slum and its irregular boundaries with surveillance towers and sensors, as well as security checkpoints for vehicles at the entrances.

The towers with their security cameras and the vehicle checkpoints maintained the illusion that Villarefu, as it was popularly known, was being kept under a certain degree of control, but the reality was very different. Although there were controls limiting the refugees' entering and leaving the camp, the same could not be said for their legal and illegal activities, which were tolerated with the aim of keeping the population just above the poverty line. Simply put, allowing them to break the law inside their slum was considerably more convenient than letting them do so outside it.

The result had been that nobody lived on the periphery of Villarefu if they had any opportunity to live elsewhere. Like crabs faced with the rising tide, part of the population of the nearby villages moved to more distant ones, leaving behind a no-man's-land of abandoned apartments where the Spaniards who had lost everything in the last crisis had settled, creating a sort of buffer zone between the shantytown and the still-prosperous city of Barcelona. A situation which, though few admitted it, had been good for almost everybody.

"My parents used to live a few blocks from here," David said suddenly, perhaps noticing Nuria's expression. "Next to the Espanyol Stadium." Nuria gave him an inquisitive look. "They went back to Galicia in 2019," he added, obvious relief in his voice. "Before everything went to shit."

For a moment, Nuria wondered whether "everything" meant the neighborhood or the world in general. She decided it could be both. "Did you go out with Gloria last night?" she asked, to change the subject.

"We couldn't find anyone to stay with the kid," her partner grumbled.

"Bummer. I've already told you that if you two want to go out, I can, you know, stay with him."

"Yeah, sure, maybe one of these days."

Nuria stared at him. "You don't trust me."

"What? No, of course not!"

"You don't trust me to look after Luisito for a couple of hours."

"No, it's just that ..." He gave her a sidelong glance. "Well, okay, you're right. You have to admit you don't exactly have a way with kids."

"Of course I do. I'm very good with them."

David burst out laughing. "Nuria," he said. "I still remember the day you cuffed one and read him his rights."

"He was aiming at me."

"With a water pistol."

"It could've been gasoline."

"But it wasn't, and he was twelve years old."

"Old enough to learn that you have to respect the police. Do you think that's wrong?"

David shook his head and gave in. "Fine. The next time we need a babysitter, we'll call you."

"No, you won't," Nuria grumbled.

David was about to contradict her but found he couldn't. "You're right." He gave her a frank smile. "I won't."

Just then the navigation system indicated that they should turn left. Nuria took the exit, entering an industrial zone of old gable-roofed brick buildings that had been abandoned to their fate, hollow corpses that had fallen victim to automation and the economic protectionism that had moved the factories back to Germany, Japan, and the United States.

But though the last crisis might have been brutal in the industrialized countries, the rest of the world had suffered much more. Starvation decimated the population from Brazil to Indonesia like a plague with no cure in sight.

Five hundred yards ahead, they reached the end of the old industrial zone. They crossed one of the bridges that spanned the river and, following a bumpy road, were soon confronted by the irregular silhouette of Villarefu, a shabby skyline of tin roofs dominated by steel towers sixty feet high, spiky with cameras. Over time, though the slum had been built by North African and sub-Saharan refugees fleeing from the war, an indeterminate number of Chinese, Latin Americans, and Pakistanis had settled there too, employing themselves in petty smuggling, forgery, and trading in anything that could be bought or sold. Wherever a particular need surfaced, someone who was ready to do business would always appear, in obedience to a law as immovable as that of gravity, or Murphy.

In front of them was the main entrance with its intimidating surveillance towers. All incoming and outgoing merchandise passed through here. It was a bottleneck where a dozen trucks waited their turn to be searched by a handful of bored private-security guards, as unenthusiastic about searching them as the drivers were to have their trucks searched.

"Hell," Nuria muttered, checking out the line of trucks between them and the main entrance. "This could take more than an hour."

"Let's go to the southern entrance," David suggested. "There's never anybody there." Nuria nodded. Without a word, she turned the vehicle around and took a detour that led them to the perimeter road. David was looking at the impressive wall. "Remember when all this was cultivated land?"

"Of course I remember. I'm not as young as that."

"If someone had told me then that years later it would turn into a fucking *favela* I wouldn't have believed it."

16

"Yeah," she agreed. "I guess despite everything, you always think that something like this will never happen near your own home."

"Until it does," David said with a trace of melancholy.

The Prius was now going eighteen miles an hour, enduring the irritating black-and yellow-striped speed bumps set every fifty yards. At that speed Nuria had time to see the changes that had taken place since the last time she'd been here, only a few months back. Almost none of the white ACNUR tents remained, the tin shacks had multiplied, and a number of the precarious cinderblock structures had risen one or even two more stories. Once the camp had reached the limit marked by the highways and the river, it had grown in the only direction it could: upwards.

"Life finds a way," Nuria murmured.

"What was that?"

"Sorry, I ... I was just thinking out loud. About what'll happen when there's no more room for the people."

"I guess they'll go elsewhere."

"Where?"

"I don't know, Nuria." David clicked his tongue. "They'll find something. It's not as if you or I can do anything about it, can we? We've got our own problems."

A half mile ahead Nuria stopped the car gently at the southern gate. It was smaller, and as they had expected, had less traffic. An obese security guard wearing a bulky bulletproof vest and carrying a scanner opened the door of his glass-paneled booth and approached the Prius with an annoyed expression. "You got a pass?" he barked at Nuria as she lowered her window. She took her badge out of her pocket, displaying it with a flourish in front of his nose.

"Oh, okay. I'd taken you for ..." The guard trailed off when he realized he was babbling. Nuria raised her brows impatiently. At once the guard stepped back and opened the gate with the remote, waving them through with the usual hand motion as if it were a display of personal magnanimity on his part.

The moment they were inside the Prius began to rattle over the patchy gravel that covered the streets of the slum. Villarefu was a city in itself, inhabited by the pariahs most deeply affected by the pandemic and the process of global warming that had driven a hundred million sub-Saharans to North Africa, desperate to escape starvation and drought.

It had been a migration the likes of which the world had never seen before, and it caused a chain reaction that ended in military coups in Morocco and Algeria. These were followed by civil war in both countries and the cherry on top, the rebirth of the Islamic Maghreb, which like Syria fifteen years earlier had taken advantage of the troubled waters to sow chaos and terror with a Koran in one hand and a Kalashnikov in the other. The next domino fell when more than a

17

million North African refugees, fleeing the war, stormed the nearby shores of Spain in whatever they could find that would float, like some desperate version of the Normandy landings.

The haphazard streets of Villarefu were as empty as they'd expected at that time of day, with the temperatures off the charts. The only evidence that the place hadn't been abandoned after some sudden emergency were the scattered groups of men in jellabas smoking in the shade of the few trees and the noise of televisions turned up to maximum volume.

Nuria noticed that the Prius's navigator screen now showed no streets or structures, as if the area still consisted of the agricultural fields it once had been. It was as if Google hadn't considered it worth the effort to update it on its maps, seeing that when all was said and done, nobody lived here legally. Nobody they cared about, at least.

Just ahead, the irregular street narrowed until it was only a little wider than the vehicle. Nuria stopped the car. "How far is it to Vilchez's house?" she asked, looking out the window warily as if they were in the middle of a minefield.

David opened his cellphone and checked the screen.

"Seven hundred ninety yards."

"Shit."

"Don't whine. Are you wearing your vest?"

"My vest? In this heat?"

"Goddamn it, Nuria!" he snapped, furious. "Don't you dare get out of the car without—" Before he could finish his sentence she grinned, raising her shirt to show the thick black material of the bulletproof vest.

"Why do you get off so much on teasing me?" he protested. "You know it pisses me off."

"But I enjoy it." Her smile widened. Putting a finger to her forehead, she added, "Besides, there's a vein right here that stands out—"

David shook his head theatrically. "Jesus Christ ... what I have to put up with." Clicking the glove compartment open, he took out his dust mask and the obligatory goggles complete with minicam and earbuds that would keep him connected every second to Nuria and headquarters.

His partner had done the same, and her voice echoed in his head. "One, two, one, two, copy?" she said, her voice muffled by the mask.

"Loud and clear. Headquarters?"

"Copy both of you. Activate cameras."

The two officers pressed a red button on the bridge of their goggles, activating the tiny recording device. Everything they saw and heard from that moment on would be recorded and would serve as courtroom evidence.

Putting on a dirty Barça cap, David turned to his partner. "Ready?"

She nodded, adjusting her chestnut ponytail, bleached golden by the sun, under her own SpongeBob cap. "Let's go."

2

Although she was expecting it, the blast of heat as she stepped out of the car met her like a punch in the face. Though the comparison was hardly original, Nuria could only think of it as putting her head in the oven. A reeking oven, in this case.

"Jesus, what a stink!" she protested at once, barely able to contain the impulse to cover her nose with her hand. David nodded toward a heap of garbage bags surrounding a cluster of containers, a flock of seagulls hovering over them.

"The odd thing would be if it *didn't* stink."

"Fuck," Nuria gasped. "With this heat and that nauseating smell on top of it … it's like someone's cooking rotten fish."

"We'll put a bad review on Tripadvisor," David said shortly. "Now let's go, so we can get this over with as soon as possible."

Leaving the vehicle behind, they set off along the route that appeared superimposed on their goggles to guide them to their destination. The dusty streets of hard-packed earth narrowed as they went deeper into that city inhabited by people with no country, no rights, and little hope. It was not a particularly dangerous place, but it did no harm to stay alert, since it was obvious from a mile away that they were police officers and there was always the possibility that some lunatic might do something stupid.

Both sides of the street were lined with one-story shacks built out of construction scraps with sheet-metal roofs, although a fair number of them boasted wooden walls. Here and there were occasional exceptions with cinderblock walls and barred windows, dwellings that, in comparison, must have looked like luxury villas to the slum's other inhabitants.

Nuria made a private bet with herself that the relative prosperity of those homeowners was owed to illegal activities, and that with a search warrant they would be sure to find drugs, dirty money, and illegal software.

But she hadn't come here for that. The goal this time was to meet with Vilchez and drag a statement out of him that would stand up in court. If it wasn't enough to put Elias Zafrani behind bars for life, at least it would keep him out of circulation for a while.

The people who worked for Elias were either very loyal or else so terrified of their boss that it was impossible to get an incriminating word out of them. They didn't even dare say his name. All this meant that the chance to obtain some testimony from Vilchez that could tie Zafrani to some crime or other was too good to pass up.

"We stick out like a sore thumb," Nuria said. Her whisper reached David through his earbuds. "There's not a soul in the street."

"In this heat, it'd be weird if there *was* anyone here."

"Either that or they saw us arrive and word's gotten around." Nuria glanced at her partner and then down at herself. "We've got *cop* written on our foreheads." They were both wearing faded jeans, old T-shirts, and athletic shoes, but anybody watching would have known they were strangers—and there was only one kind of stranger who would ever dare stroll into Villarefu so nonchalantly.

"Yeah, I know," David replied. "But there's nothing we can do about that."

"I just hope our friend doesn't scare easily. I wouldn't like to have to—" she began, eyes on her cellphone, then stopped abruptly. "Shit!"

"What?"

Nuria showed him the screen. There was no red dot blinking on it. "What the fuck?" David swore. "Headquarters! We've lost the subject's signal!"

"Affirmative. The signal has vanished. His monitor has been deactivated."

David and Nuria exchanged a look of concern. There could only be two reasons for an ankle monitor to stop working so abruptly: either because the wearer was trying to hide or because he'd stopped breathing. Neither possibility was promising.

With no need for words, they pulled out their guns in unison, adopting a defensive stance with their backs against the nearest wall. "Headquarters," Nuria called, feeling a surge of adrenaline flood through her, "send us the last known location of the signal."

"Sending," came the impersonal voice in their ears. A second later a black circle appeared on their screens, less than two hundred yards from where they were standing. Glancing briefly at each other, they set off at a run toward it, turning left and right, heedless by now of whether they were attracting attention or the fact that several heads appeared in the windows as they passed.

Three minutes of snaking through shacks and alleys brought them to Vilchez's address, a narrow cinderblock house with no room for windows boxed in between two identical neighbors.

Nuria pointed to the peeling wooden door. "This is it." A rusty lock hung from the end of a loose chain which served to keep the door closed, a sign that the owner was home.

"On three," David whispered into Nuria's earbud.

21

She nodded, then without giving her partner time to react, shouted, "Three!" and kicked the door open. Arms extended, holding her Walther PPK out in front of her, Nuria burst into the house. No lights were on, and the absence of windows meant the only illumination came from the open door. Like a spotlight at her back, it outlined her shadow crisply.

She stepped aside to let David in. As he passed, he whispered in her ear: "You and I are going to have a talk about this." Without stopping, he moved forward carefully to the middle of the space. What was presumably the living room was no more than four walls decorated with a couple of posters of Pope Pio XIII looking beatific and an outdated calendar showing a big-breasted Latina woman on a Harley. Also pinned to the wall was a solitary unframed photo of Vilchez himself standing in front of a church next to a middle-aged woman with Andean features and three children of different ages, all in their Sunday best.

The place smelled shut up, combined with the odors of mold and rotten fruit—perhaps to be expected in a house without a single window. In the middle of the room, like a pathetic little island, sat a red plastic table with a Coca-Cola logo, flanked by two grimy wooden stools. Under a pitted mirror on the opposite wall was a pile of clothes, old shoes, and garbage next to a television set on an empty fruit crate.

Like a sad white pear, a naked bulb hung from the ceiling, but there was neither a switch visible nor the time to look for one. From somewhere outside, a radio blared the latest hit cumbia of the summer:

I know I said I wasn't coming,
I know you didn't know I was here,
But look, baby, now you know
Now you know I'm here for you.

Lowering his mask, David put a finger to his lips and pointed to the hallway at the far end of the room, then turned the finger on himself and widened his eyes in a warning. This time, he would go first.

The laser beams of their guns traced two thin red lines in the darkness, dust motes glinting in the shafts of light as they pierced the shadows of the hallway. The heat inside the house was a little less suffocating than outside, but even so, drops of perspiration pearled on Nuria's forehead. She wiped them off with the back of her hand before they could drip into her eyes, but she could feel the sweat sliding down the nape of her neck and drenching her skin under the stifling bulletproof vest.

The wooden floorboards creaked with every step, making any attempt to go unnoticed impossible. Even so, they moved down the hallway slowly, side by side, sweeping the air with their laser beams, unable to see much beyond the crosshairs of their guns. The house had been crammed into the limited space separating the two buildings on either side, perhaps occupying what had been an

22

alley. It was little more than a seemingly interminable hallway whose end was unclear.

"Headquarters," whispered David, "any other signal in our location?" Silence. "Headquarters?" he insisted, raising his voice a little. "Do you copy?" A barely audible sound of static met his ears.

It was Nuria's turn to try. "Headquarters, Corporal Badal here. Do you copy?" More static. Turning toward David, she said, "Looks like we've both lost the connection."

"That's weird," he said, tapping his activity bracelet, which also lacked a signal. "This never happened to me before."

"Maybe the network's down?" Nuria suggested.

"I suppose so," he agreed. There seemed to be no other explanation.

"So what do we do? Go on?"

David nodded firmly. "Of course," he said, setting off again. Shoulder to shoulder, they ventured deeper into the house that reminded Nuria of an enormous lair. One careful step after another. Slowly. The dense, heavy air enveloped them like the last breath of a dying man as the faint sound of an African soap opera chattered meaninglessly from a distant television.

There was a surreal absence of sounds and casual voices, as if the entire neighborhood were maintaining an expectant silence, waiting for the outcome of this drama with their ears pressed to the wall. Most harrowing of all was the unbearable feeling that someone hiding in the shadows was watching them in silence. Nuria clenched her jaw, telling herself to stop imagining things, but the tremor in her partner's voice told her she wasn't the only one doing it.

"I think we ought to—" *Crack*! A snap like the noise of a twig breaking echoed at the end of the hall. "Police!" David bellowed into the emptiness. "Come out with your hands in the air!"

Silence.

"Wilson Vilchez?" Nuria shouted, her voice reassuring. "Are you there? Don't be afraid. We just want to ask you a few questions."

Silence.

They waited several seconds for a reply. In vain.

"Fuck!" Nuria muttered through clenched teeth. "To hell with it." Once again, without waiting for David, she took three long strides, reaching a doorway off the corridor, closed off by a heavy curtain. The endless hallway went on beyond her, but as soon as David arrived at her side—this time without comment—Nuria nudged the curtain aside with her gun and put her head inside.

In one corner of the ceiling a tiny opening allowed the daylight to filter into the room, revealing plastic buckets, a fridge, a gas stove connected to a butane tank, and dirty pots and plates scattered across a filthy countertop.

"Kitchen," Nuria stated briefly and immediately added: "Clear." Dropping the curtain, she returned her attention to the gloomy hallway. Narrow. Dark. Grim. Radiating the inescapable feeling that a pair of eyes was stalking them.

And there was something else. A disagreeable gurgling sound, or perhaps a muffled moan, at the edge of their awareness. Impossible to discern whether the sounds were real or a product of her imagination.

Putting the thought out of her mind, Nuria followed David as he strode forward decisively. The absurd hallway that seemed to have no end wound on, finally ending up at the doorway to another room, also closed with an oilcloth curtain.

This time it was David who pushed her to one side. There was no light in the room. Nuria moved to stand beside him. Without lowering her gun, she swept her left hand over the door-frame until she located what she was looking for: an electric cord stapled to the wall. She followed it with her fingers until she reached the switch, then turned it on. A low-wattage bulb on the ceiling blinked on, illuminating the room.

David stepped back in shock.

"Oh my God ..." Nuria muttered, holding back her nausea.

3

They'd found Wilson Vilchez. Or at least, what was left of him. On an old bed lay the lifeless body of a middle-aged man with American Indian features, tied hand and foot, staining the mattress with the blood that still ebbed from his throat that had been slit from ear to ear in a sinister scarlet smile.

But what truly horrified Nuria was that the killer hadn't been content to slit his victim's throat but had then reached in, taken Vilchez's tongue and pulled it through the cut, from where it now protruded like a macabre joke.

As soon as she was able to shake off her momentary paralysis and the urge to vomit, she holstered her gun and approached the bed to check the body's pulse. David wasn't surprised when she looked up and shook her head. Turning toward him, she said, "He's still warm."

"Headquarters," David said. "Send a forensic team to these coordinates. We have a body." No answer. "Headquarters?" he repeated. Silence. "Shit, still no signal."

Meanwhile Nuria was comparing Vilchez's image on her cellphone with the slaughtered man on the bed. "Confirmed, it's Vilchez."

"Awesome," David snorted.

For a few seconds both stood in an uncomfortable silence. Shouts on the soap opera filled the emptiness of the room like a mocking echo of what had taken place there minutes before.

"A Colombian necktie," he said.

"What?" Nuria asked. Had she heard right?

"What they've done to his tongue." David swallowed, unable to take his eyes off the corpse. "It's called a Colombian necktie. It's a message. A warning."

"A warning? Who for?"

He turned toward her. "For everyone. It's a way of suggesting what'll happen to anyone who intends to collaborate with the police. But most of all"—he passed a hand over his forehead to wipe away the sweat—"it's a message for us."

Nuria looked again at the tongue lolling out of the throat in a grotesque grimace, understanding what her partner was talking about. "You think—"

Crack! The dry sound of creaking wood interrupted her sentence before she could finish it. Instinctively, she drew her gun again and flattened herself against the wall. David did the same, taking up a position beside the door, gun at the ready. He nodded to Nuria and she covered him as he burst out into the hallway, aiming his gun into the darkness.

"Police!" he yelled. "Identify yourself and come out with your hands where I can see them!" Nuria came out after him and stood at his back, also aiming toward the entrance. There was no answer.

"The door," whispered David. It took her a moment to understand what he meant. The door to the house, the one she'd kicked open moments before, was now shut. Someone had closed it while they were inside. Someone who wanted to keep them in the dark.

"Shit," Nuria muttered under her breath. "The flashlights are in the car."

"Turn on your cellphone," David ordered.

"What—"

He cut her off before she'd finished her sentence. "Put the flashlight on and throw the phone over there."

Guessing his intentions, Nuria threw her cellphone a few yards down the hallway. The light illuminated the middle of the passage but revealed nothing but cobwebs. Both officers waited in silence without moving a muscle for more than thirty seconds.

"Maybe it closed by itself," David ventured, persuading himself, "and the noise came from the house next door."

"Maybe."

"It would be absurd for whoever did this to the witness not to have left already, seeing as he had the chance to escape."

"Of course."

"Absurd," he repeated.

For the first time in the more than two years they'd been partners, Nuria perceived a note of fear in David's voice. They'd been in worse situations, certainly, even in a couple of shootouts, but on those occasions they'd acted instinctively, without stopping to consider what they were doing. The fear had come later, when the bullets had stopped whistling through the air and the adrenaline had gone.

But now, aiming their weapons down a simple hallway enveloped in shadows, every possible evil that might be waiting to happen opened up in their minds like a sinister fan. *And at headquarters they don't even know we're in here*, Nuria thought uneasily. "What do we do?" she whispered.

In the weak light from the room behind them, she saw David close his eyes briefly and take a deep breath before saying, "There's only one thing we can do."

Moving with extreme caution, alert to any noise or movement, they retraced their steps along the twisting hallway toward the entrance. It had been a terrible idea to face an unknown situation blindly, without support. Keeping strictly to the manual, they could have stayed in the victim's room and waited for reinforcements to arrive. Officially no one would have blamed them.

Unofficially, though, it was an entirely different situation. The camera in her goggles was registering everything that went on inside the house. Anyone checking the images recorded up to that moment from their comfortable seat behind a desk at the station might conclude that they looked like a couple of old ladies scared by a door slamming.

No. There was no way they could stay hidden. They would be the laughingstock of the department and the shadow of cowardice would hang over them until the end of their careers.

"Do you see anything?"

"Not a fucking thing," David muttered. The laser beams of their guns traced erratic shapes before them, but offered not the slightest trace of information about what lay ahead. All the same, every step they took in the absence of movement or new noises made them feel calmer and more confident.

They passed the small kitchen, once again entering the space that served as a living room. The singer on the radio bawled out his absurd refrain:

Baby, you know I love yoooooou
And here I am, all of me
All of me for yoooou.....

In the living room they checked to verify that everything was the same as before, and that they were indeed alone in the house.

David lowered his gun. "All right," he said, taking a deep breath in ill-concealed relief. "That's it. There's nobody here but us."

"Fucking door," Nuria swore. She'd opened it again and was trying to prop it open with something so it wouldn't close again by itself. "You scared the shit out of us."

A cloud of dust entered the shack together with the daylight. Nuria's eyes took a moment to adjust as the heat dried the drops of perspiration on her forehead. "You know what?" she said, turning to David. "It's hard to believe that—"

The words died on her lips.

David stood in the middle of the room behind the plastic table. The square of light that came through the door reached the toes of his shoes, fading as it ascended as if lacking the courage to go further. Nuria's gaze traveled up David's jeans, passing the Toyota keychain hanging from his pocket, the belt with his gun hanging from it, his sweat-stained shirt, to his shoulders and finally, his neck. Pressed against his jugular, she saw the cold reflection of a barber's razor down whose edge ran a dark drop of blood.

27

Guided by pure instinct, before any conscious thought came into her mind, she raised her weapon. It was then that her gaze met David's. His eyes showed confusion, but even more, anger for letting himself be caught by surprise like a rookie. In them she saw no fear, but rather, an apology.

"I'm sorry," he murmured, fearing that raising his voice might increase the pressure of the blade at his throat. Nuria stopped looking at her partner and stared at the menacing blade that looked capable of slicing through David's neck without the slightest effort.

She ran her gaze along the edge as far as the handle, where a hand with thin fingers and nails smeared with Vilchez's blood led to an arm wrapped around David's torso. The arm belonged to a man partially hidden behind her partner's body. Only half his face was visible.

Unlike what they would have been in a scene from a movie, the features that half emerged were not those of some flat-nosed thug covered with piercings and tattoos, with a massive scar crossing his cheek. The man who had slit Vilchez's throat and was now holding the razor against David's jugular was so ordinary-looking he wouldn't have merited a second glance if he'd been a suspect in a police lineup. About forty years old, he had a shaved head and a delicate nose on which were propped thick-rimmed glasses that gave him the inoffensive look of a college professor. His face was framed by a thick, well-tended beard in the latest style.

Bloodshot blue eyes which, unafraid, were taking stock of her contradicted his harmless look: eyes which seemed to gauge whether what faced him was a possible threat or another victim. They were seeking to guess her reaction if he killed her partner, or perhaps calculating the time he would have to hurl himself at her before she took the first shot. Because they both knew she wouldn't have time for a second.

Taking a deep breath, Nuria aimed the red dot of the crosshairs at the center of the killer's forehead. In a soft, calm voice that surprised her, she said: "Let him go right now." The firmness in her voice left no room for any kind of negotiation. "Put your hands up, drop the blade, and take a step back. Now."

The man's only reply was an arrogant smile, showing perfect white teeth. The gesture told her he was delighted to be in this situation, his razorblade at the throat of a police officer and a gun aimed at his head from less than twelve feet away. She decided he must be a psychopath or a professional hit man. With her luck, he was probably both.

Nuria glanced for a moment at the far end of the room and realized that what had been a pile of clothes and garbage was now scattered across the floor. That was where he'd been hiding. Where he'd been waiting for them.

He'd had the chance to escape quietly, but instead had decided to wait and lure them in, as a spider might lure two stupid flies. A shudder froze her heart as Nuria understood that he'd never intended to escape.

No, he *wanted* to be there.

4

"I'm not telling you again. Drop the blade, now!"

David began to say something, but as he opened his mouth, the barber's razor slid a few millimeters, opening a thin cut through which blood began to trickle. His eyes widened.

"Shh ..." the killer said.

Nuria concentrated her efforts on speaking in an impossibly calm voice, but felt the words coming out of her mouth with a slight tremor. "Listen to me carefully. There's no way for you to escape." She couldn't show weakness when confronted with a maniac; she'd learned that on the first page of the criminal psychology manual. "But if you drop the razor now, you'll have a chance to get out of here alive." The killer smiled again, and Nuria realized she was getting nowhere. The problem was there was no other way.

The sound of distant police sirens reached her ears. Trying to keep her breathing steady as a wave of pure relief washed through her, Nuria imagined that when the signal to headquarters had been cut off they must have sent several units to their last known location.

"In two minutes this place will be crawling with officers," she said with renewed confidence. "If you haven't surrendered by then, a dozen of my colleagues are going to come in through that door keen to pull the trigger, and I can't guarantee one of them won't."

The man tilted his head like a bloodhound hearing a distant whistle, but didn't react either to her words or the ever-louder howling of the sirens. For a moment Nuria was afraid she was faced with a deaf killer. But that wasn't possible. Or was it? "Do you speak my language?" she asked.

He fixed his eyes on her with renewed intensity and the trace of a smile, but not a word came out of his mouth. At the same time he slid the razor once again along David's throat. Another thread of blood slid down his neck. Her partner's eyes seemed about to pop out of their sockets as he felt the cold steel edge penetrating his skin.

"Nu ... ria ..." he moaned unsteadily through barely parted lips.

"Don't do that, you son of a bitch!" she snarled, taking a step forward and reducing the distance between them, her weapon firm in her hands. The satisfied expression on the killer's face made her realize this was exactly what he wanted. Aware of the imminent arrival of the police patrol, he was provoking her into destroying their precarious status quo with a hasty movement. Provoking her into making a mistake.

Gazing into the bloodshot eyes of that unremarkable-looking man who had slit the throat of another man and mutilated him only minutes before and now faced a gun with the absurd indifference of a madman, Nuria realized there was no way this was going to end well. He wasn't going to surrender. He would slit David's throat with a swift cut and then hurl himself at her, and he would do it before the reinforcements arrived.

It was a question of seconds. Nuria's heart galloped in her chest. The gun she was holding suddenly seemed ten times heavier. It began to shake in her hands. A drop of perspiration slid down her forehead toward her right eye and she blinked involuntarily.

That was the chance the killer had been waiting for. Nuria saw it in his eyes a split second before he made his move. A howl of rage exploded in her chest as a cruel smirk curved the maniac's lips, and she knew that David, defenseless as a rag doll, was about to die.

Nuria did the only thing she could. Fixing her eyes on the crosshairs which shone on the killer's forehead and tensing the muscles of her forearm, she pulled the trigger. But at the exact moment when the firing pin hit the cartridge, expelling the lead bullet with a sharp crack, Nuria found to her horror that her target was no longer there.

In the tenth of a second her finger had taken to carry out the order from her brain to shoot, the killer, anticipating her reaction, had moved with impossible speed to his left, using David himself as a counterweight. When the bullet left the barrel of the gun in a cloud of gunpowder smoke, it was her partner's head which now blocked its way.

The red laser point was a herald of death, marking the exact spot between the pleading eyes of her partner, who seemed to understand at the last possible second what was about to happen.

The bullet hit him, snapping his head back like a spring. There was no chance for Nuria even to cry out. Her partner's body collapsed like a marionette whose strings had been cut. She watched as if in a dream as the man she'd shared patrols and confidences with for almost two years crumpled to the floor, lifeless, the victim of her own bullet. She stared at him without seeing him, her mind unable to process the reality of the horror.

Outside the hovel, the cumbia singer continued with his mournful, insistent lament:

Baby, you know I love yooooou ...

Overwhelmed by horror, Nuria was barely aware that the man with the razor was no longer in the same place. With inhuman agility he'd slipped out of her range of fire, crouching now in the shadows of the living room a couple of yards to her right, a predator, preparing to spring.

And here I am, all of me ...

Nuria's survival instinct guided her arm in his direction and she swung her gun toward the killer. Blinded by rage and panic, she pulled the trigger again and again before even centering her sights on him.

The razor's edge shone in the dark.

Waiting for yoooou ...

Ignoring her erratic gunshots, the predator hurled himself at her like a diabolical shadow escaped from the worst nightmare. Still shooting, Nuria threw herself backwards in a desperate attempt to distance herself from the blade that sliced the air with a sinister hiss an inch from her own neck.

Her blind leap ended when she crashed to the floor, the back of her neck hitting something blunt and hard. Nuria felt the strength draining from her and her vision darkened as if someone were drawing a curtain in front of her eyes. *Show's over*, she thought.

The last thing she saw before losing consciousness were the bloodshot eyes of the man about to kill her, dilated with excitement behind his thick-rimmed glasses. It seemed to Nuria that she pulled the trigger once more, but by that time she was unable to hear the report.

Everything faded to black.

5

"Ms. Badal?" There was no answer. "Ms. Badal?"

"Mm ..."

"Good morning." Nuria opened her eyes. The calm face of a middle-aged woman smiled cordially down at her, her hand resting on Nuria's shoulder. "How do you feel?" she asked, adjusting the pillow and raising the bed with an electric whirr.

The woman's white uniform had a blue cross on the breast and some tiny letters Nuria was unable to decipher. Her head ached as if someone had taken a hammer to it. Raising a hand to her forehead, she saw her own name written on a yellow plastic bracelet: *Badal, Nuria 57192028H.*

"My head hurts ..." she mumbled, her voice thick.

"Don't worry, it's normal considering the blow you received."

"The ... blow?"

The nurse's eyes lingered on her a second longer than necessary. "The doctor will be here presently. He'll explain everything."

Random images without apparent meaning like those from an interrupted dream she tried to remember the following morning began to file before her eyes, plunging her into even greater confusion. The image of a man with his throat slit and his tongue poking out of the gaping wound made her start and clutch the arm of the nurse who stepped back, alarmed.

"No!" Nuria cried, her heart suddenly racing. "No!"

"Calm down," the nurse said, prying Nuria's fingers from her arm and making an effort to maintain a soothing, professional tone of voice. "Everything's all right now. The doctor's on his way." Rubbing her forearm, she stepped away from the bed, focusing her attention on the drip flow and the blood-pressure and heart-rate monitors.

"What happened?" Nuria demanded, raising her voice. "How did I get here? How long have I been like this?" The nurse ignored her questions, injecting a few milliliters of transparent liquid into the IV tube. Nuria attempted to sit up. "Answer me!" But her mind clouded again and her strength failed her. Her head fell back on the pillow. "I have to speak ... speak ... to ..." Her tongue grew cottony and she could no longer remember what that important *something* she had to say was.

Removing the needle from the tube, the nurse gave her an understanding look. "Don't worry, hon. Rest a little longer and tomorrow you'll feel much better."

Nuria had no idea how many hours had gone by since the nurse had injected her with the sedative, but when she woke again, the light was slanting obliquely through the sheer curtains. It must be midafternoon by now.

The white-walled room she found herself in was modest, its only furniture a worn burgundy armchair in one corner, a folding chair, a small TV set hanging from the wall like an empty picture frame, and a small turquoise-green closet in the opposite corner. Nevertheless, the place was clean, it didn't smell of sweat or disinfectant and she had the room to herself. These observations told her she was in a private hospital and not one of the overcrowded public ones she'd visited so many times on duty, delivering victims and detainees.

Once again the images of what had happened burst into her memory. The smell of garbage, the suffocating heat, the sweat sliding down her neck, the deafening blast of gunshots, the gunpowder smoke burning her throat …

She fingered the buttons on the bedside remote until she found the call button, then pressed it again and again, her impatience growing. No more than five seconds had passed when a new nurse cracked the door and peered in.

"Nurse!" Nuria cried when she saw her. "I need to –"

"Just a moment, dear," the nurse interrupted her, raising her index finger and closing the door again.

Seeing her leave without explanation, Nuria called, "Nurse!" again. She pressed the red button furiously. A minute went by. She was ready to give up, sure that nobody was listening, when a man with thick, gelled-back, salt-and-pepper hair walked nonchalantly into the room. He looked at her over a pair of old-fashioned reading glasses, then took them off as he gave her a soothing smile.

"Good afternoon," he said with a professional air, tucking his glasses away in the pocket of his white lab coat. "I'm Dr. Martinez, and I'm in charge of your case. How do you feel?"

"Fine. I'm fine," she replied hurriedly. "Where am I? How did I get here? What … what happened?"

The doctor came over to the bed and set a hand on her shoulder as the nurse had done earlier that morning. It must be standard procedure for patients on the brink of hysteria, she thought.

"Too many questions, Nuria."

This sudden familiarity terrified her more than anything else. In her own experience it was usually a prelude to bad news. All at once, she was reluctant to ask any more questions.

Pointing to the logo at the level of his heart, the doctor said, "You're in the Valle Hebron MediCare Hospital. Yesterday you sustained a heavy blow to the back of the neck which left you concussed, and you've been under observation ever since. We haven't noticed any intracranial edema or fracture, so apart from the bump and a headache which will last for a few days, you're perfectly fine.

34

You'll be spending the night here under observation, just to make sure," he added, folding his arms, "but tomorrow morning you'll be able to go home."

Nuria listened to the diagnosis more out of courtesy than genuine interest. She couldn't have cared less about the bump or the headache. That wasn't what she needed to know with such unbearable urgency.

"How did I get here?" The memory of the razor flashing toward her throat made her shiver. "Why …?" She swallowed. "Why am I alive?"

The doctor studied her features, seemingly considering what to say. Her question must not have been one he had a cookie-cutter answer for. "I really don't know, to tell you the truth. Are you a believer?"

Now she was surprised. "I don't know … I'd say no. But what has this got to do with—"

"Perhaps nothing. Perhaps everything." Nuria now noticed the open collar of his lab coat. She glimpsed a thin silver chain and made a bet with herself that a Christian cross would be hanging at the end of it. "I don't know the details, but when your fellow officers brought you in they repeated the word *miracle* several times."

"I see …" Suddenly she was afraid she might be facing a member of the Reborn in Christ sect, with no escape in sight from his proselytizing.

Luckily for her, the doctor changed the subject. "But if you want more details," he said with a smile, "there are two of your colleagues in the waiting room. And your mother's here too."

"My mother?"

"She's been here since yesterday, waiting for you to wake up."

Nuria felt bad about not having given a second thought to her mother. The poor woman must be terribly worried. She could picture her praying nonstop, Bible in hand—she was definitely a militant Reborn—but in all honesty she didn't feel up to listening to her thanking God for half an hour, not to mention asking Nuria to the point of exhaustion whether she was *really* okay.

"Could I see … my colleagues?" The doctor blinked a couple of times, taken aback. "I need to know what happened before I speak to my mother."

"Of course, whatever you prefer. But first let me check a couple of things." Taking out his ophthalmoscope, he put it first to her left eye and then the right, checked her blood pressure on the monitor, and then, with a coldness he didn't bother to hide, took his leave, telling her he would notify her colleagues so they could come in to see her for a few minutes.

Her attempt to go and clean herself up a bit in front of the bathroom mirror was frustrated when she sat on the edge of her bed and felt her legs giving way under her when she tried to stand up. Faced with the possibility of tripping and her fellow officers walking in to find her sprawled on the floor in her hospital gown, she immediately gave up the idea. At least she could raise the hospital bed so she could sit up. She combed through her hair with her fingers, since there was no brush or ponytail holder available, and patted her cheeks to bring a little color into them.

The door opened and a man and woman in uniform came in, hats under their arms, looking formal. If she'd made a list of the officers she'd been expecting to walk through that door, these two would have been near the bottom.

"Hello, Nuria," they greeted her together as they came into the room, then bent over to kiss her on both cheeks. "How are you?"

"Carla, Raul." She looked from one to the other, making an effort not to appear nonplussed.

"Weren't you expecting us?"

"I ... no ... I mean ... how did you find out I was here?"

Carla squeezed her cap between her hands. "We were in the area when we got a call from headquarters."

"We were the first to arrive," Raul added.

Nuria could see the tension on both their faces and paused before asking the next question. "What happened?"

The uncomprehending look they both gave her was classic. "Hasn't anybody explained yet?" Carla asked.

"I've only just woken up, as they say."

"And you don't remember ... anything?"

Nuria guessed that her old fellow students from the Police Academy would have preferred to be anywhere else but there, talking to her. They must have drawn the short straw. "I remember more than I'd like to," she said, and closed her eyes for a moment. "But ... there are a lot of blanks. The last thing I remember was that madman trying to slit my throat with a razor, and—" She broke off, her face suddenly twisting into a grimace of horror. "Oh my God ... David."

6

Estela Jimenez's home was typical of someone born in the sixties, crammed with pictures on the walls, giant vases of plastic flowers in the corners, and useless gadgets—a rusty charcoal grill, a hand coffee grinder, a sewing machine, a turntable, each given its place of honor around the house: remnants of a time and place that no longer existed.

Nuria had arrived at her mother's house that morning after being discharged from the hospital. She'd sat down on the stiff living-room couch, her hands in her lap and her gaze on the ceiling fan that spun lazily over her head without saying a word. From the moment her mind had raised the curtain and shed light on the darkness of her memory she'd been absent and withdrawn, unable to weep or express the anxiety that had seized her, oppressing her chest as if someone had placed a granite slab on top of her.

She couldn't avoid seeing David collapsing over and over again, lifeless, a bullet hole in his forehead. The scene repeated itself like an ancient, scratched, vinyl record. Nuria could see nothing but his look of horror a millisecond before the bullet found his forehead. She could hear nothing but the blast of the gunshot, followed by the sound of his body crumpling to the floor.

Nuria covered her face with her hands, not to prevent her mother from seeing her expression of anguish, but in a desperate attempt to bar further images from her mind, as if they came from somewhere outside her own brain.

The bell of the microwave oven dinged like the end of a round in a boxing match and a pair of slippers dragged themselves from the kitchen, stopping in front of her. "Here, drink this. It'll do you good."

Nuria looked up and saw her mother standing there, holding a steaming cup from which dangled a label saying tila tea. A woman who spurned rejuvenating cosmetics as sinful, she looked every bit of her sixty-odd years. Her straight brown hair hung below her shoulders, framing a face that was kinder than Nuria remembered it from her childhood. Her mother's eyes were green and faded by the years, and she attempted to highlight them with a thick layer of mascara— apparently she had nothing against that type of makeup. She had a wide, thin-lipped mouth, even teeth, and a rather prominent nose by traditional esthetic standards.

For Nuria, looking at her was like looking at herself in a mirror thirty years in the future. In a way, she hated her mother for that. "Thanks, Mom," she said, taking the cup and setting it on the table. "And thanks for going over to feed Melon."

Estela accepted the thanks with a slight nod, then sat down next to her daughter and took her hand. "Are you feeling any better?"

Nuria gave her a sidelong glance. "No, Mom," she replied, more harshly than she'd intended. "I'm not feeling better."

"Would you like—"

"I don't want anything, thanks. I just need to rest."

Estela gave her a second before continuing. "I've got your room ready. If you like, you could go and lie down." Crossing her heart to emphasize her words, she added: "I promise I won't disturb you."

Nuria took a deep breath and released it slowly. Although her mother had had to buy thirty-two candles for Nuria's last birthday cake, she still managed to treat her like a child of ten. Visits to her house generally consisted of a battery of questions about what Nuria ate as Estela examined her daughter critically, muttering under her breath about how thin she was. This was inevitably followed by an interrogation about her limited love life—which implicitly included the question of whether she would one day be providing Estela with a grandchild. The icing on the cake was the predictable litany of sage advice and Christian guidelines that would have been appropriate for the middle of the last century. These were passed on by her mother courtesy of Salvador Aguirre, candidate for the Spain First party and champion of the Reborn in Christ cult.

Invariably, after ten minutes in what had once been her own home, Nuria began to lose her patience and glance toward the door like a dog waiting for its master. And this time was no different. "Thanks, Mom." She laid a hand on her mother's knee. "But I think I'll go home now."

"What? No! The doctor said you'd better not be left alone today."

"I'm fine, Mom. I won't faint in the middle of the street."

Her mother raised an eyebrow. "Yesterday you almost fell down when you tried to go to the bathroom."

"That was yesterday. Today I'm fine, and I want to go home."

Estela's eyes narrowed defensively. "*This* is your home," she reminded her daughter.

Nuria sighed. "I know … Please don't take it that way, Mom." She looked into her mother's eyes for the first time that morning. "It's just that … I need to be alone."

"But … Nurieta …" she persevered beseechingly. Only her mother still called her that. So had her father, while he was still with them. Now there was no one but her mother left to remind her of that family pet name, which saddened her even more. She had to get out of there.

"I'm sorry. I've got to go."

Her mother shook her head, staring at the ceiling fan. "Don't blame yourself," she said unexpectedly.

"What?"

"Don't blame yourself for what happened." She stroked her daughter's hand. "The Lord giveth and the Lord taketh away. He's our Maker and we're just His instruments. Our lives are in His hands."

"Yeah, but the gun was in mine," Nuria muttered. "The Lord didn't pull the trigger, Mom. It was me."

"That's what *you* think. Nothing happens unless it's the Lord's will. Don't blame yourself."

"So should I blame *Him*?" Nuria asked in sudden irritation, pointing her finger at the sky. "Or him maybe?" She gestured toward the poster of Pope Pius XIII releasing a white dove from a Vatican balcony.

"Banish rage from your heart, Nurieta," her mother said, her hand on her own heart. "The Lord works in mysterious ways. In His glory you'll find peace."

And here we go again, thought Nuria. But this time she didn't have enough energy to resist her mother's sanctimonious harangues. "I'd better go find peace in my own home," she replied, getting to her feet without giving her mother a chance to stop her. "Thanks for bringing me here, and for the tila tea."

Estela glanced at the cup that sat untouched on the table. "You shouldn't be alone today," she insisted.

Nuria went to the door and opened it, then turned. "Goodbye, Mom," she said abruptly. "I'll call you later," she added at the last moment, goaded by her conscience.

Nuria descended to street level in the elevator, hoping it wouldn't trap her in one of the many power cuts that were becoming more and more frequent. The month before, she'd spent half an hour trapped in one, suffocating in the heat and enduring the interminable chatter of two neighbors who had taken advantage of the opportunity to catch up on the news of Princess Leonor's latest boyfriend. She had no wish to repeat the experience, least of all today.

Downstairs, before opening the door and exposing herself to the heat outside, she took her phone from her pocket and called a taxi. While waiting in the relative shelter of the lobby, she decided to check the latest messages from her colleagues that kept coming in, asking her how she felt and when she was coming back to the station.

She didn't reply to any of them. What could she tell them? Even worse, what could they tell her? Nuria still hadn't handed in her official report, but the

39

previous evening she'd given her statement off the record to Commissioner Puig at the hospital while she was still in bed. Though she'd feared the moment when she would have to tell the story of what had happened in that hovel, doing so turned out to be an unexpected catharsis. There was a kind of liberation in sharing that private horror with others, putting it out there on the table. *Do you see? Do you see what I saw? Can you feel what I felt? Now this memory belongs to all of us. Let's share the horror. I can't carry it all by myself.*

Luckily, most of the "incident," as the commissioner had called it, which was okay by Nuria, had been recorded by their gogglecams and stored in the headquarters cloud, so she was able to spare herself many of the details and simply state her reactions, inasmuch as these could be explained. Commissioner Puig had already seen and heard everything in the recordings. From her point of view ... and from his own. For a moment Nuria imagined herself caught squarely in the frame, aiming and shooting her gun in the direction of the other camera. In David's direction.

Her electronic activity bracelet vibrated on her wrist. Glancing at her phone, she saw her taxi was about to arrive. Opening the door, Nuria stepped out into the street, which at that hour of the morning already seemed to be melting under the merciless sun. Luckily the suffocating Saharan dust had been dispersed by last night's wind, but the heat was still unbearable, and the few passersby who ventured out did so under wide parasols or broad-brimmed hats. They huddled in the narrow fringe of shade cast by the buildings and moved quickly. Nobody wanted to be in the street any longer than was absolutely necessary. She saw a pair of Chinese tourists looking as if they'd lost their group, an old neighbor in a camisole walking her dog who recognized Nuria and gave her a slight nod, and a couple of those blue self-driving Amazon carts making home deliveries. In this part of town there were no homeless people or refugees wandering the streets. Private security saw to that. They had no legal authority, but did have the implicit consent of City Hall, which was happy to keep the outcasts confined to the outskirts without the bother of potential accusations by the citizens' rights associations.

The yellow-and-black taxi stopped beside her. She opened the door and settled into the back seat, saying good morning. The driver, a Sikh with a purple turban and an endless beard, half turned and asked through the plastic screen: "Where to?" His heavy accent made the question sound like "Vurrtu?"

"77 Calle Verdi, please."

"Birdie?" he asked blankly.

"Verdi. Like the composer."

The Indian frowned, shook his head, and indicated the touch screen in front of her. "Write." Nuria clicked her tongue in annoyance, but wrote the name of the street and the number without comment. "Ah, Birdie!" the taxi driver cried when he saw it appear on the dashboard navigator, his tone apparently reproaching his passenger for her unclear diction.

Nuria didn't bother to reply and the taxi drove off with a buzzing sound. Tired, she let her head fall back. A sharp pain in the back of her neck reminded her of the bump she still had, so she sat up again. In front of her, on the screen where she'd written her address, the inevitable personal ads had started to appear.

"Nuria Badal," said one in a honeyed voice, accompanied by a parade of images of expert-looking doctors and futuristic medical devices. "At MediCare we have the most highly rated professionals and the most advanced technology at your service, as well as the perfect coverage for all your medical needs. Just what you need for your own peace of mind and that of your loved ones. Call now for a twenty-percent discount." An actor with a confident smile and salt-and-pepper hair peered at Nuria from the screen, suggesting she shouldn't pass up this opportunity.

"Leave me alone," she muttered in reply, lowering the volume to a minimum. The advertising screens didn't have a "silent" setting, much less an off switch, so she had to content herself with looking away while she listened to the murmur in the background offering her life insurance, anti-inflammatories, and even antidepressants. In less than twenty-four hours her medical report had been uploaded to the Internet's commercial files. This meant, without a doubt, that all the advertising aimed at her during the next few months would be almost exclusively from insurance agencies, hospitals, and pharmaceutical companies. *At least it'll be a change*, she told herself. She was fed up with ads from dating services.

In spite of the traffic, it took the taxi less than ten minutes to reach the Gracia neighborhood. The driver opened his mouth only to curse in Hindi while pointing to a driverless Uber next to him at a traffic light—at least Nuria assumed it was Hindi. He expanded on his theme, ranting in a barely intelligible pidgin about the monstrosity of those driverless cars circulating through the cities. "Take avay vork," he said. "Vy car alone? Vere taxi driver? Vere people? Take avay vork!" he repeated, turning to Nuria in search of sympathy.

As it happened, Nuria was a regular patron of the small electric vehicles that lacked both drivers and uncomfortable conversations. They never got the address wrong, never had accidents, and went back to their garages at night to recharge their batteries like funny little yellow Oompa-Loompas: more efficient and cheaper than taxis, buses, or even the subway. "Yes," she said, with no intention of debating the virtues of the system. "A real shame." The taxi driver, satisfied at having recruited one more citizen to his cause, sat back in his seat, muttered a final insult, and drove on again while the light was still red.

7

No sooner had Nuria closed the door behind her than a black-and-white cat appeared in the hallway, tail held aloft, meowing something halfway between welcome and reproach.

"Hi, Melon," Nuria greeted him. Crouching beside him, she stroked his back while he rubbed against her legs and purred, happy to see her again. "I've missed you too."

The animal stood on his hind legs and rested his paws on Nuria's knees, putting his nose to her face and sniffing it with interest. "I smell of hospital, I know," she said, and scratched his head. "Come on, I'm going to feed you." Standing up, Nuria went to the kitchen with Melon weaving between her legs at each step as if trying to trip her. Opening the cupboard, she took out a can of food for neutered cats, tipped the whole of it into his food bowl and then filled his water bowl from the tap.

"Don't eat it all at once or you'll get sick," she said, watching him. Ignoring her advice, Melon hurled himself desperately at the food. "Don't say I didn't warn you!" Cat fed, she continued to her bedroom like a sleepwalker, tripping over the Roomba on the way. It was stuck under the couch once again, the battery light yellow. But Nuria was too tired to pull it out or ask it to clean the house. Tomorrow would be a better time for that, or anything else, for that matter.

The blinds were drawn and a comforting twilight made the room look like the cave she needed at the moment. Looking at the spacious bed that took up most of the room, she was tempted to collapse onto the wrinkled sheets, hug the pillow, and let the day go by, hoping it wouldn't notice her absence.

Instead, she summoned the necessary willpower to leave the room and go into the bathroom, where she took off her clothes mechanically, left them piled on the floor, got into the shower and turned on the hot water. The red numbers on the water meter told her she had only ninety-three liters left for the rest of the week, but right then she didn't give a shit about whatever restrictions or penalties they might impose on her. She needed that shower more than she needed air.

Amid a cloud of steam she washed and rinsed her hair, which brushed her back when it was wet, then soaped herself with a sponge until she was certain every particle of dust from that shack had been banished from her body. Only when she felt satisfied with the layer of foam that covered her reddened skin did she turn off the hot water and raise her face toward the shower head.

The jet of cold water hit her hard, transformed into microscopic needles that stimulated the nerve endings of her face and body, washing away the filth, the soap, and the overwhelming feeling of unreality that had possessed her ever since she'd woken up in that hospital bed.

The gaps in her memory had been filled in and now her mind was trying to take refuge in the words of Commissioner Puig when he'd visited her at the hospital. Tall, solemn, and still muscular in spite of ten years behind a desk, he was an authoritarian figure, but one who almost from the beginning had taken a protective—on occasion almost paternal—attitude toward Nuria, perhaps projecting onto her the daughter he'd never had and substituting himself for the father she'd lost.

That afternoon Puig had had on the impeccable dress uniform he'd worn hours before at David's funeral. He still had the black mourning band on his sleeve, but he'd been sensitive enough to make no reference to the ceremony. Nor had Nuria had the heart to ask about it.

"He was a fucking junkie looking for cash for his next fix," he'd explained, sounding resigned. "The fact is, you were lucky."

"Crazy lucky," Nuria had muttered.

Puig had pulled the folding chair forward and sat down beside her. His bushy black eyebrows hovered above inquiring black eyes, intimidating whoever happened to be facing him.

"Listen," he'd told her in confidence. "We watched the recordings and you did what you had to do. The miracle is that you came out alive."

"I killed David," she'd blurted, scorning the comfort he was offering.

The commissioner jabbed his finger at her chest. "Don't you ever dare say that again."

"It's the truth."

"No, it's not. That bastard managed to put David in the bullet's path." He paused, then added, "If you hadn't managed to shoot him in the heart just before you lost consciousness, he'd have taken more of your fellow officers with him before they could stop him. In fact," he added, "I'm going to nominate you for a medal."

Nuria's expression was midway between disbelief and disgust. "You're not serious."

"Completely. And don't think my request won't be granted."

"I don't want it." She frowned. "I won't accept it. No way!"

Puig had snorted and passed a hand over his face in a gesture of weariness. "I don't give a damn whether you want it or not," he said very slowly in a tone that brooked no objections. "You deserve it and you'll accept it. That's an order."

Nuria opened her mouth, but couldn't utter a word.

43

He'd nodded in satisfaction. "That's the way I like it." Standing, he smoothed his uniform jacket. "I've been told you'll be discharged tomorrow, but take the rest of the week off. Oh, and don't forget your appointment with the counselor."

"I don't need a shrink."

"That's for him to decide."

Nuria's face took on an expression of weariness that seemed to be the signal for Puig to walk toward the door. "Commissioner," she'd called when his hand was already on the knob, "Do they have any clue as to who …?" She paused. "Junkies don't act that way. That bastard seemed to have been waiting for us. To me it doesn't make sense that he was there by chance. Maybe trailing the—"

Puig had cut her off. "Forget about it." He added, "The case is already in the hands of homicide, but stop thinking about it. He's not the first addict to kill his dealer."

"He didn't look like an ordinary junkie, Commissioner. He moved … I don't know, like a video in fast motion."

Puig shook his head. "There was nothing odd in the recordings," he said with a touch of impatience. "It's natural enough for your mind to play tricks on you after a shock like that."

"Maybe," she admitted doubtfully. "But even so, I want to help, Commissioner."

"Impossible." His refusal had been firm. "You can't work on a case you're involved in yourself, you know that. What you need to do now is rest."

"The victim we found was a possible witness in the investigation David and I were conducting on Elias. It could be that—"

"We know all about Sergeant Insúa's investigation," Puig had interrupted. "If we need you to clarify any details, we'll contact you."

"But—"

The commissioner raised his voice with a tone of finality. "I said no. You just rest and get better, and no investigating on your own." He jabbed a finger at her. "And that's an order. If I find out you're doing anything except eating or sleeping this next week, I'll give you so much grief you'll wish you were still unconscious in this fucking hospital." Bringing his face close to Nuria's, he'd said, "Is that clear, Corporal Badal?"

Nuria swallowed. "Crystal clear, Commissioner."

"I'm glad we understand each other," he said with a nod, changing his tone, a fatherly smile on his lips. "Now rest and recuperate. I want you back at the station next week in top shape … but not before. Understood?"

"I'll be there," she'd replied, trying to sound sincere. The commissioner had taken his leave, shaking her hand and leaving the room with long strides.

No, Nuria thought now, returning to reality and enjoying the way the cold water of the shower prickled her face. The truth was, she didn't believe she would be ready to go back to work the following week.

A dark, never-ending corridor. The stink of damp. Flies buzzing furiously. The beam of the flashlight barely penetrating the gloom. She reaches out, moving the dirty curtain, and puts her head inside. The cone of light penetrates the room, revealing Vilchez's body on the bed with his throat cut. But it's not Vilchez, it's David with a bullet hole in his forehead, turning to her and whispering "Please" in a voice that gurgles in his throat. Horrified, Nuria drops the curtain abruptly and turns to run, but now there's someone in front of her. A man with black, thick-rimmed glasses over bloodshot eyes who smiles perversely when he sees her, showing teeth sharp as a shark's.

Zzzzzzz!

Zzzzzzz!

Zzzzzzz!

Nuria sat up in bed abruptly, startled, waking from the nightmare like someone falling off a moving train. Gasping for air, the perspiration running down her face, she touched her activity bracelet to stop the vibration.

Under her body, the sheets were drenched. Nuria fingered them, worried about sweating so much. That was when she remembered she'd collapsed onto the bed naked, without even drying herself.

"Sofia," she called the Google assistant sleepily. "What ... what's up?"

"You have an incoming call from Flavio," the house AI system informed her. "Shall I take the call?"

Flavio's face appeared in her mind, his hair tinted pink in the latest trend, the mocking half smile on his face that was as typical of him as the cheap jokes he told at the most inappropriate moments. She clicked her tongue in annoyance, not in the mood to speak to anybody, least of all a superficial pothead ex-boyfriend.

"No," she replied. "Reject it."

"Call rejected," Sofia confirmed at once, adding in her syrupy voice, "Can I do anything else for you? Shall I turn on the coffeemaker?"

"Nothing else, thanks," Nuria said, and the assistant's loudspeaker emitted its end tone. Fixing her gaze on the paper globe that hung from the ceiling, Nuria tried to woo sleep again, but her mind wandered aimlessly. She wasn't going to be able to fall asleep. Taking a few minutes to gather her wits, she decided to get up, spurred by hunger.

At some point during the night Melon had curled up between the sheets next to her. She pushed him aside and leapt to her feet. A sharp pain stabbed her in the nape, as if someone had stuck a red-hot needle into her neck, and she was forced to sit down again on the edge of the bed until it passed.

Nuria propped her elbows on her knees and let the weight of her head fall into her hands. Rubbing her eyes, she gave a snort of annoyance. *Why me?* she wondered. Her heart felt as if it were being clamped in a vise. *Why did this happen to me of all people?* For a moment she allowed herself to be carried away by self-pity.

Then she remembered her father, that last day of third grade, when a fat, freckled boy named Pau Garcia had pushed her down the stairs. She'd broken her arm and had had to miss that year's summer camp. That same evening, when he'd arrived home from work, her father had sat her on his lap. After wiping away her tears, he'd told her the fable of a peasant whose horse had been stolen and who'd had to walk back home, sad and furious. After walking many miles in a rainstorm, cursing his bad luck at every step, he'd finally seen his humble wooden cottage in the night. But at that exact moment a massive lightning bolt had struck it like a divine hammer falling from the heavens and destroyed it.

Then the peasant understood that if he'd ridden his horse home, he would have arrived hours earlier and the lightning would have killed him while he was asleep. From the bottom of his heart he gave thanks that his horse had been stolen.

"You never know, Nurieta," her father had told her with a wink, pulling gently on her two pretty braids. "Maybe by the end of the summer you'll be thanking that Pau for breaking your arm." At the moment Nuria hadn't really understood what the story was about or what the moral was, but she liked horses and she liked it when her father told her those stories in his deep, faraway voice.

She wished he'd never left and that she could sit on his knee and cry on his shoulder until at last he would pat her on the back and persuade her that everything was going to be all right.

How she missed him.

Nuria took a deep breath, filling her lungs with the warm sticky air of the bedroom. Allowing herself one last whimper of self-pity, she set her jaw, stood up, and unhurriedly walked naked to the kitchen.

"You never know," she said to herself.

8

Around four o'clock her activity bracelet buzzed like a bee for a second time. She thought with annoyance that it might be Flavio again, but this time the name that appeared on the little black screen was Susana Roman. Nuria wondered for a moment whether to take the call or not, but in the end she asked Sofia to put her through.

"Hi there, Susi," she said, opening her smartphone so that her friend's face appeared on the screen.

Susana gave her a concerned smile. "Hello, Nuria. I just went to the hospital to visit you and found out you'd been discharged."

"Yeah, this morning," she said laconically.

"I'm sorry I didn't come before, but I had three days of double shifts, and—"

"No worries. How are you?"

Susana's freckled face smiled in confusion. "What do you mean, how am *I*?" she snorted, pointing her thumb at herself. "How are *you*?!"

"Uh … fine. I'm fine, thanks."

Susana brought her eye closer to the camera until it filled the whole screen.

"Don't lie to me …I can see you."

Nuria giggled at the sight of her friend's huge eye blinking in the palm of her hand. "I'm fine, honestly."

"Uh-huh . . ." her friend said suspiciously. She moved her eye away from the phone. "What time shall we meet?"

"Meet?"

"If you're fine, you won't mind meeting for a drink, will you?"

"Well, actually, I'm tired … and not in the mood to go out, honestly."

"All the more reason for doing it."

"But—"

"But nothing," Susana interrupted, mimicking Commissioner Puig's voice. "You've got to come out and have a couple of beers. That's an order."

Nuria couldn't help smiling, unable to resist her friend's wit. She gave in at last, admitting that it would probably do her good. "All right. Eight o'clock, the usual place?"

"I'll be there. Oh, and shave your legs and put clean undies on tonight. We're going to go out on the town."

"What? No, Susi. Today I really don't—"

"It was a joke." She brought her face closer to the screen so Nuria could see her wink. "I'll be waiting at the bar," she said. She hung up and her image disappeared.

Nuria sat staring at the empty screen. All of a sudden her good mood vanished and the heavy slab of sadness descended once more on her spirit, crushing her mercilessly. For a moment she felt an impulse to call Susana back and, without giving any further explanation, cancel their date. She would be better off at home where she could watch some old movie, eat ice cream, and let the afternoon gradually wane until it gave way to evening. She had a right to feel bad. More than that: how could she go out with a friend when less than twenty-four hours before, David had been buried?

Walking and going through the door, her father's voice said in her head.

I should go and see Gloria, she told herself instead. *I killed her husband and left her son an orphan. I need to go and see her. Let her see me. Allow her to say whatever she wants to. Everything I deserve to hear from her.*

But Nuria knew she wouldn't be able to. She still wasn't capable of summoning up the courage to look Gloria in the face and tell her how she felt, or ruffle Luisito's hair and see, in his eyes, David's terrified look the instant he understood that she was going to kill him.

Oh, God ... why did you have to fuck us up like this?

Hours later, stretched out on the couch wearing only a pair of thong underwear, Nuria idled away the time surfing the news channels without paying much attention to what they were saying.

"The Government spokesman," one speaker was saying, *"has confirmed that he will not tolerate another unauthorized demonstration by pro-abortionists at the—"*

"Next," Nuria commanded, and the image switched to a satellite photo of a sea of clouds, with a stunning brunette in a miniskirt pointing to them.

"...conditions never before seen in the Mediterranean," she was saying in a sensual voice, *"which, after reaching a temperature of 79 degrees at a depth of three feet have caused a cyclonic depression with pressures below ninety—"*

"Next."

" ... although the latest unemployment figures in Spain put the rate at over forty-two percent, the candidate for Spain First, Salvador Aguirre, has stated that if he should be elected president ..."

"Next."

"... *finishing preparations for the inaugural ceremony at the Basilica of the Sagrada Familia. A large number of distinguished visitors is expected, including the king and queen and the prime minister.*" This time the news anchor was staring fixedly at the camera, while behind him images of the placement of the final stone of the Sagrada Familia cathedral appeared in rapid succession. The cathedral had actually been completed the previous week, and the media had treated it as the most important news item since the discovery of America. "*The congregation of the Spanish Reborn in Christ group has called for a community prayer session in Plaza Catalunya this afternoon to pray that the Holy Father may overcome his health problems and be able to attend this inaugural—*"

"Fuck it. Turn it off, Sofia," she ordered. The assistant obeyed at once. Nuria sat up on the couch. Smoothing her hair back as if preparing to tie it up in a ponytail, she added to herself: "That's enough hiding for today." She stood up and went to her closet.

Two minutes later, wearing a green T-shirt with a Greenpeace logo and cutoffs that emphasized her long legs, she left her apartment and set off at an easy pace toward the Plaza del Diamante a few blocks away.

With the cooler late-afternoon temperatures, pedestrians, scooters, cyclists, and housewives on their Segways carrying their daily shopping filled the streets of the Gracia neighborhood. Although the sun still beat down on the rooftops and the temperatures hovered around eighty-five degrees, the air felt almost refreshing compared to the hundred fifteen they'd reached at noon.

As soon as she came into the little square she saw Susana, seated at a table under a patio umbrella outside the Puzzle bar. She waved and made her way to her. Her friend returned the wave, pushed her chair back, and stood up to welcome her with open arms and a sincere smile of relief on her face. "Nuria, sweetheart," she said, squeezing her tightly once she was in reach.

Their difference in height was remarkable. Nuria was more than a head taller than Susana, and from a distance they might have been mistaken for mother and daughter. They'd been friends since they'd met at the Police Academy, where Susana had ended up after a series of dead-end jobs and meaningless relationships. She had no qualms about admitting that she'd joined the police because of the pay and the job security, but to her surprise, once she'd donned the uniform and strapped on her gun, she'd discovered the pleasure of serving and protecting her fellow citizens—not to mention the shifts that allowed her to go on vacation every few months. Neither of them could have said why, but they'd become friends from the very first day.

"I'm so glad to see you," Nuria admitted.

Taking a step back, Susana took a good look at her friend's drawn appearance. "I was afraid you'd stand me up."

"To be honest, I almost did," Nuria confessed with a weak smile. "Ten minutes ago I was still lying naked on my couch, wasting time and not looking forward to going out at all."

"That's the worst thing you could've done. You need to get some fresh air and vent. Mainly, vent. Sit." She pointed to the table. "Order something and then tell me everything."

Nuria obediently did as she was told. Though she felt reluctant at first, she ended up letting herself go and explaining everything that had happened. By the time she'd finished her story, the table was littered with four empty bottles of Moritz beer and two empty plates of calamari and *patatas bravas*. She felt much better after sharing the pain and guilt that were torturing her with her best friend—better than she was ready to admit.

"I can't imagine how you must be feeling," Susana said, putting her hand on Nuria's arm. "That time I killed a suspect during a robbery I was shattered for weeks, do you remember? I spent several sleepless nights overcome by guilt, even though he was just a bastard with a sawn-off shotgun in his hand." She fixed her eyes on one of the empty beer bottles. "If I'd gone through what happened to you, I …"

Without comment, Nuria tipped her third bottle of beer up and drained it.

"Forgive me," Susana said, shaking her head. "I'm not helping much."

"You're wrong. I'm glad I could talk to you. I needed to get it out of my system."

"Great, then," Susana said, satisfied. "Don't listen to the gossip. None of it was your fault."

"Gossip? What gossip?"

Susana's eyes widened and her beer stopped halfway to her mouth when she realized she'd put her foot in it, but she did her best to make light of it. "Nothing, don't worry about it."

"What gossip, Susi?"

"Forget about it. It's just the typical idiots who always—"

"What gossip?" Nuria insisted, her face serious.

Susana hesitated a moment, then cleared her throat uncomfortably. "I … well, there are the usual morons saying that because you're a woman you got nervous and shot without aiming. That you got scared, and in the confusion you shot David instead of the perp."

Nuria was incredulous. "What? No! It wasn't like that! Anybody who watches the recording from the gogglecam can see that wasn't what happened at all!"

"I know, I know." Susana tried to soothe her. "I told you not to pay any attention to it. They're the same old dinosaurs who don't want women on the police force unless it's to scrub floors."

"What assholes," Nuria muttered, seething. "The day that recording's released to the public, they're going to have to swallow their words."

"I agree," Susana said and raised her bottle in a toast. "Let's hope it all gets cleared up quickly and you can get back to normal. By the way ..." she added after a sip, "have you spoken to Gloria?"

Nuria shook her head slowly, ashamed. "Did you see her at the funeral?" Susana nodded, but said nothing. "Did you talk to her?" Nuria insisted.

"I ... no. I gave her my condolences, of course, like everybody else. But when I went up to her, she looked at me ... I don't know how to describe it. Just *differently*—I think because you and I are friends." She picked up her bottle and saw that it was empty. "I don't know."

"Differently?"

Susana seemed to be searching for the appropriate word. Not finding a better one, she said, "Pissed off."

"Jesus!"

"Yes."

Nuria thought for a moment. "I'm going to call her," she said firmly.

"Gloria?" Susana asked incredulously.

"I should've done it the moment I got out of the hospital."

Susana laid her hand on her friend's wrist. "You're going to do no such thing," she said with all the force she could muster. "You're half drunk, and it's a really bad idea."

Nuria tried to push Susana's hand away. "I must speak to her. I've got to ask her to forgive me. I've got to—"

"Fine, but do it tomorrow. Right now you're not thinking clearly. What are you going to say to her?"

A flash of common sense cut through the haze of alcohol in Nuria's brain. She stopped struggling with Susana and patted her hand gratefully. "Yes ... you may be right," she murmured wearily. "Tomorrow. I'll speak to her tomorrow."

Susana nodded, satisfied. "It's for the best."

Nuria's activity bracelet vibrated, and Susana watched as her friend looked down at her phone to see who it was. Her face went even paler. Before Susana could ask her who it was, Nuria raised her gaze and whispered in terror: "It's Gloria." Her finger wavered uncertainly over the screen. From left to right. From the green circle to the red X.

Susana put her hand on her arm again and shook her head. "Don't take it," she said in a low voice, as if someone might hear her. "Tomorrow."

Nuria hesitated for a moment, then finally ignored the call. "Tomorrow," she repeated.

51

9

It seemed to Nuria when she opened her eyes that the lamp on her bedside table was leaning at an awkward angle. Blinking several times, she tried to correct her perspective, but both the lamp and the surface of the bedside table insisted on remaining slanted. It took her a while longer to understand that she was the one who was twisted. She was hugging the pillow, but her head was falling over the other side, her neck bent at an angle that couldn't be good for it.

Nuria tried to curse, but her tongue and the roof of her mouth felt like sandpaper. Swallowing with difficulty, Nuria's mind conjured up the image of an enormous, sweet, refreshing glass of orange juice. In fact, the immediate goal of her existence had become orange juice: to pour herself a large glass and let it slide through her lips, flooding her mouth and throat with its sweet, refreshing flavor. Driven by this desire, she lifted her head in preparation for sitting up. It felt as if someone were stabbing the left side of her neck with a red-hot poker while someone else hit her on both temples at once with rubber clubs. Again Nuria tried to curse, but the only thing that came out of her mouth was a plaintive croak.

"Ohhh, fuck …"

She lay there on her back, hands clasped protectively around her head, trying to remember why she was in this state. Her befuddled memory was able to seize on the fifth beer she'd drunk at the table outside the bar. Beyond that, there was a confusing parade of still shots of some place she couldn't recognize, but where she could hear herself shouting incomprehensible words at total strangers. Susana didn't appear in this last part, but Nuria imagined she hadn't been far away.

For a moment she thought of calling her friend and asking her what in God's name had happened the night before, but then decided to wait a few hours. If Susana had ended up in a similar state, it wouldn't be a good idea to wake her up before she was ready.

When at last Nuria managed to gather her strength enough to sit up in bed, she set her feet on the floor, realizing only then that she was still wearing the same tight shorts and T-shirt she'd had on the day before. She'd gone to bed with her clothes on. Nuria took comfort from the fact that at least she hadn't woken up in an unfamiliar bed next to a stranger.

When she felt quite certain she wouldn't faint on the way, she stood up and went to the bathroom in search of aspirin. A cold shower brought her back to life, though she was still unclear about what had happened the night before. She'd simply stopped caring, though. Her headache hadn't completely disappeared, but at least it had abated, so her next mission consisted of going to the fridge to appease her hunger and at last enjoy the longed-for orange juice.

In the kitchen, the screen on the fridge door warned her about the use-by date on the package of chicken and the fact that she was out of beer, hummus, and—naturally—orange juice. It proceeded to suggest a list of food and drink she could order from Amazon. For a moment she considered pressing the *accept* button and waiting for the food to arrive while she stretched out on the couch, but in the end she decided it would be good for her to get some fresh air, even if it was only walking to the supermarket on her own two feet, like in the olden days.

Throwing on the coolest clothes she could find, Nuria added a cap—the SpongeBob one had been left in that appalling shack—and her sunglasses, then fed Melon. Slipping on the flip-flops she kept by the door, she went to take her keys from the bowl next to the front door, and found they weren't there.

"What the hell?"

During all the years she'd lived in that flat, regardless of the state she was in when she arrived, Nuria had always left her keys in the bowl of dark wood by the door. Finding it empty was as disconcerting as getting into a car and realizing someone had taken the steering wheel.

Patting her clothes, Nuria turned in a circle while looking at the floor, just in case she'd dropped them. She gave the bowl a final glance, then with a shrug selected the key-ring app on the mirror by the entrance. A second later a muffled intermittent ring tone reached her from the kitchen door. Intrigued, she followed the sound that seemed to be coming from inside one of the drawers. She opened the first, the silverware drawer, but her keys weren't there. Opening the second, where the spatulas and large knives were kept, she saw them, the key fob emitting blue pulses in the same rhythm as the annoying ring tone.

Nuria took them out of the drawer, lifting them triumphantly into the air as if they were a mouse she was holding by the tail while wondering how it could have escaped from its cage. The keys jingled innocently when she put them in her pocket, and just before she closed the drawer she tried to remember how they'd ended up there. Though she failed to find an answer, she did, however, decide it was the last time she was going to get drunk.

It was almost noon by now and the sun was heating the air, distorting it into ghostly shreds that rose from the burning asphalt and flowed down the narrow street as though up a chimney flue. Walking unhurriedly, she came to the corner and stopped in front of the supermarket door, but didn't go in. In spite of the suffocating heat she enjoyed being in the street, and the brief walk had done more to fight her hangover than the aspirins. She decided to continue her wandering and stretch her legs a little longer; she could do the shopping on her way back.

Nuria crossed Travessera de Gracia and went on to Corcega Street, lined with banners of political parties on each lamppost, as if preparing for a parade. Here she stopped at the traffic light and looked back. What else did she have to do at home, apart from wasting time and endlessly playing the same old tapes in her head? She thought for a moment about calling Susana and inviting her to lunch, but that would only involve repeating the same conversations they'd had the evening before, and this time without any beer to muffle the bad memories.

Impulsively, she raised her hand at a driverless Uber, which pulled up with a faint hiss. The door slid open sideways, and without thinking she got into the vehicle. There were neither driver nor steering wheel, nor anything resembling them; only an empty space with four individual seats facing each other.

"Good morning, Ms. Badal," a pleasant male voice said through the loudspeaker in the ceiling, identifying her at once. "Where would you like to be taken?"

Nuria took a few seconds to enjoy the coolness of the vehicle and the comfortable seat. She wouldn't have minded asking it to drive at random around the city while she relaxed in that cool, soundproof bubble, where the chords of one of her favorite Jorge Drexler songs were beginning to sound. Those fuckers at Google sure knew how to do their job well. She heard herself say: "To La Barceloneta."

"Could you be more specific, Ms. Badal?"

"Mm ... no. Just take me there. I'll let you know when we get there."

It seemed to Nuria that the vehicle's AI took a second longer than necessary to process her request. "Barrio de la Barceloneta," the mechanical voice said pleasantly at last. "Destination still to be determined. Correct, Ms. Badal?"

"Correct, Bautista," she joked, suddenly in a good mood. "May I call you Bautista?"

"You may call me anything you wish, Ms. Badal," the AI replied as the car accelerated smoothly away. Nuria thought that if a man in a bar had said those words in that same tone of voice, he wouldn't have had too much trouble seducing her. For a moment she was tempted to ask the voice to drop the formality and call her Nuria, but if she did that her request would be sent to the commercial files and from then on she would have to put up with any operational system, from her fridge to the coffee machine at the station using her first name with tiresome familiarity. So she said nothing, leaned back in her seat, and let the conversation fade until she was alone with the music of the Uruguayan singer-songwriter.

10

After a short drive, the little Uber stopped on the Calle del Juicio in the neighborhood of La Barceloneta, an old fishermen's quarter anchored next to the sea where no fisherman had lived for decades. The long beach of golden sand that had once stretched in front of it was now only a memory. There was no money to remake the beach for the umpteenth time after the increasingly violent winter storm surges of the Mediterranean. In its place, a dam of huge concrete blocks like giant dice kept the sea at bay, protecting the neighborhood from the sea's deceptive serenity that on some stormy nights was transformed into uncontrollable fury.

The cost of the ride appeared on the armrest screen, and as soon as Nuria pressed the *Accept* icon, the door slid sideways and the system took its leave with a kind *Have a nice day, Ms. Badal*, to which she replied in the same vein. There was no need to be discourteous, she told herself, even to a machine.

On the street once again, Nuria glanced around and headed toward a nearby building with large windows and an air of melancholy, built at the beginning of the previous century. On its façade the authorities had tried without much success to remove some eye-catching graffiti demanding the end of Internet censorship. When she reached the door, she stood in front of the security camera and pressed the bell for the fifth floor.

"Hello?" came a distorted voice through the loudspeaker.

"Hello. It's Nuria." At once, the metallic-bee buzz sounded, followed by the creak of the front door opening.

"Thank you." Pushing the door further open, she entered the narrow, gloomy lobby. For some reason she dismissed the idea of taking the elevator and went to the stairs instead, in spite of the five floors she would have to climb. The effort might help calm the roiling mass of thoughts in her head.

Reaching the fifth floor, she knocked on a door whose paint was peeling. A plump mulatto woman with glossy skin and a headscarf greeted her with a wide smile of welcome. "My dear ..." she said in her singsong Dominican accent. "It's been so long."

Nuria couldn't help but respond to that brilliant smile with one of her own. She bent to kiss the woman, who barely reached her shoulder, on both cheeks. "I'm so glad to see you, Daisy."

"Come in, child, come in." Moving aside so Nuria could enter, Daisy added: "How lovely that you came."

A sweetish smell, a mixture of soap, perspiration, and antibiotics, wafted to her nostrils from inside the apartment. It reminded her of the smell in the hospital and she had to overcome the urge to step back. "Thank you, Daisy," she said instead, banishing the thought from her mind and crossing the threshold. "How's everything going here?"

"Everything's fine," Daisy replied in a tone which belied her words. "Though Miss Linda left us last week."

"Oh dear. I'm so sorry."

"She was ninety-three, poor little thing. She couldn't do anything by herself. She didn't know who she was or where she was, didn't recognize her family the few times they came to visit her." She waved her hand sadly. "Fact is, I didn't expect her to ..." Daisy's voice trailed off into silence, as if she were observing an improvised moment of silence in memory of the deceased. "Anyway," she sighed, "that means that now I have a vacancy, so if you know of anybody who—"

"Sure. I'll ask around."

"But it got to be someone trustworthy, eh?" she warned Nuria conspiratorially. "You know about our ... ahem, situation."

Nuria smiled to ease her mind. "Don't worry." As the words left her mouth, she couldn't avoid thinking that the likeable owner of the illegal retirement home would have a stroke if she knew that she herself was a policewoman. Luckily—for her as well—all that was required was a name and cash up front on the first of the month. Nobody knew or wanted to know. Together with her two daughters, the Dominican woman owned a discreet business which allowed her to get by, and those family members who either couldn't find a vacancy or couldn't afford an officially registered retirement home knew that with her their grandparents would be in good hands. It was a win-win situation.

The living room of the apartment was mainly occupied by a huge dining table surrounded by wicker-backed wooden chairs. On one side of the room was a large window, now covered by a thick curtain, while on the opposite wall, displayed in the same way a university would show its honors graduates, hung the framed photos of all those who had spent their last days in that small, clandestine home. Nuria had always thought it a macabre touch, particularly for the current tenants who knew that sooner or later their own photo would be hanging on that wall. She realized Daisy still hadn't added Miss Linda's picture.

"This way we don' forget them," Daisy told her, following her gaze. "Sometimes we look at the photo of one who's passed on and we laugh at the things they used to say or do. We remember them," she added fondly.

Nuria nodded, momentarily overcome by an unexpected feeling of desolation. If she'd died the other day, who would remember her? Who would put her photo on the wall and laugh at the memory of her anecdotes? How long would her name last in the memory of those who had known her?

Daisy took her arm. "You all right, child? You gone very quiet all of a sudden."

"Yes, I'm fine, thanks." She arranged her face into a grimace intended to pass for a smile.

The Dominican raised a skeptical eyebrow. "Well, I guess you've come to see don Pepe, eh?"

Nuria put her hands in her pockets. "Yes, of course. How is he?"

Daisy nodded in satisfaction. "Very well. He's very well." Looking toward the hallway, she added: "Although right now he's sleeping, like all of them at this hour. You know"—she fanned herself with her hand—"with this heat."

"Oh, I see." Pointing to the second door off the hallway, she asked, "Do you think—?"

Daisy widened her eyes in an exaggerated way. "Of course! He'll be delighted! Just give me a moment to let him know you're here. I'm sure he'll want to get dressed and freshen up." With a mischievous smile she added, "The older they are, the vainer they get."

Fifteen minutes later the door opened, revealing a man leaning on a cane, walking with small steps. He was dressed in a gray-striped summer suit without a tie. The corner of a white handkerchief that matched his shirt peeked from his breast pocket, and a narrow-brimmed fedora covered his disheveled, snow-white hair. He looked like one of those Italian actors from the last century who, whatever their age might be, always looked dignified and elegant.

Don Pepe's bright eyes stood out jovially in a haggard face dotted with age spots. He smiled, displaying a row of small yellowed teeth, then nodded in a satisfied way, as if Nuria had arrived punctually to a prearranged date.

"Hello, princess," he greeted her in a wasted voice.

She took his hands and kissed him on both cheeks. "Hello, Grandpa."

Taking advantage of the fact that the sun was no longer falling on the façade of the building, the old man insisted they sit on the balcony off his bedroom, where Daisy had set a folding table and a couple of camp chairs. At the moment she was laying out a small plate of olives and two vermouths on ice.

"Forgive the mess," she apologized with a wave at the scaffolding that blocked half the balcony and extended to the roof. "They're fixing the façade. I can't wait until the day they'll be finished and gone."

Nuria's grandfather waved her apology away. "It's nothing to worry about, my dear. We're perfectly all right here."

Daisy smiled and winked at them. "On the house," she said and walked away, her rotund figure swaying.

Once alone, grandfather and grandchild eyed each other covertly, avoiding open looks and compliments. Neither was much of a talker. At a nearby window a toddler called for its mother, weeping disconsolately.

Nuria took a small sip of her drink. "How are you?" she asked at last.

He smiled humorlessly. "Old. I turn eighty-seven in three weeks."

Nuria gave him a considering look. "You don't look it."

He dismissed the comment with a wave. "You're a worse liar than your mother." Nuria smiled. This was a compliment. "You don't get enough practice," he added. "Now your father, he was a good storyteller. When he was a little boy he was already spinning tales so tall I used to pretend to believe them just so I could listen to him. Do you remember me telling you about that?"

Nuria nodded, smiling. "When I was little he used to tell me stories every night. Stories he invented as he went along about princesses, dragons, and witches. Always different, and always with a happy ending."

"Your father loved happy endings."

"He was an optimist," she said abruptly, and put the glass to her lips again.

An uncomfortable silence fell over them like a layer of sound-muffling gauze. Even the baby had stopped crying.

"And how's your mother?"

Nuria shrugged, setting the glass on the table. "The same. She continues with her religious mania. More obsessed every day."

The old man saw her expression of pain and shook his head. "Don't blame her. These are difficult times. People hold onto whatever they can. Be grateful she hasn't joined some sect of apocalyptic backpaddles, the type who announce the end of the world while wearing tinfoil hats."

"Yeah, I guess so."

"So what about you?"

"Me?"

"Do you believe in anything?" The question caught her by surprise. He'd never asked her anything like that before.

"No ... I don't know," she replied hesitantly. "I'd say I don't believe in many things. Well, in nothing, really. Why do you ask?"

He skewered an olive with a toothpick before answering. "Sometimes you need to believe in something."

"I thought you were an atheist."

He raised the olive to his mouth. "And so I am. I'm not talking about religion."

"I don't follow you, Grandpa."

He smiled as though he'd just heard a private joke. "It doesn't matter, sweetheart." Setting the toothpick on the table, he crossed his arms over his chest. "On another subject, to what do I owe the honor of this visit?"

Nuria lowered her gaze, pretending to be brushing some crumbs off her T-shirt. "I hadn't come for three weeks, and since I had a day off ..."

"Are you all right?"

"Yeah, perfectly fine."

Again the smile creased the old man's face, multiplying the wrinkles on his cheeks. "You really are a terrible liar, Nuria."

She blushed under the light coat of makeup she'd applied that morning. "I ... I didn't know who to talk to. I mean, there was nobody I wanted to talk to." She looked up like a little girl seeking comfort. "Then I thought of you and ... well ..."

He leaned forward, looking concerned. "Has something happened to you?"

Nuria nodded silently, barely moving her head, thinking that if she opened her mouth to answer, her tears would betray her.

Knowing his granddaughter, Jose Badal remained silent, without insisting, protesting, or making any comment at all. He knew that just then Nuria was like a small, wary bird that might be scared off by the slightest sound.

More than a minute went by before Nuria finally met her grandfather's sympathetic blue eyes. She could no longer hold back her sobs nor did she want to, so she wept, breaking down the fragile barrier she'd managed to keep in place until that moment. Now it split like a dam behind which the pressure had been building up for centuries.

11

Ten minutes later, she'd shared aloud for the first time not only what had happened to her—as she'd done with Susana—but also how she felt in the deepest part of her. Nuria had no idea what had driven her to pour it all out to her grandfather, to make him privy to the despair that had taken hold of her insides like some repulsive parasite extending its greasy tentacles within her body, infecting every thought, every heartbeat.

If she were honest, she did know why. She remembered all the times she'd gone to visit him as a little girl when her grandmother was still alive, the house with its narrow hallways and dark armchairs where she'd sat on the lap of that man who always had a cherry-flavored lollipop in his pocket. She remembered the walks, her hand in his, to the corner café on Sunday mornings, where he would sit beside her at an outdoor table that always seemed to be free. He would drink a glass of wine and ask her with genuine interest about school and what she'd learned that week.

He would share his opinions about what she said, insisting she should believe only half of what she was told. Her grandfather often told her she should never hesitate to ask any questions that might cross her mind, even if the other children laughed and pointed fingers at her. According to him, that only proved how docile and well trained they were going to be when they grew up.

It had taken Nuria a long time to understand what her grandfather had meant by that. Now, thirty years later, sitting in a camp chair that threatened to buckle under her weight, she allowed the last tears that had built up inside her to wash away her anguish. Her grandfather had the good sense not to ask her how she was feeling.

Once she felt the knot obstructing her throat begin to loosen, she surprised herself by saying aloud that she was going to leave her job. Jose Badal seemed not to react. "I'm going to leave the force," she insisted.

The old man said nothing, instead reaching for one of the last lonely olives and putting it calmly into his mouth. The gesture seemed to her like a bit of theater prior to passing judgment on her words, but she was wrong. After chewing and swallowing the olive, he merely looked at his granddaughter and remained silent.

Surprised by his lack of reaction, Nuria asked, "Did you hear what I just said?"

"I heard you. But actually, you haven't said anything."

Nuria blinked in confusion. "What?"

He leaned forward in his chair. "I just listened to a frightened woman who's feeling sorry for herself. But that woman isn't you."

"I meant it, Grandpa."

He shook his head. "That's what you think, but it's not true. I know you too well. This is like what happened after that swimming competition, the one you came last in, when you swore you'd never get into a pool again. You were fourteen, remember? You came to my house, cried, got angry with me for arguing with you, and the following week you were already back training as if nothing had happened."

"Are you comparing that situation with this one?" she asked in disbelief.

Once again, the old man shook his head. "I'm comparing your reaction. You expect me to contradict you and try to convince you that leaving the police force would be the stupidest thing you could do. But you know that already."

"I'm not fourteen anymore."

"Then don't talk as if you were."

Nuria's incredulity wavered on the edge of irritation. "Haven't you been listening? I killed my partner!" Her voice was louder than necessary, but she didn't care. "I shot David in the head!" She put her own finger in the middle of her forehead. "Right here!"

Don Pepe waited for his granddaughter to compose herself before replying. "It was an accident," he said in a low, quiet voice. "You just told me that yourself. I know how easy it is to give in to self-pity, to sit down in a dark corner and wonder: *why me?*" He paused, and his blue eyes seemed to penetrate her. "But you're far better than that. You're not only the best person I've ever known, but also the bravest and the sanest. If you give in, then that criminal who put your partner in the trajectory of the bullet, in a way, will have won. Is that really what you want?"

He reached his hand over the table, seeking hers. Nuria hesitated, still angry, but in the end she took it and squeezed her grandfather's bony fingers affectionately. "I ... I don't know what to do," she admitted desolately, once again on the verge of tears. "Every time I close my eyes I see David staring at me while that damn bullet goes straight for his head. The more I think about it, the more convinced I am that he knew he was going to die. He—"

Jose Badal interrupted her, squeezing her hand in his. "Don't think about it."

Nuria's face was a mask of desolation. "How can I not think about it?" Her chin trembled uncontrollably. "How?"

The old man passed his gaze over the lacquered surface of the table as if looking for the answer in the coffee stains that tattooed it. Looking up with sorrow in his eyes, he said, "I don't know. Though I do know what you *shouldn't* do," he added gravely. "You shouldn't stay at home wasting your time feeling sorry for yourself. The sooner your mind busies itself with something else, the sooner you'll forget what happened—or at least, it will stop hurting so much. If you want my advice, go back to work as soon as possible."

"I … I don't know whether that would be a good idea."

"Of course it is!" he said, frowning. "Listen to the decrepit voice of experience. Call your boss right away and tell him you want to go back to work tomorrow."

Nuria made a face at her grandfather's enthusiasm. "It's more complicated than that. I still have to pass a psychological evaluation, and also there's an internal investigation going on."

"An investigation?"

She waved his fears aside. "Don't worry, Grandpa. It's just standard practice for—" She swallowed. "Never mind, don't worry. But it'll be at least a week before I can go back." She nearly added *if I actually go back*, but she didn't want to be reprimanded again.

The old man seemed to be weighing her with his gaze before answering. "And what will you do in the meantime?"

Nuria shrugged. "In the meantime, I don't know. But what I'm going to do right now," she said, standing up and forcing a smile, "is invite my favorite grandfather to lunch."

"And then you'll come with me to see how Fermina is? It's been a couple of months since I've been to see her and I can't remember the last time you did. I'm sure she misses you."

Nuria nodded, smiling. "Sure, I'm looking forward to seeing her too."

After the promised lunch at a small restaurant in the Barceloneta square, they took a taxi—her grandfather wanted nothing to do with a car that had neither driver nor steering wheel—and went to see Fermina.

Fermina was a small *Beneteau Oceanis* sailboat that measured just over thirty feet and was almost older than she was. She'd been docked at Port Vell ever since Nuria could remember. Her grandfather had taught her to sail on Fermina, and it had been during those long hours at sea off the coast of Barcelona that their deep friendship had grown. In time, it had helped to fill the void left by her father's death.

Nuria hadn't set foot on the boat for over a year, nor had she sailed since she'd started at the police academy. She always told herself she ought to go out sailing with her grandfather someday, as in old times, but in the end she invariably found an excuse for not doing so, and with each passing year, it became harder to recreate those long talks at the helm. Too many memories, perhaps.

But this afternoon, taking advantage of the fact that a cloudy front obscured the sun, mitigating the torture of being out in the open, they cleaned the deck, started the auxiliary engine, and checked the ropes as if they were getting ready to set sail. The maintenance work on Fermina helped Nuria forget her problems for a couple of hours, and when, exhausted by the heat and the effort, she sat on the aft deck to rest, her grandfather went down to the galley and came back up with two bottles of Moritz in his hands.

"They're not very cold, but it's all there is. Do you want one?"

"Are you kidding?" she said, grabbing one of the beers. "I was just about to jump into the water to cool off."

He glanced down at the layer of oil and garbage the sailboat was floating in. "Not sure that would have been a good idea."

"No, the beer's much better, for sure." She raised her bottle in a toast. "To Fermina."

"To Fermina," her grandfather repeated, copying her gesture. "To once again sailing into the sunrise."

"Hear, hear," Nuria added, and took the first swig, ignoring the little voice in her head that told her that was never going to happen again.

As dusk drew on, after leaving her grandfather in a taxi, Nuria found herself wandering aimlessly through the maze of narrow streets of the old El Borne quarter, glancing with scorn at the posters showing the candidates up for election on the first of October. She found it hard to decide which one she liked least.

Though she hesitated over whether to go into one of the cozy little cafés she passed on her way, she always ended up imagining herself sitting at a table staring into her drink, going over and over the events in her head until she fell into the well of depression and remorse once again. Her grandfather was right: she needed to keep her mind occupied.

Without knowing how she'd gotten there, she found herself in front of a Minimax cinema, located in what had previously been an official building of the now-abolished *Generalitat*. She paid for her ticket and chose a movie at random called *The Mechanical Girl*.

After buying a large bucket of popcorn and a giant coke, Nuria sat down in the last row and realized she wasn't hungry, so she set the snacks on the seat next to her. The lights dimmed and the screen lit up, showing a Spanish flag waving in the wind as the national anthem began to thunder from the loudspeakers.

The dozen spectators in the theater stood up. For a moment Nuria resisted following their example, hoping that if she sank back in her seat nobody would see her, but then the beam of a flashlight hit the side of her face, blinding her, and a faceless voice asked her to rise. Some of the other moviegoers turned to look at her. Nuria imagined their disapproving expressions, which might lead to her being reported for disrespecting patriotic symbols. It wasn't worth taking the chance and risking a corresponding loss of citizenship points, so she stood up reluctantly like the rest, waiting for the images of the royal family and the prime minister to come to an end, along with the idealized pictures of the great landmarks of Spanish history.

Nuria tried to let herself be carried away by the movie, an intricate political crime thriller set in a not-so-distant future in exotic Thailand. She'd always wanted to go to Thailand, she thought with a slight frown, but it was too late now. She should have done it ten years ago, when conflict still hadn't broken out in Southeast Asia.

In the end she enjoyed the movie so much that she stayed for the credits and was surprised to see that it was based on a book written almost twenty years before. Nuria wondered how it was possible that a mere writer could have anticipated a future in which sea level had risen more than three feet after Greenland unexpectedly melted, and that neither the UN or the IMF or any other world organization had done anything about it. Why had they only thought to swerve once we'd already missed the curve and were falling helplessly over the cliff?

The screen went black, the lights came on, and the huge fans on the ceiling slowed to a halt, inviting the few spectators still in their seats to leave the theater. One of them, a young man with a shaved head and a Spain First tattoo on his forearm, gave her an evil look as he passed her. Nuria thought she heard him muttering an insult, but she chose to ignore it. The last thing she wanted was to confront a neo-patriot looking for trouble.

By the time she came out of the theater, the sun was no longer wielding its crushing dominion over the streets and the temperature had descended to bearable limits. Once again unsure of what to do, she dismissed the idea of going into the theater again and watching another movie. For a moment she wondered whether to call Susana, or even her mother. But though she felt like talking, she realized she didn't want to do it with anybody who knew her. So she wandered aimlessly, then went into the first bar she passed, sat down, and ordered a gin and tonic.

After an hour Nuria had rejected two losers who'd insisted on buying her a drink, but the third turned out to be pleasant, with attractive amber eyes and a broad smile that he didn't hesitate to show with charming persistence. He reminded Nuria of her cat Melon. The only thing he failed to do was purr. After spending some time chatting with him she was tempted to scratch him under the chin to see whether he would.

Gradually the alcohol, the heat, and her unknown companion's charms took their effect. Not wanting to spend the night alone, she let herself be led to a nearby hotel, where she allowed his avid hands to undress her first and then take her over and over again until dawn.

When she awoke the following morning, he was no longer there and she was unable to recall his name.

Perhaps she hadn't even asked.

12

The door to the office opened and a man shorter than she was with closely cropped white hair, dressed in a studiedly casual fashion, peered out without taking his hand off the doorknob. He smiled cordially, the corners of his eyes crinkling behind his round glasses.

"Officer Badal," he greeted her, sweeping her toward his office with an eloquent wave of his hand. "Good morning."

"Corporal Badal, if you don't mind." Nuria's voice was subdued.

"Of course, of course, forgive me."

Nuria rose from the uncomfortable plastic chair in the waiting room and walked past him with the same level of enthusiasm felt by a parachutist unsure whether or not his parachute will open when he pulls the ring.

Taking a seat in front of the wide wooden desk, she glanced around. She was in a room halfway between an office and a medical examining room. On one side, a set of shelves held an extensive collection of thick, out-of-date medical books, perhaps with no other function than to show off and intimidate patients. The collection of diplomas and pictures taken with high-ranking civil servants that hung on the opposite wall served the same function.

This wasn't the first time she'd been here, but on the previous occasions she'd come here as a matter of routine, full of confidence, regarding it as a mere formality that she had to go through annually, like every other officer.

The white-haired man went to the other side of the table and sat down in his comfortable, brown-leather armchair. Above it was a bombastic diploma which credited Don Alberto Paniagua Garcia as a doctor in psychology on behalf of the University of Valladolid.

He indicated a tray of assorted drinks. "Would you like something to drink? Coffee? Water? A soft drink?"

She placed her hands in her lap. "No, thanks."

"Please relax," the doctor said, noticing her self-conscious posture. "I want you to feel comfortable."

"I am relaxed, thanks."

He nodded, not entirely convinced. "All right … You look well, Corporal Badal," he added, leaning back in his seat. "How do you feel?"

"Fine, thanks."

Doctor Paniagua seemed to be assessing this answer as though she'd given him a report a hundred pages long. This, among other reasons, was why Nuria detested psychologists.

"Hmm," was his only reply. His gaze went to the tablet he was holding. Tapping on the screen, he asked: "How's your mother?"

"My mother?" She was on the point of firing back *That's none of your business*, but she held back in time. "She's fine too, thanks."

"Apparently"—he looked up, and his gaze met her own—"you don't see her very often."

"Well, I ..."

"Why?"

Nuria shifted uncomfortably in her chair. She hadn't expected the interview to take this turn. "I don't understand the purpose of your question," she admitted. "I thought this was an evaluation to establish whether I can go back to work."

A smug smile that Nuria didn't like at all flashed over the psychologist's face. "Any aspect of our lives may be revealing as a reflection of our psyche, Corporal Badal." He intertwined his fingers and leaned forward over the table. "So tell me. What are your feelings toward your mother?"

She hesitated a moment before answering. "Well ... I love her, naturally."

"And?"

"I ... well ... she's my mother."

Doctor Paniagua did not insist. Instead, he looked at Nuria and typed a long note on his tablet. "I see," he murmured as he wrote.

For a second she was tempted to ask him what the hell he thought he saw. To tell him that in reality he didn't know shit about anything. "Work," she said instead. "Work doesn't leave me with much free time to visit her."

"Of course," he replied without raising his gaze from the tablet. The psychologist continued to write for what Nuria considered an absurdly long time. Finally he raised his eyes and asked: "Do you think you're ready to resume active duty?"

The direct question took her by surprise once again. Maybe that was his game: to unsettle the person he was speaking to.

"Yes, of course," she replied without hesitation.

"You seem very sure of that."

"That's because I am."

The pause that followed her reply suggested to Nuria that once again this wasn't the correct answer. If this had been a game show on TV, a red light on her lectern would have lit up with a blaring *beeep!*

67

"It's only been a few days since the incident," the doctor said, all condescension now. "It's normal for you to feel confused and upset. There's no need to be ashamed of it. I'm here to help you, but you have to be honest with me."

Like hell.

"I'm fine."

"You haven't had any nightmares?"

"I've been sleeping well."

"Have you been auto-medicating?"

"I've never done that."

"Drugs? Hashish? Marijuana …?"

"No."

"Do you drink?"

"Excuse me?"

"Beer? Wine? Whisky?"

"No … well, a beer or two when I go out in the evening. Nothing else."

"Have you spoken to your partner's widow?"

"What? I … I haven't …" *Beeep!* "I haven't been able to yet. I haven't found the … well, the right moment."

"Gloria, isn't it? Her name's Gloria Palau. And her son's name is …" He tapped his tablet briefly. "Her son's name is Luis. He's three years old."

"Yes … Luisito. A lovely child … he has his father's eyes. And she's a really nice woman."

Paniagua made a note on his tablet. "From what I can see, you had a close relationship," he went on without pause. "Outside of work hours, I mean."

"He was my partner and my friend."

"Nothing else?"

"What?"

"I'm asking you whether there was some kind of sentimental relationship between the two of you."

"What?" Her brain seemed to be incapable of producing any other word. *Beeep*!

"Was there an intimate relationship between Sergeant Insúa and yourself?" the doctor asked calmly.

"No!" she burst out at last, finally awakening from her daze. She sat up straight in her chair. "Never! How dare you suggest something like that?"

"Please calm yourself."

"Calm myself? Well, you stop making insinuations!"

"I haven't made any insinuations." He raised his hands in a gesture of innocence. "I simply asked you a question."

"Like hell you did!" she said, out loud this time, before she could stop herself.

Beeep! Beeep! Beeep!

"Relax, Corporal Badal. This isn't a trial, it's just an assessment to determine the suitability of your return to active duty."

Nuria opened her mouth to reply again but realized at the last moment that she was on the brink of insulting the psychologist who was evaluating her. She closed her eyes and inhaled as deeply as her lungs would allow. Releasing the air through her nose as she'd been taught in yoga class, she allowed her exhalation to draw out all her rage.

"I beg your pardon," she said in a pleasant voice once she'd calmed down. "This whole … situation. It's very hard. I'm still … I'm fine, but I still need some time to take on …" She stopped herself when she realized she was babbling. "I just *need* to get back to active duty," she finished.

"Why?"

"What do you mean, why? Because it's my job. It's what I know how to do best, what I enjoy, what I need."

"And you don't think what happened to you could affect your performance as a police officer?"

"No. Absolutely not."

"The stress might affect you and lead you to commit errors of judgment."

"That's not going to happen."

"And if you found yourself in a similar situation?"

Nuria narrowed her eyes suspiciously. "I'm not following you."

"Imagine," the psychologist said, leaning back in his chair, "that you found yourself in a hostage situation again. That an armed suspect was holding your new partner, threatening to kill him unless you dropped your weapon. That you had only seconds to decide what to do."

Nuria shook her head, denying the possibility. "It's impossible that that would happen to me again. Not to me."

"Unlikely, but not impossible," the psychologist corrected her. "You have three seconds."

"That's not—"

"Two seconds."

"But—"

"Bang!" the doctor cried, slamming both hands on his desk. "Your partner just died."

"That's not fair!"

"Life's not fair, Corporal Badal. Another partner has just died. Another widow. Another orphan. Because you froze." The psychologist's voice was a vortex that swept up the images of David bleeding to death on the floor. Staring at her out of that third eye she had put in his forehead.

"Shut up!" she yelled. "I couldn't do anything! It wasn't my fault!"

"It was you who pulled the trigger." He pointed an accusing finger at her. "You, Corporal Badal."

Without really knowing how, as if someone else had taken control of her body and she were utterly unable to prevent it, she saw herself springing up from her chair and hurling herself at the doctor, who, his eyes bulging with fear, barely had time to press the alarm button before a woman who was nearly six feet tall, deranged with fury, seized him by the neck with every intention of strangling him, screaming over and over again: "Shut up! Shut up! Shut up!"

13

The bustle in the cafeteria at the Plaza de España station somehow helped to soothe Nuria's spirits. The noise also insured that her conversation with Susana, who was sitting in front of her, still in uniform and holding a steaming cup of coffee, could not be overheard by anyone else.

"Three weeks' suspension without pay," Nuria was explaining, a little calmer after her second tila. "And a new psychological evaluation in a month to decide whether the suspension will turn into expulsion."

Her friend watched her, surprise and something more in her eyes. Taking a sip of her coffee, she ventured cautiously: "Even so, I think you were lucky."

Nuria gave her a stern look. "I'm starting to get a bit tired of people telling me I'm lucky."

Susana shook her head. "Fuck, Nuria. You were on the brink of strangling the police psychologist."

Nuria frowned. "Is that a smile I see on your face?"

Susana covered her mouth, but it was too late to deny it, so she let the smile spread across her face. "I mean, who the hell thinks of attacking the psychologist who's evaluating him?"

Indignant at her friend's reaction, Nuria protested, "That moron was just provoking me! He was asking for it!"'

"Damn it, of course he was! That's his job! He pushed you to see whether you'd explode." She laughed openly, no longer trying to hide it. "And oh my, you certainly did just that!"

"It's not funny."

"Yes, it is," Susana shot back. "You must have scared the holy shit out of the guy!"

At last a smile appeared on Nuria's lips too, as she recalled the scene with an amused gleam in her eyes. "That's true. I thought he was going to pee on himself."

Susana laughed. "I'd have paid to see that!"

"Next time I'll wear my gogglecam and upload the video to YouTube." She winked at Susana. The two friends laughed for a while, letting their tension and ill humor evaporate as it always did when they were together.

When they'd fallen silent once again, at the mercy of the conversations around them, Susana asked: "And what are you going to do in the meantime?"

Nuria shrugged. "No idea, quite honestly. He prescribed these pills"—she reached into her pocket and took out a small plastic bottle full of green capsules—"and suggested that I do plenty of exercise and find a hobby that'll help me relax."

"A hobby? You?"

"Yeah, I know. I'll have to find one. Any suggestions?"

"Does drinking beer count as a hobby?"

Nuria shook her head, smiling. "That falls under basic needs, like sleeping and eating."

Susana nodded. "You're right there." She raised her cup as if for a toast before taking another sip. "Ah, I know! How about a trip?"

"A trip? I don't know whether …"

Susana paid no attention to her friend's skeptical expression. "It's perfect! You could go to Paris. You've never been to Paris, have you?"

"Well … no."

"I wish I could come with you! I think they rebuilt the downtown after the riots. They say it's even better than before. I think they've even rebuilt Notre Dame. You've got to go!"

"Yeah, well … I don't know, Susi. I don't think it's a good idea. With everything that's happened, I'm not sure a bunch of photos of me on Instaface strolling through Paris is the image I want to present."

Susana opened her mouth to respond, but realized at once that Nuria was right. Automatic labeling meant that even if she entered the field of vision of someone taking a photo or a video for even a second, their facial recognition software would identify her instantly. That meant she would be labeled and her image uploaded to the social networks in a matter of seconds without her even being aware of it. These were bad times for anyone who wanted to pass unnoticed.

"Hmm … yeah," she admitted. "You're right. But then … what are you going to do?"

"I don't know. I might take the psychologist's advice."

Susana jabbed a finger at her. "Don't even think of it! Better drunk than hooked on those fucking pills."

Nuria smiled again and patted her friend's arm fondly. "Thanks, Susi."

Her friend raised an eyebrow. "Thanks for what?"

"For being here."

"You invited me for a coffee. There was nothing else I could do."

Nuria smiled. Bringing her face close to her friend's, she asked in a whisper, "In that case, can I take advantage and ask another favor of you?"

"Of course. What do you need?"

"Information."

"Information?" Susana repeated, puzzled by the request and the tone it had been made in. "About what?"

Nuria looked around discreetly before answering. "I've tried to access the report on my"—she hesitated, searching for the right word—"*incident*, but it's under a gag order and I can't see it."

"And what do you want me to do? If it's under a gag order, I don't have the authority to access it either."

"I know. That's why I need you to find out as much as you can. I can't go around the station asking questions while I'm suspended, but you can."

"All right." Susana sounded far from convinced. "But it's not my investigation or my department, so I don't know how far I'll be able to dig without getting the door slammed in my face."

"I know. Just find out what you can."

Her friend nodded. "Okay. But first tell me why you want to know all that."

"Wouldn't *you* want to know?"

"That's not an answer."

"David is dead, Susi," Nuria said gravely. "I need to know why, if I don't want to go crazy."

"You were just in the wrong place at the wrong time, that's all. Don't beat yourself up about it."

Nuria set her forearms on the table, leaned closer, and lowered her voice even further. "No, it wasn't chance. I think that bastard knew we were coming and he was there waiting for us."

Susana raised her eyebrows, incredulous. "Waiting for you? Why would he do that?"

"That's what I need to find out," Nuria whispered. "I don't believe he was just a junkie, as Puig insists." She shook her head before explaining herself. "The guy we were going to see, the one who got his throat slit before we arrived, was one of Elias's henchmen. We'd been putting pressure on him for some time with no results. Then suddenly he up and calls David, saying he needs to see him urgently."

"Shit, do you think he was going to betray him?"

"Very possibly."

"And you're thinking that"—she looked around warily before adding—"Elias ordered the three of you killed?" Nuria stared at her friend in silence. There was no need to answer. "I'll do what I can," Susana said. "But ... well, you know how this sort of thing tends to go."

Nuria took her hand and smiled reassuringly. "I know. Thanks, Susi."

"You're welcome." She winked at her in reply. "What are you going to do in the meantime?"

Nuria looked thoughtful. "Mm … I don't know. I might take that trip to Paris like you suggested."

Susana shook her head. "Yeah, right. You're going to stay home watching horror movies and eating ice cream, am I right?"

Nuria smiled guiltily from ear to ear.

14

When at last night fell over the city and the merciless sun grew tired of melting the sidewalks, exhausted Barcelonians took over from the tourists, gradually appearing in the doorways of the buildings like groundhogs emerging after a long winter sleep.

The sandals-with-socks crowd and the hordes of Chinese tourists on electric scooters vanished into thin air once the low-energy streetlamps no longer gave enough light to take good photos to be shared on the net. The narrow pedestrian streets of the Barrio de Gracia watched as the short-lived streams of neighbors flowed from the old modernist buildings to the squares and outdoor cafés, congratulating themselves on having survived another day of the never-ending heat wave.

The illegal batteries and solar panels on the roof of 77 Verdi Street allowed its tenants to enjoy almost twenty-four hours of guaranteed electricity, bridging the power cuts that systematically affected the city during the peak hours of heat. If found out, the tenants of the building would have a stiff fine to face for breaking the Law of Energy Usage that heavily taxed the use of solar energy. But it was either that or suffocate to death, so there wasn't much choice.

Nuria, reclining on her plush gray couch with Melon in her lap, was enjoying the air conditioning that kept the temperature at a bearable seventy-nine degrees. Digging the spoon into the half-melted tub of vanilla ice cream, she smiled to herself as she raised it to her lips, thinking about how close Susana had come to guessing how she was going to spend her days. She'd only missed the mark with the horror movies, but Nuria was currently amusing herself with a Netflix documentary about the last presidency of the United States, so she hadn't been completely wrong.

The spoonful of ice cream melted in Nuria's mouth as, eyes closed, she rolled it around with her tongue, moving it from one cheek to the other, enjoying every last trace of flavor. She finally opened her eyes again when her fifty-inch screen showed the president of the United States signing the order for the occupation of Mexican territory north of the twenty-fifth parallel, claiming it was the only way to end immigration and the drug traffic promoted by the Chihuahua and Sinaloa cartels once and for all.

"Who would have thought …" murmured Nuria, remembering the disastrous end to that story. Since her mouth was full of ice cream, though, it came out more like *Who hood ha hought ...* Just then, the symbol indicating an incoming call appeared in the upper right-hand corner of her screen. "*Ansher hall*," she called urgently to the assistant.

"Sorry," Sofia's voice said apologetically, "but I can't help you with that."

Nuria made an effort to vocalize and tried again, opening her mouth exaggeratedly as she did so. "*Ansher hall.*"

"Answering call," the assistant confirmed this time. An instant later, the image of her caller replaced the angry orange man on the screen. "*Hehho Huhi!*" she greeted her friend effusively.

Susana put her face close to the camera. "What the hell's wrong with your mouth?"

"*Ho ong ...*" Nuria apologized with a wave, making her friend wait a few seconds until she could swallow her ice cream. "There," she said, wiping her mouth with her hand. "What's up?"

"What's up is that I did what you asked me to," came the answer in a low voice.

"What I asked you?" inquired Nuria, trying to remember. "Oh yes, to access—"

"Yes, that," Susana whispered, cutting her off.

"Why are you talking like that?"

Susana glanced furtively behind her. "I'm still at the station."

"Oh, I see." Nuria lowered her own voice, although in her case it made no sense. "So what did you find out?"

Susana shook her head. "Nothing. There's nothing."

"Nothing important?"

"No. I mean nothing at all. The report isn't in our files or in the ones from the court."

"I don't understand. That's ... impossible. You must have overlooked it."

"Believe me, I searched for it thoroughly."

"But ... there has to be a report. An officer died, Susi. The subject's under a gag order."

"Well, there should be, but there isn't. What do you want me to tell you? Either somebody's deleted it, or else it was never there."

"And where else would it be if not there?"

"Perhaps they've classified it as top secret and it's on some intranet I can't access."

"Why would they classify it as top secret?"

"How do you expect me to know? Ask the commissioner."

"Good idea."

"Jesus, no. I was joking, Nuria. You can't ask him that." Susana frowned. "If you do, he'll know you've gotten into the files and he'll raise hell. Or worse still, they'll find out I did it for you and I'll take the rap."

"I can be subtle."

"Hah!" Susana burst out. "Subtle? You? You're the least subtle woman I know."

"Look who's talking."

Susana heaved a deep sigh. "Seriously, Nuria, don't do it. You won't gain anything by it apart from another black mark in your file."

"I can't just go on doing nothing, Susi."

"Well then, find some other way."

Nuria thought for a moment. In the end she nodded. "Yes, maybe you're right."

"I always am," Susana replied smugly.

"Yes, of course." Nuria smiled distractedly, her head already elsewhere. "I'll call you later."

Susana's face eyed her from the screen with distrust. "What are you going to do?"

"I don't know yet."

"Okay, but keep me informed, all right? Don't do anything stupid without telling me first."

"Of course. Count on it."

Susana snorted. "Jesus, what a lousy liar you are, Nuria."

"So I've been told." Nuria smiled. "See you later, Susi, and thanks." A second later she hung up. Susana was right. She was a bad liar.

The mere idea of going back to Villarefu, and particularly to that house, sent a shiver all the way up her back to the nape of her neck. What had happened there was still too fresh in her mind. Closing her eyes, she could almost smell the dampness, the stale air; she could almost hear the unnerving music from the other side of the street. It was a stupid idea, but she couldn't think of a better one. Without access to witnesses, evidence, or the report, the only thing she could do was go back to the scene of the crime and try to find some evidence on her own. What she couldn't do was sit at home with her arms crossed. Or rather, she could, but she didn't want to. It would be the equivalent of hiding under the bed—and really, she thought, there was no better way to overcome a trauma than to face up to it as soon as possible. So in a way, the excuse she'd been waiting for had been handed to her on a tray.

"Let's go, then," she murmured to herself. Leaving the half-eaten ice cream on the couch, she stood up, trying not to think too much about what she was about to do, just in case she suffered an untimely attack of sanity.

It took her only a moment to dress discreetly in loose dark clothes, to which she added a black scarf to cover her head. Under cover of night, she hoped it would help her go unnoticed inside the camp, where most of the women were from North Africa. Looking at her reflection in the mirror, she concluded that her disguise wouldn't hold up to a second glance, but she had nothing better on hand, and it would have to do.

Next she looked around her apartment, gathering a penknife, tweezers, small plastic bags, and anything else she could find that might be useful for collecting evidence, then put everything into a small brown leather backpack. She did the same with her regulation flashlight. Finally, she opened the safe in her closet, took out her Walther PPK with its clip holster, and attached it to the back of her belt so it was hidden under her loose shirt. She hoped she wouldn't be forced to use it while she was suspended because it would be difficult to justify, but what she knew for sure was that there was no way she was going to go to Villarefu in the middle of the night unarmed. To act stupidly was one thing, to *be* stupid something else entirely.

Now she had to solve the small problem of how to get there. Taxis and Ubers didn't go into the camp, so they were both out. She could ask Susana for her car, but in exchange she would have to lie to avoid worrying her. Finally she decided on one of the small BCNrent eSmart electric cars that rented by the hour. There was a charging station only two blocks away.

Lastly, she made a quick check, patting her pockets to make sure she had everything, and took one more deep breath to fill her lungs with eighty-degree air. Then, turning the handle decisively, she opened the door and left her apartment.

In an inversion of what happened during the hottest hours of the day, pedestrians were now thronging the squares and outdoor cafés of the Barrio de Gracia, while the number of vehicles on the streets had declined, even on the ever-busy Ronda de Dalt. When the little eSmart car turned onto the avenue, there was barely any traffic.

The light hiss of the electric engine and the absence of anybody to talk to made Nuria feel suddenly lonely. Reflexively she turned on the radio and selected a station at random to make the uncomfortable silence more bearable.

"We have a new call," the female announcer said. "This is Radio Popular. Over to you, caller."

"My name's Juan," said a man's voice, sounding upset. "I just want to say that I've had it up to here with so much politicking. The pirate attack on Formentera is unacceptable. What we've got to do is put warships all around the fucking coast and sink every boat that comes anywhere near Spain, for Christ's sake!"

"Including the dinghies carrying refugees?" asked the announcer.

"Of course!" Juan was obviously delighted to be asked the question. "It's a fucking invasion, can't they see that? The Moors are invading Spain again and as if that weren't bad enough, we're welcoming them with open arms."

"I wouldn't go as far as that."

"We let them come and stay. Isn't that far enough?"

"Let me remind you that most of them are women, children, and old people fleeing war," the announcer said. "Practically all the men are either dead or fighting against ISMA."

"I don't give a shit! It's their war, isn't it? Let them stay there and deal with it. There's no room in Spain for even one more fucking refugee, don't you realize that?"

"So you think we should use artillery fire to sink the dinghies?"

"It's the only way to make them realize we don't want them here."

"I understand that. But then ... what will happen to all those refugees?"

"They can flee somewhere else."

"What about those who are already here?"

"They ought to be kicked out. All of them. Legal, illegal, refugees ... this is Spain, right? Spaniards first!"

"That sounds like political propaganda to me," the announcer said.

"Of course it does! Salvador Aguirre is the only one with the balls to do what's necessary."

"You mean expelling all the foreigners, even if they've spent their whole lives in Spain and have jobs, children ...?"

"All of them," the caller insisted. "They've spent too long bleeding us dry and taking jobs away from the Spaniards. They can make a life for themselves somewhere else, for fuck's sake."

"But plenty of them already have Spanish citizenship and in some cases were even born here."

"Well then, if we gave it to them we can take it away! Spain's our country. It doesn't belong to the Moors, the South Americans, the Chinese, or the blacks!"

"So is your objection to all foreigners ... or only to the ones who don't have white skin?"

"For Christ's sake!" the caller snapped, fed up with hearing so many objections. "Whose side are you on?"

Nuria, tired of listening to all this, reached out and changed the station. The images proliferating in her mind of warships shooting at dinghies filled with women and children were more than she could bear.

Now a newscaster was listing the results of the opinion polls for the presidential elections scheduled for the first of October. The conservative alliance was maintaining its absolute majority, but the neo-patriots of Spain First were slipping in the polls, teetering on the edge of no longer being needed in the coalition. Nuria hoped very much that this was true. She detested their candidate, Salvador Aguirre, partly because he was the leader of a macho, xenophobic party and just as much because he was the leader of the Church of the Reborn in Spain.

After listening to a brief analysis of the electoral campaign, she turned to lighter fare such as the worrying development of a major storm in the Mediterranean and the imminent inauguration of the cathedral of the Sagrada Familia, specifically, the Holy Father's delicate health and the possibility that he might not be able to attend this long-awaited event. This particular news item was accompanied by the background noise of hundreds of faithful members of the Reborn in Christ sect lighting candles in the Plaza Catalunya and praying for his recovery.

Nuria imagined that her mother was there, kneeling in the white robe of the Reborn devotees, her forehead touching the ground in a sign of humility, praying that God would breathe health into the founder of her church.

15

As luck would have it, this evening the same overweight guard as last time was on duty in the booth at the southern gate. Nuria still had her badge in her wallet, but when she stopped at the entrance she simply put her head out the window. He recognized her and let her in. The advantage of this was that she'd avoided turning her access to the camp into something official. In any case she hoped she wouldn't be long. In and out.

As in the city ablaze with light on the other side of the river, here people had streamed *en masse* out of their overheated shacks, flooding the dusty streets of Villarefu. Under the paltry light of the few streetlamps men, women, and children wandered up and down with no real destination, dodging the rickshaw and bicycle traffic, stopping at the steaming itinerant food stands, patronizing the vendors of pens, candy, and second-hand cell phones. Nuria left the eSmart in almost the same spot where she'd parked the Prius a few days back, but this time she was alone and couldn't count on the comforting presence of headquarters on the other side of her earpiece.

With the large scarf hiding her long hair, her loose shirt and worn jeans, Nuria was a vague figure in the scant light of the street, managing to pass unnoticed in the crowd. As long as no one took an interest in a tall woman walking with her head down, everything would go fine. It wasn't that she would be lynched if she identified herself as a police officer, but she would rather not use that card unless it was unavoidable.

Nuria looked up unobtrusively every once in a while to see where she was going and made herself stop now and then just to make sure she was heading in the right direction. She didn't want to get lost, but it wouldn't be a good idea to let the other passersby see her checking her phone like some tourist lost in the Barrio Gotico.

The transformation of this place with the arrival of night was so radical she could almost imagine she was strolling through a dilapidated slum in Fez or Dakar, forgetting that she was really in a refugee camp only a couple of miles from Barcelona.

The smell of deep fat at a *buñuelo* stall stirred her appetite and she remembered she hadn't eaten anything solid since noon, but she decided it wouldn't be advisable to open her mouth and reveal her accent, so she restrained her hunger and promised herself a good dinner once she was back home.

Suddenly she realized she was in front of Vilchez's home. A large black-and-yellow sticker on the door warned potential intruders in Spanish, French, and Arabic of the serious legal consequences they would incur if they tried to gain access to the building. In spite of this, Nuria wasn't surprised to find the sticker partially peeled from the door. There was no warning in the world capable of stopping thieves, curious neighbors, or idle teenagers from taking a look at the scene of a horrifying crime.

Nuria glanced warily behind her. Once she was sure no one was paying attention, she peeled off the sticker. Taking a moment to inhale some courage, she turned the handle and entered the house.

A gust of stale, damp air hit her as soon as she shut the door and a shiver ran down her back as she relived her feelings of several days earlier. Nuria realized it hadn't been a good idea to come back with the memory still so fresh in her mind. She could still feel in her bones the horror of what she'd lived through here, the sudden understanding of the consequence of that shot, as she saw David crumple to the ground, a nine-millimeter hole in his forehead.

For a moment she felt an almost irresistible urge to turn and run. She closed her eyes and intentionally slowed her breathing to bring down her heart rate and remain calm. This was the only way she could get her rational side and her police training to take over. She reminded herself that the killer with the bloodshot eyes who appeared again and again in her nightmares was completely and irrevocably dead.

Thirty seconds later, once again in control of her emotions and fears, Nuria took the flashlight out of her pocket and pointed the beam around her. "Hello?" she called into the darkness. "Is anybody here?"

She waited, but luckily, there was no answer. She searched for a light switch, eventually finding a short chain attached to the naked bulb that hung from the ceiling less than a handspan above her head. Reaching up, she pulled it. There was a click, but nothing happened. "Of course not," she grumbled. Forgetting the light, she swept the room with her flashlight instead, then wondered if she'd come to the wrong shack. Pivoting in place, she murmured, "What the hell ..."

The room was spotless, empty. Not only had the mountain of clothes the killer had hidden himself under disappeared, so had the table and chairs. Even the TV and the fruit crate it had stood on had been taken.

Her first thought was that thieves, having decided Vilchez would no longer need any of it, must be responsible. But it didn't make sense. They might have taken the TV, the furniture, and the clothes, but the garbage as well? Nobody was as desperate as that, not even in Villarefu.

This had to have been the work of the forensic team. They'd taken the business of collecting evidence to the extreme. That meant that despite their doubts, they were taking the investigation very seriously. Nuria had never seen such diligence in the collection of evidence from a crime scene. No doubt it was a good thing they took their job so seriously. But in spite of her efforts, she couldn't shake the feeling that there was something very odd about it.

In truth, Nuria herself didn't really know what she was looking for. Seeing the state in which her forensic colleagues had left the house, it seemed impossible that they could have overlooked anything. Even so, she decided to take a look at the rest of the shack and headed to the room where they'd found the body.

The circle of white light cast by her flashlight preceded her down the hallway, oscillating from side to side as she walked, aiming it at the floor and walls, alert to any possible piece of evidence.

Reaching the tiny kitchen, she pulled aside the oilcloth curtain and looked inside. A handful of flies hovered above the dirty dishes that were still piled on the greasy countertop as if waiting for someone to get down to washing them. Apparently the diligence of the forensic team didn't go this far.

It was then that the depressing idea that perhaps this was the extent of Wilson Vilchez's legacy occurred to Nuria: an inheritance of dirty, fly-covered dishes. Firmly pushing the thought out of her mind, she allowed the curtain to swing shut and went on toward Vilchez's room.

The hallway was even darker than the last time she'd been in it, if such a thing were possible. Since it was night, there was no trace of sunlight filtering through the cracks in the building. Only the soothing beam of her flashlight prevented her from panicking and running out of the shack as fast as she could. *Easy, Nuria*, she told herself, her heart rate accelerating by the moment. *There's no one here ... keep calm.*

Summoning up her courage, she went to the end of the narrow hallway and halted in front of the closed curtain, remembering the unfortunate Vilchez, slaughtered like a pig in his bed, soaked in his own blood, his tongue lolling out of his slit throat. *Stay calm, Nuria*, she repeated. Holding her breath, she grasped the edge of the oilcloth and pulled it to one side.

Vilchez, of course, was no longer there, but the blood-soaked sheets were, tangled on the old blue-and-white mattress. A cloud of flies danced in the beam of her flashlight with a sticky buzzing, startled by the interruption. "Jesus," Nuria muttered, tugging the curtain shut and fighting back her nausea. Taking a deep breath in an attempt to restore her lost composure, she waited to open the curtain again until she was sure she wouldn't throw up.

Though the body was no longer there, everything else seemed to be in place. The drawers had been opened, the modest closet searched, that much was obvious, but clothes, shoes, and personal belongings had been left behind.

It didn't make sense. If they'd taken everything in the living room in search of evidence, shouldn't they have done the same in the rest of the house? They hadn't even taken the blood-soaked sheets.

Nuria turned back toward the hallway, looking in the direction of the front door. Why had they taken even the garbage from one room and left almost everything untouched in the other? What was the difference?

She retraced her steps along the hallway until she was back in the living room. "Why?" she asked herself aloud. "Why did you clean out this room and not that one?" Nuria swept her light across the walls, revealing that even the posters had been taken. All that remained were the holes left in the walls by the thumbtacks.

"Why?" she asked herself again. She sensed the answer was hiding somewhere in her mind, reluctant to show itself. It whispered to her that the answer was something obvious that she was unable to see.

Suddenly Nuria noticed some small discolored spots at eye level on the compressed-cardboard wall. Peering at them more closely, an unexpected smell of bleach pervaded her nostrils. Puzzled, she stood still, blinking, her light still trained on the wall. The fact that she was still able to perceive the strong smell of the bleach meant someone must have used it not long ago.

Taking a step back, she swept her flashlight across the room once more, wondering why the forensic team had disinfected the room so thoroughly. It was certainly not part of their normal protocol to clean up a crime scene after taking prints and samples.

"What were you getting rid of?" she asked aloud, running the tips of her fingers along the wall as if her sense of touch might give her the answer.

Abruptly the pieces fell into place. The explanation was so obvious she clicked her tongue, impatient with herself. "Of course," she murmured, shutting off the flashlight and turning it around. Now a small beam of ultraviolet light shone from the other end, bathing the room in a ghostly black-and-blue light that made the dust motes on her clothing and the laces of her tennis shoes shine in the dark.

But the most interesting thing about the black light, and the reason it was an essential feature of her standard-issue flashlight was that it made any bodily fluid stand out: urine, semen … or blood.

Nuria swept the black light thoroughly over all the walls and floor, with no results. The very last trace of blood had been wiped from the room. "Shit," she muttered. This made even less sense. Why remove all the blood from the living room that way? Since when did the forensic team do clean-up work? And why hadn't they done the same thing in Vilchez's room? There was certainly a lot of blood there. What was the difference?

Before Nuria had finished formulating the question in her mind, before she was aware that she knew it, the answer appeared on her lips. "It's *his* blood," she murmured, calling up the killer's spine-chilling face again. "*His* fucking blood."

Drops of David's and the killer's blood must have spattered all over the room during the shootout. For some reason, someone had wanted to wipe away every trace of that man's blood and, unable to tell it apart from David's, had wiped it all.

Nuria turned around, training the beam of light in a wide arc, confirming, despite her disbelief, that not a single drop of blood had escaped the forensic team's enthusiasm for hygiene.

If it *had* been them, of course, something she was beginning to doubt.

Someone had entered the shack and eliminated even the last trace of Vilchez's killer's blood for the express purpose of preventing him from being identified through his DNA. Nuria couldn't imagine a forensic team destroying evidence from a crime scene. It meant—incredible as it might seem—that someone else had had access to the scene later.

But who?

More important still, why?

Two good questions whose answers she couldn't even begin to guess. If someone had gone to all that trouble to get rid of the blood, it was because something in it might be important. But that didn't make sense either—given that the killer's body, no doubt at that moment on a slab somewhere in the coroner's lab, still existed.

An ominous feeling crept through her. Pulling out her phone, Nuria scanned her contact list for Margarita Font, a coroner's assistant she'd had drinks with once, and punched in her number.

Margarita's sleepy face answered, a note of concern in her voice. "Hello? What's up, Nuria?"

"Hi, Marga. Sorry to bother you, but I have a question."

Marga blinked at the phone, rubbing her eyes. "I hope it's important," she said, with a trace of reproach in her voice. "I had a terrible time falling asleep in this heat."

"I'm sorry. Next time we meet, drinks are on me."

Marga nodded. "That's a good argument. So what's the question?"

"It's about the case where ..." She realized she wasn't sure how to phrase it. "Where David ... where I ..."

"Yeah, I know the one," Marga said, rescuing her from her predicament. "What do you want to know?"

"Did they take three bodies? Vilchez's, David's, and the killer's?"

"That's right."

"And do you still have the killer's?"

"The killer's?" Marga repeated in surprise. "Why would we? David's was delivered to his family and the other two were incinerated at once."

"Of course. I understand. But were you able to identify the killer?"

Marga tried to remember for a moment, then shook her head. "The guy had medically erased his fingerprints, most likely with Capecitabine, an antimetabolite that professional killers usually inject themselves with to eliminate their fingerprints."

"Didn't you take DNA samples when you did the autopsy?"

"There was no autopsy. Cause of death was clear, and DNA samples are only taken if a judge orders it."

"Then there's no way to identify him?"

"Nuria ..." Marga's voice sounded weary, as if she were explaining something her listener ought to have known already. "Every week we incinerate two or three unidentified bodies. We take fingerprints and photos of them, but nothing else. There's no time or resources to find out who they are using DNA analysis, and in most cases it would be useless because they're usually undocumented immigrants and we'd never know who they were, even if we tried. And after all, it isn't something anybody cares about."

"But in this case, he was a murderer."

"Alleged murderer," Marga corrected her. "And as I told you, if a judge doesn't expressly order it, we don't take samples of tissue or DNA."

"I see ..." Nuria muttered, hiding her disappointment. "Thanks very much, Marga."

"You're welcome. Are you working on the case? I heard you'd been suspended over an incident with the psychologist. Are you back already?"

"Something like that." She smiled guiltily. "I have to leave you now. I'm sorry I woke you up, and thanks again. I owe you a drink."

"Make it two," Marga said, and raised two fingers in front of the camera.

"Deal. Good night." The line went dead. Nuria put her phone back in her pocket and for a long moment stood looking at the sterilized room, bathed in the black light of her flashlight.

Someone had gone to a lot of trouble to hide the identity of Vilchez's presumed killer. Someone meticulous, who knew forensic procedure better than she did herself. Someone with a reason for doing something like that.

In her mind she made a list. It turned out to be a very short one, consisting of one name only: Elias Zafrani. Vilchez's possible testimony against him was a strong reason for eliminating him, and Zafrani had more than enough resources to hire a hit man with no fingerprints—and thoroughly disinfect the scene of a crime. Nuria reasoned that if he'd gone to so much trouble to wipe out every last trace of evidence, it was because that trace could lead to him.

A drop of the killer's blood. Maybe that was all she needed to accuse Elias. Nuria crouched and swept her black light all over the rough cement floor, finding blurred spots of bleach wherever bloodstains had been wiped clean.

"You must have missed *something*," she murmured to herself. She understood at last why all the clothes and garbage in that room had been removed. It was easier than looking for traces of blood on them.

Determined not to overlook anything, Nuria mentally divided the room into squares and methodically checked every inch with the same ultraviolet light, seeking the tiniest white flash that would reveal the presence of organic matter. She searched every nook and cranny, the ridges of the uneven floor, the seams of the compressed cardboard walls, and the screws that held the metal sheets of the ceiling together, but there was nothing except spots of bleach. The place was more thoroughly disinfected than an operating room.

After almost an hour of exhaustive inspection Nuria gave up and sat down on the floor. Whoever had done this had taken a long time in order to do a perfect job. This was the work of a professional, and if she still had any doubt about the identity of who was behind all this, that fact made it clear. She could think of only one person with the interest and the resources to do a thing like this.

"Son of a bitch," she muttered as she lay back on the cement floor. "With evidence or without, I'm going to get you."

She stared vaguely at the ceiling. Her gaze settled on the useless low-energy bulb that hung naked from a wire above. Under the black light it shone, like all white objects under black light.

Like blood—if it had been spattered with it.

Without taking her eyes off the bulb, as if she feared it might vanish, Nuria got to her feet, put on a pair of latex gloves she had in her back pocket, and reached up. Thanks to her height she was able to reach it easily. Unscrewing it very carefully, she held it as if it were the chalice of Christ.

Under the black light the bulb shone as if it were radioactive, but when she switched the flashlight to white light, she saw a minuscule mote of dark vermilion on its dusty surface.

A drop of dried blood.

"Gotcha!"

16

"There are no matches," Marga said. She was sitting at her desk in the twilit lab, wearing her white lab coat. The coroner's assistant's voice sounded tired, and her eyes, reddened from weariness, underlined the impression.

Nuria tried not to show her disappointment at the news. "None in the entire database?"

"None in the whole database."

Nuria consoled herself by thinking that at least that eliminated David and Vilchez. It didn't bring her any closer to the killer, though—or to the man who might have hired him. "All right ..." she murmured, downcast. "Thanks, Marga. I owe you one."

"Wait. There's something else."

"Something else? But you just said there's no—"

"There's no DNA match to any profile we have on file," Marga interrupted her, "but there are other things in blood besides deoxyribonucleic acid."

"I'm not following you."

"I mean that in this sample you sent me so urgently, there are traces of a foreign substance."

"Define foreign."

"I've never seen it before." She paused briefly and added, "The structure is similar to that of an AMP, but a lot more complex."

"AMP?"

"Amphetamine."

"So apparently," Nuria said, remembering her conversation with Puig, "the man *was* a junkie."

Marga shook her head. "No, he wasn't. At least, not your typical junkie. This amphetamine is a kind there are no clinical references to."

"What do you mean?"

"That it has nothing to do with the usual drugs. It's something much more complex, more"—she searched for the right word—"sophisticated."

"Designer drugs are common enough, aren't they?"

"Not like this one. I've never seen an amphetamine like it."

"And the effects of this amphetamine?" Nuria asked with growing interest. "What effects would it cause in someone who took it?"

"I can't know that, Nuria. I can only speculate."

"Please do."

This time the coroner's assistant took a while to answer. "I'd say that the effects could be similar to those of an amphetamine, though looking at its structure, I would guess they would be enhanced. If I had to bet, I'd say its effect would be to quicken the synaptic response of the individual. Like a colossal kick of adrenaline to the neuromuscular and limbic system."

"Would it make," Nuria started to ask, suddenly seized by anxiety, as if she were about to place the first piece in a jigsaw puzzle, "whoever took it seem … *accelerated*?"

Marga nodded slowly. "Yes, I guess that would be a way of describing it. As long as the effect lasted, the neuronal and muscular reactions would be much faster than normal. All this is theoretical, obviously."

"Holy shit," Nuria muttered. "I was right."

"You were right?"

"Oh, nothing," she replied, realizing she'd voiced her thoughts aloud. "Just ignore me."

"Where did you get that sample?"

"I told you, I just found it."

"Come on, Nuria, don't fuck with me."

"Sorry, but I can't tell you."

"Does it have something to do with the Villarefu incident? That's it, right?" Marga lowered her voice and leaned closer to the camera. "The subject you asked me about?"

"Believe me, Marga. It's better for you not to know."

The coroner's assistant seemed to be weighing the implications of Nuria's statement. After a moment's thought, she decided there was no need for her to know.

"Can I keep the sample at least?"

"Of course. I'm just asking for your discretion. This isn't … official."

"I'd already guessed that. I found out a while ago that you're suspended."

"And even so, you helped me," said Nuria.

The corners of the other woman's eyes crinkled in a mischievous smile. "I was dying of curiosity."

"Thanks, Marga." Nuria smiled in turn. "I owe you big time."

"You can say that again. You got me out of bed at midnight to come to the lab to analyze a mysterious blood sample, overriding all the rules."

"I know. I'll pay my debt with pleasure."

On the screen, Marga nodded. "Well, is there anything else you need, or am I free to finally go home and get some sleep?"

"No, I don't need— Oh, yes. Wait. One last thing." She raised a finger. "If it's some kind of 'super amphetamine,' who do you think could be selling it? And what would their reason be?"

Marga hesitated, shaking her head. "That's a lot to speculate about."

"I know. But I'd like to know what you think."

"Hmm ..." Marga bit her lower lip thoughtfully. "A substance like that isn't easy either to make or to put on the market. If the secondary effects are anything like those of amphetamines, this drug could be a fast track to paranoid schizophrenia and psychosis. I don't think anybody would be crazy enough to take it unless it were absolutely necessary, and nobody with the money to pay for something like this is usually that stupid."

"But in theory ... a criminal with sufficient resources could distribute it, right?"

Marga thought for a moment. "In theory, yes. But who would they sell it to? Not even elite soccer players are that dumb, and besides, they're subject to regular drug tests."

"He might offer it to hit men or hired assassins," Nuria suggested.

"Well ... yes. They might be interested, obviously. But with just a few doses this drug could turn them into psychopaths. I don't know whether it would be worth the consequences, even to them."

Nuria snorted, feeling a certainty beginning to grow inside her, filling her with rage. "Thanks, Marga," she murmured, hanging up before the other woman could reply.

That was the piece of evidence she needed. Everything pointed to the same person. The person who was ultimately to blame for David's death.

"Elias ..." she muttered disdainfully.

17

Nuria waited behind the window of a Starbucks, watching the entrance to the parking lot of an office building on Avenida Diagonal, drinking cup after cup of the absurdly overpriced coffee in an attempt to clear her groggy mind and stave off the exhaustion stalking her.

Six hours had passed since she'd had her illuminating conversation with the forensic assistant. Six hours during which her mind had outlined a dozen plans of action, each more ridiculous than the one before. Six hours of trying to decide whether to forget the whole thing, inform Commissioner Puig of everything she'd found out, or act alone and try to get to the bottom of things herself. None of the three options was a hundred percent satisfactory, but the third was the worst choice by far.

Naturally, that was the one she'd chosen.

Nuria glanced at her wristwatch, realizing with a grimace that it was nearly eleven in the morning. Not that she was expecting a criminal to keep normal office hours, but this seemed a bit too much.

During the two months they'd had Elias Zafrani under surveillance, they'd established that every morning he arrived punctually at his office on the top floor of the modern office building in the Eixample. Though nobody was taken in by his carefully groomed businessman front or the golden plaque by the door of Daraya Import-Export, they'd found that Elias Zafrani could not be classified as a typical mafioso-type criminal. He was discreet and cultured, the kind of man who neither wore gold rings nor appeared in public with prostitutes hanging from his arm, a man who conducted his murky business as if it were nothing more than an efficient distribution company.

The difference, of course, was that what he distributed was clandestine computer programs and hacked personal data, together with the old standards: alcohol, contraband tobacco, illegal immigrants. And now, apparently, designer drugs as well.

While Nuria downed her third eight-euro cappuccino and watched a horde of Indian tourists entering the Starbucks as if they were planning to invade it, she detected movement in the street from the corner of her eye. Turning toward the window, she saw the garage door across from her rising, as if the building were yawning. Seconds later she saw Zafrani's mammoth Chevy Suburban with its tinted windows. Almost without slackening its speed, it turned into the underground parking lot, the garage door immediately closing behind it.

"The rabbit's in its warren," she murmured to herself, setting the cup on the table with a smile of grim satisfaction. "Now we're going to catch him."

Pushing her chair back, Nuria stood up. Conscious of the weight of the gun she was hiding in her waistband, she went out the café door, crossed the sidewalk and then the avenue, and halted in front of the main entrance to the building with its walls of mirrored glass. The irony of the situation didn't escape her: the fact that after more than six months of investigating Elias Zafrani from a distance, she was finally going to meet him in person—immediately after being suspended and taken off the case.

The double doors opened with a hiss, allowing her into the huge lobby, where a doorman in a suit and tie greeted her from his podium with professional indifference. Looking her up and down, he said, "Good morning. How can I help you, miss?"

"I'm going to Daraya Import-Export."

He glanced at the terminal in front of him. "Do you have an appointment?"

"No, but I don't need one."

The receptionist looked up at her and smiled with just the right shade of condescension. "Sorry, miss. Only visitors with a prior appointment are admitted."

Nuria had made a concession by donning non-distressed jeans and a shirt without too many wrinkles, but when she saw her reflection in the mirror behind the doorman's podium, with her ponytail coming undone and deep circles under her eyes, she realized that in this place she looked like a junkie looking for a fix. With no other alternative, she reached into her pocket, pulled out her badge, and slammed it down on the desk.

"Corporal, if you don't mind," she corrected him, enjoying his look of surprise. "And no, *sonny*," she repeated, condescending to him in turn, "I don't need a prior appointment." Without waiting for a reply, she put her badge back into her pocket and headed for the elevators.

The doorman's voice sounded behind her again. "You need to sign the register, Officer," he called, sounding more timid this time.

Nuria didn't even bother to turn around. "I'll do it on my way out," she said, stepping into the waiting elevator. She pushed the button for the top floor, turning just in time to see the doorman, his eyes still on her, picking up the phone. Before she reached the tenth floor, her imminent arrival would be known.

The elevator stopped softly at the top floor. With a tinkle of tiny bells, the door slid open, revealing an office carpeted in green with yellow-and-white walls. A smiling receptionist, even taller than she was, was waiting to welcome her.

"Good morning, Corporal Badal," she greeted her as if delighted to see her. "My name is Veronica. How may I help you?"

Nuria snorted inwardly. She had to admit that the building's facial recognition system was a good one. The elevator hadn't taken more than thirty seconds to identify her. "I'd like to see Mr. Elias Zafrani."

The young woman nodded. "Of course. Mr. Zafrani is waiting for you. Come this way, please." She turned, inviting Nuria to follow the graceful footsteps of her high heels on the green carpet.

Nuria looked down at her own feet, at her old Asics from the days when it was still possible to run in the city without a mask, and a little voice in her head told her that perhaps she ought to have tidied herself up a little better, or at least ironed her shirt.

But it was already too late for that and, truthfully, she didn't really care. So she simply followed the sashaying secretary along the carpet past individual glass-walled cubicles where executives of both sexes in business suits worked in front of huge translucent screens across which columns of data and graphics paraded. If she hadn't already known this was a company devoted to criminal activities, it would have been very easy to imagine she was in the offices of a bank. Although, when you thought about it—she reasoned—deep down there wasn't much difference between one and the other.

Distracted by the office's discreet luxury and air of efficiency, she didn't realize that Veronica had reached the end of the corridor and stopped in front of the open door of a meeting room.

"If you'd be so kind as to wait here," she said with a blindingly white smile, "Mr. Zafrani will see you in a few minutes."

Instead of answering, Nuria looked at both sides of the corridor, trying to guess which office was Elias's. Just moments before, as she'd downed coffee after coffee to counteract her sleepless night, she'd imagined herself bursting into his office and surprising him at his desk as he avidly counted a pile of bills stained with blood and amphetamines. She knew this was no more than a fantasy conjured up by her sleepless mind and that it was not going to happen that way, but there was a world of difference between her fantasy and waiting patiently with folded hands like a patient at the dentist. Losing the element of surprise before she'd even begun put her at a clear disadvantage, but there was nothing she could do now except come up with some excuse and return later, which would be even worse.

So she uttered an inaudible *thank you* before going meekly into the waiting room and sitting down. The room was mostly filled by a large oval conference table surrounded by twelve designer chairs that were so uncomfortable

Nuria thought it must be deliberate, perhaps to cut short the endless company meetings, or maybe to annoy inopportune visitors like herself. Most likely it was both.

Five minutes after Veronica had closed the door, in a pure reflex action provoked by boredom, Nuria was tempted to pair her electronic activity bracelet with the link symbol on the table, activating the thin film of graphene on its surface that would convert it to a screen. Luckily she stopped herself in time. The room was certain to be crawling with surveillance cameras, and she wouldn't be able to project the image of determination she intended if she were found surfing the web to kill time.

Nuria was beginning to realize that the combination of lack of sleep and three extra-large coffees was taking its toll. She was feeling increasingly irritated and less able to think clearly. Maybe it hadn't been a good idea to come here in such a hurry.

Once again she toyed with the idea of excusing herself on the pretext of a police emergency. She could come back some other time, rested and with a clearer mind. But right when she was reaching for her phone to pretend she had an incoming call, the door opened, admitting a forty-ish man in a sober gray suit with a black shirt and tie. Of average build, slightly shorter than she was, he had a seductive air about him, halfway between wealthy and nonchalant, which was emphasized by studiedly tousled salt-and-pepper hair and a friendly grin.

Nuria's first thought was that this man, who had begun his life in a miserable little village on the outskirts of Damascus, Syria, had done a good job learning to mimic the filthy rich of Barcelona. In her opinion, this uninhibited confidence was usually genetic and began to work its effects from the cradle. It wasn't easy to achieve, however much money a person might have. So Zafrani's attitude could only be the result of hard work and a facility for acting. But it wasn't going to work on her.

What she did have to admit was that even though she'd studied the surveillance tapes until exhaustion had set in, she hadn't realized how hypnotic his large blue eyes could be until they were fixed on her from the other end of the room.

"Good morning, Ms. Badal," he said with a barely perceptible Arab accent. Relaxed, he came toward her, hand outstretched. "I'm very glad to meet you at last in person," he said, managing to sound sincere.

It took Nuria a second longer to react. Standing abruptly so the legs of her chair screeched on the parquet floor, she corrected him, ignoring his proffered hand. "*Corporal* Badal."

Zafrani seemed unruffled by her brusqueness. "Excuse me. I wasn't aware this was an official meeting."

"It's not," she admitted as she sat down again.

94

"Well, in that case"—he smiled—"I'd prefer to continue addressing you as Ms. Badal, if you don't mind. It's less formal that way." Nuria was about to reply that of course she minded, but realized this small talk was a waste of time.

Elias Zafrani pulled back the chair next to hers and sat down with a show of insincere interest. "So tell me," he said, interlacing his fingers, "To what do I owe the pleasure of your visit?"

Instead of answering, Nuria looked at the glass walls that surrounded them. "Couldn't we speak somewhere more discreet?"

Elias nodded. Raising his voice, he said, "Windows opaque, please." Immediately the office AI responded to his request. The glass turned white until it was indistinguishable from a wall.

"Better?" her host asked. "And now, tell me, how can I help you?"

Nuria pursed her lips. Now this looked more like the fantasy she'd been elaborating for the past few hours. "My partner David was murdered," she said, her tone glacial. "But you already know that."

Zafrani nodded solemnly, the warm smile fading from his face. "I deeply regret your loss," he murmured. "Believe me when I say how sorry I am."

"Well, no, I don't believe you." Nuria exhaled forcefully. "It was your doing, and I have proof."

In a gesture somewhere between surprise and indignation, Elias threw himself back in his chair as if she'd just hit him. *He's a damn good actor*, she thought. Putting a hand to his chest, he said, "I give you my word that I had nothing to do with that."

"Bullshit!" Nuria barked. She jumped to her feet, unable to contain the rage that was mushrooming inside her.

Zafrani looked at her, his large blue eyes uncomprehending. "I swear to you I had nothing to—"

Nuria knew he was lying. Pulling out her phone, she pressed the *record* button. "Tell me the truth," she interrupted him. "Confess that you ordered a hit man to murder David and Vilchez."

Zafrani clicked his tongue impatiently. "I don't know how you think this is going to play out. But I'm certainly not going to do what you're asking."

"Do it."

"No."

Nuria reached behind her, pulled out her Walther PPK, and aimed it at Elias's forehead. "Do it," she repeated in a tone of cold determination. "Or else I'll be your judge and jury."

18

Nuria's finger hugged the trigger, tense, ready to shoot. "Talk," she hissed, nodding toward the phone she'd left on the table.

"I had nothing to do with your partner's death," he insisted again, without losing his calm. "Or Vilchez's."

"Don't lie to me, you bastard." The muscles of her jaw clenched every time she opened her mouth. "Vilchez worked for you and you had him killed."

Zafrani raised his hands, trying to calm her. "A lot of people work for me, Ms. Badal. But I give you my word, I didn't give the order to kill anybody."

Nuria's rage, instead of subsiding, was growing in the face of the Syrian's calm cynicism. "Lie to me one more time and I swear I'll splatter your brains all over this room."

Elias pointed to the ceiling. "I imagine you're aware that at this very moment everything you do and say is being recorded, aren't you?" He glanced at her smartphone on the table, with the recording icon illuminated. "Nothing I say under coercion can be used in a court of law."

"Scum like you always escape justice," Nuria said. "Your confession isn't for them, it's for me. I want to hear you say it."

A flash of understanding appeared in Zafrani's blue eyes. "You want me to confess … so that you can shoot me with a clear conscience." Nuria said nothing, but couldn't help the corners of her mouth curving slightly upwards. "But that means," Elias reasoned, "that you're not really sure what you're accusing me of, because if you were, you'd have shot me the moment you saw me."

"You ordered Vilchez killed when you found out he was going to rat you out, and then my partner and me as well, in order to put an end to the investigation. You thought we might be able to incriminate you too."

Elias tsk-tsked as if he were the victim of some enormous misunderstanding. "I'm telling you again I had nothing to do with it. The deceased Mr. Vilchez wasn't planning to 'rat me out' or anything of the kind."

"That's what you think. He'd spent months passing on information to us about your movements, evidence of your criminal activities." She closed her left hand into a fist in front of her. "We almost had you."

Zafrani shook his head slowly. "No, Corporal. You had nothing I didn't want you to have." He leaned forward in his chair without appearing to be intimidated by the barrel of Nuria's gun that was less than a handsbreadth from his head. "It's true Mr. Vilchez worked for me, but what you don't know is that he worked *exclusively* for me ... not for you. I knew you were investigating me and looking for an informer, so I provided you with one. I gave him certain pieces of information to pass on to you so he could gain your trust—tips I later supplanted with information that was false or useless. If one day we'd ended up in court, my attorneys would have shown that your accusations were unfounded and that I was the victim of unfair persecution by the police," he said, adding, "I would have sued you for falsehood and defamation, and you would have had to leave me in peace for a very long time."

Nuria shook her head in disbelief. "You're lying."

"Do you remember the stash of Chinese VR equipment you impounded at the port? That was the bait, and you took it hook, line, and sinker." He snorted, as if pointing out the obvious wearied him. "Then I threw you a couple more bones, like the truck of tobacco at La Junquera or that drone you brought down. All of it so you'd trust Vilchez. But from then on, practically everything he passed on to you was manipulated. The account books, the transit routes, the contacts, the projects ... there was just enough truth in it all to make it credible, but most of it was false information designed to show you up in court."

Nuria felt as if her heart had decided to stop pumping blood to her head. "No ... it's not possible," she muttered, dazed. She unconsciously lowered her gun. "We've been surveilling your activities for six months. We have reports."

Elias shrugged. "I'm sorry for you. I understand that you're doing your job, and believe it or not, I have nothing against the police." He paused, then added, "I admit I don't want to end up in prison, but I didn't give the order to kill Vilchez. It would have made no sense. He was doing an excellent job for me. I'm the one hurt most by his death ... after himself, of course."

This final comment made Nuria react. She aimed her gun at Elias once again. "I'm not going to let you confuse me," she said with all the aplomb she could muster. "I know what you are and what you do, and even if what you're saying were true, the drugs in your hit man's system certainly point to you."

"Drugs?" he asked. "What drugs?"

"Don't play the innocent with me."

Elias snorted in irritation. "I'm not playing the innocent, damn it." He spread his hands wide in a gesture of exasperation. "It's ridiculous to conclude that because that assassin was drugged, I must have something to do with what happened. Half the people in this city smoke, sniff, or inject some substance or other."

"Not like that one."

"Not like that one?" he asked, sounding intrigued. "What do you mean?"

"You already know."

97

Elias looked at the ceiling as though pleading for patience. "No, I don't," he said, massaging the bridge of his nose wearily. "I've already told you I had nothing to do with those deaths. You can believe me or not, do whatever you want with it, but you have the wrong person. I'm not your enemy."

"Said the scorpion, as he crossed the river on the frog's back ..."

Zafrani smiled humorlessly at the reference. "I'm no scorpion," he said. Jabbing a finger at her, he added: "Nor are you a frog, Ms. Badal. In fact, you're the one who's threatening me with a gun."

"That's right," she nodded. "And I hope you won't make me use it."

"Telling you what you want to hear?"

"I see you're beginning to understand."

"Or telling you the truth?"

Nuria sat back in her chair, still aiming at him, resting the butt of her heavy gun on the table. "This gun weighs a lot," she said, seeing Zafrani's gaze fixed on it. "And my patience is running out."

"We ought to work together," the Syrian suggested. "We could help each other."

Nuria laughed out loud. "You're kidding me, right?" Seeing his serious expression, she added: "Why would I do that? You're the fucking suspect."

"I'm as interested as you in finding out who killed them and why. If we share information, it will be easier to find out."

"Oh, sure," she said skeptically. "Now it turns out you care about the deaths of David and Vilchez. Do you think I'm an idiot?"

Elias leaned forward very slowly. "Don't take this personally, Ms. Badal," he said in a low voice. "But I don't give a shit about anybody." His tone was glacial. "What I want to know is why they were killed, and whether any of it is related to me or my business."

"Business," she repeated. "Is that what you call what you do?"

Elias waved his arm around the room innocently. "I'm just a simple businessman who offers alternative services. If there were no demand, there'd be no supply."

Nuria too leaned forward. "Don't give me that bullshit. You're a criminal."

"That's a matter of opinion. But I've never ordered anyone killed in my life, least of all Vilchez or your friend."

Nuria stared at Elias, searching his blue eyes for the truth. Scrutinizing those deep icy pools that stood out against his dark skin. She concluded she couldn't trust him. But also that—no matter how much it hurt her to admit it—he seemed to be telling the truth.

"Tell me what drug the assassin had in his system," Elias said, sensing that Nuria's confidence was about to crumble, "and I may be able to help you find the real culprits."

She pretended to consider this for a moment, but she'd understood that her ill-fated plan had foundered from the beginning. At this point she no longer had much left to lose.

"I've no idea what drug it is." She lowered her weapon, surrendering in the face of her own exhaustion and Zafrani's arguments. "The coroner couldn't identify it. But apparently it's a kind of enhanced amphetamine or something of the kind that affects neuromuscular response."

Zafrani leaned forward again interestedly. "In what way?"

"I don't know the theory. But that bastard moved incredibly fast. I'd never seen anything like it except in the movies. He practically dodged a bullet."

Elias sat back in his chair, looking alarmed. "Are you sure of that? Couldn't it be that the stress of the situation confused you?"

Nuria blinked a couple of times, leaning back in her chair in turn. Brandishing the Walther PPK in front of her, she said, "You know what? I nearly throttled the last person who suggested that. And I didn't loathe him half as much as I loathe you."

Zafrani raised his hands. "I had to ask. Is there anything else you remember? Anything odd? Perhaps … in his eyes?"

Nuria shot up in her seat like a spring. "How did you know that?"

"Were his eyes bloodshot?"

"Like tomatoes. As if he had conjunctivitis, or had rubbed them with sandpaper."

Zafrani closed his eyes and murmured, his voice barely audible, "*Ya Allah* … My God …"

Taken aback by his reaction, Nuria waited a few seconds for him to add something more, or explain himself, or say something. But his eyes were unreadable as he stared into space, his gaze unfocused. "What?" she snapped at last. "What does it mean that he had bloodshot eyes?"

Elias moved his eyes to Nuria. Instead of answering, though, he asked her, "Did this man say anything?" His voice sounded worried.

Nuria hesitated for a moment, long enough to realize there was no sense in hiding information from him. "Not a word. In fact, I even thought he might be mute, or else didn't speak our language."

"Were you able to identify him?"

Nuria shook her head. "He had no papers, no phone, no activity bracelet. Also, his fingerprints were erased and there was no matching profile in our database."

"A professional," Elias concluded.

99

"Looks like it."

"What did he look like? Describe him."

Nuria took a few seconds to summon up the memory. "Ordinary," she said at last. "Around forty, Caucasian, five foot six or so, blue eyes, thick-framed glasses, shaven head, and well-tended beard."

He narrowed his eyes. "And the body? Do you still have it?"

"Incinerated."

"Does the report mention any marks or tattoos?"

"Not that I know of."

"I see. And what was the official conclusion?"

"I haven't had access to the report," she admitted. "But the commissioner thinks it was just a junkie who killed Vilchez in order to rob him, and that when David and I arrived he went crazy and attacked us. End of story."

Hearing this, Elias sat back in his chair and folded his arms. "But you don't believe that."

"Of course not," Nuria admitted. "And I suspect you don't either. What do the bloodshot eyes mean?"

Zafrani seemed to be considering for a moment how much information he should share with this policewoman who was still holding her gun. "It's called limbocaine," he said at last. "Although most people just call it 'limbo.'"

"A drug?"

He nodded. "A very powerful amphetamine compound. Apparently it produces the effects you've mentioned: extremely fast neuromuscular reactions as well as a temporary increase in the individual's strength and speed—but the cost is massive mental and physical depletion."

"And why haven't I ever heard of this ... limbocaine? Where does it come from?"

"There's not much reliable information about it. Almost none, in fact. Mostly rumors and stories I've heard here and there, particularly from the refugees arriving from Maghreb."

"Refugees?" she repeated in puzzlement. "What do the refugees have to do with this? Are they trafficking this drug?"

"It's more that they're the ones who've suffered its effects."

Nuria sat up straight in her chair and rubbed her eyes to clear her head. "I'm getting lost here," she confessed. "Explain that."

"As I told you, all the information I have about limbocaine needs to be taken with a grain of salt," he cautioned. "But it seems to be a drug of military origin, created in an Israeli lab. The intention was to create a substance to enhance the skills of soldiers in the battlefield. It seems they succeeded ... except that the side effects turned out to be so intense they made its use nonviable."

"Side effects?"

"Schizophrenia, paranoia, psychosis … not in any way advisable for someone with a gun in their hands."

"So," Nuria mused, "do you suppose the hit man was an Israeli soldier or something like that?"

"No, I don't think so. They stopped using it there years ago, and I doubt whether any government would dare to put a thing like that into the hands of the military."

"So?"

"So," Zafrani went on, "it looks as though someone got hold of the formula and sold it to the highest bidder—to people with a lot of money who didn't care whether their soldiers lost their minds or not. Even better if they did, because then they'd gain the reputation of being terrifying and invincible."

Nuria's eyes opened wide. "You don't mean—"

Elias pursed his lips and nodded. "I'm afraid so."

"Jesus Christ, ISMA?" she asked in disbelief.

He nodded again. "It's an open secret. It's what allowed them to take the whole Maghreb region in a matter of weeks. The refugees arriving in Spain talk about insane jihadists with superhuman powers. They call them *Alshayatin aleuyun alhamra*."

"What does that mean?"

Elias leaned forward and fixed his eyes on her. "Red-eyed devils."

19

"Red-eyed devils," Nuria repeated to herself as she leaned back in the rear seat of the Uber.

The self-driving vehicle's voice surprised her. "Excuse me, I didn't understand the command," it said.

"I wasn't talking to you," she said, realizing she'd spoken aloud. "Just take me home."

"Of course," the voice replied obediently. "We will be at the destination in eight minutes."

Nuria closed her eyes and tried to take up the thread of her thoughts prior to the interruption. She was trying to make sense of the fact that someone high on a drug used by the soldiers of the Islamic State of Maghreb could have tortured and killed Vilchez. If the information Zafrani had given her was correct, the implications were so many and so confusing she didn't even know where to begin.

If the limbocaine had arrived at Villarefu in the hands of the refugees, it had probably been used to settle a score connected with the drug trade. Although Zafrani had assured her that Vilchez hadn't been dealing that particular drug behind his back, it might be that Vilchez hadn't been as stupid as he looked. He might have been playing not just two sides but three, deceiving everybody and introducing the limbocaine into the refugee camp on his own. But if that was so, Nuria reasoned, why had the killer waited for her and David instead of leaving when he'd had the chance?

Zafrani had suggested that the aggressiveness produced by the limbocaine might have led him to confront them unnecessarily, but Nuria remembered the hit man's gaze and his attitude, and neither had been irrational in the least. What she'd seen in those reddened eyes was a chilling professional coldness, with no trace of rage or any other emotion.

A shiver ran through her body at the thought that none of what had happened had been a coincidence. The fact that Vilchez had summoned them that particular morning hadn't been a matter of chance. She could imagine the killer pressing the razor against Vilchez's throat while he forced him to send a message to David setting up a meeting at his house.

But why? she wondered as the Uber threaded its way with agility through the traffic of the Paseo de Gracia roundabout. Why did that professional assassin want the two of them to go to Vilchez's house?

She had no connection with the drug trade herself, nor was there any criminal or criminal group who might benefit from her death. She was just one more officer in the National Police, and, if truth be told, a relatively insignificant one. She'd never apprehended any mafia bosses or investigated any politicians. Her career so far had been utterly humdrum, consisting of minor arrests and following her superiors' orders. All in all, she concluded, there was no reason to want her dead.

So she was no more than collateral damage, which meant that the intended victim was someone else.

David.

"Five minutes to destination," the Uber informed her solicitously. *David?* she wondered, disconcerted, ignoring the car's announcement. *Why David?*

They'd been partners for the last few years and there had been no investigation she hadn't taken part in. The most important, by far, had been the one involving Zafrani. But in spite of her certainty about his guilt, after speaking to him she'd become convinced he'd had nothing to do with the matter. At least, not directly or intentionally.

So if it wasn't about Zafrani ... maybe David had been carrying on a parallel investigation without her knowledge. She rejected the idea that he might have been involved in anything dirty, but he could have been following orders from above to keep her out of it. It was farfetched, but she could think of no other reason he wouldn't have told her anything.

Spurred by a sudden inspiration, she took out her phone and asked it to call Susana. After a few seconds her friend appeared on the Uber's screen, sounding sleepy.

"Hi, Nuria," she said. "What's up?"

"You sound tired."

"Night shift," she explained curtly.

"Sorry, I didn't mean to wake you."

Susana rubbed her eyes. "Don't worry—the phone was ringing anyway."

Nuria smiled, grateful for her friend's good humor. She was going to need it. "I need you to do me another favor."

"If it doesn't involve getting out of bed—"

"I need David's personal files from headquarters."

It took Susana a few seconds to react. "Excuse me?" she said. "I thought you said something about some personal files, but I mustn't have heard right."

"I need them, Susi."

"And I need a rich, handsome boyfriend who brings me flowers."

"I'm convinced that David's death wasn't accidental," Nuria explained. "Vilchez's murderer was waiting for us."

"Are you sure? Do you have any proof?"

"No, and that's why I want David's files. That's where I might find what I need."

There was a sigh at the other end of the line. "Look, Nuria," she began. "You know I love you and I know you're going through a hard time, but it seems to me you're taking this too far. Seriously, I don't know whether—"

"I've just been to see Zafrani."

Susana was instantly wide awake. "What? You did what?" The questions tumbled over each other as she spoke. "Have you gone completely mad? Why did you do that?"

"I went to see him, ready to get a confession out of him at gunpoint," she said when her friend stopped talking. "But we ended up having a very interesting chat."

"A chat?" Susana asked in astonishment. "With Elias? With the son of a bitch you were surveilling? Do you realize that you might have compromised the whole investigation?"

"Yes," Nuria said firmly. "And thank goodness I did."

"What do you mean?"

"I'll explain some other time. What I need right now is for you to get me those files."

"Jesus, Nuria," Susana protested. "You're asking me for a hell of a lot with no explanation. I could get suspended."

"What I'm asking is for you to trust me."

"You're making it very difficult for me."

"I know," Nuria admitted. "But all this is beginning to smell very odd. I think there's a lot more here than meets the eye. Classified reports, negligent autopsies, altered crime scenes—"

"Wait a minute," Susana cut in. "What the hell are you talking about?"

Nuria hesitated for a moment, then decided she owed her friend an explanation. "Last night I went to Vilchez's house," she said, adding before Susana could say she was crazy again, "Someone had manipulated the scene of the crime, using bleach to clean the place where I ..." She realized it was still painful to talk or even think about it.

"Are you sure of that?" Susana asked, saving her from having to put it into words.

"They left it like a fucking operating room," Nuria clarified. "They wanted to eliminate every trace of the killer's blood."

"That doesn't make sense."

"No, it doesn't," Nuria admitted. "Unless they're trying to hide something." She added, "Like for instance, the fact that his DNA isn't in any database, or that he was high on an unknown drug."

"And you know this because..."

"I found a drop of blood they'd missed and sent it to the coroner's assistant. The assassin had had his fingerprints chemically removed, and he was incinerated without having been identified."

"Sweetie," Susana said, "are you listening to yourself? I think you ought to sleep, quite honestly. You sound ... I don't know how to put it gently, but you sound paranoid."

"I'm not paranoid, Susana. The killer was a hit man, and they don't work for free. Someone hired him. Someone who wanted David dead. And I give you my word, I'm going to catch him."

Susana gave a snort, halfway between a guffaw and a reprimand. "What happened to last night's Nuria?" she said. "The one who was bored, eating ice cream and watching TV on her couch at home? I liked her better than this mad avenger version of yours."

"If they catch you, I'll say I was the one who got into the system after stealing your access code."

"Don't be silly, they won't catch me," Susana said. "I'm very good at covering my tracks."

"So ... are you going to help me?"

"Of course, you dummy. I'm hurt by your doubts."

Nuria sighed with relief. "Thank you. Thank you so much."

"Forget 'thanks,'" Susana objected. "This is going to cost you a dinner at Koy Shunka."

"Okay. I'll start saving right away." She smiled, then immediately added, "When will you—"

"I have to go to headquarters in a while. I'll see what I can do."

"That's all I'm asking."

"As soon as I have it, I'll let you know. Oh, and ... be careful," Susana added, sounding concerned. "I'm sure all this is nothing more than a misunderstanding, but just in case ..."

"I'll be careful, don't you worry about me," Nuria said reassuringly as the Uber stopped in front of her house. "Everything'll be fine." She ended the call and sat on in the Uber's plush seat, ignoring the payment notice on the screen, trying to convince herself that Susana was right and it was all just a convoluted misunderstanding.

"Everything'll be fine," she repeated. But this time, with nobody there to convince, it sounded a lot less credible.

Climbing the stairs to her apartment seemed a feat comparable to climbing the Himalayas without oxygen, and when at last she opened her door and crossed the threshold she was disappointed not to find a band waiting for her amid a cloud of confetti and placards celebrating her achievement.

"Meowww."

"Hello, Melon," she greeted the cat. Stroking his back, Nuria noticed that his food bowl was empty. Again. She took a huge bag of cat food that reeked of dried fish from under the sink. "Sorry, sweetie," she apologized as she filled the bowl to the brim. "I've had a pretty crazy few days."

After she'd made sure he had enough food and water for several days, she looked around, feeling a twinge of guilt at seeing the house in such a mess. The previous night's tub of ice cream had been forgotten on the table and as she should have expected, Melon had knocked it onto the floor and licked it clean. T-shirts and dresses she'd put on and taken off during the week as she'd entered and left the apartment were piled on one arm of the easy chair. The Roomba seemed anxious to go into hiding once again under the couch and a faint layer of dust blanketed all the furniture, motes dancing in the air in the beams of light that filtered through the gaps in the blinds. If her mother had come in just then, she would have had a fit.

Perhaps it was that thought that brought a grimace of disdain to her face. "I have more urgent things to do," she excused herself, sitting down on the couch.

As she'd told Elias, she had no knowledge of any case she'd investigated that might have driven someone to want to kill her, but it would do no harm to check. Maybe she was missing some detail, something that at the time she'd paid no attention to.

"Sofia, open my personal files on the living room screen," she told the assistant. "All cases from August 2027 to now." At once, the icons of forty-two folders, in reverse chronological order, appeared on the wall screen. *Jesus*, she thought. *I didn't remember there were so many of them.*

Calculating that this was going to take her some time, she arranged herself comfortably on the couch and asked the assistant to open the first folder.

20

The electronic activity bracelet on her wrist vibrated a couple of times, announcing an incoming message. It took Nuria several seconds to identify the sound, then a couple more to open her eyes, and finally a few more to remember why she was curled up on the couch with her clothes on and why the screen was showing a police file. Looking at the heading and date on the file, she saw it was October 2027. "Shit!" she muttered. She'd fallen asleep instantly.

The green light of a waiting message flashed on her bracelet. Swiping her finger over it, she sent it to the big screen so that it overlapped the previous image. It was a video message from Susana, and judging by what she could see behind it, it seemed to have been recorded in a restroom.

"Nuria," Susana began, keeping her voice low. "I did what you asked me, and the answer is that it's not in the system either. David's personal file has also been classified"—there was a touch of paranoia in her conspiratorial tone—"though if they did that with the one about the investigation of his death ... it makes sense they'd do it with the victim's file too, right? Well ... bottom line, I couldn't get my hands on it. But here's the good news." She brought her face close to the camera with a knowing smile. "Thanks to my sociable nature and fact-finding skills, I managed to find out who was in charge of the initial investigation into the ... um"—she cleared her throat—"the incident. Guess who!" After hesitating a few seconds to let the suspense build, she went on. "They gave it to Raul and Carla. Didn't you tell me they went to see you in the hospital?" The video finished with Susana sending her an obscene gesture and reminding her that she owed her a grotesquely expensive dinner at a Japanese restaurant.

Raul and Carla. It made sense. They'd been the first to show up. They'd claimed it was because they'd been the first to arrive on the scene of the crime, but they'd never mentioned that they were the ones handling the case. Of course, they could have been assigned the case later on and it was pure chance that they had happened to be the ones who visited her. One more coincidence.

Nuria had always thought it was stupid when people in movies said *I don't believe in coincidences*. Of course, they existed, even the ones so unlikely they seemed to be the work of some supreme being with a twisted sense of humor. Though in this particular case it was true that the coincidences were starting to pile up strangely. Without ever pointing in any specific direction or suggesting there was anyone in particular behind them, taken together, they'd begun to create a more and more distorted image of what had happened, like some cubist painting in which the elements fail to fit together.

Melon jumped onto her lap, purring and demanding her attention, looking at her with his large, round, amber eyes. Hypnotic eyes that made her think of Zafrani watching her like a predator assessing the taste of his future prey.

Shaking her head to banish the thought, Nuria focused on the matter at hand. She noticed the time blinking on the right corner of the screen and understood why the light that filtered into the living room seemed so subdued. She'd slept for eight hours.

She moved Melon from her knees and stood up, kicking off her tennis shoes and then undressing as she headed to the shower. As she stepped into it she glanced at the water meter, calculating that from that moment on she needed to use less than ten liters in each shower she took, at least if she wanted to reach the end of the month without any more penalties. She turned on the tap. Holding her hair back with both hands, she let the artificial rain fall on her shoulders and flow down her breasts and back, clinging to her hips and slipping down her legs to the floor of the shower before finally draining into the gray-water recycling tank. Nuria shut her eyes and took a deep breath, focusing only on the sensation of the water running down her skin as a means of clearing her mind and freeing her from the swirl of unnecessary thoughts.

She exhaled and inhaled. Slowly, until her subconscious receded into its proper place in the background and she was able to concentrate on the most important thing at the moment: finding answers.

The reports on the incident and David's files were classified; asking Puig put her at risk of an indefinite suspension, and Zafrani had told her everything he knew or wanted to tell her. There weren't many other sources where she could find answers.

In fact, there were only two: Raul and Carla. And she knew which of the two she could get answers out of.

Twenty minutes later she inspected herself in the mirror in the front hallway, turning this way and that to see how she looked in the diaphanous red dress she hadn't worn for so long. She checked that the waistline hugged her skin without being too tight, that the skirt was sufficiently short and revealing to do justice to her stupendous ass without looking vulgar, and that the neckline hinted at breasts that still had no need of a bra to stay in place.

Hands on hips, she leaned closer to examine the shadows under her eyes that betrayed the fact she hadn't slept well for several days now. She could do

108

nothing to counteract that except to plaster on more makeup—but her goal was to look seductive, not desperate.

"Not too bad," she said to her reflection. She still had the same athletic figure as she'd had ten years earlier, and though she'd never considered herself a beauty due to her long face and slightly large nose, her cat-like green eyes, fair hair that fell to her shoulders, and breasts that continued to defy gravity were more than enough to seduce any man who crossed her path.

"You look like a regular slut," she pronounced, a satisfied smile on her lips. Putting her keys into a small purse along with some cash, her phone, and her lipstick, she winked at Melon, who regarded her from the couch with dubious interest. "I'm off. Don't wait up for me."

Nuria called an Uber and went out the front door and down the stairs. The little car was already waiting by the curb when she reached the ground floor. They set off for Blai Street, in the Poble Sec quarter, at the foot of the Montjuic mountain.

As she crossed the city in the small, bubble-shaped vehicle, Nuria contemplated the clouds, stained red by the sunset, and thought that at last that endless day was coming to an end. She leaned back against the headrest and felt a stabbing pain in the back of her neck, a souvenir of the heavy blow that had left her unconscious. A pain that she forced herself to bear like an intimate penance for what she'd done and what she'd failed to do. David's blood was still on her hands. Only by getting to the bottom of the matter and finding the ultimate culprit could she allow herself a glimpse of expiation.

When they reached Paralelo Avenue, Nuria asked the Uber to stop and stepped out onto the pavement in her sandals, a little more than a block from her destination. She'd researched the whereabouts of her target at that hour of the evening, and she wanted to look as if she were passing the place by chance, as if on a casual stroll, not getting out of a car right in front of the door.

On Blai Street, a pedestrian walkway dense with small bars and traditional pubs, Nuria joined the crowd that moved from bar to bar, staving off their hunger with tapas and the heat with liters of beer. Unobtrusively, she peered into the bars one by one, realizing as she went that she'd made a serious mistake with her appearance. She was drawing so much attention she couldn't take two steps without having to reject some overly friendly asshole. She felt the way she had as a teenager when she'd partied with her friends and had to spend the evening evading zealous idiots who wouldn't take no for an answer.

For better or worse, a lot of water had passed under the bridge since then. Now, a warning or a meaningful glance was usually enough to nip someone's advances in the bud. If that failed, she could always use a judo hold on the guy and rub his face in the dirt in front of his friends while she explained to him that she was a police officer and that she could arrest him for resisting authority. That never failed.

Distracted by the umpteenth barfly, she almost failed to realize that the person she was looking for was leaning against the bar with a couple of friends, wearing a blue checked shirt and old jeans. He was holding a glass of red wine aloft as though drinking the health of a dead friend—or else drunk enough to raise his glass for any other reason that presented itself.

Nuria straightened her dress, pushed her hair into shape with a couple of rapid jabs, and walked decisively into the bar, attracting the eyes of all the men and women there.

The man in the blue checked shirt narrowed his eyes when he saw her, as if having trouble recognizing her. Finally placing her, he looked her up and down and with a tipsy gesture invited her to come closer. Nuria pretended to look around as though searching for someone else, then made her way toward the man with a shy smile on her lips.

"Well, well!" he cried over the music and bustle of the little bar. "What are you doing here?"

"Hello, Raul. I was going to meet a friend, but I think he's stood me up."

Openly eyeing her breasts, Raul said, "His loss." He moved aside so she could take a seat at the bar. "Can I buy you a drink?"

"I don't know …" she said, checking the time on her wristwatch.

"Come on, stay," he insisted. Turning toward his friends with a peremptory wave, he added, "They were just leaving." The friends smiled conspiratorially, apparently as drunk as he was. Honoring the universal men's code, they took one last look at Nuria's ass and left the bar.

"All right," Nuria said, moving into the space Raul's friends had left open at the bar. "But just one."

"Of course." He gestured to the waiter to bring her a glass of red wine. "Are you still … suspended?"

Nuria nodded. "That's right," she said morosely.

"I heard you gave that idiot psychologist a black eye." He smiled in admiration and raised his glass of wine again. "I'll drink to that."

"I should've blackened both of them," Nuria said. Picking up the glass that had appeared in front of her, she toasted with Raul.

He laughed loudly and patted her shoulder, passing it off as a brotherly gesture. "So you're on vacation, right?"

"Something like that. By the way," she added as if the thought had just occurred to her, "weren't you and Carla assigned to my case?"

Raul's mouth twisted. "Yeah, but it's closed now."

"Did you come up with any interesting conclusions?"

110

Raul gave a vague wave. "You know I can't talk about it," he said. "Why don't you tell me about yourself? You and I hardly ever talk. It would be good for us to get to know each other a little better … don't you think? After all, we're colleagues."

Nuria slid her hand sensually down Raul's back. "Come on. I'm curious. Puig wouldn't tell me anything."

Raul set his glass on the marble bar and snorted wearily. "Because there's nothing to tell. A junkie high on whatever killing his dealer is all in a day's work for us." He spread his hands wide as if to show that was all he had. "You were just really unlucky showing up right then, that's all."

"And the killer?" Nuria asked. "Did you identify him?"

"The junkie?"

"Yeah, the junkie."

Raul's face turned serious. "He was a fucking junkie, who cares who he was? People like that are scum."

"And that's all you got?" she insisted. "A junkie?"

Raul stared at her, intrigued. "What's all this about?" he asked and pointed at the door. "You didn't come here by chance, did you? Did you come to question me?"

Nuria closed her eyes and sighed. There was no sense continuing to lie. Raul might be a cretin, but he wasn't an idiot. Opening her eyes again, she said, "I came looking for answers. The ones nobody wants to give me."

"You're a fucking manipulative bitch," Raul growled, frowning. "I'm not giving you shit."

"I'll do whatever is necessary."

Raul's lips curved in a lecherous smile. "Whatever's necessary?" Nuria received his message loud and clear, confirming once more that men have only one thing on their minds when they're with a woman.

She nodded. "Anything."

She could read Raul's inner struggle between desire and incredulity on his face. "Why would you do that?"

"I told you. I need answers."

Raul's eyes explored Nuria's generous decolletage, his hand on her hip. "In that case … we might be able to make a deal." He moved closer and whispered in her ear, "We'd both come out winners."

"I doubt that. But I need to know what's in that report."

Raul crossed his arms, weighing Nuria's attitude. "Holy shit," he said. "You really *are* interested in this business."

"You're a smart guy," Nuria said ironically. "Now start talking."

"No, you don't …" Her colleague wagged a finger at her. "First you pay up, then I tell you what I know."

"How do I know you're not going to renege on the deal?"

Raul smiled arrogantly. "You'll just have to trust me."

Nuria stared at him, trying to judge how far she could trust him, then nodded. "All right. Let's do it."

"Fantastic." Raul took out his wallet to pay for the drinks. "Let's go to my place. We can—"

She interrupted him. "I'm not going to your place. We'll do it here."

Raul froze with the bill in his hand. Pointing at the floor, he repeated, "Here?" in disbelief.

"That's the restroom, right?" Nuria indicated a small yellow door with the sign TOILETS hand painted on it. "It's going to be a quickie. I have no intention of spending the night at your house."

"But … that's not what I had in—"

"Take it or leave it."

Raul hesitated for a moment, but between the alcohol in his system and the exciting idea of easy sex with Nuria, he made up his mind. "Fine," he grumbled. "Come on, then." He wove his way through the crowd to the restroom, closely followed by Nuria and the envious stares of half the bar.

Nuria closed the door behind her and the bulb in the ceiling lit up automatically, revealing a small cubicle whose walls were densely covered with graffiti scrawled in pen, Twitter handles, and a surprising variety of graphic depictions of sexual organs and creative postures. In the exact center was a battered but clean toilet, and Nuria pushed Raul down onto it.

"What are you doing?"

"Shut up and sit down. And unbutton your pants."

Raul hesitated again, but by then he had neither the desire to argue nor enough blood remaining in his brain to do it, so he obeyed meekly. Nuria crouched in front of him, put her right hand into his pants, and grabbed his erect member.

He moaned and threw his head back. "Oh yeah …" Nuria's hand slid along the whole length of it from glans to base, and from there down toward his testicles, seizing them, at first gently, then gradually increasing the pressure. Raul looked down. "Careful. That area's sensitive."

"I know," she said. Clenching her hand tightly, she squeezed his testicles so that Raul's eyes almost popped out of his head. He opened his mouth to cry out, but she put her left hand over it, slackening the pressure slightly as she whispered in his ear. "And now," she said with icy menace, "you're going to tell me everything there was in that report if you don't want me to make an omelet with your balls."

"You …" Raul mouthed, "you're a fucking bit—"

112

Nuria increased the pressure, cutting him off in mid-epithet. "Answers," she snapped. "Now!"

"Okay, okay." He surrendered, raising his hands. "What ... do you want to know?"

She released the pressure a little. "Who was the killer? Why did nobody perform an autopsy on him? Why did he kill Vilchez and then wait for David and me? Why did you clean up the crime scene?"

"What?" he muttered in confusion. "Where did you get the idea that we—"

"I was there. You scoured everything, right down to the last drop of blood."

He shook his head. "No, I ... we didn't do that."

"Then who did?"

"Someone from forensics must have fucked up somehow. Or maybe it was squatters, or some relative who got bored—" He raised his voice. "How the fuck do you expect me to—"

Nuria tightened her grasp and he shut his mouth instantly. "What about the report? What did you find out?"

"Nothing," he whined.

Nuria frowned and Raul hastened to add, "Nothing, I swear." He raised both hands. "It's what I told you before. A junkie who killed his—"

"The fuck he did," Nuria interrupted. "He wasn't a drug addict, he was a professional hit man. And Vilchez was a snitch on Zafrani's payroll."

"Then why are you asking? You know more than we do."

"You're hiding something," Nuria said, and sank her nails into the soft skin of his scrotum.

Raul gritted his teeth. "No, for Christ's sake! I swear to God there's nothing more!"

"In that case, why have the report and David's personal files been classified?"

"What?" he asked in disbelief. "How should I know? That comes from above."

"From who? Puig?"

"Maybe." Perspiration had begun to bead Raul's forehead, but he was in no state to notice it. "Or higher up still. Do you think they tell me anything?" he asked desperately. "They classified it and that's that, end of story. It's not the first time they've done it when an officer's died ... to cover their backs. At best, a police officer dead on their watch is inconvenient when it comes to promotion." He was breathing harder now. "Or they might even have done it to protect you. Had you thought of that?"

"Don't be a smartass."

113

"You wanted the truth, didn't you? Well, there you have it, for God's sake. You're really fucking up, you know?"

Nuria's rage was beginning to fade. Gradually the idea was filtering into her mind that—as Raul had suggested—she might be screwing things up. It was true she hadn't considered the possibility that the report might have been classified to protect her, and that the cleanup at the shack had been just a stupid mistake.

Could she have been so wrong? Elias's revelations pointed to a complex plot by radical Islamists, but ... suppose it had all been an elaborate hoax? How could she be sure she wasn't being manipulated all over again? Pursuing that thought further, she asked herself, could *he* have been the one who had gotten the investigation classified? Perhaps by bribing or blackmailing some senior officer in order to protect himself?

He'd appeared sincere, but it wouldn't have been the first time someone had tricked her by lying to her face. And if she had to believe someone ... why believe a criminal over the police? Could it be because of Elias's blue eyes that had looked at her as though they'd known her all her life? Nuria forcibly pushed the thought out of her mind. Where had all this come from?

"Are you going to let go of my balls?" Raul whined. "Or are we going to be like this all night?" His question brought Nuria abruptly back to the dirty reality in which she was holding a colleague by the balls, a colleague who had done nothing more than take her sexual hint. Slowly she removed her hand and stood up. "Forgive me."

"Forgive you?" Raul snapped as he tucked his manhood back into his pants with extreme delicacy. "There's gonna be a complaint filed against you that'll make you shit yourself. You'll never wear a badge again in your fucking lifetime."

Nuria went to the sink and turned on the tap to wash her hands. "Maybe," she admitted. "But if you do that, the whole world is going to know I had you by the balls for a good long time while you were crying like a little girl." She looked at him as she dried her hands on her dress. "I wonder what nickname they'll give you at the station."

"You're a fucking bitch," Raul bellowed.

Nuria opened the door of the restroom. Before stepping out, she turned back to him with a look of tired satisfaction, thinking of all the men who had fucked her over throughout her life. "Just doing what I can to keep up with you."

21

Her trip home was very different from her outward-bound trip. The streets were the same and even the Uber looked just like the one she'd disembarked from less than an hour before, but her mood had done a one-eighty. She no longer felt like a sharp-witted investigator unraveling a complex plot involving Islamist terrorists, drugs, and guns for hire. Now she felt like a clumsy, paranoid rookie doing everything she could to pile shit on herself, in spite of her bosses' efforts to protect her.

The more she thought about it, the more what Raul had said made sense: the fact that Puig had kept her on the margin of things, and even that the temporary suspension had been the best way for them to look out for her.

She leaned her head against the window and sighed in exhaustion, abruptly aware of all the tiredness and stress that had accumulated over the last few days. She understood that her remorse over David's death had driven her to look for culprits where there were none and to imagine complex plots that were invisible to everybody else.

She'd pulled the trigger herself. End of story.

She should have gone on vacation, as Susana had suggested. Maybe there was still time. She could go to Lisbon or Rome for a few days, or rent a car and go to the Pyrenees, where she could go for long walks alone with no phone signal, far from everything and everybody.

Yes, that was what she would do, she decided, feeling something like relief. Get away from the suffocating heat and humidity of Barcelona, away from the water restrictions, the crowds, the social networks, and the constant worry over issues that were really no business of hers.

Nuria toyed with the idea of walking the solitary mountain paths of the Aigüestortes Natural Park, accompanied only by the singing of robins and the distant murmur of the winding streams that snaked through green meadows dotted with fir trees. She saw herself contemplating some wide valley from a mountain summit, breathing the pure, fresh air sixty-five hundred feet up, pondering whether she even wanted to go back to the city of her birth that was beginning to look less and less like the one in her childhood memories.

The Uber pulled up in front of her house and the voice of the AI shook her out of her reverie, informing her she'd arrived at her destination.

Mechanically, she got out of the vehicle, entered the lobby, and mounted the stairs to her floor, her mind absent, already wandering among the snow-covered summits of Pallars Sobira.

Fully immersed in her daydream, Nuria didn't realize until the last moment that someone was waiting for her at her door: surely the last person in the world she wanted to see at that moment.

"Hello, Nuria," the woman said as she saw Nuria come to a sudden halt.

"Hello, Gloria." Nuria finished climbing the last steps to the landing and stopped in front of her partner's widow, at a loss for words. For a few interminable seconds they looked at each other in an uncomfortable silence Nuria didn't dare break. Instead, she looked into the brown eyes of the other woman with short hair and a pleasant face from whom she'd taken the love of her life and the father of her son. There were no words she could say. Even if there had been, she couldn't imagine what they might be. All the ones that occurred to her seemed banal, impersonal, or simply untimely.

It was Gloria, in the end, who spoke. "How are you?"

"I'm ... I'm fine," Nuria stammered. "How—" she asked feebly, waving a hand at her.

"Okay, I think," she nodded, her face serious. "Considering the circumstances."

Nuria took a step toward her, babbling an apology. "I ... I am ... so sorry." She put her hand on the other woman's arm. "I didn't know what to say to you. I wanted to ... I wanted ..."

Gloria closed her eyes as though counting to three in her mind. "You don't need to say anything," she said, her voice tightly controlled. "But I'd appreciate it if you offered me a glass of water. I've been here over an hour."

Nuria scrambled to take out her key. "Sorry. I'm a mess."

"No worries." Glancing at her dress, she added: "Back from a party?"

"This isn't ... isn't what it looks like," Nuria said apologetically as she opened the door and welcomed Gloria in.

Her friend glanced at her out of the corner of her eye as she passed her. "Sure ... that's exactly what I used to tell my mother."

A minute later, both women were seated side by side on the couch, Gloria downing her second glass of cold water while Nuria awkwardly straightened her inappropriate red dress.

"I ... forgive me for not calling you," Nuria said when Gloria had set her glass on the table, "and not answering your calls. I didn't know ... I don't know what to say, except that I'm so terribly sorry for your loss. I—"

"It's okay," Gloria said, cutting her off. She seemed not to want to mention the subject for fear that she might explode. "It's all water under the bridge."

116

"No, Gloria, I should have called you at once. To ask for your forgiveness, and Luisito's … to explain what happened."

"There's nothing you can tell me that can change what happened," Gloria said, her tone a mix of reproach and melancholy. "I guess this isn't easy for you either."

Nuria looked down, shaking her head. "I can't forget that it was me who—"

Gloria didn't let her finish the sentence. "It was an accident." She sighed resignedly before adding: "It wasn't your fault."

"But …" The tears were building up under Nuria's eyelids, threatening to overflow. "I'm truly sorry. So, so sorry," she murmured.

Gloria, with that maternal instinct that goes beyond reproach, felt the resentment that had filled her up to that point begin to loosen and crumble. Moving closer to Nuria on the couch, she hugged her as she would a lost child seeking comfort.

"There, there …" she whispered in her ear, stroking her back as Nuria's tears soaked her shoulder. "Everything will be all right."

When Nuria finally managed to control her sobs, she took a deep breath and wiped away her tears with the back of her hand. "It seems impossible," she said between sniffles, "that in the end you're the one who has to comfort me." She felt the sobs rising again from her chest. "It's not fair, for Christ's sake."

"It's all right, Nuria," Gloria said. She took her friend's hands in her own. "David loved his work and knew the risks. He was happy doing what he did and he always told me what a good partner you were. What happened was a horrible thing … but I don't blame you for it." And shaking her head, she added: "And you shouldn't blame yourself either."

It took Nuria a few seconds to react as she struggled to keep her emotions from overwhelming her again. "Thank you," she said simply. "Thank you, Gloria."

Her friend wiped Nuria's smudged eyeliner from her cheeks with her thumb. "Don't thank me. I was very angry with you, but in the end I realized it wasn't fair … and it wouldn't bring David back either."

Nuria made a face at the sight of Gloria's thumb, stained black. "Thanks, Gloria."

Gloria nodded and set her handbag on her lap. "You're welcome, Nuria. But actually, I didn't come just for that. There's something I … I wanted to ask you."

Nuria's heart skipped a beat. "To ask me?" she repeated, dreading the question more than a bullet aimed at her head.

Gloria lowered her voice and her gaze, looking at her own intertwined fingers. "What happened that day …" she began with difficulty. "Commissioner

Puig assured me it was an accident. That you both ran into a drug addict there who took you by surprise and ..." She looked up, as a shipwreck victim would look at his rescuer. "Was it like that?" she asked in a whisper. "Was that what happened? Just bad luck?"

Nuria swallowed with difficulty. "That's what ... what they concluded after the investigation."

Gloria leaned forward, studying her face. "But that's not what I asked you."

Nuria took a deep breath, then exhaled. "I don't know," she admitted. "Quite honestly I don't know."

Gloria nodded, apparently satisfied with the answer. "I have something to give you," she said, putting her hand into her bag.

Nuria blinked, taken aback. "Give me?"

Gloria took out a blue folder and showed it to her. "This was David's. Well, actually"—she corrected herself—"it's a photocopy of a notebook where he would jot down things from work he chose not to include in his reports. I thought that maybe they might help you find ..." She took a deep breath before finishing, "The answers nobody wants to give me."

Nuria stared at the folder without daring to touch it, as if it held her friend's ashes. "Why ..." She raised her eyes to Gloria. "Why are you giving it to me?"

"Because David trusted you absolutely."

Nuria was about to say she wished he hadn't, but she restrained herself in time. Instead she pointed to the folder, still not daring to touch it. "But ... what's in these photocopies?"

Gloria shook her head. "I don't know. I leafed through the notebook and all I saw was names, numbers, and random phrases. Nothing that made sense to me, but it might to you."

Nuria was staring at the folder as if it were a poisonous plant. Less than an hour before, she'd decided she was going too far with this business ... and now here was Gloria bringing her paranoia back to life. "I don't ..." she started to protest. "I think you ought to give it to Commissioner Puig. He's the one in charge of the investigation."

"I did. I gave him the original notebook, but I don't think he even bothered to look at it."

"That's why you were trying to talk to me?" Nuria asked, remembering how many times she'd ignored Gloria's calls.

"That's right. But you never answered, so I had to come in person."

"I ... I'm sorry. I thought you ..." She left the apology in mid-sentence. "But I still don't understand why you want to give this to me."

"Because you were his friend. And if anyone wants to find out what really happened, it's you. Am I wrong?"

"No, you're not wrong," Nuria admitted. "But the official report—"

"To hell with the official report. I need to know what really happened, and maybe the answer's in here." She laid her hand on the blue folder.

The confidence Gloria was placing in her and that handful of photocopies was heartrending. Nuria seriously doubted that anything David might have written in his notebook would be of any use, and as she'd already figured out, the same was true of anything she might find out on her own. Her mental state wasn't allowing her to think clearly, much less investigate something that affected her so profoundly. Nevertheless, she heard herself consenting, incapable of telling Gloria what she really thought.

"David never told me anything about his work," Gloria went on. "He said he didn't want to contaminate me with the filth out there ... but I do know this is where he wrote down anything important that had to do with his investigations. His 'Sherlock Journal,' he called it," she added with a sad smile, pushing the folder over to Nuria. "I'm sure you'll put it to good use."

Good use, Nuria thought, with the ghost of a grimace. She couldn't think of anything she'd made good use of in her whole sorry life. All the same, with a resigned sigh, she took the file like someone receiving a posthumous letter. Which, in a sense, was exactly what it was. "All right," she said. "Thanks, Gloria. I'll do what I can."

"No, thank *you*. This was important to David, but when I gave it to Puig he didn't seem to attach any significance to it. He glanced at it in front of me, and judging by his expression, I'm sure he threw it in the wastebasket the moment I left his office."

"I won't do that," Nuria promised. "I'll read it very carefully."

Gloria was about to stand up, but changed her mind and stayed where she was. "Do you think"—she hesitated, as if unable to articulate the words—"that David's death might have been ... deliberate?"

That was the very question Nuria had been afraid to hear from Gloria's lips. What could she say in answer? The most sensible and humane thing to do was to confirm the official version. That way they could all go back to sleeping in peace.

"Maybe," her mouth said instead, betraying her once again.

Gloria's eyes closed for a moment, as if assimilating information she knew already but had refused to accept. She stood up, too affected to go on talking about it. Indicating the blue folder on Nuria's lap, she asked in a broken voice, "You ... you'll read it?"

Nuria nodded. She too stood up and clutched the file to her bosom like a treasure. "Every word."

"Thank you," Gloria said, and this time it was her own eyes that flooded with tears.

Nuria hugged her tightly. "Don't thank me," she whispered in her ear, barely able to hold back her own tears. "I owe it to David, to you, and to your son." She sighed and added firmly, "You can count on me, for whatever you need."

"Thank you," Gloria sobbed. "Thank you."

Nuria tightened her embrace, wishing she could find the words to comfort Gloria and expiate her own sin. "If there's anything in those pages that—" she added, letting her remorse speak for her. "If I find out who's to blame," she continued, feeling the vehemence of her conviction, "I swear to God I'll make him pay."

22

Glancing at her watch, which at the moment read 2:17 a.m., as wide awake as if she had three cups of coffee in her system, Nuria understood the reason eight-hour naps weren't advisable in the middle of the afternoon. On the other hand, the advantage of not being able to sleep in spite of all her efforts was that it had allowed her to work on the contents of the folder Gloria had given her. She'd spent more than two hours studying the pile of photocopies filled with David's difficult handwriting—he'd always joked that there was no need to encrypt it—and so far she hadn't been able to find anything that made much sense.

The notes went back more than two years, and in them she'd recognized jottings on past cases as well as names and diagrams linking them among themselves. Nuria realized that the lucid reasoning David had demonstrated during some of the investigations, passing them off as bursts of sudden inspiration, were really the results of days of work in this notebook.

"You trickster." Nuria smiled, recalling how he'd made her believe he was a master of deduction. Now she understood why he'd called it his Sherlock journal. She turned another page, still with a smile on her lips, and the fact that she was thinking about the last time David had pretended to be a genius-level detective almost made her miss a name.

Wilson Vilchez.

There was no date given, but from the context she calculated that he must have made the note in June or July of that same year, when they'd begun their contact with the Peruvian—though to be exact, she remembered that it had been David who had contacted Vilchez and acted as liaison. All the information the dead snitch had had for them had been given directly to David, who had then shared it with her. Or so she'd believed until now.

Nuria turned to the next photocopy, where he'd drawn something that looked familiar. It was a diagram he'd sketched for her once, with Elias Zafrani at the top of a pyramid, the name of his company, Daraya Import-Export, below it in parentheses. From there several branches diverged according to the particular criminal area under Elias's control: one branch for software contraband, another for human trafficking, another for alcohol, tobacco, and so on. Each branch was marked with the name of the man—or woman—in charge. Question marks were penciled in where there was no face to add, which was most of the time.

Below the main branches were more numerous ones according to the scope of activity or the subdivisions of each business area, including the names of those in charge. These were further divided into smaller branches and so on, until they reached the suppliers and thugs who carried out the work at street level. These were the common criminals, the ones who were arrested so often that the police even used cut-and-paste to record their statements, but that was as far as the food chain would take them. Occasionally the police managed to nab the small fry just above them, but that was as high as they could go. The executives of that criminal enterprise were so protected by their cohort of attorneys that just sneezing next to them would have resulted in a lawsuit for police harassment.

Needless to say, Zafrani was the alpha male of that pack of white-collar hyenas. To approach him without a court order in your teeth was a fast track to a new assignment monitoring parking meters in the Monegros desert. What Nuria had done, presenting herself at the company's head office and threatening Zafrani with a gun had been an overwhelming act of idiocy. If her mention of limbocaine hadn't aroused his interest, she was sure she would already have received a call from Human Resources inviting her in no uncertain terms to resign.

The notes on the following pages were briefer and more concise, the kind you might take while on the phone with someone. In these were names, addresses, and succinct indications that Nuria recognized as the tip-offs Vilchez had given them over the course of the last few months—under direct orders from Zafrani himself.

Rage flared again in her chest as she remembered all the hours of work and surveillance that had been put into that investigation while that bastard had been laughing his ass off, thinking of all the false clues he was passing on to them.

In her irritation, Nuria began to flip through the pages faster and faster to avoid seeing all those notes, underlined and framed in ballpoint. Each of them was a taunt, a meaningless doodle Elias pinned up on their backs from his luxurious office at his headquarters on the Diagonal. So angry was she that she reached the last page almost without realizing it. She was about to slam the folder shut when her eyes fell on the final square David had drawn and the two words in it.

The first was a woman's name: Ana P. Elisabets. No address, no e-mail, no phone number. A name Nuria had never heard before. Nor could she connect it with any recent investigation.

Under the name a thick arrow led to another, or rather to an acronym. One she knew well—it had even come up in her conversation with Zafrani. One the mere mention of which inspired terror. A shiver ran down her spine as she read out the name in a low voice, almost afraid to invoke it: "ISMA."

Nuria couldn't have said how long she stared at the acronym, turning over in her mind everything implied by its appearance in David's notebook. It was the final note, penned there just two days before they'd gone to meet Vilchez that terrible morning. It wasn't hard to imagine a connection between the two things.

There was no mention on the last page of Elias Zafrani, his company, or his businesses. Only those two names in large letters, underlined again and again as though whoever had been talking to David had mentioned them repeatedly. And though the note didn't name Vilchez as its source, it was obvious from the context; there was no other name written on the page.

Nuria stopped, trying to conjure up any Ana they might have contacted or who might have been under investigation, but she knew already that she wasn't going to come up with anyone. It seemed important, but for the time being it was a thread she had no idea how to follow. She might ask Gloria later on.

On the other hand, the mention of ISMA in that notebook, after the conversation she'd had with Zafrani that same morning, was a piece that definitely fitted in some way into the whole sinister puzzle. If the substance found in the assassin's blood was limbocaine, and if the jihadists of the Islamic State of Maghreb were using it, as Elias had said, there was a clear line connecting the two, a line that also went from Vilchez to David, in which the informant might have revealed something to do with ISMA, something he'd seen or heard.

Something important enough for Vilchez to be tortured and killed. Something important enough for them to want to kill David too, for having received that call.

In her mind, Nuria imagined the chain of events: Vilchez calls David to alert him to something having to do with ISMA; the terrorists find out, torture the unfortunate Peruvian to make him confess the name of the person he told—hence, the Colombian necktie, reserved for snitches—and, before his death, force him to call David and lure him into the trap both he and Nuria had fallen headlong into.

"ISMA," she repeated to herself, still unable to believe it. "Jesus Christ ... fucking ISMA." The people who belonged to that organization, direct heirs of ISIS in the Middle East, symbolized every possible evil that could be incarnated in a human being. To say they were monsters would fall far short of the truth, not to mention be unfair to monsters. Not even the most vengeful biblical Satan would have been able to imagine a hell like the one ISMA reserved for those who fell into their hands and didn't share their unhinged vision of Islam.

The web was flooded with videos of refined tortures that lasted hours or even days, tortures whose sole aim was to inspire irrational terror in anyone who thought to confront them. The tough Moroccan guerrilla fighters who still held out in their strongholds in the Atlas Mountains always saved their last bullet for themselves in case they were captured. But not all of them were lucky enough to be able to use it, and many ended up as the unfortunate protagonists of some snuff video.

David hadn't left any other note related to that in his notebook, but there was only one activity that could be linked to ISMA: terror. If they'd arrived in Spain in spite of the surveillance along the coast, militarized as in the times of the Berber pirates, it could only be with one goal: to carry out terrorist attacks. After the last attacks in Rome, Marseilles, and Athens, it was only a matter of time before they turned their sights on Spain again.

Nuria's first thought was to call Puig and tell him what she'd found out: the drop of the killer's blood with limbocaine in it, the connection between the drug and the ISMA jihadists, and the mention of the terrorists in David's notebook. As far as she was concerned, that was more than enough to raise suspicion and begin an investigation in earnest. But when she was about to ask the electronic assistant to connect her to Puig, Nuria imagined herself explaining to the commissioner where she'd gotten the blood sample, how she'd had it analyzed, and whom she'd talked to about limbocaine and its use by ISMA.

"Shit," she said abruptly. "If I do this, I'll be totally fucked." She needed more than theories and suppositions if she was to present herself before the commissioner without being crucified on the spot. She needed solid proof that ISMA was plotting something and that David's death had been a casualty of that plan. Otherwise she would only make things worse. They would confiscate David's notes and open a new file on her, sanctioning her for altering a crime scene and meeting with a suspect under investigation while on suspension herself. She would be lucky not to end up behind bars.

Nuria leaned her elbows on the table, exhausted, and buried her head in her hands. No matter where she looked, she could see no way out. Those notes were the only concrete thing she had, and they weren't even the originals, just a handful of photocopies. She couldn't ask Susana for any more favors, and she didn't trust anyone else on the force enough to ask them to put their jobs at risk. The most depressing thing about the whole case was that even if she did talk to a colleague, she wouldn't know what favor to ask. It was like being blindfolded in a dark room with her head in a bucket. If there was any trace of light in this story, she couldn't see it.

For some reason, thinking about the light she needed brought those luminous blue eyes she'd confronted that same morning into her mind, front and center. It was crazy—she knew that the only thing she was likely to get out of it would be a restraining order—but some gut feeling told her he was precisely the one she had to speak to.

"Oh well," she said to herself, pushing the photocopies away and getting to her feet, "might as well be hung for a sheep as a lamb."

124

23

Nuria glanced at her activity bracelet. Its tiny black screen showed 3:02 a.m. She recalled her grandmother Maria saying nothing good ever happened after three in the morning. The private guard sitting in the booth at the top of Pearson Avenue recognized her without needing to see her badge. "You're alone today?" he asked, glancing inside the Uber.

"Yep, it's just me today."

"Another nighttime stakeout?"

"Another nighttime stakeout," she repeated.

"Of course, of course," the guard murmured in a show of camaraderie, as if having admitted her and David a couple of times had made him part of the team. "I'll radio the others so they don't bother you."

Nuria nodded, wanting the conversation to end. "Great. Thanks."

"You're welcome," the guard said. He raised his thumb with a grin. "If you need me, you know where—"

Nuria cut him off before he could finish his sentence, not in the mood for small talk. "Thank you. Good night." She instructed the Uber to go on, and gazed out the window as they entered the exclusive area, now restricted to residents in a clear example of the economic and social inequality that had ended up fragmenting the city, creating ghettos for the wealthy which couldn't be entered without authorization or express invitation.

The vehicle stopped a little over five hundred yards ahead, on a street that wound along the slopes of the Collserola mountain range next to impressive mansions belonging to business executives, politicians, and soccer players. Nuria stepped out of the Uber in front of an intricate iron gate ornamented with arabesques at the end of the street, the entrance to a house she'd monitored on a number of occasions with David, using drones, zoom lenses, and directional microphones.

This time, though, she was standing there in front of it, thinking that just this gate, nearly ten feet tall, must have cost more than her apartment in the Barrio de Gracia. For a man with so much money, even if he was a known criminal, someone like her was no more than a bothersome tick he would have no trouble getting rid of. Without the cover of being an officer on duty, coming here at this hour in search of answers was the closest thing to professional suicide she could think of at the moment. But there was nothing else she could do, so she rang the bell. A few seconds later, the security camera rotated to face her and a voice with a marked Arabic accent spat through the speaker: "Who are you and what do you want?"

"Corporal Nuria Badal of the National Police," she said, as firmly as she could. "I need to speak with Elias Zafrani."

The reply took a moment to arrive, and Nuria had no trouble imagining Elias's security guard studying the monitor, perusing her ripped jeans, old 2024 Paris Olympic Games T-shirt, and worn tennis shoes. "Have appointment?" the voice asked in the tone of someone who already knows the answer.

"No," Nuria admitted.

"Court order?"

"Not that either."

"I very sorry," the guard lied. "But if no appointment, no court order, can't—"

"I'll explain very slowly so you understand," she interrupted abruptly. "If you don't open this gate and tell Mr. Zafrani I'm here to see him, I'll come back within the hour with that court order, plus half-a-dozen patrol cars with their sirens blaring. Do you think that's what your boss would prefer?" The brief silence that followed suggested she'd hit the right note. She had to press on before he had time to think. "So you either open the gate right now … or you can start sending out resumes to work as a supermarket security guard for the rest of your life." She paused before adding, "Your call."

Again, her words were greeted by silence. She imagined the guard weighing her threat and wondering whether that would be worse than the consequences of waking up his boss in the middle of the night. The seconds dragged by. Nuria was beginning to fear the guard had decided to call the police himself and that the next thing she heard would be the sirens she'd mentioned, but coming for her instead.

"Come in," the speaker said, so unexpectedly she jumped. The gate buzzed and swung open like the gate to a haunted castle in the movies. Only the sinister creak of the hinges and the hooting of owls were missing.

Now that she'd gotten what she wanted, paradoxically, Nuria suddenly felt very vulnerable. Making the decision to burst into a criminal's home in the middle of the night had been easy when she was in her own living room. But now, with the gravel crunching under her feet, inviting her into the wolf's lair as if she were walking the red carpet, she began to think that—once again—she'd acted recklessly. "I hope Grandma Maria was wrong," she whispered to herself, and clenching her fists, she went on toward the house.

Activated by sensors, the lights along the path clicked on as she went further into the property. She wound through a dense grove of pine and willow trees faintly illuminated by the moonlight that kept any view of Elias Zafrani's house hidden from unlikely passersby. In this case, *house* meant a spectacular three-story, Alpine-style, stone mansion with huge tinted windows and decorative motifs in wood and slate that included a large balcony on the upper floor that ran the length of the façade. Most of these details were invisible at that moment, but she'd spent so much time watching the house with David that she knew it as well as her own.

The gravel path ended in a well-tended lawn dotted with flowerbeds, dominated by a Moorish-style fountain that vehicles had to circle after dropping their passengers at the front door. As she approached, the door opened, revealing the security guard who had opened the gate for her, a man with Arab features, biceps wider than her waist, and a decidedly unfriendly look on his face. The thug stood before her, arms akimbo, taking up the whole doorway and looking intimidatingly down at Nuria from his six foot plus of height. As she neared him, he extended a hand, palm up as if begging for money.

"Give me weapon," he ordered abruptly.

Nuria spread her arms wide. "I'm unarmed."

The thug looked her up and down distrustfully. "Have to frisk."

Nuria smiled and took a step closer so she could whisper, "If you dare put your hands on me, I'll break them." The man pursed his lips, no doubt unused to receiving threats of this kind, least of all from a woman.

"Giwan," a voice ordered from inside the house. "Let her in."

The thug still hesitated a moment, but finally took a step back to let Nuria enter. She edged her way around him sideways, keeping an eye on him just in case. When she looked forward again, she saw Elias Zafrani waiting for her in the entrance hall, wearing a gray silk jellaba that wouldn't have been out of place at a fancy dinner.

He greeted her with a formal nod. "Good evening, Corporal Badal. I must confess, I'm surprised you came to my house. To what do I owe the pleasure of seeing you again?"

Nuria searched for sarcasm in the man's voice, but he sounded disconcertingly sincere. He was standing by the staircase, looking at her with his arms folded and the corners of his mouth curved slightly upwards. To her dismay, Nuria found that she felt more intimidated by those penetrating blue eyes that were studying her with a touch of amusement than by the two hundred sixty-five pounds of muscle of the thug behind her.

"I need to speak to you," she replied with all the firmness she could muster.

Zafrani considered this brief answer for a moment, then pointed to his left. "In that case, allow me to invite you into the living room. We'll be more comfortable there."

"That won't be necessary," Nuria said defensively.

"Please, I insist. We can talk sitting down just as well."

"Fine," she said, with a show of annoyance.

Her host led her into the ample living room. It was decorated without much taste or concern with current trends: rustic furniture, paintings depicting Middle-Eastern landscapes, ceiling lamps ornamented with arabesques, carpets everywhere, and a wide white U-shaped couch encircling a traditional Moroccan coffee table.

Her host indicated the couch. "Please have a seat."

Once again Nuria hesitated imperceptibly. It wasn't because she felt threatened by this man or because she found herself in his house in the middle of the night with nothing but a handful of questions in her mind. It was a different wariness, born from the instinct that was telling her all this display of amiability couldn't be free. Perhaps it was the same feeling a mouse has when it finds a piece of cheese in front of its hole, embedded in a suspicious-looking contraption made of springs and wood that it can't quite recognize.

"Thank you," Nuria said at last and sat down, maintaining the most erect posture she could.

Zafrani sat down facing her and interlaced his fingers. "Now then, tell me what you've come for."

"I need to ask you some more questions, Mr. Zafrani."

He raised his hand to interrupt her. "Call me Elias, please."

Nuria hesitated a moment but reasoned that she was more likely to get answers if she appeared less formal and created a certain level of trust.

"All right ... Elias." Nuria plunged in. "I need you to tell me what you know about Wilson, and whether he had anything to do with ISMA."

Zafrani frowned and gave her a skeptical smile. "Wilson Vilchez and ISMA?" he asked. "Are you serious?" Nuria didn't answer his rhetorical question. Instead, she waited in silence for her host to go on. "Vilchez was Peruvian and a Christian who belonged to the Reborn in Christ sect," he said. "Not a very devout one, true, but he would never have had dealings with those people."

"But you're a Muslim yourself, aren't you?" Nuria said.

Zafrani gave her a long stare. "My father was a Christian who converted to Islam to be able to marry my mother. But in Syria, just as in my own family, religion was something almost accidental. You're not the sort of person who believes that all Muslims are fundamentalists, are you?" He sounded disappointed. "It would be like believing that all Christians belong to the Ku Klux Klan."

"No, not at all," she hastened to say. "I only meant that the Reborn are usually fanatics and not fond of dealing with other religions. So if Vilchez agreed to work for you, he might have agreed to work for other … less moderate Muslims."

Elias shook his head. "Forget that," he insisted. "I'd have known."

"Are you sure?" Nuria asked. "You live here in this … mansion, in Pedralbes." She gestured around her. "Villarefu is a long way away."

"Not far enough," he replied. "I have eyes and ears all through the camp."

Nuria leaned forward. "And yet … you say you know nothing about the hit man someone sent to kill Vilchez, David, and me."

She could see she'd scored a hit. Elias's face twisted. For the first time he didn't have a ready answer. But just then, as if he'd prepared it in advance, an attractive girl of at most eighteen, wearing a pink jellaba embroidered in gold, came in carrying a tray with a steaming teapot and two glasses filled with mint leaves. Setting the tray on the table, the girl served the tea, then without a word left as silently as she'd appeared.

When the sound of her bare feet had receded down the corridor, Nuria could not help observing, "Your niece Aya, right?"

Elias looked at her, his expression grave. "You've investigated her too?"

"Not in the least. She just appears in the report on you, nothing more than that." She picked up her glass and blew across the top to cool it before taking a long sip. "Now, back to business—"

Elias folded his arms and frowned. "What's your end game with all this?"

"I want to get to the facts: that either you know less than you think you do"—Nuria set the glass back on the tray—"or else you're not telling me everything you know."

Zafrani ran his hand through his hair in a bored gesture. "And why would I do that? I've already told you I'm the first to be interested in knowing what happened and who's behind it."

"But that doesn't mean sharing information with me. The fact is, I've given you more information than you've given me."

Elias spread his arms wide. "Well, go ahead, ask. What do you want to know?"

"I told you. I want to know what connection Vilchez had with ISMA."

"I've already answered that question: none whatsoever." He sounded annoyed. "Why do you insist?"

"Because I have reasons to believe he did."

"Reasons? What reasons?"

Nuria reached for the back of her jeans, and for a satisfying second saw fear reflected in Zafrani's blue eyes. It faded at once when he saw her take from

129

her back pocket not a weapon but a folded piece of paper. Unfolding it carefully, she passed it to him over the table.

"What's this?"

"A page from David's agenda. He probably wrote this after speaking to Vilchez on the phone."

Elias looked at it again, more closely this time. "ISMA?" he asked, sounding puzzled. "Ana P. Elisabets?"

"Shortly after he wrote that, Vilchez sent us an urgent message, asking us to go to his house immediately. I suspect he did so with a razor blade held to his throat."

Nuria could see Elias's brain starting to work, putting the pieces of the puzzle together just as she'd done. "You think Vilchez knew something about ISMA, and that's why they killed him?"

"That's exactly what I think."

Elias nodded, apparently in agreement with this conclusion. "And who's this Ana?"

"No idea," Nuria admitted. "I've searched for her online, but there's no woman with that name in the whole of Spain. I was hoping you'd know."

Zafrani shook his head. "I know a few Anas, but none with that surname or who might have a connection to Vilchez. Even less to jihadists."

"What about ISMA? Has Villarefu been infiltrated by them?"

"Impossible," Elias said, but Nuria noticed he didn't sound quite so certain now. "The refugees have come here fleeing ISMA. They'd never let them into the camp."

"They could be there without anybody realizing. Maybe Vilchez found them out, and that's why—"

Elias cut her off. "That's the line the Spain First politicians take. Trying to link the refugees with terrorism. The people in the camp loathe the ISMA jihadists more than anyone. It's highly unlikely they'd have settled in the camp without anybody finding out. Without *my* finding out."

"Well, well. It looks as though we've gone from impossible to highly unlikely."

"Let's leave it at improbable." So strong was the conviction in his voice that Nuria could see no point in insisting. Still, there was a doubt in her mind that she couldn't get free of except by putting it into words.

"How do I know you're not deceiving me?" she burst out, fixing her gaze on him.

"Excuse me?"

"How do I know you're not behind all this? How do I know Vilchez didn't find out you're a member of ISMA, tried to tell us, and you had him killed?"

Zafrani blinked in disbelief, a confusion of reactions on his face, as if he couldn't decide whether to burst out laughing or explode with rage. Pointing a finger at himself, he demanded indignantly, "ISMA? Do you think I'm a jihadist?"

"Take it however you want." She folded her arms, steeling herself against his considerable acting skills. "You've admitted you manipulated our investigation, using Vilchez to deceive us. How do I know you're not doing it again, lying right to my face? Why should I believe you?"

Zafrani exhaled forcefully, as if trying to stifle the fire of rage in his chest. "Why?" he repeated, standing up. "I'll show you why."

24

Zafrani grasped the collar of his jellaba with both hands and tore it until it slipped from his shoulders and fell to the floor, leaving him naked in front of Nuria except for a pair of black boxer shorts bearing the Armani logo.

Alarmed by this unexpected reaction, Nuria scooted back on the sofa, automatically reaching behind her in search of the gun that this time she wasn't carrying. But instead of hurling himself on her, Zafrani stayed very still, like one of those hyper-realistic statues created by 3D printers, staring at her as if waiting for something.

All at once Nuria understood that his intention was not to assault her sexually, but to have her look at him. With some embarrassment she ran her gaze along the Syrian's body, admitting to herself that in spite of being over forty, he was still in very good shape. Not like the twenty-something police officers who crowded the gym at the station, of course, but she could see in Elias the sinewy muscles of someone who'd had to use them to make a living.

A few seconds later, after basically seeing nothing, Nuria was about to ask him to get dressed when she noticed a scattering of dark marks along his torso and arms, like moles on his brown skin.

The first thing she thought was that they were scars from bullet wounds. But considering that even at first glance there had to be at least twenty or thirty of them, it was impossible he could have survived anything like that.

"Burn marks," she said, understanding at last what they were. "They're marks left by cigarette burns." Zafrani said nothing, merely closed, then opened his blue eyes in assent. He turned around and Nuria put a hand to her mouth to stifle an involuntary cry.

If Elias's chest was a field of dark craters, his back was a map of sinister canyons and crisscrossing gullies, deep gouges that attested to a painful episode in his past. "This is what they did to me the day they came to my village … just to prove they could," Elias recalled, dark rage and sorrow twisting his features. "After they'd stubbed out all the cigarettes they found in my pockets on me, they whipped me with barbed wire and …" He paused, and Nuria could see he was trying to keep that horrible memory at bay. "If I'm alive, it's only because they left me in the gutter so I'd bleed to death," he added, wrapping himself in the remains of his jellaba. He sat down again in front of her. "Others were crucified or burned alive. They stoned women to death, took the boys away to make them into soldiers, and the girls"—Elias clenched his jaw and lowered his gaze to prevent her from seeing the tears in his eyes—"the girls were kidnapped and raped and then enslaved for the troops ... until the day they put an explosive vest on them and blew them up in the middle of a market."

"Oh my God," Nuria muttered, unable to comprehend the scope of that horror.

"You can accuse me of whatever you want, Ms. Badal. You can call me a mafioso, a smuggler, a criminal—but never ... never again imply that I have anything to do with jihad."

Nuria nodded, ashamed. "I ... I didn't know."

"There are many things you don't know about me," he said. Taking a moment to compose himself, he gave a slight shake of his head. "It's all right," he murmured, looking up again. "We all have our own ghosts, right?" For an instant, Nuria wondered how well this man knew her, whether his comment had simply been rhetorical or whether he knew about the shadows in her own past.

Before she'd made up her mind to ask him about it, Zafrani said, "Why did you come to see me, Ms. Badal?"

"I told you. I need to know whether—"

Elias clicked his tongue impatiently. "Why did you *really* come?"

Nuria was about to repeat her answer, but she felt too tired to go on pretending. Leaning back against the couch, she confessed, "Because I'm lost. Because I need answers ... and you're the only one who can give them to me."

"I've told you everything I know," Elias said, spreading his arms wide.

"I find that hard to believe," she muttered, her voice barely audible.

Elias shrugged. "That's not my problem."

Nuria took a deep breath, letting the air fill her lungs before she exhaled. All of a sudden her eyelids felt as if they were made of lead and her tongue was proving reluctant to shape her words. She wanted to reply, to tell him that yes, this *was* his fucking problem, but her consciousness was draining from her like water through her fingers.

She needed to rest. To stop talking, thinking, worrying ... to close her eyes just for a moment, as though in a single long blink. That was all she needed. Yes, she decided, that was what she would do. If she shut her eyes quickly enough, no one would notice. There and yet not there.

Sinking back into the plush cushions of the couch, she allowed her eyelids to fall at last and the light to slowly fade. That was the moment, the final moment of wakefulness, when she realized there was only one empty glass on the table. Elias had not touched his tea.

133

The delicious aroma of buttered toast drifted to her nostrils, waking her just as the ringing of a bell in her ear would have done. Gradually her consciousness began to shake off sleep and begin to function, like one of those old steam engines which as they start, move their connecting rods lazily back and forth, taking their time to make the heavy iron wheels turn on the rails.

Nuria opened one eye, letting the daylight into her drowsy brain. The image she received was not at all clear, so she opened the other eye with the confused hope that using both would bring what was in front of her into focus, but it didn't really help. All she could see was a white surface, as if she were immersed in a glass of milk. Blinking in bewilderment, she put out her arm and her hand made contact with something that felt like soft leather, like the back of a couch.

"What—" she mumbled, still disoriented. A second later everything came rushing back. "Shit!" she cried, sitting up so quickly she felt a whiplash in her neck. "Ouch!"

"Slowly," a female voice said behind her. "It's not good to sit up that quickly."

Nuria whirled around, finding herself face to face with the young woman who had served her the tea the night before. This time she was wearing shorts and a summery blouse, western style. Ignoring her, Nuria jumped to her feet, but her head began to spin and she had to sit down again. She covered her eyes with her hands. "What ... what time is it?" she stammered.

"Ten-thirty," the girl replied. She pointed to the tray she'd set on the table in front of her, laden with cakes and toast. "Would you like coffee or tea?"

"What?"

The girl pointed to the table again. "Coffee or tea? To go with your breakfast."

"I don't want any breakfast," Nuria lied, praying her stomach wouldn't betray her with a rumble. She looked around and asked, "Where is he? Where is Mr. Zafrani?"

"Elias? He left for the office a while ago. He asked me to take care of whatever you needed."

Nuria frowned. "Oh, did he? Is that what he told you?"

"Also that you'd had a rough day. And not to take it wrong if you behaved rudely."

"Rudely? Me?" She stopped, realizing she'd been about to say something inappropriate. "Thanks for preparing all this, um ... forgive me."

"Don't worry," the girl said with a smile. She held out her hand to Nuria. "I'm Aya, Aya Zafrani."

Nuria nodded. "I know. Elias's niece."

"I was really his wife's niece, but as I was left without a family, he took me in and gave me his surname."

Nuria's bloated brain added two and two together. "His wife's niece?" She waved at the door. "You mean to say that he—"

Aya stared at her for a moment, as though weighing whether she ought to continue talking to her. "Didn't he tell you what happened to his family?"

Nuria shook her head. "He didn't mention it."

"But he did tell you what happened the day the jihadists came to his village, didn't he? I heard him talking about it last night."

"Yes, he did tell me that."

"And he also explained what they did to the women and children."

"Yes, he told me that—" Nuria couldn't finish the sentence. "Oh no," she murmured. Her heart contracted. The unexpected revelation hit her like a fist to the face. "He ...?"

Aya nodded solemnly. "He had a wife and two sons."

"Oh, my God ..."

"God had nothing to do with it," the young woman said. "Neither yours nor mine. It was men, evil and stupid ... doing what evil, stupid men always do."

Nuria tried unsuccessfully to shake off the image of the jihadists murdering Elias's wife and kidnapping his children. She couldn't imagine the pain, rage, and frustration that he must carry inside him, that quiet, well-bred man. None of this information had been included in their reports, and it gave a whole new dimension to someone they'd labeled as a common criminal.

"Why wouldn't he tell me?" she asked.

Aya, still standing in front of her, shrugged. "My uncle has secrets, and I guess he still doesn't trust you enough to tell you."

"Yes," Nuria admitted, remembering how aggressive she'd been with him from the start. "I guess you're right."

"Please don't tell him I told you," the girl said. She winked. "He likes you, but he'll punish me by taking away my Internet access for a week."

Nuria narrowed her eyes, thinking she couldn't have heard correctly. "You say he *likes* me?" she asked in surprise. "How ... how do you know that?"

The girl nodded confidently. "I know my uncle. I can see it in his face."

Nuria was taken aback. The only thing she could think of to say was, "Seriously?"

"Absolutely." She smiled at Nuria's confusion. "You really hadn't noticed?"

Nuria blinked in astonishment. "I ... no, not really," she admitted, mentally reviewing their earlier encounters. Maybe that explained the intensity in Elias's blue eyes every time he looked at her. "I hadn't noticed."

Aya crossed her arms and smiled. "Yes, it's pretty obvious." She nodded in amusement. "But don't tell my uncle I told you that either. Okay?"

Nuria pretended to zip her mouth shut. "Don't worry, my lips are sealed." She stood up. "Thanks for the breakfast and the conversation, Aya, but now I have to leave."

"Of course," the girl replied. With a sly smile, she added, "I'm sure we'll be seeing each other around here."

Nuria had no idea how to reply to this. She hesitated, trying to find the right words, then suddenly remembered what had occurred to her just before she'd fallen asleep. "Did you put something in my tea last night?" She indicated the table in front of her. "Something to make me sleep?"

Aya raised her eyebrows in exaggerated surprise. "Why would I do that?"

Nuria raised a hand in apology. "No reason," she said. "Forgive me, I've been a little paranoid lately." She took a deep breath and held out her hand to the girl. "Thanks again, Aya. And thank your uncle too. Tell him that … well … that I'll be in touch."

The girl nodded with a roguish air. "I'll tell him."

Nuria was on the point of asking her to wipe that matchmaker's smile off her face, but instead simply snorted under her breath and went towards the door without saying anything more.

She had a lot to think about.

25

"Ms. Badal?" called a solicitous male voice. "Ms. Badal?"

Nuria opened her eyes in confusion. "What?"

"We've arrived at the destination," the voice informed her from the speaker in the ceiling of the Uber. "I trust you've enjoyed a pleasant ride."

Nuria felt that the last sentence sounded slightly mocking, something not entirely farfetched when it came to Artificial Intelligence, which was becoming harder and harder to distinguish from the human kind. The door of the vehicle opened with a hydraulic hiss, inviting her to disembark. "Have a nice day and thanks for using our service."

"Thank you and likewise," she replied, even though she knew she was speaking to a machine, and alighted with the sluggishness of someone who's just dragged herself out of bed after hitting the snooze button. Still drowsy, she opened the lobby door to her building and started up the dark, dismal stairs with weary steps.

She hadn't reached the halfway point when she heard a familiar meow. There, on the third floor landing, she saw a black-and-white cat sitting in the middle of the hallway staring at her as if it were the most normal thing in the world.

"Melon?" she called, wondering whether she was the victim of a hallucination. "Is that you?" In answer, the cat came up to her and began to rub against her leg, purring in recognition. Nuria bent over and scooped him up in her arms. "What are you doing here? How did you get out?"

The cat didn't answer this time either, but Nuria could imagine what had happened. It wasn't the first time Melon had darted out between her legs unnoticed, or, when turning back for something she'd forgotten when going out, she'd left the door open for a moment and he'd taken the opportunity to run upstairs to the roof. She guessed that when he'd come back down, Melon had found the door closed and her gone, so he'd decided to take a stroll around the building.

"Phew," she said, tightening her grip around the seventeen pounds of cat in her arms and setting off up the last few stairs to her apartment. "As of tomorrow, I'm putting you on a diet." When she reached her landing, perspiring from the heat and the extra weight, she set Melon on the floor. Taking out her keys, she opened the door, and the lights of her apartment came on automatically.

The cat ran to the kitchen and took up his post impatiently in front of his food bowl. Nuria filled it to the brim, forgetting the promise she'd made a moment earlier to put him on a diet, then collapsed on the couch.

This demented circadian rhythm she was keeping was affecting her reasoning capacity. She needed to get back to the sensible routine of sleeping eight hours every night and eating regularly during the day so that her brain could function properly again. She felt stress and lack of sleep taking their toll in every fiber of her body. This unhealthy obsession with looking for answers where perhaps there were none was driving her to an unsustainable point of mental and physical exhaustion.

Abandoning herself to the softness of the couch cushions, she promised herself this madness would end here and now. She wasn't achieving anything except to prove to herself and others that the damn shrink was right and she was losing her marbles. She'd had enough of imagining jihadist plots, fraternizing with criminals, and suspecting everybody. She told herself that this was not her job and felt a deep relief as she did so. She was just a police officer, suspended for acting like a lunatic, and the reality was that in order to go back to her old, comfortable routine, all she had to do was follow Puig's advice: rest, and trust that people better prepared than her, with more information, would be handling the case.

Yes, that was what she would do, she decided with a sense of satisfaction. Nothing she could do would bring David back to life, so for once she would use her brain, forget everything that wasn't her business, and focus—if it was still possible—on getting her job back.

Having arrived at this conclusion, Nuria let her eyelids drift closed again. It wasn't too late yet. Letting herself be wafted away by the pleasant sensation of leaving her problems in the hands of others, she abandoned herself to unconsciousness and drifted, unresisting, toward its comfortable darkness.

And then, just as she was crossing the line between waking and sleep, her activity bracelet vibrated on her wrist, alerting her to a call with an impertinent buzz.

"Christ, this has got to be some kind of joke," she muttered. "Who's the call from, Sofia?" she asked the assistant, keeping her voice down.

"From Susana Roman," the apartment's virtual assistant answered. "Will you take it?"

Nuria sighed resignedly before answering. "Put it on the living-room screen," she said. She greeted her friend's image when Susana's pinched-looking face appeared on the wall screen. Her eyes and nose were reddened. "Hi, Susi. What's up? You don't look well. Have you got a cold?"

Her friend took a few seconds to answer. "Where are you?" Susana asked, wiping her nose with her hand.

"At home. Trying to sleep a little … until someone woke me up, anyway."

Susana ignored the sarcasm. "Are you all right?"

"Me?" Nuria said blankly, surprised by Susi's sudden interest. "Yeah, more or less. Why? What's up?"

Again Susana's reply took several seconds, but this time it sounded not so much urgent as anxious. "Something terrible's happened," she said at last.

"Terrible?" Nuria repeated. Her head cleared instantly and she jumped to her feet. "What's happened?"

"It's Gloria …" Susi said in a broken voice. "She was murdered last night."

The next thirty seconds passed in slow motion in Nuria's mind, approximately the time it took her to confirm she wasn't asleep and caught up in some horrible nightmare. She stared blankly at Susana's face.

Her friend seemed to be waiting for her reaction. "Nuria?" she asked at last.

"Yes, I …" Her voice was barely audible. "How did it happen?"

"I haven't got the details yet. But it seems … someone broke into her house, Gloria surprised him, and …" She took out a tissue and wiped her nose in front of the camera. "Luisito's fine," she added. "Luckily he was at his grandparents'. But it's unbelievable—first David and now her. What bad luck, for God's sake. What terrible, awful luck."

"No, Susi." Nuria's voice was somber. "Luck had nothing to do with this."

Susana's sobs stopped. "What do you mean?"

Nuria's first reaction was to say she hadn't meant anything, that Susi should just forget it, but whatever was going on, she knew she had to share it with her friend. Circumstances had forced her to cross a line she wouldn't have wanted to get anywhere near—but the alternative was to go out of her mind. "She was killed by the same people who murdered Vilchez and ambushed David and me," she explained with unexpected firmness.

"You're still following that line? What's it got to do with Gloria's murder?"

"It's … complicated."

"Don't give me that," Susana protested. "You can't just come out with that and then say it's complicated. Now you've got to tell me what's going on."

Nuria realized her friend was right, though she wasn't sure how much to tell her, since she didn't want to put her in danger as well. "Yesterday she came to see me," she said at last.

"Gloria? You're kidding."

139

"She brought me some of David's notes," Nuria clarified. "Some he kept at home, about the cases we'd investigated together. It was mostly ideas and data we already knew, but right at the end he mentioned Wilson Vilchez ... and ISMA."

"What? The jihadists?"

"I think Vilchez passed on some information about them to David. That's why they killed him, then tried to eliminate us too."

"Wait a moment," Susana interrupted. "Are you telling me Vilchez was a jihadist?"

"No, not that. What I think is that he saw or heard something, something he might have told David, but the ISMA people found out and ..."

Susana took a moment to process this information. Finally she said skeptically, "And you deduced all this because David wrote *ISMA* in his notes? Quite honestly ... it sounds pretty farfetched. One thing might have nothing to do with the other."

"There's more," Nuria went on. "The killer was high as a kite on a kind of amphetamine called limbocaine, a very rare drug that's used by the ISMA soldiers in the Maghreb. That links the killer to ISMA," she concluded, "and the fact that Gloria's been murdered only seems to confirm it."

"And how do you know that?"

"Zafrani explained to me that it's the drug the jihadists use in North Africa."

"What?" Susi asked in the tone reserved for someone who's just announced that they've spent their entire life savings on a lottery ticket. "Are you ...? Fuck, are you serious? Did you go see that guy again?"

"It was the only way. I thought it was his doing."

"You *thought*?"

"He's still not off the hook, but I think it's the Islamists who are behind it all."

"Jesus, Nuria, you're fucking insane," was Susana's snap diagnosis. She added, "So ... you're telling me ISMA murdered Gloria?"

"It looks like it."

"But why? Because of those notes of David's?"

"Very possibly."

Susana snorted, shaking her head incredulously. "Don't take this the wrong way, Nuria," she said after a while, "but I think you've been under a lot of pressure, what with everything that's happened, and your brain has started to look for answers where there are none." Now her eyes were gazing into the camera with something like compassion. "All this about ISMA sounds ... too complicated. There has to be a much simpler explanation for this whole crazy business."

140

"I'm sure there is," said Nuria. "But mine's the right one."

"You see? That's what I mean. I think you've made up your mind, and you'll do whatever it takes to make the facts fit your idea."

"You think I'm being delusional?"

"I think you're under stress," Susana argued, "and that isn't allowing you to think clearly."

Nuria was about to contradict her, but the fact was that her friend was right, she was under stress. But whatever Nuria said, she wasn't going to be able to persuade Susana that stress had nothing to do with her conclusions.

"How did they kill her? Gloria," she clarified unnecessarily. "Did they"—she swallowed, fighting the image that had just taken shape in her mind—"cut her throat?"

Susana shook her head. "She was shot point-blank. In the heart."

"Oh my God."

"Apparently there were no signs of a struggle," she added. "So either they caught her by surprise—"

Nuria finished her sentence. "—or it was someone she knew."

Susana nodded in agreement. "Who knows?"

"Holy shit," Nuria muttered. "And there are no clues?"

Susana shook her head. "I told you, I have very little information. It only happened a few hours ago and the investigation hasn't even gotten underway. All I know is what I told you. Oh yes," she added, suddenly remembering something, "there is something else. It looks as though the killer got scared and ran ... and dropped the gun on his way. That'll make it easier to catch him."

Nuria blinked in disbelief. "Seriously?"

"Seriously," Susana confirmed. "That's what's making them think that maybe someone broke in, got scared, and shot her without intending to."

"In the heart?"

Susana's face twisted. "These things happen, you know," she said, and Nuria knew she was referring to the lucky shot that had saved her life at Vilchez's house.

"What about the weapon? Have they traced it yet?"

"Not yet, as far as I know. But apparently it's a Walther PPK. Not a usual choice for a common burglar."

It occurred to Nuria that that was exactly the model she used herself. She'd opened her mouth to tell Susana that when all at once she froze, suddenly remembering Melon wandering around the building.

As if suspended in time, she turned her head towards her bedroom and her heart stopped in midbeat.

26

The next thing Nuria remembered, she'd left her apartment. She was unaware of having opened the door and run down the stairs or even reached the street. When her spirit rejoined her body once more, she found herself sitting on the steps of the St. John the Baptist church in Virreina Square.

Becoming conscious of her surroundings again felt like being punched in the stomach. Unable to stop herself, Nuria vomited, but as her stomach was empty, only a thread of saliva and bile fell on the gray stone steps of the old church. From the corner of her eye she saw an old couple sitting nearby, shaking their heads and murmuring something about proper civic behavior and inappropriate drunkenness. But Nuria was barely lucid enough to know where she was and why her throat felt as if she'd been drinking acid.

Everything around her seemed alien, as if it were happening in some parallel dimension: the elderly couple, the children playing ball in the square amid shouts of excitement, the pigeons pecking at the leftover grains of rice thrown at a wedding the previous day ... If they'd all disappeared into thin air, she wouldn't have been surprised.

The only thing she knew to be real beyond the shadow of a doubt was the terrifying sense of unreality that had been gnawing at her insides ever since the moment she'd opened her safe and found it empty.

How could they have stolen her weapon? That was the only thing that mattered to her. Or rather: *why* had they done it?

The answers to both questions were so painfully obvious she was reluctant even to think about them. Someone had hacked into her safe, somehow obtaining the password, stolen her gun, and used it to kill Gloria. The next inevitable question was answered by her tortured mind before she'd even formulated it: in order to pin the blame on her. That was why they'd used her gun.

Nuria had no doubt her fingerprints would still be on the grip and that no other prints beside her own would appear on the keypad of her safe or anywhere else in her home. But in spite of all this effort to try to point to her as the perpetrator of Gloria's murder, it made no sense at all in this era of permanent Internet connection. There was always a record of everything people did, where, and when.

Remembering that she was carrying her cellphone in her back pocket, Nuria took it out. She flipped it open and it switched on immediately. With a couple of touches she accessed her activity record, keyed in the last twenty-four hours and stared at the device until a brief message appeared on the screen: *No data available for this period.*

"Shit!" she said, provoking another reproachful look from the elderly couple. "Shit, shit, shit ..." Why the hell was there no data? How was it possible? Had the web crashed again, like when she and David had gone into Vilchez's house? Twice?

Once could be chance. Twice, definitely not.

Could someone have manipulated it on both occasions? Had they deleted her location from the database? All that information presumably went to some gigantic Google server somewhere in the US, in theory safe from hackers. Although it wasn't the first time Internet pirates had accessed those supercomputers and created havoc, they'd always been professional data thieves or cyber-activists. She couldn't believe she was important enough to have triggered an operation as complex as that. Nuria suddenly remembered her safe had been opened, not forced, which implied they'd found out her password, a password that wasn't registered in any physical or digital location. Nobody had ever seen her open her safe. Ever.

Nobody human, at least.

"Jesus," she said to herself. "That's not possible."

With an ominous feeling in her chest, she connected to Sofia. Her virtual assistant greeted her immediately. "Hello, Nuria. How can I help you?"

"Did anyone come into the apartment yesterday while I wasn't there?"

The reply came at once. "I have no record of that."

"What does that mean?" she burst out. "Does *I have no record* mean no?"

"It means I have no record of it."

"I see ..." She took a deep breath to calm herself, then added: "Do you have access to the password for my safe?"

"No, Nuria, I have no access. Your safe isn't connected to my systems, but if you like, I can—"

"No, I don't want that," she cut in. "What I want to know is whether at some moment you might have seen me keying in the password and whether that's been recorded in your memory."

"Negative. I have no visual record of the password for your safe."

Nuria had a sudden inspiration. "Any other kind of record? Could you have ... heard it?"

"My audio system is connected to your electronic activity bracelet," Sofia reminded her. "Under normal circumstances it can detect any sound within a range of fifteen to eighty thousand Hz."

"Is that a yes?"

"As long as the sound is produced within a range of fifteen to eighty thousand Hz."

"I don't know anything about hertz. Does that include the sound of the keypad of my safe?"

"That's right. The alphanumeric keypads of safes emit at a frequen—"

"Fine, fine ... I get it."

There was her answer. If someone had had the skill and the resources to alter her records or her signal reception while she was in Villarefu, they would also have been able to access the records of her virtual assistant to find out the password for her safe via the sound of her fingers pressing the keypad. Nuria felt a chill run down her spine when she realized it: if they could do something like this, they could do whatever else they wanted.

Whoever was behind all this was quite a few rungs above her humble capabilities. She felt like a small laboratory rat that suddenly discovers it's nothing but a tiny animal wandering through a maze under the watchful eyes of giant men swathed in white lab coats.

She went on staring at the bracelet on her wrist. They'd evolved from the old smart watches, but were similar in appearance to the activity bracelets of the previous decade that had given them their name. The bracelets not only monitored her physical state and replaced the irritating ringtones of earlier times with their vibration, they also showed the exact location of anyone who was wearing one in real time.

All of a sudden the harmless-looking device, which a couple of years before had become compulsory for any citizen over the age of fourteen, no longer looked so innocent. If her guess was correct and someone was holding the controls to her life as if it were some kind of fucking videogame, as long as she had that device on her wrist, she would continue to be at their mercy.

Nuria held her hand up in front of her face and stared at the bracelet as if she'd just discovered it was there, no doubt providing the elderly couple with irrefutable proof that the young woman with bags under her eyes was under the effect of drugs.

In a movement so unfamiliar she couldn't remember the last time she'd made it, she seized the bracelet with her left hand. After tugging hard on it, she managed to get it off her wrist with some difficulty.

The small battery that fed off the kinetic energy of her arm would last a few more hours before it deactivated. The centralized system that checked the heart-rate record on the devices would know immediately that she'd taken the bracelet off, but she would still have the advantage of a few minutes before the news reached the police.

"Enough," she told herself. Getting to her feet, Nuria raised her hand to call one of the rickshaws that were waiting for customers on one side of the square.

A moment later, a muscular Nigerian driving a rickshaw with an advertisement for Mercadona supermarkets was pedaling as fast as he could down Torrent de l'Olla with fifty euros in his pocket and the sole mission of reaching the Olympic Port and buying himself a beer to toast the health of the madwoman who had also given him a smartphone and the latest-model activity bracelet.

Meanwhile, the aforementioned madwoman was retracing her steps to her house, warily eyeing the Indetect security cameras posted at the corners of the square. In spite of her fears, though, there seemed to be no one following her. At least for the moment. While she walked, she tried to calculate how much time she had before they checked the serial number on her gun at headquarters and issued an arrest warrant for her. Not much, she concluded.

Nuria turned down Robí Street, so lost in thought it took her a few moments to realize something odd was going on. She stopped short. Her house was just around the corner, but some sixty yards ahead, his back to her, a man was raising a hand to his ear. He seemed to be speaking into his sleeve as he stared at the front of her building. Though she didn't recognize him, it wasn't hard to guess that he was a member of a much wider police operation. If they believed she was a murderer, no fewer than ten officers would be surrounding the house at that moment.

In the end, she'd had even less time than she thought.

Nuria turned around and began to walk in the opposite direction, keeping her head down. Had it not been for the ineptitude of that plainclothes officer she would have fallen headlong into the trap. By now she would be handcuffed and swearing she hadn't murdered anybody as they dragged her to the station. Praying she wouldn't come across anybody she knew, she wandered for ten minutes, concerned only with getting as far away as possible from her home and avoiding providing a clear image for either the security cameras or their facial recognition systems. It occurred to her that she ought to call Susana and warn her, but when she went to activate her bracelet she remembered it was on its way to the port.

"Damn!" she muttered without stopping. Had she been too quick to get rid of the device? But then she remembered, if the police had bugged her phone they might have intercepted her last call to her friend, and she might already have gotten Susana into trouble.

She realized it had been the right decision. The problem was that now, without the bracelet that allowed her to identify herself, anybody who wanted to earn extra civic points might call the police and report her.

"Think, Nuria," she told herself. "Think."

The first word that came to her mind was *money*. In a matter of minutes, as soon as they'd established that she'd fled, they would block her accounts and she would really be screwed. She needed all the cash she could get her hands on.

In the distance she saw the sign for a CaixaBank and hastened her steps toward it, trying not to run, praying it wouldn't be too late. Luckily, though now she only used her activity bracelet at ATMs to withdraw money, she still had her old credit card—on the point of expiring—in her purse.

When she reached the ATM at the end of the street, she inserted the card in the reader and tapped in her PIN, her heart in her throat, dreading the notice on the screen indicating that the card had been blocked, followed by the security alarm going off.

For five eternal seconds the ATM's brain seemed to be considering whether to fuck her life up or not. Nuria lowered her gaze to avoid being filmed by the security camera, cursing the fact that she was in the hands of a stupid gadget with the brain of a microwave.

Finally, with what reached her ears like heavenly music, the cash dispenser gave its characteristic rattle and a small wad of fifty-euro bills appeared in the slot. It was only a few hundred euros, all she had in her undernourished personal account, but it would have to do.

Stuffing the bills into her back pocket, Nuria left the ATM in a hurry. The fact that they hadn't yet blocked her account didn't mean they weren't already on her trail, and if they were, at that very moment a little red light must have lit up at headquarters.

She finally allowed herself to slow down when she reached the vicinity of the Sant Pau Hospital. After glancing around, she went into a Chinese-food café. The front window was full of the usual faded pictures of Chinese dishes, their prices and descriptions below in clumsy Spanish plagued with misspellings.

Inside, a dozen people were scattered at small tables covered with red oilcloth, absorbed in their morning coffees and sandwiches as they glanced at the news on their folding phones. No one raised his head when she walked in, which meant her face hadn't yet appeared in the news, but at any minute it would. And then it wouldn't be just the city security cameras she would have to hide from.

"Hey, you!" someone called behind her.

Nuria's heart stopped, knowing the voice was addressing her. In a cold sweat, she turned slowly around, fearing she would find herself facing a plainclothes officer who had just recognized her. It was only the Chinese waiter, though, looking at her from behind the counter. "What you want?" he barked with the proverbial courtesy of Chinese restaurateurs. "Want sandwich?"

"Um … no, just a black coffee," she said when she'd recovered from her shock.

The man made a face at the smallness of her order as he finished drying a cup with a filthy rag. "You sit there," he said, pointing to one of the few empty tables and wiping the sweat from his forehead with the same rag.

"Better give me a Coke," she corrected herself. "Without a glass."

27

She needed a plan.

Taking a long swig of her Coke, Nuria set it on the table, shutting her eyes for a moment and enjoying the cool liquid slipping down her throat. If they'd been in such a hurry to arrest her at home, by now all her social networks and messaging services would be under surveillance, and perhaps the people closest to her too. A depressingly easy surveillance operation, she considered resignedly, realizing it would be limited to her mother and Susana.

Luckily her grandfather was off the radar when it came to electronic surveillance, and unless her mother let her tongue run away with her they wouldn't have an easy time finding him. She hoped they wouldn't, since among other things it would mean the end of Daisy's business and a pretext on which to deport her and her daughter. No matter what happened, she needed to avoid all contact with her grandfather, however much she might need a warm hug just then to assure her that everything would be all right in the end.

With her second swig of Coke, she weighed calling Commissioner Puig and explaining what had happened, clarifying for him that everything was the result of an obscure plot to implicate her in Gloria's death, and perhaps also make her responsible for David's. It was obvious that someone with the means to manipulate her personal records on the Internet wanted to get her out of the way because of what she knew … or because of what they thought she knew. All the years she'd served under his command ought to be worth at least that.

The unfortunate thing was that she knew exactly how that conversation would go. Puig would order her to come in to the station at once, she would ask for guarantees that he would investigate her conspiracy theory, he would say that the investigation would follow the usual channels and would be evidence-based, she would reply that that wasn't enough, and when he said something like 'that's the best we can do,' she would hang up, and things would be worse than they already were.

She needed proof. She needed to show without a shadow of doubt that she'd been set up, and for that she had only two witnesses who had seen her spending the night sleeping on a couch. The problem was that the credibility of both witnesses was not only dubious but would raise further questions that would complicate matters instead of clearing them up.

The fact that the principal witness who could save her was a criminal under investigation himself was already a problem. But it was a bitter irony that she herself was the one conducting the investigation—and her alibi, that she'd been asleep at his house, was a fucking joke. A joke that wasn't even the least bit funny.

Nuria took a deep breath and leaned her head back on the chair. No doubt by now she'd been flagged as a murder suspect. All her contacts' networks would be bugged, and if she called any of them she would get them into trouble. So the list of people she could turn to and who could help her was very short.

In fact, there was only one name on it.

"Daraya Import-Export," a cultured female voice informed her on the phone. "How can I help you?"

"Good morning. I need to speak with Mr. Zafrani."

"Mr. Zafrani is in a meeting at the moment. But if you leave your number, he'll contact you as soon as he can."

"That's not good enough," Nuria said. "I need to speak to him right now."

"Right now he's in a meet—"

"Well, tell him to leave the meeting," she interrupted impatiently. "This is Corporal Badal of the police, and it's an emergency."

To Nuria's surprise, as if the admin been expecting her call, the young woman said, "Ah. I understand. I'll put you through at once." She put her on hold, leaving Nuria wondering whether the change in attitude had come because she'd presented herself as a police officer or because she'd given her name.

A few seconds later the line was connected again and she heard Elias's voice. "Ms. Badal? What's the matter?" Nuria felt an unexpected wave of relief at his tone of concern, and then immediately felt angry with herself because of it.

"I have a problem," she burst out.

"Only one?"

"This is no time for jokes," she said sharply. "I need your help."

"What do you need?" he asked, changing his tone. Nuria hesitated over what to tell him and what not to.

Elias noticed her hesitation. "If you don't tell me what's going on, I won't be able to help you."

"The police are looking for me," she said at last.

"Seriously? You?" he asked incredulously. "May I ask why they're looking for you?"

"They think I killed someone," she said. "Gloria, David's wife."

Nuria could sense Zafrani thinking at the other end of the line. "The person who gave you the notes where ISMA was mentioned?"

"That person, yes."

"But you ... you can't have ..."

"Of course not, for Christ's sake!" Nuria snapped, annoyed by the insinuation. "She was my friend."

"I see ..." Elias exhaled and fell silent.

"Are you going to help me or not?" Nuria asked when he didn't add anything more.

"Why did you call me?"

"Does that matter?"

"Of course it matters."

Nuria considered what to say, but she was too upset to tell him anything other than the truth. "Because I think you're the only person who can help me." After thinking for a moment, she added, "And because now we have a common interest. Whoever killed Gloria could be the same ones that ordered Vilchez's murder."

"Yes, that's possible," he agreed after a moment's thought. "Do you still have your bracelet?"

"No. I already got rid of it. I'm calling from a phone in a café near—"

"Don't tell me. Have you forgotten that you bugged my phone lines?"

"Oh yes ... of course," Nuria mumbled, embarrassed at not having thought of that. She herself had requested the court order. "So then ...?"

"In a few minutes you'll get a call on that number from a secure line. Wait for it."

"Understood," Nuria said. The line went dead.

Slowly she hung up the anachronistic phone next to the counter and lingered beside it, wondering what she'd done wrong to find herself suddenly being chased by the people she cared about and putting herself in the hands of someone she detested. Did it always happen this way? Was this the reason so many others went over to the dark side of society? Because someone had driven them to it?

Nuria asked herself these questions without taking her eyes off the filthy white phone on the counter. The numbers on its keypad were practically illegible beneath the countless layers of grease and grime. The waiter was looking at her out of the corner of his eye, and Nuria wondered whether he'd been listening in on her conversation with Elias. If he'd heard that the police were looking for her he might be tempted to call them and rat her out.

Glancing around her, though, she dismissed the possibility. She doubted whether he would appreciate the arrival of the police in his café. Deportation orders for foreigners were a police officer's bread and butter, and the bonuses offered to those who informed on illegal immigrants had become too great a temptation for an undocumented worker to risk attracting attention.

Distracted by her thoughts, the loud ring of the antiquated telephone gave her a start. The waiter attempted to answer it, but Nuria beat him to it. Picking it up, she said, "Hello?"

"Nuria Badal?" asked an unknown voice.

Suddenly Nuria felt uneasy and distrustful. The idea of hanging up the phone and running out of the café flashed through her mind, but she managed to stay calm enough to realize she wouldn't get very far.

"Speaking," she said at last.

"Where are you?"

"At a café near the Sant Pau hospital, called ..." She stared at the glowering waiter, who put a napkin in front of her with the name printed on it: *The Happy Chinese*. Nuria raised a skeptical eyebrow, but kept the irony to herself.

"I know it," said the man on the phone. "I'll be there in twenty minutes." Without another word, he hung up. Nuria followed suit, bestowing her most grateful smile on the waiter, whose embittered rictus remained unchanged. She wondered whether the concept of happiness was the same in Spanish as in Mandarin Chinese.

She went back to her table, followed by the curious glances of the other customers. On her way she picked up a greasy copy of *La Vanguardia*, more to hide her nervousness than out of any real interest in reading it.

Sitting down again, Nuria unfolded the paper in front of her like a spy in an old movie. She couldn't ignore the fact that the police might already have posted images of her on the networks, so the less visual contact she had with strangers, the better.

Paradoxically, having contacted Zafrani and the fact that he was helping her were making her even more nervous than she'd been before. A few minutes ago her only worry had been that the police might catch her. Now she was also wondering what price she would have to pay for the help of a criminal like Elias. Instead of feeling safer, her instincts warned her that the exact opposite might be the case. Had she ventured into the wolf's den all by herself?

Because now that she stopped to think about it ... who else but he knew she hadn't been at home the night before? Suppose, in spite of what Aya had told her, they *had* put a sedative in her tea? As soon as she was asleep, he could have given the order for someone to sneak into her apartment, steal her gun, and eliminate Gloria. He'd had plenty of time to do something like that. Besides, if anyone had the means and the paid hackers to alter her Internet files, it was him. A good part of his criminal activity took place in cyberspace: that was a fact.

So he had the means and the opportunity, but no motive. Why would he have organized something so convoluted to get her out of the way when she was asleep, defenseless, in his own living room? It made no sense. He could have buried her in the backyard, gotten rid of her like a dead pet. Even if he'd wanted her to take the fall for Gloria's murder, he could have done everything exactly the same way … and then buried her in the backyard. She would still have been a fugitive, wanted for murder, and he wouldn't have had to worry about her anymore.

But then, she reasoned, there was also the undeniable fact that Gloria had been murdered immediately after she, Nuria, had told Elias about the existence of David's notebook and his mention of ISMA. Another coincidence. One more in this whole senseless mess.

A welter of confused ideas was flying around in her brain, trying unsuccessfully to link up with each other like a flock of drunken starlings flying in a storm. Nuria could sense that beyond all the surface clutter, underneath the chaos, an image was trying to take shape in her mind, but the feeling was so subtle she wasn't even sure it was there, or that it had any connection with the case.

Once more the headache that radiated from the spot where she'd hit the nape of her neck was beginning to make itself felt. Nuria decided to stop thinking about her situation—or at least try to. She opened the newspaper and focused on articles that didn't affect her directly, like the loss of contact with the SpaceX Mayflower II that was on its way to Mars, or the walloping Barça had taken in the eSports championships.

It had been an eternity since she'd read a printed newspaper. She marveled at the tactile sensation of the paper and the smell of ink. *La Vanguardia* was one of the few that had survived the massive digitization of the press, clinging to the old ways at the cost of losing its immediacy and the common assumption that its news would already be old before it had even left the press. It had managed to survive thanks to its op-eds and in-depth analyses by old-school journalists who refused to succumb to the vortex of digital immediacy, or to streaming the news on YouTube, dolled up like twenty-somethings.

A couple of times Nuria reflexively reached for her phone, forgetting she no longer had it. She felt as though she'd lost an arm or a leg; with neither phone nor bracelet, she was as out of place as a neo-patriot in a library.

Just then, a small middle-aged man with the air of a defenseless bookworm, the sort whose school lunches were stolen as children, approached her with a smile, looking at her curiously from behind small John Lennon glasses.

"Shall we go?" he asked as if they were old friends. He had a subtle accent she couldn't identify. "The car's outside."

Nuria hesitated a moment, but having gone this far already, it made no sense to vacillate now. "Sure," she said uncertainly, dropping a bill on the table. She stood up and followed the man, who was already on his way out the door. Nuria had no idea where he was planning to take her; she'd had no chance to ask.

She realized she'd blindly put her fate in the hands of Elias, a man whom until very recently she wouldn't have trusted to hold a glass of beer for her.

She knew the circumstances had put her in this situation. She'd had no choice. Like the San Fermin bulls that believe they're free as they stampede down the street, when in reality they're being tricked into going into the bullring on their own.

Outside the cafe the man stopped beside a Lexus with tinted windows and invited her with a wave of his hand to get into the back seat. Nuria felt a shiver run down her spine and hesitated, her hand on the door handle. Once she got into that car there would be no turning back. In all probability she was making a mistake. The only unknown quantity was how much of a mistake. *Maybe it's worth finding out*, she thought. *It's not like I've got a lot to lose.*

Filling her lungs with air as if she were about to dive into the water, she lowered her head and climbed into the vehicle.

28

The door of the Lexus closed automatically the second she sat down. A moment later the man opened the driver's door and slid in behind the wheel. Turning around in his seat, he asked, "Do you have an activity bracelet or a phone?"

"I'm clean."

He took a few seconds to look her up and down. Not until he'd finished his visual examination did he nod in satisfaction. "Good," he said, facing front again and starting the electric engine.

"Where are we going?"

He glanced at her in the rearview mirror as he eased into the traffic. "I've been instructed to pick you up and take you to a safe place."

"What place?"

"A safe one," he repeated, looking ahead.

"I see," Nuria said. It was clear she wasn't going to get anything else out of him, so she decided to relax in the comfortable leather seat and wait. There was nothing else she could do.

The luxury electric vehicle cruised down Lepanto Street toward the sea. As they passed Gaudí Square Nuria caught a brief glimpse of the impressive mass of the Cathedral of the Sagrada Familia, with its eighteen towers reaching nearly six hundred feet into the sky. Its construction had taken two years longer than planned and it had cost an indecent amount of money that could certainly have been put to better use helping those in need. All the same, she had to admit the result was impressive.

The sad thing, she thought as she watched the Spanish and Vatican flags waving atop each of the towers, was that something that had been the project of a tolerant, progressive city for a hundred fifty years was now, paradoxically, going to be turned into a publicity stunt by the most reactionary government in the last several decades and the most backward-looking papacy in the last several centuries.

As the car accelerated and she lost sight of the building, she told herself she had too many problems of her own to worry about politics or religion now. There was nothing she could do about it, so there was no reason for it to matter to her at all.

From the comfortable, soundproofed interior of the Lexus, Nuria stared out at the dense traffic of electric bicycles and skateboards, weaving nervously between cars and buses like salmon between rocks in a river.

The vehicle turned right on Aragón Street. At the first red light, the driver turned in his seat and held out a piece of black cloth to her. "Put it on," he ordered.

"What?" Nuria asked, not understanding.

The driver tossed it at her and it fell into her lap. "Put it on."

Nuria unfolded it. It was a hood. "I'm not putting this on."

The driver faced front again. Though the light had turned green, he folded his arms and looked at her in the rearview mirror. "Then we're not going anywhere," he said nonchalantly, ignoring the honking of the cars behind them.

"I'm not going to put on a hood while a stranger drives me to some unknown destination. For fuck's sake, I'm not that stupid."

The driver turned in his seat again and, to Nuria's surprise, proffered his hand. "Ishmael," he said. Nuria stared at the small gnarled hand with its cleanly cut nails. Reluctantly, she shook it.

"Hello, Ishmael, I'm—"

He interrupted her abruptly. "I don't need to know. Now that you know me, are you going to put the hood on so we can continue?"

"Is it … absolutely necessary?" she asked, knowing what the answer would be.

"Absolutely."

She hesitated, convinced once again that she was making a mistake, but also that she had no choice but to go on. "All right," she said with a sigh and put the hood on, hoping it wouldn't be her final mistake.

The Lexus accelerated at once amid a recital of honks and curses from the other drivers. Although at first Nuria was able to work out where they were going, after a while she lost track and stopped trying to. She was sure Ishmael had taken a few more turns than necessary in order to disorient her.

Twenty minutes or so later the car slowed. By the echo Nuria knew they'd just entered an enclosed space. A heavy metal door slammed down loudly behind them, confirming her suspicions. The electric motor of the Lexus stopped with a hiss and Ishmael told her she could take off the hood.

Pulling it off, Nuria discovered they were inside a garage or a small locale, windowless and badly lit. Without waiting for an invitation she opened the door and stepped out, then glanced around, trying to identify the place. "Where are we?"

Ishmael indicated the wall at the far end, ignoring her question. "Come with me." Going to a padlocked door of weather-worn plywood, he opened it with a key he took from his pocket and went through, followed by a wary Nuria.

When Ishmael switched on the light, she found they were in a windowless room whose walls were stained with damp. Ancient garbage was heaped in the corners. The only furniture was a table and two chairs huddled together under the lamp, a mattress pushed against the far wall and an electric hotplate with a rusty old frying pan and a coffeepot. The air was close and reeked so much of mold and damp it was almost unbreathable. Nuria took a step back as soon as she crossed the threshold.

Ishmael indicated an open door to the left. "There's the toilet. Don't try to get out or make contact with anyone, understood?"

Nuria turned to him with a furious wave of her arm. "This must be a joke."

"A joke?"

"I'm not staying here for a single moment. This is a fucking shithole."

"Sorry, but the suites at the Ritz were all taken."

"Don't fuck with me," Nuria shot back furiously. She went up to him and jabbed her index finger at him. "I don't believe Elias told you to put me in this hole."

Ishmael was a lot shorter than Nuria, but that fact didn't seem to intimidate him, perhaps because he was armed or perhaps because he didn't know she was a green belt in Krav Maga. Or perhaps both.

"Mr. Zafrani," he explained calmly, "asked me to bring you here. It's a safe place."

"Safe for me or for him?"

"Safe for all of us. That's what it's all about, right?"

Nuria shook her head, far from convinced. "And how long am I supposed to remain here?"

"That I can't tell you. I guess as long as necessary."

"As long as necessary?" Nuria hissed. She glanced at the dirty mattress. "I don't like this at all, Ishmael. Not one little bit."

"If you like, I can take you back to where I picked you up." He jabbed his thumb at the open door behind him. "You decide."

Nuria gave a long exhale, looked around her again, and finally nodded resignedly. "I need to make a couple of calls," she told him. "I have to let people know I'm all right."

Ishmael shook his head. "No calls."

"But my mother … she doesn't know what's happened to me."

"Sorry," he said, but this time he seemed sincere.

"Shit!" she muttered to herself, beginning to understand the disagreeable turn her life was taking.

"I'll bring you water, food, and something to read," Ishmael said, and went to the door. Nuria didn't answer, her eyes fixed on a cockroach that had just

156

emerged from under the filthy mattress. "I'll be back soon," Ishmael added. He shut the door and went out.

In her stunned state Nuria didn't register the sound of the chain, and it was too late by the time she heard the padlock snap shut on it. Resigned, she didn't bother to protest.

That was when she looked down at the floor and saw myriad spatters and stains of dried blood on the smooth cement. This windowless cell with no escape route was a dungeon, a place where people had been kidnapped and tortured, perhaps even to death—and she'd entered it of her own free will. She was locked in, with no possibility of asking for help or even finding out where she was.

"Good job, Nurieta," she muttered desolately. Leaning her back against the wall, she let herself slide down until she was sitting on the floor. "You've really outdone yourself this time."

29

With neither bracelet nor smartphone, Nuria had no way of knowing what time it was or how long she'd been locked up. In fact, the absence of windows or even a crack that daylight could filter through prevented her from knowing whether it was day or night.

One thing was sure, though—she'd been lying on that disgusting mattress for hours, her gaze exploring the sinister spots of damp that covered the ceiling and the walls as she flicked off the roaches that every so often would pluck up their courage and try to climb up her legs.

She felt as if she were going mad, her mind obsessively going over and over the details of Gloria's death and the fact that someone had tried to implicate her in the murder. It couldn't be a coincidence that the murder had happened just after Gloria had given her a copy of David's notes.

As she saw it, if she discounted any involvement by Elias, there were only two possibilities: either Gloria herself had told someone she shouldn't have, which was unlikely in view of all the precautions she'd taken; or she'd been followed to Nuria's house and overheard as she gave the photocopies to her friend, which implied that her apartment had been bugged.

Nuria slapped her forehead. "For God's sake, what an idiot I am." There was no need to bug her home like they did in the old movies in order to spy on her. If they'd been able to hear the combination of her safe, it would have been no problem to follow the conversation she'd had with Gloria on the couch while she was giving her the notes.

Even worse, if they'd hacked her activity bracelet, they would know every last thing she'd said and done during the last few weeks, as well as being aware of every time she left the house, which would have made it child's play to get in and steal her gun.

She'd made it too easy for them. But knowing *how* they'd done it wasn't important; what was really important was *who*.

The mention of ISMA in David's notes and the presence of limbocaine in the blood of Vilchez's murderer made the terrorist organization, by proxy, the main suspects in everything else. The false note in that theory was that as far as she knew, the Islamic fundamentalists had declared war on technology because it went against the teachings of Allah and because it provided a way for apostasy to find its way into the minds of Muslims. In fact, the first thing they tended to do when they took over a city was to destroy any trace of technology more advanced than a spinning wheel and eliminate any form of communication with the outside world. So she found it hard to imagine one of those bearded and turbaned fanatics becoming an expert hacker capable of infiltrating her Google assistant's systems.

Of course, they might have paid someone else to do it—though that wouldn't be typical of ISMA and their methods, which were considerably more direct. Those people were more given to mass shootings in a shopping mall or detonating a truck loaded with explosives.

Nuria dropped her head into her hands in desperation. Desperate because she couldn't understand anything that was happening. Desperate because she'd been responsible first for David's death and then Gloria's, and was now a murder suspect. Desperate because she was locked up in this disgusting hole at the mercy of a man who might very well be negotiating for her head at this very moment. Everything was so confusing she felt unable to determine how far her own responsibility for what was happening went. Or had she become nothing more than a stupid puppet in the hands of a puppet master who was using her at his whim for his own ends?

She felt the despairing sobs fighting to find a way out of her throat, but she refused to give in to them. If she allowed herself to be carried away by self-pity, she would fall into a well it would be impossible to climb out of. She needed to force back the tears that threatened to come out, even at the risk of drowning in them.

Nuria was pressing the heels of her hands into her eyes in a vain attempt to block the tears when she heard the metal door to the street rise with a clang. Leaping to her feet, she assumed a defensive posture, scanning the room for anything she could use as a weapon. Unless she wrenched a leg from the table, though, she had nothing but her own fists.

She could hear an electric vehicle entering almost soundlessly. This was followed by the noise of the door descending again. Seconds later she heard the chain clinking, then the padlock being unlocked. The door opened and Ishmael's mouselike face peered in, taking on an expression of surprise when he saw Nuria in front of him, fists at the ready, crouched in the hostile stance of someone about to throw a right hook.

"Easy, miss," he said, raising his hands. "It's me."

"I want to get out of here," Nuria spit at him without lowering her fists. "I'd rather face the police than stay one single minute more in this shithole."

To her surprise, Ishmael nodded understandingly. "I understand," he said, looking around with disdain. "It was necessary, though. Now we can go."

"Go?" Nuria repeated. She hadn't been expecting this.

"That's right." The trace of a smile curved his thin lips. "We have a better place to hide you. This ... *place*," he added with a grimace of distaste, "is just for emergencies."

Now she did relax. "Good," she said. "Then ... shall we?"

"We shall," Ishmael confirmed. As if he'd only just remembered, he stuck his hand in his back pocket. "But first—" With a complicit look at Nuria, he pulled out the black hood and handed it to her.

As soon as she'd settled herself into the back seat of the vehicle with the hood over her head, the metal door rose and they drove out. Nuria resisted the impulse to peer out from under the black cloth. After a few minutes of making turns in absolute silence, Ishmael addressed her again. "If you like, you can take the hood off now."

It took Nuria no more than a second to pull it off and fling it to the other side of the seat. Looking out the window, she saw they were driving along the coast road, between the steep slopes of Montjuïc and the cargo docks of the port of Barcelona, where thousands of containers in eye-catching colors were piled up like giant Legos.

A pang of nostalgia assailed her as she remembered how as a child her father would take her to the wall of the castle on the summit of the mountain, before it was converted to a prison and closed to the public. He would point out those same containers and the ships that unloaded them, and they would play a guessing game about where they came from and what might be hidden inside them. Nuria's guess was always toys. Her father would always admit defeat and take her for an ice cream cone—strawberry and vanilla—as a prize for her perceptiveness.

The Lexus took the offramp at Exit 21, circled Drassanes Square, then took Paralelo Avenue to Nou de la Rambla and on into the Raval neighborhood, where it nosed forward slowly among the hordes of tourists, Filipinos at their food stalls, and idle North Africans smoking in their doorways.

"Where are we going?" Nuria asked, noticing the curious looks the luxury vehicle was drawing as they navigated through one of the most run-down neighborhoods in the city.

Ishmael pointed to the dot that showed their destination on the navigation screen. "To an apartment in this area. We'll be there in a moment."

"I won't let you lock me up again, I'm warning you."

Ishmael glanced at her in the mirror. "Don't worry," he said ambiguously.

Nuria was about to repeat that she was here of her own volition and that if he tried to lock her up in a hole again she wouldn't allow it, but before she could open her mouth, the vehicle glided to a halt in front of a ramshackle front door on D'en Robador Street, guarded by an aging prostitute stuffed into a leopard-print dress.

"We're here," Ishmael said. "You can get out now."

"Here?" Nuria asked, studying the manifold fauna on the street, made up of drunks, prostitutes, and drug dealers. "Don't tell me, the Ritz was full again."

The driver permitted himself a thin smile. He pushed a button and the door of the Lexus swung open. "Here's where we say goodbye."

Nuria saw that the prostitute, teetering on her heels, was approaching the open door as if it were an invitation. "And what do I do now?"

"Someone will come to take charge of you."

"Someone? What someone?"

Ishmael turned around in his seat. "Good luck, miss," he said in farewell, making it clear he wasn't going to say a single word more.

Nuria snorted in frustration. She was reluctant to leave the comfortable interior of the Lexus without knowing what the hell she was doing there, but she realized she had no choice but to get out. "Well then," she muttered, "thank you, Ishmael," sure as she said it that it wasn't his real name.

Nothing was ever what it seemed, Nuria thought as she stepped out of the car. This conclusion was reinforced when the aging prostitute approached her. Before Nuria had the chance to tell her not to bother her, the hooker looked her up and down, put her hands on her hips, and said in a voice roughened by alcohol and tobacco, "Come with me, beautiful." She winked one of her eyelids with its thick sky-blue eye shadow. "They're waiting for you."

30

Following the irregular click-click of the prostitute's heels, Nuria went up the dark, narrow stairs of the building as if climbing the steps of some Mayan temple lost in the jungle. Looking around, she reflected that all it needed was a few vines and cobwebs dangling from the ceiling to make it look like the setting of an adventure novel.

After a long, slow ascent, accompanied only by the shouts of the neighbors and the noise of gunfire from some television series, they reached the top floor of the building. Halting on a landing with the number 5 scrawled in pen on the dirty wall, the leopard-woman rapped on a door that looked as though it had been deliberately scarred.

After a few seconds the door opened and a familiar face appeared on the threshold. The man was an Arab of rather disheveled appearance with a thick beard, wearing a gray, tea-stained robe, a white crocheted prayer cap on his head. It took Nuria a few seconds to recognize him. "Elias?"

Without replying, he handed the prostitute a twenty-euro bill, which she took with the rapidity of a cobra. "Thank you, Lola," he said.

"At your service," she replied with a wink. Without further ado she turned and clattered back down the stairs.

Elias moved aside, allowing Nuria to enter. "Surprised?"

"A little," she admitted. "I wasn't expecting you to be here, and least of all"—she gestured—"looking like that."

"I like to pass unnoticed," he said. He waved her into the apartment. "Here in the Raval I'm just Mohammed. One more immigrant who keeps to himself and does what he can to make ends meet. It's easier to find out what's going on in the slums this way."

"Like that king who used to go out at night to mingle with his subjects, right?"

Elias nodded. "Something like that. But without going out on a motorbike to see his lover."

The interior of the apartment wasn't much different from its exterior. Old furniture that might have belonged to the previous tenant, torn wallpaper, sun-yellowed curtains, and a general impression of neglect, as if it hadn't been properly cleaned since the previous century. But compared to the plague-pit she'd spent the last few hours in, it was like being in a luxury hotel.

"Please have a seat," Elias said cordially, his manner relaxed as he pointed to one of the four chairs around the wooden table in the middle of the living room. "How are you?"

"Hungry," Nuria admitted, grateful for this new intimacy. "I haven't had anything to eat since yesterday."

"Of course. Forgive me. The last few hours have been total madness."

"No worries. But if I don't eat something I'm going to pass out."

Elias spoke a few words in Arabic into his phone, then looked at Nuria. "Shawarma or falafel?"

"Both," she said without hesitation. "And salad, and something to drink, and dessert." At his look of surprise, she added, "What's wrong? I'm hungry."

Elias smiled and spoke in Arabic again into his phone, giving the order. "You'll have it in ten minutes."

"Thank you."

"You're welcome." He sat down in a chair in front of her.

Nuria looked at his electronic bracelet as if it were a poisonous snake curled round his wrist. "My account's been hacked," she explained. "My records and my calendar have been interfered with, and they've been spying on me. It's very possible that someone knows everything I've said and done these past few days … including our conversations." Pausing, she added: "There aren't many people with the resources to do a thing like that." She stared at Elias.

He gave a wry smile as he understood her insinuation. "I don't have either the resources or the interest to do that," he said before she could ask. "It's one thing to hack into the police intranet, and a very different thing to infiltrate Google in order to delete personal data or spy on somebody. Don't take it the wrong way," he added, "but if I were capable of doing that, believe me, there'd be more interesting people I'd spy on."

"Well, someone's done it to me," Nuria insisted. "And they might be doing it to you too at this very moment."

He showed her his bracelet. "Don't worry about that. I use a quantum encryption system for my communications, like the one the NSA uses to control their spy satellites. The whole system cost me a small fortune"—he turned his wrist this way and that in front of him—"but it's impossible to decode."

"Okay," Nuria said. "I don't suppose you've got a spare one lying around, have you?" To her astonishment, Elias took out a bracelet identical to his own and set it on the table. "You mean it?" she asked in amazement as she stared at it.

"Don't lose it," he warned her. "And use it intelligently. Nobody will be able to track you. You can link it to a screen or a smartphone to communicate, but if you make contact with someone, make sure not to say more than you need to."

"The fact that I'm almost blonde doesn't mean I'm almost stupid."

"I'm just telling you to be careful. Any contact could be risky. For you and for the person you contact."

She put it on and felt the slight pressure as it closed around her wrist automatically. "Yes, I know. I … appreciate what you're doing." She hesitated, the words feeling foreign in her mouth. "I didn't know who to turn to."

"Never mind," Elias said, waving away her gratitude. "What's important is that you're safe."

"That I'm safe …" Nuria repeated thoughtfully. "I really appreciate it, but I still don't understand why you're doing this. What do you get out of helping me?"

"Why should I get anything out of it?"

She raised an eyebrow. "Come on. It's not that I really care, I'm just curious."

Elias nodded. Leaning back in his chair, he steepled his fingertips in front of him. "If your suspicions are confirmed and it turns out ISMA is planning something," he said after considering for a few seconds, "I want to know about it so I can prepare. I already had to flee from them once after they'd destroyed my life." He inhaled and released the breath in a long exhale, fixing his eyes on Nuria. "But that's never going to happen again. Now I'll be able to see them coming, because I have something they want."

"And what's that?" Nuria asked. Before the question was out of her mouth, she knew the answer.

Elias sharpened his gaze on her. "You."

Silently, Nuria contemplated the man sitting on the other side of the table. With his false beard, threadbare robe, and disheveled appearance, he looked nothing like the powerful criminal she'd been investigating for the previous six months. What she saw before her now was a man who had been robbed of what he most loved and who now saw the possibility of revenge—using her as bait. Seeing how his knuckles whitened from clenching his fists so hard, Nuria knew which of those two men was actually the more dangerous.

A knock sounded at the door. Nuria gave a start in her chair.

"It's the food," Elias reassured her. He got up and went to the door.

Ten minutes later Nuria left the remains of the shawarma she hadn't been able to finish on the table and took a long drink from her soft drink.

Elias looked at the ball of aluminum foil that had contained the falafel. "You were hungry."

Without taking the bottle from her lips, Nuria nodded. "You left me in that storeroom without food or water," she reminded him as she put the empty bottle down on the table.

"I apologize for that. We had to act quickly and make sure nobody was following you before we brought you here."

"I understand," she replied. She put a hand to her chest to hold back a burp. "Thank you for this, too."

"You're welcome. Is there anything else you need?"

"A shower," she said, glancing behind her at the hallway she presumed led to the bathroom. "But it can wait. Before that, we need to clarify my situation."

"Your situation," said Elias, "is that you're wanted on suspicion of murder—and your face is all over the web and on the TV news," he added. "So you shouldn't go out much for the next few days. The surveillance cameras' facial recognition system will identify you sooner or later."

"Wonderful," Nuria grumbled.

"Do you think ISMA is behind this too?"

"In that shithole I had a lot of time to think the whole business over," she said, "and they're the only ones who would have a reason for doing a thing like that. If—as it seems—they're behind Vilchez's murder and David's death, it's logical to think that they murdered Gloria too and they're trying to eliminate me from the equation as well. The only thing I don't understand ..." she added pensively, leaving the sentence hanging in the air.

" ... is why they didn't kill you too," Elias finished it for her.

"Exactly. It would have been a lot simpler to shoot me in the street, rather than make me look like a murderer and turn me into a fugitive."

"Maybe they didn't expect you to escape," Elias said. "Think about it. If they'd killed you too it would have meant two police officers, the wife of one and an informer, all murdered. Too many dead bodies, and plenty of questions in the air. Instead, if the evidence pointed to you as the woman's killer, you'd also be suspected of having killed Vilchez and David. You'd be in the news for a few days and then nobody would ask any more questions." He put his hands together. "Case closed."

"But ... in the end the truth would've come out," Nuria said, challenging him. "Even if they falsified the evidence, in the end I'd be able to prove I didn't do it. Surely there must be witnesses and evidence that prove my innocence."

"Maybe," Elias admitted. "But you'd be in preventive custody while the case was being resolved, maybe for years, and they might—"

"They might even kill me in prison, if it came to that." Nuria put her hands to her head. "Jesus ... how come I didn't see it earlier?"

165

Elias spread his hands, palms up. "Sometimes we can't see the forest for the trees."

Nuria leaned her elbows on the table and buried her head in her hands. "Shit, I'm really fucked."

"It looks like it," Elias agreed.

Nuria looked up. "Thanks for the encouragement."

Zafrani grimaced under his false beard. "I'm not here to cheer you up, I'm here to help you out of this."

"Yeah, thanks." She took a look around. "But I can't stay shut up forever in this"—she repressed an expression of disgust—"place."

"That's true," Elias agreed. "That's why we have to get ahead of the game and take the initiative. Enough escaping, don't you think?"

"What do you mean?"

"That we need to stop being the hares … and become the hunters."

She nodded. "Sounds good. But it's easier said than done. I wouldn't even know where to start."

Nuria saw a smile appear under Elias's beard. "But luckily I do." As though in some amateurish magic trick, he put his hand in his robe pocket and pulled out a folded paper which he placed dramatically on the table.

31

Nuria stared at the piece of paper on the table for a moment before stretching out a hand to pick it up. She unfolded it and read a series of meaningless numbers and letters. "What's this?"

"It's the code for a container," Elias explained. "One that arrived about two weeks ago at the port of Barcelona carrying three tons of goods, and that, according to my contacts, didn't go through Guardia Civil customs."

"And why is it special? As far as I know, most of the containers don't have to. It's a random check."

"True, but this specific one should have, because it came from a high-risk country. Apparently something 'happened' to the customs computers so that it looked as if it had gone through all the checks—when in fact it was never checked."

"Something happened?"

"They manipulated the database."

"I see." Nuria read the code on the scrap of paper again. "But I don't understand what it has to do with all this."

"The origin of this container is the city of Jeddah, in the Caliphate of Mecca."

"Okay ... and?"

Elias scratched his false beard. "You don't understand what that means?"

"Well, no, but I'm sure you're about to tell me."

"You see," Elias said didactically, "Jeddah is the main port city of the Caliphate of Mecca, the most radical of the kingdoms Saudi Arabia was divided into after their war with Iran." He put his finger on the paper Nuria was holding. "It's a theocratic, Wahhabi caliphate that has more than enough money from oil, weapons from the recent war ... and feels a deep sympathy toward international jihadist movements."

"Are you implying," Nuria reasoned uneasily, "that this container might have been sent by the Caliphate of Mecca to the jihadists here?"

"It's a possibility," Elias said gravely. "Both its origin and the fact that it's avoided customs checks are very suspicious."

Nuria was growing more and more nervous. "And what do you think they might have sent inside it?"

"In a container of almost three thousand cubic feet?" he asked rhetorically. "Well, anything. From enough rifles to arm a small army, to missiles, combat robots, or biological weapons, if they had the money to buy them. Any weapon you can think of. The Saudis bought them from the United States to use them against Iran and Yemen, and now they resell them to any Sunni jihadist group that has the money to pay, whether it's Boko Haram, Abu Sayyaf, Al Qaeda, ISIS, or ISMA. The Caliphate of Mecca only exports three things: oil, weapons, and jihad … and oil is carried in tankers."

"Combat robots? Biological weapons?" Nuria raised her eyebrows in disbelief. "Are you serious?"

"It's not very likely," Elias admitted. "To date, the fundamentalists have never used anything like that to carry out an attack. They're more inclined toward explosive vests or AK 47s, I guess because they're easier to get hold of and operate, apart from being much less expensive. On the other hand," he added, "there's always a first time for everything."

"Jesus Christ." Nuria felt overwhelmed by all this information, unable to digest the alarming turn the whole affair was taking. Even so, she made an effort to continue thinking like a cop and seek viable answers to simple questions. "Where is that container now?"

"The container was taken out of the port by a local delivery service," Elias said. "According to the driver, he took it to a rest stop on the AP7 with no surveillance, following the instructions he'd been given, then went to spend the night in a hostel. When he returned in the morning, the truck was still there, but the container was empty. He reported the robbery immediately, but the merchandise wasn't insured and the delivery address turned out to be false, so nothing came of it."

"And I suppose they have no idea who committed the robbery."

"You suppose correctly."

"Do you know whether the police questioned the driver?"

"They did," Elias confirmed. "The moment he reported the robbery. But since nobody claimed the container and there was no formal complaint, the case was closed."

"You mean to say the cops are no longer looking for what was in that container?" she asked incredulously.

Elias nodded. "That's right. "If there's no formal complaint or any suspicion of anything strange, it's quite normal for them to forget about it."

"How do you know all this?" Nuria asked, thinking hard. "I mean about customs, the theft of the container, the fact that the driver was questioned—"

"I once told you my business depends on being well informed," he said matter-of-factly. "That includes port staff, customs employees—even cops," he added casually. "The difficult thing is to connect the dots, to link facts that have no apparent connection."

"How is it possible the police haven't come to the same conclusion? How can they not be concerned about what might be in that container?"

"As far as they're concerned, apparently, it's just an administrative error by the Guardia Civil Customs. Remember, they don't have access to the same information we do."

"Then maybe we ought to give it to them," Nuria said. "They've got to find whatever was in that container."

In response Elias took out his phone and handed it to her. "Call them, then. Explain what you know, how you know it, and who you are. I'm sure they'll be delighted to speak to you in person."

"I could make an anonymous call," she objected.

"Sure you could. But if you were the officer receiving that anonymous call warning of a possible terrorist attack without offering a single piece of evidence or even a name, what would you do? How many anonymous calls of that kind do you think they get every day?"

Nuria snorted in frustration and leaned back in her seat. "You're right. But we've got to do something."

"Find it ourselves."

"Ourselves?" she repeated. "You mean *you*. I'm wanted and on the run. The moment I set foot on the street, I run the risk of being caught."

"That's true." Elias dismissed the excuse with a wave. "But despite everything, the Indetect facial recognition system used by the surveillance cameras isn't perfect. With a hat, glasses, and a little care, it would be hard for them to identify you."

"Okay ..." Nuria doubted whether it would be so easy to avoid the Ministry of Homeland Security's artificial intelligence. "But even if that were true, the reality is that we don't know what the goods in that container might have been or where they've ended up. Isn't that right? We've got nothing at all."

Elias shook his head. "Well, now ... that's not entirely true. Actually, we do have something."

Nuria blinked, taken aback. "So what were you waiting for to tell me?" she asked impatiently.

Elias sat back in his seat with his arms crossed. "You haven't said the magic word."

"The magic word?" she repeated blankly. "Seriously? Would *fuck* do?"

"You know what?" Elias said, frowning and assuming a more formal tone. "I'm beginning to get tired of your rude attitude, Ms. Badal. I've been quite

169

understanding so far, bearing in mind the pressure you've been under, but if you don't stop behaving like a spoiled brat you're going to have to start fending for yourself." He paused and added, "Have I made myself clear?"

Another insolent remark began to form on Nuria's lips, but this time she managed to contain it, realizing Elias was right. She was behaving like an idiot, in front of exactly the wrong person. She bowed her head slightly. "I apologize."

Elias nodded. "Apology accepted."

"Great ... and now that we're okay, I'd be very grateful if you stopped with the riddles and told me every fucking thing you know."

Elias shook his head. "All right," he said, sounding annoyed. "Apparently, after a few beers at a clandestine bar in the refugee camp, the deceased Mr. Vilchez mentioned publicly that he was soon going to be a hero and be in the papers."

"A hero?"

"He said he'd found out the hiding place of some terrorists in Barcelona, and that they were going to be arrested thanks to him."

Nuria's eyes opened wide. "Seriously, he said that?"

Elias nodded slowly. "That's what I heard."

"Shit," Nuria muttered as she wove the loose ends together. "That must have been what he told David, and what David meant by what he wrote in his notebook."

"Very likely," Elias agreed, with a heaviness in his voice that surprised Nuria. "The poor devil couldn't keep his mouth shut."

"Someone went to the terrorists with the story," Nuria reasoned. "They sent that man to Vilchez's house ... and before he killed him, he forced him to set a trap for David." She nodded to herself, feeling the first pieces of the puzzle falling into place at last. "I went to that house because David asked me to go with him. Maybe the murderer wasn't expecting me. Maybe he wanted to torture David the way he did Wilson ..." she mused, her gaze wandering over the surface of the table, "and I ruined his plans."

"It's possible."

"It's more than possible," Nuria corrected him. She looked up. "I'm beginning to understand what happened." She fell silent abruptly. The memory of that ill-fated day had risen in her mind again, constricting her heart like a giant hand.

Elias noticed the change in her expression. "Everything all right?"

She took a deep breath. "Yes," she lied. "Everything's fine. I was wondering," she added, exhaling, "whether Wilson ever mentioned where that lair was."

"Just that it was in Barcelona," Elias recalled. "But we don't know whether he meant the city itself or the whole metropolitan area."

"Did he say when he saw them?" she asked, trying to think like the cop she still was.

"No. But the incident at the bar was only a few days before he was murdered. So it coincides roughly with the time the container disappeared."

"Which, added to the limbocaine in the murderer's blood and the mention of ISMA in David's notes—"

"If the shoe fits, as they say."

"Holy shit!" Nuria cried, clapping her hands to her head. "We've got him. It's so simple, it has to be true."

"That's what I think too," Elias agreed, satisfied to see they'd come to the same conclusion. "But there's a question I've been turning over in my mind since I found all this out."

"The location of the terrorist lair?" Nuria ventured.

Elias nodded. "That too. But first I think we ought to answer a more important question."

"More important?" Nuria repeated, intrigued.

"Supposing Vilchez told David what he'd seen—"

"Yeah ..."

"Okay then ... but who did your partner tell *afterwards*?" He stared at Nuria. "Did he tell your commissioner? The counterterrorism division? If so, how come nobody did anything? Or perhaps"—he left the last question hanging in the air—"he kept the information to himself?"

"I don't know," she admitted. "Maybe he thought it was better to wait until he had more information before he told his superiors. Maybe he decided to risk waiting, thinking about a possible promotion. If he took the rumor to the higher-ups," Nuria speculated, "two things might have happened: either they took no notice, or else they did and passed it on to the counterterrorism division. In the end he would have gotten no credit for it. Either way, he lost."

"Would you have done the same?"

"I don't know," Nuria said after thinking a moment. "But he had a family to feed, and maybe that made him take the risk in search of that promotion."

"Then you don't think he told anybody?"

"If he didn't tell me, I don't suppose he'd tell anybody else. He didn't even tell his wife."

Elias nodded, though he looked far from convinced. "Even so, your partner's widow gave the original notebook, with his notes, to the commissioner."

Nuria crossed her arms and frowned. "What are you getting at?"

"The fact that I find it hard to believe they haven't continued to investigate Vilchez's death and your partner's. Particularly considering the mention of ISMA in those notes. And if, on top of that, you say someone cleaned

171

up the crime scene thoroughly, eliminating all the fingerprints, I wonder whether the police can really be so inept as not to connect the two."

"You're suggesting that they know, but they aren't doing anything? But that doesn't make sense. Why would they do a thing like that?"

"It does make sense." He lowered his voice and leaned toward her. "If they're the ones behind it all."

32

"You're wrong," Nuria said flatly.

"Think about it," Elias said. "It would explain everything. Why they were able to pass the container through customs, why the evidence at Vilchez's house was scrubbed clean, why your communications are being bugged ... even why you're wanted and on the run right now."

"Do you hear what you're saying?" she burst out. "A police conspiracy? Are you serious?"

"Absolutely. And if you could put your professional loyalties aside for a minute, you'd be thinking about the possibility as well."

"Like hell I would!" she spat furiously. "That's the biggest load of bullshit I've ever heard. The police would never do a thing like that. Most cops are decent, honest people who risk their lives to protect others."

"I'm not saying that isn't the case," Elias insisted. "But would you put your hand in the fire for all those officers and agents? You only need one rotten apple to spoil the whole barrel ... and let me remind you, I've got a few doing overtime for me. So don't tell me police officers aren't corruptible."

Nuria gesticulated in furious dismissal. "I tell you it's impossible, for fuck's sake! Maybe one or two may have taken your money in exchange for passing on information, but nobody on the force would participate in anything like this. Never. Not when it involves dead officers." She shook her head, refusing to accept a possibility that would undermine the foundations of her own life. "It's absolutely insane," she added, "that I'm sitting here arguing about the integrity of the police with a criminal."

"A criminal who's protecting you ... from those same cops you're defending."

"Because of a misunderstanding," Nuria added. "Someone's manipulating the evidence in order to blame me. The moment whoever's behind all this is found," she added with a note of despair in her voice, "things will go back to the way they were before."

Her tone made Elias pause and gaze for a moment into her tired green eyes. "Is that what you want? For everything to go back to the way it was before?"

Nuria was surprised. "Of course. I want all this to end so I can get my life back. My work, my friends, my home, my ca— Damn!" she cried, suddenly remembering. "Melon! I forgot about him!"

"Melon?"

"My cat! The poor thing's all alone. I have to go home!"

"That's impossible," Elias reminded her. "Isn't there anybody who can look after him?"

"Well …" She thought for a moment. "Yes, I suppose so. My neighbor can look after him for as long as necessary."

"Well then, call her," Elias suggested, with a wave at her new bracelet. "Now that there's no danger they'll locate you. Or better still, text her," he corrected himself. "There's sure to be someone listening. That way you'll avoid letting something slip."

She nodded. "Yeah, I'll do that. I guess that'll be best."

Elias soundlessly clapped his hands. "Great. And now that the serious business of your cat has been resolved, we can get back to our little problem of international terrorism."

"You're an idiot," Nuria said gruffly.

A smile appeared under Elias's thick false beard. "Come on, let's focus."

"Yeah, we'd better," Nuria said, adding, "I thought of something earlier. Which part of the city did Vilchez work in? You have your people divided into areas, don't you?"

The habit of denying everything made Elias hesitate for a moment. "The Raval," he said at last.

"This neighborhood, to be exact?" She looked around with sudden understanding. "Fuck." She pointed down with her finger. "Are we at a distribution point?"

He shook his head. "No. This is a safe house nobody else knows about— or *knew* about—until now. Not even Vilchez knew of its existence."

"But if this was his turf, it's possible that he might have seen the jihadists around, no? That their lair's somewhere around here?"

"I thought of that already," Elias said. "But nobody else has reported any strange doings in this neighborhood. We don't know what Vilchez saw or heard, but Islamist terrorists don't walk around with black flags and Kalashnikovs slung over their shoulders. If they want to pass unnoticed, it's almost impossible to find them. Particularly in a neighborhood where most of the population is North African."

"And this Ana P—"

"Ana P. Elisabets," Elias filled in the rest. "There's no mention of her anywhere on the Internet and my contacts haven't found out anything about her, but I'm still looking."

174

"Well, she's the only real clue we have."

"I know. Maybe your friend misspelled her name in his notebook?"

Nuria shook her head. "David was very careful with details like that. If he wrote Ana P. Elisabets, it's because that's how it's spelled."

"Well then, it has to be a false name. That's the only explanation for her not coming up in the databases."

"Looks like it," Nuria agreed. "And that leaves us with only one option for finding her: doing it the old-fashioned way."

"What do you mean by that?"

Nuria frowned and waved her hand resignedly. "By asking."

"Asking who?"

"Around the neighborhood, of course. If you say this is the area where Vilchez worked, it might be where we can find this Ana."

"Or it might not. He might have met her in Villarefu, which, after all, is where Vilchez lived. Or anywhere else in the city, in fact."

"Yeah, he might. But we have to start somewhere, right? And if we have to choose, the Raval's the most likely. Could you pass me your phone?"

Elias put his hand in his robe and reluctantly handed her his phone. "Is that your plan?" he asked skeptically. "To go out into the street and ask people, just like that? You're not worried about the surveillance cameras any longer?"

Nuria touched her bracelet to the smartphone to link it. "You said yourself that with a good disguise they won't be able to identify me. And in any case, can you think of a better plan?" Taking his silence as a no, she opened the Google Maps app.

"We'll have to invent a good story about a lost cousin or something like that," she went on as she scanned the map of the neighborhood. "We won't go around asking people out of the blue, as you said. Instead, we can select bars and shops across the neighborhood and ask by areas. If she's here, someone must have heard of her." Nuria looked up and saw Elias watching her curiously. "What is it?"

"Nothing. It's just that ... you're obviously in your element."

Now it was Nuria who allowed a faint smile to appear on her face. "It's wonderful to be able to take the initiative in something at last. I'm sick of running away from things all the time. And besides ... well, I'm a police officer. This is what I was trained for."

"I can see that," Elias admitted. "Where do you want to start looking?"

Nuria studied the street map for a few more moments and then enlarged a specific area with a movement of her fingers on the screen. "Unless you have a better idea, I'd begin, for example, by going ... from north to south. I'd go toward Tallers Street"—she moved her finger across the screen as she spoke—"and then head south street by street towards—" She fell silent all of a sudden, her gaze and her finger fixed on a point on the map.

"What is it?" Elias asked after a few seconds. "Is everything all right?"

"It can't be …" Nuria muttered. "Shit, this isn't possible."

He leaned across the table to see what had surprised her so much. "What's not possible? What did you see?"

Nuria's only answer was to put the phone in her pocket.

"What are you doing?" he asked. "Show me what you saw."

A sly smile appeared on her face. "That's exactly what I'm going to do." She got to her feet and stuffed the cloth napkin she'd just used into her pocket. "Let's go."

"Go?" Elias said, taken aback. "Where?"

Nuria walked unhesitatingly to the door. "You'll see," she said as she opened it. "Do you have any money with you?"

"What?" Elias got up from his chair. "Yes, of course. What for?"

"Great. Follow me."

When Elias reached the door, Nuria was already going down the stairs two at a time. "Hell," he muttered, looking down the stairwell after her. "Wait! Don't go out into the street like that!"

"Relax." She looked up to show him she'd covered her head with the napkin and knotted it under her chin. "Everything's under control."

"No, nothing's under control," Elias protested as he tried to keep up with her. "That isn't a veil, it's a fucking napkin."

"Well then, I'll buy one in the first shop we come across," she said without stopping. "Don't worry."

"Don't worry, she says," Elias muttered, gasping for breath. "Could I at least know where we're going?"

Without slackening her pace, Nuria's voice reached him from the floor below. "It's a surprise!" she replied as if it were a game. Seconds later, Elias heard her opening the door to the street.

When he caught up with her at last, Nuria was already standing in the dim light of Robadors Street, checking the phone under one of the few streetlamps that had survived the need for discretion on the part of the neighborhood dealers.

She pointed to Hospital Street. "We'll get there sooner this way. We won't even need to take a rickshaw."

"If you'd only tell me where …" Elias insisted, breathing hard as he caught up with her.

"Don't be tiresome," she recriminated him. "Just follow me."

"You're not worried about the cameras now?" He pointed to the next corner, where multiple cameras were focused on every angle of the intersection. "You might be recognized."

"Nah, it's too dark." Nuria dismissed his concern with a wave after a glance at them. "Those are old low-def cameras, and there are a lot of people. Nobody would recognize me even if I danced in front of them. And besides," she added, pointing to her head, "I'm wearing a veil."

"That's a napkin."

"That's right." She smiled again. "I trust Allah won't hold it against me." She hurried on, leaving Elias no option but to follow her.

The streets of the Raval were plastered like the rest of the city with the ubiquitous electoral posters. They seethed with tourists buying knockoff Barcelona FC bags and T-shirts from blankets on the ground. Food stands were everywhere, hawking Salvadoran pupusas and Philippine food that gave off the cloying scent of palm oil reheated too many times. Street musicians played catchy reggaeton music and a horde of Latino, North African, Pakistani, and African Barcelonians wandered about buying, selling, and greeting their neighbors now that the heat was no longer unbearable.

Elias pushed his way through the crowd so he could walk beside Nuria. "I don't like this. I don't like traveling blind, not knowing where I'm going."

"Don't worry," she said. "We're close."

On the way they stopped to buy a proper veil from a street vendor, and although Nuria still stood out in the crowd because of her height and skin color, now a shadow obscured her features in the light of the yellowish streetlamps so that no camera could easily identify her.

When she turned to Elias to answer him, he couldn't help but notice how the green veil that covered her hair matched her eyes. "I really can't understand why you won't tell me where we're going," he protested again.

Tired of the Syrian's insistence, Nuria stopped abruptly. "I know where Ana P. Elisabets is."

"What? But ... how?"

"You'll see."

"You really know who she is?"

"And where to find her."

"Damn it all," Elias protested. "You should have told me. We can't risk losing her or letting her escape. I'll call some men to help us."

Nuria put her hand on his forearm. "There's no need for you to call anybody. She's not going anywhere."

"But ..."

"Trust me, okay?"

Elias was about to extricate his wrist from under her hand, but it was as though those green eyes were capable of controlling his will. Almost without being aware of it, he lowered his hand and nodded silently. "I hope I'm not going to regret this."

"We're almost there," Nuria replied. She nodded towards a nearby alley. Before Elias could say anything more, she dodged a group of teenagers on skateboards, making her way quickly to the narrow passageway. Without hesitating, she dove into its shadows. Elias had no choice but to follow her, quickening his steps so as not to lag behind. The sight of her walking several steps ahead of him would attract the attention of anyone watching them, since the Muslim custom was exactly the opposite. He hoped nobody would notice.

When she got to the end of the alley Nuria stopped and turned to Elias with an expression of triumph. Reaching her side, he looked around. "What is it?"

Nuria's teeth showed white behind her veil. "We're here."

Elias looked around again, searching for some meaning in this statement. "Here? Where? Is this where we're going to find this Ana?"

In response Nuria raised her hand to point at the street sign just above her head. Elias looked up and read aloud:

Passatge d'Elisabets.

33

It took Elias a moment to understand the implications of the dirty white marble plaque screwed into the wall nine feet up. "It's not a person ..." he murmured, recovering from his surprise and turning to Nuria at the same time.

"P. Elisabets," Nuria recited. "Passatge d'Elisabets. It's a street."

"Incredible," Elias said. "But ... what about Ana?"

"That I don't know yet," Nuria admitted, "though I suspect we'll find her in there somewhere." She pointed back down the narrow alleyway, empty of pedestrians.

Only a couple of moribund streetlamps shone from the corners of the alley, leaving it sunk in gloom, but what caught Nuria's attention was that the camera pointing into it had had its wires cut. Someone had sabotaged it.

Without a second thought, she plunged down the dark passageway again before Elias could prevent her. He'd been going to tell her to stop and wait until they could work out a plan to find this Ana, but he realized she would take no notice of him whatsoever. All he could do was follow her.

"It doesn't look like a very popular street," he pointed out, seeing that they were alone.

"There are no shops and hardly any doorways," she agreed. She'd stopped next to the intercom of a three-story apartment building, looking for anyone called Ana among the tenants. "Nothing," she said after establishing that there was nobody of that name living there.

Elias had gone on ahead. He stopped in front of a metal door with no name or any other sign. "Look at this. It looks like the back door of a restaurant." He pointed to a garbage can filled with food scraps. The smell of cooking came from a smoke extractor in the wall.

"Maybe Ana works here," said Nuria.

"Or Ana could be the name of the restaurant," Elias hazarded. He reached for his phone to check whether he was right, then remembered it was still in Nuria's pocket. Extending a hand, he said, "Can I have my phone back now? I want to check something."

"Oh, yes, sorry." She took it out of her pocket, but instead of giving it to him, she darted past him, phone in hand.

"What the ….?"

"Shh!" she hissed. She'd stopped in front of the next locale. "Come here, quick."

Elias held back for a moment in an attempt to resist her authority, but in the end he gave in and approached Nuria. "What is it?" he asked as he watched her switch on the flashlight function on his phone.

"Look," she said, shining the light on an old metal door covered in graffiti.

"An abandoned shop," he said. "There are plenty of those in the neighborhood."

"No," she said pointedly. "Look up."

Elias raised his gaze to find a yellowed sign approximately six feet wide. Faded red lettering, eroded by time to near illegibility, spelled out *Asociación Nacional Animalista.*

"ANA," he read aloud. "It's not the name of a woman, it's an acronym." He turned to her and added admiringly, "You found it."

Nuria smiled in satisfaction. "I just got lucky," she admitted. Bending over to shine a light on the lock that secured the door, she tugged at it a couple of times to see whether it would give.

"Wait a moment." Elias bent down beside her and took the smartphone out of her hand. "What do you think you're doing?"

Nuria looked at him as if he'd asked her about his prostate. "What do you mean, what am I doing? Seeing if we can get in, of course. That's why we're here, right?"

"Of course it isn't! You found this place, which is amazing. But now we need to plan our next steps very carefully."

"There's nothing to plan," Nuria shot back. "What we need to do is get inside and see what we find."

"Into what—according to Vilchez—is a terrorist lair? That doesn't seem like a very intelligent thing to do."

"It's locked on the outside," she pointed out. "That means there's nobody at home."

"That doesn't matter."

She put her hands on her hips. "Are you afraid?" she asked challengingly.

Elias's eyes flashed in the dark. "Don't even dare suggest anything like that," he hissed, putting his face close to hers. "But what I'm *not* going to do is rush into something just because you're in a hurry."

"But we could also mess things up by waiting too long," Nuria countered. "Who knows whether they're about to do something this very minute?"

Elias thought for a moment, weighing their options. "That's true," he admitted grudgingly. "We've got to act, but we can't do this by ourselves."

"What do you suggest?"

"You go back to the safe house to avoid risk," he said after a moment's thought. "I'll call my team and they'll search this place thoroughly."

"*We'll* search," Nuria corrected him.

"They're competent people. War veterans, not neighborhood bullies. It will be better if you stay out of it and wait at the safe house."

"I'm not waiting around anywhere. I'm the only one here who knows what to search for and how to go about it."

"I give you my word I'll keep you posted on everything we find," Elias insisted. "But it's better for you to be safe. You're already running too great a risk just by being out on the street right now."

"And what do you care if I'm running a risk?"

Elias sighed as if the answer were so obvious it was tedious to explain. "Someone wants you out of the game," he explained patiently. "So as long as you're free, you're a problem for them and an asset to us. Until we know what we're up against, it's best you stay hidden. If the police catch you, we won't have that advantage any longer."

"So that's what I am? An asset?"

Elias rolled his eyes. "I didn't say that. I'm only asking you to stay safe while we find out what's going on. It's for your own good."

"My own good is my own business."

Elias folded his arms. "Well, that didn't seem to be the case this morning when you called me in a panic asking for help."

His words hit home. Swallowing her pride, Nuria acknowledged that he was right; it was the most sensible thing. She took one last look at the metal door and said, "You win. I'll go back to the safe house."

Elias gave a sigh of relief. "I'm glad you've decided to come to your senses." He reached into the left-hand pocket of his robe and took out a couple of keys. "For the street door and the apartment," he told her as he put them into her hand. "There's food and water in the fridge. Try to go unnoticed. I'll keep you informed about what we find."

Nuria nodded distractedly. "All right, we'll be in touch," she said briefly, and without another word turned and left the alley.

Elias stood watching her walk out of the dark alley. In spite of the veil that hid her hair, her tall, slim figure and energetic stride made it impossible for her to pass unnoticed. However well she might try to hide, it was only a matter of time before someone who'd seen the alerts on the web recognized her in the street or the Indetect cameras identified her habitual movements as she walked past them.

Whatever the outcome might be, they had little time left. Very little time.

34

The bells of the nearby San Agustín church tolled three times with their grave, melancholy sound as Nuria walked back to Passatge Elisabets, retracing her steps along the same streets, now deserted. She was as well covered as her green veil allowed and carried a small backpack.

As the heavy contents of the small backpack bounced on her back, it occurred to her that one advantage of being in a neighborhood full of Pakistanis was that at almost any hour of the night you could find some shop that was open and buy almost anything.

Surreptitiously, she found herself seeking out the darkest corners and the blind spots of the surveillance cameras to avoid being detected. Even if they were old-fashioned and didn't work well in inadequate light, it wasn't worth taking risks.

The flimsy stalls which hours before had been selling food amid the bustle of the street were now dismantled and huddled together against the walls. In many cases, the vendors themselves could be found in sleeping bags underneath those precarious structures, to avoid being robbed during the night or simply because they had no other place to go.

In spite of the tennis shoes she was wearing, to Nuria's ears her footsteps echoed like drum rolls in the silence of Hospital Street. It wasn't until she reached the corner of Passatge Elisabets that she felt safe from cameras and nosy neighbors. Peering into the darkness of the alley, she confirmed that, as she'd expected, Elias's people had not yet arrived.

Better this way, she said to herself. Throwing furtive glances over her shoulder, she turned into the alley and walked quickly to the metal door under the sign that read *Asociación Nacional Animalista*. Crouching, she set the newly bought backpack down beside her, drew out a flashlight, and took a closer look at the substantial lock which secured the door. "Chinese." She smiled at the sight of the characters engraved on the surface.

Next, Nuria took a pair of pliers and a couple of paper clips from the backpack. Holding the flashlight between her teeth, she straightened one of the clips with the pliers, leaving a small hook at the end, then bent the other end into an L-shape to exert pressure. First she threaded this through the keyhole as far as the other end to maintain the tension, then with her other hand inserted the lock-picking clip. One by one, she freed the four tumblers until, with a sharp click, it opened as if by magic. The robust lock that had looked capable of withstanding a jackhammer hadn't lasted even five minutes when confronted with a couple of paper clips and a bit of skill.

"Men ..." she snorted, picturing whoever had bought it asking for the biggest lock available at the hardware store.

Nuria replaced the tools in the backpack and looked up and down both sides of the alley to make sure no one was around. Praying that the gears of the door were well oiled, she hooked her fingers under it to lift it a few inches off the ground. It made almost no sound, so she tensed the muscles of her back and used her legs to push it up around a foot and a half, far enough to allow her to slip underneath. Pushing the backpack inside, Nuria held the flashlight and rolled under the door. Once inside, she stood up, turned, and pushed down the door, which made a louder noise when it hit the floor than she'd intended.

Nuria tensed, alert to any sound. Not the least ray of light penetrated the shop. Immersed in utter darkness, she waited nearly a minute, holding her breath. No sound came to her ears.

She switched on the flashlight. In her mind she'd imagined finding crates full of Kalashnikovs and rocket launchers stacked under a huge map with targets marked in red felt pen, together with the day and time scheduled for the attacks. But of course this wasn't an American crime thriller, and the bad guys were never as dumb as the Hollywood scriptwriters liked to make out.

The reality was that the shop was emptier than her own bank account. In the beam of her flashlight Nuria saw a windowless space measuring around a thousand square feet that reminded her too much of the place she'd spent several hours locked up in: dirty walls stained with smoke and a blackened ceiling. A clumsily drawn swastika on the wall provided the only decoration.

She passed her flashlight beam over the floor, shining it into the corners, searching for any detail that might reveal who'd been there lately, but only a couple of cigarette butts and an empty water bottle hinted at any human habitation—habitation that might date from ten days ago or ten years. Apart from those items, there was only the usual unrecognizable garbage in the corners and a few pieces of brown paper.

Distrusting this appearance of normality, Nuria bent over and slid the tips of her fingers along the gray slabs of the floor. Holding her fingers up in the beam of her flashlight, she rubbed them together. They were clean, with no trace of the accumulated dust you would expect to find with the passage of time. There was no doubt someone had been there recently. Whoever it was had taken great care to eliminate any trace of his presence in the shop—literally.

With this knowledge, Nuria began to search the place more meticulously, putting the water bottle and cigarette butts into plastic bags. Maybe she could find some way of getting them to the forensic lab for analysis. She doubted whether anyone careful enough to sweep the dust off the floor to eliminate footprints would make the mistake of leaving their own fingerprints or DNA on the bottle or the cigarettes, but if she'd learned anything during her years on the force, it was that—with rare exceptions—criminals didn't tend to be paragons of intelligence. And terrorists were no exception.

Satisfied with her search, Nuria decided to do one last sweep, this time in the opposite direction to make sure no shadow was hiding a clue, however irrelevant.

It was then that a noise outside stopped her dead in her tracks. It could have been a rat or a particularly clumsy cat. But it could also have been a footfall. Frozen, not moving a muscle, she focused all her attention on the place the sound had come from. She heard it again. Another footfall.

There was someone on the other side of the door.

Nuria turned off her flashlight. More footsteps approached the door now, less careful than the first. She heard whispers in Arabic among at least three people. Maybe more. Obviously they'd noticed the absence of the lock, and Nuria imagined they were arguing about whether someone might be inside or whether they themselves had forgotten to put it on. Silently she cursed the fact that she hadn't paid more attention during her Arabic language classes.

If these were the terrorists returning to their lair, they would probably be armed, whereas she had only a flashlight, a pair of pliers, and a handful of clips. Not even MacGyver would have known what to do with that.

Nuria's fears were confirmed when she picked out the sound of several safety locks sliding back. "Fuck," she muttered. There was nowhere to hide in that empty space; though at the moment it was dark, as soon as the door was rolled up she would be caught in the light like a cockroach coming out from under the sink at three a.m. She had nothing to defend herself with, nor did she have a phone to call someone—though really it was too late for that.

Desperate, all Nuria could think of was to clutch the flashlight like a club and run to one of the walls, flattening herself against it when the intruders began to struggle with the metal door.

The door began to rise, letting in the light of two powerful flashlights. Nuria took the pliers out of her backpack too. *Better be hanged for a sheep*, she thought. But no one stepped over the threshold once the door was completely open. Instead, under cover from outside, they swept the interior of the premises with their flashlights to make sure there was nobody inside.

From where they stood, the men couldn't see her. Nuria fantasized about the possibility that they would all come in at once, giving her the opportunity to slip away behind them like a lizard. That remote possibility shattered into a thousand pieces, though, when the beam of one of their flashlights swept the space in front of her feet. There on the floor, like a lowered flag, was her green veil, humiliatingly betraying her hiding place. She must have dropped it when she'd heard the men outside without realizing it.

It looks as if in the end Allah really is going to punish me, Nuria thought bitterly. The terrorists barked quick phrases in Arabic at each other, their flashlights trained on the scarf. She knew it was only a matter of seconds before she found herself with a bullet between her eyes.

"Nuria?" came an incredulous voice.

Taken aback, she was silent for a few seconds, asking at last, "Elias?" She peered through the open door. "What … what are you doing here?"

The Syrian was standing there, gun in hand, flanked by four men also armed with handguns. One of them was Giwan, the massive bodyguard she'd met at Elias's home. "Me?" he asked, sounding disconcerted. "What are *you* doing here? I told you I'd come after I got my team together."

"But I didn't think you meant this same night."

"You lied to me," Elias said sternly. "You told me you were going to wait at the safe house."

She raised a finger. "Actually, you were the one who said that. I only said I was leaving … not that I wasn't going to come back."

Elias shook his head in annoyance. "It was a stupid thing for you to do."

"Maybe," she admitted. "But what's done is done, right?"

He let out his breath abruptly. "Anyway … have you discovered anything?"

Nuria shook her head. "It's clean. Only an empty bottle and a couple of cigarette butts we might get DNA or prints from, but nothing else. These people are very careful."

"And if there's nothing … I suppose we couldn't have made a mistake?"

"Possibly. But someone's swept the floor in the past week. That doesn't make much sense in an abandoned place like this, wouldn't you agree?"

He nodded. "It's possible. Apparently the place was attacked by neo-patriots during the riots after the abolition of the Generalitat, and since then it's been empty. There's no evidence of activity in the records at City Hall, but that doesn't mean much either. If they knew it was abandoned, they might have used it for a few days and then left. These people aren't the kind who put down roots."

"It could be where they unloaded whatever was in that container," Nuria speculated. "Maybe that's what Vilchez saw."

"Could be," Elias admitted. He shone the flashlight over the interior. "But there doesn't seem to be any evidence of it. No boxes, no fragments of white polystyrene or tape or zip ties …"

"That's true. There's no trace of that. But maybe they didn't unpack anything, simply stored the crates until they could move them someplace else."

"That doesn't make much sense."

"Yes it does." She went outside and looked up. "You see? There are no working streetlights in this stretch of the alley. The surveillance camera at the corner's been disabled and there are no windows with neighbors who could look out. It's perfect for unloading at night without being seen."

Elias considered it for a moment before shaking his head dubiously. "All right," he said. "But even if you're right, we're back at square one. If there are no more clues, there's nowhere to go on looking."

"Maybe there is," Nuria said thoughtfully. "According to what you told me, you have access to the police database, right?"

He raised his hands in the air. "It's not that simple. I can manage to gain access to certain specific documents and only at certain times. I don't have access to the whole network."

She pointed to the corner of Hospital Street. "And the Indetect cameras? Could you access those?"

"The cameras?" he asked in puzzlement. "What for? Hadn't we established that they don't work?"

Nuria nodded. "I know. But I don't want images of this street. I want them of the adjacent streets, the day the container was stolen. Even if we don't have images of them unloading the container, we might get one of when they turned into the alley. There can't be that much traffic around here"—she smiled craftily—"and if we're able to find out the make of the vehicle and the plates, then who knows?"

35

The black Chevy Suburban with its tinted windows took up most of the width of the alley. When its doors were open, they nearly grazed the walls on both sides. If the area hadn't been empty at that hour, it would have been impossible to navigate the narrow streets of the Raval in the enormous SUV.

"Didn't you have a more discreet vehicle for this trip?" Nuria asked the moment she'd climbed into the back of the monstrous electric vehicle.

In reply, Elias tapped the window with his knuckles. "It's bulletproof. With the very real possibility of bumping into armed terrorists, I thought I'd come prepared."

"That's pretty obvious," Nuria commented, glancing at the third row of seats where two of Elias's men were sitting. Together with the other two who occupied the driver's and co-pilot's seats, the four made up a unique Praetorian guard: four men whose physical type fell somewhere on the continuum between Arabic and Caucasian, dressed in baggy shirts and wide pants that allowed them to hide their weapons and body armor discreetly under their clothes.

Even so, their appearance wasn't typical of those former members of the Special Forces who normally work in the field of private military protection. With the exception of Giwan, who appeared to be the leader of the group, the others didn't look like bodybuilders, nor did they wear the tattoos typical of the military. Instead, they looked like normal people in good physical shape, silent and deeply interested in everything going on around them.

"They're not neighborhood thugs," Elias said, guessing Nuria's thoughts.

"They don't look like typical mercenaries either," she replied.

"They're Kurds. Veterans of the war with Turkey."

Nuria looked at them again more carefully. "I thought they'd all been wiped out," she said, remembering the news of the horrifying Turkish biological attacks on Kurdistan.

"Not all of them," Elias said gravely. "Not all of them."

Nuria nodded. "Yes, well ... I'm glad of that." She felt an unexpected current of sympathy towards those four survivors. "When will we get the images from the cameras?"

"That depends on the hacker. I'll get in touch with him first thing in the morning and—"

"No," she interrupted him. "Call him now."

Elias stared at her before answering. Realizing she was serious, he said, "It's four in the morning."

Nuria made a face. "He's a hacker. He's sure to be playing with his console or watching porn on the Hololens. Call him."

Elias opened his mouth to tell her that all that urgency made no sense. They would be able to contact the hacker in four hours. Seeing the determined expression on her face, however, he knew he wouldn't be able to dissuade her. "All right," he grumbled. Taking his phone from his pocket, he turned aside so Nuria couldn't see the number.

After a few seconds the face of a youth with uncombed hair and a two-day beard appeared, rubbing his eyes. "*Syd Zafrani?*" he asked sleepily in Arabic. "*Marhabaan madha yhdth?*"

Elias replied quickly, giving the boy orders in a tone of voice that brooked no argument.

"*Nem sayidi,*" the young man repeated, nodding. "*Nem sayidi.*"

"*Hal fahimt klu shay'an?*" Elias finally asked. "*Hal huw adihu?*"

"*Nem sayidi,*" the young man affirmed again.

"*Eazimun,*" Elias said, sounding pleased. "*Sa'ursil lak altafasil min Spacelink.*"

"*Nem sayidi,*" the boy agreed once again, a note of gratitude in his voice. "*Sayahsul ealayha, alyawm.*"

"*Shukran ya Ahmed. 'Ana' aeulealayha,*" Elias said in farewell, ending the call.

"Well?" Nuria asked.

"As soon as he's got it, he'll get in touch with me."

"Okay, and that'll be …?"

"He works fast," Elias explained. "He's one of the best."

Nuria sighed impatiently. "Fine." Turning her attention to the streets outside the vehicle, she asked in surprise, "Wait a minute … this isn't the way to the safe house. Where are we going?"

"To my house," Elias said easily.

"Your house? Why?"

"Because you'll be safer there."

"You mean more controlled."

"Take it however you want to," he said impatiently. "But I don't want any more surprises like tonight. My men could have fired at you, or someone might have identified you."

"But they didn't."

Elias turned to her solemnly. "Look, Ms. Badal," he said, dropping his familiar tone and speaking gravely, "I'm risking a lot by helping you, but I'm not prepared to go to jail on your account." He paused to make sure she understood, then added: "So from now on we're going to do it my way, acting prudently and deciding together what steps to take. No more acting on your own or taking unnecessary risks. Is that clear?"

Nuria fixed her gaze on him. "What if I say no?" she asked challengingly.

"Giwan," Elias said, turning to the driver. "*Awqaf alsayara.*" In response, the man pulled over. "You can get out right here if you like," he told Nuria. He leaned across her and opened the door on her side. "I can even provide you with a gun and some cash." He took several hundred-euro bills out of his wallet. "What's it going to be?"

Nuria turned to the open door and put her right foot on the running board, but when she was halfway out of the Suburban she realized that she'd been a victim of her own pride. To go from nothing to depending on someone whom until very recently she'd been trying to arrest was difficult to come to terms with; the fact that he was a man made it worse, and the fact that this man treated her like a rebellious teenager was something she found almost impossible to accept.

The problem, she thought with her foot still on the running board, was that at that moment she could see no alternative, not only in order to catch the alleged jihadists—if they really existed—and prove her own innocence, but simply to avoid ending up in a cell or six feet under.

From her own experience, she knew that cops tended not to have much sympathy for anybody who had killed a partner, and if they believed she'd intentionally murdered Gloria, and before that David, it wasn't inconceivable that one of her old colleagues might send a bullet her way.

She was fucked, however she chose to look at it, but if she was capable of swallowing her pride there might be a remote possibility of escaping this nightmare or at least, finding out who was behind all this and making them pay, with interest.

Without saying a word, she sat down again and shut the door of the vehicle, staring straight ahead.

Elias glanced at her from the corner of his eye and turned to the driver. "Giwan," he said, leaning forward in his seat. "*Linadhhab 'iilaa alayt.*"

"*Nem sayidi,*" Giwan replied, and set off again in the direction of the upscale part of Barcelona.

"Coffee?" Elias asked. He waved a hand, inviting Nuria to sit down on the same couch where she'd fallen asleep the previous time.

Nuria glanced at her bracelet. "It's four in the morning," she reminded him.

"That's exactly why. I'm not going to sleep for what's left of the night. Unless, of course"—he indicated the ceiling—"you'd prefer to rest a little. I have a guest room upstairs."

Nuria considered it for a moment, then went to the couch.

"Black or with milk?" Elias asked.

"Black with ice, please."

"Right. I'll be back in a moment. Make yourself comfortable."

Nuria glanced at the soft white couch, but in the end settled for an uncomfortable wooden chair where she would be less likely to fall asleep. Even so, perhaps because the night's adrenaline rush was subsiding, or because of her accumulated exhaustion, she felt her eyes beginning to close and her chin sliding dangerously toward her chest. "No, goddamn it." Nuria fought encroaching sleep. "Not again." She stood up abruptly. Suddenly the idea of going to sleep in that guest room Elias had mentioned was looking extremely tempting. She had to move, so she began to walk around the living room as if she were in a museum, stopping to study every object there with the sole purpose of keeping her mind active.

Looking out the windows that opened onto the front yard provided little interest; all she could see were the LED lights, like a parade of fireflies bordering the high hedges that surrounded the property. Nuria smiled to herself at the memory of the many long surveillance sessions she and David had spent in front of that same house, keeping a record of entrances and exits, cursing those same hedges and polarized windows that prevented them from seeing anything from the outside.

It was ironic to think that now she could be as nosy as she pleased in that same house. Perhaps at that very moment there were another couple of officers watching the house and cursing in just the same way at the impossibility of seeing what was happening inside.

Dismissing the idea of being watched, Nuria decided to amuse herself by studying the furniture and decor of that spacious living room, hoping to draw some conclusions about its owner. She gazed around at the mahogany table surrounded by eighteenth-century chairs, the over-ornate lamp that hung from the ceiling in imitation of a lantern, the wood floors covered by plush carpets of intricate design, the rustic paintings she'd noticed the previous time, and the wall-sized bookcase crammed full of books.

Nuria went over to it curiously, sliding her fingers along the spines of the books as she read the titles, turning her head one way or the other according to whether these were written from top to bottom or the other way around.

Most of the books were in Arabic, but there were also titles in English, French, and especially Spanish, ranging from classics like Cervantes and Lope de Vega to popular essays and novels from the last few years. Unable to restrain herself, she reached for a tattered yellow volume of *Love in the Time of Cholera*, by Gabriel Garcia Marquez. She remembered the thrill of reading that novel years before on her grandfather's recommendation, recognizing the little river steamboat drawn in a corner of the cover, the one in which Fermina Daza and Florentino Ariza end up together at last, sailing down the Magdalena River.

With the nostalgic smile of someone who understands that they will never read a book for the first time again, just as there is only one first kiss, she opened it with utmost care and found a brief signature on the first page.

"The best five-thousand-dollar investment I ever made in my life," came an unexpected voice behind her. Nuria started, and the book slipped between her hands, almost ending up on the floor. "Careful, it's a signed first edition," Elias teased her.

"Jesus!" Nuria chastised him, turning around and closing the book. "Don't ever do that again."

"Sorry, I didn't mean to startle you," he said apologetically, his smile saying exactly the opposite. "Here's your coffee," he added as he offered her a tall glass with ice and coffee up to the brim, decorated with peppermint leaves.

"Thank you," Nuria muttered reluctantly, returning the book to its place and taking her coffee.

Elias turned toward his bookshelves. "Do you like books?"

Nuria nodded. "I like to read. Or rather, I did when I was younger. Now—"

"You have no time," Elias said, anticipating her answer.

"I know it's a cheap excuse. But the daily routine is so all-consuming … work, news, social networks …"

"Of course. Everything's urgent now," Elias said wistfully. "There's no time to stop and smell the flowers."

"There aren't even any flowers anymore," Nuria said curtly.

"You're wrong," Elias objected. He turned to her. "There are always flowers. You just need to know where to find them."

Nuria felt his intense blue gaze on her. Clearing her throat uncomfortably, she took a step back. "What did you do before you came to Spain?" she asked, seeking to change the subject.

"I was a professor of Spanish language and literature."

"Seriously? A professor?" Nuria asked. She was genuinely surprised.

Elias, looking directly into her eyes, took a few minutes to answer. "I was. In another life."

"Was that why you chose to come to Spain?"

The Syrian muffled a laugh at the sound of the word. "Chose?" He shook his head, amused by the idea. "I didn't choose anything. I fled my country to avoid having my head cut off and impaled on a pike. My destination was Spain, but it could just as well have been any other country. Once I was here, though, since I spoke the language better than most Spaniards, I worked hard. My organizational skills helped me do well."

"And by doing well," Nuria put in maliciously, "you mean becoming a trafficker."

"I mean surviving the only way I could," Elias corrected her. "I couldn't get a job legally because of the bureaucracy, so it was that or selling falafel from a food cart in the street. I didn't choose to do this," he added. The ice cubes jingled in his glass. "Circumstances drove me to it."

Nuria waved her arm, taking in the enormous living room of that luxurious house in one of Barcelona's most exclusive neighborhoods. "Yeah, I understand … it really must be hard, being forced to live like this."

Elias bent his head with a long sigh. "There's no way you're going to stop seeing me as just a criminal, is there?"

"Are you going to stop claiming you're not? The fact that you're a refugee and a millionaire and you read Garcia Marquez doesn't make you a better person."

"I know what I am and what I do," he admitted. "But I'd remind you that right now the dangerous criminal on the run is you."

"But in my case it's a misunderstanding, and you know that."

"True, and that's why I'm helping you, so … where does that leave me? Am I a criminal or someone trying to make sure justice is served?"

Nuria saw where he was going with this argument. "Both, I guess."

"Exactly." Elias raised his glass. "Like you, I'm trying to play the best hand possible with the cards fate has dealt me."

36

Settling himself on the couch, Elias gestured to the armchair on the other side of the coffee table, inviting her to sit down. "Make yourself comfortable. There are still a couple of hours left before dawn."

"I'm fine like this," Nuria said, standing behind the armchair.

"As you wish." Taking a sip from his coffee, he asked, "May I call you Nuria?"

"I'd say we dropped the formalities quite a while ago."

"Is that a yes?"

She turned to give her attention to one of the paintings. "Of course," she said indifferently. "Why not?"

"Okay. In that case, I'd like to know why you joined the police force, Nuria."

"Why does it matter to you?"

"I'm curious."

She turned around. "Haven't your spies found that out about me? Do you need to fill in the gaps in my file?"

"There's no file," Elias said. "I only investigated your police work, never your personal life. Besides," he added, "I answered your questions. I think it's fair for you to do the same, wouldn't you say?"

Nuria gave a weary sigh. "All right." She went to the couch and sat down in front of Elias. "What do you want to know? Why I became a cop?"

"That's right."

"My father," she said, setting her half-drunk glass of coffee on the brass table, "loved crime novels and TV series. When I was little and we were watching one of them on TV, he always ended up asking me if I wouldn't like to be one of those smart detectives who always caught the bad guys."

"And you decided to make his dream come true."

Nuria shook her head. "No. That wasn't really what I felt drawn to. I wanted to do things that were more fun. Putting on a blue uniform and being given orders all day long wasn't on my list of dream jobs."

"But—"

"But on August 17, 2017, something happened."

Elias remembered the date at once. "The attack on Las Ramblas."

"That's right."

"And that's what drove you to join the police force?" he asked in surprise.

Nuria lowered her gaze to her hands, now resting in her lap. "I was there."

"Really?"

"I was shopping with some friends on Pelayo Street. I was crossing the street at the crosswalk and happened to look at the driver of a rental van. He was looking up at the sky and praying to Allah as he waited for the light to change." Her gaze abstracted in the memory of that day, she added: "I remember he caught my attention, because the day before I'd been watching a movie where a terrorist did exactly the same thing before he detonated his suicide vest. Then"—Nuria went on with her eyes fixed on the arabesques on the carpet under her feet—"he looked right at me and smiled like a madman. His eyes were starting out of their sockets and he was sweating like a pig. His knuckles were white from clutching the steering wheel so hard. Later I found out he was Younes Abouyaaqoub, the terrorist who ran over hundreds of people on Las Ramblas immediately afterwards."

"My God."

"I was right there, standing in front of him in the middle of the crosswalk, twenty yards from Las Ramblas," she repeated insistently. "I looked around for a policeman to alert, but there were none in sight. There was only me. I was the only one that believed something terrible was about to happen … and I didn't know what to do." Nuria spread her fingers, palms up, as though she were holding her heavy burden. "Then the light changed and all the other drivers started honking their horns and yelling at me to move on …" She sighed and finished. "So I did."

It took Elias a moment to assimilate this. "But what could you have done?" he said at last. "You weren't a cop yet, and he was a terrorist. If you'd tried to stop him, he'd have run you over as well."

"Maybe. But I ought to have tried something—shouted, pointed him out, anything," she said regretfully. "But I froze."

"You were being cautious."

"It wasn't caution, it was fear."

"Aren't they the same thing?"

"No, they're not," she objected. "Caution makes you weigh the risks and use your head. Fear paralyzes you and makes you do stupid things."

Elias nodded slowly, agreeing with the definition. "In any case, I'm glad you didn't. That bastard would've run you over just like he ran all those others over a minute later."

"Maybe," she admitted. Then, raising her eyes to Elias, she concluded: "That's why I decided to join the Catalan police force a few days later. When they were still the Mossos d'Esquadra."

"To fight jihadists?"

Nuria shook her head. "So that I'd never again be that frightened girl, unable to react because she was paralyzed with fear."

All of a sudden Nuria felt she was talking too much. For some reason she didn't feel uncomfortable under the scrutiny of Elias's blue eyes. In fact, she felt very comfortable. But when all was said and done, he was still the man she'd been pursuing for the last six months. It was indescribably strange to be in front of him now, chatting and drinking coffee in his living room at four in the morning.

"And you?" she asked.

"Me what?"

"What are you afraid of?"

"What makes you think I'm afraid of something?"

"Oh, come on," Nuria snorted. "Don't give me that crap. We're all afraid of something."

Elias grimaced. "Clowns. I'm terrified of them."

"I'm being serious."

This time he took a few moments to reply. "Ignorance, I guess," he confessed. "The ignorance that drives some people to hate others because they're afraid of anything different. Cowardice, too," he added after a moment's thought. "The cowardice of those who see that something's wrong and still look the other way."

She gestured at the shelves. "And that's why you surround yourself with books? To fight ignorance?"

"No, not to fight it," he said with a sad smile. "That's a lost battle. The books are to comfort me and reassure me that in the long run, ignorance always ends up being defeated. Rome will burn, regardless of what we do, because men are like that," he said bitterly. "But books will help us rebuild it."

Nuria seemed to be considering Elias's words, but in the end she shook her head. "I still don't get it."

"Get what?"

"All that talk about watching Rome burn while you read your books ... it doesn't fit with you helping me escape from the police and hunting down jihadists."

"I'm not helping you. We're facing a common enemy."

Nuria dismissed this with a wave. "Call it what you like. But it doesn't fit with your stoic pose."

"My business with the jihadists ..." he muttered, wrinkling his nose in distaste at the mere mention of the name, "is personal."

"Because of what happened to your family," Nuria said, and immediately realized she'd put her foot in it.

Elias's face showed ill-concealed surprise. "Who told you about that?" he asked suspiciously.

"Nobody."

Elias considered this for a moment, then looked up. "Aya …" he said, guessing where the information had come from. "That young lady talks too much."

"Don't be angry with her. I was the one who got it out of her."

"Even so. She needs to be careful about what she says and whom she says it to."

"Don't you trust me?"

Elias took a moment to answer. When he did, he chose his words carefully. "Do you really believe that if I didn't … you'd be sitting there?"

Nuria shrugged. "I don't know how you usually behave toward your guests."

Elias gave a dismissive snort, gazing at her with his penetrating blue eyes. "I never have guests."

Nuria felt at a loss for words. Just then, the solemn notes of a nearby church bell announced that it was five in the morning. She checked the time on her bracelet. "Maybe I should try to sleep a little. Even if it's just a couple of hours."

Elias nodded in agreement. "Of course." He indicated the stairs behind him. "Second floor, first door on the right. That's the guest room. I'll stay here a little longer."

"All right, thanks." She got to her feet and went to the stairs. "Good night."

"Sleep well," Elias replied. He stood up and watched Nuria leaving the living room and go up the stairs. "See you in a couple of hours."

37

"Nuria. Pssst ..." a voice whispered into her ear. At the same moment someone put a hand on her shoulder. "Nuria ..."

"Huh? What's up?" she muttered, startled, sitting up abruptly in bed. A young woman was smiling at her in the dim light of the bedroom. "Aya?" she asked, recognizing her. "What is it?"

"My uncle asked me to call you."

"What for?"

"He didn't tell me. Just that he's waiting in his office."

Nuria rubbed her eyes and checked the time. "Okay, thanks." It was nearly nine in the morning, but she seemed to have been asleep for less than ten minutes.

"The office is at the end of the hall," Aya said. With a hint of a conspiratorial smile, she left the room. Nuria set her bare feet on the wood floor, then sat down on the bed again and took a moment to look around the bedroom.

Like the rest of the house, it looked like a room in one of those cute mountain chalets where wealthy skiers sport turtleneck sweaters and drink hot chocolate by the fire. Nuria wondered whether the house had been built by some Swiss expat who missed his home in the Alps and had decided to recreate it on the slopes of Collserola.

The difference, of course, was that what she saw through the window wasn't a forested mountain landscape but the city of Barcelona. It stretched to the sea in an irregular confusion of roofs and antennas dotted with occasional skyscrapers and the fabulous massif of the Sagrada Familia cathedral, bristling with tapering stone towers pointing to a sky that had dawned shrouded in unexpected black clouds.

Stretching, she looked away from the large window, which from her own experience she knew was one-way, and put on the same clothes she'd worn the day before. Going out of the room, she walked down the hall, at the end of which was a partly opened door. Beyond it she glimpsed shelves of files and the corner of a desk.

Out of habit, and because she didn't think it necessary, she'd decided not to put her shoes on. As a result, her bare feet made no sound as she walked down the hallway. Only when she opened the door did Elias notice her presence.

"Good morning," he greeted her, turning toward her and getting up from the armchair he'd been sitting in. "Did you sleep well?"

"Yes, thanks," she replied briefly. "What's going on?"

He pointed to the screen that occupied most of the desk. "Look at this."

Nuria went to stand beside him and found herself looking at the black-and-white image of a badly lit street. "Are those the images from the surveillance cameras?" she asked in surprise. "We got them already?"

"That's right. The kid was fast."

Nuria leaned on the desk. "Great! What are we seeing?"

"A camera from Bonsuccés Street." He pointed to the top right-hand corner of the screen. "The night the container was stolen, at quarter past three in the morning. Look." He touched the screen to deactivate the pause setting.

For a few seconds nothing happened. Then a large, white, unmarked van darted in front of the camera, heading down the street.

"Do you think that might be our van?" Nuria asked. She came closer to the monitor.

"I'm pretty sure."

"But we can't see the driver or the license plate."

"No, we can't."

"And neither can we see whether it turns into Elisabets. It could have gone somewhere else. It could be someone completely unrelated."

"At three in the morning?"

"That street's full of small businesses. It could have been the fruit man on his way to Mercabarna—or anybody else."

"It could be," Elias admitted. "But I'm sure it's them."

Nuria turned to him. He was hiding a knowing smile. "Okay, I'll take the bait. Why do you think it's them?"

"There's another video."

"I knew it," Nuria muttered. "Of the van turning into Elisabets Street?"

"Not exactly." He opened a new window on the screen. "From Pintor Fortuny Street, an hour later." He manipulated the image until they could see a close-up of the front of a van, taken from above.

"Is it the same one?"

"The same," Elias confirmed, putting his finger on it. "It has a dent there, next to the door."

"You can't see the driver here either."

"But what you *can* see is the license plate."

She narrowed her eyes. "I see it now. But we're talking about a distance of several blocks between one image and the other. We still don't know whether it's the same one."

"Nobody takes an hour to drive four blocks," Elias reminded her. "And besides, we know it unloaded something very heavy."

Nuria turned and looked at him curiously. "Oh yeah?" she asked, rubbing her eyes. "We know that?"

"Take a good look." He opened both video windows, one beside the other. "Look at the weight on the wheels here"—he indicated the first image— "and then here." He put his finger on the second image. "The van's much higher."

"That's true. In the first one it's carrying a heavy load, and in the second there's none."

Now it was Elias who turned to Nuria. "Weapons are usually very heavy things, right?"

Instead of answering, Nuria took Elias's smartphone and tapped a number on the virtual keyboard. "Your phone is untraceable, right?" she asked, to reassure herself.

"Yes," he said suspiciously. "But who are you calling?"

"Someone I'd rather not call, but who can help us with this," she said as a woman's face appeared on the screen.

"Hello? Who's this?" the woman asked, taken aback at seeing a call from a blocked number.

"Hi, Susi."

"Jesus Christ!" were the first words that came out of the speaker. "Do you have any idea of what's been going on around here? Where are you? Are you all right? What the fuck is going on, Nuria?"

"I'm fine," she assured her friend when the torrent of questions stopped. "How are you?"

"What do you mean, how am I? How do you think I am?" Susana answered angrily. "Worried sick, for Christ's sake! They found your gun at Gloria's house! How the hell did it get there? Half the police force is looking for you!"

"Well, let's hope it's the inept half."

"Goddamn it, Nuria, I'm not in the mood for jokes. You need to turn yourself in and clear this up in person. Being a fugitive only makes you look guilty."

"I know, but I can't risk it. They stole my gun from my safe to kill Gloria, then deleted my location record for that evening."

"They did that? Why? How's that even possible?"

"I have no idea, Susi. But I didn't even go near David's house, and if they did that with my data, they can do anything else they like."

200

"Christ, Nuria. What a mess you've gotten yourself into."

"You don't need to tell me that."

"Why don't you turn on the video? I want to see your face."

"It's better this way."

"Better? Why? Tell me what's going on, Nuria."

Nuria looked at Elias. "I'm not sure yet," she confessed. "Someone's going to an awful lot of trouble to get me out of the way, but I still don't know why."

"Someone? Who?"

"I don't know that either. But I'm trying to find out."

"Find out? How? Where are you?"

"Too many questions," Nuria objected. "My activity bracelet's encrypted, but if they question you it's better for you to tell the truth: that you don't know where I am."

"An encrypted bracelet?" Susana asked in puzzlement. "Where did you get that? You know they're illegal."

Nuria gave a sardonic snort. "That's the least of my worries, Susi. I wanted you to know I'm safe, but I also need you to do me a favor—without asking any more questions," she added.

"A favor?" Susi asked, adding after a pause, "What is it?"

"I need you to trace a license number for me. Write it down: 3867 WHH."

"Done," her friend confirmed. "What do you want it for?"

"No questions, Susana. The less you know, the safer you'll be."

Nuria heard her snort of impatience at the other end of the line. "Fine," she muttered. "I'll take a look in a while."

"Not *in a while*, Susi. I need it now."

"But—"

"You can access the traffic intranet from your computer. It'll only take you a minute. I wouldn't ask if it weren't important."

"Jesus, Nuria," Susana muttered. "You owe me a load of explanations and a case of beer."

"You can count on it."

"Okay, then … give me a moment," she murmured. After less than a minute, she spoke again. "Here it is. A Renault Master cargo van, white, a 2026 model."

"Yes, that's it."

"It looks like … it was stolen about three weeks ago. Turned up two days later in a vacant lot near Gavá, torched."

Nuria repeated Elias's whispered question. "Do you know who stole it?"

"Are you serious?"

201

"Completely."

"No. Unknown. They didn't go to the trouble of leaving a visiting card."

"I understand." Nuria closed her eyes, trying not to let this thread slip through her fingers. "Where's the van now?"

"Let me check … ah, yes. Here it is. It was taken to the city junkyard," she read off her screen. "I guess it's still there, unless they've already dismantled it for scrap."

"Thanks, Susi." Nuria remembered something else at the last moment. "The other thing I need to do is send you some fingerprints so you can put them through the database and see if you come up with a match."

For a moment it seemed that Susi was going to protest again, but in the end she gave an audible exhale. "All right," she said resignedly. "Send them."

"Thanks, Susi. You're saving my life."

"You're welcome, Nurieta. I don't know what you're doing or why … but I trust you."

Nuria felt a lump form in her throat. "Thanks," she said again in a slightly shaky voice. "I needed to hear that. You be careful out there, sweetie. Some bizarre things are going on."

"Ya think?" Susana said ironically with a humorless laugh. "Just don't let yourself get caught, okay?"

"I'll do what I can."

"You'd better," Susana admonished her. "And don't forget that case of beer."

This time Nuria's laughter was real. "See you, Susi," she said, hanging up quickly so as not to prolong the goodbye. Turning immediately to Elias, she said, "I need some talcum powder and adhesive tape to take prints from the bottle I found at the shop last night."

"I'll have them brought to you at once. Anything else?"

"We need to find out where they took whatever it was they unloaded at the shop. The place was empty, so they must have loaded it back onto a vehicle and taken it away."

Elias shook his head. "That's going to be complicated. It means a lot of days of recordings to check, and if they torched the van after the first time, it means they used a different vehicle," he reasoned. "It'll take us hours to find it."

"Well, all the more reason not to waste time." She jumped to her feet. "I'll go to the junkyard. The van might still be there."

"But hasn't it been torched? What do you expect to find?"

"I don't know," she admitted. "But it's better to be sure. They might have left a visiting card after all. I've seen stranger things."

He nodded skeptically. "All right. I'll keep checking the surveillance images. I'll get one of my men to go with you."

"I don't need a babysitter."

"I know that," Elias said, though he didn't sound entirely sincere. "But I'll feel better, and four eyes see more than two." He added, "Take Aya's small car. You won't attract so much attention."

Nuria was about to protest, reluctant to accept any kind of help, but she realized her reticence was just an absurd conditioned reflex. In fact, someone watching her back for once wasn't such a bad idea.

38

Despite her objections, Nuria could find no way of avoiding having Giwan as her companion. Nor could she argue him out of getting behind the wheel of Aya's small car, a bubble-gum-pink Model Y Tesla with heart decals on the dash.

Despite its eye-catching color, the Tesla was far more discreet than the previous night's outsized SUV. Even so, Nuria couldn't help feeling observed every time they passed under an Indetect camera, nervous at the possibility of being identified in spite of the tinted windows. From one day to the next her perception of the AI identification system that watched over the streets had taken a hundred-eighty-degree turn, and now she saw it not as an effective aid but a constant threat.

Though the Indetect system had spread throughout Spain more than two years previously, "in the name of safety and peaceful coexistence," the first protests were just now appearing, mostly due to the point system for good citizenship that went with it.

At first many people had taken it as a joke, comparing it to the points awarded for shopping at the Carrefour supermarket chain. But when they'd found out that Indetect not only added points but also subtracted them for erring against an increasingly strict norm, it stopped being so funny. And when, after losing those points, people began to lose their rights as well and suffered inconveniences such as the impossibility of getting a loan, or restricted access to certain opportunities, the whole business had become very unfunny indeed.

Shortly after they left the house, the clouds began to dump a muddy yellowish rain on them. It dirtied the vehicle's glass sunroof and forced the windshield wipers to swish back and forth at top speed to clear all the water and mud falling on them.

After leaving the busy Ronda de Dalt, gridlocked because of the rain, they took the expressway in the direction of the nearby village of Gavá, passing the irregular silhouette of Villarefu on their left, blurred behind the dense curtain of rain.

Giwan kept his hands on the wheel, although the Tesla could have driven itself perfectly well. Nuria remembered that at first she too had been reluctant to leave the driving in the hands of the autopilot. She guessed the same was true for the Kurd. "You don't talk much," she commented after more than ten minutes of travelling in silence.

The bodyguard turned his bald head to Nuria. "Little," he replied in a thick accent, after taking his time to come up with an answer.

"Have you been in Spain long?"

"No."

"No? How long?"

"Little," he said, and turned to face front again.

"I see," murmured Nuria. "And you and your friends … did you arrive together?"

"No," he answered simply.

"You don't feel much like talking, do you?"

Giwan turned to look at her again before answering, "Little."

Luckily, their destination was only a few miles down the road. They soon reached the junkyard where the van had been left for parts. Turning into the open gate of the yard, they made their way to the manager's prefabricated booth.

Giwan stopped the vehicle and was about to get out when Nuria laid a hand on his forearm to hold him back. "You wait here. It'll be easier if I go alone."

"No," the Kurd replied.

"If you come you'll intimidate the manager," Nuria argued, "and that's not what I want." She tugged her hair loose from its ponytail and fluffed it up with her hands as she looked in the mirror. "You understand? If I need you to beat up some little old lady, don't worry, I'll call you right away." It took Giwan a few seconds to understand what this tall, stubborn woman had in mind, but in the end he nodded, apparently not offended by her crude sarcasm.

"Great," Nuria said. Without another word she opened the door of the Tesla, took her small backpack and stepped out into the rain. The dirty downpour drenched her before she reached the booth, which made the white shirt she was wearing stick to her body like a second skin. *Even better*, she thought. She knocked on the door and a male voice invited her in.

Less than two minutes later, Giwan saw her exit the booth, following a short, potbellied man who was protecting himself with an umbrella. The man glanced at the pink Tesla with its tinted windows, perhaps wondering whether there was anyone inside, then pointed to a spot out of the Kurd's line of vision. The potbellied man handed the umbrella to Nuria, who took it with a coquettish moue, and hurried back into his booth, not before taking a last look at Nuria's ass when she moved in the direction he'd indicated.

Giwan smiled to himself. Men were all the same, whatever their background or age; they couldn't resist admiring a good ass. He had to admit Mr.

Zafrani's friend, though too tall, thin, and stubborn for his own taste, had a nicely molded one.

Walking in the rain in the direction the manager had indicated, Nuria found the van fifty yards or so ahead next to a pile of old tires. Unfortunately, all the anticipation generated by the discovery that it hadn't yet been recycled evaporated when she saw the charred remains dripping water in the rain.

Overcoming her disappointment, Nuria went up to the van, a model with a double row of seats and an oversized cargo area. The passenger-side door was missing and the sliding door was open. The rain poured unhindered through the openings.

"Well, that's just great," she muttered, realizing how difficult it was going to be to obtain a single print from this wreck. Even so, she closed the umbrella, put on the thick latex gloves she'd taken from Elias's kitchen and climbed into the van.

Like the outside, the inside was completely charred. The two rows of seats were a shapeless mass of twisted springs, the plastic upholstery had melted, the windows had shattered, and every interior surface was either burned or covered in a thick layer of soot.

The large cargo bay, as she'd expected, was empty. If there'd been anything there before the fire, it would be reduced to ashes now. The floor of the van, weakened by the heat of the fire, creaked under her feet as she explored the inside thoroughly, dividing walls, floor, and roof into imaginary quadrants and checking them one by one.

After making sure she hadn't overlooked anything, and taking care not to lean on anything, Nuria moved to the second row of seats. She searched among the charred upholstery remains scattered on the floor, peered under what was left of the seats, and looked in all the nooks and crannies where something might have fallen, but found nothing.

By the time Nuria finished checking the front seats, she'd become convinced that whoever had done this hadn't been satisfied with simply torching the vehicle; they'd cleaned it out thoroughly before that. These people knew what they were doing. To make matters even worse, even the remote possibility of getting a fingerprint from somewhere on the exterior that hadn't ended up charred had to be ruled out because of the rain.

Nuria's gaze landed on the open space left by the missing door. *Where is it?* she wondered, scanning the junkyard through the empty space. Climbing out, she used her hand as a visor to shield her face so she could see in the rain. A couple of yards away she spotted the door, propped against the side of a scrapped Renault Mégane.

The door had the same charred appearance as the rest of the vehicle, inside and out. She went over the window frames and the area surrounding the melted plastic handle, but there wasn't even a single square inch of clean surface.

Just when she was on the point of giving up, the persistent muddy rain getting into her eyes and irritating them, Nuria saw something that hadn't occurred to her before. There was no broken glass.

Using extreme care, she put her fingers into the empty window space. Touching the narrow slot for the glass, she found that the window was still there. Apparently it had been rolled down when they torched the van, which meant the glass was intact, protected inside the door.

Was her luck going to change at last?

Ten minutes later, under the cover afforded by a toolshed, she watched Giwan as he tried to separate the two sides of the door, using brute force. The screws were so deformed by the fire that he had no choice but to do it the hard way. Luckily the structure had been weakened, and the muscular Kurd, teeth gritted, was skillfully wielding the hydraulic shears.

At last, his bald head dripping with sweat from the effort and the heat inside the shed, Giwan loosened the last bolt. The door fell open like a sandwich, revealing the window and the system of pulleys that held it in place.

"Allow me," Nuria said, pushing Giwan aside unceremoniously. Crouching in front of the glass, she opened her backpack and pulled out a little bag of soot she'd gathered from the van itself. With the utmost care she scattered the soot over the glass until it was covered with a fine layer, then fanned it with her hand until it vanished completely. She had brought a jar of talcum powder to use for this, but the soot was much better. And unfortunately they had plenty of it.

"Shit," she muttered under her breath, and turned to Giwan. "Give me a hand with this." Between the two of them they lifted the window, holding it gingerly by the edges, and carefully turned it over. Nuria repeated the operation, spreading the soot and fanning it, but this time a faint black spot appeared at the very edge: a fingerprint that had been overlooked.

Lifting prints was a process the force's forensic department always took care of, but Nuria knew how to take prints when they were visible enough, and this one was. She took out a small notebook and a roll of adhesive tape from her backpack, applied it to the print to transfer the soot imprint, then stuck it onto one of the blank pages. The spiral design of a fingerprint was revealed in black.

"I think we got it," she said to Giwan, trying to suppress her enthusiasm. The Kurd gave her a look of complete indifference, as if she'd just boasted of making a perfect O with a straw.

On the way back, Nuria took a photo of the print and sent it to Susana so she could add it to the ones she'd sent her before leaving Elias's house and search for a match in the database of jihad suspects or sympathizers with ISMA or any of its branches worldwide. When she'd finished, she stared out at the vehicles all trying to get into Barcelona at the same time on the Diagonal.

Lifting her gaze above the electric cars, motorbikes, and tricycles, Nuria looked toward the city center, remembering that she hadn't contacted her mother or her grandfather in several days. Both of them must be worried sick. It was very likely that the police had contacted them and was monitoring them twenty-four seven, so going to see them in person was out of the question. Maybe now, though, she could call them to assure them she was all right, that she was innocent, and that there was no need for them to worry. The problem was that right now she didn't feel like facing the volley of questions that would follow and which she either couldn't or wouldn't answer yet.

Taking a deep breath, she used the car's electronic screen to send them both a brief message, assuring them that everything would soon be cleared up and she would be able to see them again. She knew this was a pitifully small amount of information, considering everything that was happening, but she persuaded herself that soon she would feel able to speak to them. Most important of all, she would have something more to offer in answer to their questions than *I don't know.*

For a moment she also considered the idea of going home for some clothes and personal items. Of course, it would be a stupid thing to do—but the police would think the same thing, which meant there was a possibility her apartment wouldn't be under surveillance simply because they'd dismissed the idea that she could be that stupid.

She'd spent the last two days in the same clothes, unable to change. When she sniffed her shirt unobtrusively she found to her horror that she was beginning to smell like a raccoon. A dead raccoon.

Unfortunately, trusting that the police would believe she wasn't stupid enough to go to her home was too risky a gamble. Especially since up to now she hadn't displayed much intelligence.

In the end, she decided she would find some way to solve the problem of personal hygiene. Right now she needed to focus on the tasks ahead of her: avoiding arrest, proving she hadn't killed Gloria, and in her free time finding out if there was a possible jihadist cell planning a terrorist attack on Barcelona.

Making a face, she concluded it was going to be difficult to find time to shave her legs.

39

Nuria waited for the door of the house's spacious garage to descend all the way before she got out of the car, secure in the knowledge that nobody could see her from outside. She went straight to Elias's office, finding him hunched over his desk monitor, taking notes.

He turned when he heard her come in. "How did it go?"

Nuria pulled up a chair and sat down beside him. "I still don't know," she admitted. "I found one print, and sent it to my friend for analysis. How about you?" She leaned toward the screen. "Did you find anything?"

"More or less."

"What does that mean?"

"It means no other vehicle went into that alley after the van, with the exception of a couple of motorbikes. In fact, practically no one at all has gone in or out, and the resolution's so bad it's impossible to make out facial features anyway."

"So how did they take the cargo out of the shop?" She pointed at the screen with the Apple logo. "Because if there's one thing that's clear in this case, it's that there was nothing there."

"I can think of several possibilities," Elias said. "Maybe we're completely wrong and we're basing everything on the false premise that that was where they unloaded everything they took out of the container."

"Or maybe this container from Jeddah had nothing special in it, an ordinary thief stole my gun and then coincidentally killed Gloria with it, and the man I killed in Villarefu was just a run-of-the-mill junkie. All that's *possible*," she concluded, "but if you put it all together, the idea that everything points in the same direction is as unlikely as me winning the lottery without buying a ticket."

"It could also be," Elias went on, "that they took the contents of the container out of the shop and carried it away in bags or backpacks. Remember, we don't have any images of the alley itself, only of the adjacent streets."

"That container was carrying several tons of cargo," Nuria said skeptically. "I find it hard to believe that something as heavy as that could have been carried away in shopping bags. To start with, assuming whatever it was could be dismantled, they'd have needed to make more than a hundred trips, risking a hundred chances of someone suspecting something or a cop asking them for ID. No," she concluded, "to me these people seem too conscientious to take a risk like that."

"Then maybe they transferred the stuff from that shop to somewhere else in the same alley."

Nuria shook her head. "That doesn't make sense either. Why would they do that? They'd simply have unloaded it there in the first place, don't you think?"

Elias leaned back in the armchair, the leather creaking under his weight. "Well, I can't think of any other explanation," he said with a long exhale. "We must be overlooking something. They can't have been swallowed up by the earth."

All at once, as occasionally happened in Nuria's brain, two idle neurons came together in a brief flash of intuition, and a clear thought crystallized as if by magic in her mind. "Jesus ..." she muttered. "That's it."

"That's what I think," Elias agreed. "We made a mistake somewhere in—"

She cut him off. "No, not that. You're right about the other thing."

"The other thing? What other thing?"

"Let me see street view on Google Maps. I need to check something."

Elias looked at her blankly, but holding his questions, he opened the app on the screen in front of them.

"Take it to Passatge Elisabets," Nuria told him. "In front of the shop."

Elias moved his fingers on the touch screen. From the satellite view of Barcelona, the image zoomed in as if in free fall, coming to a halt in front of the metal shutters of ANA. "What now?" he asked.

"Turn the camera down towards the ground." Giving her a sidelong glance, Elias manipulated the image until it showed the cobbled surface of the alley. Nuria pointed to the end of the street. "Move over there. Slowly."

"If you tell me what you're looking for," Elias suggested, "it would be easier for me to help you."

"Manhole covers."

"Manhole covers?" he repeated. "Well, there's one." He pointed at the screen.

"No, that one's square."

"So?"

"The square ones are for electricity, gas, and—" Abruptly Nuria fell silent, sat up in her chair, and put her finger on the screen. "There it is!" she cried excitedly, as if she'd just found a gold nugget in a stream. "Come on, zoom in closer!"

Elias obeyed, not yet understanding where this sudden obsession of hers had come from. He zoomed in on the image until the screen was filled with an ordinary manhole cover stamped with the emblem of the Barcelona City Council.

"That's where they went," Nuria said, nodding decisively.

"Are you suggesting ... that they used the sewers to take the cargo and escape?"

"It's what I would have done in their place," Nuria reasoned. "Down there they're safe from surveillance cameras. They can move anywhere they want in the city undetected and come out in a million different places."

"But if that's what they did," Elias said, frustrated, "then we've lost them."

The look in Nuria's eyes, far from sharing his frustration, showed a renewed fervor. She turned toward Elias. "Let's go after them."

"What?"

"Let's go there," she insisted. "Let's go down into the sewers and hunt them down."

Elias frowned, disconcerted. "Are you hearing what you're saying?" he asked her in disbelief. "Hunt them down? They would have left the shop days ago—if there even is anybody to hunt down."

"There's nothing else we can do," Nuria said. "They might have left some clue along the way. It's the only trail we have to follow right now."

"A trail? Through the sewers?"

"You never know," she argued. "We have to try."

Elias looked at the screen again, then back at Nuria, and finally shook his head. "All right," he consented, not believing the words that were coming out of his own mouth. "I'll tell the men to be prepared for tonight."

"Not tonight," Nuria said decisively. "We need to go now. We've already lost too much time."

"It's safer to wait until night."

"It's always night in the sewers," Nuria reminded him.

Elias let out a long grunt of frustration, then put his phone to his ear and issued a series of orders in Arabic to Giwan.

Nuria raised a finger. "Tell them to wear rubber boots and carry flashlights," she said.

Elias looked at her for a long moment before reluctantly adding, "*Tudhkar 'iihdar almasabih alkahrabayiyat wal'ahdihat lilma.*" Then, falsely solicitous, he asked Nuria, "Anything else? A flux condenser? A psychokinetic energy gauge?"

"Tell them to leave their sarcasm at home," she shot back with an eye-roll. "I think we've got plenty with yours."

211

Elias looked at the manhole cover again. "There's an alarm bell going off in my head right now," he muttered under his breath. "Warning me not to do what we're about to do."

"You don't need to come," Nuria said offhandedly "or your men either. I can go by myself."

"That's certainly what I should do," Elias agreed. "Act sensibly instead of letting myself be carried away by your insane recklessness."

"So why don't you?"

Elias fixed his blue eyes on Nuria's. "Sometimes one must listen to the heart and not the head," he stated solemnly. "Go astray in order to keep to the true path."

"And what does that mean? Is it an Arab proverb or something like that?"

Keeping his gaze fixed on Nuria, Elias closed his eyes and opened them again, hesitating as if debating with himself what to say next. At last he heaved a sigh, placed his hands on the table and wearily stood up.

"It means we have to get ready." Pushing his armchair back, he crossed the room, turning in the doorway to say, "We depart in fifteen minutes," before leaving her alone in the office.

40

Just like the night before, as if all they'd done was prolong their drive a little, Nuria and Elias found themselves in the middle row of seats inside the bulletproof SUV, silently gazing out at its slow progress toward the Raval district.

The four Kurds who made up Elias's security team had been equipped with night gear, weapons, and loose clothing to keep everything hidden. All waited in expectant silence except for Giwan, who was once again at the wheel. He turned to Elias during one of the innumerable traffic halts to express a laconic *Maaf,* apologizing as if the gridlock were his fault.

The rain, though less intense than in the morning, continued to fall over the city from dense clouds pregnant with mud that seemed stalled on the lower slopes of Collserola like foam on the tidemark of a beach. The media continued to repeat that still more rain was needed to compensate for the months of drought and bring an end to the water restrictions that had been imposed at the beginning of the year. According to the climatologists, though, Barcelona would never again have enough drinking water to supply its citizens; the restrictions had come to stay and would only get worse over time.

"Everything's going to hell in a handbasket," Nuria murmured, staring at the varied assortment of buckets that many Barcelonians now placed on the sidewalks in front of their houses in an attempt to gather all the muddy rainwater they could.

Elias followed her gaze and snorted. "Everything's been going to hell since the beginning of time. But while most people don't care as long as they get some benefit out of it, there are some who try to change things. People who are seeking to make this world a better place. People like you," he concluded unexpectedly.

Nuria tried not to react to this undeserved compliment, keeping her eyes fixed on the window and limiting her response to a skeptical shake of the head. "Well, I sure hope other people are better at it than I am," she said with a sigh after a few seconds, "because I've done nothing but fuck things up for as long as I can remember."

"I'm sure that's not true," Elias protested.

Nuria turned to face him. Just as she opened her mouth to tell him he didn't know her at all, Giwan announced that they were almost there. She decided to leave the reply for some other time. The SUV wound its slow way down Bonsuccés Street, Nuria praying that *Good Success* would turn out to be a hopeful omen, then turned right into Passatge Elisabets. The Suburban entered the alley slowly, like a silent black tank, its girth taking up almost the whole width of the narrow passageway. It slid to a halt in front of the abandoned shop and they disembarked.

As if performing a carefully rehearsed piece of choreography, two of the Kurds placed themselves on either side of the car while the other two pulled up the manhole cover with a tire iron and began to descend the crude access ladder without hesitation.

Elias exchanged a few words with Giwan, who pulled out his gun and offered it to Nuria. Instead of taking it, she looked at it warily.

"Sig Sauer M17," the big man told her. He released the magazine and pushed it back in. "No get stuck."

Nuria hesitated another second, knowing the implications wielding a weapon in her circumstances might have. Neither did she know whether it had been used to commit some earlier crime. Leaving her fingerprints on that grip might bring her even more problems than she already had.

"I don't think it's a good idea for you to go down there unarmed," Elias said, seeing her hesitation. "We don't know what we might run into."

After thinking about it a few seconds longer, Nuria reached for the gun. It was khaki-colored and had a flashlight taped to its barrel. As she took it, she noticed its incredible lightness and realized it had originally been manufactured for military use.

"Great," Elias said, watching her weigh the gun before sticking it into the back of her pants. "Are you ready?"

"No," she confessed. "But let's go."

Elias nodded, satisfied, and addressed Giwan in Spanish. "Look for a place to wait with the vehicle and keep your ears open," he said. "We'll let you know where to come pick us up."

The Kurd nodded and returned to the Suburban. By now, the first two men had vanished into the sewer and the third was waiting by the entrance to the manhole, keeping watch.

"Ladies first," Elias said, pointing to the dark, round hole from which issued a penetrating smell of feces and damp.

Nuria took a last deep breath. Looking up, she let the rain fall on her face for a few seconds, reminding herself why she was doing what she was about to do—and for all she knew, fucking things up yet again.

"Better be hanged for a sheep," she muttered, looking down into the manhole. It was a saying she'd repeated a little too often lately. "A shit-smeared one," she added, praying her plan wasn't one more mistake to add to her long list of previous errors.

When Nuria's rubber boots touched the slippery concrete floor, she looked up at the circle of light twelve yards above her head, from which fat raindrops were falling. Elias was already halfway down the ladder, the third bodyguard just stepping into the sewer. He slid the heavy iron cover closed over his head, gradually reducing the gray light of day like an eclipse until it disappeared.

Nuria looked around and found that they were in a narrow, brick-vaulted tunnel barely three yards wide and three yards high, lit by sickly fluorescent lights mounted on the ceiling every twenty yards. Through it flowed an evil-smelling black stream of fecal matter, plastic bags, and other remains she preferred not to identify. Only a narrow strip of concrete, barely two handspans wide, kept them above water level and safe from that river of refuse.

The current, flowing in the direction of the sea, passed between the bars of a gate a couple of yards ahead. Approaching it, Nuria found that it was kept shut by a solid chain secured with a lock. "It's very rusty," she commented when she'd examined it more closely. "I don't think it's been opened for years."

Elias, who had reached the bottom of the ladder, came up behind her to check. "You're right." He tugged the chain hard. "It's a long time since anybody came through here."

"Which only leaves us one way to go," Nuria said, looking in the opposite direction.

"Looks like it," Elias confirmed. Pointing down the tunnel, he called to the trio of Kurds, "Let's go."

In response they pulled out small Kriss Vector submachine guns from their vests. These looked both strange and deadly. Nuria had only seen them before in videogames. They turned on the powerful flashlights affixed to the short 45-caliber barrels and set off in single file down that vaulted tunnel with its strip of fluorescent lights that seemed to stretch on indefinitely. Elias gestured to Nuria, inviting her to follow them.

Noticing that only a flashlight and a radio hung from his belt, she asked, "Aren't you carrying a gun?"

Elias spread his hands as though apologizing for something. "I hope I'm not ruining my soulless-criminal image. But the fact is, I don't particularly like weapons. Besides, you're all here to protect me, right?"

Nuria raised her eyebrows indifferently. "If you say so," she said ambiguously, looking at the trio of men who were already on their way down the tunnel.

As they continued along that apparently endless underground passage, the current in the sewer seemed to decrease little by little. The slight slope of the floor was enough to encourage the flow in the opposite direction. Rain fell onto the surface through small drains from the street that emptied into the sewer halfway up the walls, drenching them if they weren't careful to avoid them.

Even avoiding them, the terrible humidity and inescapable heat meant that after only five minutes Nuria was sweating profusely, feeling her T-shirt—a loan from Aya, who'd seen her come back from the junkyard covered in soot—clinging to her body.

She licked her dry lips. "We should have brought water."

"And clothespins for our noses," Elias added with distaste.

Nuria was about to make a joke about his comment when the man at the head of the three bodyguards moved ahead of her and pointed. "Ahead. Crossing," he said in broken Spanish.

Effectively, fifty yards or so ahead, the tunnel bifurcated into two apparently identical branches. They stopped when they reached the fork while Elias consulted the diagram he'd downloaded to his smartphone.

"They seem identical," he explained as he studied the graph of colored lines. "Except that one goes northeast and the other one north."

Nuria walked over to him to see the map for herself. "Can you see any open space where they might have stashed the weapons?"

"It's a very simple map," Elias said. "It only shows the main tunnels and intersections."

"Then we'll have to separate," Nuria said. "Some of us will go down this fork and some down the other."

"That's a bad idea. Suppose we run into them?"

"After so many days?" Nuria said. "I think it's pretty unlikely they're lurking around a corner with their weapons at the ready."

"Unlikely, but not impossible."

"Well, if you're really worried about it—" she indicated the trio of Kurds—"you go down one fork with the A-Team and I'll go down the other."

Elias rolled his eyes and shook his head in annoyance. "Yihan and Yady," he ordered, "you two go down that fork. If you see anything odd, radio me before you do anything. And you, Aza—" he pointed to himself—"you're coming with us."

The first two nodded and headed down the right-hand fork without further ado, their weapons at the ready.

Nuria, who had been gazing at them, turned to Elias. "I thought they didn't understand Spanish and that's why you spoke to them in Arabic."

Elias shook his head. "They understand almost everything. But since they don't speak it very well and I speak no Kurdish at all, we're in the habit of

216

communicating in Arabic. Giwan is the only one who has a little more vocabulary."

Nuria remembered how limited her conversation with the big man that morning had been, and found it hard to imagine anyone with less vocabulary. "Good to know," she said. She turned to the seemingly interminable tunnel and took the lead without waiting for anybody. Aza looked at his boss, who shrugged. In the face of Nuria's determined attitude, they had no choice but to follow her.

After the fork, the tunnel began to climb steeply and the stream of fecal water, inches under their feet, began to flow more swiftly. Nuria couldn't push the thought from her mind that if the rain turned more intense, those black waters would reach them, impeding their forward progress.

"This doesn't make sense to me," came Elias's voice from where he was walking a yard behind her.

"What doesn't make sense?" Nuria asked without stopping.

"All this. If they did take the cargo through this sewer I can't imagine them carrying it all through here. It's too slippery, and we can barely walk in single file."

"Yeah, but up until a week ago there wasn't any rain. This must have been practically dry."

"Even so"—he pointed upwards—"they could have exited through any of the manholes we've already passed."

"That's true. But if that's the case, there would be nothing we could do. Our only chance is to hope that—"

The radio on Elias's belt crackled, interrupting her. The three of them stopped dead. Elias transferred the radio to his hand to listen more closely. After a few endless seconds of silence the radio crackled again, but no voice came out of it.

Elias pressed the red button. "Hello?" he said into the radio. "Do you copy? Over." The reply, in the form of interference, took a few seconds to arrive.

"It's got to be them," Nuria concluded. "There's no coverage down here, and the radios barely work. They must be trying to—"

"…Yihan …" crackled the radio, interrupting her explanation once again. "Quick …"

Elias and Nuria exchanged a look of understanding. "Hurry!" Nuria cried, pointing back the way they'd just come. "They've found something!"

41

Retracing their steps along one tunnel as far as the fork and then going up the other at top speed took them less than three minutes. Ignoring the danger of slipping on the moldy concrete surface and falling flat on their faces in the disgusting black water, they ran as fast as their legs would carry them. Sweat poured down their faces and the sticky humidity made their clothing cling to their bodies.

At last, after a final bend, they found Yihan and Yady standing guard in front of a metal door on one side of the tunnel. Nuria realized at once that the door was ajar and that the lock had been forced. Pointing to the twisted padlock, she asked the pair of Kurds, "Did you force it yourselves?"

Yihan's only explanation was a shake of his head. He opened the door and stepped into a dark passage. "Look here," he said.

Nuria followed him without hesitation. Yihan flipped the light switch and a string of old bulbs lit up. They found themselves in a narrow corridor where there was barely room for them to stand side by side. It led to a rusty metal ladder that took a turn to the right as it ascended.

"Do you know where this leads to, Yihan?" To Nuria's ears, Elias's voice sounded a little worried.

"No," the bodyguard replied in the purest Kurdish style.

Nuria turned to Elias. "Everything okay?"

He pursed his lips. His expression of annoyance and the sweat pearling his brow, making his hair stick to his forehead, showed he was far from feeling okay. "I don't like narrow spaces," he said, moving his hands to show he had barely enough space for his shoulders.

"Narrow spaces?" Nuria pretended to be surprised. "What were you expecting to find in a sewer?"

"Not *this* narrow." Seeing his expression of dismay, Nuria felt a mixture of sympathy and satisfaction at the sight of Elias losing the irritating aura of self-confidence he was careful to project. Hiding a malicious little grin, she faced forward again just in time to see Yihan disappearing around the bend in the ladder. Without a second thought, she climbed up after him, closely followed by Elias, placing her feet carefully on the steps that creaked under her weight.

She reached Yihan again around the bend. He'd stopped in front of a new metal door, also rusty, also forced. Nuria had only to point at the lock for the Kurd to understand the question and shake his head again.

Yihan pushed the door open, aiming the flashlight on his submachine gun into the darkness before stepping into it. Nuria did the same, taking out her gun and switching on the flashlight attached to it before cautiously following in his footsteps.

In the limited beam of the flashlights, it was difficult to figure out what the place was. The only thing they could tell was that it was quite a large space to find underground, at least a thousand square feet or so. Across it were scattered a myriad of fragments of cables in different sizes and colors, zip ties, screws, circuit components, and pieces of duct tape.

"It's like someone set up an electronics workshop here," Nuria commented. She stopped short, feeling something crunching under her feet. Intrigued, she trained her flashlight first on the floor and then the ceiling that was just above their heads. "They broke them."

"What?"

"The fluorescent lights," she clarified. "They've broken all the fluorescent lights in the room." She turned to Elias. "Tell your men to look for clues, but without disturbing anything. Tell them to let me know if they find anything."

"They're not a bunch of incompetents."

"I know. But they're not cops either … nor are you, for that matter," she added. "Tell them."

Reluctantly, Elias spoke a few words in Arabic to his men, then asked Nuria, "What is this place?"

"I don't know," she admitted, taking in the dozen or so shabby consoles against the walls, covered with decades of filth. "It looks like an abandoned control room or something li—" She broke off and approached one of the consoles. "What the hell?"

"What is it?"

Nuria almost laughed as she turned the beam of her flashlight on the contraption in front of her. "Look."

Elias was beside her in two strides, seeing the eye-catching inscription in red letters on the upper surface of the console. "*Street Fighter*," he read aloud.

As if ready to start a game, Nuria put her gun away and stretched out her hand toward the small red joystick on the dusty old control panel. "When I was a kid I used to play this on my Nintendo," she said, smiling at the distant memory. "I was really good."

Standing next to her, Elias leaned towards the dirty screen and drew his finger across the surface, leaving a black streak on it. Looking around, he stared at the dozen similar consoles lined up along the walls of the space. "I don't understand what these machines are doing down here," he said in puzzlement. "In the sewers."

"I don't think we're in the sewers any longer." Nuria swept her light over the peeling walls until her beam lit up a stretch of brick wall that filled the space where the main door must once have been. "I seem to remember reading something about this place. I think it's an abandoned shop on an old subterranean street called the Avenue of Light."

"An underground street in Barcelona?" Elias asked, incredulous. "I've never heard of anything like that."

"They shut it down before I was born," Nuria explained. She turned to him. "Apparently there were movie theaters, restaurants, shops, and—" she pointed around the large space—"videogame arcades. If I'm not mistaken, right above us is Pelayo Street and a shopping mall."

Elias looked up, as if expecting to see the street through the roof. "It's hard to believe."

"Yeah. It's one of those little secrets about Barcelona that outsiders don't know."

"*Alsyd Zafrani,*" came Aza's voice, bringing them back to the present. "Look here." Nuria and Elias turned at the same time. The Kurd was at the other end of the hall, crouched in front of one of the videogames, aiming his flashlight under it and reaching for something with his other hand. As they approached him he pulled his hand out, empty, saying apologetically, "Very small."

Nuria kneeled down beside him. When she put her cheek to the floor, she could see the beam of his flashlight picking out what looked like a piece of paper that had fallen under the videogame. "Let's hope there aren't any creepy-crawlies," she said, flattening herself against the floor and extending her arm, which was much smaller than the Kurd's. "I can't quite reach it," she muttered, straining to pinch a corner of the paper with her fingertips.

As if by magic, the machine rose into the air and she jerked her hand back. It took her a second to realize the three Kurds were lifting it up as if it weighed nothing at all.

"Now you can reach it," Elias suggested with a condescending smile.

Nuria rolled her eyes. With a grateful smile to the three men, she reached out and picked up what turned out to be a scrap of fluorescent orange paper.

"It looks new," she said.

"It does," Elias agreed. "I'd say it's part of the wrapping of a package."

Nuria turned the brightly colored piece of paper over and saw a sequence of apparently meaningless letters and numbers printed in large black type on the rough surface of the paper. "What's this?" she said. "Do you understand it?"

"It looks like a serial number."

"What of?"

"I don't know. Maybe whatever this is below it." He pointed to a long series of letters. "*Exaazaisowurtzitane*," he read aloud with some difficulty.

"Is that a word? It looks like a wi-fi password."

"Maybe, except that there are some letters missing at the beginning, see?" He indicated the place where the paper had been torn. Part of another letter was visible.

"Looks like it," Nuria agreed. "But we'll take a closer look at it when we get back to the surface." She stuck the scrap into her back pocket. "Let's keep looking. Maybe we'll find something else around here."

An hour later, Nuria was forced to admit she'd been wrong. Apart from a pile of pieces of electric cabling in assorted colors and some scraps of duct tape, they found nothing. Perhaps a specialized forensic team might have found something after a painstaking search, but there was no chance of that happening. She would have to make do with what she had: a small piece of wrapping paper.

They made the trip back through the sewer in weary silence, broken only by the sound of the foul stream. It seemed to Nuria to be more swollen than it had been when they'd arrived. By the time they reached the ladder, the black water was already licking at the soles of her boots. Nuria climbed the ladder and was irrationally glad to see the light of day, albeit dulled by the blanket of clouds, when she poked her head out at street level.

Giwan brought the vehicle into the alley as soon as they came out of the sewer, and Yihan and Aza immediately put the manhole cover back in place. There was no one in sight, so it was unlikely that anybody had seen them go in or come out.

Once again in the SUV, they set off in the direction of Elias's house, driving under the persistent rain that was forming puddles in the streets. "Can you hand me that piece of paper?" Elias asked Nuria, taking out his phone.

Sunk in her disappointment at not having found anything in the sewer, Nuria had almost forgotten about it. "Sure," she said, leaning to one side to pull it out of her pocket. She handed it to him.

"Thanks." Holding it in front of him in his left hand, Elias punched the unpronounceable string of letters into his cellphone. Immediately a concise message appeared on the screen: *There are no results for your search for exaazaisowurtzitane.*

"Are you sure you spelled it right?"

He held out paper and phone. "See for yourself."

"You did," she agreed after a few seconds. "It must be because of the missing letters."

"Or else it's some kind of code after all."

"I don't think so," Nuria said. "Look at the last part: *wurtzitane*. It sounds like something. Let's see." She pointed at the screen. "Google it."

Elias gave a skeptical glance, but keyed in the letters that reminded him of the protagonist's name in *Apocalypse Now*. To his surprise, the image of a metallic-looking rock appeared under the name *wurtzite*.

"I knew it," Nuria said. She scrolled down the webpage on the phone. "It's a mineral. This *wurtzitane* thing must have something to do with it."

"Even so, I don't see the—"

Nuria cut him off. "Look!" She read out a link under the title *Military uses*: "'Defense Technology: Briefing Bulletin.' Click on that."

Obediently, Elias pressed the graphene surface. The link took them to a Ministry of Defense website named *High Density Energy Materials*. Nuria scanned the article quickly. The word *wurtzitane* appeared, underlined in yellow, at the end of a much longer list of words, exactly as written on the piece of paper Elias was still holding in his hand.

"Hexaazaisowurtzitane," he read. "There was just an H missing at the beginning."

"Jesus, look at this," Nuria cried, grabbing the phone from him. "Also called HNIW or CL-20," she read aloud, "it is a nitroamine explosive developed at the American research facilities at China Lake. It is considerably superior to conventional explosives—" She stopped short, putting a hand to her mouth in a reflex gesture. "Oh, my God ..."

"What is it?" Elias asked in alarm.

Nuria was staring at the cellphone as if she hadn't heard him. She went on reading aloud. "CL-20 is the material with the largest capacity for destruction currently known to man"—she raised her eyes to Elias's and added ominously—"surpassed only by nuclear devices."

42

Ten minutes later, as they sat unmoving in the gridlock caused by the rain, Elias finished a conversation he'd been having in Arabic on his phone and turned to Nuria. She was still using the back-seat screen to search for information about the explosive compound.

"Apparently," he said, "CL-20 is used as a plastic explosive for mining in cases where the rock is extremely hard. It's also used by the Special Forces in some foreign countries. It's not something you can buy at your local corner store, but with the right contacts and plenty of money, you can get hold of it."

"Here in Spain?"

"No, not in Spain, but you can in other parts of Europe. A French company called Eurekol has the patent."

"So if this explosive can be bought in Europe," Nuria reasoned, "then maybe what arrived in the container from the Caliphate of Mecca wasn't CL-20?"

"Maybe," Elias admitted. "But in the contraband world, transportation routes don't usually follow the shortest path."

"What do you mean?"

"That although the logical course of action might seem simply to bring that explosive directly from France by truck, with no need to go through customs or border patrol stations, in practice it's rarely done that way. In the interests of covering the smugglers' tracks and so that whatever company is selling the contraband can plead innocence, the usual thing is for cargo like that to pass through various countries, changing hands several times, until the trail gets lost somewhere in Africa or Eastern Europe."

"And the merchandise ends up in some port like Jeddah," Nuria said, remembering. "And from there it'll be sent back to Europe with nobody the wiser."

"Exactly."

Nuria let out a long sigh and massaged her temples. Her headache was threatening to come back. "Summing up," she murmured, "it looks like we have a terrorist commando group running around the city sewers with … how much? A thousand? Two thousand kilos of CL-20?"

"In fact," Elias said with a frown, "they might also have falsified the weight of the container. In that case," he added grimly, "we might be talking about four or five tons."

Nuria put her hand to her mouth. "Holy Mother of God," she muttered. "What ... what could they manage to do with all that?"

Elias exhaled a long breath, calculating the answer. "I'm no expert, but I once saw Daesh destroy a whole building with less than a hundred kilos of dynamite. So with five thousand kilos of the most powerful explosive known to man ... who knows? They might blow up an entire neighborhood. It would be the largest terrorist attack in history."

Nuria shut her eyes. Her headache had come back and was getting worse.

"We have to stop them," she said firmly.

"I know," Elias said, the same worried expression on his face. "But all we have is a scrap of paper and a mountain of speculation. And there are no more clues left for us to follow."

Nuria half opened her eyes and gave him a sidelong glance. "There just might be," she said, touching the vehicle's terminal with her bracelet to link it. "Call Susana," she said in a low voice.

The electronic bracelet's small loudspeaker emitted a couple of buzzes, after which they heard Susana's voice. "Hello?"

"Susi, it's me."

"Nuria?" Susana asked, lowering her voice conspiratorially. "What's up? Everything okay?"

"It could be better," Nuria said evasively. "Do you have the results of the prints yet?"

"I just got them."

"And?"

"Not much," she confessed. "The print you found on the vehicle window is a partial match for one that was on the water bottle, but it's not conclusive. They would never admit it as evidence in a trial."

"That won't be a problem. Give me what you have."

"I doubt whether it'll be any use, Nuria. The list of possible matches is too long."

"How many?"

"Over a hundred, and that's just in the province of Barcelona."

"Fuck," Nuria sighed, her headache besieging her on one side and the bad news on the other.

Unexpectedly, Elias's voice asked beside her, "How many of the matches are men?"

"Who's that?" Susana asked suspiciously.

Nuria took a moment to decide how honest she ought to be. "A friend."

"A friend?" Susana repeated in surprise. "Since when do you have friends?"

Nuria interrupted her. "Enough, Susi. Trust me, please."

"You're making it difficult for me, Nuria."

"I know, but I need you to help me without asking questions. It's for your own good," she added. "Believe me."

A sigh of resignation sounded on the other end of the line. "Fifty-seven," Susana said finally. "Fifty-seven of the matches are men."

"Thanks, Susi. And how many of those are Muslims?"

"Muslims? Wait a moment while I check … Fourteen. Yes, fourteen."

"That's still too many," Elias murmured.

"Yeah, we have to reduce the circle," Nuria agreed, sounding thoughtful.

"What are you looking for?" Susana interrupted. "If you tell me, I might be able to help."

"The less you know—"

"Stop with that shit, for God's sake!" her friend snapped. "Tell me what the fuck you're looking for or I'm hanging up right now."

Nuria gave in. "All right. But you've got to swear you won't tell anybody any of what I'm going to tell you unless I ask you to."

"Okay," she said reluctantly, "I won't tell."

"I mean it, Susi. Swear."

"Jesus," she sighed. "All right … I swear. Now spill."

"I'm looking for people with possible Islamic connections," Nuria revealed. "People who"—she paused, wondering whether or not to take the final step—"might take part in a terrorist attack."

"A terrorist attack? Are you serious?"

"I'm afraid so."

"But what the fuck have you gotten yourself into, Nuria?"

"I'm still not sure," Nuria confessed. "But I think there might be a group of jihadists preparing an attack on Barcelona."

"Holy shit! You've got to contact the counterterrorism division right away!"

"No, not yet. I still need more evidence."

"It doesn't matter, they'll search for it themselves. You've got to warn them!"

"No, Susi," Nuria insisted. "Until I've got something more solid to offer them, all they're going to do is get in my way, thinking it's some maneuver on my part to let me wiggle out of things. At the moment the best chance of stopping them is to keep counterterrorism on the sidelines."

"Goddamn it, Nuria. That's not the way things are done."

"I don't have any other choice. Please help me."

225

Susana remained silent for a few moments. Even without seeing her, Nuria could picture the look of annoyance on her friend's face as she struggled with herself. Finally a *tsk* at the other end of the line told her Susana had given in. "Of the fourteen," she said, her tone resigned, "three have been investigated for jihadist connections or sympathies. But one of them's in jail," she added, "so there are only two at liberty. I'm sending you the data."

"Great. Thank you, Susi."

"I don't like what's going on at all," Susana said grimly.

"So I can imagine. Neither do I."

"Now what are you going to do?"

Nuria turned toward Elias, who had decided to remain silent. "I think I'll go talk to those two men."

"Jesus, that's stupid, Nuria. If one of them turns out to be a terrorist—"

"Don't worry, I've got backup." She snuck a look at Elias, sitting next to her in the car. "I'll be fine."

"I should go with you," Susana suggested. "That way at least—"

"No way," Nuria interrupted her. "You've done too much already. Besides, I swear I'll be careful. Nothing's going to happen to me."

"Christ, Nuria. You mean nothing *else* is going to happen to you."

"Yes, that's what I meant." Nuria smiled in spite of herself. "Just trust me, okay?"

Susana exhaled in resignation. "Fine, I'll trust you. But you have to promise me that if you find out one of those two is a jihadist, you'll get the hell out of there and warn the counterterrorism squad."

"Definitely. I promise."

"Jesus, Nuria, you're such a bad liar."

"Well, you know ... I'm out of practice."

"All right." Her friend gave in. "Be extra careful, okay?"

"I will."

"And you, whoever you are"—she turned her attention to Elias—"you'd better make sure nothing happens to her, or else I'll find you and cut off your balls, understood?"

The corners of Elias's lips lifted in the hint of a smile at the threat. "Understood."

"Enough, Susi," Nuria interrupted, shaking her head. "I have to leave you now."

"All right. Keep me in the loop."

"Of course. See you."

"Damn it, Nu—" Susana began, realizing her friend was lying again, but her words were lost in cyberspace when Nuria hung up. She went on staring at the black screen thoughtfully.

226

"Here they are," Elias said next to her, waking her from her trance. "One lives in Villarefu and the other— Well, that's interesting."

"What is?"

He looked up. "The other one lives in the Raval. A couple of blocks or so from where we just were."

43

Sitting at a table outside a popular café, sheltered from the rain under the arcade of Vicenç Martorell square, Nuria and Elias kept their eyes trained on the door of a small mosque at ground level on the opposite side of the street.

Evening had darkened into night under the leaden sky. The rain had refused to let up, as though God had forgotten to make it rain all year and was now attempting to make up for His lapse in just a few days.

Nuria set her cup on its saucer and checked the time on her bracelet: five minutes to eight.

Elias jerked his head in the direction of the mosque. "There he is."

Nuria looked up and saw half a dozen men wearing wide robes, with skullcaps covering their heads and thick curly beards. She recognized Abdul Saha at once. Completely unaware that he was being watched, he chatted animatedly with another worshipper as he opened a black umbrella against the rain.

He lifted his right hand to his chest in farewell, then turned and walked up Les Ramelleres Street, dodging the puddles so as not to get the hem of his robe wet, oblivious to the two men who had begun to follow him a few yards behind. Passing the table where Elias and Nuria sat without a second glance, he continued up the street.

"Let's go," Elias said, standing up as soon as his men had passed them. Nuria got to her feet as well. Pulling her hat down firmly over her ears, she followed in the footsteps of the two Kurds, who were walking a few yards ahead.

The touristy souvenir shops of Tallers Street were already beginning to close due to the dearth of possible customers, and only a handful of people huddled under the canvas awning of a shawarma stall. The four of them were among the few people on the street, and Nuria prayed Abdul wouldn't turn around. If he did, he would immediately realize he was being followed. Luckily, the drumming of the rain on the pavement muffled the sound of their footfalls and they reached Castilla Square without their target becoming aware of their very noticeable presence.

That was when Elias put his right hand to his ear. Pressing the inconspicuous earbud with his finger, he addressed a few words in Arabic to his team. At once Aza and Yihan quickened their pace until they were flanking the presumed jihadist. While one pretended to ask him about an address, the other took a small syringe of ketamine from his pocket. With a swift move, he jabbed the third man in the shoulder.

Abdul turned at once to Yihan, surprise visible on his face, and reached for the spot where he'd been injected, but Yihan raised his arms innocently.

Nuria and Elias had almost overtaken them when Abdul took a trembling step back. Startled, he put a hand to his forehead. Aza grabbed him by the shoulders. To anyone watching, it would have looked like the act of a Good Samaritan helping a stranger who was about to faint. This impression was reinforced when Abdul lost his balance. The two Kurds held him up between them carefully to keep him from collapsing, then sat him gently down on the ground.

A group of tourists watched the scene curiously as they dined under the awning of one of the restaurants in the square, but neither they nor any of the few passersby who had witnessed the event made any attempt to come and help.

In fact, Elias and Nuria were the only ones to approach the scene. Between the four of them they surrounded the fallen man, taking his bracelet and patting him down discreetly in search of a weapon.

"You sure it's him?" Nuria asked, suddenly concerned that they might have the wrong person.

"I'm sure," Elias confirmed, taking out his cell and quickly scanning the man's face.

A gray, unmarked delivery van came into the square and pulled to the curb beside them. The door slid open. From inside Yady urged his compatriots to hurry. Quickly, Aza and Yihan climbed into the vehicle, carrying the unconscious Abdul between them.

Nuria and Elias walked on as if none of this had anything to do with them. The van carrying Abdul and the three Kurds drove off with a squeal of tires. "I've just acted as an accessory to a kidnapping," Nuria murmured as she watched the van drive away. "This just gets better and better." The black Suburban came into the square with Giwan at the wheel, stopping in the same place the van had only seconds before.

"To make an omelet," Elias said philosophically, "you have to break some eggs."

Ten minutes later, after twisting and turning down a series of narrow streets, Giwan stopped the Suburban in front of the metal roll-up door of a shop with an abandoned air on a rundown industrial street in the Poble Sec neighborhood.

When Nuria saw Elias opening the door of the SUV and preparing to get out, she asked, "Where are we?"

"Don't you recognize it?" he answered enigmatically.

Nuria was trying to guess what he meant when Giwan pulled up the metal security door and she recognized its unmistakable screech. "You mean I don't have to wear a hood any longer?" she asked sarcastically when she realized they were at the hideout where she'd spent so many hours locked up.

Elias merely smiled conspiratorially. "Shall we?" he asked when the metal door had risen far enough to let them through. Nuria took a deep breath as if about to dive off a high dive and followed Elias into the shop as Giwan closed the metal door behind them. The gray van was already parked in the front room. Turning on the light, they went around the van to the door that opened into the real hideout.

This time there was no chain on the door. When Nuria went in, what she saw immediately chased the smell of damp and the memory of the roaches hiding under the mattress from her mind. In the middle of the room, kneeling on the floor with his hands tied behind his back and a black hood over his head—possibly the same one she'd been forced to wear herself—Abdul Saha was mumbling words in Arabic as he rocked back and forth. Nuria wondered for a moment whether he was praying or sobbing, then realized he was doing both.

Someone had poured a bucket of water on him to wake him up and his robe was soaking wet and clinging to his body, giving him an even more helpless look. Surrounded by the team of Kurds, Nuria was reminded of the images she'd seen of Iraqi prisoners in the infamous prison of Abu Ghraib.

For a few moments Elias watched the helpless man who went on mumbling prayers. With a snort of disgust, he glanced at his men and nodded heavily.

Aza went to fetch the dirty bathroom towel. Pulling Abdul's head back, he stretched it over his face while Giwan refilled the bucket with water. The other two held the unfortunate wretch by the shoulders.

Without a word, Giwan began to pour water over the towel, little by little, on the spot where it covered Abdul's nose and mouth. At first nothing happened, but after a few seconds, when Abdul was forced to breathe, he found he was unable to with the water flooding his mouth and nostrils.

With a desperate spasm he tried to shake the water out, but the three Kurds held him firmly. Mercilessly, Giwan continued to empty the contents of the bucket until the liquid reached Abdul's lungs and the unfortunate man began to convulse horribly, on the verge of drowning. Even so, Giwan carried on with his cruel ritual until all the water in the bucket was gone. The Kurds let him go and Abdul collapsed to the floor, coughing spasmodically and gasping breathlessly, desperate for a mouthful of air.

Elias squatted down in front of him. "Abdul Saha," he said in Spanish, when he saw that the man was finally able to breathe again. "Is that your name?"

"*Madha taraydaa*?" was the answer.

"I ask the questions. You answer," Elias hissed menacingly in his ear. "Are you Abdul Saha?"

"Yes, that's me," he replied hesitantly, obviously fearful of the consequences of admitting his name.

"I'm going to ask you some questions," Elias went on in the same tone. "If you tell us the truth, we'll let you go. But if you refuse to talk or lie to us ... well, we'll stay here until you die. Is that clear?"

Abdul merely nodded vehemently, seemingly without the strength to answer. Nuria imagined his face, contracted with terror under the black felt hood.

"Great," Elias said. "Now tell me, where are the explosives? Where's the rest of your group hiding? What's the target for the attack?"

In reply, Abdul raised his head in Elias's direction, as if unsure he'd heard the questions right. "What ... what attack?"

Elias passed a hand over his forehead. Without another word, he stood up and nodded to his men once again. Seizing Abdul by the shoulders again, they forced him to his knees. Aza replaced the towel on his face as Giwan went to fill the bucket.

"No! No!" Abdul screamed in terror. "I don't know anything! I don't know anything! I swear it! I don't know anything!"

The sound of the water filling the bucket muffled Abdul's cries, and Nuria felt her heart contracting at the man's raw terror. Horrified by what she was seeing, she took Elias's arm, opened the door, and pulled him out of the room. "There must be some other way to do this," she said once the door had closed behind them.

"Possibly," Elias said, "but I don't know it, and we don't have the time to research it."

Nuria pointed to the door they'd just come through. "But it's wrong. Very wrong. And suppose we've got the wrong man? Suppose he doesn't know anything?"

Elias shrugged. "If that's the case, we'll know soon enough. My people know what they're doing."

"Fuck. We're torturing him, for God's sake. I ... I can't."

"We have no choice." Elias took her by the shoulders to calm her. "We're doing what needs to be done. If he's a terrorist, there's no other way to get him to confess."

"But suppose he isn't? We'll be torturing an innocent man." She stared at him, trying to interpret his silence.

"I have to get back in there," he said. "But I think you should go for a walk." He gestured at the metal roll-up door. "You don't need to be here."

Nuria hesitated, looking towards the door and struggling against all her principles. "I know, but I'm staying," she said in a voice that didn't sound like

231

hers, then followed him back into the room. "Let's get this over with once and for all."

44

A half hour later, Abdul Saha lay huddled on the floor like a limp rag, the sopping remains of what had been a man, stripped of his dignity and the hope of seeing the next dawn, a shivering ball of trembling, pitiful flesh. He'd soiled himself out of sheer terror, in a final defensive conditioned reflex, passed down from the time when we were apes about to be devoured by a predator.

Nuria watched the scene from a corner, nauseated and mesmerized at the same time, realizing how easy it was to strip a man of his dignity, strip him of everything he believes himself to be until he becomes nothing more than a blubbering infant.

Watching Abdul Saha hugging his knees in the middle of a puddle of water and feces, Nuria understood that a human being is nothing but a series of layers, real and imagined, superimposed on each other, that we use to protect ourselves from a dangerous world. But pain and the certainty of immediate death could peel off those layers like an onion, leaving exposed what we really are: frightened animals.

"That's enough lies," Elias said, standing in front of his victim. "We know about your ties to ISMA."

Abdul had barely enough strength left to shake his head imperceptibly. "No ..." He coughed painfully, trying to expel the water inundating his lungs. "I ... don't ..."

"Stop lying and I'll make them stop. You're doing this to yourself."

"I don't ... know anything ..."

Elias crouched and put his lips to Abdul's ear. "We have your fingerprints from the van," he whispered as if confiding a secret, "and at the shop where you unloaded, which just happens to be right next to your house."

Despite his wretched state, Abdul managed to look up and frown in bewilderment. "Van?" There was desperation in his voice. "What ... shop?"

Elias grunted in disappointment, then put his hands on his knees and pushed himself to a standing position, shooting a meaningful look at Giwan, who was holding the red plastic bucket.

"Enough!" Nuria cried. "The poor guy doesn't know anything."

Elias frowned in irritation. "Don't interrupt," he said through clenched teeth. "Leave the room if you don't want to see it, but don't interrupt again."

She took a step forward. "But don't you see?" she insisted. "This man may be an extremist, but he doesn't know a damn thing about the attack."

"You don't know that."

"Damn it all, of course I know. Look at him," she persisted. "I've never seen anyone more terrified in my whole life. If he knew anything, he'd have told us by now."

Elias still looked annoyed, but Nuria could see in his eyes that he realized she was right. "All right," he conceded. Turning to the wreck of what had been Abdul Saha, he said, "I'll call someone to take care of him."

"Take care of him?" Nuria asked, alarmed. "What does that mean?"

He shook his head. "Take it easy. We'll just keep him here for a while under surveillance."

"Is that necessary?"

"That's nonnegotiable. Until I'm absolutely sure he's not a threat, I'm not going to risk letting him go free."

Nuria glanced at the abject pile of wet clothing in front of her, recognizing that Elias's plan was the most sensible one. "Fine," she said reluctantly. "So what do we do now? We still have another name on the list," she added.

Elias dried his hands on his pants. "Well, we need to go and pay him a visit."

Twenty minutes later, the Suburban was driving in the direction of Villarefu through the wide industrial streets near El Prat, keeping strictly to the speed limit. Nuria punched something into the phone and the file and photo of one Ali Hussain appeared on the screen.

"Seventeen years old," she read. "He's just a kid."

Beside her in the back seat of the SUV, Elias gave her a sidelong glance. "I've seen ten-year-old children wielding assault rifles, murdering entire families in cold blood."

Nuria didn't know what to say to that, so she turned her attention back to the phone she held in her hands. "He has priors for stealing a motorbike," she went on, "and was investigated for following jihadist groups on social networks. That's all."

"A rap sheet like that," Elias pointed out, "could apply to half the kids in Villarefu."

"Well, it's all we have," Nuria said, setting the phone down in her lap. "If it turns out he doesn't know anything either, we'll have to widen the search to include men without connections to extremism."

Elias frowned at her words. "How many are we talking about?"

Nuria looked down at the cell. "Fourteen," she read, "and that's only counting Muslims who live in the province of Barcelona."

"That's too many," Elias said firmly. "We can't interrogate fourteen possible extremists."

"I know."

"If this Ali doesn't know anything either—" He shook his head.

"What?"

Elias turned to her with an air of apology. "I think you should leave."

"Leave? What are you talking about?"

"I'm saying that if this kid doesn't lead us anywhere you ought to leave the country. Start a new life someplace else. You won't be able to do anything here except wait for the cops to arrest you."

"You don't get it, do you?" Nuria asked with a frown. "I don't want to start a new life. I want to get back the one I had before."

"No, you're the one who doesn't get it," Elias pointed out. "That life isn't coming back. Even if you found those terrorists, you'd get at most a pat on the back and be sent home—but too many things have happened for you to go back to being a cop."

"You don't know that."

"Of course I do. And so do you, for God's sake. If you want to keep lying to yourself, knock yourself out, but that's not going to change anything."

Nuria clenched her fists in fury. "And what about you? Where did all that anti-jihadist talk go? You don't care anymore that there could be an attack?"

"If I didn't care, I wouldn't be here right now," Elias said, "but I don't have a warrant on my head. Not yet, at least. I can go on investigating without impediments."

"Is that what I am now? An impediment?"

"I didn't say that," he corrected her. "But every minute you spend with me looking for those extremists all over the city makes it more likely you'll end up in jail."

"What I do is my own business."

"But it matters to me."

"Well, that's your problem," she said disdainfully. "Not mine."

Elias opened his mouth to reply, then closed it and faced front again. "As you wish," he grunted. He didn't open his mouth again until they'd arrived at the Villarefu checkpoint.

Nuria wasn't really surprised when she saw the Suburban glide through the checkpoint. A simple flash of the SUV's headlights was enough for the watchman to recognize the vehicle and lift the barrier, letting them through without even attempting to check who was inside. It was clear who the real authority in Villarefu was, and that the police would always be several steps behind Elias and others like him.

Thanks to the rain, the streets of the slum were a sea of mud. The refugees labored through the streets, their sandaled feet sunk up to the ankles in mud, while the children, oblivious to the persistent rain, played in the puddles, jumping up and down and throwing water at each another as if they were at the beach.

The bulletproof Suburban wound through the maze of poorly lit streets, finally coasting to a halt a few yards from a single-story construction of raw cinderblock with a tin roof. Under a bulb hanging in the doorway, a dozen men and women waited in front of the house, heads down, protecting themselves against the rain with raincoats or scraps of plastic that stood in for umbrellas.

Giwan, always economical with his words, pointed to the group. "There."

Elias leaned forward in his seat. "Are you sure?"

"Sure," he confirmed, showing him the location on the dashboard screen.

"What are all these people doing here?" Nuria asked.

"I don't know," Elias said. "But I don't like it." Opening the door of the vehicle, he got out, telling the others to wait. In two long strides he crossed the street to the house.

In the light of the headlights, Nuria saw him introducing himself. The group's initial reactions of surprise quickly turned into elaborate shows of respect, bordering on devotion. Elias immediately became the center of attention of everyone in the crowd. Nuria watched as they pointed to the house and shook their heads apprehensively.

"Fuck this," Nuria said. Opening her door, she too got out.

"You wait," Giwan ordered, pointing to the back seat. "Here."

"Whatever you say, handsome." She adjusted her cap and slammed the door. Dodging the deepest puddles, she sauntered over to Elias and took her place beside him, making it clear she was with him. The small crowd fell silent as soon as they saw her appear.

"I told you to stay in the car," Elias said reprovingly.

"I heard you the first time. *Layla saidda*," she greeted the group in Arabic, slightly inclining her head, then turned to Elias again. "What's going on? Why are all these people here?"

"That's just what this lady was explaining to me," he said, not bothering to hide his annoyance. He indicated an old woman with parchment-like skin, wearing a worn-out niqab, who was sheltering from the rain under a burlap ACNUR sack. "I'm afraid we arrived too late."

"Late? What do you mean? Has the boy left?"

236

"No, he's in there." Elias indicated the open door of the house through which filtered the trembling light of candles. "They're laying him out for his funeral."

45

Sheltering from the rain in the narrow doorway of the house, Nuria listened in disbelief to Elias's explanation after he'd emerged from inside.

"A heart attack?" she repeated suspiciously.

"That's what they told me."

"Someone as young as that? It's hard to believe."

"Right. Sounds odd, to be honest," Elias agreed.

Nuria looked toward the hallway leading into the house. "I'd like to examine the body. Check whether there are any marks on it."

Elias shook his head. "You can't do that. Only the family and those close to them have the right to keep vigil over the body."

"You could," Nuria said. "I saw the way these people reacted to your presence. For them, it's an honor that you've come."

"Maybe," he accepted. "But there's no way I'm going to strip the shroud off this poor woman's dead son's body."

"I will."

"I'm sure you would," Elias muttered, "but you're not going to. Forget it."

Nuria clicked her tongue in annoyance. "The fact that he was a jihad sympathizer, that his fingerprint was on the stolen van, and that he just happened to die at this particular moment—it's too much of a coincidence."

"Are you suggesting that he was killed to wipe out the trail?"

"That's exactly what I'm thinking."

"Jihadists don't usually act that way."

"Maybe," Nuria said, "but there's always a first time for everything. Maybe the boy let his tongue run away with him, or recanted, or whatever. The fact is that if Abdul Saha doesn't know anything, this is the only thread we can pull right now."

Elias nodded toward the house, from which issued the sound of muffled whispers and prayers. "Let me remind you, the boy's dead. That makes it a little difficult to interrogate him."

"Yeah, but we can check his belongings," Nuria suggested. "We might find something."

"I don't think—"

"Are you going to do this willingly?" Nuria burst out. "Or would you rather I do it myself?"

Elias pinched the bridge of his nose as if keeping an incipient headache at bay. "All right," he snapped. "You wait here." Reluctantly, he went back into the house, murmuring apologies, and came out again two minutes later accompanied by a gaunt man with sunken eyes and cheeks wearing a worn-out jacket that was coming apart at the seams. "This is Ibrahim Hussain," he said, his tone sorrowful. "Ali's father."

"My most heartfelt condolences for your loss," Nuria said, bowing her head slightly.

Elias translated her words and the man responded with a heartfelt *shukran*, putting his right hand over his heart. He led them down a dark, narrow hallway that opened into a room the size of a cell, with a tiny window near the tin roof and a bead curtain that served as a door. The austere assortment of furniture consisted of a bed pushed against the wall, a set of shelves overflowing with books, and a miniscule desk with an antiquated computer monitor and keyboard on it.

Ali's father waved an arm around the room, said something in Arabic, and went back to the wake, next to his son's body.

"This is his room," Elias said. "Was," he corrected himself.

Nuria turned in a circle, studying the collection of posters that lined the rough walls of the room, showing YouTubers, drone-racing pilots, teenage gamers with outrageous hairdos, and scantily dressed women standing next to Formula E racecars.

"This certainly doesn't look like the room of a radical extremist," Nuria commented.

"No, it doesn't," Elias agreed. He picked up an old issue of Playboy that lay on a shelf. "He doesn't even have a picture of Mecca or a verse from the Quran. I'm afraid we're barking up the wrong tree again."

Nuria clicked her tongue in frustration. "Shit," she muttered, realizing they'd come to a dead end in this teenager's room.

Elias put the magazine back on the shelf. "There's nothing more we can do here. Shall we go?"

"Wait," Nuria pleaded, reluctant to abandon this last hope. "Now that we're here, let's take a look."

"Whatever you want. The father's given us five minutes."

"So let's use them." She indicated the bookshelf. "You look there while I check the drawers."

"Fine. But what are we looking for?"

239

"I really don't know," she admitted as she bent over the desk. "Anything that doesn't fit in with a teenager."

"With a refugee teenager," Elias clarified, picking magazines up off the shelves and leafing through them before putting them back. "And one who was very interested in technology," he added after a while. "Practically all the magazines are about artificial intelligence and robotics. He's even got some technical books on the subject." He turned one over to check the price on the back cover. "Very expensive books, by the way. This one cost nearly a hundred and fifty euros."

Nuria slammed the sock drawer shut and turned to him. "Seriously?" she asked in surprise. "Where would he get that kind of money?"

"That's not the question," Elias said. Setting the book back on the shelf, he picked up another that looked equally boring. "The correct question is, why would he spend it on a book entitled *Design and Application of Sensors and Interfaces in Motor Control Artificial Intelligence*?"

"What the hell is that?"

"Something about sensors and interfaces in motor-control AI."

"Oh, right. Thanks for the clarification."

"What do you want me to say? I don't know anything about the subject either. But it's obvious that young Ali had mastered it."

Nuria looked around. "Hold on … here's a monitor and a keyboard, but where's the actual computer?"

Elias nodded. "That's true. I don't see his bracelet anywhere, either."

"That's right," said Nuria. "Do you think"—she waved in the direction of the mourners—"he might still have it on?"

"Impossible," Elias said firmly. "It has to be here somewhere. Let's do a more thorough search."

"All right." She bent over to look under the bed. "I'll look for the bracelet and the computer. You go ask the parents, in case they know what happened."

Two minutes later, Elias returned, shaking his head. "They say they don't know. Apparently he kept very much to himself. He told them he was studying something to do with the latest technology and that he was going to get them all out of Villarefu."

"And he didn't say who was picking up the tab for such expensive studies?"

Elias shook his head. "Apparently he'd also found a job, and sometimes he took a little black box of this size to work." He cupped his hands around a small imaginary lunchbox. " I guess that was the computer."

"And what job did he have?"

240

"They don't know that either. Even though he told them it had something to do with his studies, sometimes he would come back covered with dirt."

"That's odd."

"Not that odd. Teenagers can be very reserved," he reminded her. "My niece barely tells me what she does or whom she goes out with."

"Yeah, but in this case his computer, bracelet, and smartphone are missing too," Nuria pointed out. "I haven't been able to find them anywhere."

"Maybe he didn't have one."

"A teenager addicted to technology without a smartphone?" Nuria raised an eyebrow. "It'd be easier to find a Reborn without his crucifix."

"Mm," Elias admitted, realizing how little sense his suggestion had made. "I don't know what else—" he began, then broke off, his gaze settling on a small book with a brown leather cover and elaborate, incomprehensible letters on the spine. "That's strange."

"What's that? A Quran?"

"Almost. It's the *Sahih Al-Bukhari*," he read aloud as he took it from the shelf. "A book of hadith." Seeing Nuria's blank look, he explained. "Something like a compilation of sentences Mohammed is supposed to have uttered."

"And why should that seem odd to you?"

"Because it's not the kind of book people usually have in their homes. Not even believers, and this kid doesn't seem like a believer." Elias ran a hand over the cover. Its lettering was in raised gold relief stamped into the leather. "Besides, it looks like quite an expensive book."

"Let me check something," Nuria said, taking it from his hands. As Elias had said, the book smelled of money.

"Don't tell me you can read Arabic?" he asked, knowing the answer already.

Nuria ignored him, carefully turning over the first few pages of fine India paper until she found what she was looking for. "What's this?" she asked, turning the book around so he could read it.

"A seal."

"I can see that, but what kind of seal?"

"It's from a mosque." Elias read aloud, "*Ciutat Diagonal Islamic Cultural Center*."

"I know it," Nuria said. "That's a mosque built in the upper part of Esplugues, not far from where you live."

Elias nodded. "I know. I visited it a couple of times until the Saudi refugees arrived in their private jets, fleeing from their own war. The vibe got too Wahhabi for my taste."

"Wahhabi? I seem to remember you mentioning that."

"It's the least tolerant branch of Islam," Elias explained, "and the jihadist movements take their inspiration from it. It's backed and financed by the caliphates of the old Saudi Arabia."

Nuria looked up at him. "Caliphates?" she asked when she heard the word, her eyes very wide. "Like the Caliphate of Mecca?"

"That's right," he said. Looking at the book in her hands, he noticed a bookmark peeking out from between the pages. "Let me take a look at that."

Nuria handed him back the hadith, and he opened it at the marked page, where a paragraph had been underlined in pencil. *"Let those fight for the cause of Allah who are capable of sacrificing the worldly life for the other,"* he translated, following the paragraph with his finger. *"To whoever fights for the cause of Allah, whether he falls in defeat or triumphs, we shall give a magnificent reward. Why do you not fight for the cause of Allah when there are oppressed men, women, and children who say Lord! Save us from the oppressors who live in this city. Send us those who will protect and succor us."*

Elias finished reading the quotation. Closing the book, he ran his fingers again over the embossed green and gold of the cover, heaving a sigh with the bitterness of someone who finds his worst suspicions confirmed. He looked up at Nuria, but her expression was very different.

He could have sworn she was almost smiling.

46

The rain had begun to fall heavily again by the time the Suburban coasted to a gentle halt a block from the Ciutat Diagonal Islamic Cultural Center. It was a nondescript one-story concrete building without a minaret, surrounded by glass-walled office buildings and houses with front gardens. It might have passed for a simple library if not for the subtle Arabic motifs which could be glimpsed in the latticed windows.

Elias took a quick look at the building, shrouded in the rain. "It's very late. At this hour there's pretty sure to be nobody in the mosque."

Nuria looked at the discreet temple, illuminated by the streetlights whose orange light made the tiny raindrops sparkle. She unfastened her seat belt. "Well, if there's nobody, then we'll come back tomorrow. But let's make sure."

Elias turned to her. "It's just that I'm not sure that ... speaking to the imam is a good idea. I think we ought to try a more subtle approach."

"There's no time for subtlety." Her hand was already on the door handle. "If they murdered that kid, it's because, for some reason, they want to wipe out his trail. So we have to hurry. If we don't ..." She left the portentous sentence hanging in the air as she opened the door and got out.

Pulling her hat down over her ears again, she went around the vehicle and quickly covered the fifty yards that separated her from the main door of the building. When she reached the shelter of the doorway she looked for a buzzer, but there was none in sight, not even a bell like the ones in old houses.

Elias ran through the rain to join her under the overhanging roof. "Look," he said. Nuria looked up and saw a small camera hidden in a corner under the lintel. The blinking red light meant that it was activated and recording. "It's an intercom with facial recognition," Elias said. "That wasn't here before."

"A bit excessive for a mosque, surely?"

"Let's go to the back. There's a service door with a doorbell." Elias motioned for his men to wait in the vehicle. Hugging the wall to protect themselves from the rain, they walked around the building, which occupied almost half a block. Entering the alley that separated the mosque from an adjoining office complex, they found the safety door under a green emergency exit sign. There was a small intercom beside it. Nuria pressed her finger on it long and hard.

Elias threw her a sidelong glance, probably thinking this was no way to ring a bell at midnight, but as the seconds ticked by and nobody answered he refrained from comment. "Well, we tried," he said, checking the time on his watch. "We'll have to come back tomo—"

"Yes?" said a metallic-sounding voice.

It took Elias several seconds to react. Nuria took advantage of his silence to take the initiative and bent close to the intercom. "Good evening. Are you Imam"—she looked down at her phone, where the name and photo appeared on the mosque's website—"Mohammed Ibn Marrash?"

The voice on the intercom seemed to hesitate. "Who are you?" the person asked in return, with the strong accent of someone who doesn't often use the language. "What do you want?"

"My name is Nuria." She glanced at Elias from the corner of her eye before saying the lie they'd prepared on their way there. "A friend of Ali Hussain's family."

The Imam's only reply was a long silence.

"*Salam aleykum,* sheikh," Elias put in when there was no answer. "We've come from Ali Hussain's house to inform you of an unfortunate event. The boy died this very morning. You knew him, didn't you?"

"Ali Hussain?" the voice asked after an imperceptible pause. "Yes, he came here once or twice in search of spiritual guidance. Poor boy ... I knew nothing of this. We are from Allah and to Him we must return."

"Could we talk to you about him for a moment?" Nuria put in impatiently without waiting for Elias to reply.

"Who are you?" the imam asked.

"This is Nuria Badal and I'm Elias Zafrani, sheikh," Elias said. "An old worshipper at this mosque."

"I don't recall your name."

"Unfortunately," Elias said apologetically, "it's a long time since I came to pray."

This time the pause was longer. Just when Nuria was thinking he was going to suggest they come back the next day, the door opened with an electric buzz.

"Come in," the imam invited them via the intercom. "I'll be with you in a minute."

Elias and Nuria exchanged a look of genuine surprise.

"I wasn't expecting him to agree," Elias said.

"Oh ye of little faith ..." Nuria said mockingly, pushing open the door.

Elias took her arm to hold her back. "Wait. You need to put this on." As though he were a magician, the veil she'd left in the car the night before appeared in his hands.

"Is it necessary?"

"It's a mosque," he said simply.

"All right," she said with a sigh. Taking it from his hands, she put it over her head on top of her cap without checking whether a lock of hair was poking out.

They crossed the threshold and the door closed behind them with a click. Suddenly aware that they were alone, Nuria instinctively touched the grip of Giwan's gun that she still carried under her shirt, stuck into the waistband of her jeans.

The interior of the building was lit only by faint emergency lights. After walking down a corridor lined with closed doors that looked like storage rooms and offices, they came to what Nuria guessed must be the lobby of the mosque. It looked like a combined waiting room and dressing room, furnished with benches, boxes where shoes could be left and a kind of washbasin at floor level.

At the far end of the lobby, wide, wooden double doors offered access to the sanctuary. Nuria couldn't resist opening them and taking a look inside. She was surprised by the room's austerity, which matched the rest of the building. She'd had the vague idea that mosques were always decorated with intricate geometric motifs, spectacular chandeliers, and luxurious Persian rugs, but this one looked to her more like a boring conference room in some business hotel: an empty, nondescript space with halogen lights in the ceiling, gray wall-to-wall carpet, and walls painted a pale cream color. There was a discreet pulpit on the opposite wall.

"Excuse me," came the voice from the intercom behind her. She jumped. "You're not allowed in there."

Nuria whirled around to find herself facing a man as tall as herself, with a long gray beard, a calm gaze, and a beatific manner. A white taqiyah covered his shaven head, and he wore a matching wide, white robe over which he kept his hands intertwined.

"It's the men's prayer hall," he explained as he came toward them. "Women are not allowed to enter."

"No problem," Nuria lied. Offering him her hand, she added, "My name's Nuria Badal."

"And I'm Elias Zafrani, sheikh," Elias added, following her example.

The Imam took the hand Elias extended but ignored Nuria's, giving her a slight nod instead. "Mohammed Ibn Marrash," he introduced himself, once again interlacing his fingers over his chest. "But of course you already know that." Turning to Elias, he asked, "What can I do for you?"

245

"We'd like to ask you a couple of questions about Ali Hussain," Nuria intervened, annoyed by the imam's disdain.

Elias waited a few seconds, but when it became evident the imam was not going to reply directly to Nuria, he had no choice but to step in. "The family is keeping vigil over him, and they asked us to come and speak to you. They want to know whether he was a good believer."

"He was a very intelligent boy," the imam said. "But he was lost until he came here and found peace in the words of the Prophet Mohammed, may the peace and blessing of Allah be with him."

"Did you know he was a refugee?"

"That's right."

"But refugees don't usually come to this center, do they? This place is quite distant, and your worshippers are usually"—he paused, looking for the right word—"wealthier people, isn't that right?"

The imam stiffened. "All Muslims are welcome in this mosque, regardless of race or social condition. Even infidels may attend, if they so wish."

"But why did the boy come all the way to this mosque?" Nuria insisted.

The imam blinked indifferently, as if he'd heard nothing but the rain falling outside. Elias took over again. "Why do you think he decided to come to this mosque? There are several in the refugee camp, a lot closer to home for him."

"That I don't know," the imam admitted. "Perhaps someone brought him, or perhaps Allah, may His name be praised, inspired him to come to this humble house of prayer and find the peace he needed."

Elias nodded. "I see. And how did he come here? Who brought him?"

"I couldn't tell you that either," the imam said apologetically. "As you'll understand, I can't know everything about the daily life of all my congregation. I guess some kind soul with his own vehicle."

"You guess?" Nuria put in again, but the imam continued to snub her.

"You're not sure?" Elias repeated, ignoring a vibration in his bracelet which indicated an incoming call from Giwan. He had no time for that.

"I never asked him," the cleric explained. "But he attended prayers regularly, so I took it for granted."

Elias nodded. "Of course. And did you ever notice who he interacted with?"

"What do you mean?"

"Whether he struck up a friendship with anybody in particular. Did he stay after prayers to talk to someone?"

The imam spread his hands wide to show his ignorance. "I don't know. I don't check on the faithful."

Nuria was unable to hold back. "Well, you've got the mosque surrounded by cameras."

246

The imam turned to her impatiently. "That's for reasons of safety. These are bad times for Muslims. It's a rare day when there isn't another graffiti on the façade or a window isn't broken by someone throwing a stone. I have no interest in keeping an eye on anybody."

"Of course not, sheikh," Elias said, trying to soothe him. "Ms. Badal didn't mean to offend you. I beg your pardon."

"That's all right." The imam nodded and turned to Elias once again. "And now, if there's nothing else I can do to help you—"

"Actually, there is," Nuria interrupted before he could finish the sentence. Seeing Elias's questioning look, she waved her hand, imitating the movement of a surveillance camera. He looked at her uncomprehendingly until she pointed to the ceiling and silently mouthed the word *recordings*.

Understanding at last what she meant, Elias asked, "Would it be possible to see the recordings of the surveillance cameras?" he asked. "That way we could see who the boy talked to and … find more friends of his we could tell about his passing."

The imam's reply was both quick and definitive. "Impossible."

"It'll only take a moment."

"I said, it's impossible," the imam said curtly.

"But—"

"No, and please don't insist," the imam warned him. "I can't do that, nor do I want to. I hope you understand."

Elias and Nuria exchanged a look of disappointment. There was nothing more to be gotten out of him. Nuria jerked her head toward the exit and Elias nodded. "Thank you very much for your help, sheikh," he said to the imam. "I hope I haven't caused too much trouble."

"A believer visiting Allah's house, may His name be praised, is never any trouble," the cleric recited with a sideways glance at Nuria, who muttered something under her breath. Without even attempting to say goodbye, she began to walk in the direction they'd come.

"You can go out by the main door if you wish," the imam indicated with an obsequious gesture, now that they were leaving. "And may Allah, may His name be praised, guide your steps."

"Thank you," Elias replied, following Nuria rather than Allah as she strode to the door, impatient to leave the building.

"What an imbecile," she muttered, loudly enough for the imam to hear.

"True, he wasn't much hel—" Elias said, stopping short when his bracelet vibrated again on his wrist. This time he took out his phone and answered. "Hello? What's the matter, Giwan?" What he heard from the Kurd's mouth made him freeze on the spot. "Nuria!" he cried, reaching out to her.

247

"Wait!" But it was too late. Nuria, eager to leave, had already opened the main door and stepped out into the rain.

Instantly several spotlights blinked on from the other side of the street, dazzling her with their white light as she stood on the threshold, lighting her up like a rock star walking onto a stage.

"On the ground! On the ground!" a commanding voice blared through a megaphone. "Police!"

47

Nuria couldn't recall the exact number of times she'd been in that interrogation room at the station, but there had been plenty of them. She'd almost always sat on one of those chairs that were nailed to the floor and designed to be uncomfortable, her elbows propped on the metal table, firing questions at the suspect like a machine gun without giving him time to think about the answers, looking for those contradictions that would betray him.

Tonight, however, she was the one on the wrong side of the table with her hands cuffed behind her back, and it was another police officer sitting opposite her, staring hard at her as if trying to read her mind.

Adding insult to injury, the officer across from her was none other than Sergeant Raul Navarro. Wearing a blue polo shirt embossed with the emblem of the police and a Spain First activity bracelet, he was leaning back in his chair, obviously enjoying the situation.

"What are we doing here?" Nuria asked after more than half an hour of sitting in silence without a single question. "You've got my signed statement, so what are we waiting for?"

"For the Virgin Mary to appear," Raul said mockingly. "We'll see if she performs a miracle to get you out of this."

She nodded. "I see ... By the way, how are those little balls of yours? Has the swelling gone down?" Leaning over the table, she gave him a conspiratorial wink. "No hard feelings, huh? Look on the bright side, now you won't need a magnifying glass to see them."

Raul smiled humorlessly. "You're well and truly fucked," he muttered under his breath. "And I'm so going to love watching you sink into the fucking mud."

"Yeah, I guess so." She shrugged, pretending indifference. "But hey, at least I won't have to see your stupid face so often. That's what I get out of it."

Raul gave an exaggerated snort. "Jesus, *stupid?* Is that the best you can come up with? My five-year-old daughter knows better insults than you do."

"So sorry."

"Don't worry, you'll have plenty of time to learn in the slammer."

"No, no." She shook her head. "I meant I'm sorry you're a father. Poor little girl. What a disappointment she's going to suffer when she finds out her father's a douchebag."

This time Raul's cruel smile spread across his face. "Better," he conceded. "But don't—"

The door opened with a click, interrupting him. The intimidating figure of Commissioner Puig stood on the threshold, wearing his full uniform and carrying a brown folder under his arm. His stern gaze lingered on Nuria for a few seconds before moving to Raul.

"Sergeant, what is Corporal Badal doing with her hands cuffed behind her back?"

Raul was surprised by the question. "It's routine, Commissioner. When it's a murder suspect."

"Take the cuffs off right away."

"But—"

"Corporal Badal is still a member of the police force, Sergeant, and we don't treat other officers like that even if they're under arrest."

"Understood, Commissioner," Raul said submissively. He got to his feet and circled Nuria's chair.

As soon as she was free, Nuria massaged the red marks on her wrists. "Thank you, Commissioner."

"Don't thank me yet," Puig said coldly.

Raul, still holding the handcuffs, moved to sit down again.   "I'm taking charge, Sergeant," Puig said, putting a hand on his shoulder. "You're dismissed."

"Commissioner," he protested, reluctant to miss the show. "If you'll allow me, I could help you—"

Puig cut him off. "Didn't you hear me, Sergeant?"

Raul exhaled in disappointment, glancing furtively at Nuria as he headed for the door.

"Sergeant," she called. He turned around involuntarily.

Nuria was silent. "What?" he said.

"No, nothing." She gave him a farewell wave. "Ah, yes," she said, pretending to remember something. "Douchebag."

In reply, Raul blew her a kiss from the door. "Enjoy prison," he said, leaving the room. "Don't forget to write."

Commissioner Puig stood looking at the door until it closed, then turned back to Nuria. Without a word, he sat down in the chair the sergeant had occupied and laid the folder on the table, then with a weary gesture put his open palm down on it as if planning to read its contents through the tips of his fingers.

Closing his eyes and heaving a deep sigh, he looked up at Nuria. "Why?"

Nuria waited for him to say more. After a moment of silence, she opened her mouth to respond, thinking he'd finished, but just then, the Commissioner resumed speaking. "Why did you lie to me?" he repeated sadly, looking down at the folder that Nuria guessed held her sworn statement.

"I didn't lie to you, Commi—"

Puig raised a hand to stop her. "Don't make it worse."

She pointed to the folder. "Everything I said is true," she insisted.

"You lied to me," Puig reminded her. "Why would I believe your statement now?"

"I …" Nuria searched fruitlessly for a good answer, then settled for, "Because it's the truth."

"The truth?" he repeated. He opened the folder and leafed through the pages. "Hit men, traffickers, hackers, Islamic terrorists …"

"I know how it looks," Nuria protested. "But it's the truth. Down to the last word."

Puig gave her a stern look, a look that communicated disappointment and distrust. "Am I supposed to believe that while you weren't home someone broke in and stole your gun from your safe? The very same gun with which the widow of your ex-partner was murdered hours later? The ex-partner who—presumably accidentally—you'd killed days before with a shot to the head?"

"Presumably?"

"In lieu of the latest developments," Puig explained, "from now on everything that involves you will have *presumably* in front of it."

Nuria leaned over the table and rested her bare arms on the cold metal. "Do you seriously believe … that I shot David deliberately, then killed Gloria?"

"What I believe doesn't matter." He shuffled the pages of the report. "My job is to establish the facts, basing my conclusions strictly on the evidence. For the moment what we have is an agent killed while on duty under unusual circumstances, and his wife murdered days later with the same gun." He raised his eyes to meet hers. "Yours."

"But I've already explained that they broke into my house and opened my safe, and that I was at Elias's, asleep, at the time Gloria was killed. Besides, they were my friends, for God's sake! I'd never hurt them!"

"That's irrelevant," Puig said dismissively, leafing through the statement again. "When you mention Elias … you're referring to Elias Zafrani, the subject you and Sergeant Insúa were supposedly investigating."

"What do you mean, *supposedly*? You're going to doubt that too? We'd spent months on his trail, pursuing him, looking for evidence that would put him behind bars."

"But you didn't find anything."

"We couldn't," she said. "He has contacts inside the police. People who kept him informed about our investigation, allowing him to stay one step ahead of us."

"Contacts inside the police," Puig repeated. "Such as you?"

"What? No! Not me!" Nuria said. "I mean someone kept him up-to-date on the investigation."

"An investigation which, I repeat, you and Sergeant Insúa were carrying out."

"What are you suggesting?"

"I'm not suggesting anything. I'm simply tying up loose ends."

"Well then, untie them, because you're absolutely wrong. David and I were doing our job the best we could, but we didn't know he was playing us, feeding us false leads."

"I see ..." Puig was nodding, but his expression clearly indicated he didn't believe a word. "And what is your present relationship with Mr. Elias Zafrani?"

"Relationship?" Nuria frowned. "We have no relationship. We're just working together to prevent a terrorist attack."

"To prevent a terrorist attack," he repeated skeptically. "The two of you."

"We thought that"—Puig was intimidating her to the point that she'd begun to feel like a little girl trying to explain herself to the school principal—"it was too soon to alert the counterterrorism division. We wanted to get some kind of solid proof, because otherwise they wouldn't believe us."

"And did you get it?"

"Only circumstantial," Nuria admitted. "But the boy we went to see in Villarefu must have had proof, and that's why he was killed. I explained it all in my statement."

He glanced at the papers. "Ah, yes ... the boy who died of a heart attack," he murmured. "And because you found a Quran in his house, you went to the mosque to speak to the imam."

"A hadith," she corrected him, "bookmarked at a page with an underlined text, the kind of text that's used by the jihadists. That imam has to know something," she added. "That's why he called you the moment we appeared, can't you see that?"

"Actually," Puig said, "it was the facial recognition system of the exterior camera that sent your image to Central AI. The alarm was set off when AI identified you."

She waved her hand dismissively. "Fine, that doesn't matter. That imam's hiding something. I'd bet anything he's implicated somehow."

"And you know that because ...?"

"Because it fits."

"It fits?" he repeated, turning the pages of her statement. "Because of that book in the dead boy's house, which you went to on the strength of a partial fingerprint which might belong to dozens of different people?"

"I know we still don't have irrefutable evidence," Nuria said. "But we do have enough leads to—"

Puig interrupted her. "Do you know what *confirmation bias* means?"

Nuria blinked twice, taken aback by the question. "Yes, of course."

"It's the tendency," the Commissioner explained, as if she'd answered no, "to interpret information in order to confirm one's own beliefs."

"Yeah, but I don't see what that has to do—"

"That's obvious," Puig snapped. "You don't see anything."

Nuria was about to reply, but the Commissioner silenced her with a gesture. "But what *I* see," he said, closing the folder with the report and giving her a not entirely unsympathetic look, "is a good agent who accidentally killed her partner and who was affected psychologically by that fact to the point of becoming mentally unstable and imagining absurd intrigues so as not to face up to what she did. You've constructed this fantasy"—he leaned forward—"in which you're the epicenter of a complicated plot involving terrorists, hackers, hit men, and corrupt cops. A fantasy in which you're the victim and the heroine at the same time, but for which you have no evidence whatsoever." He paused and added, "Now do you see it?"

It took Nuria a few seconds to understand what the Commissioner was implying. But no, it wasn't possible. She hadn't imagined it all. She wasn't going crazy. Though deep down, she felt that the Commissioner's words did make some sense.

"But ... Elias," she protested. "He thinks a jihadist attack is being prepared too."

"Elias Zafrani?" Puig opened the folder again and took out a page, which he handed to her. "Read this, please."

"What's this?"

"The psychological evaluation of your friend."

Nuria took the sheet of paper with the forensic psychologist's letterhead on it and read the diagnosis at the bottom of the page. "*The subject*," she read aloud, "*suffers from a marked tendency to paranoid schizophrenia.*" She paused and added in a tremulous voice, "*Internment in a psychiatric facility for further evaluation is recommended.*" She raised her eyes from the page and murmured, her voice uncertain: "I don't ... I don't understand. What does this mean?"

"It means that Mr. Zafrani is insane," Puig said. "A paranoiac, obsessed with jihadists. Who first came up with the idea of Islamic terrorists? You?" He pointed to the door behind him. "... Or him?"

Nuria tried to remember her first conversations with Elias when she'd thought he was the one behind David's death. She remembered how he'd connected the drug in the body of Vilchez's murderer with ISMA, and how from that moment on the focus had shifted to a group of presumed Islamic terrorists. Terrorists for whose existence, in reality, they didn't have a single shred of evidence.

Puig was reading her expression. "Now do you understand? The two of you have been feeding each other's madness. You, looking for someone to blame for your misfortune, him giving free rein to his obsession with jihadists, dragging you into his schizophrenia. It was like pouring gasoline on a fire."

Nuria shook her head as he spoke. "No ... that's not possible."

"Of course it is. Didn't it seem odd to you that a white-collar criminal like Zafrani would put everything on hold just to play at being spies? Do you really believe that a man like that in his right mind would risk so much when there was no need to?"

"He wanted revenge," Nuria said, growing less and less convinced by her own arguments. "He wanted ... to help me."

A weary smile appeared on the Commissioner's stony face. "Help you, Officer Badal? Are you listening to yourself? Why would he want to help the very same police officer who'd been investigating him?" He waited several seconds before going on. "You were confused and vulnerable and he took advantage of it," Puig reasoned. "Mr. Zafrani is a schizophrenic. At some point, as a victim of his own paranoia, he might have come to believe you were lying to him, that you were part of a terrorist plot or some other madness, and then he would have shot you in the back of the head."

"No, he's not like that."

"Of course he is," Puig insisted, "and you know it. Right now you're suffering from Stockholm syndrome, but you'll come to realize I'm right. Not only did we arrest you," he concluded, "we saved your life."

Overwhelmed, Nuria bowed her head to avoid Puig's eyes; if truth be told, to avoid looking at anything. She couldn't believe she'd been so wrong, that everything she'd been through had been nothing more than a fantasy brought to life. But the more she thought about it, the more sense it made.

All she'd found was a water bottle, a partial fingerprint on the window of a torched car, a piece of wrapping paper from some chemical product that might have been lying there for years, and a few words David had written in his notebook that might mean anything. Everything else could be attributed to bad luck—or the confirmation bias Puig had mentioned.

"It can't be ..." Nuria repeated, like a litany. She buried her face in her hands. "It can't be ..."

The Commissioner rose from his chair and went around the table. In an uncharacteristic gesture, he put his heavy hand on her shoulder.

"I'm sorry. I'm really sorry."

48

If the holding cells of a police station have any positive attribute, it is that they simplify everything. Suddenly all distractions vanish and you find yourself enclosed inside four walls of gray concrete, where any trivial worry is relegated to the back burner. Ideas become clear and the mind frees itself of anything less solid and palpable than the steel door keeping the rest of the world on the other side.

Lying supine on her cot, fingers interlaced behind her neck, Nuria tried to recall everything that had happened over the last few days: who had said what, when, and why. She still refused to accept the Commissioner's conclusion, the one that painted her as a victim because of her need to find someone to blame for her own misfortunes, and which laid bare Elias's supposed schizophrenia. This last point in particular she was finding very hard to swallow.

Being the victim of one's own insanity is hard enough to admit. But to be the victim of someone else's brings a degree of humiliation and shame that complicates everything. Could she have been tricked as easily as that? A police officer is supposed to possess a certain mental balance and an inquiring ability to tell truth from falsehood, sanity from madness. So to have ended up being manipulated like a puppet by a paranoid lunatic was a further blow to her battered self-esteem.

Footfalls approached along the corridor and stopped on the other side of the door. A key turned in the heavy lock and the door opened with a screech of hinges. "Nuria Badal," said the officer who appeared in the doorway. "Come with me."

Nuria looked up. "Another interrogation?" she protested. "I've already testified and spoken to the Commissioner. I've got nothing new to say, and I need some sleep."

"Well then, do it at home," replied the officer. "Your bail's been paid and you're free to go."

"Bail?" she repeated, sitting up on the cot. "Seriously?"

The cop frowned. "Does it look like I'm kidding?"

"But ... who paid it?"

He pointed impatiently to the corridor. "You'll find out if you get up and come with me."

Nuria hesitated for a moment, but in the end she placed her feet on the cold floor of the cell and stood up. Obediently following the officer along the corridors of the station basement, she tried to understand how a judge could have agreed to let her go free on bail so quickly, without either speaking to her or scheduling a preliminary hearing. The only reason she could think of was that Commissioner Puig might have put in a good word to the judge, guaranteeing him that she wasn't a flight risk. Otherwise, she found it hard to imagine that mere hours after being arrested as a murder suspect, she was going to be released.

The other question was, who could have paid her bail? But as far as that was concerned, the few doubts she might have had evaporated the moment she was taken to an office where a dark-skinned man with slicked-back hair, wearing a tailored suit that must have cost what she earned in three months, was waiting for her.

Offering her his hand, he said gravely, "Good morning. My name is Raimundo Smith. I'm Mr. Zafrani's attorney."

Instead of returning his greeting, Nuria turned her attention to the window. She narrowed her eyes, surprised to see it was already morning. "What time is it?" she asked.

"Eleven a.m.," the lawyer said. Waving at one of the two chairs on the other side of the table, he added, "Please sit down."

She ignored the gesture. "Did Elias send you?"

The attorney went around the table and sat down on the other side. "Mr. Zafrani asked me to pay your bail as soon as possible," he explained as he extracted a sheaf of documents from the brown leather briefcase on the table. "Luckily the judge on duty was understanding, and although you're accused of evasion of justice, possession of an illegal firearm, and suspicion of murder, he agreed to release you on bail. So if you'd be so kind as to sign this consent form"—he took a fountain pen from the inner pocket of his jacket and placed it on the documents—"my job here will be done, and you'll be able to go home until a date for your trial has been set."

She came closer to the table to glance at the documents. "How's Elias? Is he free too?"

"Mr. Zafrani is resting at his home now. The charges against him are minor, so there was no need for bail."

Nuria was taken aback by the amount of her bail. "Two hundred ninety-five thousand dollars?" she asked in amazement. "And Elias … Mr. Zafrani has agreed to pay?"

"He insisted on it."

Nuria stared at the dizzying figure, considering the implications of accepting a favor that immense. She hated feeling indebted to anybody, least of all to a criminal with paranoid tendencies. On the other hand, if she didn't sign she would remain in preventive custody until the trial—and knowing the glacial pace at which the Spanish justice system operated, that might mean a year or two rotting behind bars.

"Okay, then," she muttered under her breath. Taking the attorney's gold-encrusted pen, she scrawled her signature at the foot of the last page. "Here you are," she added as she returned papers and pen to Mr. Smith. "Please thank Mr. Zafrani and tell him that—"

The attorney took a smartphone out of his briefcase and opened it in front of her. "You can tell him yourself. He also asked me to give you this."

Nuria touched her bracelet to the screen to synchronize the two devices. Almost immediately, Elias's blue eyes appeared on it. "Hello, Nuria," he said with a smile. "How are you?"

"Fine, thanks," she replied, feeling an involuntary smile forming on her own face. "Thank you for bailing me out. I don't—"

He dismissed her words with a wave. "Never mind. What matters is that you're free. Have you left the station yet?"

"No, not yet. I've just signed my release papers."

"Great. So come have lunch with me. You must be famished, and we have a lot to talk about."

"I really appreciate it, but actually I'd rather go home. I'm exhausted."

Elias's expression showed a brief twinge of disappointment, but he nodded understandingly. "Yes, of course. Shall we meet for dinner?"

"I … I really feel like being alone."

"Sure," he said. "It's been a tough few days, and you need to recover."

"Yes, exactly. We'll be in touch."

She reached out to end the call, but Elias spoke again before her finger could touch the key. "Is everything okay?" he asked, coming close to the camera. "You sound off."

"It's nothing," Nuria replied, too quickly. "Everything's fine."

Elias's gaze turned keener, scrutinizing her face. "Are you sure?"

"Yes, I'm sure," Nuria replied, doing her best to sound convincing. "It's just that I'm tired. Really."

Elias prolonged his silence to the point where it began to feel uncomfortable as he studied Nuria with his inquisitive blue eyes. "All right," he said at last. "We'll talk tomorrow."

"Sure, of course," she replied, ending the call before Elias could say anything more. When she looked up, she noticed that the attorney was looking at her in surprise as well. "What?" she snapped at him.

The attorney pursed his lips and shook his head as he put documents and phone away in his briefcase. "Nothing. It's none of my business."

"What's the matter?" she insisted.

The attorney finished closing his briefcase before lifting his eyes to hers again. "How long have you known Mr. Zafrani?"

Nuria was about to say it was none of his business, but she was curious about what the lawyer might have to say. "Cut the crap and tell me what you're getting at."

"All right, then. I'll come straight to the point. Mr. Zafrani doesn't like being lied to. I wouldn't do it if I were you … least of all when he's the guarantor of your bail."

Nuria frowned. "And who says I've lied? Are you calling me a liar?"

In reply, the attorney raised both hands in surrender. "I beg your pardon," he said in a tone which suggested the exact opposite. He took his briefcase and stood up. "I must have misunderstood you."

"Yes, you did," she said firmly. "Completely."

"I apologize again," he said, inclining his head slightly. Reaching the door, he rapped on it with his knuckles and turned to her one last time. "In a few minutes an officer will come to return your personal belongings and fit the ankle monitor on you. Then you'll be free to go home."

"Ankle monitor? What ankle monitor?"

"Your tracker, of course," the lawyer explained as the door was opened from the outside to let him out. "I'm afraid that as long as you're on bail, you'll have to wear one. It's the condition required by the judge in order to agree to your release."

"But I haven't given my consent for that," Nuria objected, irritated.

"Yes, you have." The attorney pointed to the copy of the documents he had left on the table. "Next time, Ms. Badal, I suggest that before you sign a document you read it carefully."

"Corporal Badal," Nuria corrected him.

The lawyer gave her a condescending smile. "Of course," he replied as he went out the door. "Whatever you say."

Less than half an hour later, Nuria left the precinct building and took an Uber to her apartment. The excuse she'd given Elias was true; she was very tired and only wanted to take a long shower and collapse into bed. She was so exhausted she wasn't even hungry, despite the fact that she couldn't remember the last time she'd eaten anything.

Before she realized it, the vehicle had stopped in front of her building. She paid by touching the bracelet Elias had given her—luckily, it hadn't been confiscated—to the vehicle's screen. Making an enormous effort, she summoned enough strength to climb the stairs to her apartment, but when she reached her floor, her heart sank at the sight of the door covered in strips of the forensic team's yellow tape. A seal covered what remained of the broken lock.

"Of course," she muttered, realizing her apartment was now forbidden territory. "I should have expected this." For a moment she felt tempted to rip off both tape and seal, but then her eyes settled on the black tracking device around her right ankle. If she went into her apartment, it was very likely that the GPS it contained would set off an alarm at headquarters and she would be back in jail before she knew it. She concluded it wouldn't be a good idea.

Nuria leaned back against the wall and slid down until she was sitting on the floor. "So now where the fuck do I go?" Taking her phone out of her pocket, she stared at the black screen for a few seconds before heaving a sigh and dialing the person she ought to have called long before.

49

"Hello, Mom," she said without much enthusiasm. "How are you?"

"What do you mean, how am I?" her mother repeated, obviously upset. "What's happening? Your Commissioner called me just now to say you're out on bail!"

"Commissioner Puig called you? Why?"

"What do you mean, why? Because I'm your mother, that's why!"

"Oh, yeah, there's that."

"What's going on?" her mother went on urgently. "Why were you arrested? I've been hearing some very strange things about you and I don't know what to think. And why haven't you called me already?"

Sitting on the cold floor of the landing in front of the taped-up door to her apartment, exhausted from lack of sleep, the last thing Nuria wanted was to have to explain things to her mother over the phone. "I should have called you. I'm sorry," she said contritely. "But I haven't done anything, Mom. It's all a complete misunderstanding."

"A misunderstanding? As far as I know, they don't arrest people because of a misunderstanding."

"Sometimes they do," Nuria replied, reluctant to offer further explanation. "What did the Commissioner say?"

"He asked me if I knew what you'd been up to these past few weeks, and of course I had to say I had no idea." She sighed theatrically. "Seeing that you never call or come to visit me."

"Okay," Nuria said, refusing to take the bait. "And what else did he say?"

"Nothing else. He just said he was worried about you, and that if I spoke to you I should tell you to be careful."

"To be careful? He said that?"

"Well, yes, that's what he told me."

"And he didn't tell you *what* I should be careful about?"

"I asked him that. He said you'd know what he meant." She paused to breathe. "Honey, what have you gotten yourself into?"

"Nothing, Mom. Don't worry."

"How can I not worry, Nuria?" her mother asked indignantly. "I'm still your mother, even if you don't like being my daughter."

"That's ridiculous, Mom."

"It's not ridiculous. You care about me less and less."

"That's not true."

"Well then, how come you never come to see me?"

Nuria was on the point of telling her that was precisely why she was calling, to ask if she could spend a few days with her until she could get her apartment back. But all of a sudden the words dissolved in her mind. She opened her mouth and her exhaustion prevented her brain from checking her tongue in time.

"It's your religious obsession," she blurted. "You're being brainwashed by that irrational Reborn in Christ movement. It makes me really sad to see what they're doing to you. That's why I don't come to see you," she added, letting it all out in a rush. "I can't stand seeing the way you've turned into a religious fanatic."

This time her mother's pause was longer. "I see," she murmured on the other end of the line.

"No, I don't think you do," Nuria said in a weary voice.

"They warned me," her mother said in a tremulous voice. "They said you'd try to make me stray from the path, but I told them you wouldn't, that deep down you're a good girl and in the end, you'd see the benevolence of the work the Reborn are doing."

"Benevolence? Come on, don't give me that crap," Nuria exploded. "They're fanatics, male chauvinists, homophobes ... they're a fucking sect, for God's sake. How can you not see that?"

"You don't know what you're talking about, Nuria. The prophet Jeremiah said it well: '*Behold, their ears are closed, and they cannot hear,*' she recited. '*They scorn the word of the Lord and do not—*'"

"That's enough!" Nuria interrupted her brusquely. "Don't give me that biblical garbage!"

"It's not garbage," her mother protested, offended. "It's the word of God."

"Whatever you say. But that's exactly why I don't come see you, Mom. God or the fucking Church comes up in every single conversation, and I can't bear to see how you've been indoctrinated. You have to choose, Mom." She took a deep breath to bolster her courage. "Either the Reborn ... or me."

"You have no right to do this to me."

"You're the one who's doing it to yourself," Nuria said curtly. "Choose."

This time the silence on the other end of the line felt eternal. Time enough for Nuria to ask herself what answer she really wanted from her mother. Time enough to understand that deep down she wished her mother would choose her sect and Nuria would never have to see her again. Time enough to realize that exhaustion and frustration had pushed her to speak the way she had. Her mother was right; she had no right to do that to her.

"Mom ..." she began.

"I've made my choice," her mother interrupted icily.

"Listen, Mom, I—"

"Goodbye, Nurieta."

"No! Wait!" she cried, but it was too late. Her mother hung up before she could say anything more. Sitting there on the cold floor of the landing in front of her door, Nuria couldn't stop self-pity from welling up in her. Tears streamed down her cheeks.

She'd ruined, perhaps forever, her relationship with her mother. She'd killed her partner and possibly caused the death of his wife. She'd thrown her police career away. She was free on bail, accused of murder, and to add insult to injury, she couldn't even get into her own home.

Leaning her elbows on her knees, Nuria dropped her face into her hands, utterly desolate. "Jesus. I'm really on a roll," she murmured to herself. Suddenly she had nowhere to go and no one to go to. Lifting her head, she thought of calling Susana and asking if she could crash on her couch, but she'd already strained the bonds of their friendship over the last few days, and showing up at her house could complicate life on the force even further for Susana. Nuria didn't want to risk Puig or Raul finding out Susana had helped her. She couldn't afford to lose her as well.

For a fleeting second she thought of going to her grandfather's house and asking Daisy for shelter. She longed to see him, listen to his advice, and let him soothe her with his love and common sense. She wanted to hug him and hear him say everything was going to be all right. But going there was another risk she didn't want to take. If she showed up at her grandfather's, her ankle monitor would betray the location of the illegal retirement home, and maybe someone would wonder why she'd gone to that particular apartment in La Barceloneta.

The pathetic list of friends she had to go to was rounded off by a moronic ex-boyfriend and a couple of contacts on Tinder she could hook up with, but no more.

"Shit," she muttered, toying with her bracelet. There was only one person she could really turn to.

Half an hour later, under a cobalt-blue sky and a scorching sun, Nuria alighted from a taxi in front of the incongruous Alpine chalet in the foothills of the Collserola range.

The door was opened at once by an attractive middle-aged man who looked at her with eyes as blue as the sky over their heads. "I'm glad you changed your mind," he said to Nuria with a warm smile of welcome as she walked up to the door.

"Yeah, well," she replied. "It was this or look for a hotel."

"How flattering."

"I really don't want to bother you."

"You're not bothering me," Elias clarified. "You can stay here as long as you like."

"It'll only be a couple of days," Nuria hastened to say. "I'll leave as soon as I get my apartment back."

"Of course, of course." He stepped aside and welcomed her into the house. "Your bedroom is ready, and I took the liberty of ordering some clothes from Amazon Express that must be about to arrive."

Nuria stopped short. "You did what?"

"It was really my niece's doing," he said defensively. "She made me see that you'd been wearing the same clothes for days and that you wouldn't be in the mood to go shopping, so she chose a couple of items herself so you'd be more comfortable. I hope that's okay with you."

Nuria wavered for a moment between gratitude and irritation that someone else was making decisions for her. If there was one thing she needed urgently, it was to feel she was regaining control over her life, and wearing clothes she hadn't chosen was certainly not a good start. On the other hand, she couldn't ignore the good intentions that had motivated the gesture, and she realized that getting annoyed about it would be absurd and unfair.

Besides, when it came right down to it, Elias wasn't wrong; she was already beginning to smell again. She needed clean clothes urgently. Forcing a smile, she said, "Thank you. You shouldn't have bothered."

"I'm only trying to be a good host," Elias said in turn. Nodding at the stairs that led to the second floor, he added, "As I imagine you must be exhausted, I'll let you rest. As soon as the clothes arrive I'll have them delivered to your room."

"Thank you," she repeated. "It's very kind of you."

Elias nodded and replied with a smile that crinkled the corners of his eyes, "My pleasure. Now I have to leave you, but if you need anything don't hesitate to ask any of the household staff." He turned toward his office. "I'll see you at dinner," he added with a wink.

To her astonishment, Nuria felt her heart rate accelerate. A blush pinkened her cheeks. Annoyed at her body's betrayal, she lowered her gaze and turned toward the stairs without another word.

What the hell was wrong with her? she wondered as she went up the dark wooden stairs. Was she going to start feeling attracted to Elias now? Didn't she have enough problems already without adding a schizophrenic criminal to the list?

Shaking her head, angry at herself, she reached the guest room. No sooner had she opened the door than she realized she'd missed it: the impeccable order and cleanliness and the masculine but welcoming décor. The feeling that someone was concerned about her only intensified when she saw that a tray containing a sandwich, some fresh fruit, and a pitcher of freshly squeezed orange juice had been left on the desk.

"Goddamn it," she murmured, realizing that in spite of herself, a completely inopportune feeling of affection was growing inside her.

50

Nuria wasn't sure exactly when she'd fallen asleep, but the half-eaten turkey sandwich next to her pillow suggested that it must have been immediately after she'd taken her shower and stretched out on the bed, wrapped in a towel, ready to relax and satisfy her hunger.

She rubbed her eyes incredulously to see that outside her window the day was coming to an end, and she had to check her bracelet twice to believe it was almost eight o'clock. How long had she been asleep? Eight hours? Nine, perhaps? This siesta business was getting out of hand.

The towel, still damp, had wet the sheets, so she eased out of it and pushed it aside, then lay there naked with her arms spread out on the bed, her gaze wandering vaguely along the ceiling, her mind blank. It wasn't until she looked down and saw the tracking device around her right ankle that reality dragged her by the hair back to the fucked-up present.

For a moment she tried to reconstruct the succession of events that had ended with her living in the house of a criminal, an ankle monitor controlling her every movement. In the end, though, she put those thoughts out of her mind; there were things it was better not to think about. Again and again she'd done what she'd thought right ... and again and again she'd been wrong.

Sometimes, she reasoned, it doesn't really matter what cards you're dealt; the result of the game is always the same. She'd followed her instincts and they'd failed her utterly, both when it came to interpreting the facts and when it came to judging people, most of all, herself.

As Puig had said, her need to find someone to blame beyond sheer bad luck had driven her to look for three feet on Schrödinger's cat. But she couldn't accuse Elias of dragging her into his own paranoia, since she was the one who had pushed him to see things that weren't there and to set off on that ridiculous hunt for old ghosts.

Nuria still didn't know how to tell him, or what words to use, but she had to confront him and get him to see they'd been wrong, that there was no Islamist cell pursuing her or preparing an attack on Barcelona. The amphetamine the coroner had found in the killer's body might not be limbocaine after all, the print on the van window could belong to a hundred different people, David's notes might have referred to a woman called Elisabets, not to an alleyway in the Raval, the stolen container might have held a load of rubber ducks, and the piece of wrapping paper they'd found under the video game in an abandoned shop underground might have been there for decades—or might mean something totally different.

Confirmation bias, the commissioner had called it. She would have to use that word to explain it all to Elias. She hoped she wouldn't have to quote the forensic psychiatrist's diagnosis to persuade him. Nobody liked to be told they were mentally ill, least of all the head of a criminal organization. A mafia-type syndicate tended not to take criticism of that kind particularly well, even less when it came from the mouth of a cop.

"An ex-cop," she reminded herself aloud, wincing.

Nuria sat up in bed, trying to rid herself of these depressing thoughts, and saw that someone had pushed a piece of paper under her door. Intrigued, she got out of bed and went to the door. Bending over to pick up the note, she read it curiously.

Open the door, it read in the carefully rounded handwriting of a teenager. Cautiously, since she was still naked, she cracked the door a few inches and found a small pile of clothes, carefully folded, with a little note on top.

Reaching for the pale pink sheet of paper, Nuria unfolded it. *I hope you like them,* it said. *I had to guess your size, but I think they'll fit. Dinner is at eight. Kisses, Aya.*

"Jesus!" she swore, looking at the time. She had less than four minutes.

Running downstairs in flip-flops almost cost her a fall, but she managed to find the dining room without losing her dignity. Trying to control a rebellious lock of hair that insisted on escaping her improvised ponytail, she entered the room to find Elias and his niece sitting at the end of a long table, laughing at some private joke. Halting in the doorway, she apologized. "Sorry I'm late."

Uncle and niece turned to her in unison, Aya with a look of satisfaction and Elias with an awkwardness he couldn't disguise in his gaze.

"You look beautiful!" the girl greeted Nuria, inviting her to the table with a smile. "That green dress suits you perfectly. It matches your eyes. Doesn't it, Uncle?"

Her uncle swallowed and nodded. "Very much so," he agreed. "You look beautiful."

Nuria lowered her gaze, shyly smoothing down the youthful dress that reached to just above her knees. "I ... thank you," she said, feeling shaken. "You must let me know ... how much I owe you for this."

"Come on," Aya scolded her. "Don't be silly. I bought it with my uncle's credit card." In a whisper, as if he weren't sitting right in front of her, she added, "He doesn't even know how much money he has."

"Oho!" Elias growled, rubbing his chin dramatically. "Now I understand where all those mysterious bills for jewelry, handbags, and shoes I get every month come from."

"That's not true," Aya said, pouting. "I've never bought jewelry."

Elias pointed an accusing finger at her. "So the rest is true?"

"Uncle, please," she said, with a gesture at Nuria. "Don't you see you're making our guest uncomfortable?"

Nuria, still standing in the doorway, raised her hands. "I don't mean to intrude," she began, pointing her thumb behind her. "I can go back to—"

"We're just teasing," Elias hastened to say. He rose and indicated the free chair between himself and Aya. "Please, sit down."

For an instant Nuria hesitated. In spite of her host's familiarity, she couldn't stop thinking she was about to sit down with a criminal—though when you thought about it, she reasoned, technically she was a criminal herself. Besides, she was starving. She went around the table and sat down at its head.

Aya pointed toward the floor. "Is it heavy?"

"What?"

"The ankle monitor. Does it weigh a lot?"

"Aya," Elias reproved her.

"It's fine," Nuria said. She glanced down at the unsightly device affixed to her ankle. "No, not much. After a few hours you forget you have it on."

"It's cool," Aya said. "Do you know if it comes in pink?"

"That's enough silliness, Aya," Elias interrupted. "Nuria's very tired, and the last thing she needs is you pestering her."

Nuria hastened to defend her. "She's not pestering me."

"Well, she is me," Elias said. "Go on, go to the kitchen and help serve dinner."

"Fine, I'm going," the girl replied. She stood and headed toward the kitchen, adding mischievously as she went, "If you wanted to be alone with her, you know, all you had to do was ask."

"You want to go to bed without dinner?"

"You wish!" Aya replied, out of sight by now. This was followed by a loud peal of laughter.

Elias rolled his eyes and spread his hands in apology. "I'm sorry. I love her like a daughter, but there are times when ..." He left the sentence unfinished, shaking his head.

"Don't worry. It's a difficult age." Looking slightly guilty, Nuria added, "I know from experience."

A brief smile curved Elias's lips. "Did you sleep well?" he asked. "Were you able to rest?"

"I'm fine, thanks. I … wanted to apologize for the way I spoke to you on the phone this morning."

"Don't worry. I understand perfectly."

"Let me finish," she interrupted. "What I want to say to you is that I really appreciate everything you're doing for me." She paused, searching for the right words. "But … I don't know how to say this …"

"You don't want to feel you're in my debt."

Nuria stared at him for a few seconds, then nodded slowly. "Exactly."

"Don't worry," he said, waving the matter aside. "You're not, nor do I want you to think you are. I just did what I thought was right."

"That's the problem," Nuria argued. "I don't know why you think you needed to help me, bail me out, or bring me to your home." She spread her arms wide. "The only thing I've done, right from the start, is cause problems for you."

Elias leaned over the table. "That's not true."

"Of course it is. The first time we talked I nearly shot you," she reminded him, making the shape of a gun with her hand, "and from then on, all I've done is put absurd ideas into your head."

"Absurd ideas?" he asked, frowning. "What do you mean?"

"Well"—Nuria was unsure how to broach the subject—"about the jihadists, for instance, the attack … You know, all that crazy stuff."

Elias looked so disconcerted it was almost comical. "I have no idea what you're talking about."

Nuria shifted in her seat, feeling terribly uncomfortable. "It's my fault," she said. "What happened to me …" The words came to her lips, but she was unable to make any sense of them. "When they killed David, I thought … I looked for someone I could pin the blame on. At first I was sure it was you, but then all that business of the drug came up and that set us off. You mentioned the Islamists and I awakened your hatred of them. We fed off each other, do you see?" She pointed to herself and then Elias. "We were unknowingly deceiving each other, creating a fantasy that fit both of us, but which was nothing more than"—she swallowed and added—"madness."

Elias was silent for several moments, trying to interpret her confused words. "Are you telling me … you believe everything we've found out up to now is a lie?"

"It's called confirmation bias," Nuria said. "It's when—"

Elias sat up straight in his chair. "I know what it is. Who put that idea into your head?"

"Nobody."

"You're lying. Who was it? Your commissioner?"

"No," Nuria said, but her tone showed he'd hit the mark.

269

"Seriously?" Elias said, frowning. "You spend ten minutes with him and he persuades you that everything you've seen is a lie? That you've had some kind of hallucination?"

"Not just me," she replied, annoyed.

"Oh, of course," he snorted. "So I've been hallucinating and inventing things too? Do you think I'm insane?" At these words, Nuria lowered her gaze uncomfortably. Noting her reaction, Elias raised his eyebrows in surprise. "Seriously?" he asked incredulously. "Do you really think ... I'm crazy?"

She made an effort to hold his gaze. "The forensic psychiatrist wrote a report on you while you were detained. The diagnosis was that you have a tendency toward paranoid schizophrenia because of ... because of what happened to your family."

"What??"

"It's not your fault," she said, taking his hand compassionately.

"It certainly isn't," he said, pulling his hand away abruptly.

"I'm the one who drove you to become obsessed with the jihadists," Nuria insisted. "If I hadn't shown up, none of this would have happened. It's all my fault," she added in consternation. "I'm really sorry."

Just then Aya burst into the dining room with a bowl in her hands and a smile on her face. "You're going to lick your fingers over my cold cream of avocado soup with—" Seeing their expressions, she stopped short and her face fell. "Is something wrong? What did I miss?"

Elias stood up suddenly, picked up the napkin on his lap, and threw it on the table. "What's wrong is that Ms. Badal needs to leave."

Aya looked from one to the other, disconcerted. "What? Why?" She stared at Nuria. "Really?"

"I'm sorry, Aya," Nuria apologized. She got to her feet and turned to Elias. "I'm really sorry," she repeated.

But Elias Zafrani was no longer looking at her. In his stiff expression, all Nuria could read was an infinite disappointment.

51

The sun had already set behind the Collserola range, so dusk found Nuria wandering aimlessly, like a ghost with no haunted castle to go to. She'd refused Giwan's offer to drive her and Aya's to call her a cab. Partly because she felt like walking, but also because she really had no idea where to go. Who was she kidding? She *had* nowhere to go.

"Why do you always have to open your big mouth?" she chastised herself under her breath, marveling at her ability to fuck things up again and again. If she'd kept her mouth shut, by now she would be enjoying a delicious dinner during which her overriding concern would be deciding which glass to use for wine and which for water. And instead, here she was, roaming around like a lost cat.

Wandering through the solitary streets of Pedralbes, where apparently the rich paid others to take their walks for them, made her feel even more wretched, if that was possible—and it had started to rain again. "You really outdid yourself this time, Nurieta," she said aloud in a disconsolate tone.

Glancing at her bracelet, she saw that the number of missed calls had grown to nine since the last time she'd looked, but she didn't want to check and see who had called. It was better not to, she told herself; she would probably end up fucking things up yet again on the same day. She put her hand back in her jeans pocket, involuntarily recalling the lovely green dress she'd left on the soft bed where she could have slept that night.

"Yep, you really outdid yourself," she said to herself again. Passing the guard booth, she nodded at the security guard and kept walking, letting her feet take her where they would. Eventually she became aware that she'd left Pedralbes and was at the foot of the old Finestrelles water tower, an ugly reinforced concrete tank on the small hill that separated Barcelona from Esplugues.

Veiled by the light rain, the city lay beneath her like an irregular galaxy of lights crisscrossed by thoroughfares that flowed to the sea like brilliant amber channels. To the left, she could make out the silhouette of the slender spires of the Sagrada Familia cathedral, lit up like Christmas trees. Directly ahead was the grim dark hulk of Montjuïc mountain, crowned by the squat castle where political dissidents and separatists were immured. To her right, between the airport and the foothills of the Garraf massif, she could trace the irregular outline of Villarefu, sparsely illuminated by its few streetlights.

What was she going to do now? she wondered, sitting down on one of the wooden benches beside the path, heedless of whether it was wet or not. With no job, no savings, and no one to turn to, it wouldn't be long before, unable to pay the rent, she lost her apartment. She would find herself on the street, the next step on the inevitable downward trend her life would take from that moment on. The points on her citizenship card would begin to dwindle quickly, hitting rock bottom when her trial date arrived and she ended up with a criminal record. If she was lucky and didn't land in jail, maybe she could find a job as a dishwasher or a dog walker.

Nuria took stock. In a matter of days she'd managed to alienate her mother, disappoint Puig, offend Elias, and abuse her friendship with Susana to the point of putting her friend's career at risk. She was out of control, and it was becoming increasingly clear that it wasn't Elias who had lost his mind, but her. She had become a danger for all those around her, like a chimpanzee with a loaded shotgun in its hands.

Suddenly she regretted having refused the gun Giwan had discreetly offered her before she'd left Elias's house. If she'd taken it, she could have solved all her problems at once with one nine-millimeter bullet. Bang, and goodbye. Fuck everything. She would have gone straight to hell for sure, but at least that way she wouldn't have run into her father and had to explain how she'd fucked everything up so badly.

"I'm sorry, Papa," she murmured, looking up at the heavens in apology, regretting that all those lessons of love and good sense he'd given her before the cancer took him should have ended up being of no use for anything except—

Her thoughts were abruptly interrupted as her gaze inadvertently settled on a poorly lit one-story building on the other side of the hill, less than five hundred yards from where she sat. Somehow her feet had guided her to the mosque where she'd been arrested less than twenty-four hours before. Sitting there in the rain, drenched again and contemplating suicide as the best way to finish out her day, it occurred to her that she might as well spend one of her final hours visiting a misogynistic cleric who was also apparently a real asshole. After all, she thought, Muslim hell couldn't be that much worse than Christian hell, right?

Strangely animated by this final mission, Nuria descended the hill from the water tower, jumping from puddle to puddle, seriously tempted to grab the lampposts as she passed and swing herself around them.

It was then, as she was trying to do a tap dance in her flip-flops, that her eyes fell on the tracking device she wore strapped to her ankle. Nuria realized that if she went anywhere near the mosque where she'd been arrested, alarm bells would go off at headquarters and in five minutes she would be in the back seat of a patrol car again, her hands cuffed behind her back.

She looked around, searching for something she could use as a tool to rid herself of the device, but apparently the street sweepers in that neighborhood were a lot more efficient than they were in the rest of Barcelona. That, and the fact that people tended not to leave bolt cutters lying around in the street made her chances of success slim. All she saw was a trash receptacle on the next corner. She approached it without much hope.

Unwilling to rummage through the garbage, she took the bag out of the basket and emptied it onto the sidewalk. It contained a handful of little black bags of dog poop, tissues, disposable coffee cups, and the remains of a sandwich still wrapped in aluminum foil.

There was no cutting tool, but the remains of the sandwich provoked a pang of hunger in Nuria, reminding her that she'd left Elias's house without having had a single bite to eat. Wrinkling her nose in distaste, she picked up the damp, half-eaten sandwich that still had several slices of chorizo in it and brought it close to her mouth, wavering between repugnance and hunger. The sandwich was disgusting and tempting at the same time. As she held it in front of her face her gaze fell on the foil wrapping and a crazy idea occurred to her.

Without a second thought, she threw the sandwich on the ground and smoothed out the aluminum foil to see if it was large enough. Confirming that it was, she murmured in satisfaction, "This might work." Foil in hand, she took shelter in a doorway, where, sitting on the steps, she rolled it carefully around her tracking device, making sure no part was left exposed.

Pleased with her skill, she stood up and turned her ankle this way and that, ensuring that her invention was secure and the ankle monitor was completely insulated.

Nuria knew she had only a small window of time before her action set off an alarm at headquarters and a patrol was sent to the last place she'd been traceable, but by then she would be a long way away, and by the time they figured out where to find her, she would already have done what she was planning to do.

Without further ado, Nuria walked briskly down the street. This time she did grab a lamppost. Swinging herself around it, she began to hum under her breath,

I'm singing in the rain, just singing in the rain …

52

This time, in order to evade the surveillance camera at the main door, Nuria approached the Ciutat Diagonal Islamic Cultural Center from behind, vigilant for any other hidden cameras. In the rain it would be very difficult for the system to identify her, even if she passed right underneath one, but it wasn't worth taking the risk.

The vague idea that had brought her here was to knock on the back door and give the Wahhabi imam what for. But the closer she came to the building the less sense it made and the more her steps dragged. It was as silly a plan as ringing the bell and running away.

In the end her steps became so hesitant that she stopped altogether a few yards from the door. Standing there in the rain that slid down her cheeks and fell to her chest in irregular streams, she bowed her head and tsked. "What the fuck am I doing?" she asked herself, staring at her toes.

Nuria stood unmoving for nearly a minute, watching the water as it flowed along the sidewalk, making a detour around her flip-flops before continuing its path down the street. In a brief flash of lucidity, she admitted to herself that not only had she lost her mother, her friends, and her sanity, she was now about to lose what little dignity still remained to her.

Feeling suddenly ashamed, she took a step back and began to retrace her steps, heaving a sigh of weariness. Just then, the buzz of the mosque door opening sounded behind her. From the corner of her eye, she watched as it slowly opened and a hand was extended through the aperture.

For an instant Nuria hesitated, standing there in the middle of the sidewalk like a soul in torment. The logical, the adult, thing would be to continue on her way or at least turn and face the imam, if in fact he was the one coming out the back door. Instead, what she did was jump over a hedge and hide in the doorway next to it.

Logical? Adult? Who was she trying to kid?

Crouching behind the hedge, she watched a boy with Arab features emerge from the mosque, followed by the imam. The first thing the sheikh did was look both ways to make sure no one could see them. Then, to Nuria's astonishment, man and boy came together in a long, heartfelt embrace.

Illuminated by the faint light filtering through the open door, indifferent to the rain, the imam stepped back, took the boy by both arms in an affectionate gesture, and spoke a few words in Arabic that Nuria couldn't understand. He gave the boy a small, book-sized package which the boy accepted with a grateful dip of his head.

After taking his leave with another short hug, the boy set off toward the street, passing in front of the doorway where she was hiding and stopping on the corner only a couple of yards from her. Nuria prayed he wouldn't turn in her direction, where he would see her easily as she crouched clumsily behind a bush like a little girl playing hide-and-seek or the most inept spy in the history of mankind.

The imam remained standing in front of the open door of the mosque, watching the boy with the melancholy expression reserved for loved ones. Nuria looked from one to the other, wondering whether Mohammed Ibn Marrash bid farewell to all the worshippers at his mosque with such affection and at that hour of the night.

Just then, the familiar white silhouette of an Uber appeared, stopping with a hiss in front of the boy. He turned to give the imam a final wave and got into the vehicle, which immediately set off.

Nuria saw the imam going back into the building. Standing up, she looked over the hedge and just managed to see the identification number on the side of the small vehicle. "What the fuck was that?" she asked herself as she tried to make sense of what she'd just seen.

Suppose, she thought, *that what this imam's hiding has nothing to do with Islamism, but rather with depraved sexual tastes?* The boy who had come out of the mosque could barely have been eighteen, and from his rather ragtag appearance he could well be a Villarefu refugee—like the deceased Ali Hussain. On top of that, the package the imam had given him as he'd bid farewell so affectionately was the same size as the book he'd given young Ali.

Nuria might have lost her ability to reason clearly, but even so, all this was just too odd. Knocking on the door of the Islamic Center and insulting the imam to his face would have been stupid and useless. But if it turned out that the man had sexual relations with minors, taking advantage of his position as a religious leader ... that was very different. Even if the boy was over eighteen and it was no longer a crime, if anything of that sort came to light she was sure his unforgiving worshippers would chase him as far as the Perpignan border.

A malicious smile spread across Nuria's face as she ordered an Uber from her bracelet. In less than two minutes a vehicle identical to the one that had just left turned the corner and stopped in front of the doorway where she was hiding, the door opening at once. She climbed in hurriedly, sat down abruptly, and glanced back to make sure the imam had not looked out again.

275

The vehicle greeted her, identifying her with its usual courtesy. "Good evening, Ms. Badal. Where would you like to go?"

"I need to go to the same place as vehicle 677RT. I have something to give to its passenger."

"I'm very sorry, but I can't inform you of the destination of another passenger, Ms. Badal. The European data protection law forbids me to."

"I don't want you to inform me," Nuria said. "I want you to take me to the same place. That doesn't violate any law."

The Uber's AI seemed to ponder the answer. Finally it asked, "Do you wish me to inform vehicle 677RT so it can wait for us?"

"No," she replied quickly. "I'd rather you took me to the same destination so that I can surprise him."

Again the AI took longer than usual to reply, probably confirming via its central computer in Silicon Valley that there was no irregularity in the procedure. "Of course," it said obsequiously after a few seconds. "We'll be there in approximately seventeen minutes."

Nuria sighed in relief and for once found herself missing the old-fashioned cabs, with no procedures for data protection or qualms about infringing any law, just as long as you put a fifty-euro note under the driver's nose. The classic *follow that car* from movies had now become history once and for all.

"Would you like to listen to some music?" the vehicle asked as it started.

"No, no music."

"The news?"

"I don't want anything," Nuria said. "Only for you to hurry."

"I'm very sorry, but I can't go over the permitted speed limit."

"I know. I just want to get there as soon as possible."

"We will reach our destination in sixteen minutes approxi— "

"You know what?" she interrupted. "You'd better turn on the news."

"National? International? Sports? Culture?"

"Whatever you like," she said impatiently, missing human cabdrivers more and more.

"Random, then," said the voice from the ceiling as the little vehicle turned toward entrance ramp 11 of the Ronda de Dalt. Fifteen minutes later, the radio was still giving her a wide assortment of news items, though returning insistently to the events programmed for the inauguration of the Sagrada Familia cathedral over the weekend.

"His Majesty Philip VI, accompanied by Princess Leonor and the Infanta Sofia," the loudspeaker whispered above Nuria's head, "will be giving a reception for His Holiness Pius XIII after the mass which will be celebrated in—"

"Turn the news off," Nuria ordered, seeing that the vehicle was now joining the B20 and then taking exit 54. Not without surprise, she realized that for once her intuition seemed to be correct: the Uber was now heading in the direction of Villarefu. This meant that the boy was also a refugee. That couldn't be simple coincidence.

At that hour of the night, traffic on the road to Villarefu was practically nonexistent, but even so, she found it impossible to make out the taillights of the Uber they were following. Even if it was two minutes ahead of them, in that darkness she ought to—

Unexpectedly, her vehicle turned left onto a narrow road that led deep into the fields that surrounded Villarefu. "Hey, stop!" Nuria called out. "This isn't the way!"

"You don't want to go to the same destination as vehicle 677RT?" the Uber asked, pulling to the side of the road and coming to a stop with a hiss.

"Yes, of course I do. But this isn't the way."

"According to my data, this is the only possible route to the desired location."

"Well, you're wrong. Can't you see Villarefu's over there?" She pointed in the opposite direction. "You'll have to turn around."

"Do you want to change the destination?"

"What? No! What I want is—" She left her sentence unfinished, seeing the lights of a vehicle approaching them through the rain. Only when it was very close was she able to see that it was an Uber with no passenger inside, just like the one she was in herself. The number 677RT was clearly visible on its side.

"Nothing. I didn't say anything." She looked back to see the vehicle pulling away from them. "Continue to the original destination, please."

She knew it was only her imagination but it seemed to her that the Uber's AI gave a barely audible snort of frustration before the neutral voice spoke again. "Four minutes to destination, Ms. Badal," it said, starting again immediately.

Through the rain, Nuria attempted to make out where they were going, but as hard as she squinted, she couldn't glimpse any light that might indicate the presence of a building. *Where the hell did that boy go?* she wondered, intrigued.

The narrow, patchily asphalted tractor track they were following led in the direction of one of the highways that surrounded Villarefu. Just when it appeared that the self-driving vehicle was about to go up a slope and through the protective fence, a small, lightless tunnel running under the highway appeared in front of them. Emerging from the tunnel, Nuria saw they were in a field with a single, lightless building at the center.

"Is that where we're going?"

"I'm sorry, but I can't—"

"Okay, okay," she cut in. "Don't give me the speech again."

The voice abruptly fell silent and Nuria peered through the window on the left side. Soon she managed to discern what appeared to be an old, apparently abandoned warehouse a dozen yards from the road at the end of a short access drive. The Uber stopped at its entrance.

"We have arrived at the destination, Ms. Badal."

"You don't say," she muttered, touching her bracelet to the screen to pay the fare.

"Thank you and have a pleasant evening," the Uber said as it opened the door. "I hope you—" Nuria got out and slammed the door on the rest of the canned farewell speech.

Taking the hint, the small electric vehicle started at once. She watched it drive back the way they'd come, leaving her alone in the middle of the night under the fine, persistent drizzle. She was in the middle of nowhere.

53

At the other end of the muddy dirt road stood what looked like a small, tin-roofed shed, the kind the farmers in the area had used to store their tractors and tools overnight before the drought had turned most of these fields into dustbowls.

The place looked as if it had been abandoned for years. Weeds were thriving amid the wreckage of a simpler, more innocent era, barely lit by the glow of the nearby highway. Nuria approached the shed, wondering where on earth the boy could have gone. There was nothing there but the small, abandoned warehouse and the refugee camp a hundred yards away on the other side of the slope up to the highway. Was it going to turn out she'd been wrong after all? That the boy wasn't a refugee after all but a boy who, for some reason that escaped her, had decided to settle in this remote spot?

Perhaps it was the accumulated exhaustion or the insistent growling of her stomach begging for dinner, but the fact was that her desire to interrogate the boy and get something dirty about the imam out of him was definitely no longer a priority. The rain seemed to be dissolving her hostility toward the cleric like a sugar cube. For a moment she wondered whether to call the Uber to come back for her. After taking a deep breath, though, Nuria decided that since she was there, it would be pointless to leave without first speaking to the mysterious boy. "Ten minutes," she persuaded herself. "Then I'll leave."

Walking up the path to the warehouse door, she found it was locked from inside with a thick chain. Rapping with her knuckles, she called loudly, "Hello! Hello! Can you open the door?" Nuria waited a few seconds, but there was no reply from within. No lights, noise, or movement. That was impossible, though. There had to be someone there.

"Hello!" she called again. "Can you help me? It's raining hard and I'm stranded!" Again she waited for a reply, and again all she heard was silence. "Shit," she muttered. Giving up on the front door, she began to walk around the building.

Boards, tools, and rusty farm implements were stacked in disorder against the wall like faithful dogs waiting for a master who would never return. Placing her feet with care, she reached the back, where she found another door, this time with a smaller padlock, barring her way. "Hello!" She hammered on the door again. "Is anybody there?"

Once again the distant noise from the highway swallowed her words. There was no answer. The rain began to grow heavier as her patience wore thinner. Nuria imagined the boy on the other side of the door, perhaps scared, perhaps laughing at the madwoman knocking on his door at that hour of the night. She wasn't sure which of the two possibilities infuriated her more, but at that moment she wasn't ready to accept either.

"This is ridiculous," Nuria said, giving the door a final glance. Retracing her steps, she picked up a mallet she'd glimpsed among the weeds, went back to the door, and unhesitatingly brought it down on the padlock with all her strength. It flew into the air at the first blow, so loudly she thought it must have been audible even in Villarefu.

Dropping the mallet, she took the chain in both hands and tugged at it until it came loose, then kicked the door open like an officer of the riot police. Without a second's hesitation, she stepped into the building and stood there in front of the door, expecting the lights to come on at any moment. Nothing happened.

"Hello?" she asked the darkness. "I don't want to do you any harm. Don't be afraid." Nothing. Not the tiniest noise. Not even the sound of breathing. Groping around on both sides of the door, she searched blindly for a light switch until finally, with a click, a bulb in the ceiling lit up and she realized she'd been talking to herself.

The outbuilding was empty. A handful of picks and shovels were tossed in a corner, together with a gas generator, an old chair, a rusty oil lamp hanging from a nail, and a couple of sloppily rolled bales of wire on the wood-plank floor. Nothing else.

A fit of wild laughter rose from her chest to her throat. Instead of trying to hold it back, she let it burst forth. A second later she was doubled up, laughing uncontrollably as if she'd lost her wits. All the absurdity, the chain of stupid decisions she'd made, had finally led her here, to an empty shed in the middle of nowhere, soaked from head to foot, with no one to turn to and nowhere to go. Even the refugees in the camp had friends, family ... something they could call home. She envied them for it, realizing immediately that if she'd reached the point of feeling jealous of a bunch of refugees, she'd really hit rock bottom.

"Jesus," Nuria muttered, directing her steps toward the chair on the other side of the shed. She felt so tired ... Abruptly the floor creaked and bowed under her weight. "What the hell ...?" she murmured. She took a step back, then stepped on the same spot again with the same result.

Squatting down, Nuria looked more closely at the wooden floorboard that seemed to be unsupported. Forgetting her woes, driven by curiosity, she slid her fingers under the edge and lifted it just enough to see that underneath was nothing but more darkness.

Then she remembered the tools in the corner. Standing again, she went to the pile, took a pick, and returned to the same spot. She slid the iron tip of the pick under the board, then used it to lever it up and move it aside.

"Holy Mother of God!" she said in amazement at the sight of the dark hole, three feet across, that opened up at her feet. The end of a ladder was poking out of it. What the hell was this? A basement? A storage room? A hideout? Most importantly, why the fuck was all this happening to her?

Nuria looked heavenward. "You're enjoying this, aren't you?" she asked. "Isn't there anybody else in the world whose life you can complicate?" Every time things seemed to be getting back to something like normality, everything tangled itself up again in the most bizarre way possible. She'd followed the boy with the idea of talking to him and finding out whether he had any connection with the imam, and instead, she'd just found a secret entrance to God only knew what new problem. Because if one thing was clear, it was that this was not a wine cellar.

Nuria's first impulse was to replace the wooden board and get out of there posthaste. She was in too much trouble already to start poking her nose into another mess. She wondered whether to call Puig and fill him in, but immediately imagined him asking her what she was doing there, why the signal from her tracking device had disappeared for half an hour, and if she was aware that she'd committed the offense of breaking and entering while free on bail. She couldn't think of any credible answers to those questions that would keep her from landing in jail again.

No. Calling Puig was not a good idea—but neither could she leave the shed as if nothing had happened and forget about the whole thing. Maybe, just maybe, she pondered as she crouched in front of the mysterious hole, if she managed to find out something valuable for the prosecution, she could make a deal and get rid of either the ankle monitor or the bail. It was a remote possibility—she wasn't as naïve as all that—but the reality was she had no more cards left to play.

"All right, then." She stood up decisively. "What do I have to lose?"

If she was going to go down there, she needed light. She didn't have her cell phone with her, nor was she carrying a flashlight or a lighter. Nuria turned her gaze to the right, where just a moment before she'd seen an oil lamp standing on a shelf. She approached it dubiously, keeping the gloomy hole in sight from the corner of her eye. The lamp, rusty and covered with cobwebs, looked as if it had been there for centuries.

"Of course," she snorted when she found there was no oil in it. Her eyes fell on the generator on the floor and she tapped it gently with her foot until she heard the sound of gasoline sloshing inside. "Good," she told herself encouragingly as she unscrewed the top of the gas tank, then did the same with the lamp.

The first problem, how to transfer the fuel from one device to the other, Nuria solved by wrenching a coupling off the generator and using it to transfer the gasoline. The second turned out to be more complicated, since naturally the oil lamp had no wick. The only dry cloth available was her own underwear, which she calculated she could roll up and poke through the corresponding hole in the lamp.

But the third problem turned out to be the really difficult one. How on earth was she going to light the oil lamp with no flame? Nuria combed the small shed from top to bottom, looking for a forgotten matchbox, a lighter, or anything else that could be made to produce fire, but there was nothing.

"Come on, Nuria, focus," she murmured to herself. "There are cars that drive themselves and you can't come up with a way to make fire?" For a moment she contemplated her bracelet, considering the possibility of opening it up and using its tiny battery to create a spark. But the truth was that though it was flexible, the activity bracelet was a device made to last. It wouldn't be easy to break it open, and even if she did, it might not be of any use. In any case, if she were to do it she would be left incommunicado. She had to think of something else.

"A spark," she said to herself. "A spark …"

That was when she realized that the generator at her feet could provide her with all the sparks she needed. Severing the electric cord with a few blows from the shovel, she replaced the coupling she'd removed and took off her thong underwear. After putting her jeans back on, she tore off a piece of cloth and soaked it in gasoline, then left it on the floor next to the lamp.

With an expression of intense concentration on her face, Nuria connected the generator. Tugging hard on the starter, she got it running on the first try. She picked up the ends of the electric cable that she'd peeled with her teeth and brought them close to the soaked wick, using extreme caution. "All I need now is to electrocute myself," she murmured a split second before touching both ends to the cloth.

The spark was so brilliant and made so much noise she gave a cry of surprise and fell backwards onto the hard floor. "Holy shit!" she cried, stunned by the unexpected explosion. The generator stopped abruptly and was smoking suspiciously, but a satisfied smile spread across Nuria's face when she saw that a blue flame now burned on the small strip of white cloth.

54

With all that noise, Nuria thought, anybody in that hole had to have realized her presence unless he happened to be deaf and blind. Which meant that if the boy she'd been following was hiding from her for some reason, he had to be waiting for her down there, hidden in the shadows.

Holding the oil lamp high, Nuria looked down into the hole. The stale air it exuded smelled of dirt and the yellow light of the lantern extended no further than a couple of yards down. "Hello!" she called. "I just want to talk to you for a moment, kid," she added. "No need for you to hide."

She waited for a few seconds, but no one answered. Not a sound met her ears. Even with the lamp ready in her hand, she hesitated, picturing herself as one of those empty-headed girls in horror movies, the kind who inevitably decide to descend alone into a dark, gloomy basement when there's no need. Didn't they watch TV? Nuria always laughed when she saw them, thinking that no one in their right mind with a minimum of cinematographic baggage would ever do anything like that.

Yet here she was, in a solitary, derelict storehouse in the middle of the night, determined to go down into a sinister well armed with nothing but a rusty old oil lamp. *And with no underwear on to boot*, she added to herself, making a mental note never to laugh at B-movie scriptwriters again.

"I'm coming down!" she announced, more to summon up her own courage than in warning. Without giving herself time to think better of her decision, she took a deep breath. Taking care not to slip, she placed her feet on the first rungs of the ladder. Soon realizing her flip-flops were more a hindrance than a help, she shook one foot, then the other, and let them drop.

The sound of them hitting the bottom reached her at once, and she calculated that the descent was no more than five or six yards. Not too much, but even so, she needed to take care not to slip, since the fact that she was carrying the oil lamp in one hand meant she had only one hand to hold onto the ladder with. Fixing her toes on each rung before moving on to the next, Nuria descended little by little until her bare feet touched the clay floor.

Holding the lamp high, she turned and almost dropped it in surprise when she saw what lay before her. She'd been wrong: this was not a basement or a hiding-place, or anything like it. In front of her, a narrow corridor extended in a

283

straight line, disappearing into the darkness beyond the halo of the oil lamp. A long way beyond.

"But what …?" she muttered, open-mouthed, trying to make sense of it. *What is this doing in the middle of a field?* she thought, perplexed. Then the memory of Villarefu, so close, came into her mind. "A tunnel," she said. "Those bastards have made a tunnel under the highway."

From what she could see in the light from the lamp, she was in an underground passage excavated in the damp earth, held up only by a few wooden beams every four or five yards. The ceiling was inches above her head, while four or five handspans separated the walls. Even so, she couldn't help being amazed by this unexpected feat of engineering.

She recalled the tunnels the Palestinians had dug under the walls the Israelis had built around them. Tunnels hundreds of yards long that even trucks had driven through, transporting weapons, people, and goods between Egypt and the colossal refugee camp that the Israelis had made the Gaza strip into.

Though this one was far narrower than its cousins in the Middle East, it was still shocking to find anything of the kind on the outskirts of Barcelona, not to mention the fact that no one was aware of its existence.

But the question Nuria asked herself the moment she came out of her trance of amazement was not how it had been built … but why. Obviously, it was to let people enter and leave the camp without going through the checkpoints, as apparently the boy she'd followed there had done—but why, exactly?

No one goes to the trouble of excavating an underground tunnel to go for prayers at a mosque in the higher part of Barcelona. Perhaps, she deduced, this tunnel was the way in for the contraband merchandise that constantly and inexplicably appeared in Villarefu.

"Jesus, Elias," she muttered, suspecting who might be behind it. What she couldn't fathom was how all this related to the imam, and what it meant for her theory about his interest in young boys. Maybe she was completely wrong, and the imam was actually part of a network of smugglers or traffickers.

The ideas bubbled up in Nuria's mind, one hard on the heels of the last, linking possibilities which grew ever stranger. Suppose the bundle she'd seen the imam give the boy in front of the mosque hadn't been a Quran but a package of drugs, or a weapon? Could the imam really be a drug trafficker? Would Elias know? Was it possible he *didn't* know? Could all this be nothing but a convoluted maneuver for getting rid of the competition?

Suddenly a muffled noise reached her from somewhere at the other end of the dark tunnel, cutting short her spiral of speculations and bringing her back to the unnerving present as if she'd abruptly fallen out of bed in the middle of the night.

Once again her two options presented themselves to her: turn around and go back the way she'd come, or continue down the claustrophobic tunnel in the pitch dark.

Nuria looked up at the mouth of the well above her head, in the direction of safety and common sense. If she went up that ladder now and called a cab, she calculated that in half an hour she could be sitting at a table in a restaurant or taking a hot shower in a hotel.

Then she looked down and saw her bare feet on the damp earth in the light of an oil lamp which might go out at any moment, a lamp that was barely capable of giving her an idea of what there might be only a few yards further on.

Her options were clear: either do what was sensible and reasonable, or make one more mistake to add to the interminable list of mistakes she'd made in the last few days. Nuria felt the same way she had the time she'd been invited to the Barcelona Casino. On that occasion, she'd approached one of the roulette tables and bet a small sum on the black. The little ball had rolled around the golden rim of the roulette wheel until, losing momentum, it had fallen into the center of the wheel and begun to bounce about in the numbered compartments until it came to rest in number three. "Number three," the bored croupier had said. "Red, odd, and manque." Nuria had made a face and, taking another chip from the ones in her hand, she'd made exactly the same bet, setting a five-euro chip on the black diamond.

Now it's black's turn, she'd thought, predicting that she would recoup what she'd lost. "No more bets," called the croupier. He threw the little white ball in the opposite direction to the spin of the wheel. A few seconds later the ball stopped bouncing and the croupier announced mechanically, "Number thirty-two. Red, even, and *passe*."

At that, Nuria knew she ought to turn around and forget roulette for the time being, but something inside her wouldn't let her give up, as if the little white ball's stubbornness were specifically aimed at her. Knowing she was making a mistake, she took two five-euro chips and placed them on the black diamond in front of her. When the ball came to rest again in a red box, she wasn't even surprised. Again, she placed four new chips on the black diamond and bought eight more.

The rounds went on. By the seventh or eighth—she had trouble remembering—she'd lost six hundred and forty euros. Calculating that the probabilities of red coming up again were one in a thousand, Nuria prepared to buy more chips in order to double her bet. Her luck had to change at some point, she'd told herself with a frown.

But it didn't. That time it was her credit limit, not her common sense, that finally made her stop. She'd gone home filled with frustration and anger, convinced that if she'd stayed for just one more bet she could have won back all her money and even a little extra with which to treat herself to a good meal. But this time there was no credit card limiting the number of stupid things she could do.

Nuria understood that up until then she'd done nothing but commit mistakes. Not only that, she'd reacted in exactly the same way as she had in the casino, doubling her bet again, making ever-greater errors in her desperate search for a lucky break that would allow her to redeem herself once and for all. Though she'd lost a month's salary, she continued to believe that on that particular occasion she'd acted correctly, and that only a conspiracy against her on the part of the law of probabilities had prevented her from going home with a win in her pockets.

What were the chances of something like that happening again? Nuria figured she'd fucked up so many times that now she could only win. Tightening her hold on the handle of the lantern, she slipped on her flip-flops and ventured forth, step by determined step, into the dense darkness.

55

As Nuria advanced through the tunnel for what felt like an eternity, submerged in utter darkness alleviated only by the tenuous glow of the lantern she held out in front of her, she began to feel stiff. Exhaustion, hunger, the damp, and the feeling of absolute isolation were starting to take their toll on her physical state, and even more on her mental clarity. With each step, she felt an imperious and growing need to sit down and rest, and it was only with great difficulty that she managed to persuade herself of how dangerous doing that would be.

She switched the oil lamp from one hand to the other for the umpteenth time, trying to calculate the distance she'd traveled through that claustrophobic tunnel. It hadn't occurred to her to count her steps from the beginning and now she had no idea whether she'd walked five hundred yards or five miles. If her exhaustion was any gauge of the distance she'd covered, she could easily have passed Villarefu by now and be burrowing under the Pyrenees.

As she switched hands yet again, her wrist and fingers aching from the awkward position, her fatigue caused the handle to slip through her fingers. "No!" she cried, but in spite of her protests she was unable to keep the lamp from falling to the ground. The glass chimney protecting the wick shattered and the improvised wick fell into the shallow layer of water covering the tunnel floor. With a desolate hiss, the flame went out.

"Goddamn it to hell!" Nuria bellowed, once again submerged in darkness. "What the fuck is up with you!?" she yelled at the heavens. "Weren't things bad enough already?" A surge of uncontrollable anger drove her to aim a kick at the place where she guessed the oil lamp had fallen, but luckily she didn't come anywhere close.

"Shit," she muttered, leaning against the wall. Dropping her face into her hands, Nuria barely managed to check the impulse to burst into tears that was rising in her chest. Desolate, she let her back slide down the rough wall until she was sitting on the puddled ground, not even noticing that her jeans were getting wet.

"Shit. Shit. Shit …" she moaned, exhausted. The willpower to go on coping with fate's booby-traps had utterly deserted her. Perhaps the best thing would be just to keep sitting there. To hell with everything. In the end someone would come by, even if it was the next day, even if it was a—

A creaking sound, as of footsteps on wood, sounded only a few yards away, cutting her pity party short. Adrenaline flooded through her. Lifting her face from her hands, Nuria turned her head in the direction of the sound. Only then, thanks to the fact that she was now in complete darkness, was she able to glimpse a tiny beam of light penetrating the tunnel from the top, a dozen yards further on.

Wiping the tears away with the back of her hand, she heaved herself to her feet and crept on in a crouch, trying not to make any more noise than she'd already made. As she neared the faint glow, a ladder identical to the one she'd used to descend to the tunnel materialized, ending in a trapdoor through which light was filtering.

With no alternative but to go up it, Nuria removed her flip-flops. Tucking them into the back of her jeans, she grasped the first rung and began to ascend very slowly, pricking her ears for any sound that might betray someone's presence.

Step by slow step, like a sloth climbing a tree, Nuria reached the trapdoor. After waiting for an endless minute to make sure there was no one on the other side, she put her hand to the bottom of the trapdoor and pushed. Unexpectedly, it resisted her efforts.

For a moment the unnerving possibility that it might be locked on the other side occurred to her, but before allowing herself to despair, she decided to try again. Hooking her toes on the rungs and using all her strength, she shoved the trapdoor with both hands. This time it gave, with so much momentum it nearly slammed onto the floor.

Abruptly her eyes were dazzled, as though someone were shining a spotlight at her face. Her eyes had grown so used to the darkness of the tunnel that she had to narrow them until she was used to the brightness and could open them slowly.

Nuria found herself in a space with concrete walls, no windows, and a flight of stairs in one corner which must lead to an upper floor. She was in a basement.

A row of fluorescent tubes along the ceiling lit up a folding table surrounded by camp chairs. Open wood and metal crates were heaped in a disorderly pile in a corner and shelves of tools, electric wire, rolls of duct tape, and small, labeled, plastic boxes lined one wall. Against the wall opposite her, illuminated by the strong light of a gooseneck lamp, was what looked like an electrician's workbench with a computer sitting on it, surrounded by technical books, voltmeters, more wires, and an old car battery.

Peeping out like a rabbit from its warren, Nuria waited a few seconds more, alert to the slightest noise. It was only when she was sure nobody could hear her that she came out of the hole, carefully closing the trapdoor behind her. Still aware that she might be stepping into the wolf's den, Nuria permitted herself a sigh of relief at having left behind the cold, damp tunnel that had led her there. Even the polished cement floor felt warm under her bare feet.

Looking down at her feet, Nuria realized she was leaving big muddy footprints with every step she took, easily distinguishable from those left by the boy she'd followed, which stopped at the foot of the stairs after crossing the room. Nuria followed those other fresh mud prints, hoping to find another exit at the top of the stairs. She no longer wanted to interrogate the boy she'd followed there nor did she care what the tunnel was used for. Instead, the sole urgent desire filling her brain was to get outside and stand in the rain, inhaling gulps of fresh air.

As she crossed the room with wary steps, though, something on the wall behind her caught her attention. When she looked back, she saw it was papered from floor to ceiling with diagrams, plans, and dozens of photographs.

Standing in the middle of the basement, Nuria hesitated, torn between the urge to get out of there and her curiosity to find out what was pinned to those massive cork panels. Her eyes lingered on the stairs and their promise of freedom, and she knew what the intelligent course of action was. But even before making her decision, she knew she wouldn't choose that option.

"Damn it all," she hissed under her breath. Turning, she retraced her steps, leaving a new trail of muddy prints on the gray cement. Going around the trapdoor, Nuria stood, arms akimbo, in front of the maze of overlapping maps, diagrams, and images, on which someone had scrawled innumerable notes with a red pen in Arabic.

At first glance the overall picture made no sense to her, but then she identified a place that appeared in several of the photos: the Nou Palau Blaugrana, home of the FC Barcelona basketball team. It was an impressive sports arena with seating for twenty thousand fans, located across from the refurbished Camp Nou on the land that had been occupied by the Miniestadi a decade before.

The photos, taken from all possible angles, all focused on a single spot, the area occupied by the Nou Palau Blaugrana as seen on an enormous map of the city of Barcelona that was pinned to the wall.

If Nuria had had a gogglecam or even an ordinary cellphone, she could have instantly translated all the inscriptions in Arabic in the margins of the panel in front of her. But even without knowing the meaning of all those notes in the language of Mohammed, it was easy to guess she wasn't looking at a tourist map.

Absorbed in the multitude of sketches and diagrams, trying to understand what they meant, Nuria failed to hear the footsteps above her head or the slight sound of the door opening at the top of the stairs. Only when someone turned a

289

heavy key in the lock from the inside did she awaken from her absorption and turn toward the stairs, her heart in her throat.

A few seconds later someone hurried down the wooden steps, making them creak. The boy she'd followed from the mosque appeared on the stairs, carrying a tray holding a steaming cup of tea and a sandwich. So concentrated was he on not dropping it as he came down the stairs that he didn't notice Nuria's footprints or the small puddle that had formed next to the opposite wall, much less the woman who was now hiding under the stairs. Setting the tray on the workbench, he turned around at a noise behind him, just in time to see a woman who was almost six feet tall materialize in front of him out of nowhere.

"Hi there," she greeted him with a smile on her lips. The boy opened his mouth in mute surprise, but before he had time to say a word, the affable-looking stranger gave him a brutal kick in the gonads that left him curled up on the floor, gasping like a fish out of water.

The woman squatted down beside him with an apologetic expression, watching his face that was twisted in pain. "I'm sorry, kid," she said with apparently sincerity. "But we need to talk."

56

By the time the boy's heart rate had returned to normal and he'd managed to fill his lungs with air, Nuria had tied him to a chair with duct tape. As she immobilized him she realized he wasn't as young as she'd first thought. He was actually in his twenties; she'd been fooled by his hairless face and juvenile-delinquent appearance. This knowledge eased her conscience somewhat about the treacherous kick she'd just given him. Sitting down in front of him on another chair, she devoured the veggie sandwich. "Mmm, it's very good," she congratulated him. "I hope you don't mind, it's just that I'm dying of hunger."

"Who the fuck are you?" the youth asked her with a slight Arab accent that turned his e's into i's. "What are you doing here?"

"I'll be asking the questions for now," she told him when she'd finished her mouthful. "What's your name?"

The young man twisted in the chair, testing his bonds. "Let me go, bitch."

Nuria wiped her hands on her jeans and shook her head in apparent disappointment. "We can make this easy or difficult. The decision's yours."

"The decision is that I'm going to fuck you in the ass and gouge your eyes out, you bitch."

She arched an eyebrow. "I see."

"No, you don't see anything," he muttered. "You have no idea who you're dealing with."

Nuria forced herself to appear indifferent to his threats. Any glimpse of fear or concern would make her lose her advantage. "Fine," she said impassively. "We'll do it your way." Standing up, she went to the table and began to look for tools that might be useful.

"I only want you to answer a few questions," she explained, selecting a box cutter, a pair of pliers, and a soldering gun. "I don't want to hurt you," she added. "But I will if I have to." As she said this her gaze fell on the battery, then traveled to a roll of thin copper wire on the table. Changing her mind, she put down the tools she'd picked up and moved the battery and the copper wire to a place on the floor in front of the young man.

He stared at the objects blankly, only gradually understanding the obscure intentions of the woman who'd just eaten his dinner. "I don't know much about electricity," she said conversationally as she unwound the wire. "But I bet if I connect the poles of the battery with this wire, I'll get some good sparks." She looked up at him. "Or am I wrong?"

"I'm not going to tell you anything," he said defiantly, but Nuria could detect a slight change in the inflection of his voice. His confidence seemed to have come down a notch.

Nuria smiled cynically, pretending she was going to enjoy the process. Holding up both ends of the wire, she asked thoughtfully, as if evaluating the consequences, "Let's see … where do you think I can hook these up to? Fingers? Under the nails, maybe? Yes, it's sure to hurt under the nails."

"Allah, blessed be His name, is my witness," he hissed, "that when you let me go I'm going to really hurt you, you infidel bitch."

"Hmm, you know what?" she added pensively. "Actually, I can think of a much better place. You wouldn't happen to be a virgin, would you?"

The young man didn't answer, but the flush that spread over his face was all the confirmation Nuria needed. "Seriously? You're threatening to rape me, and you're still a virgin? Well … I'm sorry, but I'm afraid your first time with a woman isn't going to be what you expected." Saying this, she crouched down in front of him and unfastened his belt.

"What … what are you doing?" he asked in alarm.

"Don't get too excited, kid," Nuria replied. She pulled his pants down to his ankles, revealing worn-out white jockeys with a revealing bulge in them. "Wow." She raised her eyebrows. "You did get excited, didn't you?"

"Don't touch me, whore!" he blustered in fury. "If you touch me I'll kill you!"

Nuria took the wire and wound it around the battery terminals. "You just have to answer a few questions. But if you don't want to, well—" With a shrug, she stood up and took a step back, pleased with her handiwork. "Ah, one last thing …" she added, going back to the workbench where she connected the portable radio and turned the volume up as far as it would go. The radio was set to a station of tedious Arabeat music. Turning to the young man again, Nuria raised her voice above the music. "It's for the screams, you know? You men are such whiners when someone fries your balls."

Nuria saw panic surface in his eyes and took advantage of it to insist. "All you have to do is answer a few questions and I'll leave the way I came. Well, not exactly that way," she corrected herself with a grimace. "But I'll leave and I won't hurt you. I give you my word."

The boy's teeth were chattering uncontrollably. Nuria took both ends of the copper wire. Crouching down again, she brought them close to his genitals. "We'll start with something easy," she said. "What's your name?"

"Kamal," he muttered through clenched teeth. "My name's Kamal."

She winked at him. "Great, see how easy it is? Now tell me, Kamal. What are you planning to do at the basketball arena?"

He shook his head. "I don't know."

"You don't know?" Nuria snorted. "You don't know what all that stuff behind you means?"

"No. I don't know." Kamal repeated, clenching his jaw.

"Okay then … whatever you want," she said with a shrug and prepared to pull down his underwear. "Say goodbye to your future offspring."

Kamal watched the proceedings, his eyes starting out of their sockets. The terror was clearly visible on his face, down which large drops of sweat were beginning to roll. "No!"

"Too late, my friend," she said, and exposed his genitals.

"Wait! Wait!"

"Last chance. What are you planning here?

"I … don't …" he mumbled in horror.

"All right then," Nuria said. "You asked for it."

"No! Stop!"

Nuria paused, the ends of the wires less than an inch from Kamal's testicles. "Are you going to answer me?"

"I … I don't know. Honestly," he begged, hyperventilating. "I just write lines of code … interfaces for autonomous systems …"

"Autonomous systems?" she asked, trying to remember. "Isn't that what Ali Hussain was studying … before he died?"

"I'm not sure."

"Like hell you're not sure. Why are two refugees so interested in this particular subject? And who's paying for all this? The imam you just went to see? It's him, isn't it? Tell me, for fuck's sake!"

"I don't know!"

"Don't give me that bullshit, Kamal." She brought the stripped ends of the wires close to his testicles again. "What are you planning here?"

"I just know it's some kind of action," Kamal protested. "I don't know anything more."

"Action? What kind of action?"

"I … I'm not sure."

"Don't fuck with me, Kamal," she warned him menacingly. She touched the wires together, producing several sparks.

"It's the will of Allah, blessed be His name," he added, his eyes bulging from their sockets. "I'm only a tool He uses to enact His word."

"Fuck Allah's will," Nuria spat. "Is it an attack? How are you planning on doing it? When? Who's with you?"

"Allah is with me," Kamal replied. "To whoever fights for the cause of Allah, whether he falls in defeat or triumphs—"

Nuria finished the sentence. "—we shall give a magnificent reward." Kamal's eyes opened wide in genuine surprise. "Yes, I've read it too," she clarified. "In a book at Ali Hussain's house during his funeral. The same book," she hazarded, "that the imam gave you tonight at the Islamic Center, with that quote underlined for you to read, right?" She didn't need the young man to answer to know she was right. "He's the one who's behind all this, isn't he? Is Imam Mohammed Ibn Marrash a terrorist?"

Instead of answering, Kamal asked, "Who are you?"

"A friend," she replied without thinking, "even though I might not look like one. I just want to stop what happened to Ali Hussain from happening to you."

"And why should you care what happens to me or doesn't?"

"It's my job."

"You're not a cop," Kamal said.

Nuria hesitated for a moment, then shook her head. "No, I'm not," she said sadly.

"So what do you want, then?"

"To help you."

"Help me?" Kamal snorted. "Well then, untie me."

"I will, I promise. But first you're going to tell me what you're planning here."

"Why do you think I'm going to betray my people, my imam, and my God by telling you anything?"

"Well, in the first place"—she brandished the wires she was still holding at him—"because I can still make you. But besides," she added, "that way you'll avoid ending up murdered like your friend."

"Murdered?" Kamal said, frowning. "You killed him?"

"Me? Don't be stupid. One of your people killed him, to wipe out the trail," Nuria reasoned aloud, realizing the pieces were beginning to fall into place as she spoke.

"No, that's not possible," the boy said confidently. "Ali wanted to be part of jihad."

"Jihad? Is that what this is about?"

"It's always about that," Kamal said. "It's the only fight worth dying for."

Abruptly, as if all the lights in her head had switched on at the same time, Nuria understood that she hadn't been mistaken, nor had she been led astray by Elias's presumed insanity, as Puig had made her believe. It was all true: her suspicions, her certainties … and finally, it had been fate or chance that had led her to that basement papered with answers.

Overwhelmed by her sudden epiphany, Nuria almost forgot Kamal and her line of questioning. Turning to the map of Barcelona, she dropped the wires and went to the other side of the basement, her eyes fixed on the circle drawn in red felt-tip marker over the Nou Palau Blaugrana.

Whoever was behind all this was planning something terrible. Every week there were one or two basketball games in that arena that frequently attracted more than twenty thousand spectators. Twenty thousand potential victims, in the case of an attack with explosives. It would be the largest-scale terrorist attack in history, ten times worse than the famous attack on the Twin Towers.

The magnitude of the tragedy was so colossal she couldn't even conceive of what it would mean for the city, the country, the whole world. Nothing would ever be the same if they managed to pull it off.

"That's it, isn't it?" she said to herself, heedless of whether Kamal heard her over the Arabeat music that was still blasting on the radio. "An attack, using the explosives you brought in the container from the Caliphate of Mecca. You want"—she swallowed—"to blow up the Palau."

It was then that Nuria noticed some symbols, framed within diagonal lines and surrounded by words in Arabic. It was a date, written in Arabic numerals. Nuria recognized the symbol occupying the place where the month would be. It was identical to the one used in the western alphabet: a nine.

"September …" she said, recalling that they were already at the end of the month. Turning abruptly to Kamal, she said, "You want to do it in the next few—" Nuria stopped short, realizing she was no longer alone with him. Standing next to Kamal were two men with Arab features, murderous expressions on their faces, training their guns directly on her.

One of them turned off the blaring music that had prevented Nuria from hearing them arrive. In the sudden silence, she could hear the wooden steps creaking under the weight of a man coming carefully down the stairs.

"Look who we have here," the imam said, appearing in his spotless white robe, a perverse grin on his face that stretched from ear to ear. "The impertinent infidel."

57

One of the imam's companions continued to train his gun on her while the other freed Kamal, using a knife to cut the duct tape that held him immobilized. As soon as he was free he pulled up his underwear and pants, anxious to recover his dignity. Next, he approached Nuria and spat in her face. "You're going to pay for this," he hissed through his teeth.

Nuria said nothing, but she knew he was right. She was going to pay, doubtlessly in the worst possible way. All that remained to her was the pleasure of fitting all the pieces of the puzzle together before they pulled *her* to pieces. "I knew you were behind this," she said to the cleric who was watching her from a prudent distance while his two minions busied themselves seating her in the same chair where she'd tied Kamal up. They used the roll of duct tape she'd left on the table to bind her the same way.

"I know," the imam admitted. "Pity nobody believed you."

"Who says they didn't?"

The imam shook his head. "Miss Badal … you're like a child trying to solve a problem in quantum mechanics."

"Well then, explain it to me," Nuria said, as she watched the other two men affix her ankles to the legs of the chair. "My calendar for this evening just became wide open."

"I'm glad to see you still have a sense of humor." The cleric smiled. "You're going to need it."

"Tell that to the police when they show up."

"Please don't insult my intelligence. This basement is isolated. No signal can breach these walls. Besides"—he pointed to her bracelet and ankle monitor, both destroyed by hammer blows, where they lay by her foot, pieces of aluminum foil scattered around them—"I see you yourself took care to make sure no one could locate you. So you know as well as I do," he concluded, "that nobody's going to come."

"You did."

"Because you activated an alarm in the tunnel. Did you really think you could get in here without us finding out? Curiosity killed the cat," he recited with a sinister smile. "That's what people say, right?" As Nuria watched, his eyes fell on the battery and copper wiring she'd threatened to torture Kamal with.

She followed his gaze, unable to keep a shiver from running down her spine. "I wasn't going to use it," she said. "I was only trying to frighten him into talking."

"Of course. Did he?" the cleric asked with a glance at Kamal. "Did he tell you anything interesting?"

"As a matter of fact, he didn't," she confessed. "But you don't have to be a genius to figure out what you're planning here."

"No?"

"You want to carry out an attack."

The imam smiled condescendingly. "You don't say."

"At the Barcelona basketball stadium, before the end of the month." She pointed to the map on the wall with her chin. "With the CL-20 explosive you had brought from the Caliphate of Mecca that you then took to a shop in the Raval and then hid in the sewer." The imam arched his brows in genuine surprise. "Don't you want to know how I know all this?" Nuria asked, pulling at the line so the fish wouldn't drop the hook.

"Not really, no," the imam replied, recovering from his initial surprise.

"You don't?" Now it was Nuria's turn to be surprised.

"No," he repeated, showing his teeth in a self-satisfied smile. "It doesn't matter in the least what you know or don't know. Everything is programmed now, and the will of Allah, blessed be His name, will be done regardless of whatever you or anyone else may think you know." He added, his cruel smile of satisfaction widening, "It's already too late to stop it."

"You forget I'm a cop," Nuria said. "We can—"

The imam interrupted her with a guffaw. "*We can?*" he repeated. "The police, not you, are the ones who would be here if they knew anything, don't you agree? And besides," he added, "you *were* a cop. Right now," he said, pointing to the remains of the ankle monitor, "you're nothing more than a murder suspect who's violating the terms of her bail. If you were to be found dead tomorrow, nobody would be too surprised."

"You're wrong," Nuria protested. She had no argument to counter his words, but she had to try not to let fear show in her voice.

Taking a step forward, the imam bent over and brought his face close to hers. "We'll see about that," he hissed. He addressed a few words in Arabic to Kamal and pointed to something behind her back.

Kamal disappeared from view, returning a moment later with a two-gallon can of gasoline bearing the Shell logo that he set on the floor in front of her. Nuria's heart skipped a beat at the sight of the gas can and the blood drained from her face. "What … what are you going to do?" she asked, trying to control the tremor in her voice.

Without a word, Kamal squatted down in front of the can, used the box cutter to break the seal, and unscrewed the top. The penetrating odor of gas made Nuria's skin rise in goosebumps. "You'll soon find out," the boy hissed. Picking up the can by the handle, he tilted it and poured the contents around Nuria's bare feet, creating a deadly puddle around her.

"Don't do it, Kamal," she begged. "You're not like them."

"Yes I am," he replied proudly. Nuria realized she'd pushed the wrong button. The imam gave a sinister laugh as he watched the scene in satisfaction, his hands interlaced behind his back.

"You're making a grave mistake," she burst out. "I may be suspended, but I'm still a cop. There will be an investigation and they'll end up finding out about this sooner or later."

"Maybe," admitted the imam. "But by then—" He finished the sentence by pantomiming an explosion with his hands.

"But why?" Nuria asked. "What will you gain by killing innocent civilians? Violence only begets more violence."

"True," the imam agreed. "But history also shows that violence is the only language the whole world understands."

"What do you think is going to happen after the attack? That someone's going to negotiate? Don't you watch the news?" She shook her head in disbelief. "There are politicians just waiting for the slightest excuse to expel all Muslims from Spain, beginning with the refugees. That's the only thing you're going to get out of this attack," Nuria insisted fervently. "Killing innocents is only going to make things even more difficult for Muslims in Spain and maybe the whole of Europe. Is that what you want? Because that's exactly what you're going to get."

The expression on the imam's face wasn't the one she'd expected after her impassioned speech. "Really?" he said, a satisfied smile on his face. "You don't say."

It took Nuria a few seconds to understand the meaning of that look, and several more to realize what it implied. "You already know that," she muttered in disbelief. "Jesus. You know what's going to happen. But … why?"

"Do you really think I have to explain it to you?"

"After everything I've been through? You bet I do."

"I don't see why," he said, looking bored and checking his watch. "Actually, it's getting late for everyone."

"Please." Nuria's voice was almost beseeching. "I need to understand. Grant me that at least, before …" She didn't dare finish the sentence as she watched Kamal pouring the gasoline over crates and shelves.

298

The cleric seemed to think about it for a moment. With a snort of disgust, he took a chair and sat down in front of her. "Let's see," he said didactically. "What do you think might happen if your country tries to expel ten percent of its population?"

"There would be demonstrations, protests, riots …"

"And how do you think your government would react to all that?"

"Badly. Very badly," Nuria guessed. She remembered the brutality of the anti-riot squads and the army during the student protests two years earlier. "There would be violence in the streets. A lot of reprisals."

"Exactly." The imam nodded like a satisfied teacher. "Do you see now how simple it is?"

"That's it? That's what you're looking for? Repression against your own people?"

"Does it seem like a small thing?"

"But I still don't understand. Why would you want that? The only thing you're going to achieve is to make several million Muslims suffer."

The imam shook his head theatrically, as if disappointed by her answer. "Do you know the story of the frog in the pot?"

Nuria was disconcerted by this abrupt turn in the direction of the conversation. "What?"

"If you put a frog in a pot of boiling water," the imam began, "it will jump right out to avoid being cooked to death, won't it?" Nuria was about to answer, but the imam raised a hand to stop her. "But if the frog is put into a pot of cold water and the temperature is raised very slowly, it will stay still. It will tolerate those small changes in temperature until it's too late, and it dies."

"I don't get where you're going with this," Nuria said when she saw that he'd reached the end of the story.

"The Muslims in Spain are millions of frogs that are slowly being killed. Our mission," he added, glancing at the men with him, "is to heat the pot suddenly so that they jump out."

"Jump out? Where? Most of them were born in Spain, and the rest don't have a country to go back to. They either won't want to leave or won't be able to even if they do want to, and the only thing you'll achieve will be to make the government come down harder on them."

"I see you still don't understand," the imam said. "I don't want them to leave. I want them to rebel against the oppression of the infidels. I want them to fight for the land that belongs to them by law."

"The land that belongs to them? What the fuck are you talking about?"

"Don't you know your own history? Before Spain or any other Christian kingdom existed, this place was a caliphate and Islam was its religion."

"Are you talking about al-Andalus? But that was more than a thousand years ago!"

"Just slightly over five hundred, in fact," the imam said. "Far less time than the eight hundred years during which this land was Muslim. And it's time," he added solemnly, "that it returned to its roots."

"You've got to be kidding me," Nuria said scornfully. "And you four are going to reconquer al-Andalus with your guns and a handful of bombs?"

"Not just the four of us," the imam said, raising a finger. "As you said before, there are millions of us."

"Millions who only want to live in peace, don't you understand?" Nuria replied. "Many of those people had to flee their own countries because of wars started by people like you. They'll probably end up lynching you themselves."

"It's you who don't understand," the imam insisted. His expression indicated that he was losing his patience. "When they have to defend themselves against a government that oppresses them, against the police who assault them, and against the infidels who despise them, when they're desperate, with nowhere to flee, they'll have no choice but to rise up in arms against the injustice. Then they'll understand that only jihad can save them, that only by reconquering this land will they be able to live in peace again. Exactly the way it happened in Iran, Syria, and Morocco."

Nuria shook her head and exhaled wearily. "Okay, sure. Now I understand. You're completely insane," she concluded. "That's never going to happen." She turned to the three men who had stayed on the margins of the conversation. "Don't you see he's pulling the wool over your eyes? He's talking about something that happened when people fought with spears and swords." Looking directly at Kamal, she continued. "There's not going to be any reconquest or any al-Andalus. All that's going to happen is that you're going to end up dead or in jail because of one lunatic."

In reply, the imam stood up impatiently. "I think I've wasted enough time on you," he said. He turned to Kamal and said something in Arabic.

"Wait!" Nuria protested, trying to prolong her life, if only by a few seconds. "You're making a terrible mistake!"

"My only mistake," the cleric replied, bored with the conversation, "was not getting rid of you from the beginning."

"Like you did with Gloria?" Nuria spat.

For an instant the imam seemed nonplussed. Possibly he hadn't even known the name of David's wife when he'd ordered her killed. He pointed to Nuria and said to Kamal, "*Afealha alan.*"

The boy nodded respectfully, took the box cutter he'd used to tear off the seal of the gas can and squatted down in front of Nuria. "You'd better close your eyes," he said, almost kindly.

"No!" Nuria twisted against her bonds. "Don't do it," she pleaded, her voice distorted by the anguish that was rising up in her throat.

"Close your eyes," Kamal insisted. He brought the box cutter closer to her throat. "It will be easier that way."

Understanding that he meant it would be easier for *him*, Nuria forced herself to keep her eyes wide open. "No," she said, addressing the comment to Kamal as well as the imam and his two minions, who seemed to be enjoying the show.

"As you please," Kamal said with regret, and stood up. He went around her, stopping in back of her. Clutching her hair firmly with his left hand, he used his right to set the blade of the box cutter against her throat.

58

Kamal began to recite a prayer in Arabic. Nuria clenched her teeth, praying only that she would feel no pain when the sharp blade slit her carotid artery. "You're a bunch of fucking murdering psychopaths," she mumbled, accepting at last that her fate was sealed, say what she would.

"Goodbye, Officer Badal," the imam said, casually smoothing his robe. "You've already made me waste too much time. Now Kamal will take care of—"

Before he could finish his sentence, two muffled detonations sounded from the far side of the basement. The two minions flanking the imam sprouted two red flowers on their foreheads and collapsed in a single movement as if they'd rehearsed it.

Unable to grasp what had happened, Nuria turned to look at the imam again and saw that he was as confused as she was. He turned around with a bewildered expression on his face, his bulky figure preventing her from seeing what was behind him. Hurling himself at the body of one of his men, he wrenched the gun from his dead hand and, crying "*Allahu Akbar!*" fired two shots at the other end of the room.

Before he could fire a third, there were two new detonations. The imam's body convulsed. An instant later, he crumpled to the ground next to the other two bodies, two bullet holes in his chest.

That was when Nuria finally saw that the trapdoor was partly open and the barrel of a gun was poking through it. "*La tataharak 'awsa'asibik!*" shouted a familiar voice. Kamal, still standing behind her, pulled her head back by the hair, forcing her to look at the ceiling and leaving her throat exposed like a lamb's after Ramadan. "*Al'iifraj ean alsikin!*" the same voice ordered again. Immobilized, Nuria couldn't see who it belonged to, but it sounded very familiar.

"*Iidha aqtarabat, sa'aqtuluha!*" Kamal replied, pressing the edge of the box cutter against her skin.

"Drop the knife!" the voice ordered, changing languages. "I won't hurt you. I give you my word."

"I'm going to kill her!" Kamal repeated, and Nuria felt the steel pressing into her flesh.

"Look," the voice said, calm but freighted with tension. "I'm setting my gun on the floor." Nuria heard the sound of a metal object touching the floor as the new arrival added, "You see?" Kamal's hold on her hair relaxed a little, allowing her to lower her gaze far enough to see that her hearing hadn't tricked her. It was Elias. "You see?" he repeated, raising his hands as he came up out of the trapdoor into the room. "I'm unarmed. Let her go, and we'll talk."

"Stay where you are!" roared Kamal.

Ignoring him, Elias took a cautious step forward. "I'm not going to hurt you," he insisted, his hands still in the air.

Kamal moved the box cutter away from Nuria's throat and threatened Elias with it. "I told you to—" His words were abruptly silenced by a muffled detonation, like a firecracker under a pillow. Kamal flew through the air as if he'd been kicked in the chest.

The explosion had come from the trapdoor that had been left open. A second later Giwan put his head through it. Holding a smoking gun with a large silencer attached to it with both hands, he emerged from the tunnel still aiming at Kamal where the boy lay on the floor, shaken and with a growing puddle of blood forming under his right shoulder.

"Are you all right?" Elias asked anxiously. He'd thrown himself at her the moment the shot was fired.

Nuria, still stunned, could barely focus on the man in front of her, much less comprehend what had just happened before her eyes. Breathing shakily, she finally managed to get out, "How ...?"

Elias reached for the box cutter that had fallen to the floor and began to cut her bonds. "I'll explain later," he said, sawing at a thick black zip tie.

She fixed her gaze on him. "No, now. How did you know I was here?"

Elias stopped cutting the zip tie and looked up at her. In his eyes, Nuria could read deep concern. "You still don't trust me?" Instead of answering, Nuria continued to stare at him, waiting for him to explain. With a disappointed sigh, Elias pointed to the band of white skin on her left wrist. "Your bracelet," he said. "You took it with you when you ran out of my house. When I tried to locate it, I saw the signal disappear in that shed on the other side of the highway."

"I thought it was untraceable."

"So it is." He smiled. "Except for me, of course."

"And you came to see what had happened?"

Elias nodded, busying himself with the box cutter again. "We found the tunnel, we went through it ... and, well, you know the rest of the story." Cutting her last bond, Elias remained in a crouch before her. "You have a small cut on your throat," he said, taking a tissue from his pocket and applying it to the wound. "That bastard—"

"I'm sorry," she interrupted. "About everything. I've behaved like a lunatic."

Elias arched an eyebrow. "You think?"

303

"Don't say anything," she said. Leaning forward, she took his face in her hands and kissed him on the lips. A long, deep kiss which both found hard to bring to an end. When at last their lips slowly parted, Elias still held her face as he gazed into her eyes.

Elias's faint smile mirrored her own as she whispered, "Thank you."

"My pleasure," he replied, his eyes bright with emotion.

They were interrupted by Kamal shouting, *"Luein Allah laka, almartad alkhayin!"*

Nuria and Elias turned to the young man who was still lying on the floor, his left hand pressed to the wound on his shoulder. Giwan stood in front of him with his gun aimed at his head.

"What's he saying?" Nuria asked. Until that moment she hadn't realized Aza and Yihan were also in the basement, keeping watch on the stairs and the trapdoor with their Vector automatic rifles.

Elias waved the matter aside. "That Allah will curse us, that we're a bunch of apostate traitors … you know, the same old thing."

Nuria got up from the chair with an effort, refusing Elias's hand when he tried to help her. "I can do it myself," she said, softening her words with a *thanks.*

"You've said thank you twice in two minutes?" Elias said with a frown. "Who are you and what have you done with Nuria?"

Nuria shot him a sidelong glance as she went over to Kamal, squatting down beside him to examine the growing bloodstain around him. "Looks like the shot pierced an artery," she told him, not really knowing whether it was true, but trusting that his knowledge of anatomy wasn't extensive. "If we don't stop the hemorrhage," she added in a professional tone, "you'll bleed to death."

"It doesn't matter," he muttered through clenched teeth, his voice distorted by pain. "Allah the merciful will welcome me to—"

"Yeah, yeah," Nuria interrupted him. "You told me that before." Turning to Giwan, she pointed to his weapon. "Can I borrow your gun?"

With a questioning look, the Kurd turned to Elias, who nodded. Giwan obediently proffered the grip of his Sig Sauer. She took it cautiously, the weight of the bulky silencer forcing her to hold it with both hands.

Turning to Kamal, she pointed it at his head. He gave a scornful snort, as if he found this attempt to intimidate him very amusing. "Go ahead, infidel," he said, emboldened. "Shoot. I know you're going to let me die anyway."

"You're right there," Nuria agreed. "Little shits like you have no right to live. But you're wrong about Allah welcoming you to his bosom and all that. Haven't they told you what happens to a jihadist if a woman kills him?" Kamal struggled to keep up his defiant pose, but Nuria saw a shadow of doubt appear in his eyes. "Isn't that right, Giwan?" she asked the Kurd, who was still beside her. "Wasn't there a women's division in the Kurdish army in Syria that fought against the ISIS jihadists? They were the—"—she tried to remember for a moment—"Oh yes. The YPG, wasn't it?

Giwan nodded, surprised at Nuria's knowledge. "*Yekîneyên Parastina Gel*," he said in his own language. "Brave women," he added. "If woman kill jihadist, he not go to paradise. Men of Daesh flee"—his lips curved in something like a smile—"when women of YPG arrive."

Nuria smiled and turned to Kamal again. "Now do you understand?" she asked, seeing in his gaze that he did. "If I kill you before you bleed out, no paradise, no Allah, no seventy-two virgins. You'll rot in hell, or wherever it is all the fucking jihadist losers and virgins like you go."

Elias had come to stand behind her. "She's right," he said. "If she kills you, you won't go to heaven."

"You're lying," Kamal said, but his confidence was dissolving like a sugar cube in a cup of doubt. "Just like you were lying when you said you weren't going to hurt me."

"I didn't," Elias reminded him. "He was the one who shot you"—he pointed to Giwan—"not me."

"You decide," Nuria intervened again, trying to maintain the pressure on Kamal. "Either you tell me everything you know or you're going straight to hell."

"*Allahu Akbar,*" Kamal recited. "*Ashhaduan la Ilahail-la Al-lah.*"

Nuria took a deep inhalation, trying to breathe in patience along with oxygen, then exhaled with exaggerated slowness. "Whatever floats your boat." She crouched down by his head and put the barrel of the gun to his temple. "I'll give you five seconds to save your soul. One ... two ... three ..."

To her surprise, the expression on Kamal's face was not one of terror, or even concern. Instead, the young man's lips curved in a cruel smile. Sensing something wasn't right, Nuria scooted back just in time to glimpse the small object the boy had hidden in his left hand. "Look out!" she shouted as she saw Kamal's thumb descend on the lighter, turning the tiny wheel. "*Allahu Akbar!*" he howled, waving the flaming lighter in front of Nuria, who was still soaked in gasoline. "*Allahu Akbar!*"

59

Nuria froze, unable to react. Time slowed to a stop as Kamal threw the lighter into the air. She watched, hypnotized by the tiny flame that traced a graceful arc in the air, ready to set her on fire like an Olympic torch. Part of her mind told her all she could do was bear witness to her own demise. Not moving was an easy way to end all this.

"Move!" Elias shouted behind her. Before she had time to register his words he tackled her without warning. A second later she found herself rolling on the floor in a tangle of arms and legs.

"*Hariq! Hariq!*" Yihan shouted in Arabic.

"*Indhahab!*" Aza yelled.

Disoriented, Nuria couldn't comprehend what had happened until a gust of heat struck her face. All at once she didn't need to understand Arabic to know they were shouting *Fire! Fire!*

Without giving her time to sit up, Giwan yanked her by the arm, lifting her like a sack of potatoes. It was only then that she realized the whole room had burst into flames. Fire was licking at the ceiling and spreading rapidly across the floor.

"You're on fire!" Elias shouted at her, slapping at her hair to put out the flames.

Nuria did the same, panicked by the growing heat on her scalp. Looking down, she saw in horror that the hem of her T-shirt was in flames as well. "I'm on fire! Fuck! I'm burning!" she yelled. Grabbing the hem of her shirt, she tore it off and threw it as far away as she could. The gasoline with which Kamal had soaked the basement had burnt quickly, turning every bookcase into fuel for the fire and flooding the room with an unbreathable black smoke that was accumulating near the ceiling like a malign presence.

"*Indhahab!*" Aza shouted again, running for the stairs.

Elias pulled at her. "Come on! It's the only way out!"

"Watch out!" Giwan warned from behind them. Kamal, enveloped in flames after falling into the puddle of gasoline he'd poured around Nuria, was lunging at her with the box cutter in his hand.

"Kamal, no!" she yelled at him, in vain. When he was almost upon her, she raised the gun that was still in her hands in a reflex action, pulling the trigger repeatedly.

Unfortunately, as Nuria already knew, in spite of the way it may appear in the movies, gunshots—unless they hit the heart or the brain—don't result in instant death. Generally the only thing they accomplish is to piss off the intended victim even more. This was exactly what happened to Kamal, who, in his insane rage, was beyond feeling pain. He hurled himself at Nuria, howling in pure fury and wielding the box cutter like a scimitar to the cry of *"Allahu Akbar!"*

Nuria threw herself backwards as the human torch raised his arm to strike a blow at her neck, avoiding the sharp blade by no more than a few millimeters. Kamal took another step toward her in an attempt to reach her with a reverse stroke, but a new salvo of gunshots stopped him in his tracks. The boy collapsed as though his puppet-strings had been cut, his lifeless body rolling down the few steps he'd managed to climb and landing face down at the foot of the stairs, where the fire consumed him. Nuria looked up and saw Elias above her, still aiming his smoking gun in Kamal's direction as if not yet convinced he was completely dead.

"Quick!" Giwan cried, urging them to keep going up the stairs. "Quick!" Nuria saw that the Kurd was surrounded by the flames that were licking the bottom of the stairs.

"Up!" Elias urged her. He seized her by the armpits and tried to yank her to her feet. "Up!" There was no need to say it twice. Nuria whirled around and clambered on all fours up the steps as fast as her tired legs would allow, enveloped in the unbreathable cloud of black smoke that was using the stairwell as a chimney flue. Aza was waiting for them at the top of the stairs, holding the trapdoor open and making urgent gestures neither she nor Elias needed to hurry them along.

Out of the basement at last, Nuria looked around and saw they were in a house that was filling up with black smoke at an alarming rate. Elias helped her to her feet. "Let's get out of here," he urged her again. "Open that door!" he shouted to his men. Yihan was already struggling with a solid metal door that was apparently locked.

Nuria straightened up. "The windows are barred!"

"Break it down!" Elias ordered. Yihan and Aza kicked violently at the door with their military boots. The door shook in its frame, but held.

Giwan appeared at the top of the stairs amid a cloud of smoke. *"Alaibtiead!"* he roared. *"Alaibtiead!"* Aza and Yihan jumped back as the massive leader of the team slammed into the door like a bull. With a shriek of metal hinges tearing from the wall, he burst the lock. The door flew open under Giwan's momentum.

A second later Elias and Nuria burst through the doorway, followed closely by Aza and Yihan. All were staggering and coughing, their faces blackened by the smoke.

In the rain that was now putting out the smoldering remains of her clothing, Nuria moved as far as she could from the house before falling to her knees in the mud. She had barely enough strength to stay on her feet, and a fit of coughing attacked her every time she inhaled the pure outside air. The smoke trapped in her lungs was irritating her trachea.

Looking around, she saw that the others were just as affected, trying to get their breath back in the middle of a muddy street of tin-roofed brick-and-wood shacks. It wasn't hard to guess they were inside Villarefu.

Behind her, the house they'd just escaped from looked like any other, with no distinguishing features except for the great column of black smoke that was billowing through the doors and windows and the faint glow of the fire in the basement reflected in the glass of the windows.

"We've got to get away from here," Elias said, barely able to speak for coughing. He struggled to get to his feet, speak, and breathe at the same time. Nuria looked at him blankly until she saw him glance at her ankle. Looking down, she realized what he meant. If she were linked to what had happened and they found out she wasn't wearing her tracking device, she would lose her right to bail and be ordered back to jail.

"No." She shook her head, breathing with difficulty. "There"—she was interrupted by a fit of coughing—"could still be evidence of the attack they're planning." Pointing to the house, she added, "We have to go back into the—"

The earth suddenly shook under their feet, preventing her from finishing her sentence. Nuria looked at the house. It seemed to expand for the briefest of moments as though someone were inflating it like a balloon. Then, with no warning and without giving them time either to understand what they were seeing or to seek shelter, it burst into a giant ball of flame.

Though the explosion from the basement caused the blast to go skywards, the resulting shockwave hurled shards and splinters in every direction like a deadly cloud of shrapnel. For a hundred yards around, windows burst, doors buckled, and the nearest and most jerry-built tin roofs flew in all directions. Nuria was hurled back, falling like a rag doll onto the muddy ground while tiny shards pricked her skin like a swarm of furious wasps.

The effect of the shockwave was so great it only gave her time to huddle in a fetal position, protect her head with her arms, and pray that it would be over soon. The fleeting thought flashed through her mind that this must be what you felt when you were run over by a truck. A truck enveloped in flames and laden with needles.

The explosion was immediately followed by a terrifying silence. Nuria, barely conscious, thought that the detonation had burst her eardrums, leaving her completely deaf. Unfortunately, she soon realized her mistake when the first cries broke out around her, followed at once by moans of pain, the crying of frightened babies, and desperate calls for help.

Making a superhuman effort, she raised her head and opened her eyes. Before her lay a hellish scenario of destroyed houses and rubble. At its epicenter stood the pathetic, smoking ruins of the house, hissing in the rain that was beginning to put out the myriad flames scattered around what was now little more than an empty lot scattered with debris.

"Elias?" she whispered in a barely audible voice, infusing it with all the strength she could muster. "Elias?" she repeated, looking around her. To her right, she saw a motionless form covered in dust and debris. "Elias ..." she called again. There was no reply.

Dragging herself to her feet, she stumbled over to the form and began to push aside the debris that covered him. With a deep sense of relief that surprised her, she found it wasn't him, but Aza. "Aza," she called, shaking him with no result. "Aza, wake up."

Placing her hand under the nape of his neck, Nuria straightened his head. When she drew back her hand she saw blood on it. "Shit," she muttered. She checked his pulse and found that it was beating strongly and regularly. He was alive.

"Aza okay?" a voice asked behind her. Turning her head, she saw Giwan standing there, covered in blood and mud, but apparently immune to the destruction around him.

"He's unconscious," Nuria said. "He needs to be taken to the hospital." Giwan nodded in agreement. "Have you seen Elias?" she asked.

This time Giwan shook his head. "I go look for him."

"No," Nuria said. "You stay here with Aza. I'll find him."

Giwan began to refuse, but she stood up shakily and pointed down at Aza. "He could go into cardiac arrest. We can't leave him alone." Before Giwan could respond, she staggered away, the aftereffects of the shock making it difficult for her to keep her balance amid the tide of debris carpeting the street.

Using her hand as a visor to protect herself from the rain, she turned in a circle looking for Elias, but only a couple of streetlights had survived the explosion, making it impossible to see anything further away than a few yards.

"Elias!" she called again. "Elias!" A figure stumbled up amid the remains of an adjacent house and for a second Nuria's heart beat faster. But her hope lasted only until she realized it was another man, shorter and more solid, carrying the body of an infant in his arms. Like walking dead in a zombie movie, men, women, and children seemed to emerge from amid the graves, moving uncertainly, moaning and calling for their loved ones.

Only now did Nuria begin to realize the magnitude of the devastation. There was no doubt it had left dozens dead or wounded. A tragedy she herself had unleashed, one that might never have happened had she not followed Kamal into the tunnel.

She shook her head slowly, gazing around impotently at all the victims, feeling an unbearable conviction that she'd become a sort of harbinger of death who turned everything she touched into pain and suffering. Feeling a hand suddenly laid on her shoulder, she started, but had no strength to move away.

"Are you all right?" asked a voice, heavy with concern. It took her a few seconds to identify the owner of the voice, covered as he was in blood and mud that was sliding down his face, dissolving in the insistent rain.

"Fine." She took his hand in a worried gesture. "And you?"

"I've been better." A grimace of exhaustion twisted Elias's features as he squeezed her hand fondly. "I'm glad to see you."

Nuria nodded again and turned in the direction she'd come from. "Aza is unconscious."

"I know, and Yihan's got a nasty wound on his thigh, but Giwan's taking care of them. We got out by the skin of our teeth." He took a deep breath and released it. "We were very lucky."

"Lucky? Look at what I caused!" Nuria said, surveying the destruction. "This is horrible. I—"

Elias cut her off, his tone sharp. "You didn't do anything. Those bastards must have had explosives stored in the basement and the fire set them off."

"If I hadn't come here ..." She went on lamenting as if she hadn't heard him. "If I'd stayed at your house last night ... If I'd believed you ..."

Elias held her tightly by the shoulders, forcing her to look into his eyes. "That's enough," he ordered. "You're not to blame for anything. In fact you're the only person who's done the right thing through all this mess."

"The right thing?" she repeated, frowning and freeing herself from Elias's grasp. "Look around you, does this look like the right thing? I've fucked everything up again, for God's sake!" Her lips tightened in a grimace of pain. "I fucked up," she repeated.

Elias stepped closer. This time, instead of grasping her tightly, he drew her to him gently and held her. She rested her head on his left shoulder. "That's not true," he whispered in her ear. "None of this is your fault."

Exhausted emotionally and physically, Nuria closed her eyes and allowed herself to be comforted in his arms. For the first time in a long time, in spite of the chaos and destruction around her, she felt safe. She wasn't even aware that she was holding Elias desperately as well, like a castaway clinging to a piece of wood in the middle of a storm.

"What are we going to do now?" she asked, opening her eyes again and returning to the horrifying reality. No sooner had she finished asking the question than a chorus of sirens, accompanied by red-and-blue flashing lights, became audible in the distance.

"Get out of here," was Elias's immediate reply. He took his phone out of his pocket. "And fast."

60

The black Suburban skidded in the mud as it raced toward the road exiting the slum. Yady had appeared, behind the wheel of the huge vehicle, barely a minute after Elias had called him. They had laid Aza on the third row of seats, still unconscious, and accelerated away just as the first ambulances and police cars arrived.

Elias touched Yady's shoulder. *"Abta,"* he ordered. The driver slowed at once. Elias turned to Nuria. "It's better if we don't attract attention until we're out of here."

"Where are we going?"

"If we manage to get away without being stopped," Elias said, "we'll leave Aza in a medical center. The kind that doesn't ask questions."

"And then?"

"And then to my house, naturally."

"And what happens with all this?" Nuria jabbed her thumb at the devastation they were leaving behind. "I've got to tell them the imam's planning an imminent attack. Explain what happened."

"If you do that," Elias pointed out, "you'll be the one arrested. And anyway,"—he pointed at himself, then at her—"we can't go anywhere looking like this." At his words, Nuria realized she probably looked just as terrible.

She rubbed her forehead with her hand to confirm it. "Shit," she muttered when it came away smeared with soot and blood. Looking up, she said, "I need a mirror."

"I think I left my makeup bag at home."

"I've got to look at myself," she insisted. "Lend me your phone."

"I'm not sure that's such a good idea."

"Do I look that bad?"

Elias seemed to consider his answer, searching for the right words, which alarmed Nuria still more. "Hand me your phone," she repeated.

He put his hand in his pocket, took out his phone, and reluctantly handed it to her. She opened it and clicked on the camera icon in the upper left-hand corner. A second later the face of a stranger materialized on the screen. Nuria could tell it was a woman because of the green eyes and the hair, charred and caked with filth, that fell to her shoulders. The rest of the face was covered in a thick layer of blood and filth. It took her a few moments to grasp the fact that the woman looking back at her was actually herself. "Oh, my God ..." she murmured, touching her face to confirm that it was really her. Tiny rivulets of blood flowed from numerous cuts on her forehead, cheeks, and neck, running down to her jaw and dripping onto her chest, staining her torn sports bra.

"It's only dirt and blood," Elias said at her expression, trying to make light of her distress. "Nothing that a good shower and a few Band-Aids won't fix."

Nuria glanced at him out of the corner of her eye, tempted to tell him to go to hell. Instead, she contented herself with closing the phone. "You were right," she admitted. "It wasn't a good idea to take a look at myself." Turning around and looking at the third row of seats, she saw Yihan focused on Aza, who was still unconscious. "Any change?" she asked. Yihan, whose own thigh was wrapped in an improvised bandage, merely shook his head, looking troubled.

"Don't worry," Elias reassured her. "He'll get well soon. He's tough."

"I'm so sorry," Nuria apologized again. "None of this should have—"

Elias pointed a finger at her. "Stop saying that," he interrupted her. "And now put your head down and stay quiet." He pointed ahead. "We're coming to the checkpoint, and it'll be best if nobody sees you."

Two minutes later they were driving at top speed across the fields, making for the lights of the city. Despite the sirens and alarms shrilling from every corner of Villarefu, getting out of the slum had taken no longer than the time it took Elias to exchange a few words with the security guard. The man hadn't even tried to see who was inside the car.

"Thank you," Nuria repeated yet again as they left the refugee camp behind. "All of you"—she looked at each of them in turn—"for saving my life."

"You've already thanked us," Elias said. "But the next time you plan to infiltrate some terrorist lair, let us know in advance. Please."

"I'll keep it in mind."

Elias turned to her. "And now, tell me. What happened after you left my house? How did you end up in that basement?"

"By following the tunnel," Nuria said. "Like you did."

"You know what I mean. Were you kidnapped?"

"Kidnapped? No, not at all. It was all me. I ventured into the wolf's den all by myself." She bowed her head and added remorsefully, "It was a stupid move on my part. I fucked up ... and because of that a lot of people are dead."

"No, you didn't," Elias said. "You took a great risk and you were lucky to get out of there alive, but thanks to you it's all over now."

"I'm not so sure about that." Nuria sighed.

Elias stared at her, trying to find out if she was serious. "What do you mean? We just gunned down the whole commando and blew their hideout sky-high. Do you think there's someone else still out there?"

"I don't know. Maybe not."

"So?"

"It's because of something the imam said. He wanted to make sure I understood the attack was going to take place, no matter what. 'It's all programmed.' Those were his exact words."

"Do you think they may have put the explosives in place already?"

She nodded. "And programmed them to detonate. Yes, that's what I think."

"Well, if that's the case," Elias said, "we're fucked. Heaven only knows where they might be."

Nuria raised her finger. "I know."

Hearing that, even Giwan turned to look at her from the front seat. Elias blinked incredulously. "What? You're kidding!"

Nuria shook her head. "They had a map of the city on the wall at the far end of the basement, with a mass of diagrams and photos of the Nou Palau Blaugrana," she explained. "You didn't have time to see it. But I did."

"Are you sure?"

She nodded firmly. "Absolutely. The attack's going to be there. What I don't know is exactly when. Except that," she said, remembering the date written on the wall map, "it might be during a Barça game this month. The numbers were in Arabic, but the month was definitely a nine."

"There can't be too many possibilities in that case. We're already at the end of September," Elias said. He brought his phone close to his lips and asked Google, "What matches are scheduled this month at the Palau Blaugrana?"

Almost before he'd finished the question, a soft feminine voice replied from the phone. "The only game to be held during the month of September at the Nou Palau Blaugrana will be next Wednesday the 27th at 20:45, between the Barcelona Football Club and CSKA from Moscow. The game is part of the second Euroleague conference. Would you like me to get you tickets?" she added immediately. "Would you like—"

"No thanks," Elias interrupted her, touching the screen to end the interaction.

"Fewer than five days away," Nuria calculated.

"It's an important game. The arena will be packed." He turned to Nuria, and in his eyes she saw the horror of what might happen. "It'll be a massacre."

"No, it won't," she corrected him, with a conviction that went beyond common sense. "Because we're going to stop it."

314

61

After leaving Aza and Yihan in a medical center as discreet as it was expensive in Les Corts, Yady drove the SUV to Elias's house, where his niece was impatiently awaiting them on the porch. "For heaven's sake, where on earth have you—" Aya burst out as soon as the vehicle came to a halt in front of the house. She broke off the moment she saw the state they were in. "Oh my God!" She ran towards them. "What happened to you? You look like you're returning from a war!"

"It's been a complicated night," her uncle said as he got out of the car.

The girl went up to Nuria, looking worried. "Are you all right?" she asked. "You look really awful."

"I'm fine," she nodded. "Thanks."

"I'm fine too," Elias said sarcastically as Aya fawned over Nuria, paying no attention to him.

"Come inside," Aya went on. She took Nuria's arm and led her inside, majestically ignoring her uncle. "I'll clean those cuts for you."

"There's no need, really," Nuria protested, letting herself be led away. "I—"

Aya shushed her and beckoned towards the front door. "Be quiet and come with me."

Elias, still standing beside the car, turned to Giwan with an indignant expression. "Of all the— Did you see that?"

The Kurd shrugged and raised his hands in a gesture that possibly meant either he didn't understand, or it was none of his business. Whichever it was, Elias guessed that he wasn't going to find any sympathy there. "Go and get some rest," he said to Giwan and Yady, waving at the adjoining building at the back of the property where the security team lived. "I'm afraid this isn't over yet."

The two Kurds assented. After giving them a curt nod of gratitude, Elias followed Aya and Nuria, who had already gone upstairs. "Nuria, in my office in ten minutes!" he called as he went to his own bedroom to clean up and change.

"Okay!" Aya replied for her a second before she closed the door of Nuria's room behind her. Hearing his niece, Elias knew it would be at least twenty.

His prediction was partly correct. It wasn't until thirty minutes later that Nuria appeared at the door of his office. "What are we going to do now?" she asked the moment she stepped into the room.

Elias raised his gaze from the monitor and an expression of concern appeared on his face at the sight of her face and arms, covered with scratches and bruises. Even so, he had to admit his niece had made full use of the half hour. The woman standing in front of him, freshly showered and wearing clean shorts and a loose blouse, looked nothing like the one he'd seen half an hour before, covered in mud, blood, and ashes. "How do you feel?" he asked, trying not to show too much admiration.

Nuria used an elastic hair tie to pull her charred hair back into a hasty ponytail as she sat down beside him. "What did you find out about the explosion?" she asked in response. "Did you find out whether there were any casualties?"

Elias pointed to the screen. "There's still nothing reliable. The firemen think it was a gas explosion, but there are already rumors of an attack. I hope they don't manage to link us to it."

"Link us to it?" Nuria was surprised. "What we have to do is tell them what we found in that basement. We know where and when there might be a real attack and we've got to warn them so they can cancel the event."

"Okay ... but who do we tell?" Elias objected. "And how do you plan on doing it so they'll listen? Your credibility is a little the worse for wear at the moment."

"Well then, we do it anonymously," Nuria countered. "They can't ignore a bomb threat."

Elias shook his head. "They most certainly will," he said as if it were obvious. "How many anonymous bomb threats do you think they must have received with the visits of the pope, the king, the president? Five? Ten? Twenty? An anonymous threat would be just one more to add to the list of nutjobs wanting attention."

"Well then, I'll call Puig. He'll believe me, or at least he'll listen."

"You have a lot of faith in that man," Elias said, "considering that all he wants is to see you behind bars."

"That's not true," Nuria said in his defense. "I can't blame him for doing his job."

Elias gave up. "Do whatever you want," he said, and handed her the phone. "But we'll see whether you still feel the same way when you have to explain to him why you skipped bail. Oh," he added, "don't mention me."

"Don't worry," she assured him, then asked Siri to connect her to the commissioner.

A few seconds later, Puig's voice sounded skeptically from the small speaker. "Officer Badal? Is that you?"

"It's me, Commissioner."

"Where are you? What have you—"

She interrupted him. "Commissioner, listen to me carefully. The explosion in Villarefu … I was there."

"All right, turn yourself in and we'll talk."

"Turn myself in?" she repeated. "No way, Commissioner. Listen to me. Under the house that blew up, in the basement, was the hiding place of a jihadist squad. I was able to escape by a miracle"—she glanced at Elias—"just before everything blew up. There were four terrorists, led by Mohammed Ibn Marrash, the imam of the Ciutat Diagonal Islamic Center. They all died, but the DNA tests will confirm everything I'm telling you. Now, here comes the important part, so pay attention." She paused to breathe. "This squad was preparing a major attack in Barcelona, using explosives. We think—"—she corrected herself—"I'm sure they're going to attack the Nou Palau Blaugrana during the Wednesday evening basketball game." She emphasized the last words.

Nuria fell silent, waiting for the gravity of what she'd just told him to sink in, but his reply wasn't what she'd expected. "Where are you?" Puig demanded.

"What?" She was taken aback. "What does that matter? Didn't you hear what I just said? There's going to be a terrorist attack!"

"You just said the terrorists died in the explosion," he reminded her.

"Yes, but the imam hinted that everything was already set in motion," she clarified. "I think the bombs must already be in place and programmed to explode."

"He *hinted*? Look, Ms. Badal," he said with a sigh as if obligated to explain something obvious. "All the sensitive areas are thoroughly searched before every game. Nobody could hide so much as a firecracker anywhere near the arena without the search teams finding it."

"It could also be," Nuria ventured, "that one of the terrorists survived and is planning to blow himself up with a suicide vest or a vehicle full of explosives."

"That's not going to happen either," Puig objected. "The arena will be protected by bollards and hundreds of police. When there's a game, no one can get closer than fifty yards from the entrance without first going through an exhaustive check with scanners and police dogs."

"And what about the sewers? These people moved around underground a lot."

"That's the first thing to be searched," he explained. His patience seemed to be wearing thin. "The nearest access points are sealed and the tunnels are full of infrared sensors. Any living thing bigger than a rat will set off all the alarms."

317

Nuria was running out of arguments. Just then, something clicked in her memory and the answer appeared before her eyes as if by magic. "Hold on," she said, looking up at Elias. "That's it! They're going to use drones! The two boys who were collaborating with the imam," she explained, more for herself than the people who were listening to her, "had books about drones and autonomous systems. It can't be a coincidence," she deduced. "Suppose they've loaded some drones with explosives and then programmed them to be launched into the arena during the game?" she added with growing excitement. "Perhaps that's why the imam told me the attack was inevitable. Are you listening to me, Commissioner? They're going to attack using drones!"

"I'm listening to you," Puig confirmed, "but that's not going to happen either. We use electronic countermeasures and signal inhibitors. No drone can enter the restricted airspace without being detected."

"But if they've already been programmed for a particular route, the signal inhibitors won't be—"

Puig cut her off brusquely. "There's not going to be any attack, got it? And now tell me where you are."

"Why do you want to know?"

"You know perfectly well why," Puig said. "A lot of things have happened in the last few hours, and you have to turn yourself in or tell me where you are … before things get uglier."

"I haven't done anything, Commissioner."

"You can explain that to the judge who let you out on bail."

Elias, beside her, shook his head.

"Sorry," Nuria said after hesitating for a moment. "But I can't do that."

"You're making things worse, Corporal."

"I suppose so," she admitted.

The commissioner changed his tone. "Corporal Badal," he said patronizingly. "Although you can't see it, I'm just trying to protect you from—"

"You're right, I can't see it," Nuria interrupted him curtly. "Anyway … Goodbye, Commissioner." She ended the call and stood silent for a moment, aware that she'd burned her bridges with Puig. "He doesn't believe me," she said. "He only cares about arresting me."

"I told you so," Elias reminded her. "As far as he's concerned, you've turned into a personal matter, a rotten apple that could threaten his whole career. He might have been your friend before," he added, "but he isn't anymore. Now he won't stop until he's put you behind bars." Nuria's face paled as she suddenly realized the terrible future that awaited her. "Forgive me," Elias apologized, shaking his head as he realized the effect his words had had on her. "I'm an imbecile."

"No, it's fine," she muttered, downcast, her tone contradicting her words. "It's the truth, and I'd better get used to it."

"It doesn't have to be like this," he said, inadvertently taking her hand. "I can help you get out of the country."

The ghost of a weary smile appeared on her face. "Thanks, but I don't want to become a fugitive. If I can manage to prove my innocence I'll spend some time in prison for skipping bail," she speculated, "and then I can start again from scratch. Or almost," she added, remembering that a jail sentence would bring her citizenship grades down a few notches.

"You haven't done any of the things they're accusing you of," Elias said, "plus, you've uncovered a jihadist plot. They ought to give you a medal, not put you in jail, even for a minute."

She nodded. "I know. But it might even be good for me, who knows? And in any case, that will always be better than spending the rest of my life fleeing from justice, don't you think?"

"No, I don't."

"Yeah, well," she said with a long exhale. "Luckily, it's my decision."

Elias opened his mouth to refute her words, but Nuria's green eyes fixed on his were the very image of determination. He gave in. "I hope you know what you're doing."

"Me too."

The office door opened and Aya came in carrying a tray with a couple of glasses of tea and a bowl of fruit and cookies. "I thought you might be hungry," she said, setting the tray on a side table. Looking up, she saw her uncle's crestfallen face and Nuria's barely more cheerful one. "What's the matter?" she asked, staring at them incredulously. "Have you quarreled again? Seriously? What's wrong with the two of you?" she burst out, genuinely annoyed. "Can't you be together for two minutes without arguing?"

"And haven't you learned to knock before entering?" Elias said reprovingly.

"Don't change the subject," the girl said. "You like each other a lot." She jabbed a finger at both of them in turn, like a schoolteacher. "Anybody can see that. Even that brute Giwan has noticed, for heaven's sake. So stop fooling around, face up to your feelings, and get this sorted out once and for all." She put both hands on the table and fixed her eyes on them. "Grow up, damn it!"

This said, she turned and left the office, slamming the door behind her. For several minutes both sat staring at the solid walnut door in an uncomfortable silence that neither dared to break.

"A girl with character," Nuria murmured at last, breaking the spell.

Elias turned toward her. "I've recognized it."

"What?"

"I said I've realized it," Elias repeated. "And I know you have too."

Nuria lowered her gaze and remained silent, searching for words. At last she looked up. "We can't," she said. "Let's not complicate things further, please … not now."

"We might not have an afterwards."

"No." She shook her head. "I … it's too complicated."

"It always is," he replied. "What I want … what I need, is for you to tell me whether you feel the same."

Nuria leaned her head against the back of her seat. Looking at the ceiling, she took a deep breath, held the air in her lungs, and then let it out slowly as she lowered her gaze until she met Elias's eyes, fixed on her in expectation. "Why me?" she asked after a moment. "You could have any woman you wanted. A prettier, younger, smarter one, one who isn't on her way to jail."

"I know all that. But I want you," he said firmly. "From the moment you walked into my office and threatened to shoot me, I knew I wanted to be with you."

Nuria snorted, half smiling in incredulity. "You're not right in the head."

"Look who's talking," Elias said, imitating her tone of voice.

As they gazed at each other, smiling like fools, Nuria felt her emotional armor shattering and falling to the floor like dust. Elias leaned toward her, cupped the nape of her neck, and kissed her softly, letting his lips slide over hers. It wasn't like the kiss they'd shared after their rescue, urgent and desperate. This time it was a kiss of serenity and hope. A real kiss, the kind no one had given Nuria for a long time.

Without really knowing how, she realized they'd stood up and faced each other. She let him kiss the cuts on her face one by one and explore her body beneath her blouse while she clung to his neck, drawing him to her with the urgency of someone who knows their minutes are counted.

Elias's right hand slipped under her shorts, grabbing her ass firmly while his other hand held her breast. Bending his head, he brought his lips to the hardened nipple which now peeked out over the neckline of her blouse.

She moaned and shuddered. Moving his lips from her breast, he picked her up and sat her on the edge of the desk, shoving away everything on top of it. His avid hands ran up her hips to the button of her shorts, which he undid without taking his eyes off hers. He continued to unbutton them as they gazed into each other's eyes, silly smiles on their faces like teenagers playing at being grownups.

"This is crazy," Nuria warned him, not as a reproach but simply as a statement of indisputable fact.

He laughed briefly and kissed her again. "Didn't we agree that we're both crazy?"

His laughter infected Nuria and she nodded. "That's true," she said, seeking his lips again. But before they could kiss, Elias's bracelet began to vibrate and a red light in the ceiling started to flash insistently.

"What the hell is that?" she asked, disconcerted to see him step away from her, his expression altering radically.

"It's the perimeter alarm," he announced tensely, going to the window. "We've got visitors."

62

"Visitors?" Nuria asked as she hurried to the window. "What do you mean? Who is it?"

"I don't know. But alarms don't go off by themselves."

"It couldn't have been a cat that tripped it?"

"It's an AI system that detects possible threats by analyzing someone's walk or gestures. So no, a cat can't trip it," he explained as the image on the screen split into eight separate views from the eight cameras installed around the outside of the property. "Look." He pointed to four of the small videos, their frames now illuminated in red. "They're surrounding the estate."

Nuria could see at least twelve figures enveloped in black furtively fanning out on the other side of the hedge in the rain. All of them were equipped with helmets, bulletproof vests, and assault rifles. "Fuck! It's the police Special Forces," she exclaimed as she recognized them. "What are they doing here?"

"No idea." Elias had sat down in front of the computer screen and was furiously typing instructions. "But I'm pretty sure they haven't come over for a cup of coffee."

"It has to be for me," Nuria reasoned, her gaze fixed on the surveillance cameras. "They must know I'm here."

Elias gave her a sidelong glance and shook his head. "I doubt it. They don't send Special Forces to arrest someone who's taken off their tracking device."

"Then they must be coming for both of us. They know you've got those Kurds to protect your ass, and that's why they've sent in the cavalry."

Elias stopped typing and leaned forward over his desk. "Shit," he muttered. "We've got a problem."

Nuria took her eyes off the surveillance cameras and turned to him. He was still absorbed in the other screen. What she saw paralyzed her. On the screen were two photos, one of herself and the other of Elias, under a headline in large red letters from *Elcaso.es*: *"The terrorists responsible for the explosion at Villarefu, currently being sought."*

"What in God's name—" Nuria abruptly fell silent. Now a video was playing on the same screen, apparently filmed by some witness who had happened to be near the explosion in Villarefu. In it she and Elias could be seen getting into the black SUV and driving away. They couldn't have looked more suspicious if they'd yelled "Allah is great" and waved black ISMA flags.

The office door opened and Aya appeared in her white nightgown, muffling a yawn. "What's going on, Uncle? What's that light?" She came across to him and showed him her left wrist. "And why's my bracelet vibrating?"

Elias looked up from the screen. "Go upstairs and get dressed," he ordered. "You have one minute."

"What?" she said blankly. "Why? What are you talking about?"

"We're leaving in two minutes," he clarified. "You decide whether you want to do it in your pajamas."

The girl, still wondering whether this was some joke of her uncle's, gave Nuria a questioning look. "I'd do as he says if I were you," Nuria said gravely.

Aya was still hesitating, standing nervously in front of them, when Giwan and Yady burst into the office, wearing bulletproof vests, their short machine guns hanging at their sides. It seemed impossible to Nuria that they could have gotten ready so fast unless they slept with their gear on.

"Leave. Now," Giwan ordered, with no preamble. It wasn't a suggestion. Aya took one look at the huge Kurd and ran to her room.

"All right," Elias confirmed. "Let me check the defense systems and we'll be out of here."

"Defense systems?" Nuria pointed to the image that showed the police making their way through and over the hedge. "It's the police. If you confront them, you'll only end up making things worse."

"I'm not going to confront them," he said as he stood up. "Just delay them while we get away."

Nuria looked from Elias to the security team and back. "Escape? How?" she asked skeptically. "Before Special Forces attack a house, they send drones to fly over the site and they block all the adjacent streets. Not even a lizard could leave without being detected."

"Luckily we aren't lizards," Elias said. "Are you ready?"

Nuria shook her head, baffled. "Did you hear what I just said? This isn't a joke."

Elias went up to her and took her by the shoulders. "I heard you. And this is no joke. But I need you to trust me. I know what I'm doing."

"We've got to turn ourselves in," she insisted. "All this is a massive misunderstanding. If we turn ourselves in and explain what happened, about the imam and the explosion, everything will be cleared up. That's our only way out."

"We're not going to do that," Elias argued. "We'll clear up the misunderstanding, but not locked in a prison cell while they use the antiterrorist law on us."

"But—"

"Goddamn it, Nuria," Elias interrupted her. "You're on the run awaiting trial for murder and I'm a Syrian refugee. We're the perfect suspects, can't you see that? It doesn't matter what we say. We'll be accused of collaborating with Islamic terrorists and end up in a cage in Guantanamo for the rest of our lives."

It took her only a moment to realize he could well be right. No matter how disheartening it might be, she had to admit that the evidence, albeit circumstantial, was building up against them with frightening speed. Whatever their intentions, whatever might really have happened, the Patriot Act allowed them to be imprisoned incommunicado for up to twenty-four months, and that was what the authorities would certainly do. Even if they found out what had really happened it would be easier to let them rot in a hole, using the excuse of national security, than admit the police had been wrong and had thrown them into prison unfairly. Both she and Elias were a pebble in the shoe of the system, she realized with resignation, and nobody would miss them.

"All right," she said with a long sigh. "So what's the plan?"

Elias nodded, pleased she'd finally listened to reason. "There's no time for plans. He pointed to the images on the screen. "There's only just time to escape."

Less than a minute later, twenty members of the Special Forces Quick Response Team had surrounded the house from all angles. Equipped with their cumbersome body armor and integrated NQB protection helmets crowned with antennae, they looked like gigantic black cockroaches. They darted around the garden, taking up their posts by the windows and doors, where they placed the explosive charges with which they intended to gain entry. Stationed in their assigned places, they waited for operational command, from its mobile control room, to give the go-ahead to attack the house. Drones hovered overhead, alert to any suspicious activity inside the house.

"Charges ready," Captain Lopez, head of the assault team, whispered into his radio. "Deploying bees."

At his order, the leader of each of the four groups took something that looked like a small aluminum Kinder egg out of his backpack. Instead of a plastic toy, however, the small eggs contained something that looked like a metal insect that activated automatically, spread its fine graphene wings, and flew off as if longing for freedom. But instead of flowers and nectar, these metal bees, controlled by AI at police headquarters, were in search of thermal images and sounds that would help the Special Forces team locate their targets precisely in advance of the assault.

On this occasion, though, Elias's polarized and thermally isolated windows prevented the bees from relaying the slightest information about how many people were inside or their exact locations.

"Nothing from the bees," the team captain confirmed, based on the images of his little flying robot that were live on the visor screen of his helmet. "Anything from above?"

"Nothing from the air," came the answer from the command center. "We'll have to go in blind."

"Copy," Lopez confirmed. "Rules for confrontation?"

This time the reply was delayed for a few seconds, a sign that they'd relayed the question from the mobile command post to higher authorities. "Level five," the voice said at last.

Captain Lopez, sweating under his black Kevlar armor, felt a shiver run up his spine. Level five was the technical term for shoot first and ask questions later, and it was only used in extreme cases. Headquarters must be very clear about it to give an order like that. It was the kind of order nobody who has to carry it out wants to receive.

"Please confirm level five for confrontation," the captain requested, praying he'd heard wrong.

"Level five confirmed," the command center repeated. "Initiate assault."

"Copy," Lopez corroborated, and changed channels. "Group leaders, confrontation approach: level five. Arm charges and detonate at my signal: five, four—" Before he reached three, a series of small explosions were set off all around the perimeter, shrouding the house in a dense fog of white smoke. "Cease fire!" bellowed Lopez. "Who the hell launched that smoke?"

"It wasn't us!" came the reply from one of the group leaders. "It's the people inside the house!"

Shit, thought the captain. "Be careful!" he warned his men, realizing their assault had been anticipated. "They're waiting for us!" His words were punctuated by a burst of machine-gun fire from the house. "Detonate charges!" he ordered. "Begin the assault!"

Four small C-4 charges, detonated in unison, shattered the front and back doors of the house along with the large window in the living room and the kitchen window. The echo of the detonations still hung in the air when the assault team hurled stun grenades through the openings and burst into the house, spreading out quickly and sweeping the ground floor with their laser beams, expecting to be fired on at any moment.

The assault team had taken up their positions inside the house when Captain Lopez heard the distant bang of a vehicle door slamming, followed by the deafening sound of an impact and shattering wood. "They're getting away by car!" one of his men radioed.

Lopez ran to the door they'd just come in through and saw a black SUV with tinted windows dragging a piece of the garage door behind it as it headed at top speed toward the gate.

"Son of a bitch," he muttered. He felt a touch of admiration for the skillful maneuver, which didn't prevent him from pointing to the vehicle and ordering, "Fire! Open fire!" he shouted. "Don't let them get away!"

The assault team scrambled outside and began emptying the 556-caliber magazines of their SCAR-Ls, but though most of the shots hit the target, the motorized hulk was unscathed. Realizing the reason, the captain shouted, "It's bulletproof! Fire at the wheels!"

It was too late. The Suburban charged the front gate like a black rhinoceros. With a shriek of twisted steel, it blew through it as if it were made of wire. The enormous vehicle headed at top speed for the street, where the twenty police outside opened fire with their regulation handguns with even less success. The bullets simply bounced off like rubber balls.

It seemed impossible to prevent that monster, with its two five hundred sixteen horsepower electric motors, designed to withstand the direct impact of a rocket-propelled grenade, from escaping, when all of a sudden a small black tank bearing the police logo roared out of a side street.

Hurling itself at the Suburban at full speed, the tank rammed it broadside, flinging it into the air. The SUV spun, then smashed down onto the outside wall of another property, where it lay upside-down, smoking, the wheels spinning vainly in the air as if still hoping to make a successful getaway.

63

A dozen officers surrounded the immobilized Suburban, taking cover behind other vehicles and keeping their guns trained on it as they waited for the door to open and a terrorist to begin firing at them.

"Stay back!" Captain Lopez shouted, taking off his cumbersome helmet and dropping it on the ground as he ran toward the accident with his SCAR-L in his hands. "They might have explosives!" He'd left most of his men at the house, but four of them followed him down the street as fast as they could, their weapons at the ready.

"Keep under cover!" he yelled, taking up his position behind the small tank and aiming his gun at the vehicle, whose engine, still running, seemed unwilling to give in and accept reality.

The crash had been brutal, but considering that the airbags would have inflated, the captain didn't think anybody would be seriously hurt. That meant that either they were still in shock or else in a huddle, deciding what to do.

Tactically, he thought, the best thing would be to put pressure on them to come out before they had a chance to regroup, but they wouldn't be the first jihadists to blow themselves up on finding themselves cornered. For all he knew, there could be enough explosives in the SUV to blow up a whole block of houses.

"Captain, do you copy?" came the voice from Command Center in his earbud.

Lopez put his hand to his ear. "Loud and clear."

"Report on the situation."

"Vehicle immobilized and surrounded, no sign of occupants. Request permission to throw stunners and tear gas. That'll make them come out."

The reply, once again, took some time to arrive. "Denied," the voice said. "Destroy the vehicle."

"But with tear gas, I can make—"

"Negative," the voice cut him off. "Level five of the rules of confrontation is still in effect. Proceed according to orders."

Captain Lopez was about to insist that the risk was minimal if they used tear gas, and that they still had the tank's ultrasound cannon in reserve. Employed at maximum power it could even leave them unconscious. But if one thing was clear to him, it was that the orders he was getting were coming from very high up, albeit indirectly. In cases like this the correct course of action was to keep your mouth shut and say yes to everything. It wasn't worth risking his pension, and even less so trying to save the lives of a bunch of terrorists.

"Confirm, Captain," the voice demanded.

"Copy," Lopez replied. "Applying level five." Detaching an M67 fragmentation grenade from his bulletproof vest, he raised it high in the air. Seeing this, the rest of his team immediately did the same with their own grenades. "Everybody out!" he shouted to the other officers who were surrounding the vehicle from a distance. "Get as far away as possible!" Understanding what was going to happen next, the officers wasted no time scattering and seeking cover.

"At my signal, safeties off," the captain said, hooking his finger around the grenade pin. "Three, two, one, launch!"

Five small green grenades rolled over the asphalt until they reached the vehicle, clinking as they bounced. "Fire in the hole!" Lopez warned. "Drop and cover!"

Four seconds later, five four-hundred-gram grenades containing a hundred eighty grams of explosive detonated in unison next to the battered Suburban. The vehicle vanished behind a curtain of gray smoke that slowly dissolved in the rain. When they were finally able to make out the vehicle again amid the smoke, the tires had burst, the black bodywork was pitted with dents, and the windows were shattered or cracked. Even so, the Suburban was still structurally intact, which meant its occupants would be protected from the shrapnel. But this was something Captain Lopez had already suspected. Foreseeing this, he hadn't been expecting the grenades to destroy the vehicle, only that the effects of the shockwave inside would knock the occupants out.

He pointed to the SUV. "Now!" Without waiting to see whether his men were following, he ran to the overturned vehicle, crouched down by the passenger door, and tried unsuccessfully to open it. The window was fatally cracked, though, and without further ado, the captain took out his Colt 45, pressed the barrel against the crack and emptied the magazine through it. Not a single cry of pain came from inside the vehicle. That meant that either the occupants were all dead, or else—

"Shit!" he muttered, fearing the worst. He put his eye to the hole he'd just enlarged with lead and saw his fears confirmed.

The vehicle was completely, insultingly empty.

"Son of a bitch!" he growled through his teeth, inwardly cursing the inventor of self-driving cars. "To the house!" he shouted, waving toward the eccentric alpine chalet he'd just come out of. "Search the house! They've tricked us!"

Meanwhile, not far from there, three men, a woman, and a teenage girl were climbing single file up a narrow stone stairway that branched off a secret underground passage. They navigated the route in total darkness, illuminated only by the flashlights of Giwan and Yady, at the front and rear of the group.

"Where does this lead to?" Nuria asked nervously, recalling her unpleasant experience in the tunnel a few hours earlier.

"You'll see," Elias said behind her.

"Stop with the riddles," she said curtly. "I'm not in the mood."

Aya turned to her. "It goes to an abandoned house further up the hill in the middle of a grove of trees next to the highway to Les Aigues," she explained. "Apparently the two houses used to be part of the same property"—she pointed upwards—"and this secret passage connected the owner's house with the one where the employees lived. I like to imagine," she added with a grin that was barely distinguishable in the darkness, "that the owner's daughter was in love with the son of one of the servants and they met in secret here."

"Like Romeo and Juliet."

"Something like that," Aya said with an airy wave. "But with a happy ending."

"Wait a moment …" Nuria stopped short and turned to Elias. "Is this how you went out and came back into the house without our surveillance detecting you? Is that why you bought that house?"

He smiled guiltily. "We're almost there," he said instead, and waved her forward.

Following his gesture, Nuria turned around again and saw Giwan climbing a spiral staircase, closely followed by Aya. Nuria glanced back at Elias. "You've got a lot of explaining to do."

Elias nodded in agreement. "All in good time."

She hesitated a moment, but understood that this was neither the time nor the place, so she followed Aya, anxious to get back to the open air. She'd had enough of tunnels and underground passages.

The spiral staircase led to an open door, beyond which Aya and Giwan were waiting in what looked as though it had once been a wine cellar. The small niches where the bottles had been kept were still there.

"Here's where they kept the wine," Aya said, guessing her thoughts. "We even found some bottles still intact, do you remember, Uncle?"

"Wait here," Elias said instead of answering. He went ahead with Giwan and vanished through a door on the other side of the cellar.

Nuria, not accustomed to waiting, folded her arms and tried to control her restlessness. Beside her Elias's niece, who'd only had time to put on a shirt

329

and some tennis shoes, was biting her lower lip, while her right leg seemed to have taken on a life of its own.

"Are you all right?" Nuria asked her, indicating her trembling foot.

"Me? Yeah, I guess so." She forced a tight smile. "It's not the first time we've had to leave the house with only the clothes we had on."

"It must be complicated living like this, I suppose?"

"You get used to it in the end," Aya replied with a wink that took Nuria a while to decipher. By the time she'd figured out the girl's hidden meaning, she had no time to reply, because just then Elias peered around the door and urged them to follow him. "Come on, get a move on," he said, and vanished again.

Following Aya's sure footsteps—this was obviously not the first time the girl had been through here—Nuria came out into what was definitely an abandoned house. Little more than the walls were left, and they were covered with graffiti and mold. The rubble-strewn floor, glassless windows, and ceiling full of leaks showed how long it had been since anybody had lived there.

"It must have been a beautiful house," Nuria said, seeing the size of the picture windows and the coffered ceiling that had survived a hundred years of vandalism.

"One day I'll renovate it," said Elias, who had stopped at the door to wait for them. "For the moment it's better for it to stay like this. It attracts less attention, and there's no danger of squatters taking over."

"This house is yours too?" Nuria asked in surprise.

"It belongs to a renovation firm that happens to belong to one of my proxies. An investment for the future," he added. Nuria was about to say something about that uncertain future, but she was interrupted by Giwan peering in from outside the house.

"Quick," he warned. "Still not safe."

Two minutes later they were in the midst of a dense forest of pine trees and bushes. Long ago it must have been a well-tended garden, but it was difficult to move through it now without getting covered in scratches.

"Damn mud," Aya protested. She dropped onto all fours to keep from sliding downhill. "Ugh," she added, raising her hands and seeing they were covered in mud. "Gross."

"Come on, don't stop," Elias urged her, panting from his own effort. "We've got to reach the top."

"What?" Aya asked. She looked up at the top of the rugged hill, two hundred yards above them. "We're going that far?"

"That's where Ishmael's waiting for us. It would be dangerous for him to come any closer."

"Ishmael?" Nuria asked, remembering the man who had taken her to the hideout. "Isn't that the one who—"

"That's right." Elias stopped a moment to catch his breath. "We've got to move fast and get out of here before the police start to search this area."

Nuria took a final glance back at the house, now surrounded by the flashing blue lights of police vehicles. There were several black drones flying over it, laying siege to it like flies with a piece of meat.

"Will you be able to get it back?" Nuria asked him, concern in her voice.

"The house? Yes, of course," he said confidently. "Though I'm not sure I want to go back there. Maybe the moment has come to make some changes in my life." He fixed his eyes on Nuria. The moment between them quickly passed as one of the drones began to zigzag up the side of the hill they were on like a bloodhound nosing out a trail.

"They're coming!" Aya pointed to the device. "They're searching for us!"

64

Spurred on by the growing buzz of the drone's motor that alternately swelled and faded, they climbed painfully up the muddy hill to the edge of the road, only to find no one there waiting for them.

Nuria looked both ways along the dirt road. "Where's Ishmael?" she asked. "Are you sure this is the right place?"

"I'm sure," Elias said. "I sent him my location."

"But—"

He cut her off, pointing to the right. "Shh. Listen." Above the drumming of the rain, she finally heard the distant sound of a vehicle approaching from their right.

"Back!" Giwan ordered with a peremptory gesture, while Yady aimed his gun in the direction of the sound. "Wait."

Nuria understood the Kurd's meaning: better to wait a moment longer and be sure that the approaching vehicle wasn't a police car. Her misgivings were quickly put to rest when they saw the familiar black Lexus on the gravel track.

Ishmael lowered the window as he stopped in front of them. "Did you order a cab?" he asked with his rodentlike smile.

"Come on, in you get!" Elias urged them, pointing to the vehicle, an unnecessary gesture, since before it had stopped completely the five of them were scrambling into it. Nuria found herself sandwiched in the back seat between Giwan and Yady, while Elias sat beside the driver with Aya on his lap. Without losing a moment, Ishmael turned and drove back the way he'd come, escaping the drone's field of vision as quickly as possible.

Glancing at the occupants of the back seat in the rearview mirror, he gave Nuria a passing glance of recognition. His expression quickly became downcast when he saw the amount of mud they'd brought in with them that was now smeared over the floor and the spotless black leather seats. "Everything all right?" he asked Elias without taking his eyes off the road, as if the situation were totally normal.

"Perfectly," Elias said. "Everything ready?"

Ishmael nodded. "All ready."

"Where are we going?" Nuria asked. "To the apartment in the Raval?"

Elias turned his head. "Not this time. I have a house half an hour from here where we'll be more comfortable and we can go unnoticed."

"Where?"

"A subdivision on the outskirts of Piera."

"I see," Nuria said thoughtfully. "But actually, I'm not going."

Aya turned to her incredulously. "What?"

"What did you say?" Elias asked in the same tone of voice.

"I said I'm not going. I can't go with you."

"What? Why not?" Aya snapped in annoyance.

"Let me handle this, Aya," her uncle interrupted her, shushing her with a wave of his hand. "What the hell are you talking about?" he addressed himself to Nuria. "Why can't you come?"

"The attack," she said. "I've got to do something."

"An attack?" Aya asked blankly. "Where? When?"

"Aya, please!" Elias scolded her. He turned to Nuria again. "Let's see. Nuria," he articulated slowly in an effort to keep calm. "What do you mean by *do something?* We've already done everything possible—a lot more than anyone could be asked to do." It was hard for him to turn his head with his niece in his lap, so he reached for the rearview mirror and moved it so he could look into her eyes. "You spoke to the commissioner and he didn't believe you; we wiped out the jihadist squad on our own and nearly died in the process; and as if that weren't enough, look at us now, escaping with nothing but the clothes on our backs because they think *we're* the terrorists." Aya's astonishment grew as she listened to her uncle, but she had the good sense to keep quiet.

"I know," Nuria murmured, bowing her head. "And I'm really sorry."

"I'm not telling you this for you to apologize, but so that you're aware of the real situation we're in." Pausing for breath, he added, "The only thing we can do right now is stay under the radar until the situation's clearer."

She nodded. "You're right. But I've got to do something. I can't just sit there with my arms crossed and watch all those people dying on TV."

"But didn't you listen to what your commissioner said?" he protested, his level of agitation rising. "According to him, they've got everything under control. *Not even a fly can get anywhere near,*" he reminded her. "That's exactly what he said."

"I know, but he's wrong," Nuria pronounced.

"Couldn't it be you that's wrong?"

"For God's sake, think about it!" Nuria argued heatedly. "Imagine it was you who wanted to carry out the attack. Wouldn't you consider all those variables? Wouldn't you have informed yourself about all the protective measures the police would be taking? Wouldn't you take them into account so you could avoid them?"

"I think you overestimate the intelligence of the jihadists," Elias said. "Those people usually aren't too bright." He tapped his temple with his finger. "If they were, they wouldn't be extremists. Most of them are poor dimwitted specimens who've been brainwashed."

Nuria laughed humorlessly. "Do you seriously believe some airhead would have been capable of planning and carrying out everything that's happened in the last few weeks? Look where we are, for God's sake!" she added, making a circular motion with her arm that included the whole group. "We're fucking fugitives fleeing with nothing more than the clothes on our backs. Does that look like a coincidence to you?"

"What do you mean?"

"I mean I have the unpleasant feeling that the stupid ones here are really us … or me, at least. Since David's death, I've been losing control of my life and I haven't been able to do anything about it." She fixed her gaze on his in the rearview mirror. "I've felt like some kind of lab rat being driven insane in a maze while someone in a white lab coat keeps moving my piece of cheese around just when I'm about to get to it."

"Don't you think you're exaggerating?" Elias argued. "After all, we're alive, whereas they're going to have to use a shovel to pick up the imam and his gang."

"I might be exaggerating," she admitted. "But it doesn't make sense that they were so clever about covering their tracks, yet didn't have everything ready to carry out the attack, even if they were dead by the time it happened. The more I think about it," she concluded gloomily, looking out the window, "the more convinced I am that this isn't over yet."

Elias was silent as the Lexus wound along the forest roads of Collserola in the rain toward the highway. "All right, then," he admitted, though he looked far from convinced. "Let's suppose it's the way you say. What can we do about it? Stand guard in front of the Palau Blaugrana?"

"I don't know," Nuria confessed, returning the gaze of those blue eyes watching her from the rearview mirror. "But what I do know is what I *don't* want to do: hide."

A little while later, from the open window of a cab, Nuria watched as the Lexus set off northward on its way to the safe house where, if she had any common sense at all, she would now be going herself. "You should've gone with them," she said, turning to the man sitting next to her in the back seat. "Look after your niece."

"Aya doesn't need me to look after her," Elias said. "She's a smart girl, and under the circumstances I think she'll be safer with Giwan and Yady than she would be with me."

"Even so, you needn't have stayed with me. I don't need anybody looking after me either."

Elias arched an eyebrow. "I wouldn't be so sure. But I'm not staying with you to protect you, I'm staying to help you."

"How?" Nuria said. "I'm not even sure what to do next. Honestly,"—she shook her head—"I'm pretty much lost."

"Well, in that case"—Elias brushed mud off his shirt—"I suggest we go to the apartment in the Raval, wash up, and then, once we've got clean clothes on, we can think of a plan of action. We still have"—he typed on the cab screen, activating a countdown"—"a hundred nine hours and eighteen minutes until the day of the match. We'll think of something."

Nuria studied the green numbers on the screen, then lowered her gaze to look at herself. She definitely looked like she'd been in a mud-wrestling match. "That's true," she admitted. "It's all going too fast. We need to sit down and think calmly."

"Great," Elias said. Without further ado he gave the Pakistani cabdriver the address, telling him to make sure to comply with all the traffic regulations. This was no time to be attracting attention. The old black-and-yellow Prius started with a hiss of its hybrid engine, taking the B-23 south.

"Go by coast road," the cabdriver explained, tapping the GPS. "Traffic jam on Diagonal with rain and people."

"People?" Nuria asked.

"Yes, big event today in Barcelona. Lots of people."

"No, not today," Elias corrected him. "The inauguration of the Sagrada Familia isn't till tomorrow, Sunday."

"Yes, Sagrada Familia tomorrow," the cabdriver confirmed. "Today big ceremony at twelve, people come to Spain First rally," he added. "Lots of people and cars on Diagonal. Traffic very bad."

Elias and Nuria looked at each other uneasily. Elias opened his mouth to ask more, but Nuria beat him to it. "Do you know where the Spain First rally is being held?" she asked, her heart in her throat. Before the cabdriver replied, she knew the answer.

"In Palau Blaugrana," the driver said, confirming her suspicion. He pointed to the entrance to the Diagonal. "On radio they say never so full of people."

65

"Shit, shit, shit!" Nuria put her hands to her head. "What do we do? There's less than two hours left!"

Elias was shaking his head. "I don't know."

"Fuck, people take their children to those Spain First rallies," Nuria remembered with a grimace of horror. "Often there are almost more kids than adults."

"I know," he said uneasily. "There'll be thousands of children in that arena."

"I'll call the commissioner again," Nuria said decisively. "I've got to warn him."

"Again? He's going to say the same thing he did last time."

"But I gave him wrong information," she said. "It's not going to be next Wednesday, it's going to be today!"

"I know, but think about it. Considering that it's a political rally, they'll have taken even more precautions. There must be hundreds of cops."

"Yeah, but—"

"I think you should have a little more faith in them," Elias insisted. "I'm not a fan of the police, but in general they know how to do their job."

"We just escaped a full-blown assault by the Quick Reaction Force," she reminded him. "I'm not sure it speaks very highly of them, and—" She fell silent abruptly, realizing that in her own mind she'd just crossed the line that separates police from criminals.

"Fine, I agree," he replied, unaware of Nuria's internal conflict. "But isn't there anyone else you can call? Any other reliable contact?" Nuria didn't answer, still stunned by what she'd just said, trying to understand at what point she'd gone over to the dark side.

Thinking his companion was simply trying to remember, Elias waited patiently for her to respond, finally prodding her. "Well?"

Nuria shook her head, staring at the floor. "I didn't make too many friends on the force," she muttered at last, "and obviously none of them would risk their badge to pay attention to a presumed terrorist. I do have one friend—Susana—but I don't want to get her into any more trouble. She's a beat cop and if she went to some senior officer with this story, she'd have to explain, and that would complicate her life a lot. No," she decided. "I can't do this to her."

"So what do you want us to do?"

"I have no idea." She leaned her head against the window. "I swear I don't know. Even so, I think we're missing something."

"What do you mean?"

"I'm not sure." She turned toward him. "There are still things that don't make sense. For example, bringing a container from the Caliphate of Mecca, sneaking it through customs, excavating a basement and a tunnel under the fence at the refugee camp ..." She shook her head meditatively. "All that requires careful planning over many months ... though many months ago, they couldn't have known about the rally at the Palau. It doesn't make sense," she added, "that they'd invest so much time and so many resources without knowing what they had to do or how to do it. The more I think about it, the more convinced I am that the attack is going to be carried out without any human intervention."

At the word *attack*, the cabdriver turned his head imperceptibly, obviously trying to catch the rest of the conversation. Becoming aware of this, Nuria pointed to the car radio and asked, "Could you put on some music, please?" The driver nodded and obediently switched it on, turning the dial until he found a Pakipop music station. "And turn the volume up, if you don't mind," she added with her best warning smile.

When she was satisfied she turned to Elias, who seemed lost in thought. Lowering her voice so that he could just hear her, she asked, "What do you think?"

"I'm more into classical myself," he replied in the same tone.

"Seriously, Elias," she chided him. "You still haven't told me what you think. Do you think I'm right, or have I lost it completely?"

"If I thought you'd lost it completely I wouldn't be in this cab. But the painful truth is"—he spread his hands, palms up—"that we've got nothing. Because ... let's see, what do we know for sure? That they're planning an attack on the Palau sometime in September,"—he raised his thumb—"that apparently they have explosives,"—he raised his index finger—"and that at least a couple of them knew something about programming autonomous systems," he ended, adding his middle finger and leaving all three in the air.

"It's not much."

"Almost nothing," he agreed. "Although ... there's something I've been thinking about since yesterday."

"What's that?"

He leaned back against the seat and stared at the cab roof. "I can't understand why they took the explosives from the container to that warehouse in the Raval when they had that huge underground hiding-place in Villarefu, with a tunnel they could come and go through without anybody being the wiser. Why take the risk?"

"They might have wanted to be closer to the target," she suggested. "In the city itself."

"Maybe," he said, sounding unconvinced. "But the fact is that in practical terms, it takes longer in a car to get from the Raval to the Palau than it does from Villarefu."

"That's true," she admitted, "even though it's almost twice the distance."

"And that's not all," he added, frowning. "Why would they go down into the sewers from that warehouse in the Raval? If they were worried that Vilchez had found out about them and was planning to pass their names on, they could have hidden whatever they had in the secret hideout, don't you think? What would be the sense of carrying it through the sewers? Wouldn't it have been easier to put it back in a truck and take it away?"

"Maybe they didn't want to steal another van and then have to get rid of it. Remember, that was where I found the fingerprint that put us on the trail."

"Okay, but the moment would come when they would have to load the explosives onto a vehicle all over again and take them to the site of the attack. They wouldn't stay there forever."

"Are you sure?"

He stared at her, surprised by the question. "Do you think they moved down there to live or something like that?" he asked. "I don't think—"

"No, I don't mean them," she interrupted him. "I mean the explosives. Suppose," she added abstractedly, putting the tip of her index finger to her lips, "suppose they weren't really hiding them in the sewers? Suppose what they were doing was taking them to where they wanted to detonate them?"

"From the Raval to the Palau Blaugrana?" he asked skeptically. "Why the sewers? It doesn't make sense. It's a very long way, and besides, all those underground passages and sewers around the field will have been searched thoroughly."

"True," she admitted. "But remember that the wrapper of the CL-20 we found, plus all the leftover cables and electrical material, means they were unpacking the explosives underground. So maybe they weren't just taking them from one place to another to hide them," she reasoned. "They were working on them, probably preparing them to detonate."

"All right," Elias agreed. "Let's suppose that's true. That takes us back to the fact that the police would have found them already if they'd placed them somewhere in the Palau ... or else they *have* found them, and for some reason they don't want the public to know."

Nuria waved this aside at once. "I don't think so. I'm sure that if they'd found them, someone would have leaked the information. Although if they *had*

338

found them, it's much more likely they'd have given the discovery all the publicity they could themselves. Thwarting a terrorist attack on this scale is any government's wet dream, especially the one we've got now."

"That's true," Elias agreed bitterly. "But couldn't the cops have overlooked it?"

"I don't think that's possible either," she argued. "The explosive deactivation specialists are very thorough and have the best explosive detection equipment available. They might have overlooked some small device that was very well hidden—but if what the terrorists are setting out to do is cause a massacre, we're talking about hundreds of kilos of CL-20."

"But then," he reasoned, "that would mean that the bomb's somewhere else and they'll bring it at the last moment. Although if that's the case ... how are they going to do it?" He massaged his temples. "Nobody can slip through with a suicide vest, there are barriers that make it impossible for a vehicle to approach, anti-aircraft defenses, signal inhibitors ..."

"Infrared sensors in the sew—" she added, breaking off in midsentence.

"What is it?" he asked, seeing her staring blankly into the distance.

"Jesus! That's it," she muttered, focusing her gaze on Elias again. "That's what it has to be."

"Has to be what?" he insisted. "What are you talking about?"

A look of understanding spread across her face. "I think I know how they're going to do it."

Elias sat up straight in his seat. "You know? Seriously? How?"

"Let's see." She leaned towards him. "We know they brought explosives in the container, right?"

"Most likely."

"But what if they didn't *only* bring the explosives? What if there was something else in that container? You said yourself that one as big as that would have room for a tank—so why didn't they use a smaller one?"

He raised his eyebrows. "Are you suggesting they brought a tank?"

"No, not a tank." She shook her head. "But what did Kamal and Ali have in common?"

"The two boys?" Elias asked in puzzlement. "Apart from the fact that they were refugees, young, and stupid?"

"Apart from that, yes."

He bent his head, trying to remember. "Both of them," he said at last, raising his eyes slowly to hers, "had studied autonomous system programming."

"Exactly," she congratulated him. "And that's how I think they're going to bring the explosives to the arena."

"In a self-driving car?"

"Not exactly," she corrected him. "No vehicle will be allowed anywhere near the arena, with or without a human driver. I'm talking about something programmed to move through the sewers loaded with explosives and stop just under the Palau before detonating."

Elias's eyes opened wide. "Are you talking about a robot?"

"I'm not sure," Nuria admitted. "I know the armed forces use those four-legged contraptions equipped with AI to carry equipment on the battlefield, the way they used to use mules. They're the size of ponies. Suppose the terrorists had one of those robots," she wondered aloud, "loaded it full of CL-20, and then programmed it to make its way along the sewers until it was right under the Palau Blaugrana?"

He shook his head, not at all convinced. "You're forgetting one thing. According to the commissioner, the infrared sensors can detect anything bigger than a rat."

"That's not quite right," Nuria corrected him. "He said they would detect anything bigger than a rat *with a pulse*. If it's some kind of cargo robot, one that came from the military, the kind they use to get behind enemy lines, it would be stealthy and it wouldn't have a heat signature."

"It's … it's possible," he murmured. He rubbed his temples, looking troubled. "I've seen them too, videos of those military robots that look like a dog or a cat or even a snake, slipping into buildings or caves, then blowing themselves up and destroying a target."

"That explosive, CL-20," said Nuria, "do you remember what we read about it? It said it was the most powerful conventional explosive known to man."

He nodded. "I remember. Second only to nuclear explosives."

"One of those robots," she added, "could easily carry a hundred or two hundred kilos of CL-20."

"Two hundred kilos," Elias repeated. "With that they could blow up the whole arena and everybody inside it."

"And it would explain why they went to the sewers. They weren't hiding," Nuria continued, suddenly realizing. "They were preparing the robot and adapting the explosives to it, leaving everything ready so it would get to the right place and detonate. That's why the imam said everything was 'programmed.' He meant it literally, the bastard. That's why he wasn't worried about dying or being arrested, because the robot would carry out its mission anyway."

Elias's face had paled, like a man who's just seen the ground disappear under his feet. "*Allah yahminana …*" he prayed, shaking his head softly. "May Allah protect us. If that's it … what are we going to do?"

For Nuria, unlike Elias, the revelation had seemed to provide the certainty she'd needed so desperately, like someone lost in the desert who finds a

340

map at last, even though it leads directly to hell. "The only thing we can do," she said firmly.

66

After taking the first exit at the roundabout, the cab turned and set off towards the Diagonal amid the driver's warnings about the gridlock and blocked-off streets they were going to encounter.

Ignoring his grumpy litany, Nuria and Elias studied the phone screen, where they'd downloaded the intertwined labyrinth of colored lines that was the underground map of Barcelona. Nuria pointed to the upper left-hand corner of the image. "Enlarge that area."

Elias moved his fingers over the map's surface, zooming in to see the area in detail. He put his finger on a large blue square to the north of the arena. "What's this?"

"*Reservoir for rainwater regulation in university zone*," she read on the legend. "It's an underground water tank. Here." She pointed to a large structure a bit further down the screen. "This is the Palau Blaugrana."

The silhouette of the basketball arena looked like an oval island across the street from the Barcelona football stadium. A perfectly symmetrical grid of office buildings fanned out around the two structures.

"Look here," Elias pointed out. "Since there aren't any homes in this area, there's only one sewer line that goes under the Palau."

Nuria looked at the thin blue line that divided the stadium lengthwise. "It doesn't look like much. Suppose it's just a narrow tube?"

Elias shook his head. "Think about the fact that every week twenty thousand people gather there for two hours. That's a lot of people going to the bathroom at the same time."

"Lovely image." Nuria wrinkled her nose. "But what I'm wondering is, how do we gain access to it?"

"There's just the one tunnel." Elias put his finger on the screen. "The water comes in from the north, crosses underneath the arena and comes out at the south end, carrying the sewage to the treatment plant."

"One way in and one way out," mused Nuria. "That simplifies things."

"True, but don't forget that the nearest accesses are sealed. That's going to force us to find an accessible one. To the north of the stadium, if possible," he added. "That way we'll be going with the current and not against it."

"Going with the current of piss and shit, you mean," Nuria specified.

"Better not think about that," Elias suggested, returning his attention to the image. "The sewer line goes under John XXIII Avenue and divides in two to go under the Palau."

"Yes, but all that area around the arena will be watched and the accesses sealed." She indicated the blue line. "We'll have to go in above the Diagonal."

Elias followed the line with his finger. "The line goes under Pius XII Square ..."

"Jesus, all these popes with streets named after them," Nuria murmured to herself.

"Then it goes up Pedro y Pons Street," Elias went on, "and turns right at Manuel Girona Avenue."

"Zoom in on that part," Nuria said. "At the next corner."

Elias moved his fingers on the screen so that the intersection filled it completely. "An access point," he confirmed, seeing a circle in the middle.

"It's far enough away that they won't have sealed it," she said thoughtfully. "Although, considering how much rain we've had, we'll have to make our way very carefully so the current doesn't carry us away. It'll take us a good while to get there."

"Or not," Elias added pensively.

Nuria looked up in surprise. "What do you mean?"

"That the rain might be an advantage."

She arched an eyebrow. "I don't see how."

Instead of explaining, he gave her a shrewd look and turned to the cabdriver. "Change of destination," he said, raising his voice to make himself heard over the music. "We're going to the Finestrelles shopping mall. It's less than two minutes away, on Laureá Miró, next to exit twelve of the roundabout."

"I know," the cabdriver said.

"But don't go into the parking lot," Elias specified. "It'll only take a moment." The cabdriver nodded and Elias sat back with a satisfied air.

"To the shopping mall?" Nuria asked, baffled. "Do you think this is a good moment to go shopping?"

"Trust me," was his only reply.

She was about to open her mouth to say something, but for once decided against it. It wasn't as if she could pride herself on making good decisions.

As Elias had predicted, they arrived at the shopping center a few minutes later. He asked Nuria to wait for him in the cab, which the driver had pulled onto the sidewalk with its emergency lights flashing. "It'll just be a moment," Elias said as he opened the door. He crossed the street at a run without waiting for the light to change, ignoring the honking of the drivers.

Nuria was left in the awkward company of the cabdriver, who kept sneaking glances at her in the rearview mirror. With nothing to do but wait, all she could do was stare stoically through the window, watching the passersby walking in the rain, indifferent to the catastrophe looming over the city.

Surely some of them, she thought absentmindedly, *must have friends or relatives who are attending the rally.* Suddenly, her heart missing a beat, she remembered that this was true of herself. "Mom ..." she muttered in anguish.

Salvador Aguirre, the leader of Spain First, was also the leader of the Reborn in Christ movement. The two organizations fed off each other, which meant that most of the Spanish Reborn were also Spain First voters. That meant her mother would be one of the twenty thousand who would be thronging the arena in a couple of hours.

For a moment Nuria thought of using the cab terminal to call her and warn her not to go to the rally, but then she remembered her mother had refused to use a cellphone since becoming a Reborn. They were living in an era when even toasters were connected to the Internet but—ironically—Nuria had no way of contacting her.

Frustrated at being unable to do anything except sit and wait, she switched on the screen built into the seat back in front of her, seeking something to keep herself from opening the door and running off.

On the screen appeared images recorded the previous day showing Pius XXIII, surrounded by his cohort of devotees, arriving at the Papal Palace for his stay with the Vatican retinue. The live broadcast showed the pope, his gaunt face matching the gray sky above his white skullcap, needing the help of two attendants to climb out of the white popemobile with the bulletproof glass dome that allowed him to see and be seen in safety. Apparently, Nuria thought as she watched, the prayers of the devout for his health had been effective.

The images on the screen changed. An aerial shot showed thousands of the faithful and the curious crowding the cathedral square, cheering the pope and his retinue. The television drone made a sharp descent to ground level, where it began to race along the avenue at top speed amid the applause of the spectators who were trying to attract its attention in order to appear on the news.

Tens of thousands of spectators, most of whom had no umbrellas to protect themselves, stood in the rain in their white robes looking cheerful, as if this were proof of their devotion.

Stunned, Nuria realized for the first time that the Reborn, whom she had considered up to that moment to be more or less a minority sect within the Catholic religion, were in reality a mass phenomenon capable of mobilizing millions of committed followers all over the world.

Just then, from the corner of her eye, she saw Elias running toward the cab, pushing a shopping cart loaded to the brim with large Decathlon bags. "What the hell?" she muttered, disconcerted. Reaching the vehicle, he banged on the trunk and the driver, who had been watching him with interest in the rearview mirror, reluctantly opened it.

Nuria heard him maneuvering behind her seat, putting something heavy into the trunk before shutting it with a sharp bang that raised a grunt of protest from the driver. A second later, leaving the cart abandoned on the sidewalk, he opened the door and climbed into the vehicle with his clothes soaking wet, shaking the water from his hair.

"Ready," he said, sounding satisfied.

"What's ready?" Nuria questioned him. "What the hell did you buy?"

"A couple of things I think we're going to need," he said, without explaining further. "You'll see."

The cabdriver had turned around in his seat and was watching in horror as the water dripping from Elias spread along the seat and began to form a puddle at his feet.

"Pay extra for rain," he said sullenly, "and for load,"—he pointed to the trunk—"and for stop here."

"Whatever you want, my friend," Elias said. "I'll even buy you a new cab if you want, but just get the hell out of here."

The driver held his gaze for a moment as though weighing the sincerity of the proposal. Finally, without changing his stern expression, he asked reluctantly, "Where to?"

Nuria and Elias exchanged a brief glance, asking each other silently for the last time whether they were going to do it. Nuria thought she saw a shadow of hesitation in Elias's expression. Fearing that his doubt, the forerunner of fear, would infect her, she turned to the driver with all the determination she could muster. "Eduardo Conde Street, on the corner of Manuel Girona," she said. "As fast as you can." Once the driver had turned around, she added in a barely audible whisper, "Before we have second thoughts."

67

Traffic in Barcelona on rainy days usually meant complete chaos, as if drivers were seeing water fall from the sky for the first time in their lives and had decided to drive around the city at ten or twenty miles an hour to enjoy the miraculous phenomenon. When this happened to coincide with a rally at the Palau Blaugrana and twenty thousand people were heading to the same place at the same time in their own vehicles, the gridlock at the Ronda de Dalt took on epic proportions.

But when, on top of that, thousands of faithful Reborn had come to the city to see Pius XIII and the authorities had blocked off traffic for several blocks around the Sagrada Familia cathedral in readiness for its imminent inauguration, the result was a circulatory disaster that would have spooked the toughest driver from Beijing or Calcutta.

The cabdriver apologized, pointing to the bottleneck. "I warn you. Lots of people." They were at a dead stop, surrounded by vehicles as mired in traffic as they were. The Ronda de Dalt, with its eighteen-foot concrete walls on both sides, was like the bottom of a flytrap where they'd ended up helplessly stuck.

"We're screwed," Elias said after putting his head out the window. "There doesn't seem to be any end to it, and we haven't moved a yard in the last ten minutes."

"We've got to get out of here," Nuria said. "We can't lose any more time."

"The next exit is only three hundred yards away," he calculated. "But it might just as well be three hundred thousand."

"Well then, we'll have to go on foot," she said with a sigh.

"It's over a mile to the sewer access," he reminded her. "And with the weight of my purchases, it would take us almost an hour."

"Your purchases?" Nuria jabbed a finger at the trunk. "Are you kidding?"

"We're going to need them."

"And you're not going to tell me what they are? Why the fuck are you being so mysterious?"

Elias thought for a moment before he answered. "Flashlights and neoprene suits. They'll stop the infrared sensors in the sewers from detecting us."

Surprised, Nuria blinked several times before saying, "Oh … " She nodded thoughtfully. "Good idea … yes. Good thinking."

"Thanks."

"And the big box?"

"Our means of transport when we're down there."

"Our means of transport?" she repeated. It took her a few seconds to figure out what he meant. "You don't mean—" She made an undulating gesture with her hand. "Seriously?" she asked incredulously.

"Seriously. But it won't be any use to us if we don't manage to get out of this traffic jam."

Annoyed, Nuria was about to agree with him when a motorbike grazed her window, sliding through the traffic like a salmon between rocks in a stream. Staring after the motorbike as it moved away, she turned to Elias with a wicked smile on her lips.

Less than a minute later, the buzz of a food-delivery moped sounded from behind. Nuria leapt out of the cab and placed herself determinedly in the narrow space between the vehicle and the curb of the roundabout. Raising her hand like a traffic cop, she ordered, "Stop!"

The moped driver, a delivery boy with acne and lip piercings hunched inside a raincoat bearing the McDonald's logo, reduced his speed at once, but instead of stopping, he maneuvered between the vehicles to change lanes and evade the crazy woman who was blocking his way. In the next lane, however, he was confronted with a man blocking him in the same way. The boy tried to change lanes again, but Elias darted ahead of him, making it clear he wasn't going to let him pass. "I need your moped!" he shouted at him above the noise of the rain and the honking of horns.

"Like hell!" the boy shot back, stopping dead a few yards from Elias. "Get out of my way!"

"I'll buy it from you!" Elias insisted. He took out his wallet and waved it in front of the boy's face. "I'll pay you double what it's worth!"

"I said get out of my way, asshole!" the boy insisted, keeping his foot on the brake. "I got a delivery to make!" From the corner of his eye, he saw the woman leaping over the hood of a car and coming to stand beside the man.

She shook her head. "Sorry, kid," she said. "But we haven't got time for this." Before the boy could open his mouth again, she pulled an automatic from the back of her waistband and pressed the barrel against his forehead. "As my friend already told you," she added impatiently, "we need your moped."

A moment later Nuria was driving the moped towards exit ten off the Ronda with Elias perched on the tiny back seat, precariously balancing the heavy box on his thighs while holding a sizeable bag in each hand. Behind them, the boy with the piercings dwindled in the rearview mirror, exchanging a baffled look with the cabdriver and clutching a Rolex worth a year's salary.

Nuria dodged the myriad vehicles, zigzagging through them until she reached the exit ramp. Once on the ramp, she pushed the five-horsepower electric motor to its maximum output, which turned out to be limited. The combined weight of Nuria, Elias, and his recent purchases seemed to be too much for the small vehicle. Though they'd gotten off to a good start, by the time they were halfway up the ramp they were barely managing six miles an hour. "Come on!" she demanded, leaning forward as if it might help in some way. "Up, damn you!" But the little motor had reached its limit, and was making a hoarse, ominous noise.

"With what that Rolex I gave him cost," Elias mused bitterly, "I could have bought a Harley-Davidson."

Nuria half turned with a grimace. "Even so, we're lucky it wasn't a bicycle." With enormous difficulty, the moped finally managed to climb the ramp, depositing them at the intersection of two boulevards, both equally choked with traffic. "Shit!" she cried, bringing her fist down on the handlebars. "It's the same everywhere!"

"The sidewalk!" Elias said, signaling with his chin towards the few pedestrians who were walking in the rain. "Go up onto the sidewalk!"

Nuria hesitated a moment, but realized there was no other way to get there in time. Zigzagging through the traffic would take them an eternity.

"Hold on!" she warned. Furiously twisting the right grip, she pushed the moped to a dizzying thirty miles an hour. Using the handicap ramp, she careened onto the sidewalk, leaning on the horn and shouting at the top of her voice, to the incredulity of the pedestrians who scattered at her approach, that it was a police emergency.

Five hundred yards and a thousand beeps of the horn later, after nearly running over half a dozen pedestrians, alternately experiencing terror and embarrassment in their unhinged race down Gran Capitan Street, Elias pointed to the left, holding up the Decathlon bag he was carrying in that hand. "Turn here! Left!"

The road was as dense with vehicles as it had been further up the street. Nuria jerked the handlebars and the moped leapt back onto the sidewalk, then darted into the first gap between the cars she could see.

"Careful!" Elias shouted, barely able to keep his balance as he tried to stop the box from slipping out of his arms. "It won't do us much good if we kill ourselves!"

"Don't be a chicken!" Nuria shouted back, barely turning her head for a second before flooring it and taking Manuel Girona, which was miraculously free of traffic. Taking advantage of this, they shot past the UPC campus on their left and the gardens of the Royal Palace on their right.

"From here on it's a one-way street!" Elias warned her as they reached the corner.

"I know!" she shouted back. "I'll get back on the sidewalk!"

"You can't!"

"Of course I can!"

"No! You can't! Look ahead!"

That was when Nuria noticed the mouth of the street they were on the point of turning into. Both sidewalks were blocked off by yellow barriers and strobe warning lights.

"Fuck!" she growled. "It's closed for construction!"

"I know! You'll have to take a detour!"

She shook her head. The entry point they'd chosen was directly ahead of them, less than five hundred yards away. "There's no time!"

"What there isn't is room!" he protested. There was barely any space between the cars coming from the opposite direction.

"We'll just have to fit!" she fired back. Without a moment's hesitation she drove straight ahead into the two-lane street, ignoring the alarmed honking of the drivers who were confronted with a woman, her face a mask of frowning concentration, dodging vehicles at full speed on a McDonald's delivery moped.

"You're crazy!" Elias shouted from the rear seat.

"I know!" she called without easing up on the accelerator. "I'm sorry!"

Somehow he managed to lean forward. Bringing his lips close to her left ear, he breathed, "Don't be." This time it wasn't necessary to raise his voice so she could hear him. "I love it." Though Elias couldn't see it, Nuria smiled from ear to ear, convincing the drivers coming toward her that they were being confronted by a lunatic.

Like Moses crossing the Red Sea, the moped cleaved its way through the traffic, drawing up alongside an industrial-looking brick church with a matching bell tower shaped like a chimney. "This is it!" Elias called. "It's this intersection!"

Nuria braked savagely, the wet asphalt almost causing the moped to skid. She managed to control it at the last minute, coming to a halt barely a yard from crashing into an obsolete mailbox.

Before them was a four-lane, two-way street, jammed with the usual traffic, that crossed Manuel Girona almost at a right angle. "There it is!" Nuria cried, pointing to the cast-iron manhole. "Right in the middle of the intersection!" Before the words were out of her mouth, she twisted the exhausted moped's accelerator. Forcing the oncoming drivers to brake abruptly to avoid them, she stopped dead in the middle of the street next to the round gray cover that bore the inscription *Ajuntament de Barcelona. Clavegueram.*

"This is it," she said, killing the engine and turning to her passenger. "You ready?"

"Nowhere near," Elias admitted, giving his bracelet a worried glance. "But time's running out."

68

Ignoring the annoyed honking of the drivers forced to dodge both the little moped standing in the middle of the street and the open manhole cover, Elias hastily descended the ladder to the bottom of the access well. "I'm down!" he called up to Nuria. "Throw me the box and the bags!"

"Roger that!" She peered down into the dark opening, barely a meter across. "Be careful!" Dragging the heavy cardboard box to the edge, she dropped it into the hole and watched it bump against the walls until it crashed loudly onto the bottom, raising a column of filthy water on impact as if she'd hurled a bomb.

"Shit!" Elias shouted, a dozen yards below.

She looked down, worried. "Are you all right?"

The answer took a few seconds to reach her. "I'm fine," came an annoyed voice from the depths. "But I should have bought a raincoat too."

Nuria imagined this man, accustomed to gold Rolexes and bespoke suits, soaked in stinking water, and couldn't keep a small, cruel smile from curving her lips. "Throwing down the bags now!" she called, dropping them one after the other without waiting for a reply.

"Got 'em!" Elias confirmed after a second. Looking up at her, he added, "That's everything! Hurry up, before the police turn up!"

Looking around, Nuria realized many of the drivers who were passing her, honking their horns furiously and glaring accusingly at them, might be calling the police at that very moment. There was little doubt that as soon as they gave her description and Elias's, all the alarms would go off and the counterterrorism squad wouldn't be far behind.

Resolved to get out of their way as soon as possible, she turned around and began to descend the ladder when her gaze fell on the moped's carrier box that had a large yellow *M* painted on it. Stepping off the last iron rung a moment later, she saw Elias waiting for her, covered to his waist in thick black neoprene. A current of knee-deep sewage ran between his legs. Luckily, the ladder ended on a cement pedestal above water level. The bags and the large cardboard box were resting on it.

"What took you so long?" he asked when she reached solid ground. His question was answered when she turned around and he saw the brown paper bag clenched between her teeth. "I can't believe it," he muttered. "You're going to eat now? Here?" He waved at the filth around them.

Nuria shrugged. "I'm starving." Opening the bag, she took out a Big Mac wrapped in waxed paper. "Want some?"

He wrinkled his nose. "Fuck, no."

"Is it some religious thing?" she asked as she unwrapped it and took a bite. "I don't think there's pork in it," she added as she chewed.

"It's because it's disgusting," he explained. "This place is foul."

"Oh, yeah." Nuria nodded, as if just realizing where she was. "I've eaten in worse places." She took another untroubled bite of her burger.

Elias closed his eyes, shook his head, and reached out for one of the plastic bags. "Here's your suit," he said, turning around to offer her privacy.

Nuria opened her mouth to tell him there was no need for that, but decided she didn't mind being thought of as a modest damsel. Finishing off the hamburger in a couple of bites, she pulled off her dirty, tattered clothes and climbed into the neoprene suit. Even though it was designed for a woman her size, it was so stiff it was a nightmare getting her feet through the legs.

She turned to him. "Couldn't you have found a thicker one?" she asked sarcastically. "Are we going to be scuba diving at the north pole?"

"It's a semidry five-millimeter Neotek," he said. "According to the salesperson, the best they had for holding warmth inside the suit and keeping the water out," he added didactically. "Besides,"—he opened the zipper of one of the large pockets on each thigh, put his hand in, and pulled out his gun—"it has watertight pockets."

"Yeah, sure. But I can hardly move. Here, come and give me a hand with the hood. I can't pull it up."

Elias hastened to help her. When he'd finished they looked at each other, stuffed inside suits that left only the ovals of their faces, the guns in their hands, and the flashlights on their foreheads visible.

"We look like bargain-basement astronauts," she said, gazing down at her gloved hands.

"Just wait till you see our spaceship," Elias said with a wry grimace. He bent over next to the bulky bundle that had been in the cardboard box. It looked like a lemon-yellow chrysalis cinched together by a couple of straps.

"Hold these," he said, handing her a couple of extendible aluminum oars. He undid the straps and grasped a short rope that ended in a round piece of plastic, then turned to Nuria. "Watch out."

"Watch out? What am I watching out—" Before she could finish the question, Elias had tugged hard on the rope, freeing the contents of a bottle of compressed air. The chrysalis opened abruptly like a grotesque yellow flower, unfolding and stretching its shapeless body. In a matter of seconds it became a four-man raft floating on the turbulent river of sewage.

Pushed to and fro by the current, the sides of the inflatable raft bumped dangerously against the walls of the sewer, forcing them to use the oars in an attempt to keep the raft as near the middle of the stream as possible. "If the rubber tears on some piece of glass or metal that's sticking out," Elias commented worriedly, "we'll have a problem."

Sitting beside him on the seat of the raft, Nuria pulled her oar out of the water, where it had caught on what appeared to be a huge, sticky ball of long black hair. "I think I'm going to be sick," she said, holding back the impulse to vomit as she shook the oar to rid it of the disgusting mess.

"Go ahead." Elias clenched his teeth as he used his own oar to maneuver the raft away from the wall. "It might make it smell a little better."

"Look!" she cried. "It branches off to the left there, just ahead!"

"Remember the map," he reminded her. "There's one turnoff on the left, then two on the right. The fourth one on the left is the one that'll bring us under the Palau Blaugrana."

"I remember." She shoved the wall with her oar. "But how will we know exactly when we're under the arena? There's no coverage down here."

"We'll have to eyeball it," he admitted. "It must be about a hundred yards after we take the last fork."

"Suppose we overshoot it or take the wrong turn, or the map of the sewers is wrong?"

"Well, then, we're screwed. With all the rain, I don't think we'd be able to row back up against the current."

They passed the fork. The next appeared shortly afterwards, fifty yards further on.

"You know what I was thinking?" Nuria asked, gasping from the effort of pushing the raft away from the wall.

"Surprise me," Elias panted.

"That if we're right and these people did send a military robot down here with the explosives, I'm not sure we can stop it with a couple of guns. Maybe," she added uneasily, "the thing will be bulletproof. It might even have some way of defending itself."

Elias was silent for a few moments. Then he said, "Yeah, that occurred to me as well."

"And?"

"You're probably right," he admitted.

Nuria waited for him to say something more, but they passed the second fork with no further comment from him. "Wow," she said, taking a deep breath. "I was expecting a *Don't worry*, or *I've got a plan in case that happens*."

Looking straight ahead and pushing off the wall with his oar, Elias said, "Don't worry, I have a plan in case that happens."

She opened her eyes wide in surprise. "Seriously?" she asked hopefully.

He turned to look at her. "No. Actually I don't."

"That's what I get for asking," she muttered, shaking her head.

"What do you want me to tell you?" he protested. "There are so many things that can go wrong I don't think it's even worth mentioning them." The third fork slipped by as he added, "We just need a little luck on our side."

Now it was Nuria who turned to him, arching a skeptical eyebrow. "A little?" she repeated.

"It's just a figure of speech," he said. "Or would you rather hear what I really think?"

She shook her head. "No. I'd better not," she confessed, turning to look ahead again and dipping her oar back into the water.

The weak emergency lights that kept the sewer barely above twilight visibility didn't allow them to see more than the general shape of the tunnel and the current of sewage, which was becoming ever stronger, fed by the drains and the rain that poured into it in small rivulets from the street. Nuria was sure that if the rain continued for a couple more days, the water level would reach the ceiling.

Elias pointed to the next detour on the left, a dozen yards ahead. "There's our exit. Get ready."

Unsure of how to maneuver the raft out of the main current, Nuria watched Elias try to reduce their speed by plunging his oar into the water and against the sides of the tunnel. She followed suit, but realized their speed was too great. "We're going too fast!"

Elias clenched his jaw. "I'm doing the best I can!" The opening was fast approaching. Nuria realized they would have only one chance to enter it. "Use your oar!" Elias shouted, half his body out of the raft.

"That's what I'm doing, for fuck's sake!" she protested, afraid her oar would snap from being pushed against the wall. "That's what I'm doing!"

When they were a couple of yards from the exit, it became clear that they weren't going to make it. Directly ahead of Nuria, at eye-level, she saw a black device the size of her fist, attached to the wall with a pair of screws. A tiny green light blinked from it. Without thinking, she reached out to grab it with her left hand, clutching one of the handholds on the raft with her right.

Immediately, she felt her head snap back, followed by a crunch in her left shoulder, but she held on. The runaway raft came to a dead stop, giving Elias, unaware of what had just happened, the opportunity to dig his oar in and manage at the very last minute to turn the prow of the raft into the opening of the fork.

Confused, he turned to Nuria with a questioning look. "What happened? How did you do that?" Clutching her left shoulder, she dropped the black device she'd torn from its support into the raft. Elias stared at it blankly, finally asking, "Is ... that what I think it is?"

Nuria gave a brief nod. "A sensor," she said. Her mouth twisted when she noticed that the LED light had turned from green to red. "I think we're going to have company before long."

69

"This tunnel's narrower," Elias said, noticing that there were only a couple of inches to spare between the brick walls and the sides of the raft.

"There's much less water and the current's weaker too," Nuria added. "Have you noticed how we're brushing against the bottom?"

"That's true. I hope we don't get a puncture."

"Well, we're almost there, right?"

"Yeah, I suppose we are." He looked up at the ceiling as if trying to see through it.

"Well … what do we do now?"

"To tell you the truth, I'm not quite sure," he confessed. "My plan only got to this point."

"Yeah," she murmured, as if this weren't news to her. "This stretch of sewer has only two accesses, right? The way we came in"—she jabbed her thumb back the way they'd come—"and forward."

"That's right."

"Well, from an operational point of view," she reasoned, recalling her classes at the police academy, "the best option is to separate and cover both ends of the tunnel, don't you agree?"

"No, I don't agree."

"But it's the only way the two of us can cover the perimeter."

"I don't care," he objected. "Separating seems like a terrible idea to me. We should stay together."

"But that doesn't make any sense tactically."

"To hell with tactics," he said decisively. "Besides, it's most likely to come from the south, right? That's where they prepared it, and presumably that's where it's been kept hidden until today. I say we continue this way and find a good place to wait further down."

"And suppose you're wrong and it doesn't come from the south?"

"Worst case, we have a fifty percent chance of being right," Elias argued. "But if, as seems likely, it's some kind of military robot, one of us alone won't be able to stop it, and then"—he shook his head—"the possibilities will be reduced to zero."

Nuria stared at Elias, considering his line of reasoning. "I'm not sure what you're saying makes a lot of sense."

"Neither am I," he admitted. "But either way, I'd rather we stayed together."

Nuria thought about this for a moment, then nodded in agreement. "All right. Every decision I've made has been a disaster ... so maybe it's the moment to try a different method."

"And if I'm wrong," Elias added, "you can say I told you so."

"Don't doubt that for a minute," she said with a humorless smile. "If we survive, that is."

"Well, I don't know about you," he objected, pushing with the oar to gain some speed, "but I can't die." He added solemnly, "I have a very tight schedule next week."

Nuria gave him a sidelong glance. He looked as calm as though he were rowing one of the boats in Ciudadela Park. Despite his outward appearance, though, she could see by the set of his jaw and how tightly he held the oar that he must be as nervous as she was. The fact that it didn't show on his face, though, inspired a feeling of safety in her that even if it wasn't real was nevertheless welcome.

"Look," he said, pointing ahead. "That looks like a good place." Thirty yards or so ahead, what looked like a buttress in the shape of an arch narrowed the tunnel and provided a place to hide, even if only partially.

"You think we've left the Palau behind?" she asked.

"I'd say so. Can you hear that?"

She strained her hearing, becoming aware of a noise that sounded like a rushing water coming from somewhere beyond the next corner.

"It must be the main sewer," Elias speculated. "The one we just came out of. It joins this one again after it passes under the arena."

"Well, in that case, time's a wastin'." She put her left leg over the side of the raft and sat down astride it. "Here's where we get off," she added, swinging her other leg over and jumping down as they came alongside the arch.

The sewage was only ankle-deep, so she had no trouble keeping her balance despite the nauseatingly slippery floor. Elias followed her example. Seeing her holding on to the raft by one of the ropes, he waved at her. "Don't worry about that." He traced the shape of the arch in the air with his finger. "The raft's too wide to go through."

Nuria let go. When she saw that the raft was stuck, a crazy idea began to take shape in her mind. Pointing to the yellow raft, she murmured, "Look. It doesn't fit. It's bigger."

"Yes," he agreed. "That's what I just finished telling you."

357

She shook her head vehemently. "No. I mean it's bigger than the *whole* space of the tunnel." He looked at her blankly. "Don't you see?" she insisted. Feeling hot, she drew back the hood that covered her head. "What would happen if … we upended it?" He looked at the raft again, then at the concrete arch, and finally at Nuria, realizing what she had in mind.

"Pass it through there," Elias gasped, panting with the effort, "and then through that ring that—"

"I know what to do," Nuria snapped as she passed the raft's mooring rope through a couple of rings on the ceiling. "See?" she added a moment later, sounding satisfied. "Done. You can put me down now." He flexed his knees and Nuria, who had been sitting on his shoulders, slid down his back until she was on the floor again.

"How much did you say you weigh?" he protested, rubbing his lower back.

"That's something you should never ask." She grasped the end of the rope. "Come on, don't stand there moaning. Help me pull."

Obediently, he took the rope and began a countdown: "Three. Two. One … Up!" They both pulled on the rope with all their might, lifting the prow of the raft until it was completely vertical. It blocked the entire tunnel, leaving just two fingers underneath where the water could flow unimpeded.

"Goddamn, it's perfect," she said, taking a step back to admire their handiwork.

"Couldn't be better if it were custom-made," Elias said, securing the rope. "Let's hope this fools it."

"It will, don't worry," she said with conviction. "When it reaches the other side"—she waved at the false wall created by the raft—"it will think it's a solid wall and stop. I don't think it's very smart, or that it will be programmed to bring down walls."

"That's a risky supposition," Elias said. "If you're wrong, the thing will go through the raft like paper."

"Or it might blow itself up if it doesn't see another way," Nuria argued. "But I think it's worth trying, don't you agree? We'll always have time for a shootout if it doesn't work."

"I guess so," Elias agreed as he finished tying the knot.

She tapped her wrist. "By the way, what time is it?"

He straightened up, pulled back the edge of his thick neoprene sleeve with no small effort, and checked the time on his bracelet. Looking up at her, he took a deep breath. "Eleven fifty-seven."

Peering through two tiny holes they'd made in the rubber floor of the raft, they stared uneasily down the passage that stretched on beyond them, losing itself to view when it curved to the right fifty yards or so further down.

Behind them everything was darkness. They had disabled the nearest emergency lights for fear that the rubber bottom of the raft might be translucent and dispel the illusion that it was a real wall.

"I can't see anything," Nuria whispered, looking through the same hole with each eye in turn.

"Shh ... don't make noise."

She ignored him. "It should be here by now. The ceremony started a while ago up there. Suppose there isn't an attack after all? Maybe with the explosion we somehow stopped them from activating it."

"Or maybe it's a very vain robot," Elias mused, "and it's still sprucing itself up at home, getting ready to go out."

She gave his shoulder a friendly punch. "I'm serious."

"Okay, maybe you're right," he admitted in a whisper, rubbing his shoulder. "It's weird that it hasn't appeared yet, but even so, we have to stay and wait."

"Of course," Nuria agreed. "It's just that—" He shushed her. "Hey, I'm speaking quietly," she protested.

"No, keep quiet." He put his finger to his ear. "Listen."

She tilted her head, pressing her ear against the rubber and expecting at any moment to hear heavy metallic footsteps splashing through the stream of sewage. Instead, she heard nothing but the sound of the water flowing by, and far away, a remote tap-tapping that sounded like a troop of secretaries typing on old-fashioned typewriters. "What—"

Elias's hand shot towards her mouth to silence her. Under normal circumstances, she would have responded to this amiable gesture with a loud slap across his face. But these were not normal circumstances—still less so as she became aware that the drumming sound was becoming louder. It had become a dull vibration under their feet that she could feel in her bones. Pushing Elias's hand away, Nuria peered out of the hole again, fearful of what she might see.

The reality was far worse than her imaginings. "Oh, my God ..." she breathed. Nuria watched, hypnotized, as a black tide like an oil stain rounded the corner, a threatening darkness clinging like a trembling shadow to the walls of the tunnel.

Muffling a cry of horror, she saw that the tide was made up of many individual mechanisms that moved like a single organism. They had articulated legs and segmented bodies, each with a small head armed with pincers. On each head shone a pair of red laser sensors.

Hundreds of the small robots, looking like black, cat-sized tarantulas, hugged the walls, advancing inexorably toward them.

"Robo-spiders," Elias hissed into her ear, fear plain in his voice. Nuria was opening her mouth to ask him what they were when all at once terror flooded through her.

She saw that every single one of the little monsters carried on its back a fluorescent orange packet connected with wires to its body.

70

The insidious clicking of the metal legs intensified until it was unbearable. The ground vibrated under their feet, and the sound of the sewage stream was drowned out by the tumult of that mechanical swarm.

"Don't move," Elias whispered beside her. "I read somewhere that these things are deaf, but they detect the slightest vibration."

Paralyzed by terror, Nuria didn't even dare answer as she stared through the tiny hole at the swarm of horrific machines, loaded with explosives, that were approaching rapidly, with no apparent intention of stopping. A single one of those spider-shaped devices with sensors like evil red eyes would have been disturbing enough to give her nightmares for weeks. But the sight of an army of them was like watching something that had risen from the deepest level of hell. A shiver ran down her spine and she knew that image would stay with her for the rest of her life.

The first robo-spiders reached the other side of the raft and stopped just before making contact. The others followed suit, stopping in unison, as if they were a single organism with a hive mind. Suddenly there was absolute silence, as unnerving and threatening as the racket had been a few seconds earlier.

The docile hissing of the stream echoed again in the sewer, and if she'd closed her eyes Nuria could have convinced herself it had all been a trick of her imagination. Unfortunately, her eye glued to the tiny hole, unable to drag her gaze away, the evidence was plain that it was nothing of the kind.

On the other side of that hole, time seemed to have stopped. A mere millimeter of yellow rubber was all that separated her from those mechanical monstrosities. They were so close that if they'd been able to breathe, she would have felt it.

Nuria didn't even dare blink. Her only movement was to turn her head very slightly to the right, where Elias was holding himself as still as she was. Realizing she was looking at him, he raised his finger very slowly and put it to his lips. The gesture was completely unnecessary since she had no intention of opening her mouth under any circumstances. The bugs were so close that even if they were deaf, as he'd told her, they would have detected the vibrations of her voice.

Then she heard a faint sound at the outermost limits of her hearing: the lightest tapping, followed by a brush of metal against rubber. Looking to her left, she saw one of the creatures' sharp legs feeling the raft's surface as if trying to gauge its solidity. Horrified, she now saw that, underneath the sensors on the head of each spider were razor-sharp mandibles that were opening and closing like threatening scissors capable of slicing through whatever got in their way. If they used them to slash the fragile layer of yellow rubber, it would be all over.

Somewhere in that hive mind, an AI processor would be assessing the situation. It would be wondering what the hell that wall that wasn't marked on the map stored in their memory was doing there, and deciding what to do from then on.

Nuria tried to imagine the mental process it would be following. She prayed it wouldn't come to the conclusion that this supposed wall was nothing of the kind and that they could go through it with no trouble. It might even decide it was close enough to its target to set the explosives off.

She devoutly hoped the possibility hadn't occurred to either Kamal or Ali that someone might do what they were doing at that moment—attempting to deceive their army of suicide robo-spiders.

Now dozens of spiders were imitating the first, making contact at several points, trying to find out whether there was a weak point or a crack anywhere they could slip through. Nuria held her breath, leaning her weight against the raft to keep it from moving a single millimeter, praying that the mechanical bugs weren't smarter than their living counterparts.

All at once the exploration of the rubber by the metal legs stopped, as if all the robo-spiders had received the order at the same time—or else their hive mind had determined that they couldn't get through this way. The stillness went on for what seemed an eternity. The upsetting possibility occurred to Nuria that they'd decided to camp out at that very spot. She couldn't maintain her motionless posture for much longer, not to mention the fact that an inopportune tickle in her nose was threatening to make her sneeze at any moment.

Her nerves raw with the tension of waiting, she glanced toward Elias, searching for some hope in his face, but just as she did so, the drumming of metal legs suddenly started up again. For a terrible moment, she feared they'd sensed her movement.

Paralyzed, she strained her ears, waiting for the sound of rubber being slit open and the sight of a flood of black robo-spiders surging through the opening. It was with an indescribable relief that she realized the noise wasn't growing louder but decreasing.

They were moving away.

Nuria put her eye to the hole again and confirmed that the quivering dark shadow was retreating down the same tunnel they'd come through, like a diabolical shadow withdrawing from the daylight.

It wasn't until the last robo-spider had disappeared around the corner of the sewer that she dared close her eyes. Stepping back, she leaned against the brick wall, then slid down to a squatting position and heaved a deep sigh.

"Mother of God," she muttered as she opened her eyes again. "That was horrible."

Still on his feet, leaning against the wall, Elias was showing the same signs of relief. "That was close," he gasped.

"What the ... what the hell were those things?"

He turned to look in the direction of the distant clicking, by now almost inaudible. "Military robo-spiders," he explained. "Automatons with a hive AI. They're used to infiltrate enemy buildings or caves planted with explosives, then blow them up once they're inside. It's unbelievable"—he shook his head—"that the terrorists could have gotten their hands on something like this."

"It's pretty clear there's more than just a gang of brainless fanatics involved."

"No, that much is clear," he agreed. "What's also clear is that they have people with a lot of money and resources backing them," he reasoned. "You can't just pick up those things on Amazon."

"At any rate," Nuria said, bringing him out of his sudden reverie. "Whatever the explanation is, they're gone now. What I'm wondering is, what do we do now? Do you think they'll come back?"

"I have no idea," he admitted. "But they are robots, after all. If they've decided they can't get through this way, I can't see any reason why they would try again."

"So ... that's it?"

Elias frowned and slowly shook his head. "I very much doubt it."

"What do you mean?"

"That maybe they'll try to find another way to reach their target."

She pointed toward the main tunnel. "You mean—"

He nodded heavily. "They'll take a detour."

"Shit," she muttered.

"Yeah."

"So how much time do we have?"

Elias passed his hand in its neoprene glove over his face. "Those things move fast. Maybe ten minutes, at most." He made a face. "Maybe less."

"Well then," Nuria said as she straightened up wearily, "we'd better get going. We've got to get there before they do."

He pursed his lips before answering. "Are you sure?"

363

"How do you want to do it if not that way?" she asked in surprise.

"What I'm not so sure about," he said, choosing his words carefully, "is whether both of us have to go."

Nuria took a step back, frowning in disbelief. "What?" She pointed to the tunnel. "One of us alone won't be able to stop that swarm."

"Two of us won't either," he said. "We thought we were going to be facing a single robot, not hundreds of tiny military ones. We don't have the bullets to stop even a fraction of them, and that trick with the raft won't work again."

"So what do you suggest, then?" Nuria's frown was a perfect V surrounded by deep wrinkles. "Shall we run away?"

Elias shook his head again. "No. What I want is for *you* to leave."

"What? No! No way!"

He raised his hands to the level of his chest, palms out, trying to calm her. "It makes no sense for us both to stay, Nuria," he argued as calmly as he could. "It won't make any difference whether we destroy ten or twenty of these bugs. The rest will get the job done, and our sacrifice will have been in vain."

"You may be right and it won't be any use," she said furiously, "but I'm going to try. You can leave if you want." She indicated the raft, still hanging from the ceiling. "I'll understand, this isn't your war. But I'm staying."

"You're wrong," he corrected her. "This"—he jabbed his finger at the ground—"*is* my fucking war. Plus, I'm not going anywhere without you."

Nuria looked at Elias's large blue eyes fixed on her, radiating determination, and felt an overwhelming desire to kiss him, despite the fact that he'd smeared his face with stinking mud when he'd rubbed it with his hand. Without thinking, she waded through the foul stream of black water to him. Taking his face in her hands, she put her lips to his, taking a moment to feel his skin and the moist touch of their tongues, prolonging those few moments they might never have again. *For what might be the last kiss of my life,* she thought, finally separating her lips from his, *that wasn't bad at all.*

"And what happens to Aya?" she asked softly.

"Aya's a big girl," he said. "She can take care of herself."

In spite of his answer, she asked one last time, "Are you sure you want to do this?"

"I wouldn't want to be anywhere else right now."

Nuria punched him gently on the shoulder with a weak smile. "Okay, okay." Turning to the raft, she asked, "Do we take it?"

Elias shook his head. "We couldn't even if we wanted to. It would take us forever to pull it against the current. It's better to leave it here," he added, "in case they decide to come back up this tunnel."

"Agreed," she said with a nod, and put her hand in the pocket of her neoprene wetsuit where she was carrying the Sig Sauer. "Okay then, let's go." She started to walk.

Elias stopped her. "Wait a moment." He raised a finger as if he'd had a last-minute idea. "There *is* something ... that just might come in handy."

71

With a great deal more effort than when they'd come down it with the help of the current, Nuria and Elias made their way back through the sewer, dragging their feet through the stream with difficulty and, on more than one occasion, using the oars they'd brought with them as walking sticks to avoid slipping.

"Is it just me," Nuria asked curiously, "or has the water level risen a little?"

He threw her a sidelong glance. "It's a couple of inches higher," he confirmed, "but I'm not sure it's all water." He pointed upwards and added, "The rally started a while ago."

"Ugh … you didn't need to remind me of that."

Elias grinned maliciously. "You're welcome."

She rolled her eyes and shook her head. "How much longer, do you think?" she asked, looking back and trying to calculate how far they'd walked.

Elias did the same, then pointed ahead with his oar. "A hundred yards, more or less. That corner over there looks like a good spot." He pointed to the next bend. "I think we're still under the arena." He didn't need to add that the further they were from the center of the Palau Blaugrana, the less likely it was that the robo-spiders would decide to blow themselves up.

Nuria estimated that more than five minutes had gone by since they'd set off, and that any moment now they would hear that spinechilling clicking emerging from the shadows of the tunnel. The weight of the gun in the pocket of her neoprene wetsuit reminded her of the thousands of times she'd been on patrol in uniform, with her standard-issue gun bumping against her hip in its holster. It seemed impossible that just a few weeks ago she'd been a police officer on duty, enjoying a life that was for the most part predictable and routine.

She shook her head to drive away the memory of a time that, she was now sure, was gone forever. It was ironic, Nuria thought with a bitter smile, that she was about to perform the most heroic act of her life now that she was a fugitive from justice and her face was on the *Wanted* posters at every station.

"It's funny," she murmured to herself.

"What is?" he asked beside her.

She shook her head. "Nothing ... just something I was thinking. Any idea what we're going to do when these things arrive?"

Instead of answering at once, Elias went on walking in silence, his jaw set. "No," he finally said just when it began to look as if he wasn't going to answer. He turned, a hint of apology in his eyes. "Whatever we can ... I guess."

Nuria nodded heavily; she'd known what the answer would be. The chances of stopping that mechanical horde with a couple of guns and barely thirty bullets between them were remote—and even that was optimistic. She snorted philosophically. "Oh, well ... if it's any consolation, I've had worse dates."

Elias gave her a sideways smile. "I can believe that."

She narrowed her eyes suspiciously. "What's that supposed to mean?"

"Nothing," he said defensively. "Just that I suspect you don't have a very good eye for men."

"Oh, you do, do you?" she asked indignantly. "You're thinking of yourself?"

He laid his right hand over his heart. "Exactly. Although I hope if we manage to get out of this—" He was interrupted by a shout from the shadows ahead of them.

"Stay where you are!" ordered an authoritative voice. "Don't move! Police!" Nuria and Elias froze, struck dumb with shock. "Hands up!" the voice demanded. "Now!"

She strained to see more clearly, impeded by the bad lighting, finally managing to make out several crouching silhouettes twenty yards or so ahead of them. Their camouflage uniforms made them almost invisible.

Three red laser points began to dance on her chest. Turning to Elias, she saw he was being targeted too. They exchanged a brief glance, realizing there was nothing they could do. Elias set his oar on a ledge in the wall and obeyed the order, followed at once by Nuria.

While two of the men maintained their positions, the other four, equipped with tactical gear, infrared visors, and ski masks, approached them cautiously, training the laser points of their SCAR-Ls unwaveringly at them. When they were a couple of yards away, Nuria was able to identify the Quick Reaction Force insignia on their uniforms.

"On the ground!" one of them ordered. "On your knees! Hands on your head!"

"We haven't done anything," she said as she knelt. "You're making a mistake."

"Quiet!" roared the nearest of them, bringing the barrel of his gun close to her head.

"But—"

"Where did you put the bomb?" demanded another of the hooded men with captain's stripes on his sleeve.

"There's no bomb," Nuria explained. "Well, in fact there is," she corrected herself, "but it's not a bomb and it's not ours."

Immediately, Captain Lopez took his Colt 45 and aimed it at her head. "Cut the crap and tell me where it is if you don't want me to blow your fucking head off!"

"She's telling the truth," Elias put in. "There's going to be an attack, but we've come to stop it, not commit it."

"You shut your mouth if you don't want me to blow your face away," shouted another of the officers.

"Search them!" the captain ordered.

In a fraction of a second, Elias and Nuria were pushed against the wall and patted down from head to toe. The officers soon found the guns they were carrying in their neoprene pockets.

"Weapon!" shouted the one searching Elias. He took it and stowed it away in one of the pockets of his bulletproof vest.

"Weapon!" repeated the one searching Nuria, and did the same.

Nuria turned. "There's no time for this."

"I told you to shut up!" the officer behind her barked, grabbing her by the neck and shoving her against the wall.

"Where's the bomb?" the captain insisted, his gun still in his hand. "How do you plan to detonate it? With a timer? At a distance?"

"I told you, we don't have a bomb," Nuria repeated, trying not to lose her temper. "We're not terrorists!"

The captain put his mouth close to her ear. "There are half a dozen videos on the web that show you stopping the traffic and going down into the sewer with an explosive device in a box."

"An explosive device in a box?" she repeated. Realizing what he meant, she nearly burst out laughing. "It was an inflatable raft!" The mistake was so absurd she found it hard to explain. "It's what we used to get here!"

"Oh yeah?" the corporal put in, clearly not believing a word. "And where's this supposed raft now?"

"Tied to the wall, downstream." Nuria turned her head in that direction. "We used it to fool the robo-spiders."

"To fool the—" the captain repeated, leaving the sentence hanging. "Are you making fun of me?"

"I swear it's the truth. We're not terrorists. We're here to stop an attack, the same as you."

"Yeah, yeah." He turned to the agent beside him. "Sergeant, take a man and inspect the tunnel. They could have placed the explosive device anywhere."

"Copy, Captain!" He gave a military nod, turned, and ran into the tunnel.

"We're wasting time," Elias reminded them again. "They're coming any minute now, and then there will be nothing we can do to stop them."

"I told you to keep your fucking mouth shut," snapped the cop behind him, shoving Elias's head into the wall.

"Let him speak," the captain ordered. "Who won't we be able to stop?" He went up to Elias. Nuria was sure there was a scornful grin under his ski mask. "The ... robo-spiders?"

"We tricked them, but right now they're looking for another way to get to their target. When they do, they'll destroy the arena above us." Nuria realized how crazy it sounded when she heard him say it aloud.

"I see," the captain said. "So some robotic spiders are going to blow up the Palau Blaugrana, and you two came down here with a couple of guns and ... an inflatable raft ... to try and stop them. Do I have that right?"

"When you put it like that it doesn't sound very reasonable," Elias admitted. "But it's the truth."

"You've got to believe us," Nuria insisted. "If you don't help us, we won't be able to stop them."

"The robo-spiders," the captain repeated. He seemed to be enjoying the word.

She ignored his sarcasm. "They're loaded with several kilos of CL-20 explosives each," Nuria clarified. "And there are more than a hundred of them ... maybe two or three hundred."

"In other words, there *are* explosives after all," the captain said, pleased with himself at having caught her in a contradiction.

"Robot spiders loaded with explosives," she specified.

The captain gave a humorless laugh. "Do you seriously think I'm going to swallow that load of bullshit?"

"It's the truth, for God's sake!" Nuria burst out. "My own mother will be at the rally up there! You've got to believe me!"

The captain took off his visor and ski mask, revealing a hard face that bore signs of exhaustion. The patchily shaven beard and dark circles under tired gray eyes told Nuria he was overworked and didn't get enough rest. He put his mouth close to her ear again and hissed, "I'm going to explain it to you very clearly. Either you start telling me the truth, or I swear I'll put a bullet through your heads ... and that will be that, you understand? Nobody's going to miss you."

"You can't do that," Nuria said with less confidence than her voice showed. "I'm a police officer."

The captain's mouth came even closer to her ear. "I know exactly who you two are," he said in a hoarse, threatening whisper. "You're Corporal Nuria

Badal, a police officer on suspension. There's a warrant out for your arrest. He"—
he pointed to Elias—"is Elias Zafrani, a trafficker of Syrian origin. Both of you
are suspects in this morning's terrorist attack in Villarefu. So tell me, Corporal
Badal," he added, his patience at the breaking point, "what would you think if you
were in my place and you found two presumed terrorists stuffed into neoprene
wetsuits, armed and wandering through the sewer system right underneath an
arena with thousands of people in it?"

Tying up the loose ends, Nuria realized they must have been identified
not long after they'd descended into the sewer, which was why a Quick Reaction
Force had been sent in. "I swear," she muttered, her forehead against the wall and
her voice broken with impotence, "this isn't what it looks like."

"Wow, now you're sounding like my ex-wife."

"ISMA was holding me in a house in Villarefu," she insisted, with no
real hope of convincing him. "Elias rescued me, there was a fire, the house blew
up, and we escaped by a miracle. I understand that you don't believe me," she
admitted, "but just remember, if you're wrong, if it turns out I'm right … you'll
be responsible for the deaths of twenty thousand people."

"Jesus, did you hear that, Captain?" the corporal sneered. "What an
imagination the bitch has!"

"It's the truth!" she shouted, beside herself with rage. Whipping around,
she faced the officers, intending only to shout in their faces that she wasn't lying.
Unexpectedly, though, the corporal was still turned toward his captain, and Nuria
caught him unawares. Seeing the butt of her Sig Sauer protruding from one of the
pockets of the officer's bulletproof vest, she reached for it without thinking,
impelled by instinct and desperation. A tenth of a second later she had the gun in
her hand.

The captain yelled a warning, but before the corporal realized what was
happening Nuria turned nimbly, positioning herself behind his back and aiming
the gun at his head. "Nobody move! Lower your weapons!" she shouted,
shielding herself behind the corporal's body. "And you, hands up!" She jammed
the barrel into his back.

Ignoring her order, Captain Lopez aimed at what little he could see of her
behind the bulky corporal. At the same time, the agent holding Elias against the
wall took out his weapon and forced him to kneel with his hands behind his head.

"Drop the gun," the captain hissed, his crosshairs on her head. "Don't
make me shoot."

"If you do, your corporal will die too."

"You're really fucking up," Lopez warned her. "Lower your weapon and
we'll talk."

"Now you're treating me like a moron," Nuria shot back. "You're not in
the least interested in what I have to say."

370

"Lower your weapon and I can assure you you'll have my full attention."

"He's lying, Nuria," Elias warned her from where he was kneeling with his hands behind his head.

"Shut your hole," the officer behind him threatened, pressing the barrel of the gun against his head.

"There's only one way out for you," the captain went on. "There are cops blocking all the accesses with orders to shoot to kill. So drop the gun and we'll talk about whatever you want, but don't do anything stup—"

"Captain, do you copy?" a voice interrupted from the radio at his belt. Continuing to aim his Colt at Nuria, the captain put his left hand to his earbud.

"Go ahead, Sergeant. What's up?"

"We found the raft the woman was talking about," the voice informed them. "It's sort of ... set in place to block the tunnel."

"Anything else?"

"Negative. Only shit and garbage."

"Copy," the captain confirmed, giving Nuria a sidelong glance. "Come back here at once."

"Copy, Captain."

"You see?" Nuria snapped. "We're telling you the truth, for Christ's sake!"

"That doesn't prove anything," he said impassively. "Lower your gun."

"I can't do that."

"Of course you can, and you will." He pointed to the ground with his left hand. "In fact, it's the only thing that—"

"Quiet!" Elias cried, taking them all by surprise. "Listen!"

"Shut your piehole, you piece of shit!" yelled the officer guarding him.

Elias ignored the order. "Can't you hear it?"

The officer was about to open his mouth again, but the captain gestured at him to stay quiet, turning his head slightly like a bloodhound who's heard a distant whistle.

"Captain!" came the voice on the radio of one of the men who had stayed behind. "You've got to see this!"

The captain turned to look down the tunnel they'd arrived by. "What's going on, Martinez? Report!"

"I don't know what they are!" came the alarmed voice. "But they're coming fast! Christ, there's a shitload of them!"

"They're here," Nuria said, her frustration evident in her voice.

Captain Lopez turned to her, but before he could say anything, the rattle of automatic rifle fire echoed off the walls of the tunnel.

371

72

"Martinez! Aguado!" the captain yelled to the two men he'd left protecting the rear, but his voice was lost in the desperate gunfire that echoed in the narrow passage. He looked from the gunshots to the woman who was aiming her gun at his corporal's head, trying to get his priorities straight.

Unexpectedly, Nuria stepped to the side, deliberately putting herself in the line of fire. The captain tightened his finger on the trigger, tempted to resolve his dilemma the easy way. Lowering her gun and pointing down the tunnel, Nuria said, "We have to stop those things or we'll all end up dead."

The captain stroked the trigger indecisively while the corporal who had been Nuria's hostage leapt away from her and aimed his own gun at her head. "Make your decision, Captain," she snapped, ignoring the double threat. "Are you going to shoot me or are you going to help me?"

Just then the men who had gone downstream arrived at a run, splashing through the sewage with their heavy boots. "Captain?" the sergeant panted, coming to an abrupt halt in front of him, his gaze fixed on the tunnel where the shootout was underway.

The officer closed his eyes, seeking a moment of calm to make his decision. When he opened them again a second later, Nuria saw clear determination in his gray eyes. "Motherfucking goddamn it to hell," he grunted in exasperation, returning his Colt to its holster. "Corporal, lower your gun," he barked, turning toward the shots. Grabbing his SCAR-L, he shouted, "Follow me!" He ran toward them. "Hang on!"

The laser beams bobbed in rhythm with the footsteps of the four officers, crisscrossing each other nervously. Turning the corner, all four officers stopped short as a scene more appropriate to nightmares than to the world Captain Lopez believed he'd known until that moment abruptly presented itself to their eyes.

With their backs to him, Corporals Martinez and Aguado were firing short volleys as they withdrew, taking short steps backwards. Though dimmed by the silencers, the flashes of their shots lit up the scene like pulsing strobe lights. The lights of the tunnel had disappeared, and all Captain Lopez could see were the silhouettes of his men frantically shooting at an inexorably advancing mechanical tide. Hundreds of shadows moved forward like tarantulas amid the sinister clicking of their sharp metallic legs.

"Holy shit," the captain muttered, finally understanding that the couple in the bizarre neoprene suits had told him the truth. "Defensive positions!" he ordered, forcing himself to snap out of his daze. At his direction, the four new arrivals replaced Martinez and Aguado, who withdrew to reload their weapons.

"Short bursts!" he ordered, raising his voice above the din of the robo-spiders and the gunshots. "Don't waste ammunition!" The captain was familiar with the robotic spiders, at least their search-and-rescue version. Though he'd heard of their use by the military for infiltration and sabotage, he'd never imagined they could take on an operation of this kind. What he did know was that their limited intelligence was enough to allow them to avoid obstacles and reach their objective, relying on their toughness and agility. Even after losing half their eight legs, they could move in any environment with no problem, and the solid housing that protected their control centers was so tough they were impervious to strong blows and high temperatures. As if that weren't enough, they used their powerful pincers to clear a path and defend themselves when necessary.

Luckily, the plastic explosive each of the monsters carried like a grotesque hump on its back was inert to bullets and could only be detonated by an electrical impulse, so they didn't have to worry about causing an explosion while they blew the robots up one after the other with their assault rifles. Not so lucky was the fact that the programming of the robo-spiders didn't seem to include either the possibility of surrender or any instinct for self-preservation, so even though that stretch of sewer was fast becoming a graveyard, the relentless advance of the others never stopped. They climbed remorselessly over their fallen companions, moving forward like a slow black tide.

"Last magazine!" warned the sergeant, tossing aside the empty one and inserting a new one with thirty-two bullets. His last thirty-two bullets.

"Me too!" Aguado called. "Last one!"

"Secure the targets!" the captain shouted at them, realizing they would be unable to stop them for the simple reason that there were more robots than there were bullets in their magazines. "Headquarters!" he bawled into his radio. "Do you copy? Captain Lopez here! We need backup!"

He waited anxiously for a reply, fearing that the thousands of tons of earth and concrete above their heads would block the radio waves. Finally a crackle of static sizzled through the radio.

"Headquarters," came an innocuous voice at last. "Go ahead, Captain."

"Backup, for Christ's sake!" he roared into the mike. "We need backup down here!"

"Specify, please," the voice requested indolently, as if he were calling for a pizza. "What's your status? What kind of backup?"

"My status is a fucking shit show!" the captain shouted in exasperation. "Send all available backup to my position!"

"But—"

"No buts, for God's sake!" he thundered until his voice began to turn hoarse. "Send the fucking infantry if it's around! Now!!!"

The radio went mute for a few seconds. Just when he was beginning to fear he'd lost the signal, it crackled again. "Copy," the voice answered. "ETA to your position, eight minutes."

"Make it four!" Lopez ended the call and shouted at his men, "Hang on! Backup's on its way!" He exchanged a glance with the sergeant, who shook his head and told him what he already knew: they couldn't hold out for eight minutes.

"Captain!" Martinez called, shooting at one of the robots that was practically under his feet. "They're overpowering us!"

Lopez corrected himself mentally. They wouldn't be able to hold out for even the four minutes he'd demanded. The storm of lead they'd unleashed in the tunnel had kept that mechanical tide at bay, but the moment their dwindling supply of bullets had forced them to space out their shots, the army of arachnid robots had begun to gain ground foot by foot, threatening to overpower them at any moment.

"Pull back!" the captain howled, realizing they could no longer contain them. "Pull back!"

"I'm out!" the corporal called when the firing pin of his SCAR-L clicked, but no bullet left the barrel. The captain watched as he grabbed his nine MM Glock and took out the frontal sensors of a robo-spider with a single shot. In the time it took him, nonetheless, two others slipped by on the wall beside him, overtaking him on their way to their goal. The captain fired at one of the robo-spiders point blank, destroying three of its legs before he ran out of bullets. Reaching into the side pocket of his uniform, he discovered to his fury that he had no more magazines left.

It was then, perhaps taking advantage of this momentary distraction, that the crippled robo-spider leapt with its remaining legs onto his leg. Lopez tried to shake it off, but it snapped its pincers shut with a chilling metallic clash. With a howl of pain, the captain staggered, hitting the wall with his back, a large hole in his pants and an ugly cut on his left calf. "Son of a bitch!" he roared, trying to get his Colt out of its holster when he saw the machine preparing to leap in his direction again, determined to finish the job.

At the last possible instant, Nuria appeared out of nowhere in her neoprene wetsuit. With a cry of rage, she raised the oar she was still carrying above her head and smashed it violently down onto two of the bug's remaining legs, breaking them with a loud crack and stopping it once and for all. Looking up at the captain with a savage expression, she held out a hand to him, saying, "Be careful, Captain. These things bite."

"Ya think?" he snorted, ignoring her hand and leaning against the wall to lever himself up. All around him, his men were being overpowered by the robospiders that were now leaping aggressively toward them, opening and closing their steel jaws that were capable of severing a limb. If they stayed there, their attackers would make mincemeat of them.

"Retreat!" the captain ordered, fearing for his men's lives. "Pull back!"

"No!" Nuria yelled. "We can't leave!" She pointed to the pack attached to the back of the robot she'd just neutralized. "If these things reach their goal, they'll explode! We've got to stop them!" she added vehemently. Whirling around, she hammered at another monster that Elias was fighting with. Armed only with their aluminum oars, they struck at the monster's legs until it was stumbling, with only three of its limbs remaining.

It took Captain Lopez less than a second to comprehend the situation, and less than two more to weigh up the pros and cons of believing this deranged-looking woman. Turning to his men, he barked, "Cancel retreat! We've got to stop these bugs, whatever it takes!"

"But how?!" the sergeant asked. "We're out of ammo, Captain!"

"Use whatever else you've got!" the captain shouted back. "Hit them with your rifles, or the tip of your dick if you have to! I don't care!" Grasping his assault rifle by the barrel, he wielded it like a club. "Just don't let them get past you, whatever you do!"

The shooting stopped as abruptly as it had started. All of them were out of bullets now. The rest of the team followed the example of their officer in command, raining frantic blows on the robotic horde. The muffled rat-a-tat-tat of weapons was replaced by cries of rage, the unnerving drumming of hundreds of sharp feet on the cement, and the clicks of their pincers snapping shut.

"Break their joints!" Elias called, falling on one of the spiders that had passed the officers' first line of defense. "It's their only vulnerable point!"

"We can't stop them!" the corporal shouted, leaping backwards to prevent a pair of horrifying pincers from amputating his left foot. "There are too many of them!"

"Shut your fucking mouth, corporal!" the captain barked, battering furiously at one robot's legs with the butt of his SCAR-L.

But Nuria was realizing that the corporal was right. It was like trying to hold back the rising tide with a fishnet. It didn't matter how hard they tried, in the end they would be overwhelmed.

Then the inevitable happened. Dodging the attack of a robo-spider, Sergeant Gonzalez slipped on the remains of a garbage bag, fell backwards, and lost his weapon in the current of sewage. At his cry of surprise, they all turned toward him, but there was nothing any of them could do as, paralyzed, they watched the steel arachnid leap onto his chest like an agitated puppy at the sight of its master. The sergeant crossed his arms in front of him in a reflex action at the sight of the monster opening its pincers wide to close them around his neck.

"No!" Nuria shouted as she realized what was about to happen. Horrified, she watched as the metal claws closed with a grisly snap on the sergeant's forearms, slicing them as neatly as a pair of shears would a dead branch. The sergeant's chilling howl of pain pierced her brain. She knew she would never be able to erase the image of the poor man staring at the bleeding stumps, his mouth open wide in a cry of terror.

Paralyzed by a dreadful feeling of unreality, she saw the robo-spider, still not satisfied, opening its jaws and moving in the direction of the sergeant's neck. Just when it seemed inevitable that he would be decapitated, Elias charged the robot from the side, delivering a blow with his oar that hurled it several yards away.

"Help him, for fuck's sake!" the captain roared as he saw Elias grabbing the sergeant by the armpits. "Help him!" Two other officers awakened from their daze and ran to help the sergeant, who couldn't stop screaming.

"Captain!" the corporal yelled to attract his attention. "We can't stop them!"

Lopez looked around him, at his mutilated sergeant and the two officers who were attending him, then at the other two, barely able to do more than avoid the steady snapping of jaws. He himself was bleeding freely from the open wound on his own leg. The couple he'd come to arrest were still defending them all, at the very limits of their strength, delivering ever-weaker blows with their pathetic oars.

Looking up the tunnel, he saw the black tide of robo-spiders still advancing inexorably. They'd destroyed twenty or thirty of them, and though he was aware that this was no more than a fraction of their number, they could do nothing more. If they stayed there one minute longer they would all die, inevitably and uselessly.

73

Captain Lopez clenched his teeth, refusing to accept that particular outcome for his men. "Live to fight another day," he muttered, quoting a line he'd heard in some old movie. This was a battle they couldn't win. "Pull back!" he roared, then turned to his corporal. "Take the sergeant with you!"

The corporal took up the cry. "Retreat! Retreat!"

Nuria shot the captain an inquiring look. He shook his head. For a moment she was tempted to contradict his order, to tell him that they had to resist at all costs, but a new howl of anguish from the sergeant as he was dragged away by his comrades made her finally realize that this mechanical tide was unstoppable. All they could do was escape or die there.

She saw Elias keeping a robo-spider at bay as it advanced toward him, snapping its jaws, and she knew they'd done everything they could. She'd lost too many things in her life and she didn't want to lose one more now. Somehow finding strength in her weakness, she brought her oar down on the spider again and again until, between the two of them, they managed to fracture six of its eight legs and it lay still at last.

"It's over …" she panted, dropping to her knees in exhaustion. "There's nothing more we can do."

Elias studied her for a moment, his face weary and dripping with sweat. "All right." He delivered one final blow with his oar to the robo-spider, which in spite of being immobilized was still trying to reach them with its pincers. "Let's get out of here."

The two officers carrying the sergeant were already a few yards ahead. The Captain and the other two tried to keep the robots at bay as they retreated.

"We're not going to have time," Elias said grimly, watching the officers.

Nuria turned to him. "What do you mean?"

"We won't be able to get far enough away before those things blow up," he explained, as if it were self-evident. "The blast inside the tunnel will blow us away."

It took Nuria a moment to understand what he meant. "Shit!" She punched the wall beside her feebly. "What can we do?"

He looked down, defeated. "Nothing." He indicated the narrow passage. "The tunnel will act like a fucking cannon ... and we'll be the cannon balls. I'm sorry," he added, and took her hand.

"A cannon ..." Nuria repeated, ignoring his gesture. "Jesus, that's it!" Dropping his hand abruptly, she ran to Lopez. "Captain! Captain!" A puzzled Elias looked after her as she hurried toward the other man. Equally bewildered, the captain glanced at her as she reached his side and began to speak, the words tumbling over each other, while he continued to fight desperately against the mechanical abominations.

"Get out!" he shouted in exasperation. "We're holding them off so you can get away!"

"No! Listen to me! Tell them to open the sluice gates!"

"What the fuck are you talking about?" he snapped, using both hands to bring the butt of his Vector down on the monsters. "What sluice gates?"

"The ones on the rainwater reservoir!"

The captain turned to her and she realized she must sound unhinged. From his uncomprehending frown she realized he had no idea what she was talking about. "Two blocks from here, there's a huge reservoir for rainwater!" She pointed upstream. "It must be full to the brim by now with all this rain! Millions of liters!"

Predictably, as a faithful representative of his gender, Lopez was unable to battle the machines and follow the thread of the conversation at the same time. "What the fuck does that matter?" he roared, trying to evade a pair of pincers seeking to sever his ankle.

"Call on your radio and tell them to open the sluice gates!" she shouted in exasperation. "The water will sweep them away!"

The captain looked at her again, forgetting the machines for an instant. Nuria could see in his face that his brain was processing the information. His eyes widened as the dime belatedly dropped. "Headquarters!" he barked, connecting his microphone. "Captain Lopez here, do you copy?"

"Copy," came the neutral voice, as parsimonious as before. "Go ahead, Captain Lopez."

"Cancel the request for backup, do you hear me?"

"They're already on their way, Captain," the voice said, almost reproachfully.

"Well, tell them to back off, for God's sake!" he shouted into the mike. "And I want you to open the sluice gates of the rainwater reservoir in the"—he turned to Nuria, who mouthed the answer to him—"university district. Did you get that?"

"Loud and clear, Captain," the voice said. "But I don't know whether—"

"Shut up and do as I say!" Lopez demanded. "Even if they have to blow up the damn sluice gates! I want this fucking sewer flooded right now!"

Again the reply took a few seconds, but this time the tone was obedient. "Yes, sir."

"Oh, and clear the Palau Blaugrana. As fast as you can."

"Sorry, Captain." The operator cleared his throat in disbelief. "Did you say to—"

"Clear the fucking arena. That's right, you heard right. Do it or a lot of people are going to die. Understood?" Before the voice could reply he added coldly and clearly, "Over and out." Regarding Nuria with a new expression in his eyes, he said, "I hope it works."

"That makes two of us." Pointing at the robo-spiders that were fast surrounding them, she added, "Now, if it's okay with you, let's get the hell out of here as fast as we can."

At the head of the battered group, following the direction of the current, the two officers in the best physical shape carried the sergeant. Though they'd applied tourniquets to both his arms, he'd lost so much blood he was deathly pale, his lips blue in his unconscious face.

Behind them came Nuria, Elias, Captain Lopez, and the two remaining officers, walking backwards as they did their best to keep the horde of machines at bay. All were showing signs of exhaustion, their legs marked with gashes, some deeper than others, from the sharp steel blades. Limping and bleeding, they continued to defend themselves with gun-butts and oars as they withdrew.

"They're stopping! Look!" The corporal pointed at the robots with relief. "They're not following us any longer!"

"Shit!" Elias swore. "We've got to get out of this sewer right now!"

"What? Why?" the corporal asked.

The captain looked at Nuria. "Because that means they're going to detonate. Isn't that right?"

"As soon as they get to the place they're programmed to reach,"—she shook her head, defeated—"it'll be all over."

"Well then, we're fuck—"

"The raft!" came a shout from one of his men, interrupting him. "Captain, here's the raft!"

Nuria turned her head and saw the raft still hanging in the middle of the tunnel twenty yards further ahead like a flamboyant shower curtain. She'd completely forgotten about it. "Let's get it down!" she cried, running towards it. "Give me a hand!" Passing one of the officers, she noticed the handle of a knife. Before he'd realized what was happening, she'd grabbed it out of its sheath without asking permission. Combat knife in one hand and oar in the other, she

379

reached the raft, stood on tiptoe, and cut the ropes tying it to the ceiling. The inflatable vessel fell onto the surface of the sewage water with a loud splash. Pulled by the current, it would have escaped downstream if Elias hadn't appeared next to her and seized it at the last moment.

Nuria gave him a brief glance of thanks and turned to the two police officers, gesturing to the raft. "Get the sergeant on board! Get moving!" The officers looked at Lopez, hesitating whether to obey the woman whom only ten minutes before they'd regarded as a terrorist.

The captain's reply left no room for doubt. "You heard her!" He waved his arms, urging them on. "Get the sergeant on the raft! And you too!" he added, pointing at the two agents who were limping most noticeably. "And you, Corporal Badal!" He jabbed his finger at her. "Get in there!"

"Like hell I will!" Nuria said, helping to heave the sergeant, who now looked more dead than alive, on board. "Because I'm a woman?"

"No, for fuck's sake," Lopez shot back. "Because you and your friend may be the only ones who have any information about all this, and if I have to choose between saving a police officer and a mafioso—" He gave Elias a sidelong glance. "No offense."

"None taken. I agree," Elias said. "Get into the raft, Nuria."

"No," she said defiantly.

Elias was about to open his mouth to remind her she was wasting precious time when a deep rumble behind him made him spin around, fearing that this was the beginning of the explosion. A grim silence fell among the battered group, all of whom were sure this was the last sound they would ever hear. But the seconds ticked by and there was no detonation. The brutal shock wave they were expecting didn't come.

Instead, the noise grew moment by moment, accompanied by a dull vibration under their feet, as if a subway car were coming down the tunnel. "Oh my God ... they did it," the captain muttered, proud and terrified at the same time.

It wasn't until that moment that Nuria understood. The sluice gates had been opened. Suddenly it didn't seem like such a good idea after all. "Holy shit!" she shouted, seeing the emergency lights in the tunnel going out one by one. "Everybody in the raft!" she shouted. "To the raft!"

The murmur became a roar, and a wall of white foam that reached the ceiling burst into the sewer tunnel like a derailed freight train. At the same moment, the first robo-spiders began to detonate, making the tunnel shake as if the whole city were about to collapse on their heads. The violent flood reached them, carrying off those that hadn't yet detonated and muffling the devastating effect of the ones that had, converting the effect of the shock wave into a destructive, unstoppable avalanche of water that was heading directly toward them, a shapeless monster determined to end their lives.

Paralyzed by sheer terror in the face of the wall of foam about to swallow her, Nuria felt someone shove her into the raft. She fell headlong on top of the unconscious sergeant just as someone else fell heavily on top of her. The roar of the water became a blast of thunder and the raft shot forward like a cork from a bottle of champagne.

For a few seconds the inflatable raft rode the wall of water like a surfboard. Nuria thought for a fleeting moment that perhaps, after all that had happened and against all odds, they would reach safety. But that hope lasted as long as it took them to reach the first fork. With no rudder or any way to control it, the raft shot directly and inevitably towards the solid concrete corner that divided the two tunnels.

Nuria looked desperately for something to hold on to. Her right hand found the rope she and Elias had used to attach the raft to the ceiling and she wrapped it around her wrist at the precise instant when they crashed brutally against the corner.

The raft folded in two, catapulting all its occupants into the air except for Nuria. Tethered to the rope, she thought the force of the impact would wrench her arm off. She heard a scream as someone flew through the air, but she had no time to guess who it was because the raft began to spin uncontrollably, driven by the thousands of gallons of rushing water, like a sock in a washing machine.

Nuria was forced to open her mouth to breathe. The foul water swirled into it as she whirled helplessly around, almost out of air, wrapped in the remains of the raft like a huge yellow burrito. This was the end, she realized, surprised by her last thought, which was one of relief. She realized she'd done it. She'd managed to stop the terrorist attack. Soothed by this last feeling and the lack of oxygen in her brain, Nuria saw the darkness closing in on her as she slipped into unconsciousness.

74

"One, two, three …" Nuria heard a voice saying. She felt a series of strong thrusts on her sternum. A pair of lips were pressed to her own, and just when she thought her fairy-tale prince was awakening her with a kiss of true love, she felt a gust of hot air entering her mouth and inflating her lungs to the point where she felt they might burst.

Opening her eyes abruptly, she slapped the kissing prince aside. Trying to breathe on her own, Nuria found only a tiny amount of air would enter her flooded lungs. She coughed spasmodically like a terminal consumptive.

"Roll her onto her side!" called someone beside her. Two pairs of hands rolled her over. A new spasm erupted from her lungs, this time accompanied by a surprising amount of water that erupted through her trachea and spouted from her mouth as if she were a statue in a fountain. Her throat burned as if she'd swallowed hot sauce. Nuria coughed again and again until the last drop of water had exited her lungs and she was able to breathe normally.

She closed her eyes again. Every cell in her body begged her to stay where she was, resting in the rain on the hard ground, recovering from the pain and exhaustion that were holding her in an iron grip from her earlobe to her big toe.

"Corporal Badal," said the voice from earlier. "Can you hear me?" She ignored the question, hoping they would let her sleep for a while. "Corporal Badal," the voice repeated, more insistently this time. *Maybe there's another Corporal Badal around here,* she thought hopefully. "Nuria, wake up," the voice insisted for the third time. This time it was accompanied by a slap on the cheek.

Irritated, she forced her eyes open again and found herself looking into a face that looked faintly familiar staring into her own with concern. "Are you all right?" asked the man the face belonged to. "Can you breathe?"

She opened her mouth to reply, but instead coughed as if her guts were going to come out through her mouth. The man stepped back to give her space. It wasn't until Nuria saw his torn uniform and the wound in his leg that she realized who he was. "I've had better days," she wheezed faintly. "What … what happened?"

"What's the last thing you remember?" Captain Lopez asked.

Nuria closed her eyes a moment before replying. "The water hit us, and"—she swallowed with difficulty—"I was drowning."

"You almost did," Aguado said. He was standing behind his captain.

"The raft got stuck on an access ladder," Lopez explained. "If it hadn't—" He shook his head with the air of someone who still can't believe his luck.

"And the ... bombs?" Nuria asked. "Did they ...?"

"Yes, some of them detonated. But I guess not many of them did it where they were supposed to, and besides, the water contained the explosion." He pointed behind her. "You can see the roof of the Palau Blaugrana from here, and it looks as though it's still standing."

Nuria turned and looked. As he'd said, she could see the dome that covered the arena, apparently intact and with no column of black smoke billowing from it. An indescribable wave of relief flooded her chest. She let herself fall back onto the asphalt, happy, her arms outspread. Raising her eyes to the leaden sky, she breathed out her gratitude. "Thank God."

"No, thank *you*," Lopez corrected her. "*You* saved all those people."

She shook her head. "We'd never have made it without your help. By the way," she added, suddenly remembering. She sat up. "Where are the others?"

The captain's sudden silence made her turn her head so quickly she felt a wave of nausea. "Elias?" she asked, scanning the area around her. "Elias?"

"Easy," the captain said, taking her arm. "Relax, Corporal."

"Like hell I'm going to relax!" She shook her arm loose and tried to stand up. "Elias! Where is he?" she spat at the captain, grabbing him by the uniform. "Where the fuck is he?"

His face grave, the captain shook his head very slowly. "It was only the three of us that got out," he said with the bitterness of the survivor. He indicated an open manhole close to them. "Your friend and four of my men are missing."

"What?"

"They might still be alive," he added.

"Might?" she repeated. Pushing Lopez away, Nuria stood up with difficulty, reeling like a drunkard on the deck of a ship. "Elias!" she called, stumbling in the direction of the open manhole. "Elias!"

Lopez caught her before she could plunge into the hole. "He's not there any longer," he said, trying to soothe her. "He could be anywhere. We'll find him."

"You've got to find him!" she insisted, grabbing him by the front of his shirt. "You hear me? You owe me!" She felt her legs buckling and fell to her knees on the asphalt, overwhelmed by exhaustion and emotion.

Lopez squatted down beside her. "We'll do everything possible, I swear it."

"You all owe me," Nuria insisted with a moan of pain just as a chorus of sirens burst into the street, heading toward them at top speed. "You owe *him*."

Hours later, sitting on the edge of the bed in an antiseptic, immaculate room, dressed in a standard green gauze hospital gown, Nuria looked out over the city under its veil of rain from the eleventh floor of the new and luxurious MediCare St. Gervaise Hospital.

Her left arm was in a sling and a comforting combination of tranquilizers and painkillers was running through her veins, easing the pain of her injuries and lulling her worries—though in reality, the only concern she had at the moment was Elias's disappearance. There hadn't been any news of him. Captain Lopez had given her his word they would find him and he would keep her informed, but since she'd been put in the ambulance she hadn't heard from him again, and none of the doctors or nurses who were looking after her seemed to know anything about it.

The officers of the counterterrorism squad that had taken her statement hadn't wanted to tell her anything about what was going on. It seemed that their orders were to let her know as little as possible. It was only thanks to the questions they'd asked her that she'd been able to deduce that they'd found the hideaway under the terrorists' house in Villarefu. They'd encountered large quantities of electronic material and explosives, as well as fragments of the robo-spiders from the sewer, which had turned out to be military devices manufactured by an Israeli company named Tactical Robotics. Nuria's surprise at the paradox that Islamic terrorists should possess ultramodern Israeli military technology didn't seem to be shared by her interrogators, who went on to their next question without making the least comment about it.

Even more frustrating, they'd blocked the Internet connection on her room monitor so she could only use it as a TV set now. The only thing the stations were talking about were the underground detonations that had shaken the foundations of the Palau Blaugrana and caused numerous cracks in the foundations of the arena, which would almost certainly have to be pulled down and rebuilt. There were also endless images of panic in the surrounding streets, dozens of emergency vehicles with their sirens blaring, and extremely nervous police officers fencing off the area.

In spite of the disorder outside, inside the arena the predictable scenes of panic hadn't materialized when the order to vacate had come in the middle of the rally. This was thanks in large part, a fact that was emphasized again and again in the media, to the words of Salvador Aguirre, the leader of Spain First. He'd addressed the crowd from the dais, asking for calm and for his followers to behave like brave and worthy Christians. His exhortations had yielded the "miraculous"—another word overused by the newscasters—result that the only casualties of the attack had been an elderly lady with a heart condition and a poor cat that had fallen to its death, surprised by the shock on a ninth-floor windowsill.

The official explanation given by the authorities was that the attempted attack had been thwarted by a brave unit belonging to the Special Forces. Risking their lives, they'd managed to avert the massacre at the last possible moment, though unfortunately an as-yet-undetermined number of them were missing.

Nuria switched from one channel to another. There was no mention of her or Elias. The government spokesman claimed that the perpetrators of the attempted attack were as yet unknown, but as the day wore on, a tenuous connection began to be made with the explosion in the refugee camp. Not five hours after the thwarted attack, the first voices were already demanding the dismantling of Villarefu and the immediate deportation of all its inhabitants. Nuria shook her head sadly, guessing that things were not going to end well for the refugees. Weary of it all, she decided to turn off the TV.

Her gaze lost in the raindrops tapping softly against the window, the disquieting idea occurred to Nuria that the authorities might well try to draw a thick veil over her and Elias's intervention in that sewer. Even though the captain's testimony would dispel any doubts about her innocence and clarify her role in the dismantling of the terrorist plot, it was quite likely that her superiors, both political and police, wouldn't relish looking stupid in the face of public opinion. It was very possible they would declare the whole business secret so nobody would ever know what had really happened.

What was really distressing her, though, was that they might come to the conclusion that Elias was better off dead than alive. The fact that a Syrian refugee in Spain had saved the leader of Spain First and twenty thousand of his followers from certain death could be rather embarrassing to explain against the backdrop of the movement's official position that labeled any Muslim a potential terrorist. It would be far easier for them to cover up what had happened and make sure Elias never appeared again. The more she thought about it, the more likely it seemed that they would try to assign the same fate to her.

A rap on Nuria's door interrupted her uneasy speculations. "Come in," she said without turning her head. No doubt it was the nurse coming to give her the umpteenth test in search of infections from having swallowed fecal water.

The door opened behind her. Footsteps squeaked on the linoleum floor and stopped on the other side of the bed. "Good afternoon, Corporal," a familiar voice greeted her.

Nuria spun around, finding herself confronted with the last person she'd expected to see. "What are you doing here, Commissioner?" she asked, her tone hostile, trying to cover her body in its open-backed hospital gown more adequately. "Have you come to arrest me?"

Puig came over to the bed, dropping his peaked cap on the coverlet. "If I wanted to arrest you, you'd be in a cell already."

"There are two cops at the door," she said, "and it locks from the outside."

"That's for your own safety."

"Yeah, sure."

Puig went over to the window. Clasping his hands behind his back, he stood there in silence, his gaze on the blurred silhouette of Montjuïc mountain. Turning back to Nuria, he said, "There are still a lot of things to be cleared up, and we can't risk you disappearing on us ... again."

"I'm not going anywhere," she said. "I don't have anywhere to go nor any reason to."

"Maybe," he conceded. "But even so, we're going to keep you under surveillance until we've taken your statement."

"I'm not going to say anything else until I have news of Elias."

The commissioner took a few seconds to absorb what she'd just said. "I don't think that's a good idea."

"I don't give a shit what you think," Nuria said, more calmly than she would have thought possible. "Find Elias and I'll explain everything you need to know. In the meantime, I'm not going to say a fucking word."

"This is way bigger than you, Nuria," the commissioner said in a conciliatory tone. "People that are very high up want answers, and if you won't give them to me ... you'll have to give them to others."

"Well, they can go fuck themselves." Nuria was discovering the pleasure of talking without worrying about the consequences.

Puig shook his head, apparently saddened. "I see you don't understand. The NIC, the PNU, and the ECTC want to know exactly what happened ... and they won't be as nice about it as I am."

"Is that so? And what are they going to do to me?" she asked defiantly. "Give me back my badge and then take it away again? Put me in jail for preventing a terrorist attack?" The more she said, the more rage she felt flowing through her veins. "I've saved everybody's ass—including yours, by the way—even though you've done nothing but fuck me over and try to manipulate me. So stop threatening me and being a pain in the ass and fucking find Elias once and for all!"

Though Puig didn't open his mouth during this rant, Nuria knew him well enough to know he was fuming inside. "I'll do what I can," he said at last in a restrained voice with a pointed look of reproach that she purposely ignored. Collecting his cap from the bed, he put it under his arm and headed for the door. "By the way," he added, pausing with his hand on the knob, "you have some other visitors waiting to see you."

"I don't want to see anybody," Nuria said. No doubt it was her mother. A crooked smile appeared on Puig's face. Opening the door, he left the room without another word.

Without warning or preamble, as Nuria was still staring at the door he'd left open, two bodyguards burst into the room. Each was over six feet tall and wore earbuds and mirrored glasses. After a brief search, they murmured something into the microphones hidden in the sleeves of their Armani armored suits.

Nuria stood up. "Hey, you two!" she admonished them. "Who are you, and who gave you permission to barge in like this?" The pair of intruders ignored her majestically. Indignant at the intrusion, she was attempting to find a proper insult in her mental files for this pair of gorillas with selective deafness when she realized a third person was coming in through the door.

Her new visitor was a man in his fifties of medium height, well-dressed with a neatly trimmed beard. It didn't take Nuria long to recognize him, since she'd seen him half a dozen times that same morning on television, haranguing his followers at the Spain First rally. Behind him was a second, taller man, wearing a grim, bitter expression, whose face was dimly familiar to her after seeing him once or twice in his boss's shadow.

"Good morning, Miss Badal," the tired voice of Salvador Aguirre greeted her. "May we come in?"

75

Nuria took a step back incredulously, trying to assimilate the fact that the man who dominated every news hour on television was in her room addressing her. For an instant she thought she might be hallucinating, but his slight smile when he saw her reaction persuaded her that this was real and not a mistake the doctors had made with her morphine dosage.

"You …" she stammered nervously, "you're—"

"Salvador Aguirre," he confirmed in his precise northern accent, offering her his hand. "I hope I haven't come at a bad time."

"I …" She swallowed, searching for words in the blankness of her mind. "No … no, I guess not, Mr. Aguirre."

He dismissed the formality with a folksy wave of his hand. "None of that now. Call me Salvador. That's the name my mother christened me with at birth." Pointing behind him, he added, "And this tall, stern man with me is Jaime Olmedo, my right-hand man … and very often my left-hand one too."

"Mr. Olmedo," Nuria greeted the emotionless man whose ramrod-straight bearing hinted at his military past. Olmedo replied with a curt 'good morning,' but didn't ask her to drop the *Mr.*

Nuria was at a loss for words, standing there in the center of the room in a ridiculously short hospital gown in front of the Spain First candidate and leader of the Spanish Reborn in Christ movement.

"Forgive the intrusion," Aguirre said, "but I wanted to see you in person and I have an extremely tight schedule. This was the only time it was possible for me to come. I hope I'm not bothering you."

"I … no, of course not. Though I wasn't expecting you to visit me."

"How could I not?" he said. "My only regret is that I was unable to come sooner, but after learning what happened this morning, I made sure you had the best possible care. I hope you're being well treated here."

"Yes, very well. Thank you," Nuria said, understanding at last why she was in an exclusive private hospital instead of a government one.

"No, Miss Badal." He raised a hand. "I'm the one who needs to thank *you* for what you've done. I don't know the details yet, but they say you saved us from a terrible attack by those ISMA assassins. There are no words to tell you how grateful I am," he went on, "not only for myself, but for the thousands of Christians who, if it hadn't been for you, would have died at the hands of those emissaries of Satan. From this day forward," he concluded, "you'll be in my prayers and those of all the Reborn. If there's anything I can do to help you, all you have to do is ask and I'll do everything in my power to see that it's done."

Inwardly, Nuria considered the possibility of asking him to dismantle his political party, but decided she'd already used up her quota of stupid remarks for the day. "Thank you, Salvador," she said instead. "Actually, there is something I'd like to ask of you."

"Please." With a wave, he invited her to speak. "What is it you'd like?"

"There was a man with me in the sewers. A Syrian called Elias Zafrani. Without him we wouldn't have managed to stop the attack. He disappeared down there and I haven't had any news since ..." She felt her voice failing her. "I'm not sure the police are doing everything they can to look for him," she added, "and I'd be very grateful if you could somehow put pressure on them so that they ... well, will find him."

"Of course, my dear," he said, nodding and turning the enormous gold ring he wore on his left ring finger. "We'll do everything in our power. Jaime will look into the matter." He gestured to the man behind him. "Right?"

"Of course," his second-in-command confirmed guardedly.

"You see?" the politician said. A sudden coughing fit obliged him to cover his mouth with a handkerchief he pulled from his left sleeve. "Don't worry about a thing," he added in a muffled voice when he'd recovered. "We'll make sure they find your friend." Salvador Aguirre put the handkerchief back in his pocket, but not before Nuria noticed a few small red spots on the white linen. She raised her eyes to his and found him staring at her.

Feeling as though she'd been caught cheating on an exam, she murmured, flustered, "Sorry. I didn't mean to—"

"Never mind," he interrupted, waving her apology aside. As if he'd only just remembered, he added, "Obviously, tomorrow I'll be attending the inauguration of the marvelous cathedral of the Sagrada Familia, where my good friend Pope Pius XIII has granted me the honor of saying a few words during the address on behalf of the Reborn in Christ ... which brings me to my second reason for coming to see you. It would be a great honor for me if you would attend the ceremony."

Nuria blinked, confused. "The inauguration of the Sagrada Familia?"

"That's right."

"I ..." She hesitated. "I'm not sure the police will agree." She indicated the door. "I don't think they intend to let me go free, at least not right away."

"Don't you worry about that," Aguirre assured her nonchalantly. "I'll make sure they stop bothering you and start treating you like the hero you are."

He pointed to Olmedo. "Jaime will take charge of everything. Plus, he'll reserve a seat for you in the front row. You deserve to be there more than most of the second-rate bureaucrats who are just looking for a photo op."

"Wow ... I don't know what to say."

Salvador Aguirre did something she would never have expected: he winked at her. "Say yes. Please."

"Hmm ..." She nodded. "Okay then, yes." Unable to resist his coaxing tone, Nuria was realizing, much against her will, that she was beginning to like this man she'd steadily detested since the beginning of his political career. "I'll be there."

Aguirre smiled in satisfaction. "Wonderful! I promise it will be an unforgettable day, Miss Badal. You have no idea how happy it makes me to be able to count on a hero like you."

Nuria was finding it harder and harder to connect this cheerful politician with the image she'd formed of him after listening to his virulent public speeches against everything she considered fair and reasonable. Could it be that she'd misjudged him? That her mother, when all was said and done, hadn't been so mistaken in believing in him and the church he defended?

She shooed these thoughts away and said, "It will be a pleasure, Mr. Aguirre."

"Salvador," he reminded her with another wink. "I like my friends to call me by my first name."

"Of course, sir ..." She cleared her throat. "Sorry, Salvador."

"That's better."

"I'm afraid we have to leave," Olmedo interrupted in a low voice, bending over Aguirre. "Don't forget, you have a meeting with the Holy Father in an hour."

"True," Salvador agreed. "I ignored my calendar to come and see you, but after what happened this morning, if I'm late for my meeting with His Holiness and I'm discovered in this hospital, the media will start speculating that I may have had to be hospitalized. Well," he added, taking his leave, "it's been a real pleasure to meet you, Miss Badal."

"The pleasure is mine," Nuria replied. To her surprise, she realized she wasn't lying.

"I'm sorry I can't stay longer," he excused himself again, "but you know what these things are like. I trust I'll see you tomorrow at the inauguration."

"I'll be there," Nuria confirmed.

"If it's no bother," Olmedo put in, "I'll stay with Miss Badal to arrange the details for the ceremony tomorrow."

"Of course. See you at the Episcopal Palace, then," Aguirre said. He winked at her once again as he left the room. "Until tomorrow, Miss Badal."

"Until tomorrow," she replied, and even managed a shy smile. *If your friends could see you now,* she said to herself as she watched the two bodyguards exiting the room behind the candidate to the presidency of Spain First in the upcoming elections.

The door closed behind them with a soft click and she realized Jaime Olmedo was watching her the way a hyena would look at a confused rabbit. All the cordiality and ease that had been displayed—to her surprise—by the leader of Spain First were nullified by the hieratic face and down-curved mouth of the party's general secretary.

Olmedo indicated the chair in one corner of the room. "Do you mind if I sit down? It's been a very long day."

"No, by all means," she said, praying he wouldn't make himself too comfortable.

The secretary walked to the chair, arranged his sport coat, and sat down, all his movements deliberate. He was silent for a few seconds as if meditating on what he was going to say next. "It was very brave," he said at last, passing a hand over his gelled hair, "what you did this morning."

"Thank you, but I was only doing my duty."

"Your duty?"

"It looks as though you haven't been properly informed, Mr. Olmedo," she explained. "I'm a police corporal."

He frowned in surprise. "They've reinstated you?" he asked with feigned ignorance. "I thought you were suspended."

"Well, technically—"

"And not just that," he added. "Up until a few hours ago you were wanted for violation of your probation, as a murder suspect, and for collaborating with terrorist groups."

Nuria folded her arms. Apparently they had brought him up to date after all. "What's your point?" she asked in annoyance.

"Why did you do it?" he insisted.

"I told you. I may be suspended, but I'm still a cop. That's not something that—"

"Stop all this nonsense, if you don't mind," he interrupted her abruptly, and leaned forward. "You can keep those answers for your bosses. Tell me the truth: why did you risk your life like that? From your personal file, I know you hate both our party and the Church of the Reborn. Why didn't you stay home and watch our leader and many of his supporters be blown up?"

Nuria wondered for a second whether to tell him to fuck off, but in the end she sat down on the edge of the bed and asked herself the same question. "I'm not sure," she admitted after thinking for a moment. "I guess … it was a way of settling a score."

"Who with?"

"With myself," she said without thinking, realizing at the same moment that what she'd just said was the truth.

Olmedo nodded slowly. "I see."

"Do you?"

"Better than you think," he replied enigmatically, adding, "Do you know the expression *a blessing in disguise*?"

Puzzled by the turn the conversation had taken, Nuria didn't answer immediately. "Well … yes, of course I know it."

"Of course. But do you understand what it means?"

"That something apparently bad," she said in annoyance, not in the mood for riddles, "can bring something good."

"Excellent," Olmedo congratulated her as if she were a child who had learned to say her first and last names. "In this case," he added in the same didactic tone, "your actions have placed our party in a delicate position. But in some way," he added, "you can also be part of the solution."

Taken aback, she blinked. "I … I don't understand what you mean."

"Of course you don't," Olmedo said dismissively. "Like the immense majority of people, you're not capable of seeing beyond the direct consequences of your actions. You do this, that happens, and that's that; like a dog chasing ambulances without knowing why he does it." He traced circles in the air with his index finger as he spoke. "But I carry a tremendous responsibility on my shoulders and I have to be like a chess player, Miss Badal. I have to predict what will happen many moves ahead, anticipate events that others aren't even capable of imagining, in order to correct them even before they happen."

"What?" Nuria asked in bewilderment. "Dogs? Ambulances? What the hell are you talking about?"

Olmedo ignored her. "At the same time, I'm also obliged to calculate my moves with my gaze fixed on a horizon almost no one else can see. My work consists of making decisions that are incomprehensible to the majority of people, but essential in the long run. I'm like the stern father who punishes his child, knowing that even though today it may hurt, tomorrow he'll be grateful for it." He fixed the gaze of a predator on her. "Do you understand what I'm saying?"

"Not a damn word." She was tired of listening to this pretentious Gargamel. "Tell me what you want and then let me rest," she said, lowering her voice. "It's been a very long day for me too."

"Of course." He nodded to himself. "I was just trying to … anyway, it doesn't matter. What I came to tell you is that your unthinking actions have unleashed a series of dangerous reactions,"—he leaned forward in his chair—"and if I don't do something to avert it, the consequences are going to cause a real disaster."

"Are you talking about my ... preventing the attack?" Nuria asked with a frown of disbelief. "Jesus. You say it as if you wished I hadn't." The secretary of Spain First leaned back in his chair without responding, still staring into her eyes. "You've got to be kidding me," she muttered, straightening her shoulders. "What is this? Some kind of test?" She looked around, seeking a hidden camera. "Some kind of politician's joke, or something like that? Because if that's the case, I can tell you it's not funny at all."

Olmedo ignored her tone. "You did something you shouldn't have. Now you need to fix your mistake."

"My mistake?" she repeated, unable to work out what was going on. "What mistake?"

"You meddled in events that are above your pay grade, Miss Badal," he explained indifferently. "But our Lord Jesus Christ, in His infinite grace, has also provided us with the tool to compensate for your dangerous interference."

"Tool?" Nuria repeated, humoring him while throwing a sidelong glance at the door, suddenly worried she might be locked in with a madman. "What tool?"

Olmedo grinned as though she'd just asked him an extremely amusing question, baring his teeth in a sinister grimace as if the hyena had just discovered the rabbit had a broken leg. "You," he replied softly. He got up from the chair and approached her until he was so close Nuria could smell his unpleasantly rancid breath. "Tomorrow you'll attend the inauguration, just as you promised. And once you're there, you'll make up for all the evil you've caused."

"Make up for the evil I've caused?" she repeated blankly, pointing at herself. "Me?"

"That's right," Olmedo confirmed. "You'll do what you have to do."

Nuria had reached such a point of bewilderment that she could only think of one question to ask to find out once and for all what he wanted of her. "What ... what do I have to do?" she asked fearfully.

Jaime Olmedo put his lips to her ear and whispered, "Kill Salvador Aguirre."

76

Nuria shoved Olmedo away and leapt to her feet. The secretary took a step back, contemplating the shaken face of the woman who was staring at him with a mixture of loathing and stupefaction, as though she'd just discovered a rat swimming in her toilet. It wasn't the first time someone had looked at him like that, and he liked to think it was a sign he was doing his job well.

It was a few seconds before she could speak again. Even then, the sound that came out of her mouth was little more than a whisper. "You're insane," she murmured, more to herself than to him.

Olmedo sighed as if all this made him profoundly weary. Turning around, he sat down in his chair again, leaned back, and interlaced his fingers as if the last few seconds of conversation had never taken place. "I wish that were so," he replied, his voice tinged with bitterness. "But I'm afraid it's just the opposite. I wish I didn't see what I see, I wish I didn't understand the workings of human nature and know where we're headed. Everything would be easier for me if I were ignorant of the dangers lurking around the corner and, like the rest of you, were content to react to events as they occur." He paused, then went on. "Being able to see further than others, like a lookout with a pair of field glasses stationed at the top of the mast, is the gift God has punished me with for my sins. I'm the only one who can see the reefs we're headed for, but the helmsman can't hear me and the captain is sick. Tell me,"—he fixed his gaze on Nuria—"what would you do in my place?"

She blinked, then pointed to the window. "Jump overboard," she suggested. "You'd be doing us all a favor."

"Very funny." He smiled sadly. "But I have a responsibility to the party, to the Church of the Reborn and to Spain. Even to you," he added. "I can't shut my eyes and deceive myself. It would be cowardly, a betrayal of God and country, if I didn't do what I should."

"You're a fucking lunatic." Nuria hurled the insult at him with her whole soul.

"Seriously? Do you really believe that? You're a police officer … or at least you were. Surely you've seen the well of putrefaction society is falling into. Drugs, poverty, drought, wars, separatism, terrorism," he enumerated, raising a finger for each one, "and meanwhile, corrupt politicians are only concerned with filling their pockets, passing laws to protect their cronies while hordes of infidels invade Europe because of its passivity. Just like what happened a thousand years ago, we're heading toward a new Middle Ages where twilight and darkness reign. Do you like what you see, Miss Badal?" He leaned forward. "Is that the future you want for Spain?"

"I'm not able to see the future," she said, "and neither are you."

"Well then, don't. Look at the past and the present, and tell me if we're not repeating history step by step. If you add two and two together, whether it's today or a thousand years ago," he argued, "it always makes four. I'm sure you can see that just as I can."

"The only thing I'm sure of," she answered, summoning all the scorn she was capable of, "is that you believe you're a fucking messiah, when the truth is that you're just a poor nutjob with lots of pretensions."

Olmedo shook his head, pretending sorrow. "I'm sorry you see it like that," he murmured. "I had hoped to convince you that desperate times call for desperate measures."

"And killing your leader is the solution?" Nuria snorted. "Jesus, you're a fucking loon."

Jaime Olmedo rubbed his eyes wearily. "He's already dead. Or almost," he added when he saw the surprise on her face. "He has only weeks left; days, more likely. All that vitality you saw earlier is only thanks to painkillers and stimulants. Salvador Aguirre is suffering from terminal inoperable cancer. It has metastasized throughout his body. Though he clings to the helm, knowing the elections are just around the corner, he's no longer the man he was a few years ago, and Spain First is going to be left out of the government. We've spent years keeping his illness a secret," he added, "but we know there are several parties that are already aware of it and are only waiting for the final days leading up to the vote to reveal it."

"But if he already has one foot in the grave," Nuria reasoned, trying to find an explanation for Olmedo's insanity, "why the hell do you want to kill him?"

"*I* don't want to kill him, understand that," Olmedo said. "Salvador Aguirre is … well, like my brother-in-arms. I'd give my life for him without a moment's hesitation. But the party and the future of the country are more important than him or me. Once his illness becomes public knowledge, the Spanish voters, who need a strong, vigorous leader in these times of confusion and fear, will look elsewhere." Olmedo didn't bother to hide the concern evident in his voice and expression. "And the new government, in which we will not be playing a part, will have neither the courage nor the determination to do what they must. But," he added, "if our leader dies, assassinated by Islamic terrorists, and a new candidate with the necessary experience and courage takes his place, millions of Spaniards will sympathize with us and vote for us, understanding at last that only a firm hand will save Spain from the ruin and hatred the foreigners have brought to our country."

Nuria was silent for a few moments while her mind put the pieces of this speech together. "You." She jabbed her finger at him, finally understanding. "Jesus. What you want … is to be the new president of Spain."

Olmedo nodded, satisfied with her rapid deduction. "I'm the one who's best prepared for it," he admitted, "but you're wrong if you think it's personal ambition on my part. I only do what God asks me for the good of our country."

"No," Nuria interrupted him, furious. "What you're asking is for me to do it for you."

"The best thing would have been a terrorist attack with thousands of casualties," Olmedo said. "But you took it upon yourself to ruin that opportunity. A random person shooting him in the street wouldn't have the same effect. It has to be you."

"Seriously?" She jabbed her thumb at herself. "Do you really think I fit the profile of a Muslim extremist?"

For a second, Jaime Olmedo contemplated this tall woman with eyes like a cat, unconcerned about covering herself with the brief green hospital gown. "People change," he said as if it were an accusation.

"What do you mean by that?"

"Well, we know that lately you've struck up a relationship with that friend of yours." He put a finger to his lips. "Mr. Zafrani. Isn't that his name? A Syrian refugee and a Muslim, under investigation by the police for some time. By you yourself, if I'm not mistaken," he concluded with a self-satisfied chuckle.

"Elias Zafrani isn't an extremist." Nuria was beginning to guess where all this was leading. "He's just the opposite. In fact, if it weren't for him,"—she pointed at Olmedo—"you wouldn't be sitting here right now."

"Ah, well. Actually, I wasn't at the arena this morning," he admitted. "Unfortunately for Mr. Zafrani, he's not here to defend himself. It would be very easy to link him to terrorist movements. Both him *and* you, by the way," he added. "Your meetings with the imam, the explosion at the refugee camp, your presence in the sewers at the exact moment of the attack … "

"But it was to *stop* it, for Christ's sake!" she burst out. "Everything I did was to stop the attack!"

"I know," Olmedo agreed. "But imagine how easy it would be to spin it in order to demonstrate the opposite."

Nuria clenched her jaw. "You're a fucking son of a bitch," she muttered through her teeth.

Olmedo shook his head. "I'm the will of God," he corrected her. "The humble scribe who writes his crooked lines in the history of Spain ... and you're the pen. The tool that *He* has put into my hands. You ought to be proud of that."

"Proud?" she repeated, taking a step toward him with her fists clenched. "I'm going to shove that pen up your ass, and then you'll see how proud I feel."

"That wouldn't be a good idea." With a quick movement, the politician took a small device out of his pocket. It took Nuria a moment to identify it as a weapon. It looked more like the handle of a shiny black jug. She could see no mechanism, but it had a tiny hole at one end that Olmedo was aiming directly at her. She'd seen similar weapons in some internal report or other: guns that fired tungsten needles, made from a carbon fiber resin that made them undetectable to scanners. The new favorite weapon of hijackers and assassins.

"Are you going to shoot me with that thing?" she asked.

"I hope it won't be necessary, but I will if you make me."

"I see. And what's your plan?" She smiled sourly. "To force me to kill your boss at gunpoint?"

"My plan was to convince you to do what's best for our country," he said. "But as I suspect that you don't care very much about that, I'm afraid I'm going to be forced to use more ... *persuasive* measures."

"Are you threatening me?" she snapped. "You're wasting your time. I've got nothing to lose."

Olmedo shook his head. "We've all got something—or someone—to lose, Miss Badal."

"What do you mean?" she asked, knowing what his answer would be before she heard it.

"I know you're estranged from your mother ... but I'm sure you don't want anything bad to happen to her." Olmedo leaned back in his chair, still aiming the gun at her. "To her or to your grandfather."

Horrified, Nuria put her hand to her heart, feeling it stop dead in her chest. "You wouldn't do a thing like that," she muttered, halfway between a threat and a plea. "They haven't harmed anyone. In fact, my mother's a Reborn herself, for heaven's sake. Would you be capable of harming a member of your own congregation?"

The politician's unexpected reply froze Nuria's blood in her veins. "I was willing to let thousands of them die today for a greater good," he replied in an icy voice. "Do you really believe your mother's death would mean anything to me?"

Open-mouthed, it took Nuria some time to understand the real meaning of the words the secretary of Spain First had just uttered. "You?" she stammered incredulously, taking a step back and pointing an accusing finger at him. "You knew? Holy shit!" she exclaimed, remembering the maxim that to find the culprit

397

of a crime all you needed to do was find the person who benefited from it. "Of course you knew! That's why you weren't at the rally!"

"I see you're beginning to understand." He nodded with an air of satisfaction. "Now I only hope you'll use that brain of yours to realize you have no alternative."

"You …" Nuria was still processing the implications of this revelation. "It was you the whole time, for God's sake," she murmured under her breath, bringing her hands to her head. "I knew that bunch of brainless extremists couldn't have done it alone, that there had to be people with resources and influence to help them and get rid of the evidence. Christ, now I understand why the imam looked so surprised when I accused him of Gloria's murder. My God … it was you." She took her hands away from her face and fixed her eyes on Olmedo. "You sent that assassin to kill Vilchez and David." Even as she threw the accusation in his face, Nuria still clung to the hope that he would deny it all and say something about a terrible misunderstanding.

But not only did he fail to deny it, he merely waved a hand lazily as if shooing away a fly. "I wasn't in charge of those details," he said, as if that exonerated him. "But I don't think they were counting on you showing up. If you hadn't, everything might have ended there." He clicked his tongue, regretful over that lost chance. "But not only did you survive and kill the operative, from that moment on you became a major pain in the ass, complicating everything and causing more people to die than was necessary." Noticing the shadow of guilt on her face, he delivered his coup-de-grace. "Yes, your friend died too because of your longing for revenge, Miss Badal. How does that make you feel?"

Nuria felt her heart splinter into pieces as she heard her responsibility for Gloria's murder confirmed by Olmedo. "She didn't die, you son of a bitch," she growled, clenching her fists and feeling an irrational murderous longing grow in her. "You murdered her in cold blood."

"But it was because of you," he insisted, rubbing salt in the wound. "But now you have the chance to redeem yourself. Wouldn't you like her death not to have been in vain?"

Nuria felt a powerful temptation to lunge at him and gouge his eyes out with the yogurt spoon, but Olmedo seemed to read her mind and raised the weapon to remind her of its existence.

"I hate you as I never thought I could hate anybody," she said, shaking her head and biting the words as she uttered them.

Jaime Olmedo waited a few seconds without losing his composure, finally asking with a bored air, "Are you finished?"

Driven into a frenzy by his indifference, Nuria spat, "You're a fucking monster. You're the devil incarnate, and after I kill you, your God will make you pay for all the pain you're causing."

"I'll settle my accounts when the time comes," Olmedo said. "But until then, *He* is the only one with the power to judge me."

"But I do have the power to report you," she replied.

"Go ahead." He waved in the direction of the door. "Do it, and you'll lose what little family you have left. But I'm warning you that the probabilities that anyone will believe an ex-cop with psychiatric problems, accused of murder and a likely accomplice of terrorists, are quite limited. You decide, Miss Badal." He spread his hands, still aiming the gun at her. "You'll only be hastening the death of a dying man by a few days, and in so doing you'll save not only your loved ones but also the future of your country. It will be a small sacrifice in exchange for a far greater good."

This time it was Nuria's reply that was slow in coming. She longed with all her heart to hurl herself on Olmedo and kill him with her own hands, but if she did, she would be condemning not only herself, but her mother and grandfather too. It wasn't about her anymore, it was about not causing even more pain to those who didn't deserve it. She was already doomed ... but she could still save them.

"How do I know that if I do what you want, nothing will happen to my mother or my grandfather?"

"What would I gain by that?" he asked. "Once you play your part, they won't be of the slightest importance to me. As far as I'm concerned," he added, "I can assure you they'll be safe. I'll even make sure neither of them ever lacks for anything. You have my word on that."

"Your word is worth jack shit."

"That's your problem," he shot back. "But I'll make sure your mother rises in the Reborn organization and that your grandfather spends his last days in a five-star home." Using his left hand, he tugged at a little gold chain around his neck, pulled out a small crucifix, and kissed it. "I swear it," he confirmed solemnly.

Nuria rubbed her hands over her face, beyond exhaustion. Sitting down on the bed again, she exhaled weakly, unable to continue confronting her own ill-fated destiny. "I'll kill you," she muttered, piercing him with her stare. "I don't know how or when ... but one day I'll kill you with my own hands."

In reply, Olmedo merely raised an eyebrow, impassive in the face of the threat. "So ... do we have a deal?"

77

The car that had come to pick her up from the hospital moved at a snail's pace, one more in the endless line of official vehicles that were waiting under the heavy rain to drop their distinguished passengers in front of the Sagrada Familia cathedral's Puerta del Nacimiento on the right-hand side of the building.

On the other side of the police cordon that controlled the guests' entry, a crowd of faithful Reborn from all over the world surrounded the temple, their hands raised as they gazed at the giant screens that showed the event live. Singing hymns and songs of praise above the noise of the rain and the gusts of wind that stirred their white robes, they looked like an army of ghosts assaulting a castle.

Turning a deaf ear to the reiterated pleas of the supreme pontiff and the optimistic forecasts of the meteorologists, the tropical Mediterranean depression had not only not moved north toward the Gulf of Lion, but had made directly for the coast of Barcelona, at the same time increasing in virulence to levels never before seen in those latitudes. At that particular moment, 11:32 in the morning on Sunday, September 24th, 2028, the rain and the wind were intensifying over the city as if setting the stage for the end of the world.

Nuria, in her room in the hospital, had been putting on the dress uniform brought to her from the police station while keeping the TV on to hold the nervousness that assailed her at bay. She'd seen that the colossal cyclone that had currently spread over much of the western Mediterranean, and whose eye was only a few miles offshore, had just been reclassified as a Category 2 hurricane, with steady winds of eighty miles an hour and gusts of more than ninety-three.

The Free University of Berlin, combining the names 'Mediterranean' and 'Hurricane,' and in honor of the day and place where it had made landfall, had named it *Medicane Mercè,* a name that some of the media had welcomed with suspicious enthusiasm, posting sensational headlines along the lines of *The Rage of Mercé Falls on the Catalans* or *The Hammer of Mercé Crushes Barcelona.*

All the TV stations, without exception, were alternating footage of Pius XIII on his way to the Sagrada Familia cathedral in his many-windowed vehicle with images of awnings, Spanish flags, and restaurant umbrellas whipping back and forth in the Barcelona sky like flocks of demented birds. These images were frequently interrupted by updates from the waterfront, where twenty-five foot waves were overwhelming breakwaters and flooding the lower part of the city, threatening to restore the maritime neighborhood of Barceloneta to the island status it had enjoyed many centuries before.

Nuria hadn't been able to get in touch with her grandfather, whose illegal residence was in Barceloneta, but was relieved it was on the fifth floor. She tried to convince herself that Daisy would have had the foresight to lay in stores of water and food in the face of what was coming. After all, as she'd explained on one occasion, Daisy had come to Spain after losing everything because of a devastating hurricane in the Dominican Republic—so if anyone knew firsthand how to cope with that sort of thing, it was she.

Thanks to the fact that it was a Sunday and the use of personal vehicles had been restricted except for emergencies, the city of Barcelona looked like one of those cities in North Korea where it was difficult to find even one car driving along its vast, empty avenues.

In spite of all this, it hadn't crossed anybody's mind to cancel the longed-for inauguration of the cathedral. Though the pomp surrounding the event was a bit lackluster, the program planners had gone ahead as if nothing were amiss. After a hundred forty-six years of never-ending construction work plus the two-year postponement of the inauguration due to lack of funding, not a single politician was prepared to put off the ceremony even a single day longer. In fact, a couple of hours earlier, Nuria had heard the president himself boasting to reporters that neither a hurricane nor an attempted terrorist attack would manage to defeat the will of the Spanish people. Though the already impressive security measures for the event had been redoubled, they would show the whole world their tenacity, determination, and trust in God against any adversity that might present itself. Nuria had made a face at the abject politician's toothy smile, falser than his tax return, and turned off the TV with a muttered insult.

The vehicle she was in now stopped, slamming her abruptly forward against the black leather of the front seat. Instinctively she clutched her peaked cap tightly against her chest, feeling the extra weight of the carbon-fiber gun hidden in the lining.

From the front passenger seat, a member of Jaime Olmedo's security team who had been keeping her under surveillance since the day before turned and pointed to the door of the vehicle. "You can get out now," he said, looking at her from behind his mirrored glasses.

Nuria realized they'd stopped in front of the Nacimiento façade. After waiting in vain for her guard to do the honors, she put the cap on her head, opened the door with her good hand, and emerged into the open air. Immediately, an assistant appeared with an umbrella in his hand and the absurd intention of protecting her from the rain that the wind was blowing almost horizontally. Greeting her with a 'good morning' that was almost inaudible above the wind, he struggled with the umbrella and invited her with a wave to follow him to the massive doorway in front of them, with its twenty-foot-high double doors.

With her left arm—relatively pain-free thanks to the painkillers—in a sling, and her right hand on her cap to prevent it from flying away, Nuria fought her way to the red carpet covering the stone stairway. She paused after the first few steps to look up at the four pointed stone towers that soared three hundred feet into the sky. The pinnacles of the towers dedicated to the apostles Mark and Luke were visible behind them. Towering above all the rest, nearly six hundred feet high and partially hidden by low clouds was the central tower dedicated to Jesus, crowned by a colossal stone cross from whose tips issued powerful beams of white light, blurred by the rain.

Though she'd seen it a thousand times from almost every angle, the size and shape of that astonishing building left her breathless. Like an indescribable sandcastle made by a giant child, the cathedral of the Sagrada Familia never failed to impress her every time she saw it.

In spite of the fact that the water-repellent fabric of her dress uniform was impervious to the rain, the drops that lashed her face like tiny needles made it extremely uncomfortable to stay outside. Even so, Nuria took another moment to turn and look at the crowd that filled Gaudí Square and the surrounding streets. Most of them were faithful Reborn members wearing white waterproof ponchos, oblivious to the storm that lashed their flags, some of which bore the emblem of Spain First, while others announced that the holder was a member of the Reborn in Christ sect. It was as if they were the same thing.

Nuria couldn't help thinking for a moment that her own mother might be somewhere among those thousands of worshippers, shouting hallelujahs to Pius XIII and waving one of those flags that championed the end of the separation of church and state.

The consolation for that, she thought with a bitterness that twisted her mouth, was that there was no possibility of seeing her mother again and witnessing her disappointment. She'd read enough detective novels to know that Olmedo wouldn't let her be arrested only to allow her tongue to run away with her in the course of an interrogation. She remembered Kennedy's assassination at the hands of Lee Harvey Oswald, who had been murdered before he could give his statement to the police, and she was quite certain that exactly the same thing would happen to her. There had always been and always would be people who would manipulate and sacrifice those like her with impunity to achieve their own ends. It was a fact of life.

Heaving a deep sigh, Nuria turned once again toward the entrance, joining the rest of the guests who were hurrying up the steps and trying to cross the threshold as soon as possible in their search for shelter. Most of them, she guessed, were more interested in the status gained by being one of the five thousand invited guests and in being able to parade in front of half the world's TV cameras than they were in the ceremony—a plan that had been largely thwarted by the uninvited appearance of Medicane Mercé that had turned the social event of the century into a race between Kentucky Derby-style hats in the rain.

"Identification, please," said a voice beside her.

"What?" She turned to face a member of the security team dressed in a suit with a discreet card reader in his hand.

He pointed to the badge hanging from his own neck. "Your invitation, please."

Nuria looked briefly at the guests streaming in around her, noticing that they all wore badges bearing their names and photographs. She couldn't remember anyone giving her one. Or had they? "I …" She patted her clothing. "I think I forgot it."

"Then you can't come in," the agent said curtly. "Move aside."

"No," she said, suddenly alarmed at the possibility that she might not be allowed in. "I've got to get in. Salvador Aguirre invited me personally."

"Move aside," he repeated, this time more emphatically, indicating the foot of the stairs.

"Listen to me. There's been a mistake, someone's forgotten to—"

Without further ado, the agent reached unobtrusively for the back of his pants where Nuria guessed he must carry his gun. In an instinctive response, she brought her right hand to the place where her holster ought to be, but there was nothing there. When she ran a hand over the pocket of her jacket, however, she felt something flat and rigid inside it.

"Oh, thank God, here it is!" she cried with relief. Putting her hand into her pocket, she pulled out the tag bearing her name and photo. Even so, when she looked up, she noticed that the agent was looking at her sharply, a tense expression on his face and his right hand still at the back of his belt. Nuria realized she'd been a second away from ending up face down on the ground with a gun pressed to the nape of her neck.

"You see?" she said, hanging the ID around her neck. "Here it is." With a touch of cockiness, she added, "Take a chill pill, pal."

With a deep breath, obviously biting his tongue, the guard slid the reading device along the plastic card, all the time looking daggers at her. "Go ahead," he said reluctantly, nodding toward the interior. Shooting him one last challenging look, Nuria walked through the metal detectors into the building.

But after only a few steps she stopped short, spellbound. The sublime stained-glass windows that transformed the muted daylight into an explosion of color, the soothing singing of the choir, and the intoxicating scent of incense everywhere transported her for a moment to a better world, one in which peace, serenity, and hope reigned. A very different world from the insane, stormy one that howled beyond the doors. One in which none of them had died: David, or Gloria, or Elias, or so many others. One in which she didn't have to murder someone to save her mother and grandfather.

Trying to push these dismal thoughts from her mind, she remembered that once, when she was a little girl, her father had taken her to see the cathedral. At the time it was still under construction, and because of that—and because she'd been only eight—she hadn't been able to appreciate the majesty of the columns that looked like gigantic white trees, emerging from the marble floor and branching out far above to support a ceiling that was so high it was almost invisible. Oblique rays of light filtered through the branches as though through the canopy of a forest.

This cathedral was possibly the most majestic, awe-inspiring place she'd ever been. With a bitter smile on her lips, Nuria concluded that when all was said and done, it wasn't such a bad place to die.

78

A solicitous usher showed Nuria the aisle where her seat was, but not before he'd compared the photo on her ID card to the face of the woman in front of him three times. Still annoyed by the attitude of the man at the door, Nuria was about to tell him to take a picture because it might last longer, but instead, in a triumph of self-control, bit her lip and waited until he was satisfied. It wasn't a good day for picking a fight with everyone who crossed her path.

Most of the guests at the ceremony were already in their seats, occupying almost all the available space in the nave except for the aisles. The children's choirs were in the dizzying choir stalls that jutted from the walls more than sixty feet above the congregation. In front of the main altar, in the arched presbytery, at least a hundred bishops, cardinals, and priests in their miters and white chasubles were waiting, stolid as bored statues.

Nuria walked along the side aisle toward the head of the nave, casting sidelong glances at the business leaders, politicians, and aristocrats with their gelled-back hair and dandruff, many of them with the Reborn pin on one lapel and that of Spain First on the other. *The crème de la crème,* Nuria thought as she walked between them, attracting looks of surprise as she passed their rows, ascending—in their eyes—the social ladder in the process. The nearer the front someone sat, the greater their status; it was as simple as that. She was sure that was the only thing that mattered to most of those present at the ceremony.

Finally reaching the first row, Nuria was incredulous to find there was a chair with her name on a piece of paper tucked between those reserved for the commander in chief of the civil guard and the army chief of staff. "This has got to be a joke," she muttered, tempted to switch the name tags. A single glance around, though, told her she was attracting too much attention among the security guards posted strategically throughout the cathedral.

Looking around, she noticed that many of the guests seemed to be wondering about the identity of the stranger sitting in the coveted first row, while others, to judge by their alarmed expressions, had possibly recognized her from the news as the woman who was suspected of murder and collaborating with a terrorist group. *All I need is a fucking spotlight pointing straight at my head,* she thought with annoyance. Capitulating to the circumstances, she took her seat before she attracted any further attention.

Soon after she'd taken her place, the two military officers whose seats were adjacent to hers appeared, chatting animatedly as they approached her. They stopped in surprise when they found her sitting between their own two chairs. Suddenly nervous, Nuria couldn't remember the protocol in cases like these. Should she salute? Stand up? Nod discreetly? In truth, she didn't care much what they thought, but she didn't want to attract even more attention to herself.

Luckily, the general in the army uniform took the initiative, a smile on his angular face. "It looks as though someone had the good sense to put an attractive young lady between these two old geezers," he said, pointing to the commander in chief of the civil guard. "Good morning, Corporal—"

"Badal," Nuria replied, undecided about whether to offer her hand or not. "If you like,"—she indicated the chair to her right—"we can switch places so you two can go on talking."

"None of that," the commander objected. "Stay where you are. That way I won't have to see the general's ugly mug every time I look to the side."

Ignoring the joke, the general studied Nuria. "Have we met? Your face is very familiar, Corporal."

"I was going to say the same thing," the commander said, rubbing his chin thoughtfully. "Have you been on television lately? How come you're in the first row?"

Nuria felt a cold drop of sweat slide down the curve of her nape toward her back. "I …" she stammered, fearful they would recognize her and continue to look at her. "I was told to sit here." She showed them her identification card. "I'm … I'm a friend of Salvador Aguirre's," she improvised, using her best poker face. "He invited me personally."

"Oh really? And why is that?" the commander asked.

"Enough, Blas," the general said. "Don't start interrogating the girl, can't you see you're intimidating her? The poor thing has started to sweat—look at her." He waved at the incipient drops of perspiration that had pearled on Nuria's forehead.

"It's true. Forgive me, Corporal. That was the job talking." He gave her a conspiratorial wink and added, "I'm sure you know how that is."

Nuria made an effort to put on the most relaxed smile she could manage as she nodded and said, "Yes, of course. When you're a cop, you're a cop twenty-four seven."

"Exactly," he agreed as he took the seat on her left. "And good cops," he added, giving her a last sidelong look, "never forget a face."

Not knowing how to reply to this, Nuria opted for a cautious silence and sank back in her chair, trying to remove herself from his field of vision as much as she could.

On her right, the general leaned toward her. "Don't pay too much attention to him. He loves to make young people nervous," he whispered in her ear. "Especially attractive women."

Nuria nodded understandingly, but bit her lip to avoid voicing the rude remark that had just occurred to her. Fortunately, she was saved from replying by the appearance of the minister of the interior and his wife, who passed in front of them on their way to their front-row seats. He saluted the two men with a nod, at the same time gesturing at them not to get up.

Discreetly, Nuria glanced around at the people occupying the rows directly in front of the altar. She recognized a fair number of them from the news or the gossip magazines she leafed through while waiting for her turn at the hairdresser's. Judging by the clothes they wore, their bronzed skin and almost identical haircuts, she thought they could easily all be members of the same family, or perhaps imitators of King Philip VI, Queen Letizia and their two teenage daughters, who at that particular moment were making their appearance amid murmurs of recognition and taking their seats on a separate dais to the left of the altar.

As Nuria watched the last guests arrive and parade to their seats out of the corner of her eye, she wondered idly whether everyone who attained power and wealth ended up looking the same or whether it was only those who exhibited that confident, aristocratic bearing to begin that eventually attained power and wealth.

The majestic, almost dreamlike cathedral she found herself in, the wind lashing the kaleidoscopic stained-glass windows, the dozens of celebrities sitting around her, so well-known and yet at the same time so alien ... everything seemed unreal, part of a strange dream she couldn't wake up from, a dream in which her only option was to allow events to take their course, hoping she would awaken at some moment.

Small television drones flew through the nave like brilliant metallic dragonflies, offering images from every imaginable angle to the millions of spectators throughout the world who would be following the ceremony live. From time to time one of these devices descended to ground level to take close-ups of the more important or better-known guests. One of them began to fly along the front row on the right side of the nave, stopping right in front of Nuria.

She was taken aback by the sight of the two microcameras, placed where the eyes of a real dragonfly would have been, focusing directly and brazenly on her, taking their time to study her at length. She made a mental bet that on the other side of the screen was some orange-haired cretin wondering to his followers on Instaface or YouTube about this stranger with the bruised face and serious expression, her hair with its charred tips pulled back into a crude ponytail, asking himself how she could possibly have deserved the privilege of sitting in a front-row seat.

Though she knew it would be a bad idea to call attention to herself, Nuria felt an almost irresistible temptation to swat the insidious flying camera away, but just when she was about to do so, hallelujahs began to sound from the choirs in the heights of the cathedral and a salvo of applause intensified next to the door of the Gloria façade, spreading like a wave among the congregation.

Everyone stood up, turning in unison toward the main entrance and applauding with wild enthusiasm. Nuria did the same, as much out of curiosity as to avoid attracting attention, but since her seat was almost in the opposite corner she was unable to see anything more than a cohort of bishops parading down the central aisle.

After a long minute of applause and hallelujahs, apparently recovered from his convalescence, Pius XIII made his grand entrance through the main door, sumptuously attired in a gold chasuble and miter. He was hailed by the crowd as he passed, condescendingly bestowing greetings right and left and kissing the foreheads of the children who came out to meet him, flanked by a dozen bodyguards who made sure no guest crossed the safety cordon strung along both sides of the central aisle.

Hidden as he was by the forest of guests who had risen to their feet, Nuria had to content herself with following the pontiff's passage through the cathedral on one of the huge screens hanging from the columns. It wasn't until the papal procession reached the altar that she was finally able to see him with her own eyes.

The founder and world leader of the Reborn in Christ movement who had succeeded the late Pope Francis wore his usual grave frown—understandably on this occasion, as he appeared to be almost crushed beneath his heavy, showy, sacramental robes. Nuria craned her neck in search of Aguirre or Olmedo, but was unable to find them among the guests who had stood up to wait for the High Pontiff and his prelates to finish taking their places in the empty chairs at the front of the sanctuary.

It was only then that she realized Olmedo would be watching the ceremony on TV, just as on the previous day when he'd been absent from the rally at the Palau Blaugrana. If he intended to become the new president, he couldn't afford to take the slightest risk.

Pius XIII, aided by two acolytes, took his place at the head of the presbytery under a colossal Christ on the cross suspended by invisible cables. All the choirs fell silent as the outbursts of applause died away. The five thousand attendees sat down again amid excited murmuring, like fans at a rock concert waiting for the singer to take the microphone. All the while, the storm beat furiously against the stained-glass windows, howling like a soul in torment demanding to be let in.

A sickly looking prelate in a purple skullcap rose to his feet. He approached the pope and welcomed him on behalf of all those present, then went on to enumerate the benefits his presence conferred on this, the day of the inauguration of this cathedral that was unique in all the world, rivaling St. Peter's Basilica in importance and majesty.

Hiding her hands under her cap to conceal their trembling, Nuria wished the Archbishop of Barcelona's soporific address would never end, delaying forever the moment when she would have to confront what she'd come to do.

Unfortunately, after only a few minutes, the prelate's lecture came to an end. After approaching the Holy Father and reverently kissing his fisherman's ring, he handed him the gold key to the cathedral of the Sagrada Familia amid the enthusiasm of the spectators watching the events on the ubiquitous television monitors.

Pius XIII raised the souvenir above his head as if he'd just won an Oscar. When the applause subsided, he pointed to a spot on his right and invited someone else to rise and speak. Nuria didn't need to see him to know that the person singled out was Salvador Aguirre. The leader of Spain First rose from his seat on the other side of the nave and made his way to the pulpit with a resolute air, showing no sign of the terminal cancer that, according to Olmedo, was about to end his life.

With all eyes upon him, Aguirre grasped the pulpit with both hands. Clearing his throat a couple of times, he drew several sheets of paper from the inner pocket of his black suit and spread them out in front of him.

The growing murmurs of admiration on the part of many in the audience rose now and again to encouraging cheers which Aguirre was forced to silence with a wave of his hand so that he could begin his speech. Nuria thought that perhaps in their hearts many of those present who were now cheering Aguirre actually detested him. If during the upcoming elections he was excluded from the governing coalition once and for all, there would be many who would clamor to throw him into the bonfire like a piece of old furniture. Right now, though, he stood before the cameras with his ingenuous expression, enjoying his few minutes of fame before an audience of millions of spectators throughout the world.

What none of them know, Nuria thought, discreetly opening the inner lining of her cap to extract the carbon-fiber gun, *is that his political career is going to be over even before the elections.* She felt broken inside, wishing only to run out of the cathedral and never look back. The mere thought of what she was about to do made her so sick to her stomach she could barely stifle the impulse to gag.

If she failed to go through with it, Olmedo would order the murder of her family, and that too would mean the end of her life. Nuria suddenly realized that she should have tried to kill him in her hospital room, even if it had meant losing her own life. She'd missed her chance, and now it was too late to change things.

Aguirre leaned against the pulpit, taking a few seconds before beginning his speech. "Dear brothers and sisters," he said at last in an energetic voice. "We are gathered here today in this marvelous house of God, erected thanks to a century of effort, faith, and devotion on the part of true believers." His voice echoed through the cathedral loudspeakers. "Men and women who, inspired by our lord Jesus Christ, devoted their lives to the achievement of a dream. That is why today is a day to give thanks," he added after a pause, lowering his voice. "We give thanks to the Lord our God"—he raised his eyes to the distant ceiling— "for pouring His divine inspiration into Antonio Gaudí and all those who designed this wonderful place. We are grateful to the millions of donors and to the civil and religious authorities," he continued, sweeping his gaze over the faithful and especially the first few rows with a subtle nod, "who for a hundred and thirty-six years, in the face of crises and difficulties, have made possible the construction of the most beautiful temple mankind has ever seen." Pausing once again, he concluded, "It goes without saying that of course we also give thanks to all those who have protected us from violence, hatred, and chaos." This time his gaze rested on the rows where the heads of the police and the military were assembled. "Without their will and their sacrifice, some of us would not be here today."

As he uttered these words Aguirre's eyes found hers and he nodded once again in gratitude. Nuria knew that if she waited a single minute longer, she would be unable to do it. Terrified, she understood that it was now or never.

Her heart galloping wildly in her chest, gritting her teeth to fortify herself, Nuria grasped the grip of the gun hidden under her cap and stood up to kill the man standing behind the pulpit next to the altar.

79

With Aguirre's eyes still on her, Nuria stepped forward decidedly. Though a slight murmur of curiosity rose from the audience behind her, the guests assumed this was part of the ceremony and no one made a move to stop her. Neither did the security guards nor the police officers move so much as a muscle. They'd all seen the politician apparently addressing the woman in the police dress uniform, perhaps inviting her to come forward. Aguirre didn't seem worried as he saw her walking in his direction.

Though of course none of this was in the program for the ceremony, it was Aguirre's habit to bypass the security protocol and do whatever he pleased. This allowed Nuria to arrive at the altar at a leisurely pace and stand next to the politician. Surprised, he nevertheless welcomed her with an affectionate smile.

His smile vanished a second later when Nuria drew the small black pistol from the hat she was carrying in her left hand. Aguirre showed no reaction to its appearance, only seeming to become aware of what was happening when she apologized with a heartfelt 'I'm sorry' as she put the barrel of the gun to his temple.

A few screams and cries of surprise echoed throughout the cathedral, instantly fading into a murmur of incredulity at what was happening. The guests seemed too caught up in the scene unfolding before their eyes to waste their time being alarmed.

To her right, Nuria heard the footfalls of the king and his family clicking on the wooden floor as they beat a hasty retreat from their dais, possibly remembering that they'd left a pot on the burner in the palace kitchen. Like costumed mice, the security staff burst from the dark corners of the cathedral, spreading out instantly to protect the Holy Father and the celebrities in the front rows. At the same time an epidemic of bright red spots flashed from every direction and Nuria felt dozens of laser pointers converging on her chest. The only thing preventing her from being riddled with bullets at that very moment was the fear that she too would pull the trigger in a reflex act.

According to the script prepared by Olmedo, she had to approach Aguirre during his brief speech. When she was close enough to be sure of her aim, she was supposed to shoot him in the head while crying *Allahu Akbar* with no further explanation.

If she wished to save her loved ones, all she had to do was kill him and then let herself be killed. Nuria had to admit it was a simple and effective plan. The following morning the newspapers would trumpet the news of an unbalanced woman, intimately linked with a criminal who had come to Spain as a refugee, led astray by radical Islamism to the point of murdering the leader of Spain First and the champion of the Reborn in Christ movement for being the most belligerent opponent of anything that smacked of Islam.

An unbalanced woman, a criminal refugee, and Muslim terrorists attacking a patriotic, Catholic politician, all wrapped up in the same package. The far-right journalists would be drooling over their keyboards from sheer delight.

The only problem was that, as much as Nuria wanted to protect her family, when she was standing next to Aguirre holding a gun to his head, she found she was incapable of pulling the trigger. She wasn't going to be able to kill him, shouting *Allahu Akbar* or anything else.

Nuria was at a dead end. Whatever she did from that moment on, it was clear she would be leaving the cathedral feet first and her family would suffer the consequences. There was no way this situation was going to end well.

Desperately, keeping the barrel of her gun pressed against Aguirre's temple, Nuria allowed her gaze to wander over the terrified, expectant faces of the front-row guests. Most of them were familiar to her. They stared at her in disbelief, their eyes like saucers. Abruptly, she realized she was the focus of attention not only of the thousands of people at the ceremony but of millions more all over the world who were following her every move, their hearts in their throats. Breathlessly, they waited for what she was about to do.

Or say.

Better be hung for a sheep, Nuria thought, looking around for the nearest TV camera. "Nobody move!" she shouted, stepping up to the microphone. She gave a sudden start at the volume of her voice through the speakers. "I don't want to shoot anybody," she began, lowering the volume, "but if anybody tries anything, I swear I will shoot."

Aguirre, silent until that moment, turned his head, fixing his gaze on her. "Corporal Badal," he murmured. "Why don't you—"

Nuria cut him off. "Shut up. Tell them to lower their weapons."

"But—"

"Tell them, for Christ's sake!"

Aguirre hesitated a moment, then approached the microphone, motioning for calm. "Please lower your weapons," he said in a quiet voice. Reluctantly at first, the red laser pointers began to go out one by one.

When Nuria felt sure she wouldn't be shot immediately, she placed herself behind and to one side of the politician so she could speak into the microphone while keeping the gun held to his back. Addressing the camera directly in front of her, she cleared her throat and introduced herself to the world.

"My name is Nuria Badal," she announced shakily. "Corporal Nuria Badal of the National Police," she corrected herself. "You think I'm a terrorist, and tomorrow that's what the media will say about me, but I'm not, believe me." She looked at the audience, seeing every possible expression except understanding. "I am a police agent ... or at least I was," she went on. "A couple of days ago, I discovered a conspiracy to murder this man. Yesterday a jihadist squad tried to blow up the Palau Blaugrana during your rally. But together with a group of Special Forces and my ..."—she wondered what to call him—"and Elias Zafrani, we managed to stop it, although we paid a high price for it." She lowered her eyes. "Too high."

There was a tense silence in the cathedral that she didn't know how to interpret. She wasn't expecting an outbreak of applause, but neither had she been expecting the expectant paralysis that seemed to be afflicting everyone, as if they were waiting for her to do a triple somersault in the air as a finale to the show. *Well, if it's a happy ending you want*, she thought, suddenly weary of it all, *that's just what you're going to get.*

"I know what you're thinking at this moment," she went on, studying the faces in the front rows. "You think I'm a terrorist or a lunatic in search of her minute of fame, and I don't blame you. I would think the same myself if I were in your place ... but the fact is, I'm not. Yesterday," she explained, "while I was recovering in the hospital, someone threatened to kill my loved ones if I didn't kill Salvador Aguirre today. That person," she added, "the one who tried to make me shoot this man while shouting *Allahu Akbar*, so that the whole of Spain would believe me to be a jihadist fanatic ... is the same one who collaborated with the ISMA terrorists and financed them to commit the attack we stopped yesterday at the Palau Blaugrana." She paused again, waiting for them to digest this information before she made her final revelation, "That person, whom many of you know and whose goal is none other than to win the next elections and become the new president, is"—she took a deep breath and let it out slowly before putting her mouth to the microphone once again and dropping the bomb—"the general secretary of Spain First, Jaime Olmedo."

Nuria hadn't thought even for a moment about the reaction that might be unleashed by this revelation, but what she'd never expected was that there would be none at all. She scanned the nearest faces, but could see no change in their expressions.

Disconcerted, she wondered whether she'd been speaking another language without being aware of it. There was no scandalized hum of voices, no murmuring of any kind. What she'd said seemed to mean nothing to any of them.

She turned again to Aguirre, but all he did was look back at her with the pitying gaze he would bestow on a child who had wet himself on the rug in front of his parents' guests. Nuria realized that no matter what she said, as far as everybody listening was concerned, she was nothing more than a crazy bitch brandishing a gun.

Anything that came out of her mouth would be nothing but the delusions of a deranged mind, and the more she insisted on her sanity as she stood there with a gun in her hand, talking about conspiracies and far-fetched plots, the loonier she would look.

She'd tried. Once more she'd tried to do the right thing ... and once again she'd been wrong. One final mistake, which this time would be paid for with the lives of her mother, her grandfather, and herself. Accepting that there was nothing more she could do or say to change things, she felt her strength seeping away. Suddenly the light carbon-fiber gun weighed a ton in her hands.

Surrendering at long last in the face of a stubborn, persistent fate she could do nothing to resist, Nuria heaved a long sigh and put her mouth to the microphone one more time to address David, Gloria, her mother, her grandfather, Elias ... and all those she had failed in one way or another. She looked at Aguirre and whispered, "I'm sorry."

Removing the gun from his back, Nuria set it on the pulpit like a poisonous snake, then bent toward the microphone again to address everyone there as well as those who were watching from their homes. "I didn't ..." she began to say, but was unable to finish the sentence. A succession of sharp pains in her back and side flowered into a series of brutal electrical discharges that exploded in an unbearable wave of pain, sending her muscles into an involuntary spasm. With no control over her body, her legs gave way and she collapsed, unconscious, at the foot of the altar, hitting her head against the floor like a marionette whose strings had been cut.

80

When Nuria opened her eyes after blinking in bewilderment a couple of times, the first thing she felt was enormous surprise at finding herself still alive. A bright light was shining through the mist that dimmed her pupils. It took her a couple of seconds to identify it as a light fixture hanging from the ceiling.

She realized she was lying on a sort of gurney. Turning her head to one side, she saw a white room with shelves full of flasks, plastic dispensers, and a piece of equipment for monitoring vital signs, confirming her suspicions: she was in an infirmary. For a moment she thought she'd been taken back to the hospital, but then she felt the unmistakable vibrations of an organ, accompanied by a choir of angelic voices singing a hymn. She was still inside the Sagrada Familia cathedral.

A stab of pain in her left temple made her wince, but when she tried to put her hands to her head she found she couldn't move them at all. They'd fastened both her wrists to the steel frame of the gurney with leather cinches, as they did with dangerous lunatics in mental institutions. "Shit," she murmured, intuiting that this would be the treatment she would receive from then on. Neither willing nor able to stop the tears that began to seep from the corners of her eyes and down her cheeks to the nape of her neck, Nuria wept.

She'd fucked everything up. She hadn't made a single correct decision as far back as she could remember, and the consequence of that was that she was going to spend the rest of her life tied to a bed in a psychiatric ward or locked up in a six-by-ten-foot cell, living with the pain of having caused the death of those she most loved.

The tears ran down her cheeks as she shook her head disconsolately, ruing the fact that she'd put the gun down instead of shooting herself. She'd even made a mess of that, she told herself with a snort of annoyance. Nuria promised herself she would take her own life as soon as she had the chance. She hoped that at least she would be able to do that right.

Her mind, numbed by her aching head, was weighing the various possibilities of committing suicide with her hands tied when a door opened with a slight creak and footsteps entered the room. Instinctively Nuria raised her head. The pain in her temple stabbed her like a hot poker piercing her brain. Stubbornly, she squinted her eyes and bore the pain so she could see who it was.

A tall man with a baleful gaze approached her, flanked by two bodyguards. "How are you feeling, Miss Badal?" he asked insincerely.

Nuria didn't need to see his vulturelike face to identify the repellent voice of Jaime Olmedo. "Go fuck yourself," she grunted, her voice sounding thick and garbled.

Olmedo snorted in amusement. "I see you're fine." Turning to his two companions, he dismissed them with a wave of his hand, letting them know they were to wait outside. The two bodyguards hesitated a moment, no doubt wondering behind their mirrored sunglasses whether it was wise to leave their boss alone with a dangerous terrorist. Olmedo, seeing their vacillation, pointed a finger at the door. "Out," he ordered, "Now!" The bodyguards exchanged a final look, then left the way they'd come.

The moment the door closed behind them, Olmedo turned to her again. Walking in a leisurely fashion, he came to stand immediately next to the gurney, so close that Nuria could smell his fetid breath. He shook his head reproachfully, tsking. "How could you be so stupid, Miss Badal?" he said. "I thought we had a deal."

"Go fuck yourself."

"You could have done the right thing," Olmedo went on as if he hadn't heard. "Done your country a service, saving yourself and your loved ones. But no," he added, sounding disappointed, "you had to spoil it all … and now your mother and your grandfather are going to suffer because of you."

"You'd have killed them anyway," Nuria said, forcing herself to ignore the stabs of pain in her temple every time she spoke. "But the difference is that now the whole world knows you threatened to kill them, and even if they didn't believe me, if anything happens to them it'll be proof that I was telling the truth."

Olmedo laughed softly, a muffled chuckle that reminded Nuria of an asthmatic caught in a fit of coughing. "Miss Badal, Miss Badal …" He shook his head. "It's incredible that you don't seem to know how the world works nowadays. How long do you think people will remember your words? What's more important, who will care? In a few weeks or a few months, you'll be just a dim memory and your words will have dissolved like a raindrop in an ocean of news and gossip. You had your fifteen minutes of fame today, but I can assure you that very soon nobody will remember you."

"Maybe," she conceded. "But there will be an investigation and everything that really happened will come out."

"How naïve you are." He smiled. "Do you really believe there will be an investigation?"

Nuria made an effort to hide a shiver. Of course not, there never would be. In fact, she couldn't believe she was still alive. "One way or another, the truth will come out," she said instead, trying to summon up hope in herself.

"The truth ..." Olmedo repeated, as if the word were strange to him. "The truth is a matter of perspective, Miss Badal. The whole world is lost because everybody has his own truth, and it changes from one day to the next. Out of every ten pieces of news, nine are false or exaggerated, but they're all equally credible depending on the beliefs of whoever reads them. That's why Spain needs my party and the Reborn in Christ," he explained, "because we're the bearers of certainties. We give simple answers to complex questions, and our voice is that of the Lord our God"—he pointed at the heavens, then spread his hands wide in false modesty—"expressing Himself through his humble emissaries. So ... whose word do you think will carry more weight with people, Miss Badal? Mine? Or the ravings of a deranged terrorist?"

"If you kill my mother or my grandfather, you'll prove that what I said is true."

He put his hand to his chest in a theatrical gesture of innocence. "And who says I'm going to kill them? Your grandfather's an old man, and your mother—she lives alone, doesn't she? That's quite dangerous in these times. There are so many criminals and so many refugees on the loose ..."

Hearing this, Nuria clenched her fists tightly, unconsciously straining against the bonds that held her. They didn't give an inch. She gritted her teeth in rage. "You miserable psychopath. I'm glad I ruined your fucking plans to become president."

Olmedo gave a slight shrug. "Ah, well ... It's true you've made things a little more complicated for me," he admitted, "but nothing's really changed. Even if you didn't get as far as shooting Aguirre, your presence at the previous attacks links you directly to ISMA and the refugees. An Islamic terrorist who repents at the last minute in the presence of the leader of Spain First—" he added with an air of satisfaction, "that's almost as good as if you'd pulled the trigger. Just by appearing on camera threatening Aguirre, you'll gain us millions of sympathy votes as well as prove that we're the ones the terrorists fear the most. We'll win the elections in any case, and by then it will hardly matter if our beloved leader's illness becomes known."

Impotent and desperate, Nuria had no idea what to say to this man who was watching her without the slightest trace of empathy. There was no hatred in his look, simply the indifference of an entomologist sticking a pin into an insect for his collection. It wasn't until that moment that she fully comprehended that the secretary of Spain First and the next president of Spain was a textbook example of a psychopath. She shook her head. "You won't get away with it," was the only thing she could think of to say.

Olmedo bent over her. "I already have," he hissed in confidence. "And now, if you'll excuse me ..." He straightened and pointed to the door. "I've got more important business to attend to."

417

In reply, Nuria spat into his face with all the saliva and all the disgust she was able to muster. "Go fuck yourself."

Jaime Olmedo stepped back, taking a handkerchief from his jacket pocket, and wiped his face. "Anyway," he said, "I'd say I'll see you soon—but we both know that's not going to happen. So goodbye, Miss Badal." He put his right hand over the heart Nuria seriously doubted he had. "May the Lord have pity on your soul."

He turned and went to the door. When his hand was already on the handle, Nuria spoke again. "One last thing, Jaime," she said, deliberately using his first name. He stopped instinctively, but didn't turn around. "You're going to burn in hell, you fucking son of a bitch," she spat from the gurney. Showing no reaction, the secretary simply left the room, closing the door behind him with an irritating, indifferent click.

Alone once more in the infirmary, with no antagonist to vent her fury on, Nuria could find no one else to blame but herself. In desperation, she looked around for some sharp object she could use to end her life. The agonizing pain that held her in its grip went far beyond any pain she'd ever suffered, beyond what she was able to bear.

At that moment, though, the handle clicked and the door opened once again. Four uniformed police officers entered the infirmary. Two of them stood guard while the other two busied themselves unfastening the leather straps that bound her. When they'd finished, the one with sergeant's stripes asked her to sit up on the gurney.

Nuria did so without a word, relieved to be able to get up. "Hands behind your back, please," the sergeant said, taking a pair of handcuffs from his belt.

"What precinct are you from? I don't think I've seen you before," she said.

"Hands behind your back," the sergeant repeated, obviously uninterested in conversing with her.

Aware that she could do nothing else, Nuria put her hands behind her back and immediately felt the cold steel of the handcuffs closing around her wrists. The metal rings clicked unpleasantly as the officer adjusted them a little too tightly. She looked at the four officers. "Are we done with the ceremony? Where are you taking me?"

None of them made any response. Just then, the door opened again and a tall man with a stony face wearing a dress uniform appeared in the doorway. "Good morning, Corporal," he said coldly.

In spite of his tone, tears came to her eyes at the sight of a familiar face. "Hello, Commissioner."

81

Puig dismissed the four officers with a wave. He remained rooted to his spot just inside the doorway as if, despite the physical evidence, he was finding it hard to believe what he was confronted with and wasn't sure how to react.

"Nuria," he began, shaking his head. "Nuria ..." he repeated, and the disappointment in his voice hurt her more than a Taser. "Nuria ..."

"I ... I'm sorry," was the only thing she could think to say.

"All this is my fault," the commissioner went on. "I knew something was going wrong with you right from the start, but I didn't do what I should have. I shirked my responsibility, and—well—" He waved at her vaguely. "Look at you now."

"It's not your fault," Nuria said. "What I said before was the truth. It's that damn Jaime Olmedo who threatened to kill my family if I didn't assassinate Aguirre today. He gave me the gun at the hospital. He's the one behind the attempted attack at the rally yesterday. You've got to arrest him, Commissioner, please," she implored him. The tears welled up again and began to seep from the corners of her eyes. "Don't let him hurt my family!"

Puig bowed his head, avoiding eye contact with his subordinate. "Don't make it harder for me, Corporal."

"It's the truth!" Nuria insisted. "He's the one who's been pulling the strings right from the start. He had Vilchez killed because he'd found out about the terrorists, then David because he was investigating and got too close, and then Gloria, to wipe out the trail and get me out of the way. It was him the whole time. Where do you think I got the gun while I was in the hospital? I didn't have any other visitors apart from you and him. Surely you can check that."

"It is something we'll look into," Puig said. "But the design for that kind of gun can be downloaded from the net and printed on any 3D printer. There must be one at the hospital you were in."

"But he gave it to me!" she insisted. "Aren't you listening to me? Olmedo wants to kill Aguirre so he can step into his shoes, but he needs it to look like an attack so he'll be seen as a martyr. That way he'll gain even more support for his party and be elected president in next week's elections!"

Puig closed his eyes and, uncomfortable, put his hand to his forehead. "Of course." He nodded. "I'll look into it at once."

"It's true!" Nuria burst out. "Don't keep humoring me as if I were crazy, for God's sake!"

"I just saw you put a gun to a man's head and launch into a harangue about the secretary of an ultra-Catholic political party organizing jihadist attacks against themselves. What would you think if you were in my shoes?"

Nuria exhaled a long breath through her nose and shook her head. "The same thing, I guess," she admitted, lowering her voice. "But I'm only asking you to investigate a little, Commissioner. Do you actually believe I've turned into an Islamic terrorist overnight? Don't you think there's something very fishy about all this? What does your police instinct tell you?"

Puig kept up an encouraging silence for several seconds, and Nuria thought she saw a spark of reasonable doubt taking hold in him. Finally, he said, "It's not me you have to convince."

"I know. But … do you believe me?" She was almost pleading. "I need to know."

Puig's circumspect expression remained unchanged, but she thought she saw a trace of pity in his eyes. "If you have evidence for what you say, you'll be able to present it when you have your trial. That's when it will be decided whether what you say is true."

Nuria shook her head. "Forget it. There won't be any trial. At least none with me there. Olmedo will make sure I have an accident, or some fanatical Reborn will shoot me first. That's a foregone conclusion." Puig opened his mouth to object, but she didn't let him. "I'm just asking you to investigate, and to protect my family from that monster. Please. Promise me that."

"I can't—"

"Promise me," she begged. "There's no one else I can turn to, Commissioner. In spite of all this,"—she rattled the cuffs behind her back—"I trust you. Right now you're the only one who can help me."

Puig pursed his lips, apparently struggling with himself. "I'll do whatever is possible," he said at last. "I can't promise you more."

It was the closest thing to a commitment she was going to get from the commissioner. It would have to do. "All right," she said with a long sigh. "Thank you." Puig nodded in silence, as if he found it hard to accept even this minimal show of gratitude.

In spite of the thick stone walls of the cathedral and the incessant howling of the wind, Nuria now caught the voices of the fifty thousand followers gathered outside. They were shouting some sort of repeated chant, but she couldn't make out the words. Straining her ears, she asked, "What are they saying?"

Once again Puig hesitated before answering, as if not sure whether this was information he should share with her. "They want us to hand you over, Nuria," he said in an unexpectedly confidential tone. The fact that all of a sudden Puig was using her first name again, far from comforting her, sent a shiver of unease through her.

"To hand me over?"

"To them," he explained. "Or else they'll come for you."

It took her a few seconds to understand. "Holy shit."

"The fact that you put a gun to the head of their revered leader seems to have pissed them off quite a bit."

Nuria had a fleeting image of all those thousands of fervent Reborn laying siege to the cathedral, wielding pitchforks and torches as in days of old when witches were burnt at the stake. Puig saw her look of alarm. "Don't worry, we'll get you out of here right away," he said to calm her.

"How?"

"There's no space for a helicopter to touch down, so we're doing it by land."

"With all those people out there?" she asked skeptically.

"We have an armored vehicle."

Nuria was about to point out that this would hardly be enough to stop a mob intent on lynching her when the infirmary door opened and a member of the Special Forces came in, dressed in his black uniform, with an assault rifle hanging across his back and an El Corte Ingles bag in his hand.

He stood to attention as soon as he entered the room. "Commissioner. The armored vehicle is ready and the men in position."

"Thank you, sergeant." Puig went up to him. "We'll be leaving in two minutes."

"Two minutes," the sub-officer repeated in confirmation. Handing the commissioner the bag he carried, he added, "Here's what you asked for."

"Thank you, Sergeant. Dismissed."

"Yes sir." The sergeant saluted again and left the room.

Returning to Nuria, the commissioner unexpectedly walked around the gurney and stood behind her. "Let's go," he said. Nuria's surprise grew when she felt him doing something to her handcuffs. He unlocked them with a click and her hands were suddenly free. She raised them to her face and stared at them as if she'd thought she would never see them again. "Don't get too excited," he warned her as he handed her the bag. "Put this on."

Nuria took the bag, opened it, and pulled out a large piece of white cloth that took her a few moments to identify. She looked at him in consternation when she realized what it was. "You've got to be kidding me," she said incredulously, holding up what looked like a coarse, thickly-woven sheet.

"Come on," Puig urged her. "We have no time to lose."

With a sigh of resignation, she put her head and arms through the robe and let it fall to her feet under its own weight. She checked to make sure she'd put it on correctly and that the collar of her police uniform was well hidden under the modest neckline. When she turned to the glass door of a cabinet to see whether she now looked like any other Reborn, her heart skipped a beat.

She did not. She was not simply one more Reborn. What the glass showed her was her mother's reflection. Seeing herself dressed in the same outfit her mother wore to her church meetings, Nuria was shocked at how close the resemblance between the two of them was. With a few more wrinkles and a few less bruises, she and her mother could almost pass for sisters.

"Jesus," she muttered. Seeing her own image dressed as her mother hurt. Nuria understood that in a way they'd both ended up wearing the same clothes for the same reason: to protect themselves. She from a furious mob and her mother from a reality she loathed, but both of them, in the end, trying to escape.

The commissioner's voice brought her out of her reverie. "Time to go," he urged. "You won't be in handcuffs to avoid attracting attention, but don't do anything stupid, I'm warning you." He pointed to the wall. "There are more than a thousand cops surrounding the temple, and that's not taking into account the fact that if those pious devotees out there spot you, you'll end up hanging from a lamppost or stoned to death in the middle of the street. And there will be nothing we can do to stop it. Do you understand what I'm saying?"

Her shoulders sagged. "I'm not going to run away. I'm too tired."

"Okay." He nodded, looking unconvinced. "But just in case—" Reaching into his pocket, he took out a Taser bracelet and fitted it to her wrist. Once he felt sure she wouldn't be able to take it off, he reached into his pocket again, took out a small remote control with a single red button, and showed it to her.

"That's not necessary," she said, looking at the bracelet. Apparently innocuous, it was capable of delivering a charge of seven hundred volts, leaving her unconscious all over again. It wasn't an experience she felt like repeating.

"I hope not. If I have to use it, it will draw people's attention to you, and ... well, we don't want that to happen, do we?"

"No." She sighed and shook her head. "I guess not."

Puig nodded. "All right, then." He put the remote back into his pocket. "I'll go first, but don't get more than a yard away from me, understood? Oh, and cover your head with the hood so they don't see your face."

Nuria nodded obediently. Pulling the hood up over her head, she felt suddenly as if the world had disappeared and she'd disappeared as far as the world was concerned. All she could see was the tips of her shoes and the small space of ground in front of them, as if nothing else existed.

This innocent gesture made her understand why so many women, disgusted by their circumstances, had decided to seclude themselves under that habit—or any other habit, for that matter. It was a carapace, a final place to escape and find refuge, perhaps the only way they had left to shut out everything that threatened them or made them suffer.

Puig opened the door of the infirmary and exchanged a few words with the officers guarding it. Nuria heard their footsteps moving away down the hallway to the right. "Let's go," he said. "Stick close to me and don't raise your head." Without waiting for a reply, he turned left and set off at a leisurely pace down the corridor. She opened her mouth to ask why the two officers had gone in the other direction, but just then, they began to pass other people and she decided to shut it again. Her voice had become too well known lately.

Still, with her gaze fixed on the marble tiles slipping past under her feet, Nuria was aware that there were more and more people around her, nervously whispering about what was happening. Though she only managed to grasp a few words in passing—*terrorist, hurricane, crowd*—they were enough to give her a fairly good idea of the situation. All that was needed now to turn her into the villain in a superhero movie was for her to be accused of invoking the storm as well.

"This way," Puig said. "Don't get separated." Nuria was about to reply that she was following him so closely she might as well have been stuck to his ass, but at that moment there were so many people around them she didn't even dare cough.

Suddenly a door opened in front of Puig with a creak of wood. Though she was behind him, an unexpected gust of wind lifted her hood and the rain drove against her face like a hundred needles. Caught by surprise, Nuria still had the sense to grab the edge of the hood and pull it over her head again quickly, but not before she'd realized they were standing in front of the doors of the Pasión de Cristo façade, exactly where several thousand Reborn were now shouting and raising their fists and sticks in the air in a very unChristian rage. Threatening to break the police cordon that was barely able to hold them back, they were demanding that the terrorist be handed over to them so they could execute her.

What was entirely absent as far as she could see was any kind of vehicle: no armored car, no means of transport ready for her evacuation. Nothing. Only religious fanatics filling the courtyard of the Sagrada Familia cathedral, enduring the fury of the storm and thirsty for blood.

Her blood.

Puig had betrayed her. There, under the friezes depicting Judas handing Jesus over to the Romans, Nuria realized she'd followed him trustingly, like a lamb, and he, in turn, had led her to the slaughterhouse.

82

Stunned by this final betrayal, Nuria raised her head and turned to Puig, determined to look her executioner in the eye and ask him why. He seemed to be deliberately ignoring her, though, all his attention on the hysterical crowd as he waited with his hand on the radio mike.

Just when she'd opened her mouth to ask him about his lies, he put his lips to the mike and said softly, "Puig here. Team one, go, go, go."

"Copy," said a voice from the radio. "On the move."

Nuria was still staring at the commissioner when he seemed to remember her existence and turned to her, frowning when he saw her head raised. "Bow your head, for God's sake!" he recriminated her impatiently. "If anyone recognizes you, we're screwed."

Nuria blinked at this reproach. What was the commissioner playing at? "What the fuck is going on?" she asked defiantly, not taking her eyes from his face. "Are you going to hand me over to those fanatics?"

It was Puig's turn to stare blankly back at her. "What?"

"Are you going to hand me over to that rabble?" she repeated, waving at the mob that was determined to break through the police cordon a few yards from them. "To save your own ass and the asses of everybody inside, right?"

To Nuria's surprise, his response was first one of bewilderment, followed by something very much like shame. "Do you really believe I'd hand you over to be lynched?" he asked, sounding vaguely offended. "You really think I'm as much of a bastard as that?"

Nuria swallowed. Refusing to soften her tone, she said, "If that's true, what are we doing here? And where's this armored vehicle?" She'd barely finished asking the question when something shifted among the crowd. Their disorganized shouts faded for a moment, replaced by a growing roar like a plane revving its engines before takeoff.

She turned toward them, wondering what was going on, when the roar turned into shouts. Without any apparent reason the crowd began to move, no longer charging at the police cordon, but instead dispersing to left and right as though trying to get to the other side of the cathedral as fast as they could.

"The armored vehicle is only the bait," Puig explained when he saw her confusion. "Why else would we have dressed you up as a Reborn? They'll take a while to realize you're not in it, and by then we'll be gone."

She turned her head in every direction, looking for some means of transport. "But how are we going to get away?"

"We're going to calmly walk away," Puig said, pointing ahead.

"But there are still people there," Nuria said. Though the vast majority had scattered, there were still several hundred demonstrators standing guard in front of the door, most of them wearing the white robes of the most devout Reborn. "Are we going to have an escort?"

Puig shook his head. "That would only attract more attention. The plan isn't perfect," he added reassuringly, "but we'll manage if you can pass yourself off as one of them."

It took Nuria a moment to get used to this new scenario. Two minutes earlier, she'd been thinking the commissioner was betraying her. Now he was proposing they cross a square full of fanatics who would hang her from the nearest tree if they got the chance. If just a single one of them recognized her, there would be no police presence capable of preventing them from lynching her.

She shook her head. "With all due respect, Commissioner … it's a shit plan."

"You're right," he admitted. "But we don't have a better one." Adjusting his cap, he asked, "Are you ready?"

Nuria felt her legs go rubbery from sheer terror and feared they would fail her at any moment. She had a horrible foreboding that she would end up tripping and falling flat on her face, attracting people's attention. She would be recognized and killed on the spot.

Trying to summon up her courage, she took a deep breath and looked up one last time at the enraged mob, the howling trees, and the intense downpour riddling them from above, blurring the silhouettes of buildings and people. "No, I'm not ready," she said at last in answer to the commissioner's question, then bowed her head and covered herself with the hood once more. "But let's go." She followed Puig, who didn't hesitate as he went out the main door, making straight for the police line that fortunately was now under less pressure from the demonstrators.

The rain and wind lashed at her from all directions, soaking her robe and stinging her hands and face, while the force of the wind forced her to bend forward simply to keep her balance.

"Stay close!" Puig warned, seeing that she'd drifted a couple of yards from him. Nuria was about to reply that it wasn't easy to walk into the wind with her head down, unable to see where she was going, but instead, she hastened her steps until she was right behind him.

They reached the police cordon and she heard him give a couple of orders to the officers manning it. Immediately a gap in the line was opened to let them pass. This inevitably attracted the attention of the many Reborn still in the courtyard, their righteous fury allowing them to withstand the rain under their white robes. They raised their voices above the din of the storm, demanding revenge.

With apparent indifference, Puig continued in a straight line through the shouting mob, arousing wary looks as he went that, for the moment, were only directed at him. One or two of the protestors even shouted accusations at him as he passed for not having done his duty to protect Aguirre. But the police uniform, the weapon at his belt, and the commissioner's own imposing physical presence stopped anyone from going any further.

Nuria, walking in silence behind Puig, didn't dare do anything except keep her head down and try to be invisible. All she could see in the reduced field of vision the hood afforded her were the tips of her own shoes and the heels of the commissioner's. Her world had narrowed to two objectives: to pass unnoticed through the crowd and to avoid losing sight of Puig. If she became separated from him, the commissioner might think she was trying to escape and activate her Taser bracelet, which would leave her convulsing on the ground, attracting as much attention as if she were wearing a siren on her head—which wouldn't bode well for her health.

Despite her initial fears about the insanity of the plan, Nuria was beginning to feel calmer and more confident. Glancing around from the corner of her eye, she realized they were already halfway through the courtyard and the crowd around them was thinning. She allowed herself a sigh of relief, feeling as if she'd been holding her breath up until that moment. "Jesus ..." she muttered, relaxing the tension that had been keeping her fists clenched.

But just then she felt someone take her arm in a firm grip. "Sister?" came a man's voice from behind her. "Are you all right?" Paralyzed by surprise, Nuria froze, watching Puig's feet move away from her. Apparently he was unaware of what had happened. "Are you all right, sister?" the stranger insisted. "Are you having a problem with the police? Do you need help?" That was it, she realized. Seeing her following Puig so closely and submissively had given him the impression that she was being taken into custody.

Under normal circumstances she would have laughed at the misunderstanding and solved the problem by thanking the man for his interest and telling him to mind his own business. But the circumstances were anything but normal. Merely by opening her mouth, she would run the risk of the Reborn around her recognizing her voice. What would happen if they saw her face or even suspected anything odd did not bear thinking about.

The inopportune Samaritan was not loosening his grip, though, and every second that went by increased the risk that Puig would turn, not see her behind him, believe she was running away, and press the red button on the Taser remote. She had to do something, and fast. Without turning her head, she said, "I'm fine," in a voice that sounded like a cartoon character's.

Contrary to her intention, this embarrassing performance aroused still more concern in the man. He stepped in front of her without letting go of her arm. "I can tell there's something wrong," he concluded. "Have you been arrested?"

Around them dozens of Reborn continued to shout, fists raised, demanding the handover of the terrorist, but now some of them stopped suddenly. Nuria suspected she'd become an unwanted focus of attention.

"I tried to sneak in to see the Holy Father," she improvised, modulating her voice so it sounded less artificial. "But I was discovered."

"And they arrested you for that?" he asked conspiratorially. "Well then, stay here. The policeman hasn't realized he's lost you and he'll never be able to find you among all the other brothers and sisters."

The knowledge that Puig had moved further away, far from comforting her, sent a chill up and down her spine. She would be the target of the electrical discharge any moment now. "No, I'd better go," she said, trying to free herself from this man whose face she couldn't see.

"But, sister, you—" he insisted, still holding her firmly.

"Get your fucking hands off me!" Nuria exploded, slapping his hand away and raising her voice more than she'd meant to. Her real voice. For an endless second she stood paralyzed, agonizing over her outburst and afraid that this jerk, or one of the others around her, might have recognized her. But no one said anything. A bubble of silence formed around her, quieting the shouts of the demonstrators, whose attention had now turned to her.

Though her whole body was begging her to run after the commissioner, she knew it would be a mistake. Slapping a spiritual brother wasn't proper etiquette for a good Reborn woman, and running away with no apparent reason was even less so. Nuria's brain seethed desperately. She had to find some way out that wouldn't end up with her fleeing a mob intent on lynching her.

Then came a sudden inspiration. "Death!" she shouted, turning back toward the cathedral entrance. "Death to the terrorist! Long live the Pope! Spain First!" she added, still with her head down but raising her fist, shouting with all the force her lungs could produce.

In response, those around her echoed her cries, inspired by her fervor. "Death to the terrorist! Long live the Pope!"

"Death to the terrorist!" she shouted again, finding she didn't entirely disagree with the demand. "Let her be burned at the stake!" she added without thinking, fearing instantly that she'd overdone it.

427

But a moment later dozens of voices took up the cry enthusiastically all around her. "Burn her at the stake! Into the fire!"

With a sudden shiver, Nuria remembered she was the one they wanted to burn alive, and knew she couldn't spend another second among these people. Unobtrusively, without lowering her fist, she began to walk backwards, praying she wouldn't bump into anybody and that no one would notice her discreet retreat.

But of course this was too much to ask. She hadn't taken two steps when someone grabbed her from behind and held her by her left wrist. Instinctively Nuria spun around in a fury, fed up with the Reborn misogynists who believed they had the right to hold a woman down like a dog. It wasn't a white robe that confronted her, though, but a navy-blue uniform jacket with gold buttons and stripes on its shoulders.

Looking up, Nuria saw a too-familiar face, its eyes staring at her keenly from beneath the visor of a peaked cap. "I told you not to get separated," the man said roughly.

Nuria felt a wave of relief when she recognized the inscrutable, angular features of Commissioner Puig. She had to hold herself back to keep from hugging him.

83

No one else noticed her as they left the Sagrada Familia courtyard. The clamoring crowd faded away behind them, along with the nerve-racking possibility of being discovered. Luckily, aside from the fanatics and the police protecting the cathedral against their siege, there wasn't a soul in the streets. The rest of the Barcelonians, those with a modicum of common sense, were tucked away in their own homes, sheltering from the fury of the elements. Nuria, tired of walking bent over, felt safe enough to stand up straight and raise her eyes at last.

She supposed that at any moment a police van would appear to take her to the station, so she followed Puig, who was already turning into Mallorca Street, in silence. Watching the back of the commissioner's neck, it occurred to her that if she came across some hard object she could knock him unconscious from behind, then vanish. It would be a nasty thing to do, and if she didn't knock him out with the first blow she wouldn't get a second chance. But what did she have to lose? With all the crimes she'd already piled up, attacking a superior officer would be no more than the cherry on top.

But the fact was, she was tired of running away. There was no one else she could turn to. Puig was the single remote hope she had to keep her family safe from Olmedo's threats.

As if he'd read her thoughts, he stopped abruptly and turned to her. Nuria was afraid for a moment that she'd been thinking aloud without realizing it, thereby confirming his suspicions that she was a complete nut case.

To her surprise, the commissioner didn't accuse her of planning to attack him. Instead, he pointed to the door of a silver Jaguar I-Pace parked at the curb and said curtly, "Get in." Nuria looked from the vehicle to Puig, confused. It wasn't until he'd walked around the car and opened the driver's door that she understood what he meant. "Come on," he insisted. "We're wasting time."

Nuria opened her mouth to ask what the hurry was, whether they were late for somewhere, but before she could do so the commissioner got into the car and she was obliged to do the same. The moment she sat down, her sodden robe began to drip onto the seat as though she were squeezing a sponge, wetting the upholstery and creating a growing puddle of water at her feet. "Wait a moment," she said. With a snort of exasperation, she pulled the robe over her head, opened the door, and hurled it viciously as far away as she could.

Puig raised an impatient eyebrow. "Have you finished?"

Deliberately slamming the door, Nuria shook the water from her hair. "Yes, I'm done."

He waited a few seconds as if expecting her to add something else so he could reprimand her, but she decided not to oblige him and remained silent, not looking at him and folding her arms like a pouty little girl with a strict father.

Rolling his eyes at her attitude, Puig started the vehicle without another word. The Jaguar maneuvered itself with an electric hiss into the nonexistent stream of traffic. Placing his hands on the wheel, the commissioner switched off the autopilot and drove in a straight line to Avenida Diagonal, where he turned left on Paseo de San Juan.

It seemed odd to Nuria that Puig, considering everything that had happened, would be taking her to the station in what appeared to be a luxurious, unmarked police vehicle. They were far enough from the crowds by now that there was no longer any need to hide her. After all, she wasn't just some pickpocket who had been caught in the subway.

She was tempted to ask him what was going on. Why was she sitting next to the driver rather than handcuffed in a police van with half a dozen officers holding their guns to her head? After thinking about it for a moment, though, she supposed that they wanted to move her as discreetly as possible to prevent the Reborn from knowing where she was being taken, then attempting to lay siege to that place a few hours later.

Besides, she concluded, it wasn't her problem. Perhaps this was one of those occasions when the most prudent course of action was to keep one's mouth shut.

Judging by the direction they were going in, Nuria deduced that they were taking her to the Plaza de España station, the biggest one in Barcelona. But when they reached the turnoff for the underground parking lot, Puig didn't slow down. Instead, he drove around the Plaza de España roundabout onto Maria Cristina Avenue and headed towards Montjuïc Mountain.

"Um ... haven't we gone too far?" she asked, turning around in her seat to look at the rapidly receding building with its tinted glass windows and the UNP logo. "Where are we going?" Puig didn't answer. "Commissioner?" she insisted, seeing that he made no attempt to turn around. "The precinct's back there."

"I know."

"Well then, where are you taking me?"

"You'll see. Trust me."

Baffled at his addressing her in such terms, she was silent for a few moments as the vehicle turned onto Stadium Avenue and began to wind uphill. The only things up there that Nuria knew of were the Olympic facilities, various scenic viewpoints over the city, and ... the Montjuïc Castle prison, the sinister penitentiary with its infamous history, refurbished a few years back to hold the Catalan separatist leaders. A high-security prison where it was rumored that torture and "suicides" were everyday occurrences, it was one of those places where once you went in, there was very little chance you would ever come out again.

"What ... what's happening, Commissioner? Are you taking me to the castle?" Puig glanced at her, but instead of answering, he turned off the wide avenue leading to the prison and turned into a narrow side street. She peered out the window. "But ... where the hell are we going? This doesn't lead to the castle or anywhere else."

This time Puig did turn to her, not to offer an explanation but to warn her. "Hold on tight."

Thoroughly confused, Nuria thought she must have misheard. "What?"

"Hold on tight!" he repeated, flooring the accelerator and aiming the vehicle at one of the thick poplars that flanked the road.

"No!" Nuria screamed, understanding his intentions. Anticipating the imminent impact, she crossed her arms over her face to protect herself. A second later, as if in slow motion, she watched as the nose of the Jaguar rammed into the tree, twisting around it as if trying to embrace it.

A nanosecond later the accelerometers activated the airbags. Half a dozen white bags inflated instantaneously around her, forcing her back against the seat from all directions and squeezing the air out of her lungs. The impact's brutal rebound flattened her against the front airbag. Nuria felt all her internal organs continuing to shoot forward even as her body stayed behind. A second later she was hurled back against the seat, the nape of her neck bouncing so hard against the headrest that she thought her neck would break.

The vehicle came to a final stop, the airbags deflating like punctured life preservers. Nuria fell forward once again, saved by her seat belt from smashing her forehead into the dashboard. Stunned by the violence of the crash, she hung limply, her head dangling. The earsplitting noise of the accident had given way to a ghostly silence, overlaid by the howling of the wind and the rain drumming on the remains of the car, a nagging rain that lashed her face through the shattered windshield and forced her to open her eyes as she emerged slowly from her semiconscious state.

In front of her the hood of the Jaguar was folded like an accordion and the tree trunk was disconcertingly close, almost at arm's length. The remains of the windshield, hundreds of tiny shards of glass, were scattered over the dashboard, her legs, and the floor.

"Nuria," a voice said beside her. At the same moment someone squeezed her shoulder. "Nuria," the voice said again. "Are you all right?

431

Blinking in confusion, she passed a hand over her forehead to dry it and turned toward the voice. "Commissioner?" she asked, as if wondering why she was there. "What ... what happened?"

"Are you all right?" Puig asked again.

"Yes, I ... I don't know." Moving her hands in front of her to prove to herself that she still could, she said, "I think so."

"Fantastic," the commissioner said with satisfaction, adding, "Come on, we've got no time to waste."

Nuria stared at him in bafflement. "What?"

"Get out of the car," he urged her as he opened his door with some difficulty and climbed out. "The emergency teams will be here in under five minutes."

Nuria followed him with her gaze as he went around the car. Reaching her door, he opened it like an impatient chauffeur. She didn't move. "What's going on?" she insisted. Finally putting her thoughts in order, she added, "Why did you crash the car into the tree?"

"There's no time for explanations," Puig said. Taking a small syringe from his jacket pocket, he pulled off the cap and summarily injected its contents into her neck before she had a chance to react.

Nuria put her hand to her neck, but it was too late. "What the fuck are you doing?" she protested. "What did you inject me with?" Before Puig could answer, she felt a wave of heat expanding from her neck to every other part of her body, racing headlong through veins and capillaries, reaching every nerve-ending and muscle in her.

Her heart began to race, pumping blood like a pneumatic cylinder, and her mind cleared as if a gust of wind had carried away every irrelevant thought, leaving her five senses exquisitely honed. In a matter of seconds, her body and her mind seemed to rise to a level she'd never managed to achieve in her life. A level, she realized instantly, that she'd never even imagined possible.

With her sudden clarity her breathing slowed. She turned to Puig and looked him in the eye. "You've given me a dose of limbocaine," she said with complete certainty, not as a reproach, but simply confirming a fact that was as unexpected as it was inexplicable.

84

Nuria unfastened her seatbelt and climbed out of the vehicle as a butterfly would from its cocoon; still herself, yet different. Submerged beneath an ocean of strange calm, she was keeping at bay the desire she felt in every fiber of her organism to be released, to explore, to fly with her new wings.

A little voice at the back of her brain warned her that these feelings were deceptive, that her body was still the same and that all this was a product of the limbocaine. Her metamorphosis would last only as long as the effect of the drug in her bloodstream. But the voice was muffled by the thudding of her heart in her chest and the tingling at the ends of her nerves. She felt capable of shooting rays from her fingertips. In fact, she could barely hear the voice, nor did she really want to.

"Why?" she asked once she was out of the car. She stood erect in front of Puig, for the first time in her life unintimidated in his presence. She felt powerful, capable of facing anybody. After all, in spite of his uniform and the fact that he was over six feet tall, the commissioner was only an ordinary man.

"I'll say someone must have injected you with it at the infirmary. That's the way I'll explain how you were able to cause the accident and then escape when you were my prisoner. But also," he added, "it's my way of giving you a chance to escape."

"I'm not asking you about the limbocaine," she said, indifferent to the rain trickling down her face and clothing. "I'm asking you why you're helping me."

Puig shook his head. "I'm just doing what's right."

"Do you think I'm innocent?"

He considered this for a moment before he answered. "I don't think you should go to prison."

"That's not what I asked you."

"Well, it's the only answer you're going to get," he said. "And now you'd better go." He indicated a path that led into the dense undergrowth. "If you follow that path, about a hundred yards further on you'll find an abandoned fountain, and beside it a backpack with identification papers, clothes, and some money. It's not much, but it'll be enough to let you leave the country."

Stunned, Nuria couldn't believe what she was hearing. Now, when she'd assumed everything was lost, the person she'd thought was convinced of her guilt was risking everything to help her escape. "I don't know what to say," she muttered, feeling at once grateful and disconcerted. "I don't—"

"You don't have to say anything," he interrupted. "Now get going before I change my mind."

"Will you see to it that my mother and grandfather are safe?"

"I'll take care of them."

Satisfied, she gave a brief nod, took a step back, and whispered, "Thank you," then turned toward the path. Confused by the unexpected turn of events, her brain seething under the effect of the limbocaine, she set off. Pushing through the undergrowth, she began to descend the muddy hillside.

It wasn't until she'd covered a dozen yards that a question popped into her brain with all the subtlety of a flashlight pointing directly into her eyes. Why had he decided to help her at this particular moment? Even more important, when had he left this backpack ready for her? There was no way he could have had the time, unless he'd known in advance what was going to happen. But ... how? Even if he'd suspected Olmedo's plans, she herself hadn't known what she was going to do until the last moment. How had he known she wouldn't pull the trigger, that she would be neutralized with a Taser instead of being shot, or that he would have the chance to get her out of the cathedral in disguise?

The answer was so clear, so obvious, that she stopped as abruptly as a guard dog that has reached the end of its chain. *How could she not have seen it sooner?* she reproached herself. Shaking her head, she turned around and looked back up to the beginning of the path.

As she'd known she would, she saw Commissioner Puig aiming his gun at her. Raising his voice above the din of the rain and the wind in the trees, he called, "I'm sorry."

Putting the pieces together in her mind, Nuria called back, "There's no backpack, is there?"

At the top of the slope, the commissioner shook his head and tsked in distaste. "I warned you," he reminded her. "I took you off the case, I ordered you to stay home—but no. You disobeyed my orders, and now look how you've ended up, my dear." Nuria realized that this unprecedented familiarity was his way of saying goodbye.

"You deleted my files from the cloud, hacked into my camera system, and stole my gun." As the puzzle pieces fell into place one by one, she spoke them aloud with staggering certainty. "You killed Gloria," she continued, "then pinned the murder on me to get me out of the way. My God, the limbocaine—" At last she knew the truth. "You hired that assassin to kill Vilchez and David." She pointed at him. "*You* gave him the limbocaine."

434

"I did everything I could to keep you out of it and protect you," he said without denying any of her accusations, "but I can't help you any longer."

"Help me?" she sneered. "Do you seriously believe your own words?"

"Right from the start my orders were to eliminate you," he explained. "You have no idea how much I had to insist in order to keep you alive. But you see,"—he shrugged—"in the end it was all for naught."

"Who gave you the orders? Olmedo? Is what he pays you worth David's life, or Gloria's, or mine?"

The commissioner sighed and shook his head. "You still don't understand. This has nothing to do with Olmedo—he's just one more cog in the wheel. There are far more important things at play here than the intrigues of some politician or someone's life," he clarified. "Spain is crumbling around us, and the duty of a patriot is to do whatever is necessary to save it."

"Save it from what?"

"From the Spaniards themselves," he said expansively. "From cowardice, from purposelessness, from political correctness, from people like you"—he concluded—"who think they know what they're doing and only manage to mess things up even more."

"And making me kill Aguirre or blowing up the Palau Blaugrana was going to save this country?" she spat incredulously. "Are you out of your mind?"

"That was simply going to be the first domino that would bring down all the others," Puig confirmed. "But you ruined it all. You have no idea of the harm you've caused."

"Well, I'm glad I ruined your fucking plans."

"*My* fucking plans?" Puig smiled bitterly. "This whole business is way above my pay grade. I merely receive orders and carry them out, that's all. And if you'd done the same," he said reproachfully, "we wouldn't be here now."

"Whose orders?" Nuria asked. "From headquarters? The ministry?"

"Does it matter? We all get orders from someone. Even they do."

"It matters to me."

"Ah, well ... unfortunately, I've got no time for that." He released the safety on his gun with his thumb. "I wish it didn't have to end like this."

"Wait, for Christ's sake!" she interrupted him, reading his intention to shoot her in his eyes. "You don't have to do this!"

The commissioner aimed the pistol at her head. "I'm sorry." He hooked his finger around the trigger.

Nuria knew he would fire in less than a second, but this certainty, far from frightening her, unleashed a torrent of adrenaline which spread in an instant from the soles of her feet to the tips of her fingers. The limbocaine handed over command of her system to her amygdala. Like a passenger in her own body, she saw her legs flexing and propelling her in a leap towards Puig.

Dumbfounded, the commissioner watched her rise into the air, removing herself from the crosshairs of his gun. Touching down again, Nuria zigzagged up the path toward him at superhuman speed.

Her rational mind, doomed to be a mere spectator, became less alarmed, realizing she might have a chance. The ten yards separating her from Puig shrank with every stride she took, and so far the commissioner had showed no sign of retraining the gun on her. Nuria knew that if she managed to get within three yards of him, she would have the advantage and the gun would be useless.

Even so, an alarm went off in her brain when she saw that he didn't seem at all worried as she raced towards him. His stony face was imperturbable as she made a final leap and hurled herself at him with feline agility.

That was when the commissioner opened his left hand and showed her the remote for the Taser bracelet she still wore, his thumb poised over the red button. Helpless against her own momentum, Nuria could only watch as he pressed the button. Instantly a brutal electrical discharge shot into her wrist and coursed throughout her body, which contracted violently in midair before dropping to the ground, inert, like a tigress brought down in the middle of her spring.

When the current stopped running through her veins, Nuria raised her head, gasping for breath, seemingly incapable of any other movement. She lacked all control of her limbs and was only vaguely conscious that she was lying in the mud, curled up in a fetal position.

In spite of the strength of the electrical discharge, she didn't lose consciousness, a fact she attributed to the effect of the limbocaine. But not even that drug was capable of overcoming the paralyzing effect of seven hundred volts.

That was why Puig had injected her with the limbocaine, Nuria realized. It would provide an explanation for how she'd escaped and why he'd been forced to kill her. At the same time, he could control her movements whenever he wanted with the Taser bracelet. Utterly defenseless, all Nuria could do was breathe and try to look at him, but the only thing she could see were the tips of his shoes from the corner of her eye.

She imagined him staring at her, stretched out helpless at his feet, from his perspective of six feet above, aiming his gun at her and relishing the sensation of having her completely at his mercy.

The game was over, and he, Olmedo, and whoever it was that gave him his orders, had won. That was how things had always been and how they would always be: the powerful would continue to get their way, manipulating poor idiots like her in order to achieve their goals, tossing her into the garbage once they'd got what they wanted. Nuria tried to console herself, thinking she'd done everything she could to fuck up these puppet masters' plans. Her brief moment of consolation vanished, though, when she remembered that now there was no one to protect her loved ones from the revenge of the future president. She could do nothing for them. Or for herself.

Like someone whose life flashes before her eyes as she falls from the roof of a tall building, Nuria thought about everything she'd done wrong as she lay full length in the mud, the rain falling on her like shovelfuls of earth on her coffin. She'd made so many errors of judgment she could see no sense in going through the list and lingering on her misfortune. When she thought about it, though, she found that if there was anything she truly regretted, it was not having had the chance to say goodbye to David and Gloria, to her mother, to her grandfather, to Susana, to Elias … to all the people she loved. Some of whom had paid with their lives for being too close to her, as if rather than a woman she were an infectious disease.

Perhaps she deserved to be shot by Puig. There was a certain poetic justice in the fact that her former commissioner and mentor was to be the executor of her destiny, dispensing justice for all the evil she'd done and preventing her, voluntarily or otherwise, from being able to hurt any more people.

"I'm sorry it has to end like this," came Puig's deep voice from far above her. Nuria exhaled the air from her lungs and rested her forehead on the ground, offering the nape of her neck for a clean shot. *Let it be quick,* she prayed, shutting her eyes tightly. Her hearing enhanced by the drug, she heard Puig take a deep breath and release it before repeating, "I'm truly sorry."

The shot resounded like a clap of thunder in the middle of a storm.

85

A jet of warm, thick liquid splashed Nuria on the back of her neck. Opening her eyes, she saw vermilion spots spattering the mud, dissolving into trickling streams under the rain.

What had just happened? Nuria hadn't felt the impact of the bullet. She wondered if another of the limbocaine's effects might be the absence of pain. Despite the superhuman abilities the drug had given her, it still took her a moment to realize that a shot in the back of the neck wouldn't have caused her pain, it would have killed her instantly.

But then, if this wasn't her own blood … Nuria looked up and saw the answer lying next to her in the undergrowth, an inert body in a police dress uniform. Though she couldn't see his face, she recognized Puig's shoes. Still unable to come up with a satisfactory explanation for what had just happened, for a second Nuria considered the wild possibility that at the last moment, overcome by an unbearable feeling of guilt, the commissioner had decided to take his own life. Her mind still numbed by the Taser, she concluded that that was ridiculous. Someone had shot him.

But who?

The answer came in the form of voices that seemed to be speaking in Arabic, hasty footsteps, and strong arms that lifted her roughly from the mud, slung her over a shoulder like a sack of potatoes and carried her up the path until they were back on the road. There, she was put into the back seat of a vehicle that drove off immediately.

Sandwiched between two men in the middle of a wide black leather seat, still dazed, Nuria looked in one direction and then the other to find out who had kidnapped her. What she saw left her speechless. The two men on either side of her were very familiar.

A female voice greeted her from the front seat, claiming her attention. "Hi, Nuria." She looked toward the voice and met Aya's black eyes, which were studying her carefully. "Are you all right?" the girl asked. "Are you hurt?"

"What …" Nuria stammered. "What are you doing here? How did you find me?" At the same moment she realized there was only one question that really mattered to her. "Where is your uncle?"

"That's what I'm hoping you'll tell me," Aya said, her tone unexpectedly cold.

Nuria put a hand to her chest, bewildered. "Who? Me? How on earth would I know?"

"The last time I saw him, he was leaving in a cab with you."

"B-but he disappeared," Nuria murmured. "In the sewers. I don't … Don't you know what happened? Didn't you hear about the attempt on the Palau Blaugrana? Your uncle and I were there with a Special Forces team," she tried to explain, but the words tumbled from her mouth in fits and starts. "Then those robots came. We tried to stop them"—she shut her eyes at the painful memory of the previous morning—"and to keep them from exploding. We flooded the sewers. I held onto the raft, but Elias didn't." She opened her eyes and looked up at Aya. "I don't know what happened to your uncle," she finished. "I'm so sorry."

"You say you were there?" the girl asked incredulously. "In the sewers?"

Nuria nodded. "We were trying to stop the attack."

"You two? Why? Didn't you say there was a police team?"

"They arrived later," Nuria clarified. "They saw us on the surveillance cameras and thought we were the terrorists,"—she swallowed, her mouth feeling as if she'd been sucking on a wooden spoon—"but then they helped us and …" She stopped to take a breath. "I know it's hard to believe," she added after a pause, "but it was all really confusing down there. When I woke up, they were resuscitating me on the street. I still don't know how they managed to get me out of there."

"But they did get *you* out," Aya reminded her, as if she were plunging a dagger into her. "What happened to my uncle?"

"I honestly don't know." She paused to inhale deeply; there seemed to be no air inside the car. "He was swept away by the water, like everyone else, and then I didn't …" She ran her hands over her face, tortured by the memory of a scene that was still far too fresh in her mind.

"And you don't know if they rescued him too?"

"I don't think so," Nuria said after a moment's thought. "I guess they'd have told me, even if it was just to put pressure on me."

"Then … my uncle might still be down there?" She pointed to the city spread out around the base of the mountain. "Lying in some disgusting sewer?"

"I don't know," Nuria admitted, her voice barely audible.

Aya was frowning. "Why didn't you try to get in touch with me?" she asked accusingly. "If you'd told me what was going on, we'd have started looking for him immediately."

"Because I couldn't. By the time I realized what was going on I was already in a hospital room, under surveillance and with no means of communication. I wasn't even allowed to get in touch with my family to tell them I was alive."

"They had you incommunicado and under surveillance?" Aya asked with palpable disbelief. "And the very next day you were there in the front row at the ceremony in the Sagrada Familia?"

"You saw me?"

"Did I see you?" Aya repeated incredulously. "The *whole world* saw you, Nuria. Why do you think I'm here?" she burst out. "You and my uncle disappear together … and twenty-four hours later, I see you live on television putting a gun to a politician's head."

"That's why they were holding me incommunicado. They wanted me to murder Salvador Aguirre."

"Why?" the girl asked in astonishment. "Who?"

This time Nuria shook her head. "It's better if you don't know."

"The jihadists?"

"I think the jihadists have simply been a bunch of useful fanatics in the hands of other people. It was others who were pulling the strings."

"Others?" Aya pulled a bloodstained brown leather wallet out of her pocket and opened it in front of Nuria, revealing the National Police identification badge and the commissioner's card. "Do you mean Commissioner … Puig?" she added, reading his name. "Why would a police commissioner want to execute you?"

"The less you know, the safer you'll be." Nuria put out her hand to take the wallet.

Aya pushed her hand away. "Don't mess with me, Nuria. I want to know what's going on. I *need* to know what's going on, for God's sake."

"What you need to do is go somewhere safe," Nuria objected. She leaned forward, trying to calm the girl. "It's … what your uncle would have wanted."

Aya drew back. "Don't talk about him as if he were already dead!" she hissed.

"I'm sorry, I … I didn't mean to say that."

"But that's what you think," Aya accused her. "You think he's dead." Nuria was about to say she was wrong, but then realized she couldn't do that. She closed her mouth again. "No, no, no." Aya shook her head again and again. "My uncle's alive somewhere. I know it."

Nuria nodded gently. "It's possible," she said, but her tone betrayed her true feelings.

"Don't humor me like a child," Aya protested furiously. "I'm telling you, he's alive and we're going to find him. Isn't that right?" She turned to Giwan and Yady, who each gave an imperceptible nod. Turning back to Nuria, she said, "You see? They believe it too."

440

Nuria looked at the Kurds, but didn't see the hope Aya felt in their eyes. "I hope you're right."

"Of course I am," Aya argued vehemently. "You don't know my uncle as well as I do. He's a survivor."

Nuria nodded apologetically and gave in, though she was unable to lie to the girl and bolster her vain hopes. "That's true. I don't know him as well as you do." Nor did she want to point out to Aya the fact that if Elias had survived, he would already have contacted her. "But tell me,"—she tried to change the subject—"how did you find me?"

"I told you. I saw you on TV and came to get some answers."

"I mean here, in Montjuïc. How did you find me?"

"Well … actually we had some luck," Aya confessed, bringing the tips of her thumb and index finger together. "We were just arriving at the Sagrada Familia cathedral when we saw that commissioner with a woman in a Reborn robe getting into a vehicle. If the streets hadn't been so deserted, we wouldn't have noticed. But then we saw the woman throwing the robe out the window and we realized it was you. We decided to follow you, we saw the crash … and well, you know the rest."

Nuria couldn't believe that for once, fate hadn't turned its back on her. She looked at Giwan and Yady, who were monitoring what was going on outside the car, checking for possible threats. Giwan held his still-smoking Kriss Vector between his legs. She pointed back the way they'd come with her thumb and asked, "Did you kill him?" He glanced at her and gave a curt nod. Nuria laid a hand on his knee and gave him the ghost of a smile. "Thank you."

Giwan acknowledged her thanks with a nod and turned his attention back to the world outside the car. He might have just saved her life, but he wasn't proud of having shot a man in the back.

"Thank you," Nuria repeated, this time addressing all of them. "I'm truly sorry about everything that's happening. I'm sorry Elias has disappeared and I'm sorry to have complicated your lives like this. I really am sorry."

None of them replied or accepted her apology. It was clear that though they might not consider her guilty, they certainly saw her as responsible for all the misfortunes that had befallen them since she'd burst into their lives. Even Aya, with her recent complicity and her matchmaking games, was staring at her now with the dull resentment reserved for someone who has robbed you of what you most love.

Nuria didn't blame her in the least. More than that, she shared that same resentment—except that in her case it was also directed against those who had put her into this dark well. The deep, dark well into which she'd dragged the people dearest to her and from which there was now no way out. In a sudden surge of rage, she exhaled, leaned forward again, and put her hand on Ishmael's shoulder. Looking into his eyes in the rearview mirror, she said, "Stop the car, please."

Ishmael returned her gaze. "We need to get away from here," he said. "This is going to be full of cops any minute."

"That's exactly why. Stop the vehicle and let me get out."

"No," Aya said. "I still need answers."

"But I have none to give you," Nuria reminded her. "I don't know what happened to Elias, or whether he's dead or alive. What I do know is that just by being with you, I'm endangering you all. So stop the car and leave me here."

"Let's go to a safe place where we can—"

Nuria interrupted her. "There are no safe places for me. Or for you, if you stay with me. So leave me here and go. It will be the best thing for everybody."

Ishmael turned to Aya. "She's right. If they find us with her—"

Aya's expression showed her conflicting feelings about Nuria. She vacillated, unable to come to a decision.

"Stop the car," Nuria insisted. "Let me go."

Aya debated with herself a few more seconds, then closed her eyes and nodded. "All right," she said at last. "Stop the car, Ishmael." The driver obeyed at once, pulling to the curb. "With that uniform on, you'll be recognized right away," Aya pointed out. "And you're a mess, all covered in mud. You'll attract a lot of attention." Nuria looked down at herself. It wouldn't be a good idea to walk down the street looking exactly the way she had on television. "Here, put this on." The girl took a fluorescent green raincoat from the small backpack she held between her knees. "At least you won't be recognized instantly."

"Thanks." Nuria took the raincoat. "Although I need a couple of things more."

"Like what?"

"Everything that was on Puig's body, and a weapon."

"A weapon? What for?" Aya asked. "What you've got to do is run away or hide, like we're going to do, not get into more trouble than you're already in."

"And that's what I'm going to do. But before that, there's one last thing I need to do."

"What's that?"

Nuria hesitated, staring out the car window. Just when Aya was beginning to think she wasn't going to answer, she muttered between clenched teeth, "What I should have done when I had the chance."

86

"This is as close as I can get," the cabdriver said. He had stopped the vehicle and was pointing at the police checkpoint that was blocking entry for vehicles.

"This is fine, thanks," Nuria said. She paid the cabdriver with one of the bills Aya had given her and got out without waiting for the change. Elias's niece had wisely advised her to get off at the Plaza de España, so after saying goodbye to her, Giwan, Yady, and Ishmael, she'd taken a cab there. It had left her on the Paseo Juan Borbón, next to the entrance to the Marina Vela at the port of Barcelona.

Pulling the hood of her raincoat over her head, Nuria watched the light on the roof of the black-and-yellow cab turn green as it moved off in the rain. She was standing next to a group of police that were limiting vehicle access to the Hotel W Barcelona complex, a majestic glass-and-steel construction that rose high over the sea, built in the characteristic shape of a sail and bearing a passable resemblance to the famous Burj Al Arab in Dubai.

In spite of the wind and rain and the spray thrown up by the colossal waves that battered the fifteen-foot-high seawall protecting the hotel against the fury of the Mediterranean, a small crowd of Spain First followers and devout Reborn were standing guard in front of the hotel with their flags and white robes, shouting slogans in support of Salvador Aguirre. These were carried away by the wind the moment they came out of their mouths.

Nuria raised her eyes to the top of the building, trying to imagine which of the windows belonged to the presidential suite on the twenty-fifth floor where Salvador Aguirre and his second-in-command Jaime Olmedo had set up their base in Barcelona for the weekend. Luckily, the storm had forced the airport to shut down and had even stopped the high-speed train to Madrid from running, so she was almost sure the leader of Spain First and his secretary were still at the hotel.

One hundred eighty feet below, she noticed that the city police were only concerned with controlling vehicle access and were allowing pedestrians to pass freely. That meant the real checkpoint was further in—though the more immediate problem she was faced with was how to get through that crowd of fanatics while wearing a raincoat that made her stand out like a fly in a bowl of milk. The chances that one of them would see her face and recognize her were too high. And though the limbocaine still flowing through her veins was pushing her to be reckless, that part of her that still clung to a modicum of common sense was making her realize she needed to find an alternative.

Nuria looked around in search of some way of getting into the hotel without being seen. But as it was an isolated building, almost at the end of the seawall, there were only two ways of gaining access to it: through the main entrance she was standing in front of now, or by swimming along the edge of the seawall and somehow dodging the fifteen-foot-high breakwater.

Under other circumstances, the option of swimming would have been the more intelligent one. But at that moment, with the waves lashed to a frenzy by Medicane Mercé crashing brutally against the breakwater, she wouldn't make it even with all the limbocaine in the world.

Standing in the rain in her green raincoat, attempting to figure out a way of getting through the crowd without being seen, Nuria's eyes fell on the illuminated logo of an AmazonGo24, less than a hundred yards from her. An idea took shape in her mind, and a crafty smile appeared on her face where it was hidden under the hood.

Browsing the shelves of the well-stocked mini market, she filled her basket in the pharmacy section. As she was about to pay she felt a pang of hunger and, without thinking, grabbed a handful of energy bars, adding them to the basket. She could feel her body burning calories much faster than usual, and she'd just about gone through that morning's breakfast at the hospital.

Her purchases safely in a paper bag, she needed a little privacy. "Where's the restroom?" she asked the cashier, a young Indian boy with the shadow of a thin moustache outlining his upper lip.

"Sorry, miss. Restroom only for employees."

There was no time to persuade him, so she took out Puig's wallet and showed him the shining police badge. "Are you sure about that? How about showing me your papers?"

The boy's skin paled a couple of shades on the color chart and she felt a little guilty about intimidating him. "Sorry, Officer," he apologized. He bowed his head, took a key out of his pocket, and indicated a door. "Sorry," he repeated.

"Thank you, that's okay," Nuria said soothingly. Taking the key, she went into the restroom, where she locked the door and set her shopping on the toilet lid. She looked unsuccessfully for a hook to hang her clothes on, but had to make do with dropping the raincoat in one corner, grateful for the fact that at least the little restroom was clean.

Then she got to work. After brushing her uniform to eliminate any trace of remaining mud on the water-resistant material, she took out the scissors and put them down in front of her as though hesitating about whether to use them.

"It'll grow again," she told herself. Without allowing herself time to reconsider, she grasped the ends of her mistreated hair and cut it to the level of her nape, just below her ears. It felt as if she were cutting off a limb instead of hair, but Nuria stifled a regretful sigh and went on cutting determinedly until a sizable pile of hair had formed in the sink.

"Phase one complete," she murmured, satisfied with the result. "Now let's go for phase two." Putting the scissors back in the bag, she took out a spray container of jet-black Instatint. "Onward and upward," she said to encourage herself, taking the top off the container and applying it to her hair like hairspray. She ruffled her hair with her free hand as she sprayed to distribute the tint evenly through it. Luckily, unlike its forerunners of bygone years, this particular product was based on nanoparticles and contained no ammonia or anything else that could be smelled for blocks. It also took effect instantaneously. After she'd applied it to her eyebrows, it looked passably natural.

Next she took the makeup kit from the paper bag and applied it to the cuts and bruises on her face until they were camouflaged enough to be noticeable only from very close. She outlined her eyes with mascara, applied rouge and lipstick, and finally put on a pair of dark glasses. She looked completely different from the woman those who had witnessed that morning's events would remember.

Once the transformation was complete, Nuria took a step back and stared at the face looking back at her from the mirror. She'd never dyed her hair black before, and seeing herself like this, with her hair shorter than it had been since she was a teenager, she found it hard to recognize herself. The woman who was watching her with reddened eyes and dilated pupils seemed to be interrogating her with her gaze, wondering what the hell she thought she was doing.

Uncomfortable, Nuria looked away from the mirror, put everything back in the paper bag, put on the raincoat again, and left the restroom. She threw the bag in the wastebasket before the stunned gaze of the clerk, who was now seeing a different woman than the one who'd gone in fifteen minutes before. Ignoring the boy's perplexity, she left the shop and set off briskly toward the crowd.

Fifty yards further on she passed the guards, who paid no attention to her, more concerned with the growing clamor of the crowd than with checking people walking by. Directing her steps toward the extraordinary glass-fronted building, she pushed her way through the excited mass of people. All had their eyes fixed on the hotel, which meant their backs were to her. As she passed two particularly heated Reborn, she caught part of their conversation, which was about the rumor that the terrorist who had tried to murder Salvador Aguirre had escaped.

The demonstrators now began to turn their indignation on the police, some accusing them loudly of being her accomplices and helping a murderer to escape. Others, not content with shouting insults, hurled coins at the officers

445

guarding the entrance and lunged at them with the poles their banners were attached to.

Nuria bowed her head and hurried on, anxious to get out of there before anybody noticed that under her gaudy fluorescent green raincoat she was still wearing the dress uniform of the Unified National Police.

As if the commotion in the Mediterranean had spread to solid land, the crowd began to move back and forth in imitation of the waves, pushing against the barriers that protected the hotel property and jostling Nuria in the process as she elbowed her way through. She tried to slip through the crowd as delicately as possible, being careful not to step on some screaming devotee's feet and become an unwilling center of attention.

After rowing valiantly through the sea of people for what seemed like an eternity, she managed to reach the front lines. Surreptitiously, she took out Puig's badge and showed it to the officers trying to hold back the crowd. Realizing the critical nature of the situation, one of the officers opened a gap in the barrier to let her through. By the time the demonstrators who had been beside her a moment earlier realized what she'd done, she was safe from their rage. Nuria even allowed herself the luxury of turning around one last time, shedding her raincoat with a provocative wink at those who had seen her uniform and begun to shout insults at her.

Ironically, the threat of the demonstrators managing to break through the police barrier meant that no one paid much attention to her, and Nuria was able to enter the hotel's luxurious lobby with no trouble. The polished black marble of the floor reflected the lofty ceiling that soared a hundred fifty feet above her head, an enormous gold chandelier in the form of a W hanging from its center. Despite the fact that she was surrounded by officers who might identify her at any moment, Nuria couldn't help stopping and looking up, enthralled, as if she'd just gotten off the bus from some remote village.

When she looked down again, her eyes fell on a familiar uniformed figure with her back toward her, apparently absorbed in her phone. Her heart rate accelerating, Nuria approached her cautiously until she was sure she wasn't mistaken. Then, threading her way through the remaining officers thickly scattered across the lobby, she crossed the few yards that separated them, took her arm, and whispered in her ear, "Officer Roman."

Susana turned to her, startled, and stared at her for a few seconds without recognizing her. Finally realizing who it was, her eyes opened wide, as if she'd been approached by the ghost of her grandmother who had died ten years before.

87

"What? You?" Susana spluttered in amazement. "But how …?"

Nuria gestured toward the restrooms. "Come, follow me."

Frozen to the spot, it took Susana a few seconds to react. Looking around to make sure no one else was paying attention to them, she followed Nuria, who had just disappeared behind the door of the ladies' restroom. By the time the door closed behind Susana, Nuria had already checked that no one else was inside. She waited by the sinks, a smile of genuine happiness on her face.

"Oh, Susi!" she cried, stepping toward her with the intention of taking her in her arms. "You can't imagine how glad I am to see you!"

Susana took a step back. "What are you doing here, Nuria?" she blurted. "Where did you come from? What … what the fuck is going on here?"

"It's too long to explain right now," Nuria said, stopping short, her smile faltering. "But things aren't what you think."

"Things?" Susana burst out. "You mean Gloria being murdered with your gun? Or the explosion in Villarefu where you were seen running away? Or maybe … your big hit, that duet with Aguirre? What *things* are you referring to exactly, Nuria?"

Nuria nodded understandingly, aware of how it must appear from an outsider's perspective. Any plea of innocence would sound ridiculous, even to her best friend. She appealed to their friendship, her only argument, instead. "You have to trust me. I haven't killed anybody." She paused for a second to think back. "At least not intentionally," she corrected herself. "But I swear I didn't do anything to Gloria." She shook her head. "For Christ's sake, Susi, you know me."

Her friend looked her up and down. "I'm not so sure anymore," she said.

"Someone came into my house and took my gun," Nuria explained. "Gloria was helping me solve David's murder. That's why they killed her and implicated me. They wanted to get me out of the way and pin the murder on me."

"But … who? Elias Zafrani?"

"Elias? Fuck, no! He's been helping me stay alive since then. He—" She felt as though a fist were squeezing her heart when she remembered she could no longer talk about him in present tense. "He saved me from the terrorists who were holding me in Villarefu, in the house that blew up."

"The terrorists who were holding you?" Susana repeated skeptically. "According to the reports, you and your friend caused the explosion. There are images of the two of you fleeing the scene in a car."

"No, Susi." Nuria shook her head repeatedly. "Elias rescued me. Only a few hours later, we were able to stop the terrorist attack on the rally at the Palau Blaugrana."

"You were there too?" Susi asked incredulously. "According to what I heard, it was a team of Special Forces that did that."

"That's true," Nuria confirmed. "But they were really after Elias and me. They had no idea about the attack."

"And you did?"

"When the jihadists kidnapped me, I saw what they were planning. Then Elias showed up, there was a shootout, and the house blew up. That's why I'm there in the surveillance videos."

Susana snorted, muffling a laugh. "You've got an explanation for everything, haven't you?" she said mockingly. "And what about Aguirre? Is that a jihadist thing too? Because the person I saw on television this morning putting a gun to his head looked very much like you."

"They made me do it," Nuria protested. "They threatened to kill my family if I didn't kill him in front of the cameras."

"Who threatened you? The same jihadists?"

Nuria shook her head.   "You're not going to believe me."

Susana snorted in disbelief. "Jesus, Nurieta, you haven't said a single believable thing since you opened your mouth. One more bit of lunacy won't make much difference."

"All right." Nuria spread her hands in a gesture of supplication. "It was the secretary of Spain First himself, Jaime Olmedo. He wanted me to kill Aguirre in front of the whole world while shouting *Allahu Akbar*. That would make him into a martyr and the people would vote Olmedo in as the new president."

Susana's mouth was a perfect "O," and it took her a while to close it. "You were right when you said I wasn't going to believe you," she said at last.

"I know," Nuria admitted. "It's hard for me to believe it too."

"But ... you didn't do it."

"What do you mean?"

"You didn't kill him. Aguirre arrived at the hotel a while ago, and he looked pretty much alive."

"I was going to do it. I was going to kill him. But I realized they were going to murder my mother and grandfather anyway, so I made my speech in the hope that someone would believe me."

"What speech?"

448

Now it was Nuria's turn to look taken aback. "The one I gave while I had my gun pressed to Aguirre's head, what else?"

Susana grimaced. "I don't know how to tell you this," she said, scratching the nape of her neck uncomfortably. "But a few seconds after you appeared on the scene, they cut the live feed. They only said everyone was okay and that the security forces had saved Aguirre from a new attempt on his life. After ten minutes the live feed came back on and they went on with the ceremony as if nothing had happened. They said the terrorist had been neutralized."

Hearing this, Nuria rolled her eyes and let her head fall back. "Shit," she muttered. "Now I'm really screwed. I must have looked like a fucking lunatic with a gun."

"A fucking terrorist lunatic," Susana corrected her. "Which leads me to ask, how did you manage to escape?"

"I was taken to Montjuïc so that they could eliminate me before I could talk," she explained, "but … I was lucky and managed to escape." She avoided mentioning Puig.

"Holy shit," Susana said. "But then … what are you doing here? Have you come to turn yourself in?"

"Not exactly." In her friend's face Nuria could see the puzzle pieces falling into place. She took a step backwards, bumping into the sink.

"You're not thinking—" She pointed at the ceiling. "Christ, Nuria. Don't tell me you've come for Olmedo."

"All right, I won't tell you."

Automatically, Susana moved her hand toward the gun on her right hip, resting her hand on the butt. "I can't let you do that," she warned.

Nuria looked at her, suddenly saddened. "All I want is justice, Susi."

"Don't fuck with me, Nuria. What you're looking for is revenge."

"In this case it comes down to the same thing. That bastard financed the jihadist attack. He sent the hitman to kill David and he ordered Gloria to be killed. He's a devil with a seat in the House, and if he's elected president, a hell of a lot more people are going to suffer because of him. This is the moment to stop him."

"Then denounce him," Susana snapped. "Expose him on social media. Call the press, do whatever's necessary. If you try to kill him, all you'll do is prove him right."

"That won't matter if he's dead."

"It'll matter to me, Nuria. Because what will happen is that you'll be killed."

"That's my problem."

Susana took a deep breath and drew her weapon, aiming it at her friend as the tears began to seep from the corners of her eyes. "I'm not going to let you commit suicide. If you're put on trial, you can tell the judge everything you've

449

told me. I'll testify in your favor," she added, "and so will Puig and plenty of others. You've got to have faith in the judicial system, Nuria. In the end everything will be clarified."

Nuria kept her eyes fixed on Susana, ignoring the barrel of the gun pointing at her. "It's all very clear already, Susi," she said, taking a step toward her.

"No, please …" Susana pleaded. She cocked the gun. "Don't make me shoot you."

Nuria spread her empty hands wide in surrender. "Fine. You win."

Susana's features relaxed in relief and she took her finger off the trigger. That was all Nuria needed. Her left arm shot out toward Susana's right, first deflecting the weapon, then throwing the takedown lever with her index finger and pulling the slide. Susana was still trying to work out what had happened when she found that all that was left in her hand was the bottom half of her gun, totally useless.

"What—" she stammered, looking from her right hand to Nuria's left where the barrel and the slide now were. "How did you do that? I … I didn't even see it."

"I need your help." Nuria pointed to the card pinned to the breast pocket of her friend's uniform, identifying her as an officer assigned to the team protecting the hotel.

"What?" Susana walked backwards toward the door, noticing for the first time her friend's dilated pupils and severely bloodshot eyes. "What is it you want?" she asked, her tone no longer communicating surprise, but fear.

"I'm not going to hurt you, Susana," Nuria assured her as she walked toward her. But she could see doubt had already taken root in her friend.

Susana threw a fleeting glance over her shoulder, looking for the restroom door. Nuria realized she was about to turn and run, sealing Nuria's fate. It would all be over for her, for her mother, for her grandfather—and who could say how many more.

"I'm sorry, Susi," she said. Tensing her muscles, she hurled herself at her friend.

88

Susana's ID card hanging from her pocket, Nuria left the restroom and went straight to the elevators. Anyone who looked closely would see that she and the woman in the photo looked nothing alike, but Nuria trusted that the chaos erupting outside would be keeping them all so busy no one would notice she was there.

Besides, she knew from experience that walking with an air of confidence and determination would suggest to anybody she came across that she had every right to be there. She was confident no one would stop her as long as she behaved as though she were in charge.

Nuria walked purposefully through the dozens of officers in the hotel lobby—so many it had basically become a police station with mahogany walls and designer couches—praying no colleague would recognize her. The sixty feet separating her from the elevators seemed eternal, but when she reached the bank of elevators, she found that to access the express elevator to the upper floors, she had to go through a metal detector and a card reader.

Trying to hide her nerves, she took out her gun and left it in the tray beside the metal detector, then held Susana's ID to the glass of the reader. The alarm shrieked and a red light lit up next to the sensor, almost stopping Nuria's heart. What the fuck was happening? She looked over her shoulder, but no one seemed to be paying any attention to her. Looking more carefully at the ID, she realized her mistake. "What an idiot," she murmured, turning it over and placing it correctly on the reader.

After the device had spent what seemed like an eternity thinking about it, a satisfying green light lit up on the screen and she was finally allowed to walk through the metal detector arch and pick up her gun on the other side. Not until she reached the elevator door did she realize she'd been holding her breath the whole time.

Without wasting a second, Nuria pressed the call button and heard the sound of tinkling bells a second before the doors slid open. She entered, thinking it couldn't possibly be this easy, that in spite of all the security she'd gotten this far without anybody asking her who she was. Unfortunately, when she pressed the button that would take her to the twenty-fifth floor, she discovered that she'd spoken too soon. A red light lit up on the information screen and the friendly voice of the elevator AI said "Good morning. The floor of the Presidential Suite is temporarily restricted to authorized personnel."

"I'm an officer of the Unified National Police." She held her ID up to the camera above the screen, surreptitiously covering Susana's photo.

"I'm sorry, Officer Roman," the AI apologized as it read the name on the card. "But you need a specific access card for the twenty-fifth floor."

"It's an urgent matter," Nuria objected. "I need to go up there right away."

"I'm sorry, Officer Roman," repeated the AI. "The twenty-fifth floor is temporarily restricted to authorized personnel." Nuria recognized the uselessness of arguing with a machine. She found herself missing the time when the only way computers could annoy you was by pretending they couldn't find the printer.

Abruptly, she realized that in the lobby, an officer from the squad was turning toward her with sudden interest. Her heart skipped a beat when she realized who it was. "Shit," she muttered. Her hasty makeover had kept Raul from recognizing her at once, but she knew she only had a few more seconds before he did. She couldn't afford to waste any more time arguing with the fucking elevator.

"Can I get to any other floors?" she asked urgently.

"That depends," responded the AI. "Which floor do you want to go to?"

Nuria said the first thing that came into her mind. "The twenty-sixth."

"The Eclipse Club?"

"Yes, that's it."

"The Eclipse Club is currently closed. The hours are from 6 p.m. to 2:30 a.m."

"I don't care if it's closed, for Christ's sake! This is a police matter and I need to get to the twenty-sixth floor."

"The opening hours are—"

"Take me up to the twenty-sixth floor," Nuria cut in impatiently, seeing Raul's forehead crease into an incredulous frown. "Or I'll have you dismantled and installed in a fucking vacuum cleaner."

The elevator was silent for more than a second, which in AI terms is almost equivalent to sleeping on it. Finally, the complacent voice announced, "Twenty-sixth floor. By all means, Officer." The doors slid closed just as Raul raised his arm and pointed in her direction.

The floor numbers ticked by with mind-boggling speed on the screen as her anxiety grew that at any moment the police would stop the elevator and call it back to the lobby. *Fourteen. Fifteen. Sixteen.* She counted them off mentally, wondering what she would do when she reached the twenty-sixth floor. She didn't believe the sergeant had recognized her, but it was clear she'd aroused his suspicions. If he'd raised the alarm, it was possible that when the doors opened she would find a crowd waiting for her.

452

Twenty-one. Twenty-two. Twenty-three.

Nuria put her right hand on the butt of her gun and thought of Susana, whom she'd left gagged and handcuffed to a toilet in the ladies' restroom. She'd hated doing that to her best and only friend, but at least this way Susana would be able to justify the loss of her ID and the fact that she hadn't told anyone about Nuria when she'd first seen her.

Twenty-four. Twenty-five. Twenty-six.

"Twenty-sixth floor," the elevator announced. "Have a nice day, Officer."

Nuria thought she detected a note of sarcasm in the AI's voice, and though she knew it was only her imagination, she couldn't resist answering in the same tone. "The same to you." The doors opened with a pneumatic hiss.

Instinctively she flattened herself against the side of the elevator to offer less of a target in case they were already waiting for her, but when she poked her head out she realized there was nobody there. Yet.

In front of her was a small lobby that opened into a wide, barely lit corridor that led into the club, twenty yards ahead. Stepping over the black velvet rope that blocked the way, Nuria moved down the corridor, her hand on her gun, stepping cautiously on the dark wood floor that creaked under her feet.

At the end of the corridor was a huge glass wall that looked out over Montjuïc mountain and the harbor. She could see the World Trade Center, the nineteenth-century cable-car tower and a half-dozen cruise ships moored at the docks like white whales the size of skyscrapers. Farther away, veiled by the rain, she could make out the silhouette of the Sagrada Familia cathedral, crowned by the spotlights that outlined a cross against the black clouds hanging over the city.

For a brief moment Nuria was astonished by this view of Barcelona from a perspective she'd never enjoyed before. Both the Hotel W and the Eclipse Club were far pricier than anything her police salary would have allowed her to visit. Almost instantly, though, remembering why she was there, she banished the distraction from her mind and concentrated on what she'd come to do.

The Eclipse Club was divided into two similar sections with bars, comfortable couches, and dance floors. Nuria randomly picked the left-hand section, but soon realized it didn't matter which she chose; the club occupied the entire twenty-sixth floor, and both sections came together again in front of the sloping façade of the building that looked out over the Mediterranean.

Confident there was no one else in the deserted disco, she walked across it to the sloping glass wall, currently lashed by the rain coming from the east and creaking under the gusts of wind that seemed to be on the point of cracking it. The Presidential Suite was directly under her feet, but unless there was a secret trapdoor leading to the floor below, it might just as well have been in the basement. Nuria had come to the twenty-sixth floor with no clear idea of what to

453

do next, simply trying to escape from the lobby before she was recognized. Now she had to come up with a plan quickly, because it was only a matter of time before someone found Susana handcuffed in the restroom and put two and two together.

Turning this over in her mind, Nuria walked along the entire glass wall looking for an emergency staircase or janitor's corridor, but found nothing. This meant she could only get off that floor by using the elevator again. On the other hand, there was no way she could persuade the AI to take her to the twenty-fifth floor.

Only one option remained to her. Nuria looked up at the huge windows, battered by the violent gusts of wind and rain, and calculated that they sloped at about a forty-five-degree angle. She tried to calculate the possibilities of breaking one of them, then letting herself slide down the glass to the twenty-fifth floor and the outside of the Presidential Suite, but her survival instinct, though dulled by the limbocaine, warned her it would be a suicide mission.

The problem was there was no other way. She'd come so far by now that there was no turning back. In ten or fifteen minutes tops she would be either arrested or dead. The only uncertainty was whether she would have finished Olmedo off before that happened.

Considering the idea from every angle, all her senses focused on the hurricane roaring on the other side of the glass, Nuria failed to hear the subtle jingle of the elevator reaching the twenty-sixth floor. The sound of hurried footsteps on the wooden floor finally alerted her.

"Shit," she muttered, spinning around. They'd taken less time than she'd expected. They still had to traverse the length of the corridor and then walk all the way around the club as she had in order to get to where she now was—but even if they took every possible precaution, it wouldn't be more than thirty seconds before they had her in shooting range.

Her time had run out.

Like a spirit invoked by her skyrocketing adrenaline level, the limbocaine stimulated Nuria's nervous system, imbuing her with the same inhuman calm she'd felt after Puig had injected it. Shedding the stiff jacket of her dress uniform, she took out her gun and aimed at the nearest window.

"Stop!" someone yelled at her back.

"Police! Drop your gun!" ordered another voice.

Nuria didn't need to turn to know there were only two officers there. In under three minutes, though, there would be a swarm of police, armed to the teeth. But three minutes was more than enough time. In fact, she had two to spare.

"Drop your gun!" one of the cops insisted. "Drop your weapon or I'll shoot!"

For a fleeting second, certain they would be unable to stop her, Nuria felt tempted to confront them. But the vestiges of police training still remaining to her controlled that impulse, reminding her they were just two simple officers with families waiting for them at home who believed they were doing the right thing.

"Drop the gun! I'm not going to say it again!"

She turned her gaze on them. "You won't need to," she said with absolute calm.

Hearing her voice, the two officers hesitated an instant, perhaps recognizing her as the presumed terrorist. That was all she needed to take two shots at the glass wall. The storm did the rest. Before the officers could react, the wall gave way under the pressure and imploded, admitting an explosion of wind, rain, and glass that rolled toward them like a shock wave, forcing them to seek cover.

When they got up again and looked at the spot where Nuria had been, they found there was no one there.

89

Nuria's plan had been to trick the two officers into believing she'd committed suicide by jumping out the window. At the very least, she would leave them confused for a while. But the second she landed on the sloping windows of the building's façade, she realized she'd made a grave miscalculation.

The polished surface she found herself on was like a terrifying water-park toboggan ride, so steep and slippery with water there was no way of stopping—except that instead of ending in a friendly swimming pool, this ride led to a hundred-eighty-foot drop into the void, with a reinforced concrete breakwater at the bottom. Before taking the leap, Nuria had imagined herself skating down the façade to the Presidential Suite on the floor immediately below, landing spectacularly on the small balcony like Wonder Woman.

What actually happened was that her feet flew out from under her as if she'd stepped on a soapy floor. Nuria ended up on her back, head downwards, skidding along the kamikaze slide, completely out of control. For two eternal seconds she tried desperately to grab one of the window frames in an attempt to brake her ever-increasing speed as she saw the antenna that crowned the hotel roof receding faster and faster.

Her back lost contact with the glass façade and she hung in midair for an instant before falling with a crash onto the hard wooden floor of the balcony, hitting her head and her wounded shoulder in the process. The limbocaine kept her from blacking out from the brutal impact. Feeling lucid, her pain muffled by the drug, and astonished by the fact that she'd survived her demented brainwave, Nuria got slowly to her feet, checking to be sure she had no broken bones.

Raising her eyes to the interior of the suite, she saw Salvador Aguirre and Jaime Olmedo directly in front of her, seated on a horseshoe-shaped sofa. They were staring at her, their eyes like saucers and their mouths open in disbelief at the inexplicable appearance of this woman on their balcony.

Oblivious to the storm that whipped her short black hair and drenched her face, Nuria felt a ferocious smile curve her lips. She was a fallen angel thirsty for blood. The bewilderment on the faces of the two men gave way to terror when they recognized her. They pointed at her, arms outstretched, as though they were seeing the devil himself.

Going to the sliding door that led to the balcony, Nuria opened it wide, inviting the fury of the wind and rain in with her. Together, they entered the spacious living room with its surrounding circle of columns, the storm a palpable extension of her fury.

A flash of lightning tore the sky in two behind her, turning Nuria momentarily into a black silhouette outlined against the light, her fists clenched as she moved forward.

"You!" Aguirre cried, unable to believe his eyes.

"No." Olmedo was shaking his head. "It's not possible."

Nuria stood in front of him, leaving a dark water stain on the plush carpet. "I'm the ghost of your Christmases past," she said, enjoying the terror she saw in his eyes. But the sentence was barely out of her mouth when three bodyguards, alerted by the noise, burst into the room. All three stopped dead at the sight of a woman standing in the middle of the room, black hair covering her face as rainwater streamed off her.

Nuria took advantage of their hesitation to reach for the holster at her belt, only to find it empty. She realized she must have lost the weapon either when she'd jumped out the window or when she'd hit the balcony, but there was nothing she could do about it. The bodyguards would take at most a couple of seconds to emerge from their stupor, and before another second had elapsed she would be riddled with bullets.

There was only one thing she could do: attack first. Her limbocaine-heightened senses allowed her to contemplate the scene with glacial calm, as if someone else and not she were there. Her perception of time slowed, allowing her to study each of the men in turn, assessing the immediacy of the threat he posed and choosing the course of action that would give her the greatest chance of survival.

Even before she was aware of it, her body began to move in the direction of the nearest bodyguard. Seeing her intentions, he reached toward the back of his pants where his gun was—but not even his skill and trained reflexes could match her superhuman speed as she crossed the fifteen feet separating them in the blink of an eye.

He'd barely finished taking out his gun when she reached him. Grabbing his wrist with one hand, she bent over and brutally shoved her other elbow into his face. An agonizing crunch told her she'd broken the nose of the gorilla who was a head taller and sixty pounds heavier than she was. Before Nuria could get out of the way, a stream of warm blood had showered her.

In front of her, the second bodyguard had pulled his gun from its holster and was pointing it in her direction. For Nuria it all seemed to be happening in slow motion, as if everyone but her were moving underwater. Before he could make a move, she pulled the gun from her first victim's inert fingers and, without thinking, hurled it at the second guard with all her strength. He ducked, his reflexes fast enough to allow him to avoid the impact of two plus pounds of steel, but he lost sight of her for an instant, giving Nuria more than enough time. By the time he'd regained his balance, she was looming over him like a panther in mid-spring, too quick for the eye to follow. The bulky bodyguard tried to turn toward the superwoman who was somehow next to him, but couldn't avoid her knee, which buried itself in his solar plexus, emptying his lungs of air. As he doubled over, struggling for breath, she pulled the gun from his hand.

Meanwhile, the third bodyguard had drawn his nine-millimeter Glock and aimed it at this stranger who was moving at impossible speed. While his second partner collapsed helplessly, gasping like a fish out of water, he pointed his gun at this woman who for the briefest of seconds stopped to look at him as if waiting to see how he would react. Absolutely still, she seemed as inhuman as she had when she moved faster than was humanly possible. Fleetingly, he remembered a comment a colleague had made about an experimental drug that produced an effect like this. At the time he'd taken it as a joke, teasing his friend for his gullibility and accusing him of reading too many superhero comics.

Now he wasn't laughing. With the crosshairs of his gun centered on the stranger's chest, he looked at her reddened eyes and understood the reason for the momentary unexpected truce. She was waiting for him to lower his gun—but he couldn't do that. He couldn't surrender to a woman who was threatening his client's life. His job was to protect that client. All he could do was act out the role he'd been given in this drama.

Exerting the five pounds of pressure on the trigger needed to release the Glock's safety, he fired one of the ten nine-millimeter bullets in the magazine at point blank. The detonation shut down his own senses for a tenth of a second, and when he was able to react again, he couldn't believe his eyes. The woman was no longer in front of him. Somehow she'd anticipated the shot and leaned to the left to avoid it, though she hadn't come away completely unscathed: a thin line of blood now ran across her shoulder where the bullet had grazed it, ripping away a strip of her shirt in the process.

The woman seemed not even to notice the wound or the bloodstain that now began to spread across her white shirt. Neither did she show any reaction to the pain. Her expression remained unchanged except for a slight widening of her feline grin, as if she were happy to have been shot.

"Don't fuck with me," he growled, pulling the trigger again and again, this time without taking the trouble to aim directly. The detonations of the Glock ricocheted against the walls of the spacious room, one after the next, almost automatically. Two seconds later, the firing-pin clicked, finding no more bullets to strike.

When the hurricane-force wind coming in through the open balcony door cleared the cloud of smoke and gunpowder, the bodyguard saw the woman, now so close he could see the dilated pupils in her febrile, reddened eyes. In a lightning-fast movement, her left hand shot toward his throat, striking his trachea with rigid, extended fingers and leaving him unable to breathe. He dropped his useless gun, put his hands to his neck, and collapsed onto the wood floor where a puddle of rain had accumulated. His last conscious thought was the fear of drowning in less than a half inch of water.

The fight had lasted less than ten seconds, but to Nuria's super-accelerated, limbocaine-induced perception of time, it seemed like several minutes. She looked around, first at the livid bodyguard on his knees desperately trying to breathe, then at the other two, who were in an even worse state and clearly out of commission, at least for a while.

Long enough for Nuria to finish what she'd come to do.

Behind her, still on the sofa, the two politicians' faces wore identical expressions of horror and surprise at what they'd just seen. Both of them stared at their bodyguards and then back at Nuria, trying to find an explanation.

Olmedo pointed to the fallen men. "That ... that was the work of the devil," he stammered. "The evil one is in you." His finger was now pointing at Nuria. Aguirre crossed himself, his eyes bulging from their sockets. It was clear he was in agreement with his secretary.

Nuria walked around the couch and stood in front of them. "No, Jaime." She showed him the gun she was now holding. "All this is your work, and today you're going to pay for it."

To her surprise, Aguirre stood up and placed himself between them, raising his hand to stop her. "Miss Badal." He put a hand to his chest and spoke in his best Reborn preacher's tone. "This isn't necessary. Don't do anything you'll regret."

"Regret? Do you know the kind of vermin that's standing there beside you?" She jabbed her finger at Olmedo. "He planned the terrorist attack during the rally, blackmailed me into murdering you, and threatened to kill my family if I didn't do it. *He's* the evil one himself."

"We all make mistakes," Aguirre said. "But vengeance belongs to our Lord God alone, not to you or me."

"*We all make mistakes?*" she repeated incredulously. "Seriously? Is that all you have to say? It doesn't matter to you that he ordered me to kill—" All at once the last piece of the puzzle fell into place in her mind and the words died in Nuria's mouth. Reality punched her in the face, just as it had when she was a little girl and had finally understood that her father wasn't coming back that night or any other night. It didn't seem possible. It simply couldn't be ... but it was.

Suddenly everything began to spin, as if the presidential suite had begun to revolve on its axis.

"You." She pointed at Aguirre as she took a step back, almost tripping. "Oh my fucking God … you knew it."

90

The leader of Spain First raised his hands in an attempt to pacify her. "Calm down, miss, I beg you."

But Nuria wasn't agitated. It might have been the limbocaine, or the calming effect produced by inevitable certainties, however devastating they may be, but for some reason she felt a deep serenity spreading through her. "You're scum," she said to both of them. Her tone of voice was descriptive rather than judgmental, like that of someone listing the characteristics of a virus under a microscope. "Both of you."

"You don't understand, Miss Badal," Aguirre said.

"I understand perfectly well. You're ready to murder thousands of people to obtain power."

"It isn't something I wanted to do. But it was the only way."

"The only way of getting what you wanted."

"Not what I wanted," Aguirre corrected her. "What all of us want. Do you think I'm doing all this for selfish reasons? Don't forget, I was going to be the first to die." He raised his voice and pressed his thumb against his chest. "None of this is for me, or for Olmedo ... not even for the party or the Reborn. Everything I've done has been done thinking of your future."

"My future?" she repeated in astonishment. "What the hell are you talking about?"

Olmedo took over. "Your future, and that of every Spaniard. The barbarians are at the gates, and we're the ones who opened them wide. We have to do whatever's necessary to remind people it's either us or them. If we wait a single day longer, it may be too late."

Nuria looked at them both and shook her head, unable to believe what she was hearing. "You're crazy. Both of you." Her voice was uneasy. "You want power, whatever the price, and you're justifying yourselves with all this messianic crap. But it won't fly. You're just two wretched little men who've convinced themselves their own lies are true. Pyromaniacs ready to set fire to the world if things aren't what you want them to be."

"Is that what you believe?" Aguirre asked. "That we want to set fire to the world? No, Miss Badal." He showed his teeth in a sad smile. "On the contrary.

We're the firemen who burn the weeds before the fire comes. We're the firewall against the Muslim invasion and the loss of our values."

"Jesus, now you come out with this? Is there any other topic you'd like to mention?"

"Can't you see what's going on around you?" Aguirre blurted. "Western civilization is in decadence. We need to do everything we can to shore it up. Our values, our culture, our history, our religion, even our own lives ... all these things are in danger thanks to decades of shortsightedness, political correctness, and liberal stupidity. We must do whatever is necessary to forestall disaster—and yes, if that means expelling the infidels, putting an end to licentiousness and technology, or doing away with the farce democracy has turned into, we'll do it."

"Bullshit!" Nuria shot back. "You're just a couple of old men frightened of change joining forces with a bunch of other old men who are equally frightened. You're ready to sacrifice whatever it takes so that change doesn't happen and everything stays the same. You're trying to deceive yourselves and everyone else,"—Nuria continued to vent, like a pressure cooker when its steam valve is opened—"claiming you're doing it for the common good, but that's a lie. You're doing it for yourselves, only and exclusively for yourselves," she concluded, her anger rising. "You don't give a damn about future generations." She raised her gun in their direction.

"All right, do it," Aguirre challenged her. "Shoot now. Let's get this over with." To her surprise, the leader of Spain First spread his arms wide and closed his eyes.

Disconcerted, Nuria aimed at him, but she realized she couldn't do it. Their exchange had diluted her rage, as if knowing the reasons for it all had poured a bucket of water over her rage, extinguishing it. It wasn't that she didn't still hate those two vermin. She knew the world would probably be a better place without them. It was just that she was no longer capable of pulling the trigger and murdering them in cold blood.

Aguirre lowered his arms. "You may be right. Maybe we're all wrong and you're right. But if you kill us, it will be no different than if you'd shot me this morning. Everyone will know it was you, they'll blame Muslim terrorists, and in the end some other party member will become the candidate for Spain First and win the elections."

"Maybe," Nuria admitted. "But at least this way justice will be done for everything you've done. And I'll stop you from hurting my family."

"Your family?" Aguirre repeated. "We never intended to hurt your family."

"Sure you didn't." She gestured at Olmedo with the gun. "Ask him."

"I was only trying to put pressure on you to carry out the mission I entrusted you with," he said. "I never planned to hurt your mother or your grandfather."

Nuria hooked her finger around the trigger as she remembered his threats. "Liar," she hissed through gritted teeth.

Suddenly, a woman's voice sounded next to her. "No, my child, it's the truth."

Slowly, as if in a dream, Nuria turned to her right. There, standing at the door of one of the bedrooms, white robe fluttering in the wind, was her mother, looking at her with a sad, disappointed expression on her face. "Mom?" she asked, stunned. "What ... what are you doing here? Did they kidnap you?"

"Kidnap me?" She shook her head. "What things you say. You're completely wrong about them, my dear. When they found out I was your mother, they contacted me immediately after the incident in Villarefu to offer me all the help I might need. In addition,"—she raised her hands to her chest—"in acknowledgement of my faith and devotion, I've been awarded an honorary position in the order and they invited me to accompany them while they were in Barcelona to inspire other mothers in difficult situations with their children. I didn't tell you that when you called because I know how much you hate them,"—she gestured at both men—"but they're wonderful people and they've always had you in their prayers. You wouldn't believe how much we've talked about you these past few days."

"Oh, I can believe it all right," Nuria muttered somberly, regretting that she hadn't spent more time listening to her mother and less time judging her. If she'd been closer to her instead of driving her away—

Estela Jimenez took a few steps toward her, a hint of reproach in her voice. "In that case, what are you doing here and why are you threatening them with a gun?"

"Because these two men you worship so much are the devil, Mom," she said scornfully. "I have no idea what they told you, but they threatened to kill you and Grandfather if I didn't do what they were asking me to. That's why they brought you here—to hold you hostage if necessary and to pump you for information about me."

"Well, now you can see how wrong you are." Estela spread her hands wide. "I don't think anybody intends to hurt your grandfather either. I think—"—she hesitated for a moment—"I think this is one of those times where you're getting reality mixed up with your imagination."

"No, Mom. This is real. You're the one they're manipulating."

"Wasn't it you I saw at mass this morning holding a gun to this man's head?"

"Yes, but they forced me to do it. I told you that."

463

"And they're forcing you to be here now?"

"No … I—" Nuria had always found it difficult to argue with her mother, who had the unerring ability to make her feel wrong in everything she did. "I only … wanted to protect you and Grandpa."

"Protect us," her mother repeated in a low voice. "I spoke to your commissioner a few days ago, Nuria. He was very worried about you and he asked me to let him know if you contacted me, that he was looking for you. He also explained that you were on sick leave because of psychiatric problems and that you need help urgently."

"That has nothing to do with this."

Her mother took a couple more steps toward her, laying her hand on Nuria's forearm in an attempt to pacify her. "Of course it has." She lowered her voice so Nuria could barely hear her above the roaring of the storm. "All that business about your partner David and his wife was a tragedy. It must have been terrible. It makes perfect sense that you should have looked for someone to blame. The fact that you ended up blaming Mr. Aguirre is the logical result of that, don't you see? You've always hated their party and the Reborn, and he embodies both. That's why you've created a fantasy where you've made them responsible for all your problems."

"No … that's not true. Well, yes, I did hate them," Nuria corrected herself at the sight of her mother's disbelief. "But that's got nothing to do with it. I hate the Reborn and the fascists, it's true, but Aguirre and his hit man are a couple of manipulative monsters. Psychopaths."

Her mother took a deep breath and held the air in her lungs before exhaling sorrowfully. "Psychopaths, you say?" She took Nuria's arm and forced her to turn to the TV screen that occupied almost the whole of one wall. "What do you see there?"

On the black reflective surface, as if it were a mirror, Nuria saw the image of her mother holding a stranger next to her. A woman with short black hair plastered to a bruised face with black-ringed eyes, wearing a tattered police uniform covered with bloodstains, a gun in her right hand, staring back at Nuria with reddened, unhinged eyes. It took her a few seconds to recognize herself and realize she'd turned into the very image of a dangerous psychopath. She couldn't remember when or how this change had taken place, but the evidence was there in front of her, looking back at her with the unmistakable, alienated gaze of someone who is out of control.

Staring at that stranger reflected on the screen, Nuria felt her knees beginning to buckle under the weight of the evidence and her creeping doubt about whether her mother was right and she was insane. Could she be sure everything she'd seen and heard was real? A minute earlier she could have sworn it was, but now she wasn't so sure. It was true that any lunatic questioned about his hallucinations would swear they were real and that it was others who were confused and deceived.

Was that what was happening to her? Had she gone crazy and imagined all the plots and conspiracies she thought she'd unearthed? Suppose that after all it wasn't Elias who was the schizophrenic but her? More than that ... could she even be sure Elias had been real and not a product of her imagination, or her need to have someone close to her?

"Nurieta," her mother's voice whispered in her ear, awakening her from her doubts. "Don't worry, sweetheart. You just wait and see, everything's going to be all right."

Nuria turned to her mother. For the first time in a very, very long time she saw in her eyes the love she'd always felt for her but which Nuria had refused to accept. In that face that would be her own in another thirty years, she saw understanding and forgiveness. She saw the peaceful harbor where she longed to close her eyes and curl up to rest.

Drained of the strength necessary to remain on her feet another second, Nuria fell to her knees onto the rain-soaked parquet floor. Her mother crouched down in front of her and enveloped her in a comforting hug. "Everything's going to be all right, Nurieta," she whispered in her ear, repeating the loving nickname her daughter had heard so seldom from her lips. "Everything's all right."

"True," came Olmedo's voice, unexpectedly close to her. "Now everything really is fine."

Nuria looked up to find the secretary standing beside them with a satisfied smirk on his ugly face. She passed the back of her hand over her face, wiping away the tears that blurred her vision, realizing as she did so that her hand was empty. At some point she'd let the gun fall without realizing it.

Her vision clear now, she saw the gun in Olmedo's right hand. The ex-military man was looking thoughtfully at it as if weighing it, surprised by its lightness. Nuria thought of warning him to be careful, that it was loaded.

All at once something happened that Nuria would never have imagined. Jaime Olmedo turned to Aguirre, who was still standing beside him, and put the gun to his temple.

"What ... what are you doing?" Aguirre asked stupidly, disbelief on his face.

"You had only one thing to do," his second-in-command recriminated him, "and that was to die. And even that I'm going to have to deal with myself."

"What? You're not going to—" In a useless gesture, Aguirre raised his hands to protect himself. Before he could finish, Olmedo fired. The bullet impacted Aguirre's head, which snapped backwards in an explosion of blood, bone, and gray matter.

465

Nuria was still taking in the horrifying scene that had just unfolded before her eyes when Olmedo turned to them and aimed the still-smoking gun. "I can't leave any witnesses," he said simply, without further explanation.

He pulled the trigger.

91

Nuria closed her eyes in a reflex action. In the tenth of a second it took her to understand she was about to die, she accepted her fate and relaxed her body. Weary of fighting, she hoped her death would be swift and she could rest at last.

But death did not arrive when the shot sounded. Instead, Nuria felt a violent spasm run through her, accompanied by a piteous moan. Opening her eyes, she saw her mother beside her, looking at her, her eyes glassy and her face contracted in pain. A red stain was spreading over her immaculate white robe like a flower opening its petals over her heart. At the very last instant she'd put herself between her daughter and the bullet that had her name on it.

"No! Mama," Nuria pleaded, holding her as she fell. "No, please, not you!"

"Nuria ... my baby ..." came her mother's faint voice. She reached up to touch Nuria's face as though moving away from her. "I love you ..."

"I know ... Mommy," Nuria whispered in anguish, a river of tears coursing down her cheeks. "I love you so much." With infinite tenderness she caressed her mother's face as the light in her eyes faded. Estela moved her lips, murmuring a few inaudible words, before her eyelids drifted closed for the last time. Nuria passed her bloodied fingertips over her mother's face as a blind person would do, memorizing every feature, every wrinkle she wanted to remember. She stroked her hair, her forehead, the bridge of her nose, the sockets of the eyes that would never look at her again and the lips that would never kiss her again. She traced the line of her mother's neck down over the white robe, holding the palm of her hand over the bullet-wound for a moment as she felt her heart slow, beat by beat, until it stopped.

The pain and desolation Nuria felt at that irreparable loss pierced her heart like a burning stake. All the arguments and differences she'd ever had with her mother in the past became meaningless as she held her inert body in her arms.

Like so many others, she'd died because of her. If Nuria hadn't been her daughter, Estela would still be alive. Just as Elias and Gloria would be alive if they hadn't been her friends. Even David, if he hadn't been her partner. All of them dead, murdered for the simple reason that they knew her—while she herself was still absurdly and unfairly alive. With utmost care, she laid her mother's corpse on the floor. Her blood dissolved in the thin layer of water, spreading like a rosy stain all around her.

"It's nothing personal," Olmedo said. He aimed the gun at her head, showing his teeth in a grimace that said exactly the opposite. Nuria looked up at the source of all that pain, and a dark, vengeful wrath rose from the most profound depths of her being. She calculated her chances of covering the six feet that separated her from Olmedo before he could fire and knew immediately that she wouldn't make it.

The effects of the limbocaine were waning now, almost gone. Every limb, every muscle, and every cell of her body were screaming that they'd reached the limit of exhaustion. The mere act of holding her head up now implied an unsustainable effort.

Suddenly, from some hidden corner of her mind, came the memory of something Aya had given her before they'd said goodbye. Something Commissioner Puig had been carrying that she'd put into her pocket without thinking about and forgotten until this moment.

"Goodbye, Miss Badal," Olmedo said, curling his finger around the trigger.

Nuria extended her left hand, plunging it into the water, as she put her right hand into her pocket, locating the object, which looked like a small TV remote control. Clenching her teeth, she pressed the single button on it with all her strength.

Immediately an electrical discharge ran through her battered body, arching her back in a spasm. With no control over her muscles, Nuria fell hard onto the floor. This time the limbocaine couldn't dull the effects of the shock as it had before, but at least the seven hundred volts were diffused through the water. They raced in an arc around her, reaching Olmedo's elegant, velvet—and now completely soaked—loafers.

When the charge struck him, Olmedo uttered a cry of surprise, more because of the unexpectedness of the shock than because of the effects of the limited voltage that reached him. He stumbled backwards and fell onto the couch behind him, dropping the gun.

Doing her utmost to recover from the third electrical discharge of the day, Nuria raised her head, set both hands on the floor, and made the titanic effort of raising herself a couple of inches, just enough to see that Jaime Olmedo too was recovering from the limited electrical discharge he'd received. Realizing it had been her doing, he glared malevolently at her, then began to look around in search of the gun.

Nuria saw it immediately where it had fallen on the floor just in front of her. A split second later, Olmedo too saw it. She made a superhuman effort to get to her knees, but he bent down and reached for it, beating her to it. Grasping the gun by the butt, he turned it on her, but before he could aim, she hurled herself at him, crashing into him with a smothered cry of desperation just as the secretary fired. Nuria felt the bullet graze her left ear. With a sharp movement she yanked the gun from his hand, sending it flying to the other side of the room.

Olmedo twisted his body furiously, launching a clumsy slap at her. She managed to dodge it, but his fingernails left a trail of scratches on her cheek. "You're going to pay for everything you've done, you son of a bitch," she said, squatting over him and beginning to rain punches on his face.

Blood began to flow from his broken nose and lips as he did his best to stop the blows. "No! No!" he whimpered. "Stop! Don't hit me anymore!"

Nuria ceased her blows and stared at him for a second. "You're right. There's no point in hitting you." For the briefest of moments, she saw a flash of hope in his pleading eyes—a flash of hope that lasted for the time it took her to complete her thought. "Better let's finish this once and for all," she hissed through clenched teeth. Putting her hands around his throat, she pressed hard.

"No!!" Olmedo moaned. As he struggled to breathe, he grasped Nuria's hands with his own, trying to stop her.

"This *is* personal," she muttered. The veins in Olmedo's neck began to swell as she choked off his circulation.

Abruptly, she heard the outer doors of the suite burst open. Their boots clattering on the wood floor, half a dozen hooded agents from the Special Forces entered with their weapons drawn, sweeping the room with the laser beams of their sights. "Police!" one of them yelled. "On the ground! On the ground!"

Nuria heard their voices in the anteroom of the huge presidential suite and knew that in a couple of seconds they would flood into the living room and everything would be over. What really made her furious was not the fact that it meant the end for her, but that she wasn't going to have enough time to execute Olmedo. "Shit," she muttered. The weapon was too far away, and she had no time to reach it.

In fact she had no time for anything—or *almost* anything. "Get up!" she barked at Olmedo. She grasped his lapel. Taking advantage of the fact that he was too busy trying to breathe, she seized him by the arm and dragged him toward the balcony.

"Stop!" came a voice. "Not another step!" Turning quickly, Nuria put her arm around Olmedo's neck and shoved him between herself and the soldier from Special Forces.

The hurricane-force wind and rain pounded her back mercilessly, the strong gusts threatening to knock her off balance. "If you come any closer I'll kill him!" Nuria threatened, jabbing the Taser remote control into Olmedo's back, making him and all the others believe it was the barrel of a gun.

"Lower your weapon!" the same officer roared. "Put your weapon down now!"

"I have another idea." She took a step back. "You put *your* guns down or I'll shoot."

"She killed Aguirre!" Olmedo cried in a self-pitying voice when he got his breath back. "She killed them all!"

"That's a lie," Nuria said, shoving the remote harder into his back. "This asshole is the one behind the—" All at once she stopped talking, realizing that the hooded officers in their black uniforms, the red dots of their lasers trained on her, were only waiting for the chance to blow her head off.

Suddenly, to her astonishment, the officer with captain's stripes on his shoulder who was giving the orders lowered his weapon and pulled off his balaclava. He stepped forward. "Nuria Badal?" he asked incredulously. "Is it ... you?"

"Captain Lopez?" she replied, equally surprised. "It's a small world!"

Bewildered, the captain waved a hand at his surroundings, then pointed to Olmedo. Taking another step toward her, he demanded, "What's going on here?"

"Stop right there, Captain," Nuria warned. "Don't take another step, and tell your men to lower their weapons or I'll finish him off here and now."

Lopez stopped, but without giving any orders to his men. "All right. Calm down. Drop the gun and we'll talk."

"I can talk perfectly well without dropping it."

"Well then, let the civilian go."

"Sorry, Captain, can't do that either."

Lopez shook his head in frustration. "Hell, Nuria, I'm trying to help you here."

"No one can help me."

"Come on," Lopez said. "Don't get melodramatic. Give yourself up and everything will be sorted out. I know you," he said, sweeping a hand around the room again. "I know there must be a good explanation for all this."

"There certainly is, but nobody's going to believe it."

Lopez took another step toward her. "I'll believe you," he said, sounding convinced.

"It won't go well for you if you do," Nuria said, taking another two steps back to the balcony door. The wind tossed her black hair into the air, muffling her last words.

"Do something!" Olmedo demanded, struggling to free himself from Nuria's arm that was clamped around his neck like a vise. "Stop her!"

"Drop the gun and release him!" Lopez shouted, trying to make himself heard above the wind. "Surrender and I promise I'll testify in your favor!"

Ignoring him, Nuria continued to walk backwards. On the balcony now, she climbed onto a chair and then onto one of the low tables, forcing Olmedo to climb with her. When she straightened up, the glass railing reached just below her hip.

That was when Lopez realized what she meant to do. "Don't be stupid!" he shouted, emerging onto the balcony followed by his men, who arranged themselves into a semicircle in front of her. "There's no way out!"

"There's always a way out," Nuria said, glancing quickly behind her into the void and the one hundred-eighty foot drop to the roiling sea and the colossal waves crashing against the harbor breakwater.

"I'll pay you whatever you want!" Olmedo begged, in tears. "I'll confess to whatever is necessary! I swear it! I'll turn myself in!"

"Too late," Nuria said in a tone of finality.

"Please!" Lopez begged, extending a hand to her. "Don't do it!"

"It's the only way justice will be done."

Lopez shook his head. "This isn't justice, Nuria! It's revenge!"

Seeming to consider his words for a moment, Nuria nodded agreeably. "I don't give a shit." The captain saw the determination in her eyes and leapt toward her and her hostage in a last-ditch attempt to hold them back. But before he could reach them, she leaned back over the railing and let herself fall, dragging Olmedo with her.

Lopez leapt onto the table and leaned out over the railing. As he watched, the body of the politician crashed against a lower balcony, then plummeted into the void like a broken doll, his mouth open in a scream of terror.

What the captain didn't see was Nuria falling—though he thought he glimpsed a shadow sliding down the curved façade at lightning speed. Then it was gone, hidden behind the curtain of rain, swallowed up by the storm.

92

The brutal impact as she hit the water knocked the air out of Nuria's lungs. Though she'd entered it in the same position she'd seen the Mexican cliff divers adopt, feet first and arms folded against her chest, the tremendous blow nearly caused her to lose consciousness. The worst moment, however, came when, after plunging several yards into the water, she tried to resurface. With no air left in her lungs, she moved her arms desperately, but the colossal waves forced her back under again without giving her time to take a breath.

At the very edge of blacking out, reaching for her last bit of strength, Nuria fought to reach the daylight. Just when she was about to give up, convinced she would never make it, she felt her head emerge from the water. She gulped in a desperate mouthful of air as another wave broke just over her head, engulfing her again. She spun dizzily, as if in a gigantic washing machine.

When the spinning stopped, Nuria had no way of knowing which way was up or down. What little oxygen she'd managed to hold in her lungs was beginning to fail her. She needed more of it, and fast. In that rough sea with zero visibility, never sure whether she was rising to the surface or sinking further still, Nuria fought, calling on her stubborn survival instinct and the last molecules of limbocaine remaining in her body.

Once again she managed to break the surface just as her lungs were about to burst, but this time it was through the foam of a wave that had just broken. This gave her a few seconds to get her breath back and anticipate the next wave so she could plunge beneath it before it broke above her and then resurface as soon as it had passed.

At last she could breathe more or less regularly, but this game of hide-and-seek with the waves was an exhausting one that she wouldn't be able to keep up much longer. Somehow, she had to reach the shore.

Nuria emerged on the crest of the next wave, which gave her the chance to look in the direction of land and try to orient herself. To her surprise she found that the strong current had dragged her more than a half mile to the north, parallel to the breakwater that years before had been the Barceloneta beach. To her left the unmistakable silhouette of the Hotel W receded, while to her right she saw the waves crashing against the massive concrete blocks of the Espigon del Gas breakwater. Although fewer than a hundred yards separated her from the seawall, reaching it while being buffeted by eighteen-foot waves would be a real achievement—in her battered state, nothing short of a miracle. But she had no alternative. If she didn't reach solid ground soon she would drown, and after everything she'd been through, that simply wasn't an option. She was going to reach the breakwater or die in the attempt.

Swimming against the undertow that carried her further and further away from the coast while simultaneously trying to take advantage of the forward motion of the waves, Nuria managed to move toward the dike, a double row of reinforced concrete blocks stretching a hundred yards out to sea. The waves crashed against the outermost blocks in terrifying succession, like trains colliding one after another against the buffer stops at a station.

Somehow she had to avoid that. If a wave caught her and hurled her against the concrete, they would have to use a rake to collect her remains. Her only chance was to reach the leeward side of the breakwater, where the impact of the waves was less, and once there, find a way to climb onto the barrier.

Piece of cake, she told herself, purposely ignoring the very real danger of miscalculating the distance. A series of powerful waves could detour her, the undertow could be stronger there, she could run out of strength, or a fucking bolt of lightning could strike her. Considering the luck she'd been having lately, she thought, anything was possible.

Sticking her head out of the water, Nuria dived under the next wave, trying to keep her goal in sight. Gradually she drew nearer the breakwater, gritting her teeth against the unending effort she was only able to keep up through desperation and her survival instinct.

At last she rounded the northern end of the breakwater. With one last burst of courage, striving against the undertow that tried to drag her away from her destination, she reached the relative calm of the leeward side. Though the waves didn't break directly on this side, the undertow made the approach to the concrete blocks extremely dangerous, even more so considering how weak she was. But she had no choice. Treading water a few yards away, she waited for a break in the violence of the waves. When it came, she set her jaw and climbed on to the breakwater, clinging to one of the giant blocks like a limpet.

Driven on by the possibility that at any moment a wave might flatten her against the concrete, she climbed painfully up the slippery mass of gigantic gray cubes that looked like a set of blocks left scattered around by a giant child. Finally she reached a relatively dry spot above the level of the waves.

Exhausted to a point she didn't believe possible, the rain and spray pounding her mercilessly, Nuria continued to climb, looking for handholds and slipping constantly, a millisecond from giving up.

Unexpectedly, she saw a large hole yawning beneath her, a gap between the megalithic blocks, dark and empty. Without a second thought, she slid down into it, surprised to find that it was a sort of den, a couple of yards deep and a yard high. It stank of rotten fish and cat piss, and she was sure there was a dead mouse or two somewhere in the vicinity. But under her present circumstances, that damp, rank hole felt like a luxury apartment.

"I've slept in worse places," she told herself consolingly, her voice hoarse from the effort she'd expended. Lacking the strength to blink though her life depended on it, Nuria collapsed onto the cold concrete surface and closed her eyes. In less than ten seconds she'd given herself up to the dark pleasure of unconsciousness.

When she opened her eyes at last, the aftereffects of the limbocaine hit her with all the subtlety of a sledgehammer. Nuria felt as if she'd woken up after twenty hangovers in succession to find she had neither coffee nor aspirins and that the dog had pooped in the living room.

Slowly she opened her eyes and noticed a thin ray of light creeping in between the stones. It pooled on the ground next to her, illuminating the den sufficiently to show her that it was littered with plastic and garbage. She'd fallen asleep in a fetal position in the middle of it, using her hands as a pillow.

Nuria was unable at first to remember how she'd gotten there, but eventually, the events of the previous day began to filter lazily through her memory. Her heart sank as she remembered what she'd done, and she wished she could undo it.

It was only then that she realized something extraordinary: the only sound disturbing the unreal silence outside her refuge was the peaceful lullaby made by the waves as they kissed the shore. No gale-force wind, no downpour kept her from hearing her own thoughts. There was only the lulling background melody of the waves, as if she were listening to a relaxation audiobook.

The next thing Nuria realized was that she was starving—in fact, it had been the gnawing emptiness in her stomach that had woken her up. She was so hungry her mouth watered when she recalled the story of a group of castaways who had eaten their dead companions.

Unfortunately, there was no shipwreck victim to hand, and finding food was urgent. Nuria made a move to get up and found that her body refused to respond. "What the ...?" she murmured. When she parted her lips, they split and cracked as if she hadn't opened them for a year. She blinked in confusion, even her eyelids seeming to resist her orders.

Clenching her teeth, Nuria tried again, somehow finding strength in her weakness. Propping herself on her elbow, she pushed herself up very slowly into a seated position, her head brushing the ceiling. Every cramped muscle in her body pained her as though she'd been run over by a bus, refusing to respond to her orders for the simple reason that they were unable to do so in the absence of the fuel that would enable them to function: food. Either she found something to eat in order to regain her strength or she might never be able to get up again.

Unable to turn around in her little hole, Nuria dragged herself along on her behind feet first, pushing herself with her hands. She saw, with a resigned grimace, that her shoes were missing. When had she lost them?

Laboriously covering the short distance to the hole that also served as an exit, Nuria peered out cautiously, immediately squeezing her eyes shut and covering them with her hand. Though the sun wasn't directly overhead, the sky was a dazzling cobalt blue and everything, from the windows of the buildings to the astonishingly calm surface of the sea, reflected the sunlight as though someone had polished the earth.

What had happened? How long had she been asleep? There was no trace of Medicane Mercé. Though she could see piles of wood, seaweed, and plastic bobbing against the seawall of La Barceloneta, pushed there by the waves, nothing else showed that a huge storm had passed through. There was even a flock of noisy gulls crossing the sky, screeching with absolute normality.

Still disoriented by the difference between what she'd so recently lived through and what now met her eyes, Nuria emerged from her den like a she-bear awakening from hibernation: weak, befuddled, and so hungry she could have eaten a cow, horns and all.

A black cat poked its head out of another hole. Keeping a wary eye on her, it passed in front of her and leapt nimbly onto the concrete block immediately above her head. For a brief moment she thought of all the meat on a cat. Immediately ashamed of herself, she banished the horrible idea from her mind.

Another cat walked in front of her, then another and yet another, all going in the same direction. The answer to the feline enigma came in the form of a nearby voice calling, "Here, kitty, kitty," accompanied by the sound of fingers snapping.

Desperate, casting caution to the winds, Nuria followed the cats. Clambering with difficulty to the upper part of the breakwater, she found a shabby-looking woman, surrounded by a dozen cats, filling several improvised bowls with water and cat food.

Nuria's stomach rumbled at the sight, as if she were staring at a banquet to which she hadn't been invited. Like a zombie in a B movie, Nuria began to stagger toward the woman and her cats, opening and closing her mouth as if already anticipating the moment of chewing.

Not surprisingly, the woman almost fell over backwards at this sudden apparition. She stumbled back a few steps, her eyes starting from their sockets, no doubt fearing she was about to be eaten then and there. But Nuria had eyes only for the bowls of food. Crouching down in front of them, she pushed the cats away and began to stuff handfuls of kibble into her mouth, barely chewing before she swallowed. She picked up the bowl of water and drained it with the same desperation, only then realizing she was even more thirsty than she was hungry. By then the woman had run off, terrified, looking over her shoulder as she went to make sure she wasn't being followed.

"Could you bring cheese tomorrow, if it's not too much to ask?" Nuria called after her. The woman's only reply was some sort of expletive she didn't catch. Forgetting her benefactor, she went on devouring the food. It tasted foul, but her body was as grateful for it as if it had been a free seafood buffet.

Between mouthfuls, Nuria wondered where this animalistic need for protein was coming from, then realized it was likely the toll exacted by the limbocaine. All the superhuman strength and neuronal acceleration provided by the drug must demand far more energy from the body than normally needed. This, added to the fact that she might have slept for a day or even two, explained her extreme weakness and limitless hunger.

In under five minutes, Nuria had polished off two bowls of cat food and three of water. Full at last, she collapsed onto her back, gazing up at the dazzling blue sky, its perfection unmarred by a single cloud. Meanwhile, the cats milled around her, meowing indignantly at this inadmissible intrusion.

"Now what?" she asked herself aloud. She had nowhere to go, nor anyone to go to. She couldn't go back to her apartment, nor could she go anywhere near her grandfather's house or her mother's ... At the thought of her mother, a red-hot iron fist clutched at her heart, trying to tear it from her chest. The pain was so strong, so physical, Nuria had to bite her lip to endure it.

When it subsided, she made an effort to focus her mind on her most immediate problems, returning to the possible list of people she could call on. A list that no longer included Elias—another dagger in her heart—or Aya, whom she wouldn't be able to find even if she wanted to. Nor Susana, of course. Not surprisingly, she would never forgive Nuria since she'd left her gagged in the ladies' restroom.

She realized her list of friends and relatives had been reduced to exactly zero. Now she really could say she was completely and utterly alone in the world—and this was without taking into account the fact that her face had to be on the televisions of half the planet, that the police forces of the other half would be looking for her, and that several million Reborn and Spain First patriots would be praying that their god would grant them the pleasure of flaying her alive.

Nuria had definitely had better weeks, that much was clear. Giving in to the dark humor born of the resignation felt by someone who knows that whatever he does, he's fucked, she ran her gaze over the city that fanned out behind the breakwater, from the dilapidated old buildings of La Barceloneta on her left to the new steel-and-glass skyscrapers that reared up in front of her, their skyline gap-toothed from the hurricane, to the twin towers looming over the Olympic Port, where she could even make out the white masts of the—

Nuria's eyes opened wide, her heart coming to a sudden halt as an almost-forgotten name came to her mind.

93

Sheltered in the cat-hole, that now seemed tinier and fouler-smelling than it had the night before, to avoid being seen, Nuria devoted the rest of her day to planning her next moves. It wasn't until well into the wee hours that she risked putting her head out of the hole again, once she was absolutely sure there was no one strolling, fishing, or necking on the breakwater.

Under the wary gaze of several cats who, judging by the way they were looking at her, had it in for her, she climbed up onto one of the concrete blocks. After stretching her muscles, cramped after so many hours spent in the hole, she stripped down to her underwear, filled her lungs with air, and with remarkable grace dived headfirst into the sea.

The water seemed considerably colder than she remembered from the last time, though that might have been the result of having no drug circulating in her bloodstream, but the effect was invigorating. The first thing she did was rub her skin vigorously in an attempt to rid herself of the smell of cat piss impregnating her body and disinfect her many wounds and scratches. Setting her sights on the mouth of the Olympic Port, Nuria began to swim at an easy pace.

Though the marina was only eight hundred yards or so away and Nuria was anxious to reach her destination, she reasoned that in her current state it was best to take things easy. The cat food had saved her life, but the warning light on her depleted store of energy was still on.

Changing strokes every few minutes to avoid straining her painful left shoulder further, she slowly approached the mouth of the marina, marked by a red buoy on the left and a green one on the right.

Luckily no one was bothering to watch the entrances, given how reckless it was to swim in waters so full of every type of seagoing vessel. Even better was the fact that at that hour of the night no one wanted to go sailing. Under the cover of darkness, Nuria headed for the marina.

Twenty minutes later, she slipped between the two buoys. Continuing to swim and taking care to avoid the surveillance cameras, she headed for dock six, threading her way through the floats and the hulls of the boats. What she hadn't counted on was the profusion of lines, fenders, and tarpaulins, not to mention fragments of boats torn away by the hurricane and every kind of wind-driven trash that now floated in the water, making swimming difficult.

Doing her best to keep her head above the rank layer of oil floating on the surface, Nuria found the dock she was looking for. Her heart rate accelerating, she approached the stern of a sailboat with the name *Fermina* in stylized blue lettering on its side, its rigging jingling against the mast in the gentle sea breeze. After making sure there was no one in sight, Nuria climbed up the stern ladder and onto the deck.

At first sight the boat appeared to be in good condition, its fenders in place, protecting it from the hulls of the boats on either side. Untroubled by the fact that she was in her underwear, Nuria tugged at the mooring lines, checked the shrouds, and tested the knots. When she was satisfied, she put her fingers into a hole in the boom and took out a small key that her grandfather kept there the way other people might keep an extra key under the welcome mat on their porch.

Going to the wooden hatch that led to the boat's interior, she unlocked it and descended to the cabin, the steps creaking under her bare feet. Feeling for the light switch, she flipped it.

The cabin, barely three yards wide by two high, with its wooden walls and floor, pictures of nautical knots on the walls, old books about sailing, old-fashioned lamps and cushions, and its faint scent of engine oil, flooded her with such a deep and unexpected feeling of home that Nuria burst into tears of pure joy. All at once, she felt safe and protected, even if it was only by the thin carbon-fiber layer that sheltered her from the outside. This boat was impregnated with her grandfather's presence and the good memories of times spent with him as if with a layer of resin. The *Fermina* was not just a sailboat, it was a fragment of memory: a physical, palpable memory of all the love and laughter that had filled it. There, standing in the middle of the *Fermina's* cabin, with nothing left to her in the world but the bra and panties she was wearing, Nuria allowed herself to smile for the first time in a very long while.

To avoid taxes, the boat had been registered in the name of an old company of her grandfather's that had gone bankrupt decades earlier. This meant it couldn't be traced to her unless the connection was thoroughly investigated. As long as she was discreet, she could use it as a refuge until she decided what to do next, and no one would come looking for her.

Calm and confident in a way she hadn't been for weeks, Nuria stopped worrying about whatever might be happening outside the boat and went to the austere shower in the main cabin. Here she finished undressing, turned on the hot water, and soaped herself thoroughly, standing motionless under the stream of water until she'd drained the heater's ten-gallon tank. When she'd finished, she wrapped herself in an old beach towel and began to look through the pantry. She set all the cans she could find—pickled mussels, stuffed olives, sardines and cockles in oil, as well as a few bags of potato chips and bread sticks—on the table. She and her grandfather always had enough snacks on board for a birthday party, and though at that moment she would have killed for a quattro formaggi pizza or a good hamburger, all this was still better than the disgusting cat food.

At the bottom of the fridge she found several cans of beer. Without bothering with such niceties as plates or silverware, Nuria sat down on the couch in front of all that food. Opening the bags and cans one by one, she began to devour them systematically, as if there was a prize waiting for her once she'd finished them all.

She was already on her fourth can, so concentrated on what she was doing that she was startled when she heard a voice quite near her say, with a note of reproach, "I definitely like you better with long hair."

Redemption

Nuria's heart nearly leapt out of her chest at the shock. The mouthful of cockles she was chewing at the moment shot out and stuck to the bulkhead in front of her like buckshot. She turned toward the voice with her heart in her throat, almost passing out from astonishment when she saw a face peering through the hatch, a face she'd thought she would never see again.

There, crouching at the top of the ladder, Elias was watching her in silence, his white teeth showing in a radiant smile.

Nuria leapt to her feet. "I can't believe it! You're alive!"

"Looks like it," he said. Coming down the wooden steps, he spread his arms wide. "I'm so happy to see you, Nuria."

Nuria stayed where she was, happy, confused, and angry in equal parts. "But ... what ...? How ...?" she said, her words tripping over each other. Jabbing a finger at him, she asked, "Where the hell have you been?"

"I see you're happy too," he said ironically, his smile unaltered.

"I thought you were dead!" Nuria said, still in a state of shock.

Seeing he had no option but to explain, Elias made himself comfortable by leaning on the small card table. "You and everybody else," he said. "Until yesterday evening I wasn't able to contact Aya safely to tell her I was alive."

"Is she all right?"

"Yes, perfectly," he said. "Aya's in good hands with Giwan and Yady."

Nuria lowered her head, distraught. "I ... I'm sorry. I've really complicated your life."

"Complicated my life?" he snorted. "Far from it! Thanks to you, I'm officially missing, and in a few months I'll be presumed dead. And that, in my current circumstances, turns out to be extremely practical."

Nuria realized Elias didn't look much better than she did. He was dressed in an old hoodie to hide from the surveillance cameras, and one of his hands was bandaged. A multitude of cuts and scratches covered his face and arms, crowned by an ugly bruise on his temple. She felt an irresistible urge to go to him and caress his wounds with her fingertips.

Approaching him slowly, she brought her face close to his until their lips met. Gazing into each other's eyes, they held each other in a long, silent embrace. Tears of relief ran down her cheeks, wetting Elias's neck and shoulder. Feeling them, he held her tighter still.

"I thought I'd been left all alone," she whispered.

"You're not alone," Elias murmured softly, "and you'll never be again as long as you want me by your side."

Nuria tried to smile as she wept, producing an effect something like a snort. "Everyone who gets close to me ends up dead," she warned. "It's like there's a curse on me."

"Well, in a sense I'm dead already," Elias joked, "so your curse won't affect me. Anyway, it's a risk I'm willing to take."

Nuria took a step back so she could look directly into his eyes. "You're crazy."

He arched an eyebrow. "Says the woman who jumped out of a twenty-fifth floor window."

She gave him a guilty smile. "It was really a balcony. But yes, it was a crazy thing to do. I still can't believe I did it."

"They're also saying you took out an entire security team,"—he sounded more serious now—"and then Olmedo and Aguirre."

"No, that's not true," she protested. "Not all of it, at least." She shook her head. "But I don't want to talk about that now."

"I can imagine."

"What about you?" she asked. "How did you get out of that sewer?"

Elias waved his hand, making light of it. "Nothing as spectacular as what you did," he clarified. "I had a rough time. I thought I was going to drown down there, but in the end I managed to grab hold of a ladder and ended up surfacing somewhere in the Sants neighborhood, with only a couple of bumps and cuts that weren't that serious. I went to the safe house," he added as if describing a boring day at work, "and stayed there until it was safe to come out."

"But ... how did you find me?" Nuria asked, suddenly realizing. "I never told you about this boat."

"No, but you did tell me about your grandfather."

It took her a few seconds to understand what he meant. "Did you talk to him?" she asked excitedly. "Is he all right?"

"Perfectly well. He wasn't difficult to find. He sends you his love."

"Oh my God." She dropped her face into her hands, sobbing. "I thought he ... that he'd been ..." she babbled incoherently. "They threatened to kill him if I didn't—"

"Shh." He put his arms around her again to soothe her. "I arranged for the house to be watched in case you went to see him. Your grandfather's safe."

"Thank you," she whispered, then took a small step back. "But he must think I'm dead. I have to tell him I'm not."

"Your grandfather?" Elias sounded amused. "He was the one who convinced me you were alive. He insisted again and again on what a good swimmer you were. He told me more than once that a few little waves wouldn't get in his Nurieta's way."

New tears of joy ran down Nuria's face. She could no longer hold them back, nor did she wish to. It was over, her pretense of strength; if she needed to cry, she would cry until she was dehydrated.

When all her tears had been shed and her burden lifted, she asked, "What now? What are you going to do?"

"What are *we* going to do," Elias corrected her.

She shook her head, sensing that he wasn't listening to her. "I'm completely fucked," she insisted. "Right now I'm sure I'm number one on the most wanted list of the National Police and Interpol. It's a pretty safe bet the Church of the Reborn and Spain First have a contract out on me, and who knows who else is going to be looking for me to silence me."

"You're not wrong there." He winked at her. "You've become pretty popular lately. Try not to let it go to your head."

"Do you think it's funny?"

Elias was unable to suppress a damning smile. "Yes, I do, a little," he confessed.

Nuria tried to look angry, but ended up following his example. "It's true," she admitted. "It *is* funny in a way. But that doesn't make it any less dangerous to be anywhere near me."

He was suddenly serious. "I wouldn't want to be anywhere else. And you're not going to get me to change my mind, so don't insist."

"I'm going to have to spend the rest of my life on the run."

"And you think I'm not?" he reminded her. "But don't worry about that. Right now, the best thing is for everybody to think we're dead. In a year's time nobody will be looking for us anymore. With a radical change of image to fool the cameras and some fake documents, you'll be able to stroll through Plaza Catalunya again if you feel like it."

"A year?" she repeated. "What are we going to do in the meantime?"

Elias ran a hand over the card table and glanced around him. "This looks like a good place," he said appreciatively.

It took Nuria a moment to follow his thoughts. "Do you … do you want to stay here?"

"Not exactly. You know how to pilot it, don't you?"

"What about you?"

"I'm a fast learner."

Nuria shook her head a few times to clear it. "Um ... are you suggesting we go away?"

"Why not? We've got a boat, and money won't be a problem."

"And your niece? Your business?"

"I've left my business in good hands, and Aya's going to Paris with Giwan and Yady as soon as it's safe to spend a year there studying and squandering my money. I can assure you, it wasn't difficult to persuade her."

"What about Yihan and Aza?" Nuria asked, suddenly remembering them with a twinge of guilt. "Are they all right?"

"Better than we are. They're being given the royal treatment at a private hospital."

Nuria nodded in relief and crossed her arms, considering his proposal. "So ... you're serious about this."

"Absolutely."

"Oh well ... what the hell." She gave a dry laugh. "Okay then, come give me a hand." Disentangling herself from his embrace, she began to climb the ladder. "You get the bow mooring ropes and I'll get the stern ones. I'll turn the outside lights on and start the engine to warm it up."

"What?" Elias asked, bewildered, not moving from where he was. "You want to set sail now? It's the middle of the night."

She looked back down through the hatch. "You have something better to do?"

He gave her a roguish look. "Well ..." He rubbed his neck. "Actually, I can think of a couple of things."

Nuria rolled her eyes. "There'll be time for that later. We need to take advantage of the darkness."

Elias nodded after a moment, realizing the need for discretion. "Of course," he said reluctantly. "There will be time." He followed her up onto the deck.

In a couple of minutes they'd cast off. Nuria took the helm, throwing the twenty-horsepower engine into reverse. After maneuvering the *Fermina* out of her berth, she steered slowly toward the mouth of the harbor.

"Wouldn't it be more discreet if we unfurled the sails?" Elias suggested. "This engine sounds like a batucada concert."

"First lesson in sailing: it's compulsory to use the engine inside the harbor. Apart from the fact that in narrow spaces like this, it would be very hard to control the sail."

"Ah, I see."

"What I do need you to do is bring the fenders in, please." She pointed to the sides of the boat.

"Bring in the what?"

"The fenders," she repeated. "Those rubber things hanging over the sides of the boat. Bring them up on deck."

"Sir yes sir." He mimicked a military salute. "At your command."

"You're supposed to say *Aye, aye, Captain*, cabin boy," she said, trying to suppress her giggles. "And hurry up, I need it done today!"

Giving her a sidelong glance, Elias gave a theatrical snort as he followed her order, muttering loudly enough for her to hear, "Maybe it wasn't such a good idea to go sailing with you after all."

Nuria smiled again, feeling absurdly happy as she steered out of the harbor mouth and set an easterly course, leaving the city of Barcelona behind the stern. The groundswell began to rock the sailboat up and down, making it sway slightly with the waves. "Hey," she called when Elias had finished pulling the last fender on deck. "Come here."

Holding on to the shrouds to avoid falling overboard, he went to the cockpit and jumped down beside her. "Anything else, Captain?" he asked mockingly. "Should I swab the deck? Polish the railings?"

"Take the helm," she told him, moving aside.

He looked at her in surprise. "Are you sure? I've never—"

"Sure." She smiled. "Come on, take it."

Elias shrugged. "Okay," he said. He put his hands on the enormous aluminum wheel and gazed steadily ahead to where the night sky was tinged with indigo and violet. "And now?"

"Now all you have to do is keep the bow facing into the wind, following the course we've set, while I hoist the sails."

"Done. Anything else?"

"Try not to crash into anything."

"Very funny."

"I know." She winked at him and got down to unfurling the mainsail and the genoa jib, tightening knots and coiling loose ropes in exactly the way her grandfather had taught her. When she was satisfied, she went back to Elias, and after checking to make sure they were on course, asked, "How are you doing?"

"Very well, to tell you the truth. The feeling of independence is amazing. As if there was nobody else in the world."

"True," Nuria agreed. She paused, then added, "I've been wondering about something."

"What's that?"

"Well ... why?" she said. "Why me? Looking back, it seems that ever since we met you've been helping me, and now you say you want to be with me, when all I'm going to do is make more trouble for you."

"I guess I'm a glutton for punishment."

"No, I'm serious."

Elias thought for a moment before answering. "What do you want me to say?" he asked without taking his eyes off the bow. "Since the day you came to my office, I knew I wanted to be with you. Every second by your side has been exciting and dangerous, but you've made me feel alive like I've never felt before. With you I've left the past behind," he added somberly. "You brought me back to the present at last. You taught me to make the most of every moment, knowing it could be my last. I'm no longer worried about what might happen to me tomorrow," he finished, "only that I might not be able to spend whatever time I have left with you."

Nuria's lips curved into a smile. "That's the most beautiful thing anyone's ever said to me."

He winked at her. "And I haven't even seen you naked yet."

"Well, that's easily solved." She untied the knot in her towel and let it fall to her feet.

"Holy shit!" Elias cried, overwhelmed by the sight of her naked body next to him. "Jesus, don't do this to me now. Don't you see I can't let go of the helm?"

"Of course you can," Nuria said with a sly smile. "The autopilot's been on from the beginning."

"What?" He lifted his hands from the helm and saw that the boat remained perfectly on course. "Why did you trick me?"

"It kept you busy with something," Nuria apologized. "But now I'd rather keep you busy with something else."

Forgetting the helm once and for all, Elias approached her as if she were a unique and fragile human being. Caressing the curve of her hip with his fingertips, he came closer and immersed himself in the sea-scent of her skin. A promise of salt, love, and freedom.

"You can't imagine how often I've dreamed of this," he whispered, letting himself fall into her incredible green eyes.

"Me too," Nuria confessed. "But it's not a dream any longer."

"It still seems like one," Elias said. "You, naked in front of me, steering a sailboat to—" He stopped, realizing the truth of what he was saying. "You haven't even told me where we're going."

For a second Nuria turned her head to the bow, where the sun was beginning to appear on the horizon like a beacon of hope and redemption. "Towards dawn," she said, thinking that everyone deserves a happy ending. Even her. "Always towards dawn."

Nuria

Nuria Badal Jiménez is a real person. Or rather, she was.

A police officer from the Mossos d'Esquadra who was exactly as I've described her: noble, shy, generous, and as beautiful inside as out, doubtless one of the best people I've ever met. One of those angels fallen from heaven who somehow land in our lives, one of those we can proudly boast about having met. Nuria was a wonderful, unique woman. With this humble novel I wanted you to know her too. But this story, obviously, is not hers.

Although ... now that I think about it, it might be.

Nuria left this world bereft of her presence one ill-fated day in July 2012. But if the theory is true that infinite parallel universes exist in which everything is possible, not only is she still alive in one of them, but just like in this novel, she's a hero who has saved thousands of innocent people and is now sailing toward the dawn in her grandfather's old sailboat.

Personally, if I have to choose, I choose to think of her in that universe, alive and happy, because it's sure to be a more just, more beautiful place, a better world to live in.

Thank you for coming with me to visit her there.

Fernando Gamboa
Barcelona-Chiang Mai

Author's note

If you enjoyed *Redemption*, I invite you to post a review—however brief—on the book's Amazon page. It will take you only a moment, but for me it's very important because it will encourage other readers to discover the novel.

In exchange for those two minutes of your time, I'll personally send you a short story related to this novel called *Pump 16*. All you have to do is email me at *gamboaauthor@gmail.com* and I'll send it to you immediately with my most sincere thanks.

Oh, and if you like, you can also follow me on my author's page on Amazon and be the first to know about future book launches.

See you in the next adventure!

Fernando Gamboa

Acknowledgments

I want to thank all those who made this novel possible, starting with my family and friends—you all know who you are. I'm also grateful to my alpha readers, Diego, Noelia, Xose, and Jorge Magano for their judicious suggestions; to Rosina Iglesias for her editing, and especially to Teresa Márquez for her constant patience and support during two exhausting years of work. Saints have been canonized for much less.

I would also like to extend my thanks to all my followers and friends on social media who are always there, supporting me and urging me to keep writing, spurring me on every time I take a break. I hope you'll finally allow me to take a good rest now!

Of course I can't forget Carlos Liévano of KDP, Pablo Bonne of Audible, and Gonzalo Albert of Suma de Letras for their blind faith in my work. The same goes for all those booksellers who have found a space on their shelves for this humble novel. I grew up wandering through bookstores, running my fingers over the bindings. For me it's a pleasure to be part of that wonderful universe that smells of ink and cellulose again.

But if there's anyone I need to thank for being able to devote myself to writing, it's you. You, the person who's reading these last lines right now, squeezing the very last drop out of the novel—you are the person to whom I owe everything I am and everything I have. Without you, Fernando Gamboa the writer would not exist, and the truth is, that would be a pity, because I've begun to grow quite fond of him.

So, from the bottom of my heart, thank you for reading me. I send you a big virtual hug. See you on the next adventure!

Fernando Gamboa

Printed in Great Britain
by Amazon

69386115R00293